The Dolls

KIKI SULLIVAN

To James, Chloe, Eddie, and Colton:
I can't wait to see who you grow up to be

First published in the UK in 2015 by Usborne Publishing Ltd., Usborne House, 83-85 Saffron Hill, London EC1N 8RT, England. www.usborne.com

Text © Kiki Sullivan and The Story Foundation 2014

First published in the US by Balzer + Bray, an imprint of HarperCollins Publishers, 195 Broadway, New York, New York 10007.

The right of Kiki Sullivan to be identified as the author of this work has been asserted by her in accordance with the Copyright, Designs and Patents Act, 1988.

Illustrations © Usborne Publishing 2015

Author photograph by Melixa Carbonell

The name Usborne and the devices 🏆🎈 are Trade Marks of Usborne Publishing Ltd.

A CIP catalogue record for this book is available from the British Library.

ISBN 9781409584001

J MAMJJASOND/15   03484/1

Printed in Chatham, Kent, UK.

ONE

WHEN I OPEN MY EYES and blink into the milky morning sunlight, there's no longer snow on the ground outside the car. Instead of the brown-grey tableau of a New York winter, endless cypress trees line the road, their branches heavy under the weight of trailing Spanish moss and their green leaves catching the first rays of dawn.

As I struggle upright from a deep slouch in the passenger seat, it takes me a second to remember exactly where we are: Louisiana – or en route to Louisiana, anyhow. I'd fallen asleep just before midnight some eight hundred miles into our drive. Now, just after six a.m., thick white fog swirls around us, making it seem like we've been swallowed whole by a silent, drooping forest.

"Good morning," I croak, unwinding a tangle of red hair from my watch band.

"Morning, sleepyhead," Aunt Bea replies without turning. She's focused intently on the road ahead as if expecting other cars to suddenly appear, though the woods appear entirely deserted. "Did you sleep okay?"

I glance at my watch. "I guess I did," I say. "How are you feeling?" She's been awake for at least a day, running on coffee and Red Bull.

"I'm hanging in," Aunt Bea says, her face taut with exhaustion. "We'll be there soon."

"Cool." I try to smile, but it comes out as a grimace. I still don't understand why we're doing this.

Three days ago, my life was normal: winter break was almost over, and I was getting ready to celebrate my birthday and start the second semester of junior year. Then Aunt Bea – my legal guardian since I was three – announced over coffee and Cheerios that we were moving back to Carrefour, Louisiana, the town we left fourteen years ago right after my mom killed herself.

"I miss Brooklyn already," I murmur as I look out the window again.

"Give Carrefour a chance, Eveny. Believe me when I say you'll fit in fine."

"You don't know that." The thing is, I've always felt a half step different from everyone else, more at home in gardens and with plants than with real people. Still, I managed to develop a small, tight-knit group of friends back in New York. Starting over feels daunting.

"Carrefour isn't exactly new to you," Aunt Bea says, reading my mind. "People will know who you are."

"That's what I'm afraid of: being the girl whose mom offed herself by driving into a tree."

"Oh, Eveny," Aunt Bea sighs, "no one's going to judge you for that. If anything, they'll feel bad for you."

"I definitely don't need anyone's pity." After all, my memories of my mom are all good ones – up until the day it all ended.

"You know, it's okay to let people in," Aunt Bea says after a pause. "Your mom being gone is still hard for me too. But you deserve to know who she really was. I think being in Carrefour, where people knew her, will be a good thing."

She looks miserable, so I force a smile and say, "Moving back will be good for you too."

Aunt Bea's been dreaming for years about opening her own bakery, but in New York she could never afford to do it. In Carrefour, she'll be leasing a kitchen space downtown and is already making plans to open within the next week and a half. As frustrated as I am about this move, it will be positive for her, at least. And that's something.

I take a deep breath and add, "If you think this is the right thing, I'm on board." I spend the next hour of the drive trying to convince myself the words are true.

It's 8.46 in the morning and I'm texting with my best friend Meredith when Aunt Bea announces, in a voice that sounds oddly choked, that we're almost there.

I look up in surprise as we approach an impenetrable looking iron gate. On either side, as far as I can see, a stone wall ten feet tall extends into the swampy forest. Above the gate is a rusted sign that says *Carrefour, Louisiana: Residents Only* in swirling script.

"Residents only?" I ask. "How are we going to get in?"

"We're residents, Eveny." Aunt Bea shifts the car into neutral and steps out into the foggy morning. She rummages in her purse for a moment before pulling out an antique-looking bronze key. She inserts it into an ornate keyhole and hurries back to the car just as the gate begins to creak loudly open.

"What the...?" I say, my voice trailing off as she gets in and begins driving through. I turn around and watch as the gate closes slowly behind us, its hinges squealing in protest. "What *was* that?"

"My key to Carrefour," she says, like it's the most obvious thing in the world. "Every family has one. It's the only way in or out."

"Weird," I murmur. We continue through a swampy area that gets darker and darker as more tangled branches stretch overhead. Mist is rising from the shallow water surrounding the road, and as we break through a clearing, my confusion deepens. I thought I'd recognize Carrefour right away, but this place doesn't look at all familiar.

The town that lives in my memories is southern, Gothic, and filled with old mansions and stately, moss-draped cypress trees. But what's rolling by my window is a lot plainer than that, making me wonder if I've imagined everything. Bland row houses line the paved streets, and kids play in a few of the yards. I see a yellow car jacked up on bricks in front of one of the homes and a cluster of plump, middle-aged women wearing dresses and wide-brimmed hats sitting on a front porch of another. A tangle of little boys kicks a soccer ball lazily around the end of a street, and two girls ride rusted bikes in circles at the end of a cul-de-sac.

"This is Carrefour?" I ask.

"Technically, yes," Aunt Bea responds. "But you didn't spend much time out here in the Périphérie."

The name rings a vague bell, but I can't place it. Spanish moss hangs from hickory branches that arch over the road like a canopy. Above them, the sky swirls with the dark clouds of a coming storm. Behind the row houses, I glimpse marshy wetlands, gnarled cypresses and a stagnant creek. My aunt tells me this is the bayou; a wide, slow stream under whose pale green surface lurk crawfish, shrimps and – sometimes – alligators.

I look out the window again, feeling a little sad. "I just don't remember the town looking like this." Not that I'm judging. I loved the cluttered disarray of Brooklyn. But I'd always thought of Carrefour as so opulent – and so wealthy.

"This was always the…less privileged area of Carrefour," Aunt Bea says, her brow creasing. "But it seems like it's gotten a whole lot worse since we left."

"Because of the bad economy?" I guess as the road leads us past the last dilapidated house and into a deep, misty forest.

"Maybe," she says slowly. "But I'd be willing to bet central Carrefour is doing just fine."

As we round another bend and emerge from the woods, sunlight suddenly streams in from all directions. In under a half mile, we've driven into an entirely different world.

Just beyond the final creeping cypress tree of the Périphérie sits the edge of the most perfect-looking town I've ever seen. As we begin making our way through a neighbourhood, I see immaculately manicured lawns, houses with picket fences and matching shutters, and gardens blooming in brilliant colour even though it's January. "It's like one big country club," I say.

I stare out the window as Aunt Bea takes a left, turning into what appears to be Carrefour's downtown area. On the corner there's an ice cream parlour flanked by a café with an old-fashioned *Enjoy a Coke* sign out front, and beside it a little French bistro called Maxine's. A half dozen shops that look like they belong in an Atlantic seaside resort town – not middle-of-nowhere Louisiana – extend down the left side of the street.

"That's where my bakery will be," Aunt Bea says, pointing to a sliver of storefront next door to a boutique called Lulu's. "It used to be a little walk-up hamburger stand when your mom and I were kids."

Perfect canopies of blue and white stripes shade the sidewalks of the main street – which is actually called Main Street – and the store windows are all cloaked in curtains of sea-foam green and pale yellow. The buildings are a uniform clapboard white, and the people strolling along look like they've been plucked from Martha's Vineyard and dropped here in their shirt dresses, khakis, and button-down shirts.

"They know it's winter, right?" I ask as I watch two women emerge from the market with a wicker picnic basket. "And that they're not actually on their way to a clambake?"

Aunt Bea laughs. "Roll down the windows. It won't feel like winter here."

I give her a sceptical look, but by the time my window is halfway down, I realize that it must be in the low seventies outside. "But it's January," I say.

"It's Carrefour," she says without explaining.

"Does everything here look like a postcard?" I ask, wriggling out of the sweatshirt I've been wearing since we left New York.

"Wait until you see our house," she says, and, suddenly, I feel uneasy. The last clear memory I have of this town is standing in our front hallway with my mother's two best friends, Ms St. Pierre and Ms Marceau, as the police chief arrived to tell me the news. *Honey, your mama killed herself,* he'd drawled. *Drove right into a tree.* I'd screamed and screamed until I passed out.

"There's your school." Bea cuts into my thoughts as we pass a sprawling brick building with an ornate sign that reads *Pointe Laveau Academy* in Victorian script, just like the entrance gate. The parking lot is full of expensive sports cars, and two impossibly thin girls in white oxfords, maroon plaid skirts, and knee socks walk across the lawn, deep in conversation.

"Isn't there a public school in town?" My skin itches just thinking about wearing a uniform, never mind fitting in with a bunch of rich kids.

"There is," Aunt Bea answers lightly, "but your great-grandmother founded Pointe Laveau Academy, and it's where your grandma, your mom, and I went."

I'm about to argue, but then I look out the window and realize the sun has slipped behind the clouds, casting long, eerie shadows over the cemetery we're about to pass on the edge of town. Suddenly, a vivid memory hits me like a punch to the gut.

It's my mother's funeral, and I'm standing among soaring white tombs, my eyes sore from crying. A man with sandy hair and dark sunglasses slips from the shadows and bends to speak to me, his voice low, his words fast. "You must listen to me, Eveny, I don't have much time." He's a stranger, but there's something familiar about him. "They're coming for you. You have to be ready." He melts back into the shadows before I can ask what he means...

I gasp and push the image away as I try to catch my breath.

Aunt Bea looks at me sharply. "What's wrong?"

"Nothing," I say. "Just a weird memory." I hesitate. "Of Mom's funeral."

"Honey, you were only three then," Aunt Bea says gently. I don't think I'm imagining the concern on her face. "What are you remembering?"

I feel silly, because how can I recall someone I've never met, someone who left before I was even born, someone I've only seen one picture of in my life?

"I think my father was—" I start to say, but the words get caught in my throat as I notice a shirtless guy jogging around the outer rim of the cemetery, his head bent, his caramel-coloured skin glistening with sweat. He looks up as we pass, and for an instant, our eyes meet, and it feels like the world slows on its axis. Then, just as quickly, we're moving past him towards the south side of the graveyard.

"Who was that?" I ask, spinning around in my seat to look out the back window. The guy has stopped running and is standing in the middle of the road, staring after us. His muscular chest rises and falls as he catches his breath.

"Who?" Aunt Bea asks, glancing in the rear-view mirror.

"That guy running around the cemetery," I say. "He was about my age."

"Honey, we've been gone fourteen years," she points out gently. "He would have been a toddler last time we were here."

"Oh, right." My heart sinks a little.

I turn back around as the road winds up the middle of three small hills that sit on the south side of the cemetery. Ahead of us, at the top of the slope, looms a huge white house, a mansion really. As we follow the drive around to the front, I take in the Gothic columns, the enormous *Gone with the Wind* porch, the steps leading down to a sprawling, immaculately maintained lawn. A thin veil of fog swirls around the property.

"This is…ours?" I ask. But I already know the answer. I remember my mother teaching me how to ride a tricycle in the driveway; I remember doing lopsided cartwheels in the yard; I remember being happy here. How had I managed to mostly block this place out? And more importantly, why have we been living in a tiny Brooklyn apartment when we own a place like this?

"Actually," Aunt Bea says, "it's yours." When I turn to look at her, she's already watching me closely. "Welcome home, Eveny."

Two

I'M STILL STANDING OUTSIDE THE passenger door of the car, staring up at my house – my mansion – when I feel a warm hand on my arm. Startled, I spin around and see an old man peering at me.

"Eveny," he says in a low, rumbly voice. His dark brown skin is a sharp contrast to his snow-white hair. He must be at least seventy-five, but his wide grey eyes are startlingly clear.

"Where did you come from?" I ask, my heart still pounding.

He beams at me. "From the garden. I didn't mean to scare you, dear. Do you remember me? I'm Boniface. Boniface Baptiste."

"Boniface? Geez, of course," I say. He was the house's caretaker when I was little. He was around all the time, and he even used to babysit me sometimes when my mother and Aunt Bea ran errands together. "You still work here?"

"I live just out back in the caretaker's cottage. I've been looking after the Cheval mansion for practically as long as I can remember. Come on," he says, gently placing a hand on my back and leading me towards the house. "Let me show you around."

Aunt Bea has already vanished somewhere, so it's just me as Boniface talks slowly about how he took the sheets off the furniture, shook the dust out of the curtains, and scrubbed the beautiful hardwood floors before we arrived.

"I miss your mama all the time," he says abruptly as we come to the front door. "You're the spitting image of her, you know. Same red hair, same green eyes, same lovely smile."

He opens the huge black front door for me, and I feel a pang the moment I step over the threshold. I stand frozen in the front hallway as I'm hit with a barrage of hazy memories. But it's not until I look to my right and see a set of closed double doors painted a sombre red that I feel the breath knocked out of me. "That's the parlour," I say softly.

"You remember it?"

"I don't know…" I'm confused. I don't recall ever being inside the room, but something about it lurks in a far corner of my mind. Suddenly, my heart is racing and my lungs are constricting. I reach for the big bronze door handle, but Boniface steps in front of me.

"It's locked, I'm afraid. Haven't seen the key in years." He's already walking away by the time I can breathe again.

"What is it with this town and keys?" I mutter.

"Just wait until you see your bedroom," Boniface calls over his shoulder. "I took the liberty of decorating a bit. I wanted you to feel at home here," he's saying as I catch up to him on the wide wooden stairway.

Upstairs, Boniface pushes open the door at the end of the hall and motions for me to step inside. The bedroom, which last held my little twin bed and the big armchair where my mother read me stories at night, has been transformed.

The walls have been painted sky blue – my favourite colour – and are lined with colourful photos of flowers. There are framed shots of lilies in a field, lavender in a garden, sunflowers in a white pitcher on a farm table, and cornflowers in a vase. Pushed up against the right wall is a teak sleigh bed with a fluffy white comforter. Above it, a beautiful wreath of dried poppies and peonies hangs from the wall. To my left is a huge picture window framed by gauzy white curtains.

"It's perfect," I breathe. In fact, it's nearly as large as our entire apartment in Brooklyn.

"Your aunt called and told me all about your interest in

botany." Boniface is smiling at me. "Well I'll let you get settled, then."

As he leaves, I feel myself beginning to warm to the place. But then I make the mistake of wandering towards the window, which is arched and beautiful and diffuses the rays of soft morning light. I'd forgotten that it overlooks the cemetery we passed earlier, and as I gaze out now at the sprawling, fog-shrouded field of ornate crypts, I feel a chill go through me. Even when I back away and try to focus again on my great room, my veins feel like they're filled with ice.

I'm sitting on the deck just after sunset, trying to figure out how it's seventy degrees here in the dead of winter, when my phone rings.

It's Meredith, who launches into an off-key rendition of "Happy Birthday" as soon as I say hello. "So how's Nowheresville, Louisiana?" she asks when she's done assaulting my eardrums.

"Well, it's not New York. And this whole town is surrounded by a big wall, so it's like we're completely trapped." I feel a million miles away from my best friend as I hear laughter and honking horns in the background. The sounds of the city sure beat the silence out here in the middle of nowhere. Aunt Bea and Boniface have gone into town to pick up some things for the new bakery, and I feel like I'm the only person left on earth. I absent-mindedly flick on and off the flashlight I'd grabbed from inside, watching the deck alternately illuminate and plunge into darkness.

"You won't believe how crazy the wedding was today without you," Meredith says.

"The Michaelsons?" I ask, trying not to sound as sad as I feel. "Or the Harrises?" For the last year and a half, Mer and I have worked for Blossom and Bloom, a florist in our neighbourhood. The owner, Pauline, always said I had a sixth sense about which flowers fitted which brides. Working for her is one of the things I'll miss most.

"The Michaelsons," Meredith replies. "It was just me and Pauline because David called in sick. We ran out of lisianthus and had to figure out what to sub in."

"What'd you use? Texas bluebonnets?" I lived for those emergencies, the ones where you ran out of the blooms you were intending to use, so you had to find something else, something that fitted both the bride's vision and your own sense of the couple.

"We only had purple statice."

"I'm sure that worked great," I lie. Purple statice is a filler, so the substitution would have changed the whole feel of the bouquets. I'm so dorky – I'm the only person in the world who would care about something like that.

"Anyway, what did you say about there being a wall around the town?" Meredith asks, and I'm relieved for the change of subject because it momentarily stops me from thinking about the life I left behind.

I quickly recap what Aunt Bea told me about the gate. Then I tell her about the weather, the cemetery just beyond the garden wall, and the strange, swirling mist.

"No offence," Meredith says when I'm done, "but Carrefour sounds crazypants."

I'm surprised to realize I feel a bit defensive. "It's not so bad."

"Whatever you say. Anyways, what're you doing for your birthday?"

"Nothing yet." In fact, I'm beginning to wonder if Aunt Bea has even remembered, because it's just after eight p.m., and she hasn't wished me a happy birthday. No cake. No ice cream. No singing. Nothing.

"Maybe Bea's planning to surprise you."

"Maybe." I turn the flashlight off and tap it absently against my knee.

I'm about to tell Meredith about the intimidating-looking Pointe Laveau Academy when something darts across the backyard. I blink into the darkness and sit up, my heart pounding. Meredith launches into a story about how Jon Dashiell hit on Holly Henderson right in front of her boyfriend, but I'm not listening. "Shhhh," I finally manage.

"Did you just shush me?"

"I think I heard a noise," I whisper. "There's definitely something in my backyard."

"Kind of like how you always thought you saw some guy lurking in the shadows here in Brooklyn?" she asks, laughing.

"No," I mutter, feeling stupid. Three months ago, I'd begun to notice a slender man with white-blond hair loitering behind me wherever I went. I'd be walking home from school, and I'd catch a glimpse of him in the shadows, or I'd be window-shopping in SoHo with Meredith and see his reflection in a glass storefront. When I finally told Meredith about it, she'd laughed for a full minute. Like she's doing now.

But I tune her out as I strain to see across the darkness. The moon is half full, so it's casting light over my mother's rose garden, which Boniface has so carefully maintained. Beyond that lies her vegetable garden, lush with greens, tomatoes, and herbs. It backs up against the cemetery wall edging our property. That's where I see a shadow slinking along now.

I squint, then draw in a sharp breath as I realize it's human-shaped. I blink a few times and can just make out the faint silhouette of a person methodically picking something from one of the plants near the wall.

"Hey!" I drop my phone and call out. "Hey you! Stop!"

I'm dashing across the backyard in defence of my mom's beloved garden before I realize how stupid I'm being. How do I know it's not some creepy guy waiting to rob our house – or worse?

Suddenly, there's a thud, and the person goes down hard.

"Damn it!" comes a curse in the darkness, and I'm hugely relieved to realize the voice is female. I almost trip over her, and as I beam my flashlight down, I see a girl about my age with wild, sun-kissed blonde waves. She's in a white cotton dress, and her feet are bare.

"What do you think you're doing?" I demand.

"Who in the hell are you?" the girl shoots back in a thick southern accent.

"I *live* here. This is my yard. What are *you* doing in it?"

She looks perplexed. "But this is the Cheval mansion."

"Yeah, so? I'm Eveny Cheval."

The girl stares at me like I've just told her I'm the President of the United States. "Huh?" she manages.

"I just moved in," I say, growing more confident. "And I want to know what you're doing on my property."

"Uh, picking herbs," she says, adding defensively, "My friends and I pick stuff here all the time. It's no big deal."

"What do you need herbs for?"

"Recipes and stuff," she mumbles.

She's obviously lying. "What, is Boniface growing pot out here?"

The girl laughs and unfolds her left hand. "Not that I know of," she says. I peer at her palm. Indeed, I see only lavender, thyme and lemongrass.

"Told you so," she says. She sticks out her right hand to shake mine. "I'm Glory Jones."

Her grasp is warm and firm, and she grins at me as I help her up. "So you must be starting school in Carrefour?" she asks as she brushes the earth off her dress. When I nod, she asks, "Pointe Laveau?"

"Not that I have much of a choice."

Glory shrugs. "It's not so bad. You get used to the uniforms. Plus, it's fun to accessorize." She jiggles her armful of bracelets and bangles.

It still sounds like torture to me, but I find myself smiling anyhow. "You go there too?"

"Yeah. Maybe we'll have some classes together. Do you know what you have for first period yet?"

I shake my head. "I actually don't start until next week."

"How come?"

"I think the days off are my consolation prize for my aunt dragging me halfway across the country on my seventeenth birthday."

"You're seventeen?" she asks in a small voice. "When? Today?"

"Yes…" I say slowly.

"Oh." Glory gives me an uneasy smile. "Well, it was

nice to meet you, Eveny." She's already backing up. "I've got to go meet my friend Arelia now. I guess I'll see you at school next week. And, um, happy birthday."

I stare after her as she hurries away. I'm still trying to figure out what just happened when she pauses and turns to face me. "Listen, Eveny," she says solemnly, "be careful." And then she's up and over the back wall.

I blink into the darkness, then shake my head. Glory Jones was weird. But I like weird.

By the time Aunt Bea arrives home a couple of hours later, I've called Meredith back twice, but her phone's going straight to voicemail. I try not to feel hurt that she's out celebrating my birthday without me.

Aunt Bea brings me a chocolate cake from the market in town, and although it tastes a little like cardboard, I'm grateful for the effort. "I wanted to bake you something special," she tells me, "but my pans and mixing bowls haven't arrived yet. I promise, I'll make you whatever you want next week."

She finds a single, dusty candle in a drawer, and she and Boniface sing "Happy Birthday" to me as she sets the cake down atop the little table on the back porch. Boniface flips a switch inside the house, and the garden is illuminated by a hundred little fairy lights overhead. I take a deep breath and prepare to make a wish, but a gust of wind sweeps in and snuffs the flame for me. I shiver, even though it's not cold outside.

"Happy birthday, sweet girl," Aunt Bea whispers into my hair. She walks away without another word, leaving Boniface and me to eat our cake in silence.

That night, I lie awake in bed for hours. The wind howls angrily outside my window, and I swear I can hear sirens in the distance. Finally, with Glory Jones's odd words of caution ringing in my ears, I drift off to sleep.

I rarely dream, but the images that assault me tonight are as clear as the vision I had of my mother's funeral. First, I see the hallway outside my bedroom door, then the stairway leading to the front hall. As I begin making my way down the steps, I'm hit with the sudden, powerful scent of rusted iron in the air, and that's when I see it: blood beginning to pour out from beneath the closed parlour doors, pooling thick and nearly black on the hardwood floor.

I gasp and begin to run back up the stairs, but the crimson ocean is rising fast, and soon I can feel it, hot and sticky, licking at my ankles and then my legs. "No!" I cry out. The faster I retreat up the stairs, the faster the tide advances until there's nowhere else for me to go. The whole house is filling with blood…

I wake with a jolt, screaming. Aunt Bea rushes into my room and turns on the light. "What happened?"

"A nightmare," I gasp as I try to catch my breath. My legs still feel wet and sticky. "There was so much blood…"

"It was only a dream." She strokes my back, and my heartbeat begins to return to normal.

After she's gone, I stare at the ceiling for a long time. It's not until the first rays of dawn begin to filter through my windows that I finally drift off into a dreamless sleep.

THREE

STORMS POUND THE BAYOU ALL WEEK, making it impossible to venture out on one of the old bikes from the shed in the backyard. Like many people who grew up in New York City, I never learned to drive, and Aunt Bea is too busy setting up her bakery to teach me now. She's making several trips a day into town to prep her kitchen space, in hopes of opening sometime next week. I keep offering to help, but she insists this is something she has to do on her own.

Now I have nothing to do but explore the house while the rain comes down in a steady, driving rhythm. I try to imagine my mom walking these same halls when she was my age, but I can only visualize her as she was when she died: twenty-eight years old, already worn down by life, the premature lines around her eyes suggesting the weight she must have felt on her shoulders before she killed herself.

I wander from room to room, trying to piece together my family's past as lightning illuminates the cloud-speckled sky. In the living room, I see black-and-white photos of a woman in a flapper outfit – my great-great-grandmother, perhaps – and of two teenagers listening to an old-time radio in what looks like the early 1960s.

In one of the photos on the wall alongside the staircase, Boniface is holding my mom and Aunt Bea as little girls, one on either shoulder, as he grins at the camera. He doesn't look much younger than he does now, although the photo must have been taken thirty-five years ago.

I continue up the stairs to a big piece of glossy, polished wood hanging from the wall. The words carved into it are so ornate that I have to squint to make them out.

For each ray of light, there's a stroke of dark.
For each possibility, one has gone.
For each action, a reaction.
Ever in balance, the world spins on.

Weird, I think. It sounds almost like a warning. Or maybe I'm just taking it that way because I can't shake my creepy dream.

I spend the next few hours searching every picture in the

house for an image of my dad, the piece of my family history I understand the least. I've only ever seen one photo of him: a faded picture where he's standing in my mother's rose garden, holding one of her purple Rose of Life blooms and grinning at the camera. Aunt Bea hates his guts, though she's made a point of telling me that his leaving right before I was born had nothing to do with me. "He just wasn't the man we all thought he was," she always says.

By Wednesday evening, the only place in the house I haven't explored is the room off the front hall with the blood-red doors, the one from my nightmare.

"I'm still looking for the key," Boniface keeps telling me.

There's a sharp knock on the front door at two thirty Thursday afternoon, just as I'm in the middle of texting with Meredith about a bag she's debating buying at Michael Kors.

I bet it's the UPS man with my Pointe Laveau uniform, I text as I get up to answer the door.

I can't believe you have to wear a uniform, she texts back. *CRAPTASTIC!!!!!!*

I want to be insulted, but I completely agree. Plaid and a white oxford shirt are not exactly the fashion statement of the year.

But when I swing the door open, it's not the UPS man

at all. It's a guy my age with brown hair, muddy hazel eyes, and a deep tan.

"Eveny?" he asks, staring at me like he's seen a ghost.

"Yes…" I'm wondering why he seems to know me. He's in a black suit with a pale blue shirt and a dark grey tie; he looks like he's on the way to a prom.

"It's Drew Grady." His baritone has an appealing southern twang to it. "Don't you remember me?" He grins, and suddenly, I do.

"We used to play together," I say. His mom was friends with my mom, and they'd sometimes get together to chat while we chased each other around the playground on Main Street. "I used to dump sand in your pants."

"Every time our moms' backs were turned," he says with a laugh.

"So what are you doing here?"

"My mom heard you and your aunt had moved back. I didn't believe it, but I was walking by and saw all the curtains open."

"Dressed kind of formally for a walk, aren't you?" I ask.

From the way he's shifting around, and the fact that the suit doesn't quite fit in the shoulders, I'd bet that he's more of a Levi's kind of guy. He looks itchy.

His face registers surprise, as if he's just remembered what he's wearing. "Oh, right. Well, I'm on my way to a funeral."

"Geez, I'm sorry. Whose funeral is it?"

He looks down. "A girl at Pointe Laveau Academy. Same year as us."

"Really? That's so sad."

Drew shrugs and clears his throat. "Well, um, it was good to see you, Eveny. I'll come back at a better time."

"Wait!" I call as he starts to walk away. "Can I come with you?"

"Um…" he begins.

"It's just that I've been stuck here all week." I realize how odd my request sounds, but I'm desperate to go *anywhere*. "I'm completely bored."

"You want to go to a stranger's funeral with me?" Drew asks.

Sure, it's probably not the most appropriate thing to do, but I'm going to go crazy if I don't get out of the house. "Please?" I venture.

"Yeah, okay, it'll be nice to have some company," Drew says after a moment.

I ask him to hang on for a second then race upstairs to throw on a grey dress and a black sweater, which are the most sombre pieces I spot in a scan of my closet. I shoot Meredith a text to tell her I'm going out and will talk to her later, but she doesn't reply.

When I get back downstairs, Drew points to my ballet flats. "You're going to want something other than those.

It's really muddy after all the rain this week."

I settle for the battered motorcycle boots that saw me through last winter's snowstorms in New York, and although I feel stupid wearing them with a flouncy dress, Drew gives me a thumbs-up. "You look real pretty," he says, his cheeks turning a cute colour of pink.

I leave a note for Aunt Bea, then hurry out the door. "So what happened to the girl who died?" I ask as we trudge through my backyard.

"I can't believe you didn't hear," he says. "She committed suicide. The way she did it was awful, actually." He points to a spot in the cemetery wall where a few bricks are missing, and he offers me a hand to help boost me up and over. I land with a wet thud, and mud flies up around me, staining my dress.

"Why, what did she do?" I ask as he splashes over the wall too. I'm trying not to think of my mom and her suicide. "Apparently she drank a bottle of vodka, then stabbed herself in the chest. Right through the heart."

"Through the *heart*?"

Drew looks down at the soggy ground as we begin walking again. "The medical examiner told the paper she was probably dead within seconds. But what a horrible way to go."

I shudder. "The police are sure that she did it to herself, that it wasn't murder or something?"

Drew looks at me sharply. "Of course not. Things like that don't happen in Carrefour." His tone is final. "Anyway, I heard the police found a suicide note. There's a rumour that it was some kind of a satanic ritual or something."

"You've got to be kidding me."

Drew shrugs. "Let's just say that this is a place where things sometimes happen without an explanation. Strange things."

"Oh, great," I mutter. *What has Aunt Bea gotten me into by moving us here?*

The ceremony has just begun as we approach, and we're careful to tread quietly. People still turn and stare, though, and I'm not sure whether it's because I'm the new girl in town or because sloshing into the middle of a funeral is plain rude.

"Sorry I made you late," I whisper to Drew as the minister begins to read from the Bible in a monotone voice.

"Don't apologize." He reaches for my hand and squeezes. "I'm glad you came."

He lets go, and I can feel my heart thudding. I don't exactly have a ton of experience in the boy department. Back in Brooklyn, Meredith was usually the one at the centre of attention while I played wingwoman, which was fine by me.

My mind wanders as I scan the crowd, wondering

which people here will be my classmates at Pointe Laveau.

And that's when I see them.

Across the group of mourners, two impossibly beautiful girls are staring right at me. One is a gorgeous honey blonde with perfectly tanned skin, ridiculously long legs, and huge blue eyes. The other, who's even more stunning, has glistening cocoa skin, a model's body, and mounds of wildly gorgeous ebony curls that surround her like a halo. Both are dressed in clothes that are obviously designer and expensive; the blonde is in a black lace minidress plus open-toed stilettos and loads of pearls, while the dark-haired girl is wearing a form-fitting leather sheath, fishnet stockings, and leather spike-heeled boots that come up over her knees. Both have nearly identical black stones with jagged edges hanging from long chains around their necks. They're surrounded by three guys and two other girls, all of whom are also gorgeous, but not as much so as the two in the middle.

The dark-haired girl's eyes burn into mine, and I look quickly away, embarrassed to have been caught gawking. There's something vaguely familiar about them that I can't quite put my finger on. "Who are *they*?" I whisper to Drew.

"Everyone calls them the Dolls," he says, and I sense disgust in his tone. "The whole group of them. They all go to Pointe Laveau too."

"Oh." My heart sinks. I hoped to make a fresh start here; I'd even hoped that coming from New York City might make me seem a little edgy. But with girls like that at Pointe Laveau, my dream is fading fast. In the cool department, I obviously don't hold a candle to them.

"I call that one Medusa," Drew adds in a whisper. He nods slightly towards the girl with the cocoa skin and the killer curls, the one who's still staring at me.

"Because of her hair?" I vaguely remember the story of Medusa from Greek mythology; she was a monster with serpents growing out of her head.

"Sure, that's one reason."

I'm trying to puzzle out what he means as the minister asks everyone to bow their heads and pray. As he begins to read from the Bible, I sneak a look back at the Dolls and am unsettled to see the Medusa girl still staring at me. She holds my gaze for a moment then reaches into her purse and whispers to it. Something moves inside, and I clap my hand over my mouth when I realize it's a fat black snake, which is weaving back and forth, its eyes fixed on her face. I take a big step back, nearly tripping over Drew's foot.

"Drew!" I whisper urgently, pointing shakily in the direction of her purse. "She has a snake!"

"Like I said," he replies with a laugh. "Not just her hair."

I shoot him a look; I don't see anything funny about this.

"Who in their right mind would bring a snake to a funeral?"

"Who says she's in her right mind?"

My heart is still pounding when I notice something else; although Medusa and her blonde friend have finally looked away, and most of her group appears to be paying attention to the ceremony, one of the guys is staring directly at me, an indecipherable expression on his face.

Suddenly, I recognize him: it's the gorgeous jogger I caught a glimpse of the day we moved to Carrefour, and he's even hotter than I'd originally thought. He has smooth caramel skin, close-cropped dark hair, and pale blue eyes, and judging from what I saw that day out the car window, he has a hot body hidden under his crisp charcoal suit. I can feel the heat rising to my cheeks, but I'm finding it impossible to look away.

The minister puts the Bible down then and begins to speak. "It is with great sadness today that we lay to rest one of this town's daughters, only seventeen years old. She was a member of our church, and I knew her as a kind, good-hearted young woman. I pray that the Lord is welcoming Glory Anne Jones into his kingdom."

My heart skips a beat, and I momentarily forget all about the hot jogger. "Wait, it's *Glory Jones* who died?"

Drew looks surprised. "You knew her?"

"N-not really," I stammer. "We just met once. She was

picking herbs in my yard on Saturday night and I interrupted her. She seemed...nice. Happy. Not like she was planning to kill herself."

"Wait, you saw her Saturday night?" Drew asks. "What time?"

"Maybe eight, eight thirty."

"Eveny," he says, his voice hollow, "that was the night she died. You may have been the last person to see her alive."

FOUR

THE REST OF THE CEREMONY goes by in a blur. I'm reeling as the minister drones on about how much Glory will be missed, and leads the group in a closing prayer. All I can think is, *The only new person I've met so far in Carrefour is dead.*

After the funeral, I'm still deep in thought and staring at the tomb where Glory has just been interred when I hear Drew say, "Brace yourself." I look up to see the group of four stunning girls and three perfect guys approaching. I open my mouth to say hi, but the girl in the middle, the one with the Medusa curls, speaks first.

"You're new," she says bluntly. "And very under-dressed."

Up close, she's even more stunning. Her dark skin is flawless, and her eyes are a startling violet. I glance uneasily at her big black bag.

"You have a snake," I reply and immediately feel like a fool.

After a tense silence, she surprises me by laughing. "You're very observant, new girl," she says, her silken voice dripping with sarcasm. "What's your name?"

I take a deep breath. I'm not ready to be marked as the poor little daughter of the suicidal lady just yet, so I shoot back, "What's *yours*?"

She looks caught off guard. Behind her, I see the guy with the blue eyes hide a smile. "You must be the only person in a hundred-mile radius who doesn't know," she says.

"I must be," I reply, trying to sound a lot more confident than I feel.

When she replies, her words are clipped and cold. "Have it your way. I'm Peregrine Marceau, and this is Chloe St. Pierre." She jerks a thumb at the Barbie doll girl beside her and adds, "Obviously."

"Wait, I know you. I mean I *knew* you," I clarify.

"What are you talking about?" asks the blonde. Her tone is aggressive, but I have a feeling she's trying to sound tougher than she is to match up to her friend.

"We played together when we were kids," I say. Their mothers were my mother's best friends, the two women who accompanied the police chief the night he told me my mother was dead. And their families are, if I remember right, the two other founding families of Carrefour.

"What on *earth* are you babbling about?" Peregrine asks in a bored voice.

"I'm Eveny Cheval," I say.

The girls' eyes widen, and behind them, I hear the gorgeous guy draw a deep breath.

"Eveny *Cheval*?" Chloe repeats in a whisper. She touches the black stone hanging from her neck and looks at Peregrine.

"Sandrine Cheval's daughter?"

"That's me," I say weakly. It's just like I thought; everyone knows I'm the girl with the dead mom. The two girls behind Chloe and Peregrine are whispering furiously and shooting me strange looks. The guys are standing silent, but all of them are gazing at me too.

"Eveny," Peregrine says after a moment. "Why yes, of course." She pauses then shoots me a dazzling and undoubtedly fake smile. "Our mothers will be thrilled we ran into you. They'll want to see you immediately."

With that, she whirls on her stiletto heel and whisks away.

"Well, welcome home," says Chloe, giving me an odd look before following Peregrine. The other two girls skitter after them, while the three guys take turns sizing me up as I stand self-consciously glued to the spot. The first guy, who has floppy hair and hazel eyes, waits only a moment before running after the others and grabbing Chloe's hand.

The second, who's smarmily handsome in a Clark Gable kind of way, shoots me a knowing look before turning. But the blue-eyed guy stands as rooted to the ground as I am before Peregrine calls for him. He looks back once with a confused expression on his face before following after the rest of the Dolls.

"Well, that was bizarre." I feel strangely breathless after they're gone.

Beside me, Drew snorts. "Welcome to Carrefour."

We walk back to the house in silence as I think about the perplexing reaction of the girls I remember vaguely from childhood. I'd expected a weird welcome, since I'm sure everyone in town knows the tragic story of my mom, but they'd stared as if I were a movie star – or a murderer. There must be something I'm not getting.

"You want to sit outside for a bit?" I ask once we've climbed over my back wall. Drew agrees, so I dash inside to grab two Cokes from the refrigerator before leading him out to the garden. Boniface is there trimming rosebushes and humming to himself, but when he sees us, he says hello, winks at me, then makes himself scarce.

"Well, that's about the welcome home I'd expect from that group," Drew says once we're alone.

"I thought they might judge me for what happened to

my mom," I say as we sit down on the edge of one of the rose planters. "But that felt like an overreaction, right?"

"They're just weird. It's not about your mom's death as much as it's about them thinking they're better than everyone. They're only giving you a hard time because you're new here and they can."

"Well, they sound delightful," I reply. "This school year should be great."

Drew laughs. "Hey, Carrefour's not all bad. Wait until you come out for a day in the Périphérie." He pauses. "In fact, how about Sunday? There's a crawfish boil at my buddy's place."

He launches into an elaborate explanation about how it's a big Louisiana tradition, and although it's early in the season for fresh crawfish, he has a friend who flash-freezes them each year so he can host big blowout parties in the winter. "There's corn, potatoes, onions, sausages, hot sauce…" He keeps going, but I tune out when he begins listing beers.

I find myself thinking instead about the cute guy from the funeral and feel immediately foolish when I interrupt Drew's story to ask, "Who was that guy, anyway?"

Drew stops mid-sentence and looks at me. "What guy?"

I swallow hard. "Sorry," I say. "Just the one from the funeral who was looking at me funny."

"Eveny, they were *all* looking at you funny."

"But I mean the one with the blue eyes," I mumble.

"The light-skinned black dude?" Drew asks.

I hesitate, not quite liking the face he makes as he says it.

Drew rolls his eyes. "Oh, that's Caleb Shaw," he continues. "He's, like, a genius at school or something. I heard he got a perfect score on his PSAT in the fall, but he's a little...odd."

"Meaning what?"

"I don't know. Like he's always leaving town for a few days at a time. Most people in Carrefour only leave once or twice a year, if at all. But it's like Caleb thinks Carrefour isn't good enough for him." I think Drew's being critical until he adds, "Though I kind of admire the guy for realizing there's more out there than what this town has to offer."

"Do you know where he goes?"

"Nah. He kind of keeps to himself." He gives me a look as he adds, "Every girl in Carrefour is in love with him. Don't tell me you are too."

"Of course not," I say quickly. "I don't even know him."

"Well, I'm sure you'll have a crush on him soon enough, just like everyone else." He studies me for a moment. "So you want to know about the others too?"

"Sure." I'm embarrassed that he apparently thinks I just

want to hear about Caleb, although that's exactly what I want.

"The guy with the dark hair who looks like a model is Pascal Auteuil," he begins. "Rich as sin, and the biggest manwhore in town. Rumour is he's even slept with a few teachers."

"Ew," I say, wrinkling my nose.

"The other dude's Justin Cooper. Never heard of him a year ago, but now he's always there, following Chloe around like a lost puppy. In case you hadn't guessed, pretty much every guy in town lusts after her and Peregrine."

"Do…you feel that way about them too?" I hate that I sound jealous, because I'm not exactly. I just don't want to hear that Drew is also under the snake girl's spell.

Drew's eyes bore into mine as he says, "No. I appreciate it when a girl is kind and down-to-earth." He pauses and adds, "Like you."

I look away, flustered. "So who are the other two?"

"They're impossible to tell apart – not that you really have to. I've never seen them separated from each other – or from Peregrine and Chloe. Out in the Périphérie, we call them the Clones, but their real names are Margaux and Arelia."

"Arelia?" It takes me a moment to realize why the name rings a bell. "Wait, that's who Glory said she was going to meet the night she died."

"She did?" Drew blinks a few times. "Did she say anything else?"

"Not really." I shudder. "I still don't understand it. She seemed like she was in a good mood. We talked about school. She was picking herbs. Why would she be doing that if she was on her way to stab herself through the heart?"

He hesitates. "I have no idea. But Glory, she was a cool girl. Not like the rest of the Dolls." He checks his watch and stands up. "Listen, I'd better be going. But how about Sunday? The Périphérie's always a good time. I promise, you'll have fun."

I tell him I'm in, and he says he'll pick me up at five thirty. But as I walk him out of the garden towards the front yard and we hug goodbye, I'm only thinking about Glory and what she could have been doing the night she died. And despite myself, I'm also thinking of the guy with the brilliant blue eyes, the intriguing Caleb Shaw.

That night, I dream again of the parlour off the front hall. I'm walking down the stairs, but when I look at my feet, I'm surprised to find that I'm floating. In a panic, I grab for the railing, but my hand goes right through it. I'm being carried towards the parlour, powerless to stop.

I smell blood in the air, and there's the scent of roses and fire too. As I float across the front hallway, the parlour doors creak open, and blood oozes out. I hear crying from inside the room and as I move through the doorway, I see a little girl standing off to the left, her back to me, the bottom of her nightgown soaked in blood. There's something beside her on the ground, and I strain to see, but it's hidden in the shadows.

That's when the girl turns. Her hands are stained with blood, and her face is streaked with tears. My whole body goes cold as I recognize her immediately.

It's me, as a child.

"*Please help*," she whimpers.

I wake up with a start. It takes me an hour to fall asleep again, and the smell of blood and death are still with me when morning comes.

FIVE

By the time I finally drag myself out of bed the next morning, Aunt Bea is gone. She's left a note saying she went out early to receive a big shipment of bakery supplies, scribbling on the bottom, *Only five days to go until the opening!*

I pour myself a bowl of cereal and settle at the kitchen table with my laptop, determined to find out more about Glory's death. I Google her name, but nothing appears. I try *suicide + Carrefour*, thinking that maybe Glory's name wasn't printed in the paper because she was a minor. But I strike out there too.

I backspace again and this time, I type in *Carrefour newspaper*. But when I press enter, I'm only hit with a long list of meaningless options that have nothing to do with this place.

I'm still staring at the screen, trying to decide what to search for next, when I hear Boniface's voice from the back garden. I look out the window and see him talking to two women wearing expensive-looking black dresses and heels that make their legs look miles long. I recognize them immediately – not just from my foggy memories, but also because they look exactly like their daughters.

Annabelle Marceau and Scarlett St. Pierre. I haven't seen them since the night they accompanied the police chief to deliver the news that changed my life. *Honey, your mama killed herself. Drove right into a tree.*

Boniface's eyes meet mine through the windowpane, and as he approaches the back door, I see him grimacing.

"Eveny, we have a couple of visitors," he says. He lingers uncertainly for a moment before walking back towards the garden.

"Ms St. Pierre, right?" I say, smiling at the one whose honey-blonde hair cascades over her shoulders just like Chloe's. "And Ms Marceau?" I ask, glancing at the one who looks like a slightly older version of Peregrine, but with short, spiky black hair.

"I *knew* she'd remember us, Annabelle," trills the blonde. "And I'll be damned if you are not just the *spitting* image of your mother!"

"Thanks," I say awkwardly. "Want to come in?"

"Don't mind if we do," Peregrine's mother says, already

sweeping past me like she owns the place. "It's been ages since we've been inside this house, hasn't it?"

Chloe's mother hands me a white cardboard box wrapped in an intricately tied purple ribbon. "This is for you, sugar," she says. "It's a lemon and herb cake."

"We baked it for you last night," Peregrine's mother adds. "A little welcome-home treat!"

They stand there smiling at me for so long that the silence grows uncomfortable. "Would you like a cup of coffee?" I finally ask, trying to be polite. I turn and walk towards the kitchen, and they click-clack after me in their impossibly high heels.

"Have a seat," I say, gesturing to the kitchen table. I pull out a filter, line the coffeemaker with it, and scoop in several tablespoons of Folgers.

"Don't you have any chicory coffee?" Chloe's mother asks.

"Just the Folgers," I tell her as I add water, push the start button, and grab three mugs from the cabinet. "This cake looks delicious," I tell them.

"Oh, it is!" Chloe's mother bubbles. "It has rosemary to ward off evil, cloves to help foster friendship – with our daughters, of course – huckleberry to help you remember your dreams, and just a pinch of cinnamon to help promote good taste, because, let's face it, you're in Carrefour now."

"Okay…" I say slowly.

"Of course it's nothing like the cakes your aunt bakes," Peregrine's mother adds. "We can't *wait* to have her little bakery open! What's she calling it?"

"Sandrine's Bakeshop. After my mom."

"How lovely. I remember your mama and your aunt baking up a storm when we were your age." She gets a faraway look in her eye and adds, "We miss her so much, Eveny, we really do."

"Yeah. Me too." I pour three cups of coffee and ask if they want cream and sugar. They decline.

"So, Eveny," Peregrine's mother says a moment later as I hand steaming mugs to them. "All those years you were gone, did your aunt tell you much about Carrefour?"

I shake my head.

The women exchange looks. "I see," Peregrine's mother says. "So she hasn't explained any of the…customs of the town or anything?"

"Customs?" I ask blankly.

"Oh, Annabelle, stop putting Eveny on the spot," Chloe's mother says quickly. She turns to me. "I think what Annabelle is wondering is whether you'd heard of the Mardi Gras Ball. It's coming up in about a month, you know."

"Sorry, doesn't ring a bell. My aunt and I didn't spend a lot of time talking about this place. I think it reminded her of my mom."

"Your aunt never was a big fan of Carrefour," Chloe's mother says with a sigh. "But we'll change that yet, right, Eveny?" She claps her hands in a way that reminds me of a preschool teacher trying to coax a child into singing along.

"Sure," I say. I glance down at my computer. "Listen, while I have you here, do you know the website for the local paper?"

"The local paper?" Peregrine's mother asks.

"Yeah. I was trying to read more about what happened to Glory Jones."

"Why on earth would you want to do that?" she asks.

"Well, I met her the night she died, actually."

Chloe's mother goes suddenly pale, and Peregrine's mother freezes. "Did you?" she asks.

"She just didn't seem suicidal to me," I continue. "I thought maybe if I read about what happened, it might make more sense. But I can't seem to find anything about it on the internet."

Peregrine's mother takes a second to recover before speaking. "Of course not. We're not on the internet, dear."

"What's not on the internet? The whole town?" When she nods, I add, "But that doesn't make any sense."

"We like our seclusion from the world, Eveny," Chloe's mother says. "It's one of the wonderful things about living in Carrefour. We don't air our dirty laundry. We don't get unwanted visitors. Everyone knows everyone, and nothing bad ever happens."

I shake my head in disbelief. "What about Glory dying? What about my mother dying?"

"Those were both very unfortunate incidents," Peregrine's mother says, looking out the window.

"Try your cake, sugar," Chloe's mother urges.

I clear my throat and take a bite, even though I'm not hungry. "Delicious," I say politely. And actually, it is – it tastes a bit like the lemon cake they served in the Polish deli below our apartment in Brooklyn, but with a spicy, herbal twist.

"Really, Eveny, there's no reason to go looking into poor Glory's death," Peregrine's mother says after I've taken a second bite. "It's a tragedy, but it's all very straightforward."

But the more they brush off my questions, the more I'm convinced they're hiding something. "My friend Drew said there was a rumour about something satanic going on."

Both women laugh. "Satanic?" Peregrine's mother asks. "That's a new one."

"In any case, enough talk about death!" Chloe's mother says brightly. "Let's talk about you! I understand you're interested in botany?"

"Yeah." I nod. "I always have been. I was in charge of our community garden back in Brooklyn, and I worked for about a year and a half for a wedding florist."

"Your mother would have been so proud," Chloe's mother says. "She was very passionate about flowers and herbs." She glances at Peregrine's mother and adds, "We all are. Annabelle, me, our daughters…I think you'll find that this is a wonderful place to live if you're interested in gardening."

"Great," I say, forcing a smile. I can't exactly imagine their supermodel daughters in muddy jeans and canvas gloves, digging in the dirt. "Must be nice to have good weather year-round."

The mothers eat their cake and drink their coffee quickly as they chatter about all the social gatherings I can get involved with now that I'm back. Apparently, I just haven't *lived* until I've attended the annual Mardi Gras Ball.

"You are *so* lucky, Eveny," Peregrine's mother says as she finishes the last of her cake. "It's *the* social event of the year. It'll be a wonderful welcome home for you!"

"Thanks for the coffee, sugar," Chloe's mom says. She stands up and brings her mug and plate to the sink.

Peregrine's mom hands her dishes to me. "We're sure we'll be seeing a lot more of you."

"You must promise us, Eveny, that you'll spend some time with our daughters," Chloe's mom says. "They're *ever* so delighted that you're back, and they can't wait to get to know you."

I want to tell her that based on the way Peregrine and

Chloe were looking me up and down at the funeral like I was yesterday's garbage, I'm not expecting a call from them anytime soon.

"Sure, I'd love to hang out," I say, forcing a smile as I walk them to the door.

"Make sure you eat that cake, now!" Chloe's mother says brightly. They both air-kiss me on their way out, and a moment later, they're vanishing down my long driveway in a sleek silver Bentley coupe.

Later that afternoon, I'm wobbling down Main Street on a 1970s cruiser that Boniface found for me in the storage shed. Its red paint is chipped in places, and I've managed to convince myself that the rust stains and loud rattling noise aren't all that obvious until people start to turn and stare at me. I'm relieved when I spot my aunt's bakery, which now has a purple sign above the front door that says *Sandrine's Bakeshop*.

"Aunt Bea?" I call out as I head inside, where the air is soft with cinnamon and chocolate. She's painted the walls pale pink and decorated them with a dozen ornate French-style mirrors in various shapes and sizes. As I step up to the polished silver counter and the big glass case, I think how proud my mom would have been to have her name on a place like this.

"Eveny? That you?" I hear my aunt's voice from the back, and a moment later she emerges wearing a flour-streaked blue apron over jeans.

"Aunt Bea, the bakery's beautiful!" I tell her. "I can't believe you put this together in a week."

"I hoped you'd like it." She smiles at me. "Want to try one of my chocolate lavender cupcakes? I have some cooling."

"Maybe later. I just had some lemon herb cake."

She looks confused. "Where did that come from?"

"Peregrine's and Chloe's mothers dropped by to welcome us to town."

I expect her to be pleased, but instead her face darkens. "What did they say?"

"That their daughters are positively *thrilled* to have me back." I roll my eyes. "Doubtful."

"I suspect you'll have more in common with them than you imagine," she says. "Now, would you mind helping me frost some cupcakes? I want to take them home for Boniface to thank him for all his hard work."

She brings me a tray of unfrosted cakes and a piping bag, setting them on a table in front of the bakery window. "I'll be in the back if you need me."

I spend the next few minutes distributing caramel cream onto little pillows of chocolate. As I work, my head is swirling with a thousand questions about my mom, prompted by my brief visit with her two best friends. I've Googled her before, hoping to find some information about her death, but not even an obituary popped up. Just like with Glory.

"Hey, Aunt Bea?" I ask when I'm finished, setting the tray of frosted cupcakes on the counter in the back. "Does Carrefour have a newspaper?"

"Sure, it's a weekly one. Why?"

"I'm trying to understand what happened with Glory Jones. I don't get what would make someone who seemed so happy kill herself."

She studies me briefly before saying, "Try the library. Mrs Potter, who runs the place, prides herself on keeping perfect town records. Or at least she used to when I was growing up here." She walks me to the door and points down the street. "It's just past the theatre, on the left side."

"Thanks," I say, but she puts a hand on my shoulder to stop me.

"I know you're going to look up your mom's death as well," she says. "Just don't read too much into it. Things in this town are never quite what they appear."

She heads back inside without explaining more. I'm still puzzling over her words as I make my way up Main Street towards the library.

"Can I help you, dear?" asks the old woman behind the front desk as I walk in.

"Do you keep archives from the local paper here?"

She peers at me over her glasses. "I haven't seen you around before. Are you from the Périphérie?"

I'm not sure what that has to do with newspaper archives, but I reply politely, "No, ma'am. I live on the other side of the cemetery. I just moved back to town."

Her eyes widen. "You're Sandrine Cheval's daughter, aren't you?" she breathes. "Well, I'll be damned."

"You knew my mom?"

"Honey, everyone knew your mom." She seems to gather her composure as she gestures for me to follow her. "How nice to see you back in Carrefour."

She leads me down a hallway to a small room, explaining as we go that it's a bit old-fashioned but that they still keep the archives on microfiche. "I find that the tried and true way is often the best way," she says confidently. "Now, what can I help you find?"

"Actually, I was wondering whether I could see this week's paper. And" – I pause, a little embarrassed – "if you have the paper from the week my mom died, I'd like to read that too."

"You don't want to go reading something like that, honey."

"But I do," I say, not sure why I'm explaining myself to a stranger. "So if you could bring me the articles, that would be great."

She purses her lips and leaves, returning less than a minute later with three slides.

"Here's this week's paper, which I just put on microfiche yesterday, and the...older ones. You just move them under the glass there," she says, gesturing to a microscope-like device on a desk, "and they'll show up on the screen." I thank her and she walks out, muttering to herself as she shuts the door behind her. I use the knob on the side of the machine to focus the lens and begin reading the article from the front page of the most recent *Carrefour Weekly Chronicle*, titled "Local Girl Stabs Self".

According to the paper, Glory was a well-liked, straight-A student who lived in Carrefour her whole life. Her mom is quoted as saying, "There was absolutely no indication that something like this could happen." Peregrine and Chloe are both quoted too, with Peregrine describing Glory as, "a true, trustworthy friend", and Chloe saying – apparently through sobs, according to the reporter – that she'll always blame herself for not protecting her friend.

Protecting her? Seems like a bizarre way to talk about a suicide.

Glory's body, the paper says, was found in a wooded area along Cyprès Avenue on the north side of town by a possum hunter from the Périphérie who was trolling the woods before dawn. The police were called right away, but it was too late. The medical examiner estimated the time of death between 11.00 p.m. and 1.00 a.m. the night before.

Just a few hours after I'd met her.

"It's definitely a suicide, although the manner of death was highly unusual," the chief of police, Randall Sangerman, told the paper. "No prints on the body or on the knife, except for her own. Our department sends its deepest sympathies to her parents."

I search the rest of the newspaper, but there's nothing else about Glory, nothing that puts me any closer to understanding why she'd take her own life.

Confused, I pull out the slide and insert the first one from fourteen years ago, the one from the day after my mother's death. I take a steadying breath, adjust the viewfinder, and begin to read.

Sandrine Cheval, 28, died when her car slammed into a tree along the bayou on Route 786, on the outskirts of the Périphérie, near the town wall. "Death occurred when a shard from the windshield sliced open the carotid artery in her neck," the medical examiner told the reporter. *"Ms Cheval likely died almost instantaneously."* The newspaper promises more information in its next issue.

I sit back, the breath knocked out of me. I've never heard the detail about her neck being cut open. It makes me profoundly sad, and I sit there for a moment wondering what could have been going through her mind in those final seconds before she died so horrifically.

I clear my throat before loading and focusing the next slide. The front-page headline screams, "Carrefour Mom's Death Ruled a Suicide". The police chief at the time told the paper, "*Based on the lack of brake marks on the road, the speed at which she was travelling, the fact that Ms Cheval had to have turned the wheel very sharply at the last minute, and the lack of any intoxicants in her system, we've concluded that Ms Cheval's death wasn't an accident but rather a self-inflicted incident.*"

The article concludes by saying that Sandrine Cheval is survived by a younger sister, Beatrice, and a daughter, Eveny, age three.

I look at the screen for a long time through eyes blurred with tears. I've heard bits and pieces about my mother's car crash from Aunt Bea, but it never seems to add up. Seeing it in black and white makes it even more confusing. My mother was happy and loving, with a whole life in front of her. Why would someone like that deliberately drive her car into a tree?

I switch the screen off, and stand up. It's irrational to search for answers that don't exist.

I shake my head, grab the microfiche slides, and walk out to the librarian's desk.

"Did you find what you were looking for?" she asks.

"Not exactly," I tell her. "But thanks for your help." Her eyes look sad, and I can feel her watching me as I walk out the front door.

I'm in a fog, puzzling over the new details of my mom's death, as I head back out onto Main Street. I'm so caught up in my thoughts that I don't notice the guy rounding the corner of the library building until I run straight into him.

"Oh my gosh, I'm so sorry!" I exclaim. "I wasn't looking…" I'm about to ask if he's okay, but my breath catches as I look up and realize that the solid, muscular chest I've just collided with belongs to the guy from the cemetery, the guy with the blue eyes. Caleb Shaw.

"It was my fault too." He reaches out with both hands to steady me. "You okay?"

His voice is deep and warm, just like I imagined it would be. I blush as I look down and realize the hairs on my arms are all standing on end. "Uh-huh," I finally say.

He looks unconvinced. "You sure?"

"Uh-huh," I manage to repeat. *Brilliant conversational skills, Eveny.*

He stares at me for a minute, and at the same time we both realize that his hands are still on my arms, holding me upright. He pulls away like he's been burned. "Well, I'm just headed into the library to check out a few books," he says.

"Yeah, reading's cool," I mumble. I immediately want to smack myself. *Reading's cool?*

I can see a smile tugging at the corner of his perfect mouth. "Sure," he says.

"Cool," I manage to say very uncoolly.

"Right. So see you later then?"

"Later," I squeak.

He gives me a long, searching look and then vanishes through the library door.

I stand there frozen in place for a moment before shaking myself out of it.

"*Reading's cool?*" I say aloud. "Who *says* that?"

I can feel my cheeks flaming in embarrassment the whole way home.

Six

"I don't even know if it's a date," I tell Meredith on Sunday evening as I put make-up on in the bathroom mirror. I'm wearing a long-sleeved black T-shirt, my old leather jacket, and a pair of skinny jeans, which I'm hoping are appropriate for the crawfish boil Drew's taking me to tonight. At Meredith's insistence, I've swapped my Converse for a pair of cowboy boots.

"But you said this Drew guy's cute?" she prompts. I have her on speakerphone, and the way her voice fills my room, as if she's right here with me, makes me miss my old life in New York so much it hurts.

"Very," I tell her. I put the tube of mascara down and concentrate on dusting some blush on my cheeks.

"So do you like him?" she asks.

"I don't know," I tell her. "The thing is, there's this other guy…"

Meredith is silent as I tell her about Caleb and the way our eyes met across the cemetery on Thursday. I refrain from telling her about our spectacularly dorky encounter Friday outside the library.

"Girl, for all you know this Caleb guy is gay. He could have been staring at Drew," Meredith points out. "Go for the guy who's already into you. How cool will you be if you start at a new school already having a boyfriend?"

I shrug before realizing she can't see me. "I don't even know if he's interested. Besides, the girls I was telling you about don't seem to like him."

"Well, they sound like snobby little rhymes-with-witches," Meredith sniffs. "So who cares?"

"I guess you're right. But they're from my past too. Everything feels totally complicated here."

"Or maybe you've just been reading too many angsty novels," Meredith says. "You don't need to have every step planned out. Just do this crawfish boil, have a good time, go with it, and make out with the Drew guy if you want to."

I swallow hard. I wish it were that easy. I wish I weren't thinking about Caleb. I wish I hadn't spent the last twenty-four hours daydreaming about being pressed up against the solid chest I'd collided with outside the library.

The doorbell rings, snapping me out of it. "That's him. I've got to go."

"Have fun!" she replies. She makes some kissy-kissy sounds, then I hear the phone click and she's gone.

"Eveny!" Aunt Bea's voice wafts up from the front hallway. "Drew's at the door!"

"I'll be right down!" I take one last look in the mirror, spiral my fingers through a few errant curls, and head for the stairs.

On the drive over to the crawfish boil in Drew's pickup truck, I once again note that the Périphérie is practically the polar opposite of central Carrefour. In my part of town, every building sports a fresh coat of paint, every neighbourhood looks like it could have been lifted from *Better Homes and Gardens*, and every person strolling by looks like they've been styled for a photo shoot.

But as soon as we make it through the thick tangle of trees that surrounds the centre of town, it's like we've driven into a new universe.

"It's so different out here," I say, hoping that I don't sound like a snob.

Drew looks amused. "Poor, you mean."

"No, that's not what I meant," I say quickly. "It actually seems like it has character."

"I think you mean decay."

"Not at all. It's just odd that there'd be such a big divide between the two sides of town."

Drew raises an eyebrow. "You have a lot to learn about this place."

"Even the weather is different," I add. Indeed, outside Drew's pickup, clouds swirl against a dark, ominous sky, and it feels like the temperature has dropped twenty degrees since we emerged from the trees. I shiver and roll my window up.

"I heard once that the temperature variation between the two areas has something to do with water vapour from the bayou," Drew replies. "I'm no meteorologist, but it never made much sense to me."

We arrive at Drew's friend Teddy's house a few minutes after six. Most of the guys are wearing sweatshirts and jeans, and about half of them are in maroon and beige letter jackets that I assume are from Carrefour Secondary. Most of the girls are in cowboy hats and jeans or denim miniskirts. The only piece of my outfit that fits with this crowd are the cowboy boots Meredith insisted I wear.

There's a bonfire blazing in the middle of the yard with a few dozen people clustered around it, talking, laughing, and occasionally sloshing their drinks out of red plastic cups. On the side of the house, two huge pots at least three feet high and three feet across are simmering on big propane burners, sending giant puffs of steam shooting skyward.

"What are those?" I ask, pointing at the pots.

"That's where they cook the crawfish."

Just then, a guy with green eyes, freckles, and a cleft chin, all shaded by a giant cowboy hat, materializes next to us. "It ain't crawfish season yet, but we got a whole load of those daddies in the freezer from last year's catch, and we got to use them up before we can start getting 'em fresh again. That's why I'm calling this my Clean Out the Freezer Crawfish Boil." He sticks out his hand and adds, "You must be Eveny. Real pretty name. I'm Teddy. Welcome to Freezer Night."

I laugh, shake his hand, and thank him for inviting me.

"Thank this guy," he says, clapping Drew on the back. "He's been raving about you since you got back into town. We've all been dying to meet you. So this is your first crawfish boil?"

"It is." I can't help but grin at him. He's a ball of happy energy.

"Sweet! So what'll you have? We got beer, or there's something my girl Sara over there made called Swamp Punch. No idea what's in it."

"I'll stick with the beer."

"Smart girl," he says with a wink. "I'll be right back. You want a beer too?" he asks Drew.

"Just one. I gotta get this girl home safe."

"He seems nice," I say to Drew as we watch Teddy bound off towards the back deck, which is lined with three rusted-looking kegs. "He goes to Pointe Laveau too?" I'm already imagining a new life where I hang out with the down-to-earth people from the Périphérie even if I go to school at Snob Central.

"Nah," Drew says, kicking the dirt and looking down. "Pointe Laveau is kinda reserved for *your kind*."

"Excuse me?"

"The people who live in the privileged part of town. People with money. Out here, none of us can afford the tuition, so every year six merit-based scholarships per grade are awarded to Périphérie kids. I guess it's some kind of philanthropic gesture."

I'm quiet for a moment. "Just so you know, my aunt Bea and I weren't rich when we lived in New York."

"Eveny, you live in a mansion. Your family founded this town. You're probably one of the richest people in Louisiana."

I don't know what to say.

Finally, Drew sighs. "Maybe your aunt was trying to raise you with some values. Most of those spoiled rich kids don't have any."

I swallow the urge to defend the Dolls. In a strange way, I feel as much a part of them as this life out here, because even if we're polar opposites now, we share a past. I don't know whether I'm rich or poor, refined or casual, city or country. But I have the uneasy feeling that living in two worlds isn't going to be easy for long.

The crawfish boil turns out to be a blast.

Even though I worried I wouldn't belong, everyone is being really nice. Drew leads me around the sprawling yard, his hand lightly resting on the small of my back, and he introduces me to so many people that I start forgetting names. There's a raucous game of cornhole – which apparently involves throwing beanbags into a board with holes cut out – going on near the bayou, and in the yard another group is playing beer pong. There's country music blasting from speakers on the back deck, which has turned into a dance floor.

Everyone shrieks with excitement when Teddy announces the crawfish are ready to boil, and Drew excuses himself to go help. I stand alone and clap along with everyone as Drew, Teddy, and two other guys dump huge cases of crawfish into the boiling pots, which are already simmering with red potatoes, corn, and spices like garlic powder, onion powder and cayenne pepper. The air smells sweet and spicy, and I find myself getting hungrier and hungrier.

"Thirty minutes till we eat!" Teddy announces. "Y'all better work up your appetites!"

The crowd cheers, and the dancing on the deck gets more frenzied. When Drew comes to find me a minute later, his cheeks are flushed and he's grinning. "Man, I love a good crawfish boil," he says. "Want to go take a quick walk down the bayou while we wait for the food?"

"Sure." His enthusiasm is contagious, and I find myself smiling too.

We grab a flashlight from the deck and stroll towards the back of the yard, where it dissolves into a mess of dying cypress trees, brown Spanish moss, and darkness. When Drew grabs my hand, I don't pull away.

It only takes a few minutes for the noise of the party to vanish behind us. Out here, the night is thick, and the buzz of mosquitoes is a steady soundtrack.

"So," he says after we sit down in the grass, "do you remember the time you and your mom came out to visit us and my mom made her special gumbo?"

I shake my head sadly. "I wish I did. I think maybe I blocked out most of my memories of being a kid here."

"But you remember your mom?"

"Yeah. I still think about her a lot." I pause. "She died a long time ago, though. Sometimes I wonder if there's something wrong with me for not moving on."

"Eveny! That's crazy! She was your mother. Of course you're still thinking about her."

I look out in the blackness. There's rustling in the trees and splashing in the water, and although I don't know what's out there, I realize I feel safe with Drew.

"She's just on my mind a lot more since we've moved back. I think—" I hesitate. "I think I still can't wrap my head around the idea that she took her own life."

Drew studies me for a long time and then pulls me into a hug. "I'm so sorry you went through all that, Eveny."

I'm relieved that he understands and grateful when he abruptly changes the subject, chattering about a science project he's working on until we're called to eat.

As we stroll back to Teddy's house, he tells me all about his band, which is called Little Brother and plays something called bayou fusion rock music.

"Bayou fusion rock?" I repeat.

He laughs and says it's their own form of banjo-driven rock 'n' roll. "Like if the Eagles, the Avett Brothers and a New Orleans jazz band got together and had a music baby. I play the guitar," he adds. "Teddy's our drummer; he thinks we'll get a record deal if we can just get in front of the right people."

"Is that what you want to do with your life, go into music?" I ask.

"Who wouldn't want to be a rock star, right? But I'm not

a total idiot; I know those things don't always work out. I'm going to go to college too, so I have a back-up plan."

"Where do you want to go?"

"LSU," he says instantly. "No doubt. But I'll have to get a scholarship or take out a bunch of student loans. It's not like my parents have the money for something like that any more."

"Any more?"

He shakes his head. "Let's not talk money right now. Too much of a downer. So how about you? Planning to go to college?"

"Yeah, NYU," I answer without hesitation.

"You want to go back to New York?" he asks in surprise.

"No offence, but this isn't home. New York is."

"Well," Drew says, "we'll see about that. This town has a funny way of sinking its teeth into you."

Ten minutes later, I'm standing in Teddy's backyard again, watching as the guys pull giant metal strainers out of the huge pots, shake them dry, and dump them on long picnic tables covered in newspaper. A sea of what look like miniature lobsters pours out alongside hundreds of potatoes and ears of bright yellow corn that have been cut into thirds.

"Dig in!" Drew shouts at me across the yard as he carries one of the strainers towards the back deck, where Teddy's already hosing them off.

I laugh as the crowd descends on the tables, piling big handfuls of crawfish, corn, and potatoes onto styrofoam plates. Drew arrives at my side a moment later and leads me over to scoop up my own dinner, then we retreat to a quiet corner of the yard, where we sit down, leaning our backs against a big oak tree. Drew teaches me how to eat the crawfish, which is kind of a gross process: you twist them in half, suck the heads, and then squeeze the tails to get the meat out.

"You're a natural," Drew marvels after I've decapitated my fourth crawfish.

"Maybe I belong here after all."

"I guess we'll see," he says, suddenly serious. "You've got some potato on your face." He reaches over to gently brush a speck off my chin, and from the way he pauses and looks at me, I have the uneasy feeling he's going to make a move. But then he pulls back and looks down. "Glad you liked everything," he says. "I'd better get you home once we're done eating before your aunt skins me alive."

SEVEN

I'M NERVOUS THE NEXT MORNING as I get ready for my first day at Pointe Laveau. Even with Aunt Bea's tailoring, my uniform looks terrible. My white oxford shirt is boxy, my maroon plaid skirt comes down just past my knees, and my white socks and black oxfords make me look suspiciously like a seventy-five-year-old orthopaedic patient.

"You sure these are the shoes we have to wear?" I ask Aunt Bea as I round the corner into the kitchen.

"That's what the school guidebook said," she tells me apologetically. "For what it's worth, I think you look cute in a retro kind of way."

I text a photo of my uniform to Meredith, hoping she'll make me feel better, but she doesn't reply. It takes me a few minutes to remember that Louisiana is an hour behind

New York, so she's probably already at school with her phone off.

At breakfast, Aunt Bea seems even more nervous than I do. She spills her coffee, knocks over her juice, and drops her toast on the floor twice.

"You're going to have a great first day!" she tells me with a smile that looks as fake as it probably is.

"You're acting a little weird," I say. "Everything okay with the bakery?" Her grand opening party is scheduled for Wednesday night, and the closer it gets, the more scatterbrained she's becoming.

"It's you I'm concerned about; I remember how tough first days are. But you're going to do great."

"Sure I am," I reply drily. "What could possibly go wrong in a school full of beautiful rich people?"

"Stop worrying," she says, but she's chewing her lip the way she always does when she's uneasy. I'm relieved when she drops me off in front of the school twenty minutes later because her nerves are rubbing off on me.

Pointe Laveau Academy must have been built right around the same time as my house, because it has the same kind of dramatic, neo-Gothic construction. The main building has narrow, arched windows, steep gables, and a bell tower, and the outlying buildings, which are clustered around a green space I can barely see from the street, are flatter versions of the same design. The complex looks like a cross between a church and an old prison. I shudder as I walk up the front steps and lose the sunlight.

Just before I enter the building, my phone dings with a text message. It's from Drew.

Sorry, he says, *but I won't be at school. Woke up sick this morning. Hope you didn't get my germs. Have a good first day!*

My heart sinks. He's my only friend here, and now I'll have to brave my debut alone. I text him back, *Aw, feel better!* then I switch my phone to silent and head inside to start my new life.

"Eveny Cheval," the pudgy school secretary says flatly as I enter the front office, which is decked out in regal-looking furniture with eggplant-coloured cushions.

I nod, wondering how she knew it was me.

"We never get new students here," she remarks, answering the question I haven't asked. She fluffs her bleached-blonde curls and purses her bright pink lips at me. "Except scholarship kids from out in the Périphérie once in a while. But I know all of them in advance."

"Oh, do you live out there, in the Périphérie?" I ask, trying to be polite.

"Are you being smart with me?" She glares back.

"What? No, of course not."

"Well, last time I checked, I wasn't sitting on a mountain of gold coins in a mansion like you people," she says. "But I'm certainly not from out *there*." I just stare at her, wondering how I've managed to piss off the first person I've encountered. "Now go on," she says, handing over my class schedule. "Your books are in your locker."

I take a deep breath and head into the main hallway, which is teeming with students. The first thing I notice is that although all the girls are wearing the same uniform I am, every single one of them is pulling it off way better. None of them are in clunky loafers; they seem to be wearing everything from ballet flats to cowboy boots to strappy heels. My heart sinks as I realize the first impression I make here will be one of dorkiness.

The guys are all wearing pressed khakis and pale purple oxford shirts with the initials of the school emblazoned on their left breast pockets. They, too, seem to have skipped anything resembling an official dress code. I spot a few purple and gold letter jackets, but most of the guys are dressed in pieces that smack a bit more of individuality – leather bombers, a few blazers, a handful of hoodies.

Everyone is streaming by in a hurry, and nearly all of them are shooting me curious glances, but no one stops to help. I look down at the schedule again. It says on the top that I've been assigned to locker 445.

Yet I have no idea where locker 445 might be, or how I'll find my first class. I look around, hoping I'll spot Peregrine or Chloe or another one of the Dolls, because at least they're not complete strangers.

That's when I notice that the hallway is draped in black crêpe ribbons. Signs that say *We love you, Glory* and *We'll miss you, Glory* are taped on walls, and I spot a few photographs on a pinboard nearby, framed in black. I step closer and see Glory Jones's face smiling out at me.

"You look lost." A voice comes from the right, startling me, and I turn to see a slender girl with a heart-shaped face, big brown eyes, and thick dark hair. She's wearing a purple tissue-weight cardigan and faded purple Converse hightops with her uniform, almost as if she's trying to look anti-glamorous. I like her instantly.

"Yeah. It's my first day, and I have no idea how to get to my locker," I admit. "Or my first class. And I'm beginning to feel like an idiot."

"It was super rude of Mrs Perkins to send you off without telling you where to go. I'd blame it on all that tacky hair bleach going to her head, but around here, if you're not one of the chosen ones, you can forget about anyone giving a crap about you."

"The chosen ones?"

She laughs, although it sounds a bit like a snort. "You'll see." She squints at my schedule and says, "All right, let's get you to your locker." We begin walking, and she adds, "By the way, I'm Liv."

"Eveny," I reply.

She reads my schedule as we dodge other students in

the hall. "Cool, we have physics together sixth period," she says. "Other than that, our classes don't match up. But I'll show you where your first period is."

We reach a row of lockers, and she points to one near the middle. "Here we are. Locker 445."

I look at the slip of paper, which tells me the combination is 16-7-13. I turn the dials, and the door pops open, revealing a neat stack of books – and a name scratched into the inside panel: *Glory Jones*. I freeze.

"This was Glory Jones's locker?" I ask.

Liv peers inside and sees the curvy letters too. "Can't believe they'd reassign it so soon. Then again, Glory was one of the nice ones. She'd probably want you to have it."

I grab my textbooks for English and trig, my first two classes. But what I'm thinking is that, nice or not, Glory would probably prefer to still be here, using her own locker.

The bell rings. "Here we go again," Liv mutters. She points down the hall and says, "Your English class is that way. Fifth door on the right. Mrs Shriver. You'll be fine."

I take a deep breath, clutch my books to my chest, and begin walking, relieved that I've now met at least one potential friend who's not dead.

The second bell rings a millisecond before I walk into English, which makes me officially late.

I feel two dozen pairs of eyes on me as I hand Mrs Shriver my schedule and mumble that I'm new here.

"Oh yes, Eveny Cheval," she says. "We were expecting you. You can take that empty seat in the last row."

"No." I hear a languid voice from the back, and I turn to see Peregrine, decked out in thick eyeliner, dark lipstick, and a lacy black silk camisole under her standard-issue oxford shirt. The same stone necklace I noticed at the funeral dangles in her cleavage, and she's wearing a close-fitting black quilted leather vest. "Eveny will sit right here." She gestures daintily to an empty chair beside her.

I hesitate, wondering if she's just being nice to me because her mother said she had to, but she snaps her fingers, gestures to the seat, and says, "We don't have all day, Eveny. Chop chop."

"Go on, take the seat, dear," Mrs Shriver says, seeming to recover a bit as I move down the aisle towards Peregrine.

"Nice shoes," Peregrine says, raising an eyebrow at me after I sit. "Did you borrow them from a nursing home?"

"The dress code said we had to wear black loafers and knee socks," I say, glancing down. She's wearing strappy black platform stiletto sandals on her bare, perfectly pedicured feet. I feel ridiculous.

"Eveny, you'll soon learn that *we* don't have to do anything," she says. She turns away without elaborating.

As Mrs Shriver begins to talk about *The Great Gatsby*,

which I read last year in my American Lit class, I spot Chloe sitting beside Peregrine, wearing a dark fur stole. She's paired her oxford with a set of Chanel pearls featuring a diamond-encrusted, interlocking double *C*. Her high-heeled Mary Janes are studded with what look like diamonds, and her hair is artfully mussed.

"Yoo-hoo, Eveny!" she says, waving at me pleasantly. "Welcome!"

I wave back to Chloe vaguely as I realize that no one seems to be paying any attention to Mrs Shriver. A cluster of skater-looking guys in the back of the room have pushed their desks together and are playing games on their iPhones. I recognize Arelia and Margaux sitting just behind Peregrine and Chloe, dressed in matching leopard-print cardigans and sky-high heels. There are a few guys wearing purple and gold letter jackets near the centre of the room and three cheerleaders who, even in their short-skirted uniforms, look frumpy compared to the Dolls.

I glance down and realize suddenly that Peregrine's big, studded designer tote, which is lying half open on the floor beside her desk, appears to be moving. I let out a strangled gasp as her snake pokes its head out and blinks its beady eyes at me. Mrs Shriver's monotone monologue about Daisy Buchanan and Nick Carraway screeches to a halt.

"Is there a problem, Ms Cheval?" Mrs Shriver asks.

"Uh, no." I'm pretty sure I've now turned as red as my skirt. "Sorry."

"Oh, relax, Eveny," Peregrine says in a bored voice, examining her nails. "It's just Audowido." She looks up at Mrs Shriver and says, "Don't worry. Everything's under control. You can resume your lecture."

Mrs Shriver shrugs and begins droning again. I turn to Peregrine. "You bring the *snake* to *school*?"

She looks at me blankly. "Of course." She pauses and adds, "His name is Audowido, by the way. Addressing him simply as 'the snake' is so impersonal. He really dislikes it."

"Oh," I say helplessly.

"I accept your apology," Peregrine says.

I spend the remainder of the class sneaking occasional glances at Audowido, who just keeps staring at me with his unblinking little eyes.

The rest of the morning goes by uneventfully – and thankfully without any other reptilian appearances. There's no one I know in my fourth-period economics class, so when the bell rings and everyone begins flowing towards the cafeteria, I let myself get swept up by the current. The whole way there, I'm hoping I won't have to eat alone.

It's Liv I want to run into, but I see Peregrine and Chloe first, mostly because they're impossible to miss. Not only are they undoubtedly the most gorgeous girls in school, but they're being trailed by a crowd of adoring-looking guys as they sweep into the cafeteria in a cloud of expensive perfume.

"Eveny!" Peregrine exclaims, whisking over to where I'm standing in the caf line, trying to decide between the fried chicken and the gumbo. "What on earth are you doing?"

The cafeteria seems to grind to a halt. Everyone is staring at us, and I can hear a few whispered voices asking who I am and what I'm doing talking with the Dolls.

"Getting ready to order lunch?" I venture.

Both girls laugh like I've said something hilarious. "Oh, nonsense, Eveny," Chloe says. "You'll eat with us in the Hickories, of course."

I open my mouth to reply, but Peregrine beats me to it.

"Seating in the Hickories is by invitation only," she says. "And we have a very exclusive list. Obviously you'll want to join us."

It's admittedly nice to have someone asking me to hang out with them, but not for the wrong reasons. The last thing I need is their pity. "Look, just because your moms knew my mom doesn't mean you have to invite me to eat with you," I say stiffly. "I'm fine on my own."

"Oh yes, you look like you're already an *enormous* social success." She gazes around pointedly to underscore the fact that I'm all by myself. "Well?" she prompts. "Are you coming, or are you expecting an engraved invitation?"

"Fine. I'll come find you after I order," I mutter.

"Eveny," Chloe says slowly, looking at me like I'm a mental patient, "we don't *order* our food here. Our lunch is *catered*. Come on."

Confused, I follow them up the grassy knoll behind the school, where I spot Arelia and Margaux spreading out a huge blanket in the shade of an enormous, swooping hickory tree. The grassy patch is surrounded by a dozen smaller hickories, all dripping with sun-dappled Spanish moss. I notice Pascal lounging against one and Justin standing beneath another. He gazes adoringly at Chloe as we approach. "Hey, baby doll," he drawls, stepping out to wrap his arms around her.

She kisses him chastely and steps back to Peregrine's side.

"Gin and tonic?" Arelia asks eagerly as she smoothes a corner of the blanket. It's cashmere, I notice. "Or would you prefer champagne today?"

I'm expecting Peregrine and Chloe to laugh like this is some kind of inside joke. But Peregrine chirps, "G and T," and Chloe says, "Same for me."

Arelia turns to me next, looking confused. I stare right back, trying to figure out how they're planning to drink alcohol out in the open on school property.

"Arelia?" Peregrine begins. "Aren't you going to ask Eveny what she'd like?"

"Seriously?" Arelia says. When Peregrine nods, she turns and says in a tight voice, "Eveny, would you like a gin and tonic too?"

"Uh," I say. Chloe nods encouragingly, so I add, "Sure, okay. Thanks."

Arelia makes me a drink, muttering to herself, as Justin wanders over and drapes himself over Chloe's shoulders like a scarf.

"I missed you today," he says, nuzzling her ear.

"Honestly, Justin, I just saw you three hours ago," Chloe replies with a roll of her eyes, but her expression is delighted.

Five minutes later, we're all seated on the soft blanket, holding crystal tumblers full of ice, liquor, lime wedges, and what look like tiny purple verbena flowers. "Cheers to old friends returning," Peregrine says, holding up her glass in a toast. We all raise our glasses, and everyone turns to look at me.

"And to happy reunions?" I say.

"Hear, hear!" Chloe says cheerfully as Justin plays with her hair. We clink glasses, and I watch as everyone takes a long sip of their drinks. I sniff mine suspiciously. Call me crazy, but it doesn't seem like the first day at a new school is the time to start with a liquor habit.

Fortunately, no one seems to notice I'm not drinking. I watch as Chloe wriggles free of Justin to whisper something to Peregrine. Pascal leers at them while licking his lips, and Justin watches Chloe's every movement like his life depends on it. I'm so intrigued by the fact that Margaux and Arelia are unpacking a full lunch of tea sandwiches and salads from a giant picnic basket that I don't notice anyone else approaching the Hickories until a shadow falls over us. I look up and my heart nearly stops.

It's Caleb Shaw, and in his Pointe Laveau uniform, with a charcoal grey hoodie and navy Chuck Taylors, he's even more gorgeous than he was outside the library.

"Oh," is the first thing he says when he realizes I'm sitting there. I could swear that there's some sort of accusation in his eyes as he stares at me.

"Um," I reply, feeling my cheeks heat up.

"Titillating conversation, kids," Peregrine says, looking amused.

I try to think of something to say, but his gaze is turning my brain to mush.

"I think I'm going to eat in the caf today," Caleb says, refocusing on the group.

"Don't be ridiculous, Caleb," Peregrine says. "Or are you just being pissy because you didn't get to go away this weekend?"

"No, I think being pissy is your thing, not mine."

Peregrine rolls her eyes, but she's smiling.

"You eat with us *every* day," Chloe says. "You're not going to be rude to Eveny, are you?"

He glances at me uncertainly.

"Of course not." But he avoids looking at me as he settles on the far end of the blanket.

Peregrine must notice the same thing, because she's looking back and forth between us with a small smile on her face. "Well, then," she says finally, looking at Chloe.

I cast sidelong glances at Caleb while Arelia and Margaux quickly pile sandwich quarters and spoonfuls of macaroni salad onto gold-rimmed bone china plates and hand them out.

I'm the last to receive my food, which Arelia shoves at me. I take a bite of an egg salad sandwich, which is soft and delicious, as the others take big swigs of their cocktails.

"So, how do you concentrate in the afternoon if you drink these at lunch?" I ask after a moment, holding up my drink.

"We don't have to *concentrate,* silly!" Chloe trills. "Besides, that's what the verbena flower is for. It enhances concentration."

I look at her in confusion. When I was a kid, my mom used to make up funny bedtime stories about herbs and their magical powers – which is probably one of the things that got me so interested in botany – so I'm no stranger to superstition. But do these girls truly believe that the verbena is having some sort of effect on them? I recall the strange words of Chloe's mom as she handed me the lemon cake last week, and I realize that maybe the answer is yes.

I watch in silence as they continue to sip and eat. Even in the humidity of midday, everyone's hair is perfect, and the girls' make-up hasn't budged. I'm sure that I, on the other hand, look like I've stuck my finger in a light socket, frizzing my hair and insta-melting the foundation off my face. Yet no one has said anything biting about the way I look, although I'm expecting Peregrine to be full of snide remarks.

Margaux spoons second helpings of macaroni salad on to Pascal's plate as the conversation turns to the Mardi Gras Ball.

"It's the pinnacle of Carrefour social events," Pascal says, settling down next to me as he digs into his salad. He reaches over after a moment and runs a finger up my spine, which makes me shiver. "Maybe you can be my date."

"Maybe," I say non-committally, trying to figure out why an impeccably dressed, smarmily handsome guy like Pascal would have any interest in a human frizzball like me. Perhaps because I'm new?

As if she's reading my mind, Peregrine smirks and says, "Pascal, maybe *you* can refrain from attempting to bang the new girl for at least a few days."

I feel eyes on me again, and this time when I look up, Caleb holds my gaze for a long moment before looking away.

Pascal eventually scoots over to flirt with Margaux, and I see Arelia beginning to gather up the dirty dishes on her own. No one makes a move to help, so I stand, grab a few empty plates and glasses, and make my way over to the picnic basket. I'm about to ask where we wash them – I'm still confused that they eat on china and sip from crystal in the middle of school – but Arelia silences me with a dirty look.

"Just so you know," she says under her breath as Peregrine and Chloe chatter behind us, "it took Margaux and me *years* to become Dolls. So don't make the mistake of assuming that just because you're a Cheval, every door in the world is going to open for you. You still have to work your way up."

"I'm not assuming anything," I reply. I have no idea what she's talking about.

As Arelia snatches the dishes from my hand, I see Caleb stand, hitch his backpack onto his shoulder, and nod goodbye to everyone. As he begins to trudge down the hill, I grab my bag too and quickly thank Peregrine and Chloe for the invitation to eat with them.

"Where are you going in such a hurry, Eveny?" Peregrine asks knowingly.

"Just to class."

"Nothing to do with the cute boy you're chasing after?" Peregrine sing-songs. I can hear them laughing as I dash down the hill to catch up with Caleb.

"Hey," I say, pulling up beside him.

He turns and looks oddly nonplussed to see me. "Oh. Hey."

"So," I begin awkwardly, "I'm Eveny."

"I know." For a moment he looks straight ahead, and I have the feeling he's not going to say anything else. But then, as if he's conceding something, he adds, "The girl who thinks reading is cool."

"Well, it is," I say defensively, which makes him laugh.

But his smile is gone as quickly as it appeared, replaced with an expression that looks inexplicably frustrated. "I'm Caleb," he says.

"I know," I reply. A loaded silence stretches between us. I can't figure out why I'm feeling uneasy, or why he's acting almost stand-offish. "So, what class are you headed to?" I ask.

"American history."

"Oh, me too!" But he doesn't say a word, and we sink back into silence.

This time, it's Caleb who breaks it. "So you moved from New York?" His tone is reluctant, like he doesn't want to be talking to me at all.

"Yeah, really suddenly. It was right before my birthday last week, and my aunt was just like, 'Hey, we're moving back to Louisiana'. I didn't even have time to prepare for it, you know? I mean, one second, I live in New York, the next second, I'm in the passenger seat of a car headed a thousand miles away…"

I realize I'm babbling. I clamp my mouth shut, embarrassed.

"I've always wanted to go," Caleb says a few seconds later, as if I haven't just sounded like a rambling idiot. "To New York, I mean. It looks like it would be a pretty cool place. Millions of people. More restaurants than you could visit in a lifetime. Something for everyone."

I'm hit with a pang of longing. "You'd love it there."

"You miss it, I take it?"

"I do. It's home."

Caleb doesn't reply right away. Finally, he turns to look at me. "I thought you'd be back in Carrefour sooner, to be honest."

The change of topic catches me off guard. "What do you mean? You knew who I was before I got here?"

He half smiles at me but doesn't elaborate. "Anyway, happy birthday," he adds after a pause. "Seventeen's the big one."

"Well, not as big as eighteen," I say.

"Not around here."

EIGHT

CALEB SITS ACROSS THE CLASSROOM and doesn't acknowledge me once during the entire fifty-minute period. When the bell rings, he strides out without looking back, and by the time I make it into the hallway, he's completely gone. I hate that this leaves me feeling so disappointed.

I'm relieved to find Liv, the girl from this morning, saving a seat for me in physics, my last class.

"How was your first day?" she asks as I sit down beside her.

"Honestly? Kind of weird."

"That's pretty much every day at Pointe Laveau. I found that out last year when I transferred from Carrefour Secondary. You might as well know I'm from the Périphérie."

"Cool. My friend Drew lives there too. Actually, I was just out there last night with him for a crawfish boil."

"Drew Grady? How do you know him?"

"Our moms were friends when we were kids."

She stares at me oddly as the bell rings. The middle-aged, bespectacled Mr Cronin welcomes me to class and launches into a lecture about action and reaction. When he finishes and assigns us to review chapters six and seven with a partner, Liv and I resume our conversation.

"I'm sorry, you said you went to the Périphérie last night?" Liv asks.

"Right," I say. I don't get why she's reacting like I've told her I went to Mars.

"But you live on this side of town, don't you?"

"Yes," I say slowly.

"It's just that usually people from this side of town don't spend much time on the other side of the bayou." She shakes her head. "Anyway, Drew's a cool guy. Did he tell you about his band?"

"I think I heard the term 'bayou fusion rock' fifty times last night."

She smiles. "He's a little obsessed. He kind of considers music his ticket out of this town. I've got to say, I think he's kind of onto something."

"His band's good?"

"They're awesome. I'm planning to go to school for music production someday, and I think it would be pretty cool to work with a group like that." She pauses. "Anyway,

I know how you must feel, being new and all. I started at the beginning of sophomore year, and it was like no one wanted anything to do with me. Newcomers aren't exactly welcomed with open arms."

"I'm noticing that," I tell her. "So how did you wind up here?"

"The kid with the scholarship before me flunked out. When the spot was offered to me, my dad wouldn't even listen."

Her tone is bitter, but only a little. "Switching to this school, it's like crossing a line. People expect you to be different, so it's harder to hang out with everyone back home. But I don't fit at Pointe Laveau because I'm from the Périphérie."

"People really judge you for that?" I ask.

She looks at me like I'm nuts. "Dude, it's the *poor* side of town. That means everything in this place." She pauses. "So what brought you to Carrefour anyhow? We never get new people."

"I'm not exactly new." I tell her what happened with my mother and moving away.

"Your mom's the one who committed suicide? Man, I'm sorry. I remember hearing about that." She looks genuinely sad.

When the bell rings at the end of class, everyone scrambles to grab their bags and dash for the door. Liv walks out with me and hands me a slip of paper with her phone number.

"It's nice to have someone new here," she says. "Other than my best friend Max, who I'll introduce you to tomorrow, and Drew, who's cool, this whole school is really lame."

"What about Peregrine and Chloe and their friends?" I ask carefully.

Liv snorts. "If you're into staring at yourself in the mirror, getting wasted, and maxing out your mother's credit cards, then yeah, they're awesome."

As if on cue, the Dolls round the corner in a cluster. "Eveny!" Peregrine exclaims, stopping in front of us and ignoring Liv entirely. The whole clique draws to a halt behind her. "How was your first day, darling?" Then, without waiting for an answer, she rolls on. "Listen, Chloe and I have a surprise for you! We're getting you a haircut and a makeover on Thursday after school. We've already scheduled an appointment for you at Cristof's Salon."

"But—" I begin to protest, weakly reaching up to touch my tangled mass of red curls. Much as it would be nice to look a little better than I do now, I think I have a grand total of about seventeen dollars in my bank account at the moment. I'm guessing Cristof's services cost more than that. "I'm not sure I can afford it."

"Don't be ridiculous. It's our treat," Peregrine cuts me off.

"We won't take no for an answer. Consider it a happy birthday and welcome-back-to-town gift."

Before I can reply, the Dolls are already walking away. Arelia casts me a dirty look over her shoulder, and then they turn the corner and are gone.

When I look back at Liv, she's staring at me suspiciously. "You're friends with *them*?"

"My mom was friends with their moms," I try to explain.

"That doesn't answer why they seem to think you're their new BFF."

"I know," I say helplessly. "I don't understand it either."

"Right," she says. "Well, I'll see you tomorrow." As she walks away, I know a wall has gone up between us. I wonder if the Dolls have done something cruel to Liv, and suddenly, I feel guilty. But even though all the logic in me tells me I should steer clear, I'm feeling more and more drawn to them by the day. It's like they hold the key to who I once was – and who I'm supposed to be.

Everyone else is roaring out of the parking lot in their expensive cars, but Aunt Bea left a voicemail saying that she's tied up with something at the bakery and can't reach Boniface to ask him to get me, so I'm stuck walking home. I don't mind, actually. I used to walk all the time in

New York; it was a chance to be alone with my thoughts, even in a sea of people.

But fifteen minutes later, the sun disappears completely, the humidity becomes oppressive, and the clouds turn black. I quicken my pace, but I'm only halfway around the cemetery when there's a deep, earth-shaking rumble and the skies open up.

I curse and begin running towards my house, but the rain is coming down in driving torrents, soaking me to the core, and the road is getting muddier by the second. Lightning is flashing everywhere, sending electricity crackling through the air. The wind is holding me back, and I look up nervously at all the arching oak and cypress trees over the road; any of them could be a lightning rod in a storm. It would be just my luck to have survived my first day of school only to get electrocuted on the way home.

As I trip and fall over a branch in the road, sending mud splattering all over my uniform, I notice a black Jeep Cherokee with a faded surfboard strapped to the top pulling up on my left.

"Get in!" yells the driver through the open window. It takes me a moment of wiping the rain out of my eyes to realize it's Caleb. I scramble ungracefully to my feet, slosh through a puddle, yank the door open, and tumble inside.

"Sorry about your seat," I say as my drenched skirt squishes loudly against the vinyl.

"It'll dry," Caleb replies. As soon as I shut the door behind me, he guns the engine and continues up the road without another word.

"Thanks for stopping," I say. I smooth my hair a little but suspect it doesn't help. "So you live out in this direction too?" I have to raise my voice to be heard over the roar of the downpour.

He nods, and for a moment I'm afraid he's not going to answer. Then he says, "Other side of the cemetery from your place."

"How do you know where I live?"

"Eveny, everyone knows. Your family is as legendary in this town as Chloe's and Peregrine's." He doesn't elaborate, nor does he look at me.

"So," I say, bridging the silence. "I heard you aced your PSATs." And then, because I apparently have some sort of disease that makes me blurt out idiotic things in front of handsome, enigmatic guys, I hear myself add, "Rock on."

I can see him hiding a smile. "No big deal," he says gruffly. But then he adds, "Does that mean you've been checking up on me?"

"What? No. Of course not." I can feel my cheeks turning red. "But I did notice that you surf." Outside, there's a huge roll of thunder, and lightning crackles across the sky.

"How do you know that?"

I point upwards. "There's a board strapped to the roof."

He laughs. "Right. Yeah, I take my board out whenever I get a chance. Or I used to, anyhow. I won't be going much any more." A muscle in his jaw twitches as his expression hardens.

He probably wants me to shut up, but it's not every day you meet a hot surfer who also happens to be a mysterious PSAT-acing genius, and I'm desperate to know more about him. "So, surfing, huh? I thought we were pretty landlocked here," I say.

"We are." For the first time since I've met him, his face relaxes a little. "I actually drive to a beach in the Florida Panhandle called Sailfish Island, which is about four and a half hours away." A faraway look crosses his eyes for a moment as he adds, "You wouldn't believe the way the sunrise looks over the Gulf from the east side of the island."

"Sounds beautiful," I say, embarrassed that I'm suddenly picturing myself with Caleb on a beach watching the sun come up. Stupid overactive imagination. "So you think you'll get out there again soon?"

Everything in his face immediately shuts down. "Things are different now. It's a long story." He stares straight ahead, and I have the strangest feeling he's suddenly mad at me.

I try to make casual conversation as Caleb turns onto the road leading up the hill towards my house, but his only replies are one-word answers.

By the time he pulls up my driveway and sweeps the Jeep around in front of the house, the silence and tension in the car are so thick I can feel them.

"Well," I say awkwardly, grabbing my sopping backpack from the floor, "thank you again."

When he doesn't reply, I get out into the rain, which is pounding down so hard that I barely hear him say, "Rock on, Eveny," in that perfect, deep voice of his, just before I slam the door closed.

And then, before I have the chance to react, he's already pulling away.

NINE

THE STORMS HAVE PASSED BY that evening, but the humidity lingers in the air, making it hard to breathe. Drew is still out sick, and I try calling him a few times but it goes straight to voicemail. I remind him he's invited to Aunt Bea's bakery opening on Wednesday night, but he texts back that he's not sure he'll feel well enough to be there.

I eat lunch Tuesday and Wednesday inside the caf with Liv and her friend Max, a scrawny, smart guy who wears thick hipster glasses and announces right away that he's gay. "Just so you don't accidentally develop a crush on me," he adds quite seriously. "It's been known to happen." He tells me that he's from central Carrefour instead of the Périphérie, but that he's always been kind of different from the other kids at Pointe Laveau, so he has that in common with Liv.

"You may have noticed," he says stiffly, "that unless you get a blessing from Peregrine and Chloe, you might as well not exist around here."

Liv chomps angrily on her burger and says, "Eveny *hasn't* noticed, considering the Dolls are, like, totally fixated on her."

And as bizarre as it seems, she's right. Peregrine and Chloe beam at me in English class, wave hello to me in the halls, and seem bewildered when I say I'll be eating in the caf instead of the Hickories.

"But no one *ever* turns down an invitation to eat with us," Chloe tells me Wednesday, looking truly baffled as she wanders away from me and heads outside.

The thing is, even though I know it's supposed to be some kind of huge deal to be invited into the Dolls' inner circle, I'd prefer to eat with people I like. And I like Liv and Max. They remind me of my friends back in New York, but more than that, they're *normal*. The Dolls, on the other hand, seem like they're from Planet Glamour. I look out the window at their tree-shaded spot overlooking the school, and I see both Peregrine and Chloe gazing at me coolly, as if they can read my mind.

"Told you that you couldn't just automatically become one of us," Arelia trills as she passes me in the hall on the way to fifth period.

"I never said I wanted to," I reply sweetly, although she's

already disappearing around the corner with Margaux. But I feel a little annoyed that she apparently thinks I've been banished from the Hickories for not being cool enough.

Caleb Shaw is the one flaw in my plan, because if I exile myself from the glamazons in the Hickories, I'll be writing myself out of his life too. He doesn't even look at me in American history, the one class we share, though I have the weirdest feeling he's aware of my every move. He shifts in his seat each time I shift in mine, and sometimes I swear I can feel his eyes on me even though he's always gazing off into space when I turn around.

Boniface picks me up after school on Wednesday and drives me the short distance to Aunt Bea's bakery for the opening.

"Any luck finding the key for the parlour doors?" I ask him on the way. I still can't shake the nightmares I've had twice now, and I've begun to think that the only way to convince myself they're just dreams is to get inside the room.

"Not yet, Eveny," he says, and the uneasy feeling sticks with me as we drive the rest of the way to Main Street in silence.

Aunt Bea is rushing around like a flour-covered maniac when we get there, and the bakery smells heavenly. The plan for the opening night party is that she'll have miniature versions of a dozen of her signature pastries circulated by two waiters. Because the shop is so tiny, the celebration will spill out onto the street, so Boniface heads outside to set up a few high-top tables and tablecloths while I go into the back to help frost miniature cakes.

"Did you invite any of your new friends?" Aunt Bea asks hopefully as she hands me a pastry-decorating bag filled with lemon-thyme icing for the olive oil cakes.

"A few," I tell her as I carefully pipe the pale yellow icing. "I texted Drew, but he's been out sick. There's a girl Liv at school who might make it, and maybe this guy Max too."

The timer goes off on one of her ovens, and she turns to remove a baking sheet full of chocolate mint meringues. "And how about Peregrine and Chloe?"

"I didn't ask them."

"They might come with their mothers," Aunt Bea says lightly. "I felt like I needed to invite them since they were such close friends of your mom's."

"Makes sense."

Aunt Bea peers at me curiously. "You aren't getting along with them?"

"I'm not *not* getting along with them," I hedge. "They've actually been pretty nice to me. It's just that they're so…different." She waits for me to continue, and after a moment, I add, "I guess I don't really get why they want to be friends with me. They're completely opposite from me in every way."

Aunt Bea turns away and begins to frost a big trayful of chocolate lavender cakes. "Tradition means a lot in this town," she says.

"Everyone keeps saying that," I say, "but I have to be friends with them just because my great-great-grandma liked their great-great-grandma?"

"It's more than that. But I'm glad you're a little sceptical. It's important that you remember who you are and how I raised you."

Three hours later, the bakery and sidewalk out front are filled with at least a hundred people. Everyone seems to know Aunt Bea and Boniface, and I watch with pride as they circulate among the crowd.

Along with the chocolate lavender cakes, the lemon-thyme olive oil cakes, and the chocolate mint meringues, Aunt Bea has also prepared butter sage cookies, rosemary popcorn balls, pear and bay leaf tarts, and several other herb-based confections. "I wanted to honour my sister, Sandrine, whom many of you knew," Aunt Bea says in an impromptu speech on the front step just past six thirty. "She loved flowers and herbs, so we'll specialize in just that: baked goods with an herbal or floral twist. I hope you enjoy tonight's party, and please do come see me again soon."

The crowd applauds and goes back to chowing down. I feel proud of Aunt Bea and especially connected to my mother as I jump behind the counter and help the two harried waiters fill up champagne flutes. Liv and Max make a brief appearance and thank me politely for inviting them, but they disappear soon after, Liv mumbling that this isn't exactly her crowd. I don't have time to feel bad, though, because Peregrine, Chloe and the other Dolls sweep in a few minutes later.

"So sorry we're late, sweetie," Peregrine says as she glides over to me. She's wearing a floor-length leather coat, a leather miniskirt, a sheer silk blouse, and leather stiletto heels that lace up to her knees. Her stone necklace catches the pale light of the bakery and shimmers against her dark skin. "But it's dreadfully tacky to arrive on time, don't you think?"

I open my mouth to reply, but Chloe beats me to it. "We really did mean to be here earlier," she says. "But Pascal couldn't decide on a pair of shoes."

He looks offended. "I have over a hundred," he says. "And I wanted to look just right."

"You look nice," I say. And aside from his smarmy expression, he does. He's in a tailored black suit with an eggplant-coloured shirt that's unbuttoned at the collar. The expensive-looking tasselled leather loafers he's wearing complete the look.

"They're Italian," he says, gesturing to his shoes. "Custom made."

Chloe looks like she's channelling vintage Carrie Bradshaw in a frilly pale pink tutu made from a hundred layers of tulle. Her legs look long and tanned, and she's wearing camel-coloured stiletto ankle boots, a tight, military-style camel leather jacket, and an intricately beaded white tank top to complete the look. Like Peregrine, she's wearing her black stone necklace. Justin, in designer jeans and a suit jacket with a lime green pocket square, is draped on her arm like an accessory. "This place is gorgeous, Eveny," he tells me before asking if that was Max and Liv he saw just a few minutes ago. He looks weirdly disappointed when I tell him they've already gone.

Arelia and Margaux are there too, wearing nearly matching little black dresses.

"Where's Caleb?" I whisper to Chloe as the others move towards the bakery counter to grab drinks.

"Ah, so you *do* like him," she says knowingly. "Peregrine was right."

"No." I can feel myself turning red. "I mean, I barely know him. I just thought he was always with you guys."

"Not always," she says. "He goes away a lot."

"Surfing, right?"

She looks surprised. "I see you've talked to him." When I nod, she looks troubled. "Just so you know, he kind of broke Peregrine's heart last year."

I feel like she's dumped a bucket of water over my head. "He and Peregrine dated?"

But then Chloe leans closer and says, "Don't tell Peregrine I told you, but I don't know if I'd call it dating exactly. She was in love with him for ever, and they finally went out on a few dates, but nothing ever happened."

"Do you know why?"

"I just don't think he was that into her."

"Come on. That's impossible."

"No, Caleb's different. I think that's what drove Peregrine nuts: the idea that he wasn't automatically attracted to her like every other guy in the world." The corner of Chloe's mouth twitches, and I have the feeling that she was at least a little bit glad to see someone reject Peregrine. "Anyway, she hasn't dated anyone since then."

"But she's surrounded by guys every time I see her."

"I didn't say she doesn't make out or have fun with them. She just doesn't let them in any more."

"So she still likes Caleb?" I wonder if being interested in him makes me a traitor to the girl who's inexplicably trying to befriend me. Not that I owe Peregrine anything.

"They're just good friends now. But I think she's still pissed that she couldn't have him. Anyway, I'd be careful, that's all."

She lingers for a moment like she wants to say more, but then she drifts away. Shortly thereafter, she and the

Dolls leave without saying goodbye.

It's not until the party is winding down and the last few stragglers are finishing their champagne that I spot him. Or at least I think I do. He's standing outside the bakery window, dressed in jeans and a tight grey T-shirt. But his face is obscured by the shadows, so I'm not one hundred per cent sure.

I hurry out the front door of the bakery. "Caleb?" I call. But the street is empty, and I feel foolish. I've reached a real low point if I'm conjuring imaginary images of the guy I'm developing a very real crush on.

"Ready to head home?" Aunt Bea comes up behind me and puts a hand on my shoulder. "I'm beat. I can do all the clean-up tomorrow morning."

"Sounds good," I reply. "Mom would be really proud of you, Aunt Bea."

She gives me a hug. "She'd be proud of you too, honey," she says. "In so very many ways."

I'm wound up from the party and confused about Peregrine and Caleb's dating history and Chloe's warning, so it takes me until almost two in the morning to drift off into an uneasy sleep.

For the first time in almost a week, the strange nightmare returns. I'm floating down the stairs again, and just like before, the hallway begins to fill with blood. But now there are voices too, coming from behind the closed doors.

For each ray of light, there's a stroke of dark.
For each possibility, one has gone.
For each action, a reaction.
Ever in balance, the world spins on.

The voices fade away as I float into the parlour, which I now notice has walls lined with broad crystal mirrors. When I blink into the darkness, I can just barely make out the shape of the toddler version of myself standing in blood, crying.

"Eveny!" I call to her, but she can't hear me. She falls to her knees in the darkness, still sobbing. "Eveny!" I cry out again, and this time she turns, her face and hands streaked with blood...

I awaken with a start, drenched in sweat. The visions are getting more and more vivid; this one was like watching a movie on a high-definition screen. I've never dreamed like this before. *What the hell is going on here?*

I try to go back to sleep, but it's impossible. After a while, I glance at my clock and see that it's 2.36 a.m. I flick my bedside light on and get up. Maybe I'll feel better if I can get into the parlour and reassure myself that the dreams aren't real.

I rifle through my bag until I find a couple of paper clips in a side pocket, then I quickly bend one so that it's a single long piece of metal and the other so that it's folded over once on itself: a picklock, like Mer taught me to make last summer when I was locked out of my apartment. I shove both makeshift tools into the pocket of my sweatpants, grab a flashlight, and head out my bedroom door.

I creep down the stairs, keeping my flashlight aimed low. In the front hall, I bend to inspect the floor just outside the parlour. This is the spot where the blood always pools in my nightmare, but of course it looks completely normal now. *It's just a dream, you dork,* I tell myself. But then I touch the ground to get my balance as I stand up, and for the quickest of instants, I catch a flash of crimson staining the beautiful hardwood.

"You're seeing things," I tell myself aloud. But when I reach tentatively for the floor again, the dark stain reappears the moment my index finger makes contact. I hold it there this time long enough to notice two tiny, child-sized footprints in the faded stain. I stand up, and the floor returns to looking normal.

"What the…?" I whisper. I reach for the thick brass handle of the parlour door, but I pull away as soon as my fingers make contact. It's burning hot. I try again, holding on tighter as I tug hard, and when I yank my hand back, my palm is a scalded red.

My hand shaking, I pull the paper clip tools from my pocket and prepare to insert the longer one into the lock on the door. But the second metal touches metal, I'm struck with a jolt of electricity so sharp that I'm thrown backwards.

Completely weirded out, I scramble to my feet and place my palm against the wood of the door, trying to steady myself. But the instant my skin makes contact, I'm hit with a vivid image.

There's blood everywhere, and suddenly, a shadow in the corner of the parlour catches my eye. Before I have a chance to call out or see who it is, the figure slips out the door in silence...

I yank my hand away. "This can't be happening."

I take a deep breath and reach for the door once more, tentatively, but nothing happens. I pull away and try again, but when my finger connects with the door, there's nothing unusual about it, no uninvited images of blood and shadows.

Slowly, I back away. Am I losing my mind?

But when I look down at my right palm, it's still red, throbbing, and painful – proof that I'm not imagining things.

Something's going on, but whatever secrets this house is holding, it's not giving them up tonight.

* * *

After smearing Neosporin on my hand, I wander into the living room, my heart still racing wildly.

I sit on the sofa and reach for the framed photo of my mom on the coffee table to the left. Thinking about her always helps centre me, and I feel as off-kilter now as I ever have. "What the heck is going on in this house, Mom?" I ask the photo, which was taken on her wedding day. She's standing in the garden, wearing a beautiful gown of layered lace, her red hair done up in an elaborate twist. She's laughing and looking at someone off to the side of the photo, but I can't see who it is. Curious, I turn the frame over and gently begin to slide the photo out. As I do, another picture, which was hiding behind the wedding one, flutters to the floor.

I bend to pick it up, and I'm so surprised that I almost drop it. It's a photo of me when I was two or three months old, my red curls so vibrant that I look like a Raggedy Ann doll. My mother is holding me, her expression serene and happy, but what shocks me is the sandy-haired man beside her, his arm slung around her shoulders, staring down at me lovingly.

It's my father – the father Aunt Bea always told me left before I was born and never returned.

"That's impossible," I say aloud. But the image is unmistakable.

I turn the photo over after a moment and am even more surprised to see a note scribbled on the back.

I'll watch over Eveny always.
— Love eternal, Matthias

Not only had my father come back to see my mother and me, but he'd made her a promise that he'd always watch over me.

The image from the cemetery, the one that hit me so vividly as we entered Carrefour last week, flashes through my mind again as clear as day. *They're coming for you*, my father said. *You have to be ready.*

So was the cemetery recollection a dream, or had he really been watching over me like he promised? And does Aunt Bea know he'd come back at least once? I'm still staring at the back of the photo in confusion when something outside catches my eye.

I blink into the darkness beyond the back window. For a moment, I think I'm imagining things, but then I see it: three faint beams of light bobbing through the gloom of the cemetery beyond the garden wall.

I jump to my feet and press my nose against the glass as I peer out into the blackness. There's no mistaking it: three shadowy figures are making their way through the maze of tombs beyond our back wall. Suddenly, I have the crazy sense that whatever's going on out there is connected to the dreams I'm having and the weird mystery of my own house.

Before I can question my own sanity – and let's face it, I'm pretty sure I'm losing it anyhow – I grab my flashlight and stuff my bare feet into an old pair of Aunt Bea's ballet flats I find lying in the laundry room. I'm careful to open and close the back door as quietly as possible, and I keep the flashlight off. The moon overhead provides just enough light to see.

It's only once I've landed in the mud on the cemetery side of the wall that I realize exactly what I've done. I've dashed out of my house without leaving a note, climbed into a creepy cemetery in the middle of the night, and am pursuing a group of people sneaking around in the darkness – all because of a completely baseless theory.

"Brilliant, Eveny," I mutter. I'm just about to turn back when I hear it: a faint, female voice in the distance, singing words I'm beginning to know well.

For each ray of light, there's a stroke of dark.
For each possibility, one has gone.
For each action, a reaction.
Ever in balance, the world spins on.

Just like in my dream and on the hallway wall.
Now I'm desperate to know what's happening. My heart hammers faster as I make my way deeper into the cemetery, the light of the half-moon growing fainter above

the thick canopy of trees. I can clearly see the three beams of light now, bouncing towards a small clearing up ahead. I flatten myself against a tomb and pray that no one is looking in my direction. Carefully, I peer around the edge.

I notice three things at once in the pale light of the moon.

First, there are at least two dozen candles flickering on the ground, laid out in a circle.

Second, the three people standing in the middle of the circle, eyes closed, hands raised to the sky, are Peregrine, Chloe and Pascal.

And finally, Audowido is winding his way slowly down one of Peregrine's outstretched arms, his scaly body reflecting the moonlight as he hisses into the silence of the night.

TEN

I WATCH IN SHOCK AS Audowido slithers to the ground and Peregrine begins calling out loudly to someone or something called Eloi Oke – El-ooh-ah Oh-key. "Come to us now, Eloi Oke, and open the gate. Come to us now, Eloi Oke, and open the gate. Come to us now, Eloi Oke, and open the gate."

She pounds on the ground with a big, gnarled stick, while Chloe holds up a huge silver triangle dangling from a string and strikes it once before dropping it. I half expect the earth to open up beneath them, but all that happens is an unnatural calm settles over the cemetery as the air goes completely still.

Peregrine releases the stick and joins hands with Chloe and Pascal, whose eyes are closed. All three of them look like they're in some sort of trance, and I wonder for a moment if they're drunk, or maybe even high. Peregrine says something else, in a language I don't understand, and then she repeats the phrase twice more.

Chloe and Pascal begin to dance slowly, their feet thudding against the ground in an unhurried, deliberate rhythm, their hips swaying in time. After a moment, Peregrine joins in too, and I realize I can hear a distant, musical tinkling sound. Then I see the moonlight glinting off tiny bells attached to all of their wrists and ankles. The breeze that has picked up out of nowhere carries the sound skywards.

The dancing gets faster and wilder as Peregrine chants more urgently in a sultry, velvety voice. Soon Chloe is singing along with her, her voice sweeter and higher. Pascal is the last to join in, his voice gravelly and low. Audowido is coiled in the middle of the circle now, and as the song gets louder, he begins to rise up towards the half-moon, his body weaving in time. Suddenly, he turns his head towards me and freezes as his eyes lock with mine.

It takes all my self-control to keep from screaming. If I didn't know better, I'd think the damned snake had just cracked a small, satisfied smile. After a long moment, he turns his gaze skywards and begins swaying to the music again. I fall back against the tomb as Peregrine, Chloe and Pascal abruptly let go of each other's hands and open their eyes. Audowido retreats back into the studded leather bag, and Peregrine waits for him to vanish before she kneels in the dirt and begins digging with her bare hands. After a moment she stands and brushes her hands off.

"It shall be done," Chloe says solemnly. She pulls a cloth bag out of her pocket and sprinkles some sort of black powder in the shallow hole.

"It shall be done," Pascal echoes, pulling a cloth bag from his own pocket and doing the same thing.

"It shall be done," Peregrine says solemnly, sprinkling powder of her own into the hole.

They join hands again, and this time, while their chanting is louder, I can't understand most of the words.

"*Fantom nan sot pase a, tande sa pledwaye nou an,*" they say together. "*Move lespri a sot pase a, tande sa pledwaye nou an.*"

There's a sudden chill in the air, like the temperature has dropped twenty degrees. I shiver and begin to back away slowly, but I stop in my tracks when I hear them say a familiar name – Justin Cooper. I also hear them chant the name of a guy I don't know, someone named Beau Fontenot. I squint into the darkness to see what they're doing, and my eyes widen when I see each of the girls holding up a small rag doll.

They throw the dolls into the shallow hole, then kneel on the ground and smooth dirt back over the open space. When the ground is flat and the dolls have been buried, each of them spits on the earth. Once they're standing again, Peregrine begins to chant: "Dandelion and mojo beans, sandalwood and lemon balm, we draw your power. Spirits, open the gates of Carrefour on Saturday night." She holds up a handful of herbs to the sky, then she drops them on the ground, reaches for the stone that dangles around her neck, and joins hands with the others.

I hear them say twice in unison something that sounds like "*Mesi, zanset.*" But before they can say the words a third time, Chloe pulls away.

"We can't do this," she says. "It's wrong."

Peregrine rolls her eyes and tries to grab Chloe's hand. "Oh come on, goody-two-shoes," she says. "You don't have a problem when we're making boys fall in love with *you*, but now you don't want to complete *my* charm?"

Goosebumps prickle up and down my arms as I try to process what they're saying.

"This is different," Chloe says in a small voice. "Especially after Glory…"

Peregrine laughs, and the sound cuts through the still night air like a knife. "Glory's death had nothing to do with this."

"But don't you think we should be trying to figure out what happened to her instead of playing?" Chloe asks.

"You don't think I'm doing that?" Peregrine demands.

"I'm exhausted. There's no harm in creating a teeny, tiny exception to the protection charm so that we can have a little fun as a reward for all our hard work."

"I just really, really don't think it's a good idea," Chloe replies.

Peregrine's eyes narrow, and she says, "Well, I didn't think it was a good idea to cast a charm on Hazel Arceneaux when she tried to hit on Justin, did I? But I did it because it was important to you."

"That's different," Chloe mumbles. "Justin's my soulmate."

"You're being a hypocrite," Peregrine says calmly. "Now are you in, or am I going to have to throw this party all by myself?"

I wait for Chloe to fight back, but instead she says something under her breath, grabs the hands of Peregrine and Pascal, and says along with them in a low voice, "*Mesi, zanset.*"

"There," Peregrine says, dropping Chloe's hand. "Was that so bad?"

"I hate you sometimes," Chloe says, but I can see a small smile on her face, and Peregrine begins to laugh.

Pascal is watching them with his arms crossed over his chest. "Are you sure it worked?"

Peregrine glares at him. "Of course it did."

"I was really looking forward to the idea of hot

sorority girls arriving on our doorstep like pizza delivery," he continues. "But usually we can feel it if a charm works, and I didn't feel a damned thing this time."

"Me neither," Chloe agrees. She hesitates and adds in a small voice. "Maybe we're running out of power."

"You two are so tiresome." Peregrine sighs.

"Don't you think it's maybe time we get Eveny involved?" Chloe asks.

What the...

"It's not like we have a choice," Peregrine mutters.

"So we'll talk to her tomorrow?" Chloe asks.

"You better hope you're right about her," Pascal says, "or everything goes to hell around here."

Without waiting for a reply, he strides off into the darkness, away from where I'm standing.

"I don't think she knows anything yet," Chloe says stiffly after the sound of his footsteps has faded. "At all."

Peregrine makes a noise. "Well, her hippie aunt is completely useless. What do you expect?"

Chloe kicks at the dirt. "I don't know. In a way, it must have been kind of nice to have a normal life all these years, don't you think?"

"A normal life?" Peregrine repeats. "I can't think of anything more pointless. Not when you have powers like ours."

She grabs her bag from the ground, stomping off before

Chloe can respond. After a moment, Chloe scrambles after her.

I stand still for a good five minutes to make absolutely sure Peregrine, Chloe, and Pascal are gone. Then I give in to the weakness in my knees and slowly slide down the tomb until I'm sitting in the dirt. I can't understand why they'd mention Aunt Bea and me.

I knew the Dolls were odd, but is it possible they actually believe they have some sort of magical powers? Though as much as I want to dismiss what I just saw as some sort of sorority ritual, I can't deny the way the air got deathly still the instant they began their ceremony, or how a breeze picked up as soon as they began to dance.

I struggle to my feet and creep into the clearing, which is bathed in lemon meringue moonlight. It appears to be a well-defined crossroads. Three of the four corners are grave plots, filled with shadowy, aboveground tombs and mausoleums of all shapes and sizes. The fourth corner, where I saw them bury the dolls, sits entirely empty, except for the handful of herbs Peregrine threw to the ground. I bend to look at them and am startled to realize they're an ashy, burned black. I could have sworn they were alive when she let them go.

I take a deep breath and begin digging with my left hand; my right is still throbbing from grabbing the parlour door. Side by side in the hole lie two dolls, each with a name written across it, a lock of hair glued to it, and a feather pinned to it. The one that says *Justin Cooper* has a pale pink feather, and the one that says *Beau Fontenot* sports a bright red feather. The dolls have crudely sewn *x*'s where their mouths and eyes should be. Like the real-life Justin, the miniature version has brown hair and is wearing pants and a shirt that vaguely resemble the Pointe Laveau uniform. Beau is sporting a purple letter jacket.

I can't possibly piece together everything I just saw while squatting in the middle of a cemetery, so I shove the Justin doll in my pocket and push the dirt back over the other doll. I stand up, my legs shaking, and make a run for it towards my house, no longer caring if I make noise.

ELEVEN

A FEW MINUTES BEFORE SEVEN the next morning, I sit down across from Aunt Bea, who looks wide awake and cheerful after her successful opening. "Morning, hon," she says through a mouthful of Cheerios. She's reading the New York Times on her iPad, just like she does every day at the breakfast table. She looks up at me and the smile falls from her face. "What's wrong?"

I take a deep breath. "Aunt Bea, there's some seriously strange shit going on in this town, and I want to know what it is." I do my best to look threatening.

She sets her iPad down. I can tell she's trying to appear casual as she says, "What would make you say that, Eveny?"

"Drew said something about satanic rituals in town, and I thought he was just being dramatic until I saw

Peregrine, Chloe and Pascal perform a ceremony in the cemetery last night."

She blinks a few times. "What were you doing in the cemetery?"

"You're missing the point."

"Okay." She looks at the table. "Well, first of all, I can assure you that nothing like satanism is going on here. That's just idle gossip."

"Oh come on. This town is cut off from the outside world by a big, creepy gate! Everything's in bloom, even though it's January! But you drive a half mile away across the bayou, and it's winter again." I'm ticking things off on my fingers as I go. "I've been having bad dreams about the parlour, and last night I burned my hand trying to open the door. And now, the daughters of Mom's best friends, who look and dress like supermodel gabillionaires, are sneaking around in cemeteries at night, casting spells on people! You're going to tell me nothing's going on?"

"Charms," my aunt murmurs. "Not spells." As she takes a bite of her Cheerios, her hand is shaking so hard I can hear her spoon clattering against her teeth. "Why are you so sure I'll know the answers, anyhow?"

"Because I heard them mention you – and me. Not to mention the fact that you've been walking around since we got here saying cryptic things about how I have so much more in common with these girls than I realize. What, am

I supposed to be out there with them, dancing around with snakes and burying voodoo dolls?"

"They're not voodoo dolls," she says right away. When I continue to look at her, she sighs and says, "Look, before we get into an explanation, I need you to tell me that you won't get sucked into all of this before you've had a chance to understand what it's all about."

"I'm not making you any promises until you start being honest with me," I shoot back.

"Well, I guess that's fair." She studies her cereal for a moment. "Okay. To start with, I'm guessing that what you saw in the cemetery was a zandara ceremony."

"A what ceremony?"

"Zandara. It's a kind of magic only practised here in Carrefour."

She stands up from the table and takes her bowl to the sink. I stare at her in disbelief as she washes her leftover cereal down the drain then turns on the disposal. When the rumbling is over, the silence feels dead and all-encompassing.

"Aunt Bea?" I prompt.

"I don't even know where to begin."

"How about at the beginning?"

She nods slowly, and when she speaks again, her voice is firm and steady. "At one time our ancestors were very powerful practitioners of voodoo. But in 1863, they, along with Peregrine's and Chloe's ancestors, struck their own deal with the fates because they felt voodoo was getting too commercialized. The final straw came during the Civil War, when your great-great-great-great-grandmother learned that a Confederate general was purchasing potions and using them to defeat Union soldiers in battle.

"Our ancestors didn't want any part of that," she continues, "so they sought out a powerful spirit named Eloi Oke, who agreed to serve as a gatekeeper between this world and the world of the spirits, and—"

"That's the name I heard them say in the cemetery," I interrupt.

She nods. "He agreed to help in exchange for letting him and some of his friends possess them once a year on Mardi Gras so that they could experience life in human form again. A small price to pay for the power he opens them to."

"Oh yes, being possessed by a ghost," I mutter. "Such a small price to pay."

Aunt Bea ignores me. "So zandara developed as a way to trade for what the queens wanted through communication with different spirits. All the magic centres around living things that grow from the soil, because they're a direct link between life and death. Zandara queens just need to find a spirit who's willing to help them channel the power of those plants once Eloi Oike opens the gate to the nether."

It feels like my head is spinning as I try to keep up. "What's the nether?"

"The world between life and death, where some spirits are stranded for a while. It's people who did something wrong in their lives and can't move on to a peaceful death. They long for human comforts because they're closer to the human world than most spirits. That's how queens barter with them, by providing those things through occasional possession ceremonies."

"And you're saying zandara only exists here in Carrefour?"

"It's where the queens decided to make their home, for their own protection." Aunt Bea's expression grows serious. "Just before the turn of the last century in New Orleans, seven French immigrants who believed the magical arts were evil founded a group called Main de Lumière. They zeroed in on zandara and began a 'Crusade of Light'."

Aunt Bea draws a deep breath before going on. "They started murdering practitioners who were part of your great-great-great-grandmother Eléonore's group, claiming they were cleansing the world of evil.

"In early 1903, a Main de Lumière soldier killed Eléonore's younger daughter, who was three years old at the time." I gasp as Aunt Bea continues. "If he'd killed her firstborn, as he believed he was doing, he would have destroyed zandara for ever. You see, only the firstborn daughter of each of the three queens inherits power, generation after generation, so that the balance of power will never change. Killing a future queen would have ended that family's magical bloodline.

"Eléonore and the other zandara practitioners had to leave New Orleans immediately if they were to escape Main de Lumière's bloodlust," Aunt Bea continues. "They chose the land we're on now because it was out in the middle of nowhere. Crossroads are very powerful in zandara – symbolic of the intersection between this world and the nether – so the queens built a crossroads in the cemetery and performed the founding ceremony of Carrefour there, imbuing the town with power and protection.

"Over the years, the queens and their descendants have let in a few thousand carefully screened outsiders to ward off suspicion," she says. "If they had kept Carrefour to only themselves and their *sosyete* – the small group of trusted insiders they practised their magic with – a town so tiny would have looked suspicious. But allowing the town to grow slowly in a very controlled manner has let Carrefour look from the outside like a typical small bayou town. Most of the families here have no idea that magic is keeping Carrefour afloat, so for a long time, the town existed without raising Main de Lumière's suspicions."

"Wait, Main de Lumière still exists?"

"Unfortunately." Aunt Bea's expression is grave. "In fact, I think it's possible they found you in New York. The way you described the man you thought was following you – pale face, blond hair, slinking around in the shadows – it fits what we know of Main de Lumière soldiers."

"And they're after me because…?"

"As this generation's direct descendant to Eléonore, you're the next in line to the throne."

My mouth goes dry. "I'm a…zandara queen?" I manage.

She looks down for a long time before answering. "I wanted to protect you as long as I could, because I think your mother might still be alive if it wasn't for zandara. And because I wanted you to have better values than this town would have given you. You're different from Peregrine and Chloe, Eveny. They may be your sister queens, but that doesn't mean you have to become one of them."

"This isn't possible." I shake my head. "I've never felt powerful or magical or capable of anything close to what you're talking about."

Aunt Bea frowns. "A queen comes into her abilities on her seventeenth birthday, which means that you wouldn't have begun feeling anything magical until last week."

I stare at her in disbelief. I'm not sure what to ask first, so I settle for the simplest question. "Okay, I can see why we had to leave New York if you thought some Main de Lumière guy had found me, but we could have hidden somewhere cool and far away like London or Paris or the Siberian tundra. Why come back to Carrefour?"

"You're safest here. The whole town is under a protective charm. Unless someone is in possession of a key, which is passed down through generations and bestowed on new families only by the queens, they can't enter. It's like there's an invisible barbed wire fence all around us.

"In fact," she adds, "we believe Main de Lumière has finally found Carrefour after all these years because, without your mom to complete the triumvirate, the protective charms have weakened. Peregrine's and Chloe's mothers have been able to continue performing the annual Mardi Gras Possession ceremony, so they've accrued *some* favours from the spirits, but their power has greatly diminished and so has the protection around the town because there aren't three queens."

"But now that I'm back…" I say in a hollow voice.

"You, Peregrine, and Chloe are all seventeen. That means you're queens now and can begin casting together, restoring the full power of a triumvirate to Carrefour. But," she continues, her face darkening, "I don't trust them, Eveny, and I don't trust their mothers. They've used their magic selfishly and carelessly, drawing power in ways that are strictly forbidden. The town is dying because of it."

"So what am I supposed to do?" I ask desperately.

"I don't know, I really don't." She leans in to kiss me on the forehead and adds, "Remember, there are only a handful of people in town who know about this. You must keep all of it a secret, or you'll put us in terrible danger." She checks her watch and grimaces. "I'm sorry, but I have to go. We can talk more later."

She walks out of the room before I can get another word out.

A moment later, I hear the front door open and slam closed, then the sound of her car's engine being revved in the driveway. By the time I make it to the front window to look outside, she's already gone, leaving me alone with a thousand questions I don't have the answers to.

I stay home from school that day because I can't go off to Pointe Laveau and pretend that things are normal after everything I've just learned. Besides, my brain feels as muddled as if I'd just downed a half-dozen lunchtime gin and tonics in the Hickories. I go out to the garden to try to talk to Boniface, but he's not in his cottage, and I can't find him anywhere on the grounds. I search the house for books or notes that might be related to zandara, but I come up empty on that front too.

I consider calling Peregrine or Chloe, but I realize I have no idea what I'd say. There isn't exactly an approved script for the hey-I-saw-you-performing-a-creepy-ceremony-and-now-I-know-you're-a-queen conversation I'd need to have with them. I pull the Justin doll out and stare at it for a while as if it might be able to provide some answers, but its *x*'s for eyes begin to creep me out, so I shove it back in my desk drawer.

By mid-afternoon, I'm still going crazy over Aunt Bea's crazy revelations when the doorbell rings. I squeeze my eyes shut and hope that whoever it is goes away, but the bell rings again and again. Finally, I hurl myself out of bed and slouch down the stairs. By the time I get to the front hallway, the doorbell has sounded a sixth time, and I'm ready to punch whoever I find standing there.

But when I yank open the front door and see Peregrine and Chloe, my jaw falls. I'm not ready for this yet.

"Why hello, Eveny!" Peregrine trills. She's still wearing her Pointe Laveau uniform, which she has paired with black, thigh-high perforated leather boots and blood-red lipstick. Her smooth black stone with the jagged edge hangs just above the ornate hook and eye of a black fur capelet. She's carrying a huge quilted leather Chanel bag. "We certainly hope we didn't wake you. We were concerned when we didn't see you in school!"

"You were?" I ask sceptically.

"Of course, sweetie!" Chloe chimes in. She's dressed nearly as outrageously in platform ankle boots and a long sable coat that I swear I saw in *Vogue* this month. Her black stone necklace shines against her smooth, tan skin. "Are you all right? Do you need anything?"

I'm not surprised to see that their smiles don't reach their eyes.

"So?" Peregrine prompts after a moment. "Why did you miss school?"

I debate what to say but settle on the truth. "I saw you last night, in the cemetery."

The colour drains from Chloe's face, and Peregrine's expression hardens.

"What is it you think you saw, exactly?" Peregrine asks carefully.

"I saw you practising zandara," I tell her.

Their mouths open into identical *o*'s of surprise.

"You know what zandara is?" Chloe asks. "We figured your aunt hadn't told you yet."

"She hadn't," I say. "Until this morning."

They look at each other and then back at me. "Remarkable," Peregrine breathes. Then she shoots me a dazzling smile.

"What I mean to say is, *perfect*. Chloe and I have been studying for years, so there's no one better to learn from than us.

"But first things first," she adds, leaning forward. "Now that you know the truth, let's go have some fun."

TWELVE

FIVE MINUTES LATER, I'M FOLDED uncomfortably into the back of Peregrine's cherry-red Aston Martin DB Mark III hatchback, after she has sworn up and down that she's left her creepy snake at home. She guns the engine and roars down the hill towards the centre of town while Chloe turns around in the passenger seat and stares at me.

"What?" I finally ask.

"It's just amazing, that's all," she says. "To grow up with no idea about any of this. I can't even imagine what you must be thinking!"

"I don't know what to think."

"Well, I'm sure you have questions," she says excitedly. "Ask us anything!"

"Okay." I hesitate. "How do we cast spells, for example?"

Peregrine rolls her eyes at me in the rear-view mirror.

"They're not *spells*, Eveny. You are not a character in *Bewitched*. They're called *charms*."

"Ignore her," Chloe says. "There are a few things to know: First, all charms have to start with asking Eloi Oke to open the gate so that we can talk to the spirits. Second, they all have to involve herbs or flowers, because we channel our power from them. Third, they always have to be specific. Like you can't say, 'Make all the boys fall in love with me'. Instead you'd have to ask for your own beauty enhancements, or ask for the love of a specific guy. Or both."

"Assuming you're completely lame and believe the best use of your immense power is to make boys love you," Peregrine says with a snort.

Chloe turns red. "Peregrine thinks that only losers fall in love," she tells me.

"No, I believe that only losers use their powers for something so entirely pointless." Peregrine glances at me in the rear-view mirror again. "But while we're on the topic of losers and powers, Eveny, why don't we have you do a little charm with us today? Our strength is much greater when there are three of us, so really, this should be no big deal. It's just to open the gates of Carrefour for one teeny, tiny night so that we can have a fraternity party."

It's the charm I overheard them trying to cast in the cemetery, the one Pascal thought didn't work. "Look, I'm all for the idea of bringing a bunch of hot college guys to town, but are you sure we should be opening the gates if a bunch of magic-haters are out to kill us?" I ask.

"I told you she'd be a nerd about this," Peregrine sing-songs.

"Maybe a better question is why Main de Lumière is after us in the first place. Or didn't your aunt tell you that?"

"Peregrine—" Chloe says in a warning tone.

"It was your great-great-great-grandmother Eléonore's fault," Peregrine says, cutting her off. "*Our* great-great-great-grandmothers were wise enough to realize that if they had this kind of power, they shouldn't waste their time on something as pointless as falling in love. But Eléonore decided she was above all that. She fell for a man and let him get to know her daughters, and look what happened: he killed one of them."

"The murderer was Eléonore's boyfriend?" I ask.

"She was engaged to marry him," Peregrine says smugly. "When she and our ancestors fled to Carrefour before he could finish the job, he vowed that he'd find us, no matter how long it took. It's revenge, pure and simple, passed down through the generations, all because of Eléonore's stupidity."

Chloe takes over. "What she's trying to say, Eveny, is that after Eléonore made that mistake, the queens vowed they'd never let their hearts get in the way again. They need to give birth to continue their bloodlines, but they decided it was easier to have one-night stands and then use zandara to make the men forget. It just uncomplicates things."

It takes me a second to grasp what she's saying. "Wait, your fathers don't have any idea you're their kids?"

"We don't even know who our fathers are," Peregrine says. "And when you don't know someone in the first place, they can never deliberately let you down, like your father did. I mean, our dads don't know we're theirs, but yours *chose* to abandon you."

Peregrine obviously thinks she's pushing my buttons, but I'm not about to waste my time and push back. Instead, I return to the more pressing topic. "So everyone thinks Main de Lumière has found us? Why?"

The question is greeted with silence. Finally, Chloe says, "Because we're fairly certain they killed Glory."

My blood runs cold. "I thought she killed herself. Didn't she?"

"The police chief is part of our mothers' sosyete," Chloe says. "He helped cover up her murder and make it look like a suicide."

"Otherwise it would have panicked everyone, made them leave town. We can't afford for people to be leaving right now, especially in the Périphérie. Our power has to come from somewhere," Peregrine adds.

"What?"

"What Peregrine's trying to say," Chloe interjects, "is that in every great society, there are people of privilege and people who make sacrifices for the people of privilege. You need that separation to keep things balanced. Though we totally make life as comfortable as possible for the people who don't live in central Carrefour!"

"But you don't treat them as equals," I say. When neither of them says anything, I push down my annoyance at their snobby attitude and ask why they suspect Main de Lumière of killing Glory.

"Their pattern is always the same," Chloe explains. "They stab practitioners of magic through the heart, because that's the source of our greatest power. And that's how Glory died."

My mind flicks to my mother. If Glory's suicide was staged, is it possible my mom's was too? But her wounds were to her neck, not her heart... I fight off a sense of disappointment and say, "I thought the charm around the gates was supposed to protect us from intruders getting in."

"Main de Lumière could only have gotten to Glory if they recruited someone who already lives here in Carrefour," Peregrine says. For the first time, she looks worried instead of just smug. "In other words, someone who grew up in town, maybe even someone we're friends with, has turned their back on us and joined Main de Lumière."

I gape at her. "No offence, but with all of this going on, doing some sort of charm to let strangers into town doesn't exactly seem like a genius move."

"First of all, opening the gates isn't going to have any impact on the person who's already here," she snaps. "Second of all, we only invited the very hottest fraternity guys from LSU, and they've all passed their background checks with flying colours. Plus, we'll have Oscar and Patrick, two older guys who work for us, checking IDs at the gate. No one will get in if they're not on the list.

"Besides," she adds, "if Carrefour gets any more boring, there'll be no point in protecting it anyway. Don't you see, Eveny? We can have anything we want. Good grades. Fabulous clothes. Immunity from teachers' punishments. Control over everything. Lust and love from whatever boys we choose. It's all ours. Doesn't that interest you?"

I feel a surge of excitement, despite my trepidation. "Of course it does."

"So you'll join us?" Chloe asks.

"Well...yeah." I suspect I don't have much of a choice, and I have to admit, the possibilities of what this means are tempting.

Peregrine pulls into a space on Main Street, parallel parking in one impressive attempt. I unfold from the backseat and launch myself onto the sidewalk.

"Welcome aboard," Chloe says, linking arms with me

and pulling me towards a pair of pink double doors on the corner. "Now let's get you looking like the queen you are."

Cristof's Salon is opulent and gold-trimmed on the inside, with mirrors lining all the walls, like the parlour of an eighteenth-century French palace. A small, slender man with a goatee and several tiny stud earrings emerges from behind a velvety purple curtain in the back and exclaims, "Dah-lings!" as he rushes over and kisses Peregrine and Chloe on the cheeks. He turns to me. "And *you* must be Eveny." He leans in to kiss me on both cheeks too. "I am Cristof!" he says grandly. "I see you're not a moment too soon. But don't worry, doll, that's what we're here for. We'll fix you up real nice and pretty.

"Sharona!" he yells at the top of his lungs, startling me. A moment later, a round middle-aged woman with rosy cheeks and spiky purple hair emerges from the back wearing a smock. "Sharona," Cristof says, "this here is Eveny, Sandrine Cheval's daughter." The colour drains from Sharona's face as Cristof goes on. "Obviously we have great raw material here, but we have a lot of work to do."

My cheeks continue to flame as Sharona's eyes rake over me. "Dat's a fact," she says in a thick accent.

She takes me over to a chair, leans me back, and begins to wash my hair while Peregrine and Chloe talk in hushed tones with Cristof. By the time Sharona has blotted my hair and led me over to a chair facing a huge oval mirror, the girls have settled into seats behind me.

"So, my dear, what can I do for you today?" Cristof asks as he approaches.

Peregrine answers for me. "She'd like a gloss treatment, of course, and those shaggy split ends will have to go. Also, if her bangs could sweep to the side rather than cut across her forehead like she's a second grader, that would be ideal."

I turn. "I like my bangs," I say. "They're ironic."

Peregrine just looks at me. "They're hideous."

Cristof chuckles. "The gloss, I can do. The bangs, well, that's your department. I cut. I don't make hair grow."

"Right," Peregrine says. She exchanges looks with Chloe, and together, they get up and walk towards me. Peregrine grabs my right hand and Chloe grabs my left. With her free hand, Peregrine reaches up and plucks a single strand from my bangs.

"Ow!" I exclaim.

"Oh give me a break," Peregrine says, rolling her eyes. She grabs my hand again and gestures for Chloe to do the same. In her right hand, she holds up the strand of hair. "Cristof? A flame, please?" she asks.

But he's already approaching with a lit red candle. He hands it to Chloe, who thanks him and thrusts it towards

Peregrine. They squeeze my hands tighter as Peregrine holds my strand of hair over the flame.

Chloe fishes in her pocket for something. Finally, she withdraws a handful of squished herbs, which she hands to Peregrine as she looks towards the ceiling and begins to speak in a low voice. "Come to us now, Eloi Oke, and open the gate. Come to us now, Eloi Oke, and open the gate. Come to us now, Eloi Oke, and open the gate."

There's a subtle shift in the air after she speaks the last word. The room is silent and heavy. Chloe takes a deep breath and continues in a sing-songy voice:

Rosemary roux, marigold dust,
Violet leaf, we draw your power.
Spirits, let there be bangs where there weren't before,
Beauty for Eveny, let it be done.

They release my hands, and as soon as they do, I feel a gust of wind blow through. The herbs in her hand turn to black dust, and the flame on the candle goes out. "*Mesi, zanset,*" she murmurs.

"Not bad," Peregrine says.

"See for yourself." Chloe turns my chair so that I'm facing the mirror.

My jaw drops. My hair is still damp from the shampoo, but I can plainly see that my choppy Bettie Page bangs are no longer there. In their place, there's an elegant swoop that skims across my forehead, grazing my right eyebrow and falling ever so slightly over my left eye. "How did you do that?" I whisper.

Peregrine rolls her eyes. "Seriously?" she asks. "You're impressed with *that*?"

"But you made my bangs grow," I say in astonishment.

"Oh for goodness' sake," Peregrine says. "Get your big girl pants on. This is nothing."

"*I* think you look pretty," Chloe whispers, meeting my gaze in the mirror.

"All right, Cristof," Peregrine says, waving a hand at him. "Do your thing."

"Of course!" Cristof says, sweeping over to us dramatically with a pair of scissors. He reaches for my long bangs and holds them up. He lightly snips the ends and lets them fall gently back on my forehead. "Now, let's get a conditioning treatment on you."

He smears a gel that smells like lavender all over my head and then rolls a big hairdryer over. It looks like a giant helmet, and he instructs me to sit under it for five minutes while the conditioning treatment warms up. "Then we'll rinse and work some magic," he says, winking. "Well, stylistic magic."

He heads towards the velvet curtains in back, leaving me alone with Chloe and Peregrine.

"I thought we weren't supposed to practise zandara in front of people," I say as soon as he's gone.

"Cristof is one of us," Peregrine says.

"Sharona too," Chloe adds.

"They have powers?"

The girls laugh. "No, silly," Chloe says. "But they're both members of our mothers' sosyete. It's fine to work magic in front of those who are part of the sosyete because they're sworn to secrecy, punishable by death."

Peregrine adds, "Not that it's ever come to that. The sosyete members don't have powers of their own, but they're in on the Secret of Carrefour, and they help increase the queens' power as they channel the power of the spirits."

"So if the sosyete members don't have their own powers, what are they there for?" I ask.

"The spirits like to know they have humans who will do favours for them," Peregrine explains. "So only the queens can call upon the dead or use the power they give us, but the sosyete members can enhance our strength during ceremonies just by chanting or dancing along with us. Plus, when they allow themselves to be possessed, the spirits are more likely to help us."

"So in our sosyete it's us three plus Arelia, Margaux, Pascal and Justin," Chloe adds. "Oscar and Patrick, who you'll almost never see, work with us sometimes. Oh yeah, and Caleb Shaw."

I can feel myself flush at the mention of Caleb. I look away as Peregrine raises her eyebrows at me.

"Everyone in our sosyete is a descendant of people who have been involved with the Secret of Carrefour for generations," Chloe goes on. "Once we're a little older, we get to add a few new members too, people we pick and choose. But that doesn't happen until after we've all turned eighteen."

Cristof re-emerges from the back room then, brandishing a pair of scissors. "Ready to be transformed, Eveny?"

I take a deep breath. "Ready as I'll ever be."

Forty minutes, one zandara-charmed facial mask, and one cut and blow-dry later, I look like a different person.

My frizzy hair is gone, replaced with shiny waves that cascade over my shoulders, down to the middle of my back. My bangs sweep perfectly to the side and frame my glowing face. My pimples have all vanished, and my skin looks like it's lit from within. Even my eyelashes, which usually need multiple coats of mascara, have turned dark and lush, and my lips have become pinker and fuller.

"Not bad," Peregrine marvels.

I just stare at myself in the mirror as Chloe squeals, "Eveny, you're gorgeous!"

"I don't even look like me," I say.

"Exactly the point," Peregrine says smugly. "Now, we've taken the liberty of picking out some shoes and accessories for you. The way you've been styling your school uniform" – she pauses and shudders – "just won't do. They should be at your house by the time you arrive home."

"Oh," I say awkwardly. "You shouldn't have done that. What do I owe you?"

"It's our treat," Peregrine says. "Now, let's work on that charm and see what you can do."

They lead me behind Cristof's purple curtain, where several candles flicker in the corner of a small room. Sheer gold scarves are draped over lamps, and incense burns from a small pot on a coffee table. I see three tiny bells, each hanging on a long piece of string, sitting on a chair. Beside them is a cluster of various flowers and herbs.

"Aren't you excited?" Chloe asks. "Think about it, Eveny. You have the power to give yourself anything you want."

"How do you even know I'll be any good at this?" I ask.

Peregrine shrugs. "We don't." She slips a bell on a long piece of twine around my neck. "But there's only one way to find out."

Thirteen

My heart hammers as Peregrine and Chloe grab each other's hands and then mine, so that we're standing in a circle of three.

"I can feel it already," Peregrine says, a dangerous gleam in her eye. "Power."

Chloe turns to me. "Just relax, Eveny, we'll do all the work. Clear your mind and think of this as a two-way street back and forth from the spirit world. It'll just be an easy little ceremony."

Like I saw them do in the cemetery, Peregrine and Chloe call out three times to Eloi Oke to open the gate. Chloe stomps her right foot and the room suddenly goes still. The air feels thick and heavy, as if we're underwater. It's hard to breathe for a moment, but when Chloe and Peregrine release my hands and begin to dance slowly, the air thins out again. Their feet move in a steady right-left-right, left-right-left sashay, with their hips swaying gracefully. I try to follow, and although I feel clunky, I'm sort of getting the hang of it.

As the three of us move in time to Peregrine's voice, I feel a breeze picking up. The candles are snuffed out, and we're plunged into near darkness, the only light coming from a lone scarf-draped lamp in the corner.

"Dill, fern and five-finger grass, we draw your power," Peregrine chants. "Spirits, please open Carrefour's gates to the outside world Saturday night until the hour just before dawn."

Chloe takes over the chanting. "Dandelion and mojo beans, sandalwood and lemon balm, we draw your power. Spirits, please make all of our LSU visitors forget they were here after the gates have closed again." She pauses and adds, almost as an afterthought, "And coriander and cumin, I draw your power. Spirits, please keep Justin faithful."

Peregrine snorts in the darkness but joins Chloe in reciting, "Spirits, open our gates. Spirits, open our gates. Spirits, open our gates. *Mesi, zanset. Mesi, zanset. Mesi, zanset.*"

They stop abruptly, and I'm about to tell them it isn't working when I feel a rush of icy coldness wrap around me. Something solid pushes on my skull from the inside out, and my head throbs. When I try to pull away, I find that my hands are frozen, as if my brain is no longer firing impulses to my limbs. I begin to tell the girls to let me go, to reverse whatever they've done, but my mouth isn't working either. I'm getting colder and colder until my entire body is prickling with icy pain. The room begins to look blurry, and I wonder fleetingly if I'm dying.

Suddenly, something moves inside me, and my fear turns to flat-out terror. It's like there's another person fighting for room in my body. Before I can do anything about it, I hear myself whisper in a thick southern accent, "My killer is among you."

I'm a puppet, a shell; someone else is moving my jaw, speaking through my mouth. I scream, but no sound comes out. Through my blurred vision, I see Peregrine and Chloe staring at me. *Get out!* I cry in my head to whatever's inside me.

"Glory, who did it?" I hear Peregrine ask, but she sounds muffled and far away. "Who killed you? Was it Main de Lumière?"

I feel the spirit inside me gathering its strength to reply. "Yessssss," the voice hisses.

"Did you see your killer?" I hear Peregrine demand, a desperate edge to her voice. "Is it someone we already trust?"

The only thing that comes out of my mouth is, "In your midst."

The coldness begins to fade, and I can once again feel the tips of my fingers and toes. *Eveny*, says an urgent voice in my head just before the icy chill is gone. I recognize Glory's drawl immediately. *I didn't see my killer, but it was someone who knew exactly where I'd be. It must have been a friend.*

And then she's gone, and I can move again. I jerk away from Chloe and Peregrine. "What the hell just happened?" I demand. My tongue still feels thick and heavy, but at least I have control of it.

"You were possessed," Chloe whispers. Her face has gone pale, and she's looking at me with wide eyes. "Glory must still be in the nether."

"How remarkable," Peregrine says.

Chloe clears her throat. "It's not the possession itself that's so unusual…"

"It's that we've never seen it happen so easily before," Peregrine says. "And we've never seen it happen uninvited like that."

"I can't believe you didn't tell me that would happen!" I'm out of breath, dehydrated, and weak. I don't know whether to be excited or terrified.

Peregrine's eyes narrow. "Power to communicate with the spirit world like that is a great gift. It figures you wouldn't appreciate it."

I want to ask them what Glory meant when she said her

killer was in our midst, but my eyelids are growing heavy, and it's getting harder to stay on my feet. "Guys?" I say. "I think something's wrong with me."

"That's what it feels like after you've been possessed," Peregrine says. "The spirits take your energy with them."

"We should get her home," Chloe suggests.

Peregrine nods. "Well, the good news is that we know she's definitely one of us. She's a natural."

I see Chloe's forehead crease in concern, so I ask the obvious question. "And the bad news?"

Peregrine's tone is sombre as she turns her attention back to me. "The bad news is that now you're definitely a target for Main de Lumière too."

My house is dark and silent when Peregrine and Chloe drop me off, and I head straight upstairs. I'm swaying on my feet by the time I finally make it to my room and collapse into bed.

That night I dream again of the parlour and blood pouring out from beneath the doors. But this time, the images are blurry and vague, as if my brain can't muster the energy to form them whole.

Still, I wake up with my heart racing, the alarm clock blaring on my bedside table next to me.

I haul myself out of bed and head towards the bathroom.

As soon as I catch a glimpse of myself in the mirror, I stop in my tracks and stare. It would be no exaggeration to say that I look like a model. The so-called magic mask seems to have continued working overnight, making my lips even fuller, my skin even more luminous, and my eyelashes even thicker. My hair, which is normally creased and wild when I wake up, looks like it's been professionally dried.

I dress quickly in my school uniform, then dig into the box of accessories Peregrine sent to my house and pull out a pair of huge diamond studs. I've only ever had the fake kind you can buy at stalls in Chinatown, though I have the feeling these are the real thing. I put them on and study myself in the mirror, admiring the way they catch the light. I'm about to venture back into the box to see what else is there when Aunt Bea's words from yesterday flash through my head. *They may be your sister queens, but that doesn't mean you have to become one of them.*

I'm hit with a surge of guilt. Am I doing something wrong by embracing the advantages zandara can give me? Then again, my ancestors risked their lives so that we could have this kind of power. After a minute, I close the box up, but I keep the earrings on.

Downstairs, there's hot coffee in the pot on the counter, and Aunt Bea has left a note saying she had to get to the bakery and will see me this afternoon. I guess that means

I'll be walking to school. I shoot Meredith a text saying, *You'll never believe the makeover I got*, toast a Pop-Tart, pour myself a paper cup of coffee, and head out the door. Maybe the walk will clear my head.

But Peregrine's Aston Martin is already idling in my driveway. "Get in," she says through her open window, looking me up and down. "No, on second thought, go back inside, change your shoes, and get in."

I glance down at my loafers then back at her. "What are you doing here?"

"Giving you a ride," she says calmly. "Unless you insist on wearing *those* hideous things. The least you can do after we went out of our way to help you yesterday is to wear some heels."

"But I don't *want* to wear heels."

"There are at least six pairs in the box I sent," she says. "Seriously, go. The purple stilettos will look perfect with your skin tone."

I retreat back inside and throw the shoes on, grateful that Aunt Bea isn't here to see this. When I totter back out, Peregrine calls from the car, "Now roll up your skirt. What are you, a nun?"

I suppose she has a point, so I roll it once at the waistband, raising the hem an inch from my knees.

"Roll it again!" she commands.

I shake my head vehemently. "I'm not a nun," I grumble

as I climb into the passenger seat, "but I'm not a prostitute either."

She makes a face. "This would be so much easier if you'd just accept my fashion advice." She revs the engine, puts the car in drive, and roars down the hill towards town. It's only when I glance absent-mindedly at the backseat that I realize her creepy snake is sitting there, his eyes fixed on me. I shriek, and Peregrine swerves.

"Crap, Eveny, what's the problem?" she snaps. "You're going to get us into an accident!"

I flatten myself against the door. "Your snake is staring at me."

"So?"

"So it's creepy," I say.

"Oh for goodness' sake, grow up. Snakes are an important part of zandara. Did you know that in some parts of the world, people who practise magic even worship them?"

"You're never going to get me to worship your snake."

Peregrine laughs. "Of course not. If anything, *he* worships *us*." I look back at Audowido, who's still staring at me with his beady little eyes. I shiver as his tiny tongue darts out of his mouth.

"Aw, he likes you," Peregrine says. "That's his way of blowing kisses."

Peregrine laughs, and I could swear that I can see Audowido crack a small, snakey smile.

* * *

As I walk down the hall towards first period flanked by Peregrine and Chloe, people turn and stare. And it's not the who's-the-new-girl? stares I got on Monday or the what's-she-doing-with-the-Dolls? stares I got Tuesday. No, these stares are disbelieving and appreciative. A few guys whistle at me, and I feel myself turning red.

As we take our seats in English class, everyone turns to look at me. A cheerleader is openly glaring at me from the front of the room, and a guy wearing a Pointe Laveau baseball uniform and glasses is actually drooling.

"You're welcome," Chloe says, beaming at me.

"This is all because of my makeover yesterday?" I whisper.

"Maybe you're underestimating how unfortunate you looked before," Peregrine says.

I grit my teeth. "So this is your secret? You cast charms on yourselves, and boys just fall all over themselves with lust?"

Peregrine pouts dramatically. "You say that like it's a crime! You're forgetting that *we're* both beautiful to start with, so it's not like we need as much work as you do."

"Leave her alone, Peregrine," Chloe says wearily. "You know she's pretty." She turns to me and adds, "Just between us" – she gestures to her ample cleavage – "this is magic too!"

"Your chest?" I ask incredulously.

"Our whole *bodies*," she replies. "Our moms created a charmed floral mud; the effects last about six weeks. It works amazingly."

"Maybe if you play your cards right, we'll let you have one too," Peregrine says. She looks meaningfully at my chest and adds, "Your A cups will thank you."

As much as I'd love to magically have the perfect body, Aunt Bea's warning echoes in my head again. But can I really turn down something like this? I settle for saying, "Let me think about it."

Peregrine snorts. "Suit yourself. But don't blame me when the frat boys at our party mistake you for an eight-year-old girl."

When I slink into my seat in third-period French class with Mrs Toliver, trying to avoid the catcalls in the hall, I'm surprised to see that Drew's back.

"Hey! I didn't know you had this class with me!" I say. "Are you feeling better?"

But Drew just stares. "What happened to you?" he asks. I'm not sure whether the question is appreciative or critical.

"A little makeover. No big deal."

"Whoa," is all he says. But the smile doesn't quite reach his eyes.

I clear my throat. "So you were out sick?"

"Yeah, must have been a stomach bug or something. I woke up Monday morning feeling totally gross. So how was your first week?"

"It was okay. I made some friends."

"At this school? You must have magical powers or something."

He's just joking, but knowing how close he's come to the truth makes me flinch. "Liv Jiménez is nice," I say. "She says she knows you."

"Liv? Yeah, we went to grade school together."

"You don't hang out with her now?"

"Not at school too much, just because we have different classes. But she comes to see my band play sometimes. She knows a lot about the music industry, actually. She's a real cool girl."

The bell rings, and Mrs Toliver tells us to quiet down. Drew takes the seat beside me and scoots his desk a bit closer. "So what other classes do you have?" he whispers.

I dig my class schedule out of my backpack and hand it to him. "Bummer," he says. "This is the only one we have together. Figures you'd be in all those smarty-pants AP classes."

"Eveny? Drew?" Mrs Toliver asks. "Think your conversation could wait until after class is over?"

"Sorry," we say in unison.

After class, Drew walks me to my locker. "So," he begins as I pull out my economics book and stuff it in my bag, "my band's playing at this bar tonight. I was wondering if you might want to come." He looks nervous and hopeful.

The truth is, I want to stay home and think about all the bizarre developments that have come with moving back to Carrefour. But I have to admit, it would be nice to have a few hours off from my weird new reality.

"Sounds cool," I say. "Where is it?"

He jots down the name and address of the place. "It's in the Périphérie, though. Is that going to be a problem?"

I look at him blankly. "Of course not. Why would it be?"

"I don't know." He looks me up and down. "You just seem to be adjusting real quickly to this side of town."

FOURTEEN

I'M STANDING IN LINE IN the caf when Liv and Max walk by without so much as a glance.

"Liv!" I call out.

She turns and does a double take. "*Eveny?*" she asks. "What happened to you?"

"Holy facelift," Max says.

I look down. "I just got a haircut and a facial. No big deal."

Liv looks me up and down and waits for me to meet her gaze. "You look like a different person," she says flatly. It's not a compliment.

I open my mouth to explain, but I'm interrupted by Peregrine's voice behind me.

"Eveny?" she trills. "Why in the world are you standing in line?"

"Yeah, come on," Chloe, who of course is standing beside her, cuts in. "Up in the Hickories, Margaux and Arelia are serving smoked salmon blinis and caviar, and they brought Veuve Clicquot today."

"Veuve what?" I ask.

Peregrine makes a face. "It's a brand of champagne, Eveny. Obviously."

How was I supposed to know that? "Well, can Liv and Max come eat with us too?" Liv is glaring at Peregrine, and Max just looks nervous. His eyes dart back and forth between Liv and me.

"I'm sure Liv and Max would prefer to eat with their own people," Peregrine says. "Isn't that right, Liv?" Somehow, Peregrine manages to make her name sound like a dirty word.

"Whatever," Liv mutters, calling Peregrine a few dirty words of her own under her breath. "See you in class, Eveny. Have fun with your new friends." She storms off, dragging Max behind her.

I start to follow after her, but Chloe grabs my arm. "Let her go," she says gently. "She's a nice enough girl, but this is bigger than her. She's not one of us." She and Peregrine begin walking away without waiting for me. I glance after Liv and Max, but they're already gone.

After a moment's hesitation, I follow Chloe and Peregrine towards the Hickories. I know it's where I'm supposed to belong, but I can't help feeling like I've just made a mistake.

Arelia and Margaux openly glare at me when I sit down, but when Peregrine tells them to pour me a glass of champagne, Arelia grudgingly does so, and Margaux shovels a spoonful of caviar onto a plate and thrusts it in my general direction. My nose wrinkles when I taste it; it's salty, and the texture is peculiar.

"Take a sip of your drink," Peregrine advises. "It brings out the flavour."

I take a small sip of champagne and am surprised to realize she's right.

"You forgot the verbena in Eveny's champagne!" Peregrine says, shooting daggers at Arelia.

"Sorry." But Arelia doesn't look sorry at all as she grabs a sprig of purple flowers, leans across the picnic blanket, and shoves it into my drink.

I'm about to ask her if she needs help refilling people's glasses, but I'm interrupted by the arrival of a cute guy with huge, broad shoulders, dark hair that curls at his ears, and empty-looking brown eyes. His sleeves are rolled up to reveal bulging muscles, and he has a letter jacket slung over his left shoulder. "Hey, baby," he says dully, plunking down next to Peregrine. He doesn't look at anyone else;

he immediately busies himself with giving her a shoulder massage while sniffing her hair adoringly.

"Oh sorry, Eveny, perhaps you haven't met Beau yet," she says. "Beau, this is Eveny. Eveny, Beau."

Beau grunts what I assume is a greeting, but he doesn't tear his eyes away from Peregrine for even a millisecond.

"Beau Fontenot?" I ask. It's the name I heard them utter in the cemetery on Wednesday night. I realize in an instant that this is what his part of the charm was about: making him fall blindly in lust with Peregrine.

"Yes." Peregrine narrows her eyes at me. "Anyhow, as I was saying, people who aren't in on the Secret of Carrefour are not welcome to eat in the Hickories. This is *our* place."

"Well, what about Beau?" I ask.

Beau goes on massaging her shoulders lovingly. Peregrine laughs. "Oh, Eveny, he's so enthralled with me that he's not listening. Isn't that right, Beau?"

"Baby, you're hot," Beau mumbles robotically.

"See?" Peregrine says.

I glance at Chloe and realize she's not paying attention to us at all. She's staring at Justin, who's sitting down in the courtyard outside the cafeteria, laughing with a few other guys. I turn my focus back to Peregrine. "I thought you didn't believe in using zandara to make people fall in love with you."

"Love? Don't be ridiculous. This is just lust, which is

much easier to control. Besides, you've been in Carrefour for, like, thirty seconds. I don't think you're exactly in a position to judge me."

"Whatever." I scoot away from them and towards Chloe. "What's the matter?" I ask her as I reach her edge of the blanket.

The expression on her face is mournful as she watches Justin. He's grinning, and from the way the three guys around him are laughing as he talks, I'm guessing he's telling a joke, which surprises me because this is the first time I've ever seen him exhibit anything resembling a personality.

"Did something happen with you two?" I venture.

"I don't know what's wrong," she says. "He's totally ignoring me."

"At least he's not hitting on other girls," I point out. I'm trying to think of something else comforting to say when I realize that his behaviour is probably my fault. If Peregrine cast a charm to make Beau fall in love with her that night, Chloe was surely doing the same with Justin. When I dug his doll up, I must have reversed it. "Um, sorry if this is a personal question," I say, "but did you cast some sort of charm to make him like you?"

Chloe looks at me sharply, but then her face softens and there are tears in her eyes. "Maybe," she says. "But he liked me before that. I just helped things along. He's really shy."

I look up at Justin, who's carrying on an animated conversation.

"Shy with girls," Chloe amends, following my gaze. She sighs heavily. "Anyway, things were really good between us. And now…I don't know what I did to screw things up."

I swallow hard. "Sorry."

She gives me a watery smile. "Oh, Eveny, it's not your fault," she says, which makes me feel even worse. She turns back to watching Justin with a dreamy, troubled expression on her face.

I open my mouth to reply, but Pascal interrupts our conversation with a long, low whistle as he makes his way up the hill to the Hickories. "Damn, girl!" He's staring at me with a predatory grin. "You look *fine*."

I notice Peregrine's attention snap in our direction. Her eyes narrow at Pascal as he sits down next to me. "You're the hottest chick in this whole school now, Eveny," he continues. "What do you say we spend a little alone time in the teachers' lounge?" He makes air quotes over *alone time*.

"No thanks," I say.

"Ignore him," Peregrine says coldly. "He's just trying to get in your pants. He's exaggerating. *Obviously*."

"About me being the hottest girl in school?" I ask with mock innocence. I know that's exactly what she's talking about; her eyes burn with jealousy.

"She's not as beautiful as you, Peregrine," Arelia says, shooting me a smirk.

"Not nearly," Margaux adds helpfully as she gazes in adoration at Peregrine.

To my surprise, Peregrine seems unmoved. "Give it a rest, girls," she says. "She's one of us. She has been long before you two joined the sosyete."

Arelia's and Margaux's heads swivel towards me in surprise. "But she's new!" Margaux whines.

Peregrine narrows her eyes at them. "For goodness' sake, you *know* she's a queen. Now quit being ridiculous and pour me another glass of champagne."

I turn away from them in annoyance just in time to see Caleb walking up the hill towards us. My heart does a little flip-flop, and I feel colour rising to my cheeks. I glance away as our eyes meet, but a second later, I look back and realize he's still gazing evenly at me.

"Hey," I croak.

"Hey," he replies. He settles on the far side of the cashmere picnic blanket, facing away from me.

My heart hammers, and I'm not sure whether to be grateful that he doesn't appear to be impressed by my magically enhanced looks, or disappointed that he's obviously still avoiding me.

Peregrine purses her lips at our exchange. "So, Caleb, catch any good waves lately?" she asks, turning to him.

"I heard conditions are supposed to be ideal in the Gulf right now."

"Since when do you follow the surf forecast?" Caleb asks suspiciously.

"I've always been interested in your hobbies," she says sweetly.

"You know I haven't left town, Peregrine," he says. "Give it a rest."

She laughs as he turns away, and I have the feeling she's not as over him as she wants everyone to think.

Twenty minutes later, I sit down next to Caleb in American history, expecting his usual inexplicable silent treatment. So I'm surprised when he says, "I see Peregrine and Chloe have gotten their hands on you." His voice is deep and warm, and it makes my stomach feel like Jell-O.

My cheeks heat up. "You could say that. It feels... different." I take a deep breath and ask, "So what do you think?"

"You look pretty," he says, and for a moment, my heart both soars and sinks at the same time. "But I thought you looked pretty before too."

He doesn't say another word for the rest of class, and he strides out of the room at the end before I have a chance to talk to him. But his words stay with me and echo in my head for the rest of the afternoon.

* * *

I call Meredith on my walk home, but she doesn't pick up. I swallow back a lump in my throat and leave her a message saying that I miss her. I call Liv next, because she avoided me in physics and was gone by the time I reached the hallway.

"Look, I'm sorry about lunch today," I say to her voicemail when she doesn't answer. "I don't know why Peregrine and Chloe are so picky about who eats in the Hickories."

I spend the rest of my walk hoping that Caleb will pull up alongside me like he did my first day of school, but only a few cars whizz past, and none are his. I try not to feel disappointed.

When I arrive home, I wander around the rose garden looking for Boniface, but he's nowhere to be found, nor is Aunt Bea.

Liv calls back at four, and before I can even say hello, she says, "There's no law saying you have to eat with the Dolls just because they invite you."

"I know," I reply. "I'm sorry." I wish I could explain to her that like it or not, I'm linked to Chloe and Peregrine for ever. But of course Liv's not in on the Secret of Carrefour, so all she sees is that I'm choosing popularity and power over real friendship.

She's silent for a moment, then she says, "No big deal," but her tone tells me she's still pissed off.

"Hey, so Drew invited me to go see his band play tonight," I say.

"At Domion? Yeah, I was planning to go."

"Cool. So would you want to go together, maybe?"

"What, are Peregrine and Chloe busy?" The bitterness is creeping back in.

"I didn't ask them," I tell her. "I'm asking you."

"Oh." She pauses. "Yeah, all right. And I'll come get you. But dude, you need to get your driver's licence."

"I know."

"And Eveny? Don't invite the Dolls, okay?"

"Don't worry," I tell her. "I definitely won't."

FIFTEEN

AUNT BEA GETS HOME FIFTEEN minutes before Liv is due to arrive, her navy T-shirt and skirt smudged with flour. She looks surprised to see me in skinny jeans, boots, and a flowy top, all dressed for a night out.

"Don't tell me you're meeting up with Peregrine and Chloe," she says, looking at me suspiciously.

"No, my friend Liv is picking me up. We're going to see Drew's band play in the Périphérie."

She chews her lip. "Who's Liv? One of the girls in Peregrine and Chloe's sosyete?"

"Actually, she pretty much hates Peregrine and Chloe."

Aunt Bea's expression relaxes a little. "Well, I was hoping we could talk."

"Me too. But Liv'll be here in a few minutes."

"The morning's fine, I guess," Aunt Bea says. She kisses

me on the cheek and walks away without another word.

Five minutes later, I hear a horn honking outside. I look through the peephole and see Liv sitting in a pale blue VW Bug with rusted bumpers.

"I'm heading out!" I call up to Aunt Bea, who doesn't respond. "Back by eleven!"

I lock the front door behind me and climb into the passenger seat of Liv's car. "Hey," I say, but she doesn't reply. My heart sinks; she's obviously still annoyed about today. "Look," I say after she's pulled out of my driveway and is sputtering down the hill. "I know you don't like Peregrine and Chloe."

She snorts. "Understatement of the year."

I glance down. "It's complicated with them, Liv. I knew them when we were kids. They're kind of part of my life whether I like it or not."

Liv's shoulders relax a little. "I don't want you to get sucked into their little circle of clones, that's all."

"Just because I'm hanging out with them doesn't mean I have to *become* one of them." But the words taste like a lie, because of course I *am* one of them.

Fifteen minutes later we're walking into Domion, a run-down looking restaurant heaving with people. At least half the crowd inside is our age, and I tag along after Liv as people come up to her to say hi. A few of them I recognize from the crawfish boil, but most are unfamiliar and don't pay any attention to me.

Liv seems completely in her element. Dressed in a denim miniskirt, faded leather cowboy boots, and a sheer blouse with a cami underneath, she also appears more relaxed than she does at Pointe Laveau.

"You see why I don't exactly fit in with your new friends?" she asks as we settle into seats at a high-top table to the right of the stage. "Unlike them, I realize there's more to life than looking hot and messing with guys' heads."

Liv's smile is bright, but her eyes are hard. I wish I could explain that their snubbing her has nothing to do with money and everything to do with birthright. But of course I can't, so I settle for changing the subject. I ask Liv about her family, and she tells me she has a little brother named Davy, a freshman at Carrefour Secondary, and that they live with their dad; their mom left when Liv was three.

"My dad disappeared before I was born," I tell her. "So I get it."

She looks up at me with an expression of surprise. "I didn't know that," she says. "Where did he go?"

"No idea. I only know that he's from somewhere back east and that my aunt hates him." I hesitate and add, "I've been thinking about him a lot since we got here, actually. My aunt says I've never met him, but I found a photo of us together, and I have a weird, hazy memory of talking to him at my mom's funeral."

"So you've never heard from him other than that?" she asks.

I shake my head.

Liv studies me for a moment. "Maybe Peregrine and Chloe know something about what happened to him, since their moms knew your mom."

"Maybe," I agree. Truthfully, I hadn't thought to ask.

Liv is looking at me differently now. "I guess I can see why you'd want to hang with them sometimes," she says grudgingly. "Even though I still think they're pretty worthless human beings."

I open my mouth to answer, but I'm interrupted by a mash-up of guitar strings behind the small stage. A moment later, Teddy, the guy who threw the crawfish boil, bounds out and hurls himself into the seat behind an impressive drum set. He begins banging the cymbal with a drumstick, and a moment later Drew runs out with an electric guitar, and two other guys I don't recognize come out playing a banjo and a bass guitar. Teddy whales on the drums while the guy with the banjo leans towards one of the microphones and begins to sing in a low voice that reminds me of John Mayer.

Drew looks up and grins at us after the first verse is over.

"They're good, aren't they?" Liv says once he looks away. "Good chord structure. Good hooks. They've got a good look too." She pauses and adds, "Especially Drew."

I realize she's staring at Drew raptly as he launches into a solo to begin the second song. I see a blush creep up Liv's neck, and I wonder for the first time if she likes him as more than a friend.

We both clap along as the band rocks out to the next song, which reminds me a bit of an Irish drinking anthem with a hard rock rhythm and a smattering of banjo strings.

"I'm Tallon Duchovny!" announces the banjo-playing singer after Drew has strummed his last chord. "And we're Little Brother, from right out here in the Périphérie!"

The room explodes into applause, and Drew grins at us again as he strums a few chords to lead off the third song. Tallon is singing lead again; the lyrics are about a girl who goes around breaking hearts. After the chorus, Drew and Tallon lean towards each other and engage in a few minutes of duelling licks; Tallon plucks out complicated melodies on the banjo, which Drew mimics while Teddy and the bass player keep time.

"I've never heard anything like this before," I shout to Liv over the music as Little Brother launches into a fourth tune.

"They're something special!" she shouts back.

After their first set, Teddy bounds over to our table, still clutching his drumsticks, while the other guys head into a back room to put their guitars down.

"Hey, Eveny!" he says. "Hey, Liv!" His forehead is

glistening with sweat, and he's grinning. "Anyone want to go do a shot with me at the bar?"

I say, "No thanks," at the same time Liv says, "Sure, why not? There's something I want to run by you anyway." I give her a look, because after all, she's the one driving home after the show.

"They're not real strict with IDs in this town, are they?" I ask.

Liv and Teddy both laugh. "The Dolls aren't the only ones who can get away with breaking the rules," Liv says. I watch as she follows Teddy, giggling about something he's said.

I turn my attention back towards the stage just in time to see Drew emerge without his guitar. He heads straight for me.

"You came to my show," he says, giving me an awkward half hug.

"Yeah, me and Liv both." I gesture towards the bar.

He glances her way then grins at me. "You look beautiful tonight, Eveny. Really."

"You looked pretty good up there yourself." I change the subject before it gets uncomfortable. "I'm really glad we came. The band's amazing."

"Thanks!" He launches into a long explanation of how they're trying to get a record deal with some New Orleans-based music label, and I'm listening until a familiar deep voice somewhere off to my left catches my attention. I do a double take when I see who's sitting there.

It's Caleb, all by himself at a table near the back of the room, giving a pretty waitress his order.

I feel my heart leap into my throat. *What's* he *doing here?*

Caleb catches me staring and half raises his glass in greeting, then turns away as if he has no interest in interacting with me at all.

As I force myself to refocus on Drew, I feel a river of heat flowing through me, and I hope it's not showing on my face. Drew's still talking, and when he leans in and touches my arm to make a point, I pull away and feel instantly guilty when a hurt expression flickers across his face. But what if Caleb thinks I'm *with* Drew?

Drew makes it worse a second later by giving me a peck on the cheek. "Seriously, Eveny, thanks so much for coming out tonight. It's really cool of you."

Then Tallon beckons from the stage, and Drew says sadly, "Looks like I have to go. But see you in a few, okay?"

Liv sits down next to me a moment later holding two drinks. She pushes one towards me. "They're both Sprite," she says.

I thank her, and I'm about to open my mouth to ask what she thinks Caleb is doing here when she asks eagerly, "So did Drew say anything about me?"

I look over at Caleb's table. He's deep in conversation

with the waitress, who's in short shorts, a tight white T-shirt, and cowboy boots. I shake off a surge of jealousy. "He's really glad you came," I tell Liv.

"Awesome," she says.

The band begins playing, and we turn back to the stage. Drew keeps grinning at us, and Liv is squirming in her seat. Meanwhile, Caleb doesn't appear to be paying the slightest bit of attention to me. I'm puzzled that he's here, considering that the Périphérie isn't exactly the Dolls' domain.

"So would you think I was totally crazy if I told you I'd offered to help Drew's band?" Liv asks after a few minutes.

"Help them how?"

"I was thinking I'd offer to manage them," she says. When I shoot her a confused look, she hurries to add, "I know it sounds kind of nuts. But I'm always listening to indie bands and reading *Spin* and *Rolling Stone* and all that. I've been saving up for this program that'll basically turn my Mac into a home recording studio – what if I offer to cut a song for them?"

"You know how to do that?"

"I'll learn," she says confidently. "Then maybe I can get out of this town and take Drew and his buddies with me. I mean, look at those guys." She points at the stage. "Girls will go crazy for them. They're all really cute, right?" Her eyes linger on Drew several beats too long.

"You sure this isn't just a way to hit on Drew…?"

"No!" she exclaims. Then she shoots me a guilty look. "Maybe. But only a little. If you tell anyone that, though, I'll have to kill you."

I laugh and settle back to watch Little Brother's set. Just before the band finishes, Liv grabs my arm and says, "Wait, is that *Caleb Shaw*? What's he doing out here?"

I sneak a glance at his table again. He's reading the menu like it's a fascinating book. "I don't know," I say, trying to pretend I don't care.

Liv stares at me. "Wait, do you *like* him?"

"No," I protest unconvincingly. "He's just, uh, a nice guy, you know?"

"You don't have to lie. Every girl in Carrefour has had a crush on Caleb Shaw at some point. *I* even liked him for thirty seconds. But sooner or later, everyone realizes he just doesn't date."

"But I thought he used to date Peregrine."

Liv frowns. "That was really short-lived. I wasn't at Pointe Laveau yet, so I don't know all the details, but I hear he just wasn't that into her, and everyone sort of knew it except her."

I'm embarrassed by how happy this makes me. But then something occurs to me. "Maybe he's gay," I say, my heart sinking a little.

"No. Believe me, Max has asked. Several times."

I laugh, but before I can say anything in reply, Liv's already standing up.

"I have an idea," she says before waving her hands dramatically in the air. "Caleb!" she yells across the bar. "Over here!"

He hesitates before getting up and walking slowly in our direction. I can feel the hairs on my arms standing on end as he comes closer.

"Hey," he says in a low voice. His sky-blue eyes flick to me for an instant and land back on Liv. "What's up?"

"Well first of all, Caleb, I didn't know you hung out in the Périphérie."

"I do sometimes."

"But you live in central Carrefour, right?"

"Right."

"So Caleb, I was wondering if you could do me a favour," she continues. "I picked Eveny up, and I don't *mind* driving her home. But seeing as you live right by her, maybe you'd be willing to do it?"

Caleb looks startled, so I jump in to say, "Liv, that's really not necessary."

"Oh, but Eveny, I have to talk business with Drew and the band." Liv turns to Caleb with a faux-serious expression. "Plus, I've been drinking," she says. "Like, a *lot*."

"Liv, I'm sure Caleb is busy. And you said yourself you only did one shot."

"Caleb, are you really that busy?" Liv asks immediately. "I mean, you're going home anyway, right?"

"Uh, yeah, sure, that's fine," he says. "But I was about to leave, actually. I don't want to cut your night short." I feel like curling up and vanishing; it's so obvious he doesn't want to give me a ride.

I open my mouth to tell him to forget we even asked, but Liv elbows me in the ribs.

"Would you excuse us for a minute, Caleb?" I ask. He looks uncertain as I grab Liv's arm and drag her a few feet away. "What are you doing?" I demand.

"Just getting you a little alone time with the hottest guy in Carrefour."

"I didn't ask you for that!" I exclaim.

"You didn't have to," she says with a shrug. "Besides, I was kind of hoping this would give me some time to talk with Drew."

"Talk? Or make out?" I tease.

Her cheeks turn a little pink. "To talk about the *band*, Eveny."

I'm about to argue further when Caleb comes up behind us. "You ready to go?" he asks.

"If you're sure you don't mind taking me."

Liv's already slinking away from us. "Later, you guys," she says, winking at me.

"My Jeep's this way." Caleb begins walking towards the

exit without waiting for me, and even when I hurry to catch up, he keeps a few feet of distance between us.

"I'm sorry about that," I say. "I didn't ask Liv to do that."

"I know."

"What are you doing here, anyhow?" I ask when he opens his passenger door for me.

"Driving you home," he says in an even tone. "We're neighbours, and Liv asked me to, in case you don't remember."

He waits for me to get in and buckle my seat belt, then he shuts my door and goes around to the driver's side. Once he's buckled in and has started the engine, I say, "What I mean is, what are you doing *here*? At Domion?"

"Listening to music, same as you," he says. "Why, are you implying I'm following you?"

"No, of course not!" I feel like an idiot.

For a moment, I'm sure he's about to say something else.

But he puts the car in gear, mumbles something to himself, and backs out of his parking space.

It's not until we're almost out of the parking lot that I realize I've walked out without saying goodbye to Drew.

SIXTEEN

THE FIRST FEW MINUTES OF the drive are silent. I feel nervous and tongue-tied in Caleb's presence.

"So, Liv and Drew? I didn't know she liked him until tonight," I say in an attempt to cut through the awkwardness.

"Yeah," Caleb says, his eyes glued to the road.

"I mean, Liv seems so tough sometimes, like she doesn't need anyone," I add when it's clear he's not going to say anything.

"Yeah."

I take a deep breath. "But when you think about it, they're kind of perfect for each other."

"Yeah."

This is getting ridiculous. "Okay, so the way that conversation works is that I say something, and then you say something back – preferably something other than 'yeah'."

This finally elicits a reaction from Caleb. He chuckles.

"Yes, I know what a conversation is." He hesitates and adds, "I'm sorry. I'm not making this very easy, am I?"

"I just don't understand why you're avoiding me."

"I'm not," he says instantly.

I continue to stare at him until he clears his throat and says, "All right. Maybe I've been avoiding you a little."

The words hit me harder than I expect. "Why? Does it have something to do with zandara?" I ask after a moment of silence.

He hesitates. "It's hard to explain. I think it's better if we just don't talk about this."

"Look," I say, "I didn't even know anything *about* the Dolls or the sosyete or anything until two days ago. I wasn't raised with any of this, so you can't hate me because of it."

"I don't hate you," Caleb says immediately. His voice is husky as he turns and repeats, "I don't hate you."

"Well, it sure feels like it," I reply.

"It's not that. It's just…" His voice trails off. "It's just that certain people in town have certain responsibilities. And feelings make those responsibilities that much harder."

"*Feelings?*"

"Oh, that's not what I meant."

"Right," I say, feeling foolish. "Me neither."

"It's just…" He hesitates and starts again. "There are some things in this town that you don't understand."

I grit my teeth. "You know, I'm getting pretty tired of everyone talking in mysteries and riddles over my head."

"Eveny…" For a moment, I think he's going to tell me what he means. But instead, what he says is, "It's complicated."

"Seriously, no explanation? Are you *trying* to drive me crazy?"

"No," he says quickly. "I'm trying to warn you. This town, it sucks you in. It's like all your choices start to disappear, and you realize your life's been planned out for you long before you got here."

"Well, that makes everything a lot clearer," I say sarcastically. I realize that he actually looks upset, so I soften my tone and add, "That's why you disappear to go surfing, isn't it? You're just trying to get out of here."

He looks surprised. "You remembered." When I nod, he continues, "I love that feeling of anonymity when I'm out there alone in the water." He pauses. "But now that I'm not going as much any more, it sometimes feels like this town is closing in on me."

"Because of the Dolls?"

"I just have this feeling that there's a storm coming, and they're the ones bringing it here." He hesitates. "They told me about the possession at Cristof's. You should be worried too."

"Gee, thanks for making me feel better."

"This is life-and-death stuff, Eveny. I know Peregrine and Chloe think this is all fun and games, but I need to know that you know better. Tell me you know better."

"Of course I do."

He's silent for a moment before changing the subject. "So Drew. Has he said anything to you about Glory?"

"Drew?" I repeat, surprised. "No. Why?"

"I think he was seeing her," Caleb says. "I was just wondering if Liv knows."

"Caleb, that's crazy," I say. "The Dolls act like Drew's not even alive. Besides, Drew would have told me if there was something going on."

He shrugs. "I saw them together. A week before she died."

"Saw them doing what?"

He clears his throat. "It just seemed like they were together, okay? I thought it was great that something was going on between them, being that she was a Doll and he's from the Périphérie. About time someone shook things up around here. But then she died, and he kept right on acting like he didn't know her."

I shake my head. "Are you sure they were together? Like *together* together?"

"No. Not one hundred per cent."

"So don't you think you're being a little unfair?"

"Then ask him, Eveny," Caleb says. "I just want to make sure Liv is aware. She's your friend, and if she's interested in him, she deserves to know that something might have been going on."

We're pulling into my driveway now, and I feel a sense of disappointment. Even if we're disagreeing, I want to keep talking to Caleb. For ever, if possible.

"I'm only being cautious, Eveny," he says as he puts his car in neutral. His eyes are wide and concerned as he turns to me. "You should be too."

I open my mouth to respond just as he leans forward to jiggle my door handle. "It sticks sometimes," he explains. Our eyes meet, and for a moment, as he goes still, I have the weirdest feeling he's going to kiss me. But then he retreats to his own seat and looks out the windshield with his hands gripping the wheel, like he can't wait to get out of here.

"Bye," I say softly as I climb out of the car.

He doesn't reply. Instead, the moment I shut his car door, he guns the engine and pulls away.

But he lingers at the bottom of my driveway until I've unlocked my front door and slipped inside my house. I watch from the window as his taillights disappear.

* * *

Aunt Bea is already in bed when I get home, but I'm not even slightly tired. I sit down at the kitchen table and dial Meredith's number.

When she answers on the third ring, all I can hear at first is club music pumping through the earpiece.

"Mer?" I ask loudly. I repeat myself a few times, until I hear her voice faintly over the music.

"Eveny?" she yells. "Hang on, I'll go outside!"

A moment later, the music fades and is replaced by New York street sounds: people talking, car horns honking, brakes screeching. I realize with a pang just how much I miss being there.

"Hey, girl!" she says excitedly.

"What are you up to tonight?" I ask.

"Nick and Holly heard about a party in Chinatown," she says. "So Colton and James and I grabbed a cab and came out here. This place is amaze, Ev! No cover, and the door guy didn't even look twice at my ID."

"Sounds cool."

"Totally wish you were here! What're you doing tonight?"

"Just got home from seeing a friend's band play," I tell her.

"Ooh, you have a friend in a band?" she asks. "Is it a *boy*?"

"Just the guy I told you about the other night. The one I knew when I was a kid. But the other guy drove me home."

"Who?"

"Caleb. The one who's insanely gorgeous."

She makes a noise. "Girl, the hot ones are the ones you've got to look out for." She pauses. "So are you coming back to visit soon, or what?"

I think about it for a minute. A few days ago, I was dying to return to New York. Now, I feel like there are a thousand answers I need to figure out here in Carrefour first. "Probably not," I tell her. "Not for a while, at least."

"Seriously?" she asks. "Why, your aunt won't give you money for a plane ticket?"

"It's not that. It's just that so much of my family's history is tied in to Carrefour." I try to stay as vague as possible. "I know it sounds crazy, but I think I belong here for now."

"In the sticks?" she asks with a laugh.

"It's not so bad," I say, actually meaning it.

"Well, in that case," Meredith says after a moment, "I've been meaning to ask you a question."

There's something in her voice that makes me pause.

"What is it?"

"Do you still like Trevor Montague?" she asks quickly.

"I guess." I've had a crush on Trevor for as long as I can remember, though nothing ever happened between us. "Why?"

"Well, he kinda asked me out," Meredith says.

"Trevor, who I used to ask you for advice about on a daily basis? Trevor, who I used to draw pictures of in my notebook in middle school? Trevor, whose name we carved into that tree in the park in ninth grade?"

"Yes," Meredith replies, her voice flat.

"Well, you said no, right?"

"Not exactly."

The silence is heavy between us. "You didn't?"

"It's not like you're coming back, Eveny. You just said so yourself. And I've liked him for a while too."

"No, you haven't," I protest. "You've never said anything about liking him."

"Well, maybe I do!" Her tone is defiant, and it wounds me. I close my eyes and try not to think of them together. After all, she's right; I might never be coming back. But that doesn't mean my best friend has to go out with the guy I've liked for ever.

"Meredith—" I begin, trying to sound calm.

But she cuts me off. "You don't get to call dibs on someone if you're not here."

She hangs up without another word. I try calling her back, but it goes right to voicemail. Finally, I settle for texting Drew. *Your band was awesome*, I tell him. *Did you and Liv have fun?*

But there's no reply.

When my phone stays silent, I head up to bed, feeling more alone than ever.

I wake up the next morning to a return text from Drew.

Thanks again for coming, he writes. *And yeah, Liv is cool.*

I grab my phone and text back, *Anything happen with you guys?*

Nah. We just talked about music and stuff. There's a pause, then he writes, *So I hear you went home with Caleb Shaw??*

My cheeks heat up as I text back, *He only gave me a ride cuz I was on his way.* But even over text, I can sense Drew's jealousy. I feel like adding, *Caleb acts like the very thought of me is offensive, so you don't have to worry,* but instead, I settle for, *Call me later,* before I head down to the kitchen.

Aunt Bea is sitting at the table, sipping a cup of coffee, when I round the corner.

"Morning," she says. Her eyes flick up to meet mine, and I realize they're bloodshot and underlined in deep blue half-moons.

"You okay?" I ask.

"I didn't sleep well last night," she says. "A lot on my mind."

That's when I notice a small purple jewellery box and a yellowed envelope on the table in front of her. She follows my gaze. "I picked this up yesterday while you were at school," she says.

"What is it?"

Aunt Bea just shakes her head. "Sit down," she says, sliding the envelope and box over to me. "They were left in a safe-deposit box for you many years ago. Your mom wrote the letter the year you were born, in case anything ever happened and she wasn't here when you turned seventeen."

She pauses and looks down at the table. "I should have given them to you on your birthday, but I was hoping to prolong the sense that our lives are normal. Now that zandara has found *you*, though..." Her voice trails off, and there are tears in her eyes when she looks up again.

"You knew it would when you brought me back here, didn't you?" I ask, turning the box over in my hands.

"I was doing what I had to do." She nods at the envelope, and with shaky hands I open it carefully. A dried rose flutters out first, and I recognize it as one of my mother's gold-tipped Rose of Life blooms. There's also a single piece of thick paper, yellowed at the edges. I unfold it shakily and begin to read.

My dearest Eveny, my mother writes.
Happy seventeenth birthday. If you're reading this, it means I am no longer with you, and

for that, I am sorrier than I can ever say.

As I'm sure you've realized by now, Carrefour is full of secrets, and only you can make the decision about what's right for your future — although I suspect others around you will have opinions of their own. Remember that zandara can be used for good or evil, selfishly or selflessly. But one thing remains true: it exists always in balance with the universe.

Dark times are coming, and in order to survive, you'll have to tap into everything inside of you. You have the chance to become the greatest queen the world has ever known.

I have always loved you, Eveny, and I always will. I hope that one day, you'll understand everything.

Then, in verse form, she has printed the poem from the front hallway:

For each ray of light, there's a stroke of dark.
For each possibility, one has gone.
For each action, a reaction.
Ever in balance, the world spins on.

But there's a second verse too.

Blood of my blood, in dreams I will come
To show you the way, soul to soul.
The pieces are shattered, a puzzle undone.
You must piece them together to make it whole.

Beneath the second verse, the letter is signed simply,

Love for ever, Mom.

When I finish reading, tears cloud my vision. I slide the letter over to Aunt Bea. "I don't understand. Why would she write all this if she was going to kill herself?"

Aunt Bea doesn't reply. Instead, she looks up from the letter a moment later with tear-filled eyes and pushes the box towards me. "Open it," she says.

I take the top off gently. Inside, a smooth black stone with one jagged edge hangs from a long, thin gold chain. I pick it up, and as my fingers touch the stone, a jolt of electricity shoots through me. "It's just like the necklaces Chloe and Peregrine have," I say.

Aunt Bea is watching me closely. "It's a third of the Stone of Carrefour. When the town was founded, Eléonore and the other two queens channelled a huge amount of magical energy into a piece of obsidian. And when they cast the protective charm, the stone itself was so laden with power that it split into three. The reigning zandara queens in Carrefour each have one, passed down to them on their seventeenth birthdays.

"Only a zandara queen can harness its strength," she continues. "Once you put it on, it will hang from your neck until you die, or until you pass it on to your own daughter on her seventeenth birthday. If someone tries to take it from you, the magic within the stone burns them. And as long as you're wearing it, it's all you'll need for minor charms."

"You've lost me," I say, confused.

"As long as you're touching the stone with your left ring finger," Aunt Bea explains solemnly, "you can channel any herb or flower, without actually having it in your grasp. The queens designed it that way so that they didn't always need access to their gardens. Actually holding the plants in your hand always makes a charm stronger, but the stone is sort of like a back-up plan."

I touch the stone, and it throbs with possibility and foreboding.

"If you channel a specific herb while you're using it, somewhere in the world, one of those herbs dies," Aunt Bea continues. "Zandara always requires balance, which means power always comes from somewhere.

"Now," she adds, looking up at me, "about your mother's letter—"

"It sounded like she knew what might happen with

Main de Lumière," I cut in, "and like she thought I should do all I could to learn about zandara."

"But that's an easy thing to say in the abstract, Eveny. You were just a baby when she wrote this. She never had the chance to know you as a young woman, and she didn't have a chance to see you blossom outside of this town. She assumed that your choices were already made for you, like hers were for her."

"But my choices *are* made, aren't they?" I ask. "If I walk away, the town will get weaker, until Main de Lumière figures out a way to destroy us."

"On the other hand, perhaps if zandara wilts here, we'll fall off Main de Lumière's radar," Aunt Bea says. "Maybe losing its magic is the one thing that will allow Carrefour and zandara to survive."

SEVENTEEN

THAT EVENING, I WANDER OUT to the garden, the place I
feel closest to my mom.

I have no doubt that Aunt Bea has my best interests at
heart, but in the last fourteen years she has watched her
sister take her own life, assumed custody of a child she
never expected to raise, and left behind everything she ever
knew. All because of zandara. It's no wonder that her
feelings about magic would be less than glowing.

But if my mom wrote me a letter telling me that the
only way through the storm is to stay strong and tap into
everything inside of me, there must be a reason. Suddenly,
it occurs to me that there might be a way to ask her
directly.

My heart thudding, I stand up and put my left ring
finger on my Stone of Carrefour like Aunt Bea told me

to do. "Come to us now, Eloi Oke, and open the gate," I say uncertainly. "Come to us now, Eloi Oke, and open the gate. Come to us now, Eloi Oke, and open the gate."

There's an almost imperceptible shift in the air, and a small gust of wind picks up around me, swirling like a miniature cyclone. I take a deep breath and realize I don't know what to do next.

"Eveny?" A concerned voice from behind me startles me, and I release the Stone of Carrefour and whirl around. In an instant, the air pressure regulates and the air stops spinning.

It's Boniface, and he's holding pruning shears and staring at me worriedly.

"Oh, hey," I say casually, trying to act normal.

"Sweetheart, what were you doing?"

"I was trying to talk to my mom." I feel suddenly silly and childish.

His expression is sad as he shakes his head. "I'm afraid you can't. Her spirit has moved on. Zandara queens can only communicate with spirits in the nether."

"Oh," I say.

Boniface puts his shears down and pulls me into a hug. "What brought all of this on?"

"Aunt Bea gave me a letter from my mom, and I was just trying to find some answers."

I sit down on the edge of one of the big rose planters,

and Boniface settles beside me. After a moment he says, "This is all very new to you, isn't it?" When I nod, he adds, "And very unsettling."

"I don't know what I'm supposed to do," I tell him, "or how I'm supposed to become this great queen my mother thinks I'll be."

Boniface seems to consider this for a moment. "I've been around these parts – and your family – for quite some time now. I reckon I've picked up a few things. How about you learn to work a bit of magic on your own?"

I feel a flutter of excitement. "Really?"

"For something minor like charming roses, you don't need the herbs themselves as long as you're touching your stone with your left ring finger and as long as you're thinking about the herbs you've chosen." He strokes his chin for a moment and appears to be thinking. "You always want to look for herbs and flowers associated with what you're hoping to achieve. For this one, let's invoke squaw vine and master root. They're both used to foster growth. Are you familiar with both plants?"

"Yep," I say, and Boniface looks impressed.

"Great. Start with something simple, like, 'I draw the power of the squaw vine and the master root'. Then command the roses to grow."

I take a deep breath and touch my Stone of Carrefour as Boniface and I say in unison, "Come to us now, Eloi Oke, and open the gate. Come to us now, Eloi Oke, and open the gate. Come to us now, Eloi Oke, and open the gate. Come to us now, Eloi Oke, and open the gate."

Boniface nods to me, and I take a deep breath. "I draw the power of the squaw vine and the master root," I chant, touching one of the rosebushes with my right hand. My stone hums against my breastbone. "Spirits, please grow this rose, raise its height."

Nothing happens. I try again but still nothing. "What am I doing wrong?"

"The words you say don't matter as much as the things you're channelling as you say them. You touch the stone with your left ring finger because people believed in the *vena amoris,* a vein that runs from the ring finger to the heart. That's one of the reasons that finger is used for wedding rings, you know."

I look down at my ring finger and touch it to the stone again.

"Touching the stone with your ring finger links your magic to your heart," Boniface explains. "It has to do with harnessing specific memories, times when you've been filled with love. Harnessing feelings that pure can enhance a queen's magic tenfold. Love is power."

"Then how can Peregrine be so powerful?" I mutter. "She doesn't exactly seem like the warm and fuzzy type."

Boniface chuckles. "Love of oneself is also a very powerful emotion, not to mention love of material things."

He leans in and adds, "What she's missing, though, is the power of someone loving you in return. That can magnify your magic too.

"So think of a memory in which you loved and were loved," Boniface says, "and try again."

I close my eyes. When I recite the invocation, I think about my mother smiling proudly at me in our front yard when I was a little girl as I showed her the cartwheels I'd just learned to do. I feel a sizzle shoot from my left ring finger through my heart to my right hand, which is touching the rose. I open my eyes and see that the bush has grown a foot taller and has sprouted three new rosebuds.

"So somewhere out there, a squaw vine shrub and a master root plant just died?" I ask.

He nods. "*For each action, a reaction, ever in balance, the world spins on.* Now try again."

I touch another rosebush. This time, I reach even further back, to my oldest memory of my mom. I'd fallen in the driveway and skinned my knee, and when I looked up, there she was, with a look of concern on her face so deep that I felt instantly soothed. I recite the words and crack my eyes open.

"Even better." Boniface looks approvingly at the second bush, which is blossoming in a rainbow of colours now. "You were thinking of your mother again?" When I nod, he says, "Try again, thinking of someone else."

This time, I'm intending to think of Aunt Bea and everything she's given up for me, but when I close my eyes what I see is Caleb leaning across me to open the passenger door of his Jeep last night, during the split second in which I thought he was going to kiss me.

When I open my eyes, not only has the bush I was touching grown and sprouted dozens of new blood-red roses, but every bush *it* was touching is flourishing too. I pull my hand away.

"Who were you thinking of?" Boniface asks.

"Um, Aunt Bea," I lie.

"Hmm. Well, she clearly loves you very much." He checks his watch. "In any case, I must get inside. I have a few things to do tonight. Besides, I'm guessing you're tired; working zandara can be exhausting."

I yawn and thank him. As much as I want to keep going, to keep learning, I have the feeling he's right. And even though it's only a few minutes after eight, I feel like I could crawl under my covers and sleep for the next sixteen hours. As I head off to bed, all I'm thinking about is Caleb and the power that surged within me as he flashed through my mind.

It feels like I've barely drifted off when my phone begins ringing. I swat at it to silence it and snuggle deeper into my covers, but it rings again. I reach for it on the third cycle and, still half asleep, mumble into the receiver, "Hello?"

"Eveny? It's Peregrine. Where on earth are you?"

I yawn. "Sleeping," I mumble. "Good night."

I start to hang up, but I can hear her yelling something, so I reluctantly hold the phone back up to my ear. "Are you there?" she's asking angrily.

"Hmm mmm."

"Are you seriously in bed? It's eleven p.m. on a Saturday, you lame-o!"

"I'm tired," I tell her. I don't really care if she's judging me or not.

"Boy, you must have been the life of the party back in Brooklyn," she says, her voice dripping with sarcasm. "Nevertheless, I need you here, pronto. Frankly, I'm rather disappointed in you for not making this a priority."

Now I'm confused. "You need me *where* pronto?" I ask.

She lets out a frustrated huff. "Our *party*, Eveny! You know? Frat guys in togas? Hunch punch? All sorts of secluded corners to make out in?"

I sit up in bed. "What does that have to do with me?"

"Seriously, Eveny? This is your first party as a Queen of Carrefour. Your sosyete needs you."

"But—" I start to protest.

"I'm not taking no for an answer," she says. "Be here in twenty. Your toga is hanging by my front door."

"I don't even know where you live."

"Geez, Eveny, do you need me to spell everything out for you?" When I don't reply, she sighs heavily and says, "Walk out your front door and turn right. We're the mansion next door, just down the hill and up the next one. Obviously."

She clicks off and I'm left holding a dead phone. A moment later, against my better judgment, I haul myself out of bed, slouch into the bathroom to brush my teeth, and head back to my vanity mirror to add a bit of mascara and lipstick. Thanks to the facial mask from Cristof's, my face and hair are otherwise perfect, so I'm ready to go in under five minutes.

Aunt Bea is snoring in her room at the end of the hall, so I don't bother disturbing her. Instead, I leave a note on the table in case she wakes up before I'm back.

As soon as I'm outside, I can hear the party. Loud music and muffled laughter float through the trees, and as I begin to walk down the driveway on the back side of the hill, I can see Peregrine's house glowing. As I get closer, I realize there are blazing torches all over her property, casting shadows and light everywhere.

There's music blasting from the speakers on the grand, columned front porch when I arrive, and since the door is open, I don't bother ringing the bell. I squeeze inside past a big group of hot, toga-clad guys.

"Eveny!" Peregrine exclaims, emerging from a hallway off to the right. "It's about time!" She's wearing sky-high chocolate leather stilettos and a white toga so short that I'm pretty sure it's supposed to be a top, not a dress. "Come in, come in! Here's your toga!" She grabs a slip of white, drapey fabric from the coat hook beside the door and thrusts it at me. "I'll show you where to change. Follow me!"

As she leads me down the front hall, through a throng of muscular, square-jawed guys whose eyes follow her, I look around in awe. The Marceaus' mansion is a little smaller than ours, but it's a thousand times fancier. The front hallway is all ivory marble with gold leafing and gold trim. An enormous crystal chandelier hangs over the entryway, sending little rays of light cascading everywhere.

As we emerge into a larger room, which Peregrine calls the ballroom, I suck in a deep breath. The chandelier here is even larger than the one in the entryway, the floor is all done in black and white marble, sleek white furniture hugs the walls, and the ceiling soars several storeys high. There are torches blazing everywhere, and the place is teeming with guys and a handful of girls, all of whom are wearing togas too. I recognize Arelia and Margaux gyrating on the dance floor, but the rest of them are strangers.

"Pascal appreciates the sorority girls we added to our guest list," Peregrine says as we whisk past. "It's nice to be able to appease your friends."

Indeed, I spot him grinding on a leggy blonde whose toga has ridden up almost to her crotch. A tall black girl with perfect features and close-cropped hair is pressed up against his back. "Well, he definitely looks appeased," I say, and Peregrine laughs.

She leads me into a huge, sprawling bathroom. "Change in there," she orders.

I slip inside and quickly shrug into the tiny swathe of fabric Peregrine has shoved into my hands. I'm unsurprised to see that it hits above mid-thigh, but at least I'm not flashing anyone. I tug it down uncomfortably and, clutching my own clothes in my hands, open the door.

"You look hot," Peregrine says. She snatches my clothes and adds, "I'll put these away. On second thought, perhaps I should burn them, since bootcut jeans are totally passé."

"They're comfortable," I protest, but she just snorts. "Why are we wearing togas, anyhow?"

"Parties are so much more fun when they're themed," she says. "And since Chloe and I went through the whole Greek system at LSU and chose only the hottest people, we figured Hot Greek would be a great theme for our little soirée. Try to keep up."

Back in the ballroom, Peregrine drifts away and I stand against the wall awkwardly until Chloe walks up wearing a toga even shorter than mine.

"Have you seen Justin?" she asks over the music. The dance floor is full of hot guys ogling Arelia and Margaux and casting looks at Chloe and me in the corner. I feel conspicuous, and I tug on the too-short hem of my toga again.

"No," I say. "Isn't he with you?"

She shakes her head. "He keeps disappearing with this group of frat guys," she says miserably. "Do you think he's doing drugs?"

"Doesn't seem like the type," I tell her.

"At least he's not trying to get with the sorority girls," she says.

"Yeah, I think Pascal seems to have the monopoly on that." We look back to the dance floor, where Pascal's gyrating sandwich seems to have grown. There's a girl with long brown hair giving him a come-hither look and a girl with the biggest fake breasts I've ever seen jiggling pointedly in his direction. He looks delighted. "Is Caleb here?" I ask uneasily.

"Maybe he's with Peregrine," she suggests. My stomach swims.

Chloe snaps to attention as soon as Justin strolls in from the direction of the front hallway. "I have to go," she says quickly. "Have fun."

She's already making a beeline across the dance floor before I can reply. I'm about to turn and go look for Caleb when I feel a hand brush against my arm. "What are you doing standing over here all alone?" says a male voice in my ear.

I turn to see a blond guy with brown eyes and glasses smiling at me.

"Just hanging out," I tell him.

"Well, you want to just hang out with me?" he asks. He doesn't wait for an answer before introducing himself. "Blake Montoire, Lambda Delta Epsilon."

"I'm Eveny," I reply.

"Which sorority are you in?"

"I'm not. I live here in Carrefour."

"Wow, cool," he says. "Pretty amazing town you've got. I've never seen houses this gorgeous. Built around the turn of the last century, right? Maybe 1904 or so?"

"How'd you know that?"

"I'm majoring in architecture. Although I have no desire to talk about school tonight. I'd rather talk about you."

He looks down at me flirtatiously, and I can feel my cheeks heating up. I'm flattered by the attention, but there are fifty guys here and only a dozen girls; maybe he's just run out of other options.

"I'm going to go get a drink," I tell him.

His expression falters. "I'll come with you. Protect you from all those other guys who'll want to hit on you."

"Thanks, but I'm good," I tell him, already inching away. "I'll be back in a little while."

Instead of returning, I circulate around the party for the next hour, feeling a bit like a character from *The Great Gatsby*. Champagne's flowing from a big fountain out back, people are getting drunker and wilder, and the dance floor heaves with more frat boys every few minutes. I would have thought that a bunch of partygoers in togas would look sort of dorky, but because Peregrine and Chloe only invited the hottest people, the backyard is filled with Adonis look-alikes. I'm scanning the party for a glimpse of Caleb when I spot Arelia and Blake disappearing upstairs together. So much for his interest in me.

By one in the morning, I'm ready to go. I find Peregrine to thank her for the party and ask where my clothes are, but she's too busy making out with a tall, muscular guy with a tattoo of a tiger on his arm to say anything other than, "Just wear the toga home, for goodness' sake, Eveny."

Arelia, Margaux, and Chloe are in the corner of the ballroom whispering to one another, so I say a quick goodbye to them before heading out the front door.

Blake is sitting on the step and jumps up as I walk by. "Hey, Eveny, where are you off to?"

"Heading home," I say without stopping.

He hurries to catch up with me. "I'll walk you. You

never know what might be lurking out there this time of night."

"I'll be fine," I tell him. I can't resist adding, "Maybe Arelia could use an escort back to her place, though."

He looks surprised. "She was just showing me around the house. Nothing happened." He grasps my forearm as he adds earnestly, "You're the girl I've been thinking about all night."

"Eveny?" comes a voice from the darkness behind me. I turn to see Caleb striding out of the house. Somehow, the toga looks better on him than it does on anyone else at the party. "What are you doing?"

I open my mouth to answer, but Blake beats me to it. "Hey, man, I was just about to walk her home."

"I'll do it," Caleb says instantly. He walks right past Blake and offers his arm to me. "C'mon."

"Look, man, I was talking to her—" Blake begins, but Caleb cuts him off.

"She's my girlfriend," he says, which makes my cheeks immediately heat up. "And I'm taking her home."

He turns and begins striding down the driveway, pulling me with him, before Blake can respond.

"Hey," I say, my heart fluttering madly as soon as the sounds of the party have faded behind us and we're alone. "Where'd you come from? I haven't seen you all night."

"I was around."

"You called me your girlfriend," I say after a minute. I'm thankful for the darkness, because he can't see me blushing.

"Oh," he says. "I didn't mean it, obviously."

I shake my head. "Yes, because that would be horrible."

"Sorry," he says. "That came out wrong."

I blink a few times. "Well, if I'm so repulsive to you, why did you drag me away from the perfectly nice, cute guy who was hitting on me?"

He stops walking and looks at me in surprise. "You were interested in that guy? I thought I was saving you from him."

"I didn't ask you to save me," I snap.

"And you're not repulsive," he says after a pause. "At all."

"Gee thanks," I say. "I can't think of the last time someone said something so flattering to me."

"Eveny—" he begins, but he stops as I pull my arm away from his.

"I can take it from here," I say, already quickening my pace towards my own front porch, which is visible on the hill up ahead. "Goodnight."

"But—" he begins to protest.

"I said goodnight," I say stiffly. I double my pace and continue ahead without looking back.

That night, the dream about the parlour returns, and it's even more vivid than last week. I hear screaming and crying as the blood pours out, and I see someone creeping from the room, hugging the shadows. I can't make out his face or any of his features in the darkness, so I follow him as he walks through the front door.

But the moment I leave the house, it begins to crumble. I run into the yard, but I lose the man in the darkness as I turn in horror. My beautiful mansion, the one my ancestors built, disintegrates, its bricks and stones crashing to the ground with a mighty roar. "No!" I cry.

But the tide of blood from the parlour is rising around me now, hot and sticky. I try to run from it, but as I get to the edge of the cemetery, it drags me down and pulls me under.

Eighteen

On Monday morning, I wake up to a missed call from Meredith. When I play back her message, I grit my teeth as I listen to her chirp, "I hope you're not still mad at me. What Trevor and I have is special, and I know you'll be a good enough friend to understand." What irks me about her behaviour has little to do with the feelings I once had for Trevor. With the distance of a few weeks and a thousand miles, and with destiny and power swirling around me in ways I never could have imagined, Trevor feels irrelevant.

What bothers me more is how easily Meredith has rejected the idea that my feelings could be hurt. The reality is, she simply doesn't care.

I'm still grumbling to myself as I head out the front door, and I almost trip over Caleb, who's inexplicably sitting on my doorstep. He hastily stands and brushes his hands off. "Sorry, I didn't know if your aunt was up yet, and I didn't want to wake anyone."

"What are you doing here?" I ask. Even though I have bigger things to worry about, his instant dismissal of me on the walk home from Peregrine's still stings.

"I wanted to explain what I meant on Saturday night."

"Oh, I think it was pretty clear," I tell him. I lock the door behind me and start walking down the driveway. "Let me recap: you could never imagine dating me, even though you don't find me *entirely* repulsive. That about the gist of it?"

He falls into step beside me, even though his Jeep is still parked in my driveway. "You don't understand."

"Don't I?"

"Eveny—" He attempts to interject, but I'm on a roll.

"I know I'm an outcast here. I know I don't really belong with the Dolls. But if you're not interested in me, why do you keep lurking around being all sexy and intriguing?"

He stops walking. "You think I'm sexy and intriguing?"

I groan. He's missing the point.

After a moment, he hurries to catch up with me. "Eveny, I'm not trying to jerk you around."

I snort. "Yeah, well, your social skills could use a little work."

"I know." He hesitates. "The thing is, I do like you. A lot."

This time, I'm the one who stops walking. "What?"

"I like you, Eveny."

A whole fleet of butterflies invades my stomach. I try to keep my face neutral. "Well, you have a funny way of showing it."

"The thing is, I'm trying my best to stop having these feelings for you."

The words hit me hard, and I start walking again so that he can't see my face. "Gee, sorry to be such an inconvenience."

He grabs my arm and spins me around. "Would you stop being sarcastic and listen to me?" He takes a deep breath and blurts out, "I'm not *allowed* to be in love with you. I'm not allowed to date you. I'm not allowed to be feeling this way at all."

"What are you talking about?"

"I'm your protector, Eveny," he says. "For as long as Carrefour has existed, my family has protected your family."

"My protector?"

"It was all established in the town's founding ceremony," he explains. He looks miserable. "There's one protector for each queen. We're specially charmed and trained to guard you, and there are rules that go along with it, just like there are rules dictating everything else in this damned town."

I realize what he means. "And one of the rules is that you can't have feelings for the person you're protecting."

He nods. "As long as you're inside Carrefour's walls, I'm supposed to be able to sense when you're in danger. But the more I feel for you, the fuzzier the protectorate link gets. Like, I don't know, the way Wi-Fi slows down when there are too many people using it."

I choke out a laugh, despite everything. "You're comparing your feelings for me to a slow internet connection?"

"Maybe not the best analogy ever." He half smiles, but the expression quickly disappears as he adds, "Look, I'm sorry. But if I keep letting myself feel this way, I'm putting you in danger. And I can't do that."

I take a deep breath, trying to absorb what he's saying. "But what if I'm willing to risk not being protected?"

"Why would you do that?" he asks, his voice catching.

"Because I like you too," I say, "and I'm getting sick of some ancestral pact controlling my life."

There's sadness etched across his face as he says, "I can't run from who I am any more than you can. I'll just have to figure out a way to stop having these feelings." He pauses and says, "I just thought I owed you an explanation."

Without another word, he walks back up the hill and gets into his Jeep. I stay glued to the spot as he guns the engine and comes down my driveway to where I'm standing. "Get in," he says as he pulls up alongside me.

"I'm okay walking," I say, trying not to think of the first time I climbed into his car, when electricity crackled between us and anything felt possible. It feels like an eternity has passed since then.

"Eveny, you know I have to keep an eye on you. It'll be a lot easier if you're in my passenger seat."

"Fine," I say after a minute, climbing into his car and slamming the door behind me.

We ride the rest of the way to school in silence, and when he drops me off in the parking lot, he says that he has to go.

"Go where?" I ask, surprised.

"Training," he says, his jaw stiff, "with Patrick and Oscar, Peregrine's and Chloe's protectors."

"Oh," I manage. "What does this training involve, exactly?"

"It's part intensive workout, part martial arts, part reflex training and speed. But the biggest thing is reviewing years' worth of intel our fathers, their fathers, and their fathers' fathers have gathered on Main de Lumière. It's about knowing exactly how they might hurt you and staying one step ahead."

"So you're training to be a killing machine?"

I expect him to laugh, but instead, his mouth straightens into a thin line. "We're trained to kill, but that's always the last resort."

"I was joking."

He looks sad. "I know. So I'll see you later, okay?"

"Wait," I add. "All this protector stuff. Why tell me now?"

He hesitates for a moment before saying, "All these years, I figured I'd hate you, which would make protecting you easy because there wouldn't be any feelings involved. But then I saw you for the first time, and I felt exactly the opposite. I still do." He drives off without another word and my Stone of Carrefour, which is hidden under my standard-issue oxford shirt, heats up against my chest.

I'm floating down the hall in a fog of my own making a few minutes later when I hear Mona Silvestre from my French class saying to a guy near her locker, "Holy crap, did you hear what happened to that guy from LSU?"

"I heard he was murdered right outside the gate to Carrefour!" the guy replies.

I hurry to my own locker, where more people are gossiping around me as I grab my books. "Dude, some frat guy was stabbed to death," a soccer player named Phil Demetroux is saying. "I heard it was so gruesome that the police chief hurled all over the crime scene."

By the time I make it to first-period English, I've managed to piece together the full story through snippets of hallway gossip, and I'm chilled to the bone.

Apparently, sometime on Saturday night, one of the LSU guys on Peregrine's guest list was stabbed to death just outside the city walls. But since his car wasn't found, police speculate that someone stopped him on the road, perhaps pretending to be injured, and killed him to steal his car.

"What the hell?" I hiss at Peregrine as soon as she takes her seat beside me in class. "You said nothing bad would happen if we opened the gates for a few hours!"

She looks at me defiantly. "I don't know what you're talking about."

"Someone is *dead*!"

"Quiet down, okay?" I'm surprised to see Peregrine looking tearful. "I didn't mean for it to turn out this way. I swear, Eveny, I don't know what could have happened!"

Chloe slides into her seat then, looking equally disturbed.

"Eveny's pissed at us," Peregrine mumbles.

"We didn't know," Chloe says miserably.

"Well, this should really help us keep Carrefour off Main de Lumière's radar," I mutter. "Nice work."

Chloe and Peregrine spend the remainder of class staring straight ahead. When the bell rings, they pick up their things and dash out without another word. My Stone of Carrefour continues to hum against my chest.

* * *

In third-period French, before the bell rings, Drew pulls his desk over to mine and whispers, "You heard about that dead frat guy?"

I nod without looking at him. I don't want to give anything away with my eyes. "Pretty awful."

"Doesn't it seem kind of strange to you that someone would be stabbed to death right outside our gates for no apparent reason?"

I shrug and look away. "Totally strange."

"What was he even doing here?" Drew asks.

I'm saved from answering as Mrs Toliver calls the class to order and begins talking about irregular verbs. Drew reluctantly scoots his desk back, but I can feel his gaze on me all through class.

At lunch, I deliberately avoid locking eyes with Peregrine or Chloe; instead, I grab a lunch tray and get in the caf line with Liv and Max, who look surprised to see me.

"You're not eating with the Dolls today?" Max asks.

"I'd just rather eat with you guys."

"See?" Liv says to Max. "I told you she wasn't one of them."

Max shrugs. "Yeah, but who wouldn't want to be? *I* even want to be a Doll."

Liv rolls her eyes at him, and I force a laugh. I order some gross-looking lasagne from the cafeteria lady, grab a carton of chocolate milk, and follow Liv and Max to a table in the centre of the caf once we've all paid. I've just taken my first bite of the lasagne, which isn't as bad as it looks, when a shadow falls over me. I know without looking who's there.

"Eveny?" It's Peregrine, her voice hushed. "Can I talk to you for a minute?"

Beside me, I hear Max drop his fork. He and Liv stare, and I'm not sure if it's because she's gracing us with her presence in the cafeteria, or because even with her Louboutin boots, a fitted fur vest, and perfect make-up, she looks terrible.

"About what?" I ask. I take another bite of lasagne and do my best to ignore her.

"You know," she says. She's being uncharacteristically meek, and it's freaking me out a little. "Please?"

"I'm eating now," I say stiffly.

She leans down and whispers in my ear, "*Please?* There's a serious problem."

"No kidding," I reply.

"What's the problem?" Max pipes up eagerly from across the table. His eyes dart over to Peregrine. "If you need help with something, I'll help you."

Liv smacks him on the back of his head, but Peregrine acts like she hasn't heard him. "Just come talk to me for a minute, Eveny. I'm asking nicely."

I slam my fork down. "I'll be right back," I say. I stand

up and follow Peregrine outside. She begins to head for the Hickories, but I say, "No. I'm eating with Max and Liv today. If you have something to say, say it to me here."

She looks wounded. "How come you don't want to eat with us?"

"For real?" When she doesn't reply, I say, "Look what you've done! You wanted to have a party so you could have more hot guys than usual drooling all over you. And someone ended up dead because of it!"

"But I didn't mean for that to happen!" she protests.

I look back towards the cafeteria and see through the window that Drew has arrived at the table and is deep in conversation with Liv. Max is staring at us with wide eyes. "Well, Liv, Max and Drew don't create situations where innocent people die," I say.

"This isn't totally my fault," she says. "Look, I know I screwed up. But there's a bigger issue here. The guy they found dead was killed *before* my party."

"So?"

"*So*, everyone at the party was accounted for," she says urgently. "We had a guest list at the door. Every single person signed in. So how did that happen if one of them was already lying dead outside the gates?"

My blood runs cold. "What are you saying?"

"That someone stole the dead guy's identity and used

it to get into town. Into *our party*. For all we know, he's still here."

"But the gates are closed again, right, so we're protected?"

"Not exactly," she says miserably. "If someone got into town when the gates were open, he'd still be able to do what he pleased here. Including kill us."

"So fix it!" I cry.

"I *can't*," she says. "Not alone, anyway. Just like I couldn't open the gates on my own, I can't restore the protection by myself either."

I shake my head. "I should never have taken part in this," I say, more to myself than to her.

"You didn't know," Peregrine says. "Please, Eveny. If you, Chloe and I work together—"

"Why should I trust you?" I interrupt her.

Peregrine looks at me blankly. "What are you talking about?"

"I know there are more important things to worry about, but you're obviously keeping things from me. Like, couldn't you have clued me in about the fact that Caleb's my protector? Or were you having too much fun watching me make a fool of myself?"

"So he told you." The corner of her mouth twitches. "Well, it was kind of amusing watching you stare at him like he was God's gift to earth." When I just glare at her, she adds, "Fine, so Chloe and I thought it might be too much for you to handle along with everything else, okay? In case you haven't noticed, we've been trying to ease you into this whole zandara thing. It's obvious that you like him, so why hurt your feelings right away by telling you that you two can never be together?"

"Yes, you're a benevolent angel," I say drily. "So while we're on the subject, is there anything else you're keeping from me? Any other secrets about my own life I should know about?"

"Now you're just being a drama queen." She sticks out her lower lip in a dramatic pout. "So are you going to keep yelling at me, or are you going to help us fix this?"

"Obviously I'm going to help you. Tonight?"

Her shoulders sag. "It'll take us a day or two to put together the necessary herbs to render the intruder powerless. We'll need the help of the whole sosyete too. This is a big deal."

"I don't understand," I say. "Can't we just reverse the charm we cast to let him in on Saturday?"

"We have to find out who the guy is first. As long as one of us in the sosyete actually saw him at some point that night, as long as we know what he looks like, we can harness that memory in a ceremony and cast against him."

"And we can't just cast a charm to learn his identity?" I ask.

Peregrine purses her lips. "You don't think we would

have done that already if we could? No, the spirits rely on our eyes. If we didn't see something, the spirits won't know it either. It's exactly why we have no way to learn who killed Glory. No one saw what happened, except for Glory herself and the killer."

The words send a shiver down my spine. "Well, what's the name of the guy who was killed outside the gates?" I persist. "Obviously the killer used his identity to get in."

"The police haven't released his name yet. But I'll keep trying to find out."

"You do that," I say tightly. I can't resist adding, "I don't believe this is happening. All because you wanted to have a party."

Peregrine's eyes narrow. "You can quit blaming me, Eveny. You know *nothing* about how this town works. Nothing."

With that, she spins on her stiletto heel and walks away towards the Hickories.

Back in the cafeteria, Max, Drew, and Liv stare at me as I slide into my seat and pick up my fork. I take a bite, but the lasagne's cold. I've lost my appetite anyhow. "What?" I ask after a moment.

"Did you just stand up to her?" Liv asks.

"She had a question she needed to ask. It was no big deal."

"It's like she thinks she runs this town, like she thinks

she's *so* much better than the rest of us," Liv mutters. "It's about time someone lets her know she's not the queen of the world."

Liv returns to chatting with the guys, and I watch them for a moment, feeling like I'm miles away. Although Peregrine may not be the queen of the world, she *is* one of the Queens of Carrefour. And like it or not, I am too.

NINETEEN

THAT AFTERNOON AFTER SCHOOL, I'm changing into jeans and a T-shirt in my room when I spot my mother's letter lying on my desk. I pause and sit on the corner of my bed to read it again. It feels like the answers to the question of what I'm supposed to do should be there in her words. Then again, maybe that's the wishful thinking of someone who's just stepped into the weirdest situation of her life.

I head outside to look for Boniface, who I'm hoping will be able to help me understand. He's not in the rose garden, but I eventually find him in the toolshed, organizing a rack of hammers and screwdrivers. He turns when I enter. "Hi, honey," he says. "How was school?"

"I need to talk to you," I say instead of replying.

He stops what he's doing and looks at me with concern. "What is it?"

"We think there's a Main de Lumière soldier in town," I tell him. "Not just the one who killed Glory. But someone from the outside."

"That's not possible." He looks suddenly unsteady on his feet. "How would they have gotten in?"

I reluctantly explain the fraternity party and the guy whose body was found outside the gates. "I know it was the wrong thing to do," I conclude miserably, "but at the time I thought it was a harmless sort of wrong."

"Of course you did," he says. "But Peregrine and Chloe, they know better. They've gotten out of control."

I pull my mother's letter out of my pocket and hand it to him. "I feel like there's something in here I'm supposed to understand, something connected to what's going on now. Can you take a look?"

"Of course." He unfolds the letter, and a shadow crosses his face as he begins to read. "This sounds just like her," he says when he's done. "God rest her soul."

"What do you think the two verses are supposed to mean?" I ask. "Or her line that dark times are coming?"

"She knew her sister queens well enough to realize that if she was gone, they might resort to practising zandara in a way that defies your ancestors' rules. And she knew enough to be afraid of what that might lead to."

"I don't understand."

"The universe is like a seesaw – when one side is lifted

up, the other has nowhere to go but down – and zandara exists in the middle. Action and reaction. But when your mother died and Carrefour lost its triumvirate, her sister queens' power was greatly reduced, and they could no longer cast with the strength they were accustomed to. In other words, they can use herbs, but there's nothing to magnify their power any more."

"Right, it's why the protective charms around the town are crumbling. I know all that."

"But did you ever stop to wonder why the wealth of central Carrefour hasn't crumbled too?" Boniface asks.

My stomach swims uneasily as he continues.

"A few years after your mother died they realized there was another source from which they could draw power," he says. "They're still able to execute small charms with herbs and flowers, and they do so when they can. But the bigger things – new cars, great wealth, unnaturally good looks – those have to come from somewhere else. So they tapped into the Périphérie."

"What do you mean?" I have a bad feeling about this.

"The Périphérie was always less privileged than central Carrefour, but it wasn't like it is today," he says. "That's a result of Annabelle Marceau and Scarlett St. Pierre realizing they could achieve great things by taking from the other side of town. Casting a charm to get a new sports car, for example. Because they can't draw a large amount of power from flowers and herbs without having three queens working together, they cast using the Périphérie's good fortune instead. So they get their car, but something of value crumbles in the Périphérie, the same way a herb dies in the world when it's drawn for a simple charm. That's an overly simplistic explanation, but you get the idea. There's always a balance, and when it doesn't come from plants, it has to come from somewhere."

"So they've been taking from the Périphérie all these years, making themselves richer while people out there get poorer and poorer?" I whisper.

"Yes. I don't approve, and neither do most of the people in the sosyete. But they're the queens. They don't need our permission. And until you came back, Chloe and Peregrine were doing the same thing. Now they won't have to; they have you."

My mind is spinning. "But look at all the destruction they've caused."

Boniface nods, and that's when I realize he hasn't addressed the second verse my mother wrote. "What do you think the rest of her letter means?" I ask.

He looks away. "I'm not sure."

I take the letter back from him and read it. *Blood of my blood, in dreams I will come to show you the way.* And suddenly, I know.

"I need to get into the parlour, Boniface," I say. "There's

something in there I'm supposed to see; I think that's what the verse means." I quickly explain the dreams I've been having and the way the door burned my hand when I tried to open it.

"My mom's letter specifically mentions blood and dreams," I conclude. "That can't be a coincidence."

He looks into my eyes for a long moment, like he's trying to figure something out. Then he sighs and says, "There's no missing key, Eveny. The room is charmed. It hasn't been opened in fourteen years."

Well that explains the burning-hot handle. "Who charmed it?"

"Ms Marceau and Ms St. Pierre closed the parlour off years ago. It holds memories that they wanted to forget – but that they couldn't afford to lose altogether."

"Memories connected to my mother?"

"I think I'd better call Annabelle and Scarlett," he says.

"No." I shake my head. "I'm going to uncharm the room myself." I don't trust the mothers, especially now that I know they've been destroying the Périphérie. If they're hiding something connected to my family, I have to find out.

I stride towards the house, and Boniface follows me.

"Please, Eveny, I think you should wait until someone can be here to explain things to you."

"Explain *what*?"

He looks uneasy, but he doesn't answer the question. Instead, he says, "How about I call Peregrine and Chloe? Perhaps they should be here for this."

"*They* know about the parlour too? Unbelievable." Once again, everyone has been keeping me in the dark. I feel a surge of anger as I storm away, my mind spinning through the herbs and flowers I've studied over the years.

What comes to mind as I reach the closed parlour doors is something I once planted in our community garden. Its technical name is *Euonymus americanus*, but it's more commonly known as bursting-heart or burning-bush. Superstitious people put it over their doorways to repel unwanted magic.

It may not be the perfect plant for what I'm trying to do, but it should work. I stand in front of the doors and ask Eloi Oke to open the gate. Then I take a deep breath, think of my mother, hold my left ring finger against my Stone of Carrefour, and say, "Bursting-heart, *Euonymus americanus*, I draw your power. Please, spirits, open this door to me and reveal the secrets that lie inside."

For a moment, nothing happens. Then I hear a click, and one of the doors opens a crack. Musty air escapes in a whoosh, and I drop my stone and reach for the handle, my heart racing in anticipation as I push it open.

As my eyes adjust to the dim light, I realize the room is exactly as it appears in my dreams – except now enormous spans of cobwebs hang from the chandeliers, and the mirrored walls are covered with a film of dust and smoke so thick that the images blinking back at me are dark and hazy. Candles still stand, half melted and covered in dust, on big candelabras.

I walk across the room to the spot where I've seen my toddler self standing in my dreams. I bend to touch the floor, and as I do, I can see a huge, dark stain on the hardwood. It vanishes as soon as I pull my hand away. A chill sweeps through me, and I turn around slowly to find Boniface looking at me.

"This is blood, isn't it?" I ask.

"Yes," he says sadly.

"Whose?" I ask. But the look on his face tells me all I need to know. "My mom's?" I ask in disbelief. "But she died miles from here. Didn't she?"

Boniface frowns. "Eveny, I really think you should wait until your aunt comes home. She'll explain everything."

"If she'd wanted to explain," I say, "she would have already." I clench and unclench my fists. "Are there herbs that will let me see what happened in this room?"

"Eveny, your aunt will be furious with me," he says.

"Please!" I exclaim. "I promise, I'll tell Aunt Bea you tried to stop me. I deserve to know what happened."

"Yes, I suppose you do." He crosses the room and stands in front of the bookcase for a moment before pulling a narrow, leather-bound volume from the shelf. He flips through it, seems to find what he's looking for, and returns to me. "I believe peppermint leaves and flax seed will call the past into focus."

"What's that book?"

"Your mother's herb journal. It's incomplete, but she took notes on herbs and charms that worked particularly well for her. It's yours now." He hands it to me. "I hope this is the right thing. Good luck. But I can't be here for this," he says as he walks out of the room.

I put the journal down on the coffee table and take a deep breath. I again call on Eloi Oke to open the gate, then, with my left ring finger on my Stone of Carrefour, I invoke peppermint and flax seed and ask the spirits to show me what happened here. As the wind picks up, the candles around me flicker suddenly on, their flames growing and shrinking like the room itself is breathing. Suddenly, all of the flames go out, and I'm plunged into darkness. I hear the faintest of whispers, a woman's voice saying, "*It shall be.*"

When the candles flicker on again, the cobwebs are gone and the parlour looks entirely different. It's just like it was fourteen years ago, just like it has looked in my nightmares the last few weeks. Suddenly, three figures appear in the middle of the floor. They're hazy at first, but they quickly materialize, and I gasp as I recognize my mother and younger versions of Peregrine's and Chloe's mothers. All three are dressed in long, gauzy gowns that catch the candlelight and make them look like ethereal fairies.

"Mom!" I cry and take a step forward. The women don't hear me, though, and when I reach out to touch my mother, my hand goes right through her. It's like I'm watching a projected image on a movie screen.

The three mothers begin to chant and dance, and then the candles flicker out again. I hear a panicky voice ask, "What just happened?" I'm pretty sure it's Chloe's mother.

Another voice – Peregrine's mom – replies shakily, "I don't know. It must have been the wind."

Then there are heavy footsteps and the sound of something sliding. "Who's there?" says a voice I recognize as my mother's. Hearing her after all this time pierces my heart.

There's silence for a few seconds, then a pealing scream and a soft thudding sound before footsteps retreat and a door slams. A moment later, the overhead light flickers on, and I see Peregrine's mother near the light switch, blinking into the sudden illumination. "Sandrine!" she cries.

I follow her eyes to see my mother lying with her neck sliced open in a rapidly spreading pool of her own blood.

I sob uncontrollably as the rest of the scene unfolds. Peregrine's and Chloe's moms are screaming. Chloe's mom tries to revive my mother, but she's drifting in and out of consciousness. "We have to go get Bea," Peregrine's mother says.

Chloe's mother stands up, and when she does, I see that she's covered in my mother's blood. Her mascara is running down her face in teary rivers. "And Boniface," she adds weakly. She turns back to my mom. "Sandrine, we'll be right back. We're going for help. Hang on, sugar."

They run out of the room and, in the sudden quiet, I can hear my mother gasping for air. It breaks my heart. I move towards her, and that's when I see my younger self amble into the room, blinking in confusion. She's wearing the same nightgown from my dreams, and I know this is the moment I've been seeing. I watch as she rushes over and wraps herself around my mother, trying to fix her, trying to stop the blood.

My mother whispers something, and I can just barely make out her words: "You're the only one who can save us all. I live on in you," she says, and then her whole body goes limp.

"Mommy?" I hear three-year-old me ask in a small voice. "Mommy, wake up!"

I'm full-out sobbing as the images slowly fade away and the room returns to the present. Dazed, I stumble out of the parlour and into Boniface's waiting arms.

"You saw everything, didn't you?" he asks gently as he rubs my back.

"I saw my mother die," I sob. "She didn't kill herself. She was murdered. Why has everyone been lying about it all these years? Lying to *me*? Why has everyone let me believe my mother took her own life?"

"Honey, no one knows exactly what happened that day. But we couldn't have the police asking questions, not if her death was linked to zandara. So a decision was made to stage a car crash. It was for the good of the sosyete, and it made sense at the time. Your aunt asked that everyone play along for your sake too. She didn't want you to remember your mom dying this way."

"It was better that I think she'd killed herself?" I whisper incredulously. "That I'd think she deliberately abandoned me?"

"Bea was just trying to protect you. While Peregrine's and Chloe's mothers took care of staging the accident, your aunt and I calmed you down, got you back into bed, and convinced you it was just a bad dream. Chloe's and Peregrine's mothers gave you a charmed potion to make you forget what you'd seen."

"They should never have done that."

"But no child should ever, ever grow up with that kind of sad memory, and we were all afraid that if the police were called, you'd let the cat out of the bag about the ceremonies that were going on here. The police chief was a member of the sosyete, but none of the officers were.

We couldn't take the chance of anyone finding out."

"So who killed her?" When he doesn't answer, I add, "Was it Main de Lumière?"

"You didn't see her killer in your vision?" he asks. When I shake my head, he sighs. "At first we assumed it was Main de Lumière, but tradition and ritual are very important to them, and none of us really believed they'd kill your mother by slitting her throat instead of stabbing her through the heart."

"So if it wasn't them…" I say.

"No one knows what could have happened," he says simply, looking away.

"Okay, I get why no one wanted a little kid to have a horrible memory like that," I concede. "But I'm seventeen now. Why hasn't anyone said anything?"

Boniface looks sad. "It wasn't my place to tell you, honey. I can't speak for the others."

I clench my fists, a wave of frustration rising within me. All the lies, all the half truths – I'm suddenly furious. "Peregrine and Chloe knew, didn't they? They've known all along."

I don't wait for an answer; my blood is boiling. "I'm going over there."

"Eveny—" Boniface begins, but I'm already on a mission, already moving towards the front door. I have to confront them, to find out what else they've been hiding from me. "Wait, Eveny!" Boniface calls after me. "Come back!"

"I can't," I say as I shut the door behind me. I take off running towards Peregrine's opulent mansion on the next hill over.

TWENTY

I POUND ON PEREGRINE'S FRONT door with both fists and am surprised when she and Chloe answer together.

"You lied to me!" I cry, still breathless from my run.

They look at each other and then back at me. "Lied about what?" Chloe asks.

"About the night my mother died!" I say. "Your mothers were there. I just charmed the parlour and watched the whole thing play out. Your mothers saw *everything*. You knew all along, and you let me keep believing my mother had left me on purpose!"

"Calm down, Eveny," Peregrine says crisply. "Anger isn't getting you anywhere."

But her words only make me madder. "Could you cut the whole icy superiority thing for a minute and be honest with me? Or is that too much for you?"

Chloe takes a step forward and reaches for me without saying a word. At first I pull away, but she just steps closer and stays there until I crumple. She folds me into a hug as I start to cry. "We're sorry, Eveny," she says. "We're sorry we didn't tell you. And we're sorry about what happened to your mom." She pulls away after a moment and tilts my chin up so that I'm staring right at her. "If you come inside, we'll tell you what we know."

I reluctantly follow her in, glancing at Peregrine as I go. She's being strangely silent, and her lips are set in a thin line.

"Are your mothers here?" I ask once we're seated in the living room.

Peregrine shakes her head and looks almost apologetic. "They're at Chloe's house. We can wait until they're back if you want…"

"No," I say immediately. "I want to know the truth. Now."

"What did you see?" Chloe asks gently.

"Wait, go back," Peregrine interrupts. "You said you charmed the room? How?"

"I used my Stone of Carrefour."

The eyes of both girls widen. "You have your stone?" Chloe asks in a whisper. "We thought it was lost with your mother."

"This is a huge deal," Peregrine says flatly. "I can't believe you didn't tell us."

"Kind of like you didn't tell me that my mother was murdered?" I say through gritted teeth.

Chloe puts a hand on Peregrine's arm and says to her, "We can talk about the stone later. Right now, Eveny's trying to tell us about her vision."

I recap what played out in the parlour. The ceremony. The plunge into darkness. The screams. My mother gasping for breath as Peregrine's and Chloe's mothers ran for help. My mother dying.

"Our mothers aren't sure whether your mom was a target because of something personal, or whether it was someone trying to weaken the power of Carrefour by eliminating the triumvirate," Chloe explains when I'm done.

"Without your mother," Peregrine adds, "our mothers were greatly weakened, and it's been harder for them to..."

Her voice trails off and she adds, "Harder for them to cast their magic."

"So I've heard," I say stiffly. "Somehow you've all managed to convince yourselves that it's fine to use the Périphérie to keep your own lives floating along perfectly."

"You don't understand; they owed it to us," Peregrine says right away. "Our ancestors have been providing for the people in the Périphérie for over a century."

"That doesn't justify taking from them now!" I exclaim. "All the crumbling houses, the people who have lost their money, the dead lawns, the decaying trees… That seems right to you?"

"We had to keep central Carrefour up somehow," Chloe says in a small voice.

"Even the weather?" I ask.

"The sunshine on this side of town doesn't create itself," Peregrine says. "We don't use it every day, though. You can see there's a storm coming now." Peregrine's eyebrows knit together in annoyance. "You can't expect us just to stop *living*."

"I don't," I say. "But you have no right to live in luxury that's built on other people's lives falling apart. That's disgusting!"

Chloe quickly picks up the thread of Peregrine's argument. "It doesn't have to be that way any more, Eveny. That's the great thing about you being back. We have a triumvirate again. We can start drawing our power purely from plants. We can even restore the Périphérie."

"If you join us," Peregrine says, "our lives can be just as we want them to be. You seem to keep forgetting what a gift this is." She reaches out to take my hand, but I pull away.

"But you and your moms have already destroyed so much. You can't possibly justify that."

Peregrine rolls her eyes. "Whatever," she says. "Don't goody-goody us. You've adjusted quite well to the perks of zandara since you've been back, haven't you? Your beautiful house, your huge property, your instant popularity, the money to attend Pointe Laveau. It's all zandara, Eveny. All of it."

"We don't deserve those things," I reply. "None of us do."

I stand up and look at the two of them. They're perfect on the outside, exactly what any girl would want to look like. Perfect hair, perfect skin, perfect bodies, perfect *everything*. But none of it's real. It never was. "I can't do this," I say. "Not until I've figured out what's right and wrong here."

"Do you have any idea how much you'd be walking away from if you turn your back on us?" Peregrine demands.

"None of those things matter to me," I say. "Besides, if we stopped – no magic, no charms – Main de Lumière wouldn't have a reason to punish us any more."

"Sure, it's possible they'd stop coming after us," Peregrine says, "but in the meantime, we'd have nothing! We'd be like everyone else."

"That's better than being dead," I tell her. I take a deep breath. "You've gone too far, Peregrine. You know that. I'll do the ceremony with you whenever we figure out the identity of the Main de Lumière soldier who snuck in during the party, but after that, I quit."

"You can't quit!" she cries.

"Watch me," I say.

With that, I stride out of Peregrine's perfect mansion, slamming her perfect front door behind me as I go. I don't look back.

Boniface is sitting in the parlour with his head in his hands when I storm through the front doorway of my house a few minutes later.

"Eveny?" he asks, standing up right away. "Are you okay?"

"Just peachy." I move past him without making eye contact.

"I never should have let you into the parlour," he says, wringing his hands together and following me into the room.

I stop and look at him. "I wish someone had told me before."

"Eveny—" he begins.

"Any other secrets you're keeping from me?" I interrupt. "How about my dad? Is everyone lying to me about him too? I know he's been back since I was born."

"Yes, he's been here, Eveny," Boniface says slowly. "But he's gone now."

"Where?" I demand. "Where did he go?"

But Boniface just shakes his head. I throw my hands up in frustration, grab my mother's herb journal from the coffee table where I left it earlier, and head upstairs to my room without saying another word. I can feel his concerned gaze on my back as I go.

I flip through the little book until I find a page in my mother's hand entitled *The Removal of Charms from Inanimate Objects*. She's written that you must focus intently on the specific things you want uncharmed. I fold the page and dash downstairs. I don't know if her charm will successfully remove magic from this house, but I intend to try. It's the first step to making things right again.

I close myself in the parlour, and with the herb book open in front of me, I ask Eloi Oke to open the gate to the spirit world. The air in the room shifts, and I touch the Stone of Carrefour with my left ring finger. I focus on our house and property as I read the words from my mother's charm.

"Mint, nettle, and rue, I draw your power," I say. I pause and try to feel the request with my heart, like Boniface advised. "Spirits, magic killed my mother, and it's destroying this town. I want it gone from this house."

For a moment, nothing happens, but then I notice my Stone of Carrefour getting colder and colder, and something begins leaching from the parlour. I can feel it, like the air is being sucked out. The lights flicker, and a huge, crimson stain appears on the hardwood floor, just where my mother died. I stifle a scream, and it takes me a moment to realize that her blood had never really been gone at all; someone had simply cast a charm to make it disappear.

I run towards the door and pull it open, but the moment I stagger into the hallway, I almost fall over. I stare around me in horror.

It's not the same hallway I entered through just a few minutes earlier. Or rather it is, but it appears that the hall hasn't been touched in decades. It's caked with dust and cobwebs, the marble floors are cracked and chipped, and the walls sag under the weight of the house. Above me, the chandelier hangs at a precarious angle, like it's going to crash to the ground at any moment. The front door is splintered, and light slices through in jagged beams. Several of the windows are broken, and wind whistles in.

"What have I done?" I whisper, but I know the answer to my own question before the words are out of my mouth. I hadn't thought it through enough to realize that the mansion itself is mostly a product of magic. Without zandara, it's just a dilapidated old shack, and the room where my mother died still looks like a crime scene.

I have to fix this. And I'm certainly not going to turn to Peregrine or Chloe for help. Boniface will know what to do. In a panic, I run across the rotting floorboards of the living room and out the back door, which is hanging from its hinges and swaying in the breeze.

As soon as I'm through the doors, I stop dead in my tracks. My mother's beautiful rose garden, her pride and joy, is dead and decaying. The few roses that still cling to vines are wilted and grey; the rest of the garden looks like it hasn't been tended in decades. It's overgrown with weeds and smeared with mud.

"Boniface?" I cry out. But then I see him, and for a moment, I'm so stunned I can't move. He's lying motionless beside one of the rosebushes, a pair of garden shears still in his hand. "Boniface?" I whisper. I run to his side, but when I bend to help him, my breath catches in my throat, and I scramble backwards in terror.

Not only has he collapsed, but he looks like a skeleton with greying skin stretched haphazardly over the sharp juts of his bones. He's gasping for breath, but his skin is so thin and decayed I can see his lungs rising and falling inside his chest. He looks like a rotting corpse. "Eveny…" he rasps. "Help me." It sounds like a death rattle.

Boniface's eyes close and as he goes still, I back away, horrified, sure that I've somehow killed him. I'm sobbing with my hands over my mouth when Peregrine and Chloe stroll into the rose garden, looking as glamorous and unperturbed as usual.

"The front door was unlocked — well, more like

unhinged – so we let ourselves in," Peregrine says casually, her stilettos clicking across the stone path as they approach me. "Come to think of it, you're looking rather unhinged yourself."

"What did you do to Boniface?" Chloe asks, staring at his collapsed, sunken frame. "We came over because we figured you might do something rash after our talk, but we didn't think you'd hurt someone."

"I didn't mean – I mean, I didn't want – I didn't know…" I'm still stammering nonsensically, my teeth chattering, when Peregrine holds up a hand to stop me.

"Just tell us what you've done," she says calmly. "Quickly, before Boniface expires."

I take a deep breath and quickly recap what happened. "I was only trying to get rid of zandara's influence in my life," I say. "H-how did I hurt Boniface?"

"Well," Peregrine says coolly, "it's probably because in actuality, he's one hundred seventy-six years old, and zandara is the only thing keeping him alive. Or it *was*, anyhow, before you cleverly removed it. Nice work."

My whole body goes cold. "What?"

Chloe interrupts in a gentler tone. "Eveny, Boniface is one of several people in town who rely on the zandara queens to extend their lives. He's been in his seventies for more than a century now."

"Same with our groundskeeper, Milo, and Peregrine's

groundskeeper, Samuel," Chloe explains. "When the town was founded, they made a bargain: they'd help watch over the Queens of Carrefour and continue to keep up our homes without pay, in exchange for lodging and continued life."

"Like indentured servants?"

"Not really," Chloe says. "They could leave at any time."

"But if Boniface leaves, he'd die?"

"Yes, unfortunately he would, when the magic wears out," Peregrine says nonchalantly. "That's one thing zandara *can't* reverse – death. Once someone has expired, it can't be undone."

I gape at them. I have a hundred questions I want to ask. But first: "Please, help me save him," I whisper.

"Of course we'd be happy to help you," Peregrine says sweetly.

"But you have to agree to join us," Chloe adds. "We need you, Eveny. It's the only way."

"We know it's a lot to absorb," Peregrine says diplomatically. "But we promise you'll like it. And you'll have a one-third vote in how we handle things from now on."

"Like, I can tell you I think you're a real snob, and you treat people outside your sosyete like crap?" I ask coldly.

Peregrine looks surprised, but she laughs. "Eveny, I can't be wonderful to *everyone*. I simply don't have the time."

I just glare at her until she sighs heavily.

"Fine," she says. "I'll try to be more decent to your little friends. Are you happy now?"

I look down at Boniface, whose breathing is growing shallower by the moment. "Fine," I say. "I'll do it. Just help me fix this."

"Wise choice, Eveny," Peregrine says. "Come on."

She and Chloe lead me reluctantly away from the gasping Boniface and back into the parlour. While Chloe lights some candles, Peregrine asks me to remember exactly which herbs I invoked. When I tell her, she walks out the door.

"You'll have to focus your energy on this house and the grounds like you did when you cast the original charm," Chloe says while we wait for Peregrine to come back. "Feel the energy as deep in your heart as you can."

Peregrine returns a moment later with a handful of mint, nettle and rue. "Fortunately, you didn't destroy the herb garden entirely."

"Casting with the herbs themselves instead of only relying on your Stone of Carrefour to channel the herbs will help make us stronger," Chloe explains. "Now put your left ring finger on your stone, and your right hand here."

I do as she says, reaching for my stone and then folding my right hand over Peregrine's, which is upturned and clutching the herbs. Chloe's hand comes down over ours, and as soon as she touches us, I feel a surge of power. "When Peregrine's done, you'll recite the words *Mesi, zanset* with us," Chloe instructs. "It's what finishes an important charm."

"What does it mean?" I ask.

"*Thank you, ancestors,*" Chloe replies. "It's Creole. When our great-great-great-grandmothers founded Carrefour, they dealt with a lot of Haitian immigrants who had lived and died in this swamp. Some of their words became a part of zandara."

"Are we going to have a history lesson here," Peregrine asks, glancing from Chloe to me, "or are we going to fix what you messed up?"

I take a deep breath while Peregrine calls on Eloi Oke. I feel the air in the room shift, and then Peregrine chants:

Mint, nettle and rue were invoked to cast a charm.
Reverse it now, oh spirits, before it's too late.
A mistake was made here, and it must be righted.
We humbly beg you for your sympathy and assistance.

Together, the three of us say, "*Mesi, zanset. Mesi, zanset. Mesi, zanset.*"

I feel a whoosh of air, and suddenly the whole house is shifting beneath our feet. The walls straighten, the crimson pool of blood vanishes, and the peeling wallpaper turns vibrant and new again.

When Chloe pulls away a moment later, her eyes are wide.

"Did you feel that?" she whispers to Peregrine.

Peregrine nods, looking just as shocked. "Power," she whispers.

I felt it too, but I don't have time to dwell on that. "I have to make sure Boniface is okay." I run out of the parlour towards the backyard.

I find Boniface sitting on the ground, rubbing the back of his head. I exhale in relief when I see that he looks like he's seventy-something again instead of a hundred and seventy-something. He appears to be breathing normally.

"I don't know what happened there!" he says, looking up as I approach. "I must have fallen and hit my head. I feel a little woozy."

I hurl myself at him and wrap my arms around his solid body. "I'm so glad you're okay," I tell him.

"Well, that sure is the best greeting I've gotten in a long time," he replies, hugging me back.

Peregrine and Chloe step out on the deck and call to me. "Come on, Eveny!" Peregrine says impatiently. "We have things to discuss!"

My stomach twists itself into a knot as she turns and disappears inside, followed by Chloe.

"When did they get here?" Boniface asks.

"Just in time," I tell him in a shaky voice. With a heavy heart, I stand up and head towards my fellow zandara queens.

TWENTY-ONE

PEREGRINE IS STANDING IN MY living room filing her nails when I re-enter the house. Chloe is applying lipstick in the mirror on the wall.

"You're welcome," Peregrine says as I linger in the doorway, watching them.

I give her a look. "I don't remember thanking you."

Peregrine shrugs. "I assumed that was just an accidental lapse in manners on your part. After all, I *did* just save your house and Boniface's life."

"So I made a mistake. But can we agree that we won't do any more big charms without consulting each other? Like I won't destroy my house, and you won't endanger everyone just because you've run out of guys to make out with?"

Peregrine glowers at me. "You're being awfully bossy for someone who's new at this."

Chloe elbows Peregrine. "Eveny's right," she says. She turns to me and says, "We'll scale it back until we know for sure what happened to Glory and that frat guy. Deal?"

I nod.

Peregrine doesn't look happy. "I still get to work zandara on guys, though."

I open my mouth to protest, but Chloe cuts in. "Don't bother arguing," she says to me. "Peregrine would wilt without male attention."

Peregrine walks out of the room without another word to me. "I'll be in the car, Chloe!" she calls over her shoulder.

I hear the front door open and close a moment later. I turn back to Chloe, expecting that she'll leave too, but she's just standing there. She shifts from stiletto to stiletto for a moment and twirls her honey-blonde hair nervously as she stares at me.

"What?" I finally ask.

"Look, I'm not accusing you of anything, but did you dig up the Justin doll? In the cemetery that night that you spied on us?"

"Oh, crap," I say. "I'm sorry. I was just trying to figure out what was going on."

"You need to put him back." She looks like she's about to cry. "You don't mess with another queen's magic! I mean, I know you didn't know, so I'm not mad this time.

But Justin's been acting weird, and I had no idea why. Just rebury him before I have to break up with him, okay?"

"Chloe," I say slowly, "is *everything* between you and Justin magic?"

She gives me a look. "Not everything. It's just easier when there's a little charm involved. I don't have to worry about stupid stuff like him checking out other girls."

"It's called real life," I say.

Chloe makes a face. "But why would I want to go through that if I don't have to?"

"Maybe because it would be great to know that Justin likes you for you, and not just because you've forced him to?"

She studies the ground. "But he wouldn't like me," she says so softly that her words are almost inaudible. "He'd like Peregrine."

"You don't know that."

"Every guy in town is into her, Eveny. And I've been in love with Justin for a really long time. I can't lose him."

She looks miserable, and I feel sorry for her. It's not worth arguing about. "Fine. I'll rebury the doll tonight."

"Thank you so much. I'll write down a super easy reinstatement charm."

She grabs a pen and notepad out of her Louis Vuitton bag, jots something down quickly, then rips out the page and hands it to me. I stuff it in my pocket. "You have to mix damiana with balm of Gilead buds," she says. "When you use them together, they strengthen a charm's ability to bring back a drifting lover."

"You sure you want to do this?" I ask.

"Of course, Eveny." She pauses, then brightens suddenly.

"Hey, want me to write a love charm for you too?"

My mind immediately goes to Caleb and how drawn I feel to him, how many things stand in our way. "Nah," I say. "Thanks, but I think I'll do it the old-fashioned way."

Chloe looks perplexed. "Suit yourself," she says and disappears out the door to find Peregrine.

Exhausted from working the charms in the parlour, I go to bed early and set my alarm so I can make a quick trip to the cemetery on Chloe's behalf under cover of darkness.

At nearly two a.m., clutching the Justin doll, I slip out the back door and over the garden wall by the light of the moon.

"Don't freak out. Don't freak out," I say to myself as I move past fog-draped tombs. I don't think there will ever be a time when I'm not nervous to be in a graveyard in the middle of the night. But I promised Chloe, and I'm eager to see if a charm like this works when I do it alone.

Standing at the crossroads, I touch my Stone of Carrefour and call on Eloi Oke. I feel the now-familiar change in air pressure, and I know the door to the spirit world has once again opened. I take a deep breath and quickly skim the words Chloe has jotted down. I shake my head in amusement when I realize she's written them in rhyme, then I chant them quickly aloud.

> *The magic lifted, and some were hurt.*
> *I restore it now, back in the dirt.*
> *The charms of Chloe will work through this doll*
> *On Justin's heart, through it all.*

I rebury the Justin doll and a flannel sachet of damiana and balm of Gilead buds along with it. As I kick the dirt over the doll, concealing him completely, I feel a quick whoosh of wind, and the dust settles.

I stand there for a moment, then bend and touch the dirt again. I reach for my Stone of Carrefour with my left ring finger and say, "Also, spirits, if you're still listening, if Justin isn't a good guy, or if he doesn't care about Chloe at all, please make her realize that before he breaks her heart."

I hastily straighten up, brush my hands off, and turn to walk back towards my house, and that's when I suddenly hear pounding footsteps getting rapidly closer. I gasp and flatten myself across a tomb. Someone's running towards me, and I'm out here in the darkness all alone. I curse my stupidity. What if it's the faux frat boy who's unaccounted for, or the person who murdered Glory?

A moment later, a figure shrouded in darkness bursts into the clearing less than a foot away from me, breathing hard. I scream before realizing that it's Caleb Shaw – a shirtless Caleb Shaw, with ripped biceps, taut abs, and caramel skin sparkling with moonlit perspiration.

He whirls to face me and pulls out his earbuds. "What are you doing out here?" he demands. "You scared me to death!"

"*I* scared *you*?" I manage. Just as quickly, my heart is racing for a different reason entirely.

He wipes his arm across his forehead and then puts his hands on his thighs as he catches his breath. He's wearing olive-green running shorts, dark grey running shoes, and nothing else. "You shouldn't be out here, Eveny," he says. "It's not safe."

"Well, what are *you* doing out here?" I counter.

He looks a little embarrassed. "I like running in the cemetery at night when I can't sleep," he says. "My dad's buried here, so I kind of see it as my time to visit him."

"Oh, I'm sorry. About your dad, I mean. I didn't know."

"I don't talk about it much."

I study him for a minute. "How old were you when…?"

"Four," he says. He wipes the sweat from his brow again, and the moonlight highlights the tendons and muscles in his arm. "Not much older than you were when you lost your mom." He scratches his head and says, "What are you doing in the cemetery anyways?"

"A favour for Chloe."

He grimaces. "Zandara?"

"Yeah."

He gazes at me for a moment but seems to accept this. He leans beside me against the tomb, and suddenly I'm acutely aware of his near-naked body just inches away.

"You shouldn't be here all by yourself," he says, and I have the strange feeling that he's as nervous as I am.

"Nothing happened," I mumble.

"But it could have." He shakes his head and changes the subject. "So Peregrine and Chloe have swayed you to the dark side?"

"I don't know that I'd call it dark, exactly."

"I'm not sure this qualifies as light either. You're standing in a cemetery in the middle of the night, all alone."

"But now you're here," I say before I can second-guess myself.

For a moment, we just stare at each other. In the silence, I can hear both of us breathing rapidly.

"So this protector thing," I say after a minute. "I don't get it. Before I got back to Carrefour, you weren't responsible for me?"

"We're only officially responsible for our queens when they're inside the gates. But before you got here, it was kind of like sitting around, waiting to be called into active duty in the military. There was always a good chance I'd have to step up." He half smiles. "You know, the day I heard you and your aunt were returning, I was out on Sailfish. The waves had been epic that day, so I was feeling great. But then I got home, and my mom was crying. She told me you were on your way back to Carrefour, and she kept telling me I had to figure out how to get out of this."

The words wound me. "I'm sorry. If you know a way out – if there's any way to get you out of the obligation—" I begin, but he cuts me off.

"No, you don't understand," he says. "I didn't want to do this. Not at first. But it's in my blood, same as being a queen is in yours. And then I saw you at Glory's funeral and a day later, I talked to you for the first time." He shakes his head and says, "When you said, 'Reading's cool,'…"

He trails off, so I say, "You realized I was the biggest dork you'd ever met?"

He laughs. "No. I realized you were different from the rest of this town. You weren't trying to be anything you weren't. It was the moment I realized I wouldn't be able to forgive myself if I ever let anything happen to you."

"But you can't have feelings for me," I say softly.

"That's the rule," he says.

We're silent for a little while. Finally, I move us into less depressing territory. "So what do you want to do with your life, anyways? I mean, after we graduate next year."

He looks surprised. "No one in this town talks about life after school. Everyone just...stays."

"Is that what you want?" I ask.

He turns to look at me, and we're so close that I can feel him breathing. For a moment, all I want him to say is *No. You're what I want.* But of course he doesn't. Instead, he says, "No one's ever asked me that." He hesitates. "The truth? I just want to go somewhere else. I want to have a future that hasn't already been picked out for me. I want to go to college and live in a big city and have a normal life. But I can't just run from the responsibilities I have here."

"But you didn't choose the responsibilities."

"Neither did you. But here we are."

"Here we are," I murmur. And this time when our eyes meet, we look at each other for a long, frozen moment, and then Caleb leans down slowly, very slowly, until his lips brush against mine. He kisses me gently, weaving his hands through my hair as he cradles the back of my head. He tastes like cinnamon. I couldn't have imagined a more perfect moment.

But suddenly, he pulls away, and when I blink up at him in confusion, I see pain in his eyes. "What?" I ask, still breathless.

"Shit. I can't believe I just did that." He shakes his head. "That can't happen again. Do you understand?"

Before I have a chance to reply, he's already running away, back in the direction he came from.

I stand still in the cemetery, touching my lips, my heart hammering, until the sound of his footfalls has faded into the darkness.

Twenty-two

It takes me until the beginning of fourth period the next day to realize that Caleb isn't at school, which makes the knots in my stomach twist even tighter. Either he's off training somewhere with Oscar and Patrick again, or he just doesn't want to see me. Regardless, I'm reminded just how much my arrival in Carrefour has disrupted his life.

On the way to lunch, Peregrine and Chloe flank me in the hallway. Peregrine's in thigh-high leopard-print stiletto boots, and Chloe's wearing elaborately spiky platform heels that add a good six inches to her height. I see Audowido poke his head out of Peregrine's studded tote bag, and I shiver and inch away from him.

"So?" Peregrine asks in a sour tone. "I suppose you're off to ask those little peons to join us?"

"Who?" I ask.

"Liv, Max and Drew." She makes a face. "After your big speech yesterday, I figured that I was supposed to be more *decent*, or whatever it was you said. So here I am, acting like a nice person by inviting your grimy friends to eat in the Hickories."

I try not to show my surprise. Instead, I say evenly, "My friends aren't grimy."

"Well," she says haughtily, "let's just say I've already asked Arelia to dry-clean the cashmere picnic blanket after today's lunch."

I just give her a look and she giggles and walks away.

Chloe lingers for a moment longer. "So you did it?" she asks furtively. "The charm? Justin?"

"Yes."

She looks relieved. "I thought so. Thanks, Eveny. See you in a few!"

Liv, Max and Drew are all in line for food when I enter the cafeteria a moment later. "Unless you're dying for congealed mac and cheese," I say, shooting a glance at the orange globs the caf lady is lobbing onto plates, "you should all come eat with me in the Hickories today."

The three of them just look at me. "Wait, what?" Drew manages.

"The Hickories," I repeat. "You can eat up there today, if you want."

"Us?" Liv asks blankly. "In the Hickories?"

Max lets out an excited whoop and dashes out before I can say anything else. Drew and Liv follow several paces behind, looking stunned.

"You're sure this isn't just some trick the Dolls are playing on us?" Drew whispers, hurrying to catch up with me.

"I'm sure. Things are going to be different now," I tell him.

"Sure they will," he says under his breath.

Liv hurries to catch up with us too. "Why, exactly, have Peregrine and Chloe deigned to allow us to eat with them?"

"No idea," I lie. "But Peregrine invited you herself. Anyways, it's really not a big deal."

But judging from the horrified expressions on the faces of Margaux and Arelia as we approach, it *is*, in fact, a big deal.

"What are *they* doing here?" Margaux demands, not even bothering to address Liv, Max or Drew directly. Liv and Drew glower at her, while Max walks around, checking out the picnic basket, the china, and the champagne bottles with a huge grin on his face.

"This is amazing!" he declares.

Margaux glares at me. "Well?"

"Peregrine and Chloe are fine with it," I say.

Margaux opens her mouth to retort, but Peregrine cuts

her off. "Seriously, Margaux, give it a rest, and pour me a drink, would you? I'm completely parched."

Margaux opens her mouth then clamps it shut almost comically. "Just don't expect me to serve *them* lunch."

"They are our *guests*, Margaux, and you *will* serve them," Peregrine snaps.

"But—" Margaux begins. She trails off when Peregrine's eyes narrow even further. "Fine," she grumbles. "Champagne?" she asks Liv, Drew and Max, her voice dripping with bitterness.

The three of them accept and follow me to sit beside Peregrine and Chloe.

"This is, like, the best day of my entire high school career," Max enthuses once we've toasted and taken sips of our bubbly. Arelia and Margaux are both glaring as they prepare a platter of sandwiches for us to share.

"Here," Margaux barks, shoving the platter so hard at us that a few sandwiches topple over the edge.

Max seems oblivious to their coldness, though, and begins chattering away a mile a minute, asking if they're going to the Mardi Gras Ball, what they're wearing, and where they got a cashmere blanket this big. Eventually, Margaux and Arelia seem to warm to him. In fact, they even look vaguely amused.

But though we're all eating together, Liv and Drew sit on one side of the blanket, staring suspiciously at Peregrine and Chloe, who stare suspiciously back until they're distracted by the arrival of their guys. Justin immediately drapes himself over Chloe, and they spend the rest of the lunch hour making out. Peregrine, not to be outdone, has charmed a skater named Tyler into fawning all over her today.

"They are *so* gross," Liv says. "It's like watching porn."

"Uh-huh," Drew agrees vaguely.

"Hey, hotness." Pascal interrupts my train of thought as he approaches from the other side of the Hickories. He grins at me lasciviously and then turns to Liv. "I see you've brought someone new to lunch. Hey, baby."

She wrinkles her nose, and I see Drew stiffen beside her.

"She's with me," Drew says.

I exchange looks with Liv, who looks thrilled that Drew has come to her defence.

Pascal gazes at him evenly. "And you are…?"

"You know who I am, man," Drew says stiffly. "We've been in school together for years."

Pascal looks amused. "Well, *man*, I can't notice everyone. But this pretty thing, well, with a little make-up and a wardrobe makeover, she'd be damn fine. Just the kind of woman I'd like to get to know in a special way."

Liv opens her mouth to reply, but Drew beats her to it. "I *said*, she's with me."

Pascal crosses his arms. "I'm sorry. Did you not

understand that I don't give a damn about that?"

Drew glowers back. "Did *you* not understand that you can't just take whatever you want?"

Pascal's eyes flicker for a moment, and then he chuckles. "Dude, you really have no idea. I'll have her if I want her. And there's nothing you can do about it." He calls over to Peregrine, "Hey, who invited this douche up here anyhow?"

"He's with Eveny!" Peregrine sing-songs, breaking away from her make-out session long enough to smirk at me. "I told her it was a bad idea."

Pascal turns back to me. "Way to go, Eveny. We have a firm no douchebag rule in the Hickories."

"Then how do *you* manage to eat lunch here every day?" I ask evenly.

His face darkens for a moment, long enough to make me feel uneasy, but then he laughs. "Touché," he says. "But seriously, babe. You can't just let commoners up here." He turns to Liv and adds, "Although *you're* welcome anytime. Preferably with fewer clothes on."

He shoots Drew a challenging look, but I put a hand on Drew's chest and say, "Don't."

Drew appears to relax after a moment, turning to Liv. "I've been meaning to ask you: would you be my date to the Mardi Gras Ball?"

Liv turns pink. Her eyes dart to me for a second and then back to Drew. "For real?" she squeaks.

Drew grins at her. "I'd love to take you."

"I mean, I guess, yeah, that would be fine." She's trying to play it cool, but when her eyes meet mine, I can see her fighting a grin.

"Oh, puke," Pascal says, rolling his eyes. "Eveny, you want to be my date to the ball?"

"Not a chance," I reply sweetly.

On the walk back to class after lunch, as Drew and Max head towards the north wing of the building, Liv catches up with me, grabs my hand, and asks, "So did you hear Drew ask me to the ball?"

I nod and give her hand a squeeze before letting go. "That's awesome."

"You think?" Her brow creases with worry. "What if he was just asking me to piss off Pascal?"

"He wasn't. He likes you."

"How can you be so sure?"

"I just am," I tell her.

She grins. "So how about you? Do you think you'll go to the dance?"

Caleb flits across my mind, but I dismiss the thought. If I'd had any hope that we could get around the protector rule, it was dashed last night, when Caleb swore me off then literally ran away. "Probably not," I say.

"You shouldn't miss out on it," Liv says. "What if you and Max go together? As friends, I mean."

"Maybe," I say. "I'll probably just skip it."

Liv looks disappointed but lets it go. "So that was weird today, huh? In the Hickories?"

I laugh. "That's a pretty normal day up there."

She wrinkles her nose and shakes her head as the bell rings. "They all creep me out. Those cookie-cutter girls and those guys who don't seem to think for themselves—"

"So what's going on with Drew's band?" I interrupt her brightly.

She stares at me for a minute. "You're changing the subject."

"Yeah, you caught that," I say with a smile.

She laughs. "All right, have it your way." And as she starts to tell me about a gig they're trying to book in New Orleans, and a producer who's expressed some interest in them, I relax into the conversation and appreciate what it's like to talk to someone whose life isn't already prewritten.

My cell rings at five thirty that evening, startling me. I'd been poring over my mother's herb journal, trying to memorize the plants, roots and potions that seemed most important to her. Lemon for protection. Blackberry to send evil back to enemies who try to inflict it upon you. Wormwood to prevent car accidents. Bayberry for good health. Chia seed to quell gossip.

I reach for my phone and see Liv's name on the caller ID.

"What are you doing right now?" she asks after I've said hello.

I look at my mother's journal, open on my lap to a hand-drawn sketch of a zandara doll. "Not much," I tell her.

"Good," she says. "Come out with me and Drew, then."

"You and Drew?"

She's silent for a minute. "He just called and asked me to dinner tonight. I already had plans with Max, and I don't want to just bail on him."

"Sooo…" I prompt.

"So could you be Max's platonic date for the night? It would really help me a lot. Plus," she adds, "I kind of want to get your read on whether Drew's actually into me. Please come?"

I'm about to say no, but then I think about Meredith and how different Liv is from the girl I'd always thought of as my best friend. Liv may not approve of everything in my life – and I can't exactly blame her for disliking the Dolls – but she's never been unsupportive of me. I've only known her for a few weeks, and I realize that already, the friendship I have with her means more to me than the one Meredith is so casually tossing aside. The least I can do is have her back.

I close my book and push it to the side. "Okay, I'm in."

"Woo-hoo!" she cheers on the other end of the line. "You rock, Eveny. I owe you one. Can you meet us at Cajun Eddie's at seven? It's out in the Périphérie, and it's Drew's favourite."

"Sure," I agree. I check my watch. I know Liv's not thinking about the fact that I don't have a car, and I don't want to bug her while she's getting ready for a date. The weather's supposed to be nice out, and I should have enough daylight left to ride my bike. "Just text me the address."

"You're the best!" she says before hanging up.

I cast one last reluctant glance at the herb book. As I head to the bathroom to put on some make-up for my "date" with Max, I'm repeating some of my mother's favourite herbs in my head in an attempt at memorization.

I've just started applying tinted moisturizer when my cell rings again. Drew's name flashes on the screen, so I pick up. "I hear we're doing dinner in an hour," I say.

"Word travels fast. Liv said you're meeting us, but I know you don't have a car. Want me to come get you?"

I pause. "You don't have to," I tell him. I don't want Liv to get the wrong idea if I show up with Drew.

"I don't mind," he says. "How else would you get here, anyhow?"

"Bike?" I venture.

He laughs. "I'm not making you ride your bike all the way to the Périphérie when it'll barely take me any time to swing by your place."

I'm ready to go ten minutes later in a black tank maxidress and a striped cardigan with ballet flats. While I wait for Drew, I boot up my laptop and check my email, which I haven't done in days. Along with a few dozen junk messages and a bunch of ads for Sephora, *Glamour* magazine, and some online bookstores, there are a few forwarded chain emails from Meredith, which I delete instantly, and a note from a guy named Ross I had a few classes with back in New York asking whether I want to go see a movie with him. I laugh out loud at that; a date with a guy who hasn't even noticed I'm gone doesn't sound like the best idea.

I check the time and see that I still have a couple of minutes, so I pull up Google and enter *LSU newspaper* into the search box. It sends me to the site of the *Daily Reveille*, the official school paper. I enter *Carrefour* into the search engine and am relieved when nothing comes up. Then I type in *murdered + fraternity*, and one result, from earlier today, is returned. I click on the article and begin to read.

The body of a Louisiana State University senior was found early Sunday afternoon in the Fantome Swamp region of Louisiana, about an hour outside Baton Rouge, after Louisiana State Police received a call from the man's fraternity brother Sunday morning. I nearly drop my laptop when I get to the next line: *Blake Montoire, 21, a member of the Lambda Delta Epsilon fraternity, was stabbed several times before his car was stolen, police say.*

Blake Montoire was the name of the guy who was talking to me at Peregrine's party, the guy who tried to walk me home before Caleb stepped in. But the grainy photo featured on the website doesn't match the person I met, except for the glasses, which can only mean one thing: I was talking to Blake's killer. Worse, he'd seemed overly interested in getting to know *me*.

"Eveny?" Aunt Bea's voice from the door startles me. I look up to see her staring at me suspiciously. "What were you reading?"

"School assignment," I lie as I quickly shut the computer.

"You look awfully freaked out for an assignment," she says.

"Math scares me," I say as innocently as possible. I know that if I tell her there's a Main de Lumière soldier inside our gates who's set his sights on me, she'll insist we leave Carrefour. But if I go, the town will have no chance of surviving now that the enemy has gotten in.

Like it or not, this is my fate. And I have no choice but to face it head-on.

TWENTY-THREE

I SHOOT PEREGRINE AND CHLOE a quick text telling them that I saw the probable killer – the fake Blake Montoire – then I shut off my phone and try to forget about zandara and death for the evening. There's nothing I can do for the next few hours except be on guard.

Drew arrives at 6.45 on the dot, and when I open the door, he grins. "You look real pretty," he says. Once we're in his pickup, he turns to me. "You know I wanted to ask you out, right? When you first got back to town?"

"What? No!"

He gives me a look as we rumble down the hill. "What'd you think that invitation to the crawfish boil was?"

"I thought it might be a date," I admit. "But then you kind of acted like we were just friends."

"Admittedly, I don't have the smoothest mackin'-on-the-ladies moves," he says.

"Mackin'-on-the-ladies moves?" I repeat, stifling a laugh.

"Fine, so maybe I'm not good at talking about my moves either," he concedes. "But then you came to my show, and I figured, hey, girls go for musicians, right? But you disappeared with Caleb Shaw before I could do anything."

"I'm sorry," I say. I want to explain to Drew that our shared history makes him feel more like a brother to me. But I have the feeling that'll only make things worse.

Before I can say anything, he says, "I guess I was stupid to think you could like someone from my side of town."

"That's not it at all!" I say instantly. "Look, if I did anything to hurt your feelings—"

He cuts me off. "I wasn't trying to make you feel bad, Eveny. I was just saying that I'm glad. I mean, it worked out the way it was supposed to. I hadn't really thought of Liv like that, but then I kept running into her because of you, and…" He shrugs and says, "Well, anyway, I'm really happy she said yes to going with me to the Mardi Gras Ball."

"She's a great girl," I tell him.

We're halfway out to the Périphérie when I finally ask the question that's been on my mind since Caleb mentioned it. "Before she died, were you dating Glory Jones?"

Drew looks at me in surprise. "Where'd you hear that?"

"It doesn't matter," I say. "And I don't care if you were. I just want to know."

"No," he says after a pause. "But we were friends. Really good friends, actually."

"So why did you act like you barely knew her at her funeral?"

"Because I promised her I'd keep our friendship a secret. I'm still trying to honour that, Eveny, so I'd appreciate if you didn't say anything to the Dolls." There's bitterness in his voice, but there's pain there too. "You know about the line between people from central Carrefour and the Périphérie."

"If she liked you, if you two were friends, she should have been open about it. People would have had to be okay with it."

"I used to tell her that. But it meant a lot to me to have her in my life at all. I don't have a lot of good friends, and I didn't want to hurt her by making Peregrine and Chloe turn their backs on her because of me."

"You really think they would have done that?" But I know the answer to my own question. They treated people from the Périphérie like sources of power, not human beings.

"Peregrine and Chloe aren't the people you think they are, Eveny," Drew says. "They're not nice, they're not good people, and I think they were ruining Glory's life. She died before I had a chance to figure out how to help her."

"You must miss her."

"Sure I do," he says. "All the time. But we were from two different worlds." He clears his throat and adds, "Kind of like you and me."

"I'm not from a different world than you are," I say instantly.

"Could have fooled me, with that big mansion of yours."

"I'm sorry," I say, but I'm not even sure what I'm apologizing for. "I'm not like them, you know. The Dolls, I mean."

Drew glances at me as he turns onto a side street in the Périphérie, but he doesn't reply.

The silence between us stretches long and thick until we pull up to the restaurant, close enough to the town wall that you can see the bricks and stones that separate us from the outside world. "Welcome to Cajun Eddie's," Drew says as he puts his truck in neutral and turns off the engine. "You're going to love this place. Best jambalaya on the planet."

Liv and Max are already waiting by the hostess stand, and although a flicker of worry crosses Liv's face when she sees me and Drew arrive together, she relaxes when I hug her and whisper in her ear, "He talked about you the whole way here."

Twenty minutes later, I'm staring down at the first bowl of jambalaya I've ever ordered.

"You've got shrimp, chicken, andouille sausage, onions, peppers, celery and all sorts of amazing Cajun spices," Liv explains enthusiastically as she eyes the piping hot mixture on my plate.

"Go ahead," Drew says, smiling at me as he pushes my glass of water towards me. "Try it. But it's gonna make you thirsty."

As I take my first bite, my taste buds tingle with the assault of flavours. But I have to admit, it's smoky and delicious.

The others dig into their own meals: fried oysters for Drew, a blackened fish sandwich for Max, and a Caesar salad for Liv, who nibbles nervously while looking at Drew out of the corner of her eye. *Relax*, I mouth to her when Drew's distracted by a debate with Max over the merits of the Beatles versus the Rolling Stones. *He likes you.*

Thanks, she mouths back, visibly calming.

As we eat, we talk about having lunch with the Dolls in the Hickories, our upcoming tests in French and physics, and the fact that we're all weirded out by the death of the fraternity guy just outside our gates. "I don't get what happened to him," Drew says, glancing at me. "It's so odd."

"Beats me," I say as innocently as possible as I wash down another spicy mouthful of jambalaya.

By the time we're done, Drew and Liv are gazing at each other with googly eyes, and I'm trying not to feel jealous. It's not that I'm interested in Drew at all, and of course I'm glad that he likes Liv. I just wish someone would look at me that way. Specifically Caleb. Instead, I evidently inspire cursing and fleeing.

"Earth to Eveny," Max says. I realize I was so lost in thought that I'd spaced out for a moment.

"Sorry. What were you saying?"

"Just asking if you had a date to the Mardi Gras Ball," he says.

I shake my head. "No. Do you?" I'm hoping he won't ask me to go as friends, because I'm holding out hope that something will change with Caleb.

So I'm relieved when he says in a stage whisper, "I'm thinking of asking Rob Baker." When I look at him blankly, he adds, "He's in my Spanish class. I'm, like, ninety per cent sure he's been flirting with me lately."

"Do you like him?" I ask.

"I guess. He's a nice guy. And he'd be fun to pass the time with until Justin Cooper stops pretending to be straight."

I gape at him. "Wait, what? Justin who's dating Chloe?"

He leans in conspiratorially. "I don't know what's up with him. He and I were flirting like crazy for a year. He finally told me he was going to officially come out to his parents over the summer. Next thing I know, he's dating Chloe St. Pierre."

"No way," I whisper. I'm absolutely positive Chloe has no idea about Justin's sexual orientation. "What do you think happened?" I ask carefully.

"Maybe his parents weren't cool with it, and he felt like he had to pretend to be straight? Whatever it was, though, he's not worth it. If he can't be true to who he is, I don't need that."

I see sadness in his eyes behind the forced nonchalance.

"Maybe there's an explanation," I begin, but when Max gives me a questioning look, I realize I can't explain further.

"What, that he'd rather be popular than be with me?" Max asks bitterly.

Drew interrupts us then to ask how we want to split the bill. As Max and I dig in our wallets for cash, Max leans over and says, "Don't say anything, okay? Liv's the only one who knows what happened. I figure that whatever's going on with Justin is his business."

I agree to keep Max's story to myself, but I know it's on me to fix this – not just for Max and Justin, but for Chloe too. As the four of us walk out together, I think how lucky Liv and Drew are to have a chance at a relationship. Whatever's between them is real. Max deserves that too.

* * *

Drew and Liv hug awkwardly in the parking lot, then Drew gestures towards his pickup. "You ready?" he asks me.

I nod and say goodbye to Liv and Max before following after him.

"That was fun," I say once I'm strapped in and we're pulling out of the parking lot.

"Liv's a great girl. And Max is kind of growing on me."

"Growing on you?"

"I always thought he was sort of eccentric, with his Buddy Holly glasses and all those vests he likes to wear. But he's okay." He pauses. "You know, now that you have friends like that, I don't know why you'd want to keep hanging out with the Dolls."

I glance at him but don't say anything. Defending Peregrine and Chloe to him is getting old. I get that he's probably still hurting over losing Glory, and blaming the Dolls for making her life complicated is an easy thing to do. But the more I find out about this town, the more I realize that there are no clear-cut lines between right and wrong, good and bad.

"So, anything new with your band?" I ask, changing the subject. "Liv says you have a producer interested."

"Yeah, he wants us to come to New Orleans and meet with him, maybe play him a few of our originals."

"For real?" I grin at him. "Drew, that's a huge deal! Why didn't you say anything?"

"I'm just trying not to get ahead of myself," he replies, but he looks excited. "Besides, I have to tie up a few loose ends here before I can even think about getting out of this town."

We've just turned on to Cemetery Road when Drew's truck pulls sharply to the right, sending us skidding off the shoulder into a muddy embankment. I cry out and reach for the door to steady myself as Drew struggles to regain control.

"What the hell was that?" I demand once we're back on the street. His face is pale, and his knuckles are white on the wheel.

"I have no idea," he says unsteadily. "Something's wrong with the steering."

The words are barely out of his mouth when the truck jerks to the right again, but this time Drew loses the fight with the steering wheel, and the truck goes spinning wildly towards the cemetery. I scream and do my best to brace myself between the dashboard and the door. Drew tries desperately to overcorrect, but we're only spinning faster.

Just as the driver's-side wheels of the truck begin to lift off the ground, and I can feel us starting to flip, I'm hit with a wave of calm and clarity. I can save us.

I touch my Stone of Carrefour and say, "Lemon and wormwood."

I don't even have to talk to Eloi Oke or think of what I want to ask the spirits, because every cell in my body knows what it wants: to live through this accident.

And then, as suddenly as the truck started to career out of control, it slams back to the ground and skids to a halt with the passenger door – my door – mere inches away from a huge oak tree. Another few feet and I would have been crushed.

We're silent for a moment as the car's engine hisses and dies. My breath comes in ragged gasps.

"Eveny," Drew says, turning to me with a horrified expression on his face. "I don't know what happened. I-I could have killed you."

"But you didn't," I reassure him in a shaky voice.

We scramble out of the truck. Drew's hands are trembling as he grabs his phone and calls 911. I hear him tell the police officer that he's had an accident. "Are you hurt?" he asks me, covering the mouthpiece with his hand.

I do a quick once-over and am astonished to realize that aside from my rapidly thudding heart, I'm physically fine.

"No," I tell him. "Are you?"

He shakes his head and reports to the officer that we're both okay. He hangs up after explaining where we are. I watch as he sinks to the ground and puts his head in his hands.

"How did you survive that?" he asks in a hoarse voice.

"I don't know," I whisper. But against my chest, my Stone of Carrefour is burning. *Lemons for protection and wormwood to prevent car accidents*, I think, sending a silent *thank you* up to my mother for having the foresight to include both of those plants in her herb journal. "*Mesi, zanzet*," I add.

"What did you say?" Drew asks, but I just shake my head.

As we wait for the police to arrive, I see a flash of something in the cemetery, and for a second, I'm sure it's Caleb, out for his nightly run. But the figure doesn't stop, and a moment later, I have the strange feeling that we're being watched.

TWENTY-FOUR

THE NEXT DAY, THE BUZZ around school is all about my accident with Drew. Apparently, his truck is still stuck in the cemetery, and lots of people saw it lodged against the massive oak on their way to school today. Everyone keeps telling me they can't believe I walked away unscathed.

As for the Dolls, they're all quiet and on edge, which I suspect is because tonight's ceremony to disempower the killer inside our gates is a big deal. Even lunch in the Hickories is subdued and mostly silent. It's only the chatter of Max, Drew and Liv, all of whom have joined us on the cashmere blanket again, that breaks up the monotony. Caleb glares openly at Drew and entirely ignores me all through lunch.

On the way out of American history, Caleb catches up with me and puts a hand on my arm. "I'm really glad you're okay," he says, and the depth of concern in his eyes holds me captive until he turns and hurries away.

After school, I tell Aunt Bea that I'm working on a school project with Liv and spending the night at her place. I'm expecting her to be suspicious, but she's too shaken up by the accident to guess that I'm lying.

"Eveny, what if someone was trying to kill you?" she asks. "What if someone saw you arrive with Drew and cut the steering fluid line or damaged the brakes of his truck or something?"

"Relax," I tell her firmly. "It's just an old pickup truck. Nothing sinister."

I'm not sure I believe my own words, but I don't need Aunt Bea freaking out on top of everything else. She'll never allow me to leave the house tonight if she thinks I'm in danger. "Besides," I add, "I'm fine. Drew's fine."

"Because of a stroke of good luck," she says.

"No, because of zandara," I reply. "I used my Stone of Carrefour."

She blinks at me, her expression darkening. "Well, it sure didn't take you any time to become an expert, did it?" she asks. Without another word, she strides out the front door, slamming it behind her. A moment later, I hear her car's engine rumble to life.

I'm still thinking about Aunt Bea's reaction when I head

down our driveway just after eleven. I arrive at Peregrine's mansion twenty minutes later, wearing a flowing, gauzy emerald dress of my mother's that I found buried in the back of my closet. I feel beautiful in it, and I hope it will make Caleb see me that way too.

But when the door to the Marceau mansion opens, my heart sinks. I'm dowdy in comparison to Peregrine and Chloe. As usual, they both look like supermodels in five-inch heels, perfect make-up, and slinky designer dresses. Peregrine's is a black leather sheath with a diamond-encrusted snake-shaped zipper, and Chloe's is a gold lamé minidress that catches the light and makes her skin look even tanner.

"What look, exactly, are you trying to achieve?" Peregrine asks. "Thrift store hippie?"

"It was my mom's," I say defensively.

"I think you look pretty," says a low voice from behind Peregrine and Chloe. I look up to see Caleb gazing at me. In a crisp charcoal suit, he's too good to be real. Locking eyes with him hits me so hard that I can't breathe until he turns and walks away.

Peregrine rolls her eyes and air-kisses me dramatically. "Well, come on in," she says, nearly shoving me inside. "We don't have all night. Are you feeling better after your accident?"

"Still a little freaked out," I say. I follow Chloe and

Peregrine into the house. The rest of the Dolls are mingling around, all of them as dressed up as Peregrine and Chloe. Arelia and Margaux are in matching hot pink minidresses with sky-high heels, and Pascal is standing behind them, leering at their legs. He's in a black suit with a silvery shirt and a black tie. A few feet away, Justin lounges on an armchair, looking uncomfortable in a navy suit and a yellow tie, which he keeps tugging at.

I clear my throat as Peregrine announces, "Eveny's here! Someone get her a drink!"

Margaux purses her lips but makes a move towards the bar.

"Gin and tonic?" she asks in a bored voice. "Or champagne?"

"Neither, actually," I say quickly. I want to stay as sober as possible.

Peregrine makes a face and rolls her eyes. "Fine," she says. "Someone go get Eveny some sweet tea instead."

Margaux hustles off towards the kitchen as quickly as her stilettoed feet can take her. Not to be outdone, Arelia scrambles after her.

A moment later, Margaux reappears at Peregrine's elbow and thrusts a tall glass of iced tea at me. "Happy?" she grunts.

"Thanks," I say, put off by her weirdness as usual. I take a few long sips, then set my glass down on a coaster.

The grandfather clock chimes midnight, and the energy in the room shifts.

"It's time," Peregrine says solemnly.

I'm the only person who seems not to know what this means, but I follow the others towards a pair of closed double doors, which remind me a lot of the parlour in my own house. Peregrine and Chloe pull open the doors, and I follow the others into a large, dark room lit with candles that send flickering shadows dancing across the walls and ceiling.

The group moves silently into a circle in the centre of the room. I'm surprised when it's Caleb who winds up on my left side and even more startled when his large, warm hand folds around mine. I'm elated for a second until I look up and realize that everyone in the circle is joining hands. In the centre of the circle sit a bottle of bourbon and the coiled form of Audowido. I swallow back my discomfort, and I keep a close eye on him as his tongue darts lazily in and out of his mouth.

"What's happening?" I whisper to Caleb.

Caleb looks at me with concern. "The girls didn't explain this ceremony to you?"

I shake my head.

"It's a possession ceremony called a *Renmen Koulèv*." Caleb's voice is flat and grim. "They probably thought it would freak you out."

"Why? I've already been possessed."

"It's—" He hesitates, as if searching for the right words. When he looks back at me, his expression is pained. "This ceremony is weird to watch. We use a snake – Audowido in this case – to call the spirits in from the nether. Then Peregrine and Pascal will allow themselves to be possessed by two spirits who already do a lot of favours for us."

"And it's weird to watch because…?" I ask.

Caleb clears his throat. "Because it's kind of…sexual. The spirits don't get to do things like smoke and drink and have sex any more. So the sosyete banks favours by letting the spirits take over their bodies for a while."

"Wait, Peregrine and Pascal are going to have *sex*?"

Caleb shakes his head. "Not quite. But things get pretty…hot." Even in the dim lighting, I can tell he looks embarrassed. "It's the best way to gather power in the short term. If everything goes right and the spirits get what they want, they'll help us, and the Main de Lumière operative who killed the fraternity guy will be powerless again. He'll become immediately paralysed the second he tries to use a weapon against any of us. We'll all be safe. This is something we have to do."

He squeezes my hand tighter just as Peregrine steps into the centre of the circle beside Audowido. Chloe grabs my right hand and Justin's left to complete the ring.

Pascal breaks away from the group to strike a large

triangle that hangs nearby. The sound reverberates throughout the room, and as Pascal rejoins the circle, Peregrine closes her eyes and looks skywards.

"Come to us now, Eloi Oke, and open the gate," Peregrine chants. "Come to us now, Eloi Oke, and open the gate. Come to us now, Eloi Oke, and open the gate."

She takes a small bundle of herbs, strikes a match, and sets them on fire. She drops them on the marble floor, and as soon as they're done smoldering, she says, "Ashes to ashes."

She begins to dance, slowly at first, then more rapidly in the silence. I watch as Audowido uncurls and inches towards Peregrine. He begins to coil himself around her left leg just as she starts to chant again, but she doesn't seem to notice; she appears to be in a trance as she sways, moves her feet, and claps, while singing over and over in a high, sweet voice, "*Move lespri, pran kò mwen. Move lespri pran tèt mwen.*"

Caleb leans in to whisper to me, "She's asking the spirits to take her body and her mind. But in order for this to work, we all have to focus on the ceremony. I promise; I won't let anything happen to you."

His voice is deep and soothing, and I believe him entirely. I close my eyes and try to focus on Peregrine's words and on the melody. Then she abruptly stops chanting, and I open my eyes to see what's going on.

Peregrine is standing in the middle of the circle, completely still, with Audowido wrapped up her left leg and down her left arm. The snake looks like he's become a part of her. I can see him breathing, his skin expanding and contracting.

"Just follow along," Caleb whispers as Peregrine returns to chanting. This time, on her second verse, the whole room begins to hum along with her. Peregrine starts to dance again, and when she does, everyone else in the circle begins swaying to the music too. I do my best to join in as the movements get more and more frenzied. Audowido is slowly unwinding himself from Peregrine now, and he, too, appears to be moving in time to the beat.

Suddenly, Peregrine stops singing and cries out. Everyone else's eyes are closed, but I keep mine open a sliver to watch what's happening. The air in the room has changed, and my Stone of Carrefour is suddenly so hot it's burning me. My heart thuds as I watch Pascal step silently into the circle. But he doesn't look like himself any more; his body moves fluidly, like a rubber doll's.

He bends to pick up a pale purple handkerchief from the ground, where Audowido is slowly slithering in a wide circle.

Pascal takes one end of the handkerchief and puts it into his mouth. Peregrine steps closer, until she and Pascal are just inches apart. She slowly takes the other end of the handkerchief and puts it in her mouth too.

The second she does so, the others in the circle resume their dance. Chloe starts chanting the now-familiar *Move lespri, pran kò mwen. Move lespri pran tèt mwen.* As she begins singing faster and faster, Peregrine and Pascal move closer and closer to each other until their bodies are touching. Caleb's hand is warm and reassuring in mine, but as Peregrine and Pascal's dance grows more sensual, I feel uncomfortable. I continue moving my hips from side to side, but as I watch, Pascal begins to touch Peregrine. She responds by pulling him closer and grinding against him. It looks like they're about to start ripping each other's clothes off.

Suddenly, goosebumps prickle up and down my arms, and I can feel my hair standing on end. There's something different in the room now, a shift in the equilibrium, and once again everyone instantly stops chanting and dancing. We're plunged into silence, and for a moment, it's as if the room is entirely frozen.

Then, Pascal suddenly breaks away from Peregrine and grabs the bottle of bourbon from the floor beside Audowido. He rips off the cap, tilts his head back, and drinks the entire bottle without taking a breath.

My jaw drops. "Did he just drink a *whole bottle* of alcohol?" I whisper to Caleb. But Caleb doesn't respond; his eyes are closed, and he looks just as out of it as the rest of the group. I begin to pull away – I want to get out of here – but Caleb's grip on me is like a vice. I'm feeling woozier by the moment, and my legs are unsteady beneath me. It's similar to the exhaustion that swept over me at Cristof's after Glory possessed me, but far worse.

My heart thuds even faster as Pascal begins mumbling what sounds like nonsense. Peregrine remains in a trance as Pascal approaches and begins peeling her clothes off, right there in the middle of the circle. First, he removes the shawl she has wrapped lightly around her shoulders, then he roughly pulls her dress over her head, so that she's standing there in only a shell-pink bra, matching panties, and her five-inch heels.

Pascal and Peregrine begin to kiss now, sloppily and aggressively. Pascal's hands tangle through Peregrine's ebony curls and I feel weaker and weaker as their movement grows more frantic. It's almost like my own energy is being sucked out of me and funnelled into the centre of the circle. I look at Caleb again, and when I see that his eyes are open now, I feel a surge of momentary hope. But my heart sinks when I realize he, too, is possessed by whatever spirit is filling this room. I look around and see that everyone else appears as blank and wide-eyed as he does. I seem to be the only one who hasn't succumbed to the magic.

I don't have time to think about it, though, because in that instant, Pascal lets go of Peregrine and swings in my direction. I'm frozen in place as his eyes rake me over. Then he grins, a big, sloppy grin that doesn't look a thing like the carefully controlled Pascal. *It's not him any more*, I realize. *It's the spirit who's in him.*

In his eyes, I can read evil and foreboding. His grin melts into a sneer. "Eveny Cheval," he slurs in a deep Louisiana accent that doesn't sound at all like Pascal's aristocratic drawl. Then he begins to laugh. Suddenly, the sneer vanishes from his face, and I feel a chill run through me.

"They're coming for you," he says in a flat voice, staring directly into my eyes. "Bang bang, you're dead."

TWENTY-FIVE

TERRIFIED, I USE THE LAST of my strength to rip my hand out of Caleb's grip. My arms and legs feel like they're made of sand, but I manage to stumble away from the circle and towards the door. I land in a heap in the living room while behind me, Pascal is still cackling maniacally. I can hear him saying again and again in a sing-song voice, "Bang bang, Eveny's dead! Bang bang, Eveny's dead!"

The moment I'm outside of the ceremonial room, my body feels more normal. My limbs aren't as heavy, and I can move again. I lurch towards the front door of Peregrine's mansion, pull it open, and land face down on her front porch. The air outside is cool and crisp, and I drink it in hungrily as I try to gather the strength to run.

I struggle to my feet and head for the cemetery. It creeps me out to think about cutting across it in the dark of night, but it's the quickest way home. I'm still woozy and unsteady, but Peregrine's house doesn't have a wall separating it from the cemetery like mine does, so I only have to climb over a waist-high picket fence. I land on my feet and plunge into the darkness between a cluster of tombs. Far away, I can see my back porch light glowing like a beacon.

As I move down Peregrine's hill, deeper into the cemetery, the tree cover grows heavier overhead, and I begin to lose the moonlight. The further I go, the heavier my feet feel. My brain is foggy, and I stumble over exposed roots that I can't see in the darkness. I wince in pain as I come down hard on my left knee, slicing it open. I smell blood in the air as I struggle to my feet, and I can no longer see the light from my house. The graveyard is swallowing me whole.

I pause to catch my breath, and when I do, I hear footsteps somewhere behind me, moving fast. I stifle a scream. I can't get Pascal's words out of my head: *Bang bang, Eveny's dead.*

But maybe it's Caleb. My heart soars for a second in relief. I begin to turn towards the sound, but my heel catches on another root, and my knees buckle beneath me, betraying me. I go down hard. The last thing I'm aware of is the sharp pain of hitting the back of my head on a grainy tombstone as the world goes black.

When I wake up, my head is pounding, and I'm not sure how much time has passed. I blink into the darkness, and the first thing I realize is that I'm still in the cemetery, lying in a patch of grass.

"Hello, Eveny," says a smooth voice just to my right, and I jump, startled. My neck aches and my head throbs anew as I turn. I scream and struggle to sit up when I realize there's a man in a dark jacket bent over me, peering at me like I'm a specimen in a jar.

It takes me a moment to recognize him.

"Blake Montoire," I whisper. His pale face seems to glow in the dappled moonlight, and his eyes, which had appeared to be a normal shade of brown at the party, are now a chilling shade of almost translucent ice blue. He must have been wearing contacts so that he didn't look so freakish.

"That was just the name I used at that silly little party of yours," he says. "Very frat-boy chic, if I do say so myself." His accent, I realize, is vaguely French.

"I wouldn't know," I mutter. "So I'm guessing you're the Main de Lumière soldier who killed the real Blake Montoire outside our gates." My pulse is pounding, but I'm trying to appear calm.

"Main de Lumière *soldier*?" he repeats. "Heavens, no. I'm a Main de Lumière *général*. In other words, I'm in charge of the Louisiana division of our little organization.

And you, Eveny Cheval, are our biggest problem."

I begin to inch away, but he puts an ice-cold hand on my arm, and I find myself pinned to the spot.

"What do you think you're doing?" I demand, trying to sound brave.

He chuckles, and it reminds me for a moment of Pascal's evil laughter. "So impolite," he says. "That's no way to greet an old friend, Eveny."

"You're not my friend, you murderous asshole," I tell him. "Besides, I don't even know your real name."

His mirthless laughter chills me to the bone. I struggle again, but his vice-like grip becomes tighter. "Of course. How terribly rude of me. I'm Aloysius Vauclain."

"No wonder you decided on an alias," I say under my breath.

He ignores me. "Now, before you waste any energy trying to get away or calling for help, understand this: I will not hesitate to strike down anyone who comes to your aid. Is that clear?"

I swallow hard, thinking of Caleb. I glare at Vauclain and say, "You're powerless now anyhow. We've restored the protection of the gates."

Concern flashes across his face for a split second but vanishes just as quickly, replaced by a smirk. "Oh, but you don't know that for sure, do you?" he asks. "You fled before your little ceremony was over."

He's right. For all I know, I disrupted the power of our circle by breaking away from it. I curse myself for being so stupid.

"Now, Eveny," he says smoothly, releasing my arm. "I was hoping we could speak for a moment like rational adults. Do you think you can handle that?"

Instinctively, I reach for my Stone of Carrefour, but Vauclain's hand shoots out again at lightning speed, his cold fingers wrapping around my wrist.

"Ah ah ah," he chides. "Don't even think about it. Using magic right now would be a very, very bad idea. I'll have no choice but to end your life."

"Get it over with, then," I say. "If you're going to kill me, just do it."

He smiles. "But what's the rush, Eveny? The small talk is my very favourite part."

"Well, gee, don't let me stop you."

Vauclain laughs again, and the sound makes my blood run cold. "A sense of humour, I see. I like that. But then, I already knew you had wit. We've been watching you for years, and I must say, we've been very impressed with your aunt's resolve not to introduce you to zandara."

"I don't see how that's your concern."

"She's a wise woman, Eveny. She's kept you from magic because she finds it detestable. Yet you seem not to have inherited her intelligence, for here we sit in a cemetery, just after you've performed a serious zandara ceremony."

"It wasn't some magic joyride," I say. "It was a ceremony to fix what we screwed up last week when we opened the gates for that party. We were trying to get rid of *you*."

He chuckles again. "How very foolish and small-minded of you to assume that taking care of me would remove the threat to your town. You must know by now that there's someone on the inside who wishes you dead. After all, an attempt has already been made on your life."

"Drew's truck," I say softly. "That wasn't you?"

He looks offended. "I would never end your life in such an unimaginative way. Plus, of course, there are the far-too obvious parallels with your mother's staged suicide. But this, conversing with you in the very cemetery where your ancestors lie just before I end your life, well, it's much more poetic. When I recall your death later, these are the moments I'll savour."

A chill runs through me. "So I suppose you've spent a lot of time savouring the details of Glory Jones's death too."

He laughs coldly. "I didn't do that myself, of course. I would never get my hands dirty with someone with no real power of her own. And to be honest, it wasn't part of the plan, but she was, how do I put it, *uncooperative*. Although I admit, the soldier who killed her has gone a bit rogue. It's rather amusing to watch the unravelling."

"Did one of your soldiers kill my mother too?" I ask. The words are thick and sour in my throat.

He looks surprised. "Of course not. It would be pointless to kill a queen without stabbing her through the heart," he says, as if it's the most logical thing in the world. "Her murder wasn't our style at all, although we're certainly grateful that someone else chose to do it."

He begins to explain that stabbing a queen through the heart prevents her from taking power on to the afterlife and seeking revenge, but I tune him out, realizing that as he's talking, his grip on my wrist is relaxing. I scan my brain for an herb I can channel if I'm able to touch my Stone of Carrefour. The only thing that comes to mind is an image of wishing on dandelions with my mother when I was a little girl. It's not perfect, but it will have to do.

I silently ask Eloi Oke to open the gate, and then, just as Vauclain is concluding his explanation of how a queen's heart is her greatest source of magic but also her greatest vulnerability, I twist my left hand away from him and punch him across the face with my right.

In the seconds it takes him to recover, I grab my Stone of Carrefour and say, "Dandelion, I draw your power. Spirits, please grant my wish and render Aloysius Vauclain incapable of following me. *Mesi, zanset.*"

He's already grabbing for me, and I have no idea if the charm worked, but I don't wait to find out. I begin to run back in the direction of Peregrine's house, my head throbbing and my mouth dry with fear. I trip over a root and scramble to my feet again.

Once I'm out of the clearing, I run for my life, branches scraping my face. Their gnarled fingers reach for me in the darkness as I stumble into the tombs that rise from the soft, decaying earth. The ground rolls beneath my feet, and I can't trust my own steps.

The only thing I do know is that Vauclain is somewhere behind me, his long jacket making him one with the black shadows of the cemetery. I can hear his footsteps in the darkness. The jagged edge of a broken tombstone appears just ahead, and I stumble, landing flat on my face. A buried rock slices into my cheek, and I feel blood as I scramble to my feet.

"Help!" I cry, hoarse with terror as the mansion on the edge of the graveyard comes into view. It glows in the blackness, but I fear I won't make it that far.

I just have to get out of the cemetery, I tell myself. I struggle to my feet once again. I want to live. I have to live. I hold so many lives in my hands.

It feels like an eternity passes before I can see Peregrine's back fence. I turn to glance behind me and as I do, I collide hard with someone warm and solid who lets out a startled "Oof!"

I scream, sure that it's Vauclain, that he's somehow

materialized in front of me to kill me within sight of salvation.

"Please don't!" I cry.

"Eveny?" says a deep voice, and that's when I realize it's not the Main de Lumière general. Relief floods through me as I look up to see Caleb's face creased with worry.

"Caleb," I breathe, collapsing into him.

He holds me for a moment, then pulls away, steadying me by putting his hands on my forearms. "Eveny, what is it?"

"The frat guy," I begin, but I'm barely able to get the rest of the words out. The ceremony-induced exhaustion I've been fighting for the last hour is overtaking me. "It was the Main de Lumière guy," I finally manage. "The one from the party."

He's already scooping me into his arms and carrying me towards Peregrine's house. "I thought he was going to kill me," I say weakly, my voice muffled against the soft nub of his shirt.

"Eveny, I'm so sorry I wasn't there." Caleb's voice is rough with emotion, and it looks like he's about to cry. "I tried to follow you, but possession ceremonies take all the life out of you. By the time I got to the door, you were gone, and…"

"Caleb, if you'd been there, he could have killed you."

We've reached Peregrine's back door now, and Caleb

gently sets me back on my feet. "Are you okay? Can you stand?"

I nod, but before I can say anything, he pulls me towards him, and I melt into his strong chest, already feeling safer. "How can I ever ask you to forgive me, Eveny?" he whispers into my hair.

"It's not your fault," I say softly, and Caleb makes a deep guttural sound in the back of his throat.

"Eveny—" he begins, but then he stops.

"What?" I whisper.

"It *is* my fault." He looks away from me and puts his hand on Peregrine's back door. "It's just like I said. My feelings for you…I didn't know you were in trouble until it was too late."

"But it wasn't too late," I say, and I pull him back towards me. "I'm here. I'm okay." I never want him to let me go.

But then the door flies open, and the moment is over as Peregrine and Chloe stumble out. Their eyes focus unsteadily on Caleb and me, and Peregrine's mouth opens into a little *o*.

"Eveny," she begins, her eyes flicking uncertainly between Caleb and me. "I didn't mean for you…" Her voice is slurred and she trails off.

"We're sorry, Eveny." Chloe's voice is stronger and clearer, but she doesn't sound normal either; it's more like she's just run a marathon and is weak and out of breath. "We didn't expect the spirit to say what he did through Pascal," she says. "But whatever it is, we'll deal with it together."

It takes me a moment to realize that she and Peregrine think I'm shivering in fear because of what happened during the ceremony. "It's not that," I tell them. "I…I tried to run home, but in the cemetery, I was attacked by the guy from Main de Lumière." I add pointedly, "The one who was posing as Blake Montoire at *your* party."

I watch as their eyes widen into saucers, and I realize for the first time how dilated their pupils are. "Wait, what?" Peregrine whispers.

"Are you sure?" Chloe asks at the same time.

"Positive," I say and recap my encounter in the cemetery.

"Well, he was just bluffing," Peregrine says when I'm done, her eyes darting nervously to Chloe, who's chewing her lip. "The ceremony worked. He's powerless in Carrefour now."

"But he confirmed that there's already an operative here," I tell them. "Someone we trust. Someone who killed Glory. Someone who *isn't* powerless because they have a key to Carrefour. It's just like we thought."

Peregrine grabs my right hand and Chloe my left, and before I know it, I'm being pulled away from Caleb. The moment I'm out of his arms, I feel cold and exposed.

"We'll call our mothers now," Peregrine says. "Let's get inside."

Caleb steps back into the darkness, and I hesitate. "Aren't you coming in?" I ask.

"There's something I have to do." His jaw is set, and I realize what he means.

"You can't go after him, Caleb," I say. "It's not safe."

"I'll be fine." He doesn't give me a chance to argue. He turns away and strides towards the cemetery, his fists clenched.

"Caleb!" I cry out. But Chloe and Peregrine hold me back as he vanishes into the darkness.

"He'll be okay," Peregrine says. "Don't worry."

"Don't worry?" I demand. "You just let him go after a Main de Lumière general!"

"A Main de Lumière general who's powerless now," Peregrine corrects. "Caleb can take care of himself."

I don't believe her. I call out once more for him, but the only answer is the cawing of a raven from somewhere beyond the cemetery wall.

TWENTY-SIX

"YOU PERFORMED A CEREMONY WITH Eveny without bothering to explain it to her first?" Peregrine's mother demands twenty minutes later once we're all gathered in her living room. She and Chloe's mother came right away from a cocktail party on the other side of town. Peregrine's mother has her black hair done in a thousand tiny braided extensions, and she looks impossibly slim in a shimmery silver dress. Chloe's mother's sleek blonde hair is pulled into a chignon at the nape of her neck, and she's wearing a black cocktail dress that hugs her slender curves. They're both clutching flutes of champagne, which the maid handed to them as soon as they walked in the door.

"We thought it would make it easier on her if she didn't know what was going to happen," Peregrine whimpers, looking at the floor.

"Easier on her?" her mother asks, her eyes flashing. "Or easier on *you*?"

"I—" Peregrine begins, but her mother cuts her off.

"Enough," she says in a voice that's deadly calm. She looks at me. "Eveny, on behalf of my daughter, and of both sosyetes, yours and mine, I apologize. What Peregrine and Chloe did was inappropriate. You're one of us, and you deserve a full explanation from now on."

"Chloe knows better too," Chloe's mother pipes up, looking nervously at her daughter, who, like Peregrine, is staring at the floor like it's the most interesting thing she's ever seen.

I shrug uncomfortably. I don't need an apology – particularly not from the mothers whose carelessness has nearly destroyed the town. "What about Caleb?" I ask. "He's out there all alone."

The mothers exchange looks. "He's not alone," Chloe's mother says. "Oscar and Patrick are with him."

"Besides, it's certainly not your job to feel such concern for him. Quite the opposite," Peregrine's mother says. "Now, on to the more pressing matter at hand. Main de Lumière. Eveny, what did you find out?"

As I tell them about the conversation with Aloysius Vauclain, everyone in the room stands completely still. There's a collective gasp when I tell them how easily he admitted to Main de Lumière's involvement in Glory's murder, and another gasp when I say that he disavowed any Main de Lumière involvement in my mother's death.

"We need to figure out who the Main de Lumière operative in Carrefour is," I conclude. "If we find out who killed Glory, we can protect ourselves."

"You know," says Arelia, "the only new people in town in *years* have been Eveny herself and her aunt."

I open my mouth to defend Aunt Bea, but Peregrine's mother beats me to it. "Arelia, I don't care for Bea Cheval either," she says stiffly. "But to accuse her of being affiliated with Main de Lumière is taking things too far."

"And how do we know it wasn't you?" I hear myself say to Arelia. I hadn't meant to confront her, but her blind accusation of my aunt makes me furious.

"Eveny," Peregrine says in a warning tone.

"No," I say, turning to her. "Glory said she was meeting Arelia only hours before she died." I look back at Arelia. "Do *you* have an alibi for the night she was killed?"

I expect Arelia to have a retort ready, but instead, her face crumples, and she looks away. It's Margaux who steps forward and says, "She was with me. I swear it on our sosyete."

"Well, there you have it," Chloe's mother says, clapping her hands together enthusiastically. "I take it that will be the end of that discussion." She turns to me and adds in a lower voice, "In Carrefour, the women of the sosyetes stick together. They don't accuse each other of things."

I'm being chastised. I don't have a response, but I shoot a suspicious look at Arelia, who's glowering at me now. Peregrine takes a step forward. "I say we hold a ceremony tomorrow night to cast as many protective charms over our sosyetes as we can."

"I disagree. I think we should stop practising zandara for now, at least until the big Mardi Gras ceremony," I say immediately.

"This again?" Peregrine asks.

"I'm just suggesting we stop until we figure out what the situation is and who's after us," I say. "We're a target as long as we keep practising magic."

"You're assuming that this Vauclain person was being truthful with you about Main de Lumière's motives," Peregrine says.

"I don't think he would have bothered lying if he thought he was about to kill me," I point out.

"I agree with Eveny," Chloe says. "It doesn't mean we won't be ready if there's an attack. But there's not much we can do without knowing the identity of the traitor."

"But we can't just stop doing zandara," Margaux protests. "That's who we are."

"Which is all well and good until another one of us winds up six feet under," Peregrine's mother says sharply.

"I agree," Chloe's mother says. "For now."

"There we have it," Peregrine's mother says crisply. "This means that for the next few days at least, no zandara in Carrefour. We must avoid calling attention to ourselves until we know what we're facing."

"But Mom—" Peregrine begins to protest.

Her mother cuts her off. "That means you, girls."

"So what now?" asks Arelia.

"Now," says Peregrine's mother, "we attempt to make contact with a few magical sects we trust in other parts of the country."

"And in the meantime," adds Chloe's mother, "we lie low and keep our eyes open for signs that something's not right."

"But—" Peregrine begins.

Her mother interrupts again. "This isn't open for discussion."

Peregrine seethes in silence as the meeting draws to a close.

After I say my goodbyes, I head out the front door, thoroughly exhausted. I'm worried about the walk home, but Peregrine's mother hands me a sachet of protective herbs and promises that she'll cast a charm so that she'll know if I'm in any danger. "Besides, you'll be fine," she says. "Caleb and the boys are taking care of things."

I'm too tired to argue, plus I'm glad to get away from the sosyetes for the night. Still, I'm relieved when I hear Caleb calling my name. I turn to see him emerging from the cemetery, his shirt ripped on the right side and dirt streaked across his left cheek.

"Hey," he says, falling into step beside me.

"What happened?" I ask.

"We caught the guy who attacked you." Caleb hesitates. "He won't be bothering you any more."

Something cold wraps itself around my heart. "You killed Vauclain," I say softly.

"We had to," Caleb says. His voice breaks, and he pauses before continuing. "Patrick was the one who caught him, and Oscar was right behind him. He was already dead by the time I got there."

"He was their leader," I say. "They'll want revenge even more now."

"We didn't have a choice," he says. "If anything had happened to you…" He trails off, sending a shiver up my spine. "Eveny, I never would have forgiven myself."

He stops walking, and a few steps later, I stop too. I look up at him, and he puts a warm, rough hand on my cheek. We stare at each other for a long moment. He leans in, and I'm sure he's about to kiss me, so I close my eyes. But his lips never meet mine, and when I open my eyes a moment later, I feel like an idiot.

He's just staring at me. "Eveny. Have you made plans for the Mardi Gras Ball yet?"

"No." I hold my breath.

"Do you think… What I mean is… Would you want to go with me?"

My heart leaps into my throat, but there's something about his expression that feels off. "You don't have to ask me if you don't want to, you know," I say.

"I know. It doesn't change anything between us, but," he says, looking into my eyes, "I want to. So is that a yes?"

"Of course it is."

"Good." He clears his throat and looks up at the moon. "Now come on. Let's get you home before we lose the light."

I walk inside to find Aunt Bea pacing the living room. "There'd better be a good explanation for what happened tonight," she asks, but before I can open my mouth, she adds, "Because this isn't the way I raised you, Eveny. You have no idea what you're dealing with here."

I open and close my mouth before I finally settle for, "Who called you?"

"Chloe's mother," she says. "I *told* you this was the sort of thing that could happen if you got involved in zandara, Eveny!" Aunt Bea slams her fist against the wall.

All of a sudden, a wave of calm rushes over me. "Aunt Bea," I say, "I can't run away from this."

"But *I* can. And I can make you come with me. We're going back to New York. I never should have brought you here."

They're the words I would have given anything to hear a few weeks ago. But now, everything's different. "No."

"*No?*" she repeats.

I shake my head. "It's not what Mom would have wanted. I know things are messed up here, Aunt Bea, but I think I'm the one who's supposed to fix them."

Her eyes are suddenly awash with sadness. "But Main de Lumière *killed* your mother," she says. "You want to wait around and have the same thing happen to you?"

"But Main de Lumière *didn't* kill her," I say, explaining what Vauclain told me in the cemetery. "I don't think he was lying. He had no problem admitting what they did to Glory."

"Well, if they didn't kill your mother, who did?"

"I was hoping you'd have some idea," I reply. "Vauclain said I should be worried."

Aunt Bea looks down at the floor. "That doesn't make any sense."

"Maybe it was my dad," I venture after a pause.

Her head snaps up. "Where would you get an idea like that?"

"You despise him. You refuse to talk about him. And he's completely vanished."

Aunt Bea looks away. "Your father didn't kill your mother, Eveny. We are not living in an episode of *The Jerry Springer Show*."

"You hate him so much, though."

She gazes out the window. "Yes, because he left. Because your mother always believed he'd done the right thing, even when he abandoned you. Because he can't run from who he is, or who he was born to be."

Something inside me lurches. "What do you mean? Who was he born to be?" My pulse quickens; I have the feeling that whatever she's about to say is important.

But her face goes blank, and she looks away. "It's none of your concern, Eveny," she says tightly. "It has nothing to do with you."

"Of course it does," I reply, but Aunt Bea is already striding away, her heels echoing on the hardwood floors. "It has everything to do with me!"

But there's no reply. She's already gone.

TWENTY-SEVEN

A WEEK PASSES AND EVERYONE in the sosyete is on edge. True to their word, Peregrine and Chloe stop practising zandara, but in the meantime they're assembling a stockpile of herbs and furiously poring over charms from their mothers' notes. I stay up late and cram too, trying to memorize the uses of all the herbs my mother lists in her journal. "We have to be ready," Chloe keeps saying.

"I hate sitting around and waiting for some traitor to come get us," Peregrine whines on Thursday as we sit down on the cashmere blanket in the Hickories. "This feels like a ridiculous waste of our powers. I mean, have you seen my skin? I really need a refresher."

"We just have to figure out who the Main de Lumière person is, and then we can go back to normal," Chloe says, holding up the list we've been working on each day.

There are already thirty-five names on it, everyone from Mrs Perkins in the main office to the head cheerleader to Mrs Potter at the library. Arelia forced us to put Bea's name on there, so I put hers on too, which has earned me countless snarls.

I glance towards the caf to see Drew, Liv, and Max coming our way. They've been eating with us all week, which Peregrine and Chloe accepted without complaint after I mentioned that if the Main de Lumière insider is a student or teacher, the presence of non-sosyete members will make it obvious we're backing off. I know I have to speak quickly before they arrive. "The ban on magic is temporary," I remind Peregrine. "Besides, it's about time you had a breakout. Welcome to the real world."

"I hate the real world," she moans. "How do people live like this?"

The conversation ends abruptly as Drew, Liv and Max sit down on the opposite end of the blanket. Margaux, who looks like she's developed a beer belly in the last week, and Arelia, whose thighs seem to be expanding, just stare at them. "There's not enough to feed the three of you today," Arelia says sourly.

"Don't be rude, Arelia," Chloe chides half-heartedly. "They can have mine. And from the looks of it, you two shouldn't be going back for seconds either."

Arelia and Margaux glower at her, but they pile smoked

salmon blinis onto plates without further complaint.

"What's up with all of you perfect people?" Drew asks as he takes his meal. "Everyone's looking a little rough around the edges this week."

"Drew!" Liv says. But she appears delighted as she shoots Peregrine and Chloe a look of triumph. The Dolls just glare back.

"Perhaps your friends would be more comfortable eating in the cafeteria in the future," Peregrine says tightly, turning to me.

"Oh, he didn't mean it!" Max says eagerly. When Drew doesn't say anything, Max adds, "Seriously, man, apologize!"

Drew shrugs. "Sorry."

"Can't everyone just get along?" I ask. But from the dirty looks I get in reply, I'm guessing the answer is no.

By the next morning, though, something is different. Peregrine is keeping her head down in English class, and I can't help but notice that her curls are bouncy, and Chloe's hair looks like silk. When Peregrine finally looks up and meets my eye at the end of class, I know for sure by the guilty expression on her face.

"You used zandara!" I hiss as I catch up with them leaving the classroom.

"I don't know what you're talking about," Peregrine says haughtily. But her skin is clear, and the circles under her eyes have vanished.

"Chloe?" I ask.

She looks at me ruefully. "We should have called you, I guess."

"You *guess*?" I repeat. "How could you two do this after everything that happened? And after what your moms said?"

"Oh, get off your high horse, Eveny," Peregrine says. Two guys whistle at her as we pass. "This is who we are. I told you that. And we did it the old-fashioned way, with herbs. No harm to your precious Périphérie."

"But the danger—" I begin.

"The danger may not be real," Peregrine says sharply. "For all you know, Vauclain was bluffing. Not to mention that he's dead now."

"He wasn't bluffing," I say flatly. "And I'm sure there are a lot more Main de Lumière soldiers out there. His being dead doesn't mean we're safe."

Peregrine ignores me. "This town relies on us. We couldn't just turn our backs on it."

"Really? You're worried about the *town*? Not your pimples?"

Peregrine gives me a dirty look.

Chloe clears her throat. "Besides, our moms got back from New Orleans last night. They talked to a few voodoo priestesses there, who said the best way to get Main de Lumière to lose interest is to ignore them and go about our business. If we give in to their demands so easily, they'll know they have the upper hand."

"Did these priestesses have any first-hand experience with Main de Lumière?"

"Not that I know of," Chloe says.

"Then this situation is different!"

"Quiet down, Eveny," Peregrine says. "People are staring. This isn't the place."

I'm so angry I don't care. "So your mothers know you did this?"

"Yes," Chloe says.

"Our mothers feel, as do we, that we've been given this gift for a reason, and it's our right – our *duty* – to use it," Peregrine whispers.

"Just because you want better skin," I say. "And better grades. And better hair. And better boys."

"But now that you're back, we're not drawing our power from the Périphérie any more," Peregrine says. "Things are in complete balance. I don't see what's so wrong about what we're doing."

"Everything's wrong with it, Peregrine. And I'm really afraid we're about to find that out." I walk away quickly before she can say anything else, but a moment later, I realize Chloe is following me.

"What?" I whirl to face her. "There's no way to justify what you've done. This was a decision we were supposed to make together, the three of us, and you and Peregrine just did what you wanted!"

That's when I realize she looks like she's about to cry. "It's not that," she says. "It's…it's Justin. I need some advice."

I realize with a surge of guilt that between the car accident with Drew and Main de Lumière, I'd forgotten to say something to Chloe about him. "I've been meaning to talk to you about him too. Want to go outside for a bit?"

She nods, and we head out the door as the bell rings to start second period. No one seems to notice, but then again, I'm getting accustomed to the rules being different for Dolls like us.

She looks at her hands once we're sitting on a bench facing the Hickories. "So I've been thinking a lot about what you said. About how maybe I should let Justin make up his own mind about me."

I wait for her to go on.

"The thing is, I'm scared. Do you think he'll want to keep dating me without a charm?"

I hesitate. "I think that's a chance you have to take."

"I'm scared he's in love with another girl," she mumbles.

"I'm sure he's not," I answer honestly. "But if there's someone else he's meant to be with, you're taking that possibility away. If he's supposed to be with you, he will be."

"It could mean losing him," she says almost inaudibly.

"But it could also mean opening the door to someone who's right for you. If you're in the wrong relationship, your eyes won't be open for the right one."

She's quiet for a moment. "Eveny," she says, "you're in love with Caleb, aren't you?"

I can feel myself turning red. "I don't know. Maybe. Why do you say that?"

"It's just the way you get when he's around. Like you're a little nervous, but also happy. Like seeing him makes you feel better."

I consider this. "That's pretty much exactly how I feel."

"But you know you can't be with him. He's explained that to you."

"I keep hoping he'll change his mind."

She looks sad. "It's more complicated than that for him. I think he's trying to do the right thing." She hesitates and adds, "You know, you could cast a charm on him to make him see things your way."

"It's tempting," I reply. "But whatever would come of it, it wouldn't be real."

"I guess." After a moment, she stands up. "Wait, what were you going to say? You were going to tell me something about Justin."

I hesitate. "I just wanted to say I know you'll do the right thing."

"You too, Eveny." She walks away without another word.

In her wake, I'm left wondering exactly what that right thing is, though, and how I'll find my way there.

I spend the afternoon reading and rereading my mother's letter, studying her herb book, and trying to figure out what I'm supposed to do.

It takes me until late that night to come to the conclusion that although zandara has gotten terribly off track in Carrefour, it's still who we are. I've been so focused on making sure the Périphérie isn't harmed any more and making sure Main de Lumière doesn't have a reason to attack us, that I'm losing sight of our gift.

Sure, zandara can be misused. But that's the case with everything. If I walk away now, the inevitable result is that the scales will one day be tipped too far, and who knows what could happen then? I can't fix anything by turning my back on it.

It's nearly midnight when I show up at Peregrine's house unannounced to tell her I'm not going to run from who I am any more. I expect to find her alone, but instead, when she opens the door wearing a low-cut caftan that shows off her cleavage, I see Caleb standing in the shadows of her front hall.

"What are you doing here?" I ask, looking back and forth between them as my stomach drops.

Peregrine just rolls her eyes. "Don't you call first, Eveny? It's rude to drop by unannounced so late without a warning."

"It's not what you think," Caleb says quickly. "We were talking about you."

"You were?" I ask uncertainly.

"Oh for goodness' sake, don't be so melodramatic, Eveny," Peregrine says. "We're not *banging* each other, if that's what you're asking. Not yet, anyhow," she adds. "Stop being so theatrical and come in."

I close the door behind me and follow the two of them into the living room. Peregrine settles onto the sofa and folds her long legs under her. A moment later, Audowido slithers out from behind a pillow and slinks into her lap. She pets him absent-mindedly like he's a cat.

"So why are you here?" Peregrine says, once Caleb has taken a seat in an armchair and I've perched uneasily on an ottoman. "More criticisms about how I'm horrible and selfish and superficial?"

"I came to tell you I'm in." I glance at Caleb, who looks troubled.

"Meaning...?" she says.

"Meaning I know I have to embrace this. I have to be the queen I was born to be."

"I knew you'd come around," Peregrine says. "Chloe will be so thrilled. So what do you want to do first?"

"What do you mean?" I ask.

She gestures to me. "Well, we could fix your hair or make your legs look longer. Or maybe we should start with your boobs. I'm sure Caleb would prefer C cups to A cups on you."

I can feel my cheeks heating up. "I'm not here for a new body."

She stops petting Audowido and waits for me to continue.

"I'm here to say that I'll work zandara with you, but we've got to stop being so careless. Could you just hear me out for a second?"

Peregrine snorts. "Oh, this should be good."

"Look, I know you think I'm being a goody-goody. But we have to fix what's been done already, or it's only a matter of time until we're destroyed."

"I see you've appointed yourself queen of the queens now?"

I ignore her. "You've only been using your power to make your own lives easier. Maybe once we stop being selfish, we'll have a little more perspective on what to do about Main de Lumière."

Peregrine studies me for a moment, then she leans forward so that Audowido can slither up her arm. When she stands to look at me, she looks positively creepy with her violet eyes blazing and her snake wrapped around her shoulders. He hisses at me, and I look away. He's the one thing in this town I know I'll never get used to.

"You know, it occurred to me as you were speaking how little you really know," she says slowly. "And it seems to me that someone who's so ignorant about things isn't exactly qualified to give other people advice on how to run their lives."

"I know I'm new at this—"

She cuts me off. "No, not that. I'm not referring to your little do-gooder speech. I'm talking about how clueless you are about your own life and how horrendously underqualified that makes you to judge mine."

"Peregrine—" Caleb says, but this just makes her turn on him.

"Caleb, I know it's your job to protect her, but this is a little much, don't you think? You don't get to shield her feelings too." Peregrine smiles at me, her eyes glinting. "Like, for example, it might hurt Eveny to know the real reason you're so fixated on the rules is that your father let her mother die, and now you have to salvage your family reputation."

A knot forms in the pit of my stomach. "Caleb?" I say softly. "That's not true, is it?"

But he merely hangs his head, and I realize in an instant

that Peregrine must be right. I can't believe it didn't occur to me before: if my mother's dead, that means her protector – Caleb's dad – didn't do his job.

"So Caleb probably didn't tell you that when your mother was being stabbed to death, his father was at home having a good ol' time with his wife and son?" Peregrine says with a cold smile. "He sensed the danger, but by the time he got back to your house, your mom was already dead."

"Peregrine!" Caleb says, his voice choked.

Peregrine ignores him. "He also probably didn't mention that the guilt and shame drove his father out of town. And that his mother always blamed your family for destroying hers. So, you see, Caleb's not just torn about his responsibilities as your protector. He's torn because he was raised to hate everything Cheval. It all gets rather complicated, doesn't it?"

"Caleb—" I whisper, turning to him.

Caleb doesn't answer; he just stares. And so without another word, I turn to go. I've heard enough.

"Oh, Eveny, one more thing!" Peregrine calls out as I stride towards her front door.

I stop, because even though I can't stand to hear another word, I know I have to. I need to understand everything.

"The thing about our protectors is that if they let you die, they'll die within a year themselves. Our ancestors designed it that way to make sure they always stayed loyal."

My breath catches in my throat as she goes on.

"So if Caleb doesn't protect you, he's dead, which is exactly what happened to his dad," she says. "Now you can see why he's so motivated to hang out with you. He's confusing self-preservation with feelings. Or maybe it's just that he wants you to believe he likes you, so that you care about keeping him alive too."

"Eveny," Caleb says, "that's not true!" But I'm already walking away.

"Just let her go," I hear Peregrine coo in her syrupy smooth voice. "She'll be fine. Come here. I'll make you feel better."

I slam the door behind to shut their voices out. The whole way home, I try very hard not to think about the fact that the things I thought mattered were all in my head.

Twenty-eight

I LOCK MYSELF IN MY room the next day and dodge five calls from Chloe and one from Caleb. Aunt Bea knocks on my door around seven to ask me to come down to dinner, but I tell her I'm not hungry. Finally, around eight she knocks again, and I open the door reluctantly.

"Did one of the Dolls do something to you?" she asks bluntly.

"Peregrine told me about Caleb Shaw and the fact that his survival is tied to mine."

Her expression shows me she already knew, which makes me feel even more betrayed. "Oh."

"Why didn't *you* tell me?" I demand.

"I don't like to talk about the Shaws."

"Because Caleb's father let Mom get killed," I guess in a flat voice.

Aunt Bea looks surprised. "No. I've never blamed him for that. Neither did Peregrine's mother or Chloe's mother. Whoever got to your mom got through every one of us." She shakes her head. "That poor man always blamed himself. He felt he'd failed to uphold his family's end of the pact. He left town soon after, and about a year later his body was found in Savannah."

My blood runs cold. "What happened to him?"

"The police never solved the case. Rumour is that he was stabbed over a gambling debt. But of course his death was tied to the original pact," she adds. "It was inevitable."

It takes me a second to realize what she means. "He died within a year of Mom because he failed to protect her," I say.

"I'm afraid so. I think Peregrine's and Chloe's moms felt guilty, like they'd driven him away. They gave Caleb and his mother some money to get back on their feet, and they continued paying Charles's salary until Caleb was old enough to take over."

I blink. "Charles's *salary*?"

"Part of the deal the Shaws made with your great-great-great-grandmother was that they'd be rewarded financially for protecting Cheval queens, plus they would always be members of the sosyete and be provided with whatever they needed to live comfortably. Caleb's mother should be a sosyete member too, but after her husband's death, she became a recluse. She didn't want anything to do with zandara."

"Poor Caleb. Having to carry on a tradition that destroyed his family…" I shake my head. "He should hate me."

"I think that's the last emotion he feels for you." She pauses and changes the subject. "I'll make you a plate and bring it up. I don't want you going to bed hungry."

But for the rest of the night, I can't stop thinking about Caleb's father. My mom's death was at the hands of a random murderer, but his dad's death would for ever be tied to my mom – and to an obligation he never asked for.

I'm attempting to catch up on some homework Sunday afternoon when the doorbell rings. Aunt Bea pokes her head into my room a moment later to tell me that Peregrine and Chloe are here.

"I have nothing to say to them," I tell her without looking up.

She hesitates. "I think Peregrine's here to apologize. With things as dangerous as they are right now, maybe it can't hurt to hear her out."

"Fine," I grumble.

I follow her downstairs and find Peregrine and Chloe waiting in the front hall.

"I'll leave you girls alone," Aunt Bea says. She narrows her eyes at Peregrine before slipping away.

"What do you want?" I say once Aunt Bea is gone.

Chloe looks at Peregrine, who's still staring at the floor. After a pause, she nudges her.

Peregrine looks up and blinks at me a few times. "Look, I'm sorry, okay?" she says. It seems difficult for her to get the words out; I assume she's not used to contrition.

Chloe nudges her again. "Go ahead, tell her the rest."

Peregrine glares at Chloe for a moment, but then she looks up again and says, "Fine, I *might* have been a little jealous. Caleb's the only guy I've ever really liked, and he rejected me. Then you get to town, and he's all over you. And not only that, but our sosyete's supposed to bend over backwards to do what's right now that you're here. It doesn't seem fair."

"You think this is what I want?" I demand. "Besides, it's not like anything's ever going to happen with me and Caleb anyhow." I wave my hand distractedly and try my hardest to pretend I don't care. "What matters is that we're in danger."

"Exactly my point. That's why we have no choice but to do the ceremony. Think you can get your panties out of a twist long enough for that?"

"The Mardi Gras ceremony?" I ask.

Peregrine's expression turns reverent. "The Mardi Gras *Possession*. The single most important ceremony we hold each year. If you do it with us, Eveny, it can protect us entirely and restore Carrefour's power, which has been draining away for the last fourteen years. It'll even bank us enough power to start to fix the Périphérie."

I hesitate. "If it's the only way, I'm in." I don't like it, but I know I don't have a choice.

"Wonderful. We do it right after the Mardi Gras Ball next Tuesday," Chloe explains. "After the ball ends, our sosyete caravans to New Orleans."

"Mardi Gras is the craziest day of the year in New Orleans, so everyone will be out in the streets partying," Peregrine says. "We'll do a mass possession ceremony soon after we arrive, then join the party."

"It's like the ceremony that freaked you out at Peregrine's," Chloe cuts in, "but everyone gets possessed by a different spirit, so that each of our bodies become vehicles for them. It's the best way to draw power to us. Eloi Oke and the other spirits that possess us have free rein to party, drink and be among real people for the first time in a year. It's the greatest gift we can give them, and in return they give us tremendous power."

"But leaving Carrefour means leaving the protection of the town," I point out.

"It's a chance we have to take," Peregrine says. "If we

don't do this ceremony, we won't be able to fix anything that's gone wrong. And that could destroy us."

"The ceremony has to take place in New Orleans?" I ask.

"It's the only place the spirits are entirely free to revel in public without anyone blinking an eye," she says. "Our defences might have been down before, but they're not any more."

"Eveny," Chloe says, "I don't like this either. But I think we're out of options."

Caleb is gone from school Monday and Tuesday, which makes me feel sadder than it should. I know he's off training with Patrick and Oscar as the Mardi Gras Possession approaches, but I miss his presence. There are times I glance out the classroom windows and see flashes of someone in the woods that I'm sure is him, but I know I'm imagining things.

He does call twice, but he doesn't leave messages, and I don't bother calling back. What is there to say? There's undeniably something between us, but he simply wants those feelings to go away.

An eerie calm settles over Pointe Laveau the next several days, and even those who aren't in on the Secret of Carrefour seem to sense that something's wrong.

"The Dolls are being even weirder than usual," says Drew as we head up to the Hickories on Wednesday.

I try to appear nonchalant. "I hadn't noticed."

"Don't be so dramatic," Liv says, nudging him gently. They're flirting, and it's cute. More than that, though, I'm glad they're distracting each other. As long as they're sneaking adoring looks, they won't be thinking too hard about the peculiar behaviour of the Dolls.

"What happened between Chloe and Justin?" Max whispers to me on the way back to class that day. "He hasn't been up here in the Hickories since last week."

"I don't know," I tell him honestly, but I'm hoping Chloe did what she said and released him from her charm. "Do you think they broke up?" he asks.

"I hope so. It would be the right thing."

On Friday, Peregrine's not in school, but Chloe offers me a ride home in her little white BMW so I don't have to wait in the rain for Aunt Bea to pick me up.

"You know," she says as we pull out of the parking lot, "you still have to go to the ball with Caleb. It's safest that way. If Main de Lumière knows about the Mardi Gras Possession we do each year, that's going to be a dangerous night. You need Caleb to protect you, now more than ever."

"Great," I mutter. "So he's obligated to take me to the ball. How delightful for him." Thunder rolls outside, and lightning flashes across the sky, illuminating dark, hulking clouds.

"He *wants* to take you, Eveny."

I snort and look out the window. The rain is coming down in sheets, and the world has turned black.

"Things are different with you two," she adds after a minute. "Seeing you with him made me realize that I needed to let Justin go."

"Did you do it?"

"Yes," she says. "He's still part of the sosyete as long as he wants to be. And he'll still be my date to the ball, because he's coming with us to New Orleans. But after that, we're done." She pauses. "You know, it's true that Caleb had no choice about protecting you unless he wanted his family to lose everything. But he did have a choice about falling in love with you."

I look at her in disbelief. "You think Caleb is in *love* with me?"

But Chloe isn't laughing. "You're different from the rest of us. Maybe it's because you didn't grow up here. Maybe it's because you're just a different kind of person. But I think Caleb sees you for *you*."

I ponder this in silence for a moment. "It doesn't matter, though. He's making a choice, and the choice is to distance himself from me."

"You're not being fair to him," she says. "It's not like

he's being a jerk. He's trying to do the right thing."

"Only because his life depends on it," I say.

"No!" Chloe exclaims, and I can tell she's getting frustrated with me. "It's because he's a good guy. It's because he understands that you're in danger. It's because he would do anything to protect you – including staying out of your life."

"He's just doing his duty," I say softly. "That's all."

"Look, never in the history of this town has there been an incident of a protector falling for one of the queens," Chloe says after a pause. "It's forbidden. This wasn't supposed to happen. But it did. That means something."

My heart thuds as I turn to look out the window again. "Can he sever his obligation to me if he wants to?" I ask.

"Well, technically, he could stop protecting you at any time," she says. "But he'd instantly lose everything his family has ever had. He and his mom would be out on the street. And of course if something happened to you…"

"He'd die too," I fill in.

"Yes."

"But I can release him from the obligation," I say.

Chloe looks startled. "That wouldn't make any sense. You'd be putting yourself in serious danger."

"Humour me. Is it possible? If I did it, would it free him from his fate being tied to mine?"

She hesitates. "I guess so. But it would be crazy to do

that now, Eveny, with Main de Lumière after us. Caleb has been training his whole life to protect you. Besides, think about future generations. If you sever the protectorate, you leave your children, your grandchildren, and their children unprotected."

My stomach lurches at the thought, but there's no justification for protecting myself and my family at the expense of Caleb and his. "I need you to tell me how I'd do it," I say.

Chloe's grip tightens on the steering wheel, but after a long pause, she begins to explain. And by the time she drops me off at my front door, I'm beginning to have an idea of how I can change everything – if not for everyone, then at least for the future of the one person in my life who's willing to sacrifice everything for me.

Twenty-nine

THAT WEEKEND, I IGNORE CALLS from everyone, including Liv, who seems to think she's done something to offend me. I shoot her a text telling her that I'm just worried about the ball, but the truth is, I don't have the energy to make up another story about why the Dolls are acting so strange.

I go to bed early Saturday night, hoping that I'll dream of my mom. The more alone I feel in this town, the more I long for her advice and comfort. But my sleep is annoyingly dreamless. I wake up frustrated, wondering what good my powers are if I can't call upon my mom – or at least someone helpful – when I need to.

Aunt Bea and I eat grilled cheese in silence on Sunday, and afterwards, I shut myself in my room. I tell her I'm studying for a test, but in reality I'm leafing through my mother's herb book, hoping there's something there I've missed. Perhaps a "How to Save the Whole Town from Impending Disaster" charm? No such luck.

It's nearing twilight when I head out to the garden to think. It's the place where I most feel my mother's presence, and tonight I want to do everything I can to channel her wisdom, in hopes that I can find some answers.

But all I'm left with are the cryptic words of her letter. *In order to survive, you'll have to tap into everything inside of you. You have the chance to become the greatest queen the world has ever known.*

I keep searching my heart for the insights she seemed to think would be there, but all I can find are betrayal and loss. My mother is gone. My father is gone. The truth about Caleb has come to light. Everything is wrapped in secrets and lies.

I'm still sitting in the garden a few hours later, no closer to an answer, when a rustling from behind the rosebushes startles me. I turn and see Boniface approaching.

"Oh," I say, putting my hand over my heart. "It's you."

"Sorry, honey," he says gently. He gestures to the bench beside me. "Mind if I sit for a minute?"

I shake my head, and he settles down next to me. I haven't seen much of him since the incident in the garden where I nearly killed him, and although I feel like I should be freaked out by the realization that he's been alive for more than a century and a half, I'm not. This town is weird, and after a while, the weirdness becomes the norm.

"It seems like you have some decisions to make," he says.

I look at him in surprise. "How do you know?"

He chuckles. "Do you think I'm just here to care for the house? I'm here for you too, Eveny. You're my family, just like your mom was."

"I keep wondering what she'd do right now if she were in my shoes."

He puts a hand on my back. "You know right from wrong. You realize it's your job to stand up for the right thing. I don't think you have to expend so much energy wondering what decisions your mother would make. They're the choices that are in your heart already."

"So what do I do?" I ask. "How do I protect everyone? How do I do what's right?"

"Is your sosyete still planning to do the Mardi Gras Possession on Tuesday night?"

"That's the plan."

"Then go to New Orleans and work your magic. You must." He stands, and for a moment, I think the conversation is over and he's walking away, but then he gestures for me to follow him. "I have something I'd like to give you."

He leads me into his cottage, which is lit by a dozen

squat, dripping candles. "Have a seat," he says, gesturing to two wooden chairs beside a small table. I settle into one of them while he disappears. He returns a moment later with something clutched in his hand.

"After your aunt moved you to New York, she asked me to go through your mother's things," he begins. He sits down in the chair opposite me and leans forward. "Everything I held on to is stored in the attic for you. But this, I took down a few days ago." He unfolds his palm, and I peer at what he's holding.

"Lipgloss?" I ask.

He chuckles. "It belonged to your mother."

"Oh. Thanks." I force a polite smile. I'd hoped he was going to give me something that could help me, but I appreciate him trying to make me feel better. "It'll be nice to think of my mom when I wear it to the ball."

"No, you misunderstand," he says. "I'm not giving you this to remind you of your mother. I'm giving it to you because once upon a time, she imbued it with power."

I look at him and then back to the tube of gloss.

"She spent months working desperately to come up with the right combination of herbs," he explains. "This sort of thing is difficult, because in zandara herbs are used in the moment, in ceremonies, not to give inanimate objects power of their own. But just before she died, she told me she thought she'd done it; she added ground alder leaf to uncover someone's true motives, thyme to reveal a liar, and peony to bring the truth to light. She never had a chance to charm it, though."

He hands the tube to me. "It's meant to show you betrayal around you." I roll it over in my palm while he continues. "It will be clear on your lips, and it will be clear on people who are being honest with you. But if you charm it correctly, it will show up blood red on the face of the person who's lying to you about the night Glory Jones died. And only you will be able to see the mark of the traitor."

"Are you sure it will work?" I ask.

"No," he admits. "But it may be your best chance."

I consider this for a moment. "What made my mom so desperate to perfect this before she died?"

He frowns. "She had the feeling she was in danger, and she wanted to find out if there was someone here in Carrefour lying to her." He puts his hand on my shoulder. "Your mother's magic didn't save her. But it could be the thing that saves you."

Mardi Gras arrives crisp and clear in Carrefour, the first cloudless day we've had in a while. Pointe Laveau is closed in honour of the holiday, so I don't set my alarm, but I'm up before five thirty anyhow, my nerves on edge.

The first thing I do is cross to my window and look out at the garden. I'm startled to see Caleb sitting in the pre-dawn darkness on the bench beneath my mom's favourite roses, staring up at me.

I open the window. "Come inside," I call down.

He shakes his head. "Thanks. But I'm okay."

"Caleb, you don't have to do this."

He looks down at the ground and then back up at me. "I'm fine, Eveny. Go on with your day."

I pause and say, "You've been avoiding me all week. What are you doing here now?"

I'm hoping he'll say he's here because he wants to be. But instead he says, "It's Mardi Gras, Eveny. The most dangerous day of the year for our sosyete."

I stare at him for a long time before nodding and closing the window, a lump in my throat. He's here because he has to be; that's all. But that doesn't stop me from being touched. Or from making him a cup of coffee once I'm dressed and bringing it out to the garden. I hand it to him and sit down on the bench next to him with a mug of my own. I try not to notice as he scoots away.

"You know, you don't have to take me to the ball tonight," I say.

He turns to look at me as the steam rises from his coffee mug, blurring his face for a moment. "I want to," he says bluntly.

"Of course you do," I say, trying not to sound bitter. "It's your job."

He seems to choose his words carefully before speaking. "I'm obligated to protect you, not to take you to the ball. I *want* to take you to the ball." He doesn't look at me, but he takes a sip of his coffee, which feels a bit like an acceptance of my olive branch. "That's why I asked you," he adds a moment later.

We sit in silence for a long time. Finally, he says, "I'm sorry," in such a low voice that I almost don't hear him.

"For what?" I ask in disbelief.

"For everything. For all of this. You didn't ask for any of it."

"Neither did you," I say.

He nods and takes another sip of his coffee, and I take a sip of mine. Around us, the world comes to life as the sun rises, turning the sky a million beautiful shades of watercolour blue.

I lock myself in my room that afternoon and, after poring over my mother's herb journal and thinking a lot about what Boniface said, I take a deep breath, hope my mother was right about the lipgloss, and call on Eloi Oke.

"Alder leaf, thyme and peony, I draw your power," I say. "Spirits, please imbue this gloss with the truth that could save our lives tonight. Let it show up blood red on the face of the person who's lying about the night Glory Jones died." The air pressure shifts, and I feel a breeze as I murmur, *"Mesi, zanset. Mesi, zanset. Mesi, zanset."*

I call Peregrine when I'm done and ask if she can conference Chloe in. When they're both on the line, I hastily explain my mother's lipgloss and the charm I just cast over it.

"How do you know it will work?" Peregrine asks.

"I don't," I say. "But do you have a better idea?"

"No," she admits. "But you're the only one who will see the mark of the traitor?"

"That's what Boniface said," I tell her.

"Can't hurt to try," Chloe says. "Let us know the second you see anything, okay?"

"Of course," I say. "Don't tell anyone, though. I know you two aren't the ones who betrayed Glory, but it could be someone else we trust."

"Like one of your unfortunate little friends from the Périphérie?" Peregrine asks sweetly.

Chloe surprises me by saying, "Lay off, Peregrine. It could be anyone. And Eveny, I agree. We don't know who to trust. Your secret's safe."

"Peregrine?" I ask.

"Whatever," she says. I hear a doorbell ring in the background and Peregrine says, "Cristof is here. I'm getting my hair done. See you tonight."

I hear a click, then Chloe's voice. "You still there?" she asks.

"I'm here." I pause. "Will you call Caleb and tell him about this too? I don't think I can handle talking to him right now."

"I'll do it." She pauses and adds, "Good luck, Eveny. I hope this works."

"Me too."

Liv comes over late that afternoon so we can get ready for the ball together. She's so excited about her dress – a slinky purple satin sheath – and her date with Drew that she doesn't seem to notice how quiet I'm being.

"Do you think Drew'll try anything tonight?" she asks as she curls her hair in my bathroom mirror. I'm standing beside her, putting on my eye make-up. "I think he likes me, but this will be our first date-date. We've been talking on the phone every night, though, and our chemistry is pretty insane. Am I being totally lame?"

She's talking so quickly I can barely keep up with her, but her enthusiasm is just what I need to keep my mind off what might happen later.

"You're not being lame at all. And I bet he'll try to kiss you," I say.

Liv laughs. "Maybe." She fluffs her curls in satisfaction, turns to look at herself from both the left and the right in the mirror, then unplugs the curling iron. "How do I look?"

"Gorgeous."

"You okay, Eveny?" she asks, watching my reflection in the mirror closely.

"Me? I'm fine!" I overenthuse.

"You're nervous about Caleb." Her expression is sympathetic and concerned. "I know I keep saying this, but I don't think you have anything to worry about," she says. "Just kiss him!"

I look down at the tube of charmed lipgloss, which lies on the bathroom counter. "I will."

I finish putting on mascara, then add a dusting of peach blush, which makes my skin look luminous. My hair falls around my shoulders in gentle, rippling waves, and the beautiful champagne-coloured dress I've pulled from my mother's closet complements my colouring perfectly.

The last thing I do before leaving the bathroom is to uncap the charmed gloss, slick it over my lips, and glance once more at the mirror. *Thanks, Mom*, I think as I set the gloss down on the bathroom counter.

I take a deep breath, pray that Liv isn't the one I need to worry about, and give her a kiss on the cheek. I sigh in relief when no mark appears. "I'm so glad we're friends," I tell her.

"Me too, Eveny." She looks at me more closely. "Ooh, let me grab some of that gloss," she says, reaching for the tube.

She runs it over her own lips before I can stop her.

Liv hands me back the tube, and I shove it into the little beige purse she loaned me for the evening, hoping she didn't affect the potency of the magic.

"You okay?" I ask uncertainly.

"Of course. Why wouldn't I be?"

The doorbell rings before I can answer, and Liv's eyes widen. "They're here!"

She's already barrelling out of the bathroom before I have a chance to reply. I say a little prayer that nothing bad will happen to her tonight, and follow her downstairs.

Liv blows me a kiss then pulls the door open. Drew and Caleb are standing there side by side, each of them clutching small, clear boxes with corsages inside.

"We pulled up at the same time," Drew says, gesturing to Caleb. "Although now I'm thinking we should have coordinated." He refocuses on Liv and holds out the corsage, which is white with little green ribbons. "You look really pretty, Liv."

Caleb looks at me with sad, almost desperate eyes while Drew slips the corsage onto Liv's left wrist. When Drew is done, Caleb holds up his little box. "For you," he says, handing it to me.

It's a beautiful cluster of white roses, a white lily, and a sprig of baby's breath, wrapped with a deep green ribbon trimmed in gold. "It's gorgeous," I say.

"Well, put it on her!" Liv urges with a laugh.

Caleb clears his throat and steps forward.

"Roses for strength, a lily for peace and baby's breath for hope," he whispers. As his fingers touch my wrist, I feel a jolt of electricity shoot through me. From the way he looks at me, I know he feels it too.

"Thank you," I say once he slips the corsage onto my wrist and looks away. I take a deep breath and lean in to kiss him on the cheek. I exhale in relief when nothing shows up on his face.

He offers me his arm and I lock the front door behind us. I feel like I'm floating down the driveway as we head towards his Jeep.

"I'll let them pull out first," Caleb says, after he shuts the passenger door behind me and climbs into the driver's seat. We watch as Drew helps Liv into the old Nissan he's borrowed from his mother. Liv giggles and blushes, and Drew almost trips over his own two feet as he hurries to the driver's seat to get in. "They're kind of cute together," Caleb says.

Drew starts his car up, and the two of them head out

without looking back. I look over at Caleb, expecting that he'll turn the key in the ignition too, but he just sits there staring straight ahead.

"Caleb?" I ask after a moment.

He turns to look at me. "Eveny," he says after a pause. "You really do look beautiful." He stares at me for another long moment, then he leans across and touches my cheek so gently I can barely feel it.

"I wish things were different," he says. He doesn't wait for me to respond before starting the car. We drive into town in silence.

THIRTY

THE BALL IS EVEN MORE spectacular than I imagined. I attended Homecoming my sophomore year in Brooklyn – Mer and I went stag together – and I suppose I'd expected an upgraded, Carrefour-ized version of that: a punch bowl, streamers hanging from the rafters, maybe a DJ. But the Lietz Theater on Main Street has been transformed into a wonderland of cascading gold sheets, deep purple uplighting, and a million twinkling lights overhead. The oval dance floor is a deep ebony, and instead of a DJ, there's a small orchestra in the corner. Tuxedoed waiters circulate with trays full of champagne flutes and appetizers.

"This is amazing," I say. The whole town seems to be here. I even recognize a bunch of Drew's friends from the Périphérie, and I assume that many of the adults clustered near them are their parents or their parents' friends. The men are all wearing tuxes or dark suits, and the women around the room are all in elaborate ball gowns. It's decadent, outlandish, ritzy, and over the top.

Peregrine's and Chloe's mothers both make a beeline for Caleb and me as we walk through the door.

"Your aunt isn't here, is she?" Peregrine's mother asks once they've both hugged and air-kissed us.

I shake my head. "I don't think she's coming."

Peregrine's mom makes a tsk-tsk sound. "I wish she had even a little of your mother's courage."

I feel a surge of annoyance in defence of my aunt. "Maybe she doesn't feel like it's her duty to fight your battles."

Peregrine's mother looks at me. "Honey, this is your battle as much as it is ours. And she's your blood. You'd think she'd want to help you."

Chloe's mother cuts in. "Or perhaps she just knows things are in your hands now and there's nothing more she can do."

I bite my tongue and resist the urge to tell them that maybe if they and their daughters had practised even a little self-control, we wouldn't be in this mess. Instead I kiss both of them on their cheeks, just in case. When no lipstick mark shows up, I excuse myself and hurry away.

I spend the next hour greeting everyone with cheek kisses and reapplying my lipgloss every few minutes. I'm sure I look like a crazy person, and I'm beginning to wonder if maybe I am. Maybe it's madness to have put my faith in an old tube of gloss, but I know Boniface cares as much about the fate of this town as I do, and that has to mean something. Plus, I trust my mom. If she believed this would work, then I do too.

It's not until nine o'clock that it occurs to me for the first time that the traitor might not even be here, rendering the whole issue of the charmed gloss moot.

"I love that you're finally loosening up tonight and kissing everyone. It's very sexy." Pascal interrupts my thought process by sidling up behind me and putting a hand on my waist. I turn to find him leering at me. "If you're looking for someone to make out with, look no further." He puckers up as I roll my eyes.

"I'm here with Caleb," I say.

"Who, might I point out, is nowhere to be found," he replies.

"He went to the bathroom ten seconds ago. He'll be right back."

"And in the meantime, if you want to make out with me…" Pascal says.

I grit my teeth and dive in to kiss him on the cheek, which seems to shock him. I'm relieved when I don't see any red mark develop.

"Seriously, Eveny, if you're into it, we could slip outside

for a few minutes," Pascal says, his eyes darting around like pinballs.

"Pascal," I say calmly, "I wouldn't slip outside with you if you were the last guy on earth."

"That's just because you haven't had any of this body yet," he says, gesturing proudly to himself.

"That must be it." I turn to walk away before he has a chance to say anything else. My shoulders sag in relief as I see Caleb coming towards me from across the dance floor.

"How you doing?" he asks, his forehead creased with concern. He puts his right hand gently on the small of my back, and for a moment, it feels like everything is okay. Then, he quickly pulls away like he's done something wrong.

"I'm fine," I say, looking at the floor. "Just confused."

Caleb clears his throat. "About me?"

"About everything."

"I'm right here," he says after a minute.

"I know."

Caleb stays protectively by my side all evening. To anyone who doesn't know us, who doesn't understand what's happening, I'm sure we look like the perfect couple. He keeps a hand gently on my waist or my back all night; he dances with me to the slow songs; he even pushes my hair out of my face when it tumbles over my shoulders.

He's so close, so *mine*. But none of it's real.

This year's Carrefour Mardi Gras king and queen are supposed to be crowned at ten, and just a few minutes before that, I ask Caleb if he'll step outside with me for a minute.

He hesitates. "Sure."

We duck out a side door, and as we do, I catch Liv's eye. She's slow dancing with Drew, her head resting on his shoulder. She waves, and I force a smile back. Drew turns to look at me too. Liv says something to him, and he gives me a thumbs up. I'm sure they both think we're heading into the alley to make out.

"Before you say anything, I need to tell you how sorry I am," Caleb says once the door has shut behind us and we're alone. "I know I should have told you everything sooner. But I was afraid you wouldn't understand. I guess selfishly, I didn't want anything to change between us…"

"I understand perfectly, Caleb," I say. "I just hope you can forgive me too."

His face clouds. "Forgive you for what?"

Instead of answering, I place my right hand on his cheek. It's warm, and the stubble on his jaw tickles my hand. I look at him for a moment, then I touch the Stone of Carrefour hanging from my neck and ask Eloi Oke to open the gate.

"Lemon balm to release you, saltpetre to change your fate, rue to reverse a charm," I say quickly, before he has a chance to stop me. "Spirits, please grant the Shaw family a return of their free will."

"Eveny, what are you—" Caleb begins to say.

But I cut him off by continuing with the brief incantation Chloe taught me. "*M'lage ou. M'lage ou. M'lage ou,*" I say quickly, the Creole version of *I release you.*

There's a brief swirling wind in the alley, and then everything goes still.

Caleb pulls away. "What did you just do, Eveny?"

"I let you go," I tell him. "Officially. So you're not obligated to protect me any more. You and your family have your life back. And if I die, you still live."

His eyes get even bigger. "Eveny, no, you don't know what you're doing!"

"I know exactly what I'm doing."

"But you just broke the bond between us! That means I won't know where you are if you're in trouble and you need me!"

I take a deep breath. "I know that. So you're free now. Get on with your life."

"Eveny!" he begins again, but I shake my head.

"It's all taken care of," I say quickly. "Chloe told you about the lipgloss, right? We'll find the killer tonight, and then you'll have nothing to worry about any more."

"What if it doesn't work?" Caleb asks. "And what about the future? The threat to you won't end tonight."

"But your responsibility to me is over," I say firmly. Then I steel myself for the lie I'm about to tell. "I don't need you any more, Caleb."

He begins to protest, but I don't stay to listen.

I run back inside and stand in the doorway for a moment, expecting him to come after me. Although I fully intend to push him away if he does, I'm still disappointed when the door behind me doesn't open at all.

But there's no time to think about it, because they're announcing this year's Mardi Gras king and queen, and the crowd is going wild. Pascal is already on stage, wearing a crown and a sash that says *King of Carrefour*. I'm not surprised; apparently he won last year too, and if I were a betting woman, I'd say that he probably asked the spirits for some favours during a possession ceremony.

"And now, it's time to announce this year's Mardi Gras queen!" says the announcer, a silver-haired, faux-tanned man in a tux. Someone hands him an envelope, and as he opens it, his expression changes. He looks back at the crowd and says, "Well, this is unusual! For the first time in the history of this town's Mardi Gras Ball, we have a dead tie for queen. We've split the winner's bouquet in half, but we only have one crown and one sash, though, ladies, so you'll have to share!"

The crowd laughs lightly and then quiets down again in anticipation.

"This year's first Mardi Gras queen should be no surprise to any of you, since she was last year's queen too," the man says in his booming voice. "Let's welcome Peregrine Marceau!"

The crowd erupts in applause as Peregrine glides towards the stage in a slinky black dress and red-soled Christian Louboutin heels. She accepts the small cluster of roses handed to her, as well as a kiss on the cheek from the host.

"So, queen number one, would you prefer the sash or the crown?" The host holds up a sparkly tiara in one hand and a pretty purple sash in the other.

"The crown," Peregrine coos into the microphone without missing a beat. "I've brought my own sash."

The crowd gasps as Chloe appears at the foot of the stage and hands over Audowido. He wraps himself around Peregrine and hisses at the audience while the host nervously holds out her crown. She laughs and puts it on as Audowido slithers around her shoulders.

"And now, for the announcement of the second queen," the host says, inching away from Peregrine. I glance at Chloe, because who else could it be? I know the voting is fixed by the sosyete. She's lingering near the front of the stage, smiling up at the host.

"Drum roll, please!" the host says, and the drummer in the small orchestra acquiesces with a slow snare roll. "Tonight's second queen is…Eveny Cheval!"

For a moment, I'm sure I've heard him wrong, but when I look up at Peregrine, she's smiling at me knowingly, and I realize this is her version of making peace with me. She's somehow fixed it so that I get to be her co-queen, which she's expecting will mean a lot more to me than it actually does. As applause echoes around the room, Margaux appears from somewhere behind me and gives me a not-so-gentle shove towards the stage. "What are you waiting for?" she hisses. "Go on!"

My feet carry me through the cheering crowd towards the stage. The announcer squints at me as I walk up. "Are you Eveny Cheval?" he asks.

"Yes," I say, glancing at Peregrine, who looks triumphant, as if this moment is the answer to all our problems.

The announcer offers his hand to help me onstage, and after ascertaining that I don't have a reptile concealed anywhere on me, he drops the sash over my head and hands me a bouquet of roses before retreating. Peregrine squeezes my hand and leans towards my ear. I expect her to say something sarcastic, but instead, she whispers, "If I've got to share this with anyone, it might as well be you."

I look at her in surprise just as Pascal slides between us. "Looks like we're a threesome tonight, ladies," he says in a

Barry White voice as he drapes his arms around our waists.

"You're truly disgusting," Peregrine says cheerfully, wriggling out of his grip. I do the same, smacking his roving hand away.

"Well, folks," the host cuts back in. "Thanks for coming tonight. Please get home safely!"

The band launches into a slow version of "New York, New York", which makes me homesick, and above us, the house lights come on. "It's only ten thirty," I say, puzzled.

Peregrine shakes her head at me. "The ball always ends early so that the controlling sosyete has plenty of time to make it to New Orleans. The rest of the town just thinks it's because the Main Street district has an eleven o'clock noise ordinance curfew.

"Meet us outside in ten minutes," Peregrine adds before disappearing into the crowd.

I'm escorted offstage, and I head over to find Liv, who's been dancing with Drew all night. She's smiling in disbelief as I approach.

"Congratulations, girl!" she exclaims.

She hugs me, and I hug tightly back. "Thanks," I say, a little embarrassed. "It's no big deal."

"I beg to differ," she says. "Dude, you just got crowned queen of the biggest ball of the year!"

"Co-queen," I say.

"A mere technicality," she replies.

I change the subject. "So where'd Drew go? I wanted to say goodbye to him too."

"He just went to the bathroom. He'll be right back. Where's Caleb?"

I frown. "I don't know."

"Did you two have a fight?"

"Something like that," I mumble.

"Do you need a ride home?"

"Peregrine and Chloe can drive me," I promise. "But enough about me. So has Drew kissed you yet?"

She looks so excited that I can't help but smile as she exclaims, "Yes! Totally! And Eveny, he is *such* a good kisser! I think there's really a future in this."

I pull her into a fierce hug. "I'm so happy for you," I murmur. I hold on just a moment longer than I have to, because who knows what will happen tonight? "Thanks for being my friend," I say.

She pulls away and looks at me with concern. "What's wrong, Eveny?"

I shake my head. "Nothing."

I turn to walk away and collide with Arelia, who's hurrying in the opposite direction. "What, now that you've been voted the queen of the ball, you're too good to watch where you're going?" she demands.

I realize that she looks like she's been crying. "What's wrong?" I ask. "Are you okay?"

"What do you care?" she asks, sniffling.

That's when I realize that she's one of the few people at the ball I haven't kissed yet. Knowing she'll think I'm completely nuts since I've already seen and ignored her several times tonight, I dive in and give her a quick peck on the cheek.

"What the hell?" she demands, her hand flying to her face like I've burned her.

But I'm too frozen to reply. That's because a raspberry-red mark has bloomed on her cheek, exactly where my lips met her skin.

"It's you," I breathe.

She narrows her eyes. "*What's* me?"

"You're the one who killed Glory," I say, my voice hollow with disbelief.

Her gaze slides away from me. "Oh, honestly, Eveny, haven't we been through this already? Just because Glory mentioned my name doesn't mean anything."

"No," I say. "But the red stain on your cheek does. You've been lying about what happened that night."

She reaches up and touches her face in confusion just as I spot Caleb across the room. "Caleb!" I cry, gesturing wildly.

He looks confused, but he hurries over.

"You okay?" he asks.

"It was Arelia," I tell him tersely.

He looks at her, and she winds her finger in a circle around her ear to indicate that I'm crazy. "What are you talking about, Eveny?" he asks.

"The red mark from my lipgloss," is all I need to say to make him understand.

"She's obviously losing her mind," Arelia begins to protest.

But Caleb interrupts her, his eyes blazing. "You're absolutely sure?" he asks me.

"Positive," I say.

"Okay, I'll take care of it," he says, already grabbing her arm. She's struggling and trying to tell us something, but we both ignore her. The red mark speaks for itself. "Hurry. Go join the others and explain. I'll be along as soon as I can," he says.

I hesitate. "Will you be okay?"

"I'm fine, Eveny. Just go. Tell Peregrine and Chloe what's going on."

I pause and look Arelia in the eye. "I don't know what your game is, or what you hoped to accomplish here," I say. "But it's over. You're done."

"Eveny, you have to let me explain!" she cries, but Caleb is already dragging her away.

He looks back once, and as our eyes lock, he mouths, *Go*.

I run outside, where Peregrine's Aston Martin is idling at the kerb.

"What took you so long?" Peregrine calls out the driver's-side window. Chloe, Oscar, and Patrick are wedged in the backseat.

"It's Arelia," I say quickly. I cross in front of the car and get into the passenger seat quickly as they all stare at me. "She's the traitor," I say as I buckle my seat-belt. "She's from Main de Lumière."

"The lipgloss?" Chloe asks.

I nod as Peregrine guns the engine. "I can't believe it," she says in a tight voice as she roars away from the kerb. "Damn it!"

"Where's Caleb?" Chloe asks after a minute. "He should be here with us, protecting you."

"He's not my protector any more," I tell them. Peregrine gasps and Chloe sighs in realization.

"What?" Oscar asks.

"She let him go," Chloe answers sadly for me. "Eveny, do you realize what you've done?"

"Yes. I've given him his life back," I say.

"Or you've doomed us all," Peregrine whispers after a moment.

She floors the accelerator, and as the speedometer creeps past ninety, we all stop talking.

We roar through the bayou towards New Orleans and our date with destiny.

THIRTY-ONE

WE'RE ALL MOSTLY QUIET ON the way to New Orleans as we digest the revelation about Arelia. "I just can't believe she'd betray us like that," Peregrine says four times before falling silent again.

It's not until we get to the edge of the city that Oscar speaks up. "You know, Patrick and I were suspicious of her all along. I mean, the way she was always lurking around and glaring at everyone…"

"You never thought to mention that?" Peregrine asks.

"You never listen to us," Oscar says. "You act like we don't have brains."

Chloe jumps in before Peregrine makes the situation worse. "Oscar, Patrick, we're very grateful for your protection. Peregrine's just on edge."

"Of course I am," Peregrine says sharply. "This girl

who's been acting like our friend for years has just been lying in wait to murder us. It's a lot to digest."

"I just can't understand her motives," I say. "She had everything she wanted."

"Not everything," Peregrine says. "We were always going to be more powerful, more beautiful, and more privileged than her. We're queens, and she's not. Some people can't handle coming in second."

I think about my first day in the Hickories, when Arelia snapped at me that it had taken her years to become a Doll, and I had no right to assume that doors would open for me just because of my family name. "She did seem jealous," I admit. "It's just a long leap from envy to joining Main de Lumière and murdering innocent people."

"You said yourself that Glory mentioned Arelia's name the night she died," Peregrine says.

"I know," I reply. "I guess I should have listened to my gut all along, but it seemed so far-fetched. I'm an idiot."

"You're not an idiot," Chloe says as Peregrine begins to weave her Aston Martin swiftly through the city streets towards the heart of the French Quarter. "If anything, we're the ones who talked you out of suspecting her. But let's try to forget about Arelia for the time being and focus on what we have to do, okay? Tonight's important, and our minds have to be clear."

"Fine," Peregrine says.

I look out the window and feel a little dazed as I try to turn my thoughts to the task at hand. The streets of New Orleans are heaving with people, many of them wearing hundreds of strings of beads as well as elaborate masks and, in some cases, feather headdresses. The city itself is saturated in bright colours, its soundtrack a cacophony of blaring trumpets, banging drums, and laughing revellers. People swig huge beers and bright red drinks, trip over each other, fall on the pavement, and sing off-key as we inch past on some of the side streets that aren't closed to traffic. Peregrine's jaw is set, and her lips are pressed together in a fine line as she drives.

"I've never seen anything like this," I say as a woman near our car screams up at several men hanging off an ornate balcony, pulls up her tank top to flash them, and receives a shower of beads and catcalls in reply.

Peregrine finally makes a right turn on a side street and pulls the car into a disabled parking spot along the kerb. As we get out and head towards the back door of a big mansion, Chloe explains, "We were here last year to take part in the ceremony with our mothers' sosyete – that always happens when a sosyete is a year away from inheriting its power – but this year, we're the ones with the control." The words make me shudder. Control seems like the wrong way to put it when we're really just players in a game set up long before we were born.

Peregrine unlocks the mansion's back door and flips on the lights inside. A huge, opulent parlour, all done in black and white marble, is illuminated before us.

"Beautiful place," I say.

"It's ours, you know," Chloe says, turning to me. "This mansion."

"Ours?" I ask.

"Yours, mine and Peregrine's," she responds. "The great-great-great-grandmothers willed it to us. It's our haven for practising magic in New Orleans."

"And," Peregrine says, "our occasional place to get hammered and hook up."

Chloe nudges me. "You and Caleb should come here some weekend. It's really romantic."

I swallow hard. "I'm pretty sure Caleb and I are done."

Chloe pats my back. "Don't give up on him yet. What you two have…" She doesn't finish her sentence.

"We don't have anything," I say after a pause.

"You're wrong," she says. "And now that it's not his responsibility to protect you any more…"

Peregrine gives me a sour look over her shoulder as she leads us into the kitchen, which has beige marble countertops and state-of-the-art stainless steel appliances. In the corner sits a teak bar with several bottles of liquor on top. "Chloe," she says, "I think it's pretty clear Eveny has ended things for ever with Caleb." My heart lurches, and I feel ill as she turns and says sweetly, "Champagne, guys? We're fully stocked, and hello, we've just escaped a murderer! Shouldn't we be celebrating?"

I look into the fridge, where the top shelf is lined with at least a dozen bottles of champagne with bright yellow foil wrappers.

"I'll have a glass," Patrick says.

"Me too," Oscar adds.

"Me three," Chloe says quickly. "Eveny'll have one too. Right?"

"Um," I say weakly. I should be feeling relieved, but instead, I just feel oddly uneasy. Knowing that Arelia was acting like our friend while she planned our murders unsettles me. It also reminds me that the deepest threats can come from the people you trust the most. I wonder if the person who betrayed my mom was someone she trusted too.

Peregrine plugs her iPhone into a pair of silver speakers and pulls up a playlist. A moment later, there's music blasting, and Chloe, Patrick and Oscar head into the kitchen to do shots.

"For one night, Eveny, do you think you could stop being so lame?" Peregrine asks, handing me a flute of champagne. "Let loose. Have fun. We deserve this."

* * *

Margaux, Pascal, and Justin arrive ten minutes later, just as Peregrine is joining Chloe, Oscar, and Patrick for another round of tequila shots in the kitchen.

"The traffic was killer," Pascal reports as he strolls in and tosses his keys on a coffee table.

"Maybe if you hadn't stopped and leered at every topless girl we passed, we would have gotten here faster," Margaux says. She pauses and looks around. "Hey, where's Arelia? I thought she was with you guys."

Chloe and Peregrine emerge from the kitchen, looking uneasy. I turn the music down, and for a moment, we just stand in uncomfortable silence.

"What?" Margaux demands. "What happened? Is she okay?"

"Margaux," Chloe says gently. "Arelia's the one who killed Glory."

"That's impossible," Margaux says instantly. "This is some kind of a joke, right?"

"I'm afraid not," Peregrine says. She quickly recaps the story about the lipgloss and the crimson stain on Arelia's cheek. Before she finishes speaking, Margaux is already shaking her head vigorously.

"No, no, no, no," she says. "This is all wrong." She turns to me, her eyes blazing. "What did you say in your charm? Tell me the *exact* words!"

Startled, I explain that I asked that the gloss turn blood

red on the face of the person who was lying about the night Glory died.

Margaux puts her hand over her mouth, and for a moment, she's silent. "She *was* lying about that night," she says finally. "But it's not what you think. She didn't kill Glory. She *loved* Glory." When we all stare at her blankly, she exclaims, "She and Glory were dating, you morons! They thought you guys would ban them from the sosyete if you found out." She turns to Peregrine and adds, "You're not exactly the most tolerant people in the world."

We gape at her. "Are you sure?" It's Chloe who finally speaks. "Maybe she and Glory got into some kind of fight—"

Margaux cuts her off. "Just like I've already said, she was with me at the time Glory was killed. I swear on the graves of my ancestors." She turns to me. "You kissed my cheek too, didn't you? You know I'm not lying!"

"She's right," I say uneasily.

"Kiss her again," Peregrine demands. When I hesitate, she says, "Do it!"

I give Margaux a quick peck on the cheek, and nothing happens. A knot of dread is forming in the pit of my stomach. Margaux's telling the truth; it wasn't Arelia, which means the real killer is still out there.

"I told you so," Margaux says, her face pink with anger.

"We have to let Caleb know we screwed up," I say.

"*You* screwed up," Peregrine corrects, turning to glare at me.

"I'll call him now," I mutter. But I dial his number three times, and each time, it goes directly to voicemail.

"We just have to wait for him to get here," Chloe says.

"I'm so sorry," I whisper.

"You should be," Peregrine says. "Not only is the Main de Lumière traitor still out there, but now we're down one sosyete member for our ceremony at a time we could use all the help we can get. Excellent work, Eveny."

Caleb arrives forty-five minutes later, just after twelve thirty, his suit rumpled, his eyes wild.

"I was wrong about Arelia," I blurt out as soon as he walks through the door.

He glances at me as he greets Peregrine and Chloe. "Yeah," he says, running his hand distractedly over the top of his head. "I know. She told me everything."

"What happened to her?" I ask in a small voice, my heart hammering.

"She's fine. She's with Boniface. She was too shaken up to come along."

"She must hate my guts," I say.

"You were only doing what you thought was right,"

Caleb says after a minute. "I don't think she blames you. She knows she lied."

"But that was her secret to keep if she wanted to," I say.

"The bigger problem," he says, "is that the killer is still out there."

Peregrine comes over and whispers something to him, and he disappears for a few minutes with her. I'm sitting by myself in the corner of the room, nursing the same glass of champagne I was handed an hour ago, when he gets back, a tall glass of what I assume is gin and tonic in his hand. He doesn't look at me once as he joins the group.

"Loosen up, baby," Pascal purrs at me as he makes his way to the kitchen for another cocktail. He's slightly unsteady on his feet. "This is supposed to be fun."

"Don't you understand?" I shoot back. "We could die tonight. We don't know who's trying to hurt us."

He snorts. "Nothing's going to happen here. Geez, Eveny, could you just give the let's-save-the-world crap a rest for once?"

When the clock strikes one, the whole group moves upstairs and out to the huge balcony overlooking Chartres Street, two blocks away from the famous Bourbon Street. The road below us is still throbbing with people, and I back against the wall, my whole body tense, as Peregrine and Chloe lean over the rail and flirt with guys, and as Pascal throws beads out to the dozens of girls who seem all too happy to show him their breasts.

"I love Mardi Gras!" he shouts, laughing, as a pair of twins flash him enthusiastically. I catch Caleb's eye for a millisecond and am heartened to see him looking as uneasy as I feel. I brace myself and head over to him.

"Hey," I say. "Are you mad at me about Arelia?"

"No, of course not," he says. "But why did you release me from being your protector?"

I'm startled at the anger in his eyes. "I was trying to help you."

"I didn't ask for your help."

"You didn't have to. It wasn't fair to you, Caleb. The whole system of you having to put your life on the line for me? I can't ask you to do that."

"That wasn't your decision to make." He walks away before I can say anything else.

I turn to see Peregrine staring at me with an indecipherable expression on her face. She looks away after a moment and claps her hands. "People!" she yells, and then when everyone just goes right on revelling, she whistles loudly, and the conversation on the balcony comes to a halt. "It's time," she says.

The world below us on Chartres suddenly seems far away and disconnected as she leads the group into the house and into a huge chamber that looks like a much larger and more ornate version of my parlour. Several crystal chandeliers hang in the shadows on the ceiling, and blood-red candles flicker everywhere.

Peregrine asks us to join hands, and Caleb winds up on my right side. His grasp is so warm and comforting, it makes my heart hurt.

Pascal grabs my other hand and says, "Just go with it. Open yourself. There's nothing in the world like being possessed. On Mardi Gras, it's supposed to be positively *orgasmic*."

I play along as Peregrine moves to the centre of the circle, lights a cluster of dandelion and anise seed and calls to Eloi Oke. Chloe steps into the middle of the circle as she and Peregrine raise their hands to the sky and begin to dance in the centre of the room. They're chanting softly, and as the tempo picks up, the rest of the group begins chanting too.

"Open yourself, Eveny," Margaux hisses at me across the circle just before her eyes turn empty. "Don't be so selfish as to think you're above all this. It's your fault Arelia's not here to help us."

I glance at Caleb, but his eyes are already glazed over; he seems to have slipped into another level of consciousness along with everyone else.

One by one, around the circle, I see people's expressions go blank. Everyone's still singing the same phrase over and over – something like, "*Esprits du passé, entre en moi.*"

I search my rudimentary French knowledge; they're saying something along the lines of *Spirits, enter into me.*

As a breeze picks up inside the room, I feel something pushing at the corner of my mind. I know without asking that it's a spirit trying to get in; it feels like the pressure just before Glory's spirit slipped into my body at Cristof's. I push the presence away; I have to keep my wits about me tonight.

Move aside, girl, a hissing voice in my head says suddenly. *I want to use you.*

"No," I say aloud. Caleb glances quickly at me and then goes back to looking blank. Everyone else in the circle seems lost in his or her own world; they're all stumbling around now.

They're all possessed.

Move aside, I said! The voice in my head is more insistent now, and I mentally push back. The spirit trying to get in is stronger than I expected. *Do you really think you can stop me?*

I summon all my energy and push back. "Yes," I say aloud. "I do." There's a sharp pain on the left side of my head, and then, all is quiet, and the pressure is gone. The spirit has moved on.

Soon, the rest of the Dolls begin acting like they've gone crazy. I watch, my breath caught in my throat, as Margaux flings herself to the ground, wailing and rolling around.

Peregrine's eyes are wide and her limbs rubbery as she contorts into positions that no human body should be able to move into. Justin is lying on his back, languidly making snow angels on the marble floor, while Pascal and Chloe are draped all over each other, their hands roaming each other's bodies. Even Patrick and Oscar are dancing in the corner with blank expressions, and Caleb is leaning against the wall, moaning softly with his eyes closed.

I take a deep breath and pretend that I'm possessed too, so that the other spirits won't get suspicious.

I cringe as Oscar begins to rub up against me. I take a deep breath and let it happen for a moment, playing the part. Then I begin to dance, as if the spirit inside of me would rather do that than be groped. Oscar follows, grunting at me, but then he loses interest and moves over to Margaux, who's rubbing herself against a chair now.

Peregrine finally writhes over to the giant triangle in the corner of the room, picks up the wand that lies beside it, and strikes it. The sound reverberates through the house, and everyone stops what they're doing instantly and heads in a single file line towards a door in the corner of the room. Peregrine opens it, revealing a big walk-in closet containing at least a hundred silk robes in varying shades of gold, green and purple. One wall is filled entirely with elaborate feathered masks propped on long, wooden shelves.

Without speaking, the others begin shedding their

clothes with a complete lack of self-consciousness. Margaux simply steps out of her dress, bra-less, and casually grabs a robe from the wall, cinching it around her waist. Chloe and Peregrine are both wearing elaborate, lacy lingerie sets, but they don't seem worried about anyone seeing them as they shed their dresses too and step into robes. Everyone is still possessed, as evidenced by the completely empty looks on their faces, and my heart thuds faster as I realize I'll need to take off my clothes too.

For an instant, I could swear Caleb's hesitating. But then his face goes blank, and he begins taking his suit off slowly. *At least he's not really in there*, I tell myself as I unzip my dress.

I try not to look as he peels off his jacket then his shirt, revealing abs that look like they've been chiselled from stone and arms that ripple with strength. I bite my lower lip as he unbuckles his belt, unzips his trousers and takes them off, revealing a pair of charcoal grey boxer briefs. I hurry to shrug off my own dress as he throws on a green robe from the closet. It feels like Caleb is watching me, but he goes back to swaying languidly as soon as I look in his direction. I swallow hard, slip into a rich emerald robe that matches Caleb's, and cinch the belt tightly.

Once everyone is done donning robes, Peregrine grabs a mask – an elaborate white one with gold swirls and black feathers – and pulls it on. Everyone quickly follows suit, so

I take a deep breath, pick up a gold mask with long white and green feathers, pull it over my face, and watch as Caleb puts on a black mask trimmed in gold.

Peregrine makes a grunting sound, then she emerges from the closet and strikes the triangle again. Everyone instantly lines up and follows her down the stairs and towards the front door of the mansion. I fall into line, just in front of Caleb, and when I feel his hand on my hips through the cool silk of my robe, I have to remind myself that it's not really him, that he's not really there. Still, his touch sears me.

The front door opens ahead of us, and as it does, the sounds of the outside world pour in. The street is still overflowing with drunken revellers, and many of them turn to stare as we move out of the house and into the crowd.

"I told you this is the place with the sluts in robes," I hear a rough-looking bearded guy in a stained T-shirt slur to his friend. "I call the hot black chick with the crazy hair."

"I'll take the blonde," his friend growls back.

I watch in horror as the two men move towards Peregrine and Chloe and begin trying to talk to them. When Peregrine and Chloe don't respond and instead just continue swaying their way down the street, the rougher-looking one who'd called dibs on Peregrine reaches for her, his hand roughly grazing her breasts. She doesn't react at all. *They're not really in there,* I tell myself. *They don't know this is happening.* But then Caleb comes out of nowhere and barrels into the guy groping Peregrine.

"What the f—?" the guy growls, turning to Caleb. But Caleb is flailing wildly now and catches the bearded guy square in the jaw with his elbow. An instant later, his knee connects with the other guy's crotch, sending him sprawling and wincing in pain.

"Dude, he's just as effed up as they are," says the guy on the ground, clutching his crotch protectively and rolling away from Caleb. "Maybe he's their boyfriend or something."

Caleb sways unsteadily away from the men, and if I didn't know better, I'd think he was herding an oblivious Peregrine and Chloe in the other direction.

"Caleb?" I call out, suddenly sure that he's faking it too. But then he goes back to writhing strangely, and my heart sinks.

The group stays loosely together as we turn left, heading towards the bigger crowd on Bourbon. One by one, members of our group begin drifting off, and I resist the urge to try to protect them from the crowd. I remind myself that they've all come here willingly. I cringe as strangers reach out from the crowd to grope me, and I cinch my belt tighter.

The closer we get to Bourbon Street, the wilder the

crowd is. I'm losing sight of more of the members of our group, and I feel a sense of panic setting in. The only Dolls in my eyesight are Pascal and Margaux, and both of them are up ahead, getting swallowed in the sea of people.

"Wait!" I cry out before clamping a hand over my mouth. I'm supposed to look possessed. I take a deep breath, heart thudding, and continue to play along, although I dance through the crowd more quickly now, trying to catch up to the others.

I feel a pair of hands grab my waist, and as I try to wriggle away, the grip grows tighter. I feel a lump of fear in my throat as I pull harder and the hands begin pulling me back.

"Let me go!" I cry, dropping the possessed act. When I feel myself being dragged forcefully away from the street, I begin to scream.

All around me, people are too caught up in their own drinking, partying, singing and making out to notice me. I grab a man's hand as I'm dragged past, but he merely shakes me off. "Help!" I scream, clutching at a group of guys with bloodshot eyes, who are swaying on their feet as they discuss what to do next. The only one I make contact with brushes away the spot I'd grabbed like he's swatting a fly. I cry out once more, struggling against the person behind me, who's dressed all in black. He's pulling me towards a darkened alley.

"Just come quietly," he says suddenly in my ear. "I have a knife, Eveny, and I'm more than happy to use it on anyone who tries to save you."

"Who are you?" I struggle to turn around in the shadows and see his face, the top half of which is totally covered with an elaborate silver mask. Just then, we pass beneath a street light and I gasp. His mouth is completely covered in crimson stains, just like the single one that showed up on Arelia's cheek. But how? I haven't kissed anyone on the lips tonight.

I realize suddenly, though, that Liv did. While wearing my gloss. "Drew," I breathe.

The pieces tumble into place quickly. The way Drew happened to show up at my door right after I arrived back in town. The eagerness with which he kept hanging around even after he realized I was interested in Caleb. The way he moved on seamlessly to Liv, which still kept him in my immediate circle of trusted friends. The truck crash that would have most likely killed me if I hadn't reached for my stone.

He's the Main de Lumière soldier, the one Aloysius Vauclain said had gone rogue.

There's only one question left. "Why the hell are you doing this?"

"What, did you think we were friends?" His laughter is coarse and cruel. "I know all about you and your slutty sister queens. I know how you've been making yourselves richer at our expense. You're everything that's wrong with this society, but it stops tonight."

"You don't understand, Drew," I protest as he drags me further into the alley. "You're making a mistake."

"Shut up, Eveny," he sneers. "And try to relax. It'll only hurt for a minute when I stop your heart."

THIRTY-TWO

DREW PULLS ME TOWARDS THE end of a long, closed passageway between two dilapidated buildings, and as he does, the sounds of Bourbon Street become more and more muted behind us. As Drew jerks me closer, he presses the knife deeper into my side in warning. He's already sliced through my robe, and I can feel the blade cutting into my skin.

"I've been training for this moment for a long time," he says as we move deeper into the blackness. He shoves me against a wall. "Nothing's getting in my way tonight."

Hands shaking, I reach up and rip his mask off. I'm unprepared for the wide range of emotions I see playing across his face. His features are twisted in anger, but I also see sadness and regret.

"How long have you been part of Main de Lumière?" I ask.

He tears off my mask too and pins me against the wall. "They came to me when I was thirteen and told me everything: the way you zandara whores destroy the balance of the universe; the way you keep getting richer while people like me suffer; the way every little thing in your pathetic lives is fake."

"They're just using you, Drew. Don't you realize that?" This earns me a slap across the face. "You don't know a damned thing. We're not in Carrefour any more. This is my game now." He calms down after a pause and resumes his story. "They told me that ending your life was the only way to fix things. All I had to do was learn Main de Lumière's tactics and wait for you to come home."

Something in his eyes flickers, and he looks away.

"But you didn't even know I'd be back," I say.

"Of course I did. Main de Lumière knew. It was only a matter of time until your aunt decided you'd be safer in Carrefour. And I was paid handsomely to train in methods of murdering zandara practitioners while we waited for your return."

I reach for my Stone of Carrefour, but Drew sees me and grabs my hand before I can get to it. He pins both of my arms against the wall above my head and sneers at me. "Really, Eveny? You really thought I'd let you use your evil magic on me?"

I struggle to get away, but he holds me tighter. Finally, I relax my arms. "I don't understand how you could hate me so much."

"It's not really about you," he says. "It's about the bigger picture."

I take a deep breath. "You were my friend when we were kids – my mom was friends with your mom – and you threw that all away because they fed you some lies about zandara and promised to pay you?"

He glares at me. "You're stupider than I thought. Of course it's not just for money. Once they told me about who you really were, I began to understand how much you queens are screwing with fate and the lives of my friends and family. I saw the good Main de Lumière was doing by eliminating people like you from the world. And you know what? I wanted to be a part of it."

"How can you say that?"

"There's a balance to the universe," he says flatly, almost as if he's reciting something he's memorized. "And you and your slutty, greedy friends have been violating that balance. We're restoring the world to its natural order."

"Murdering people isn't the answer."

He casually twirls his knife, studying it as it catches the light of a street lamp. "I don't see another way, and neither did Général Vauclain. My orders have always been to kill you as soon as you started using your powers. And if I let you go back to Carrefour, I won't have another chance."

"Why me?" I demand. "Why wouldn't Main de Lumière just have you go after one of the other queens years ago?"

For the first time, he looks genuinely surprised. "Because of how powerful you are, of course."

"But Peregrine and Chloe are way more powerful than I am," I protest in confusion. "I'm only just beginning to learn."

He studies me for a moment, then laughs in disbelief. "You don't know?"

"Know *what*?"

He grabs a handful of my hair and pulls, jerking my head to the side so hard that I wince in pain. He holds the knife to my throat. "It's because of your father, stupid." I can see him searching my face to discern whether I know what he's talking about.

"Drew, I don't know my dad," I say desperately. "You know that."

"I thought you were lying," he says, almost to himself. "Well, you may as well hear the truth since you're about to die anyhow. Your deadbeat father is a very powerful king in the world of dark magic."

My heart thumps against my chest as I wait for him to say more.

"He's the leader of a sosyete in Georgia that practises andaba, which is like zandara, except they use bones instead of flowers to commune with spirits, and men have the power instead of women."

"That can't be true. My aunt would have told me. *Someone* would have told me."

"Apparently not. Your dad fell in love with your mom, married her, and boom, you were conceived. Her sister queens didn't trust him, though, and he didn't trust them. He thought they were irresponsible with how they practised magic, the way they were so generous with themselves and so inconsiderate of those less fortunate."

"Less fortunate people like you and your mom," I whisper.

Drew steps closer and his expression grows more menacing. He presses me against the wall and draws a small line across my chest with his knife. I gasp in pain as my own blood streams, hot and wet, down my robe.

"You know *nothing* about my mother," he growls. "Let's just get that straight."

I'm already feeling light-headed. I struggle to maintain my composure. "Go on," I manage.

"The three queens – your mom, Peregrine's mom, and Chloe's mom – were actually close to listening to your dad and changing their selfish little ways," Drew continues. "And then one day, he just up and left. He left your mom;

he left you. And they realized he was using them, drawing on their power to enhance his."

"That can't be true," I say. "My mother loved him until the day she died."

"Then your mother was a pretty stupid woman. Face it, Eveny, you and your mom didn't mean anything to your dad."

The words cut deep. "But he came back," I protest. "He promised to look after me."

Drew guffaws. "Well, he's doing a superb job of that right now, isn't he?" He presses me against the wall and holds the knife just below my collarbone. "You see this?" he asks, nicking the skin of my chest with the tip of his blade. He pulls the knife against my skin, and I watch dully as he opens up a large wound. A thick trail of blood begins a steady descent down my body.

"This blood," he continues, staring at the wash of crimson sliding down my chest, "makes you the most powerful queen in the *world*. You're the only one we've ever known who has a king for a father and a queen for a mother. There's no telling how powerful you could be if properly trained. But right now? I have *all* the power, and you have none. And when I kill you, I'll be restoring balance to the world. I'll be a hero."

"Don't you understand that I agree with you? We made some mistakes, but now I'm trying to make things right."

Drew snorts. "By performing your most powerful ceremony of the year?"

"It wasn't to gain anything for ourselves! It was only to protect Carrefour against Main de Lumière! And to restore the Périphérie!"

"You really think I'm that stupid? Eveny, it was to gather favours so your sosyete could continue to make themselves richer and us poorer."

"That's not true." My voice is growing weaker. The world around me is starting to swim. "Was it you who killed Glory?" I whisper.

He looks down instead of meeting my gaze. "She figured out who I was. I was trying to turn her to our side, and it went wrong."

"But she was your friend," I say.

"So are you, supposedly. But unfortunately that doesn't change a thing," he says casually. He looks at his watch and sighs heavily. "I'm afraid we're nearly out of time. It's been nice knowing you, Eveny, it really has. But you're an abomination of nature. You're of the devil. And I'm afraid I'm going to have to kill you now."

His words are smooth and determined, but something flickers in his eyes as he says them, something like regret, and I use his moment of indecision to muster the last of my strength and pull away. The blood covering my body makes me slippery enough that he loses his grip, but I only manage to stumble a few feet down the alley before he's on top of me. His knife glints angry in the light again as it slices through the air towards my heart, but I twist at the last minute and it lodges deeply in my upper left shoulder instead.

I cry out in agony. This cut finds muscle, and the pain is excruciating as he removes the knife and prepares to bring it down again.

Once again, I roll out of the way just in time, so that his knife clatters against the pavement instead of cutting through to my heart. But this only makes him more furious, and he's far stronger than me. I try to touch my Stone of Carrefour, my only hope, but he sees me going for it and grabs my wrists.

"You're not using that damned thing again," he growls. "Not like you did when I tried to kill you in the truck crash." He pins my arms above me against the ground using his left hand, and with his right, he raises the knife again.

I can no longer move. The blood is flowing out of me too quickly. My eyelids are growing heavy. My whole body throbs. And as Drew holds the knife over me, mumbling something about my heartbeat being silenced so that evil can be stricken from the world, I close my eyes and prepare to die.

But suddenly, out of nowhere, something springs from

the darkness and pounces on Drew, knocking him off me. My eyelids are fluttering, and I'm finding it hard to breathe. I can hardly see. In fact, it's not until I hear the shape mutter a curse that I realize it's a man. All I can see are shadows, blurs.

"It's going to be okay, Eveny," he says, and for the first time, I realize that it's Caleb. Caleb has come back for me.

"Watch out," I croak. "Drew has…knife…"

My voice is fading with my consciousness, but I'm aware of Caleb grunting, "I know."

The shadows rise and fall around me, and I can hear fists connecting with faces, heads hitting pavement, grunts of pain. I muster all my strength and reach for my Stone of Carrefour.

My heart is full of only one thing: a fierce desire to protect Caleb. And when my fingers brush the stone, that's enough to invoke some kind of magic, even without words or herbs. I watch in frozen surprise as a bubble with a faint greenish tint surrounds Caleb. Drew attempts to stab him, but the knife just bounces off like the bubble is made of iron, not air. Both guys look momentarily confused; I know I'm the only one who can see the protection surrounding Caleb.

"Caleb," I say, and what I'm trying to tell him is that the magic isn't strong enough, the bubble is already starting to fade. But he seems to realize it too, and this time, as Drew slices towards him again, the knife gets through and gashes through Caleb's upper arm. I hear him cry out, but just as quickly, he spins away and grabs the knife.

Drew rolls over and tries to come after him. He cries out as he lunges forward, his features twisted in anger.

And that's when his chest meets the tip of the knife Caleb is holding unsteadily in his hand. Later, when I try to reconstruct it all in my mind, I'll remember Caleb's eyes widening, his hand going slack, the knife remaining wedged in Drew's chest as he staggers backwards and falls.

But right now, the world is still growing dim, and all I know is that Drew has stopped moving and is lying on his back, his eyes wide, the knife lodged deep in the left side of his chest. He makes a gurgling sound, gasps for air, and then goes still.

"Caleb?" I whisper into the nothingness. The noise of Bourbon Street is still very far away. I feel like we're surrounded by overwhelming silence.

"Come on, Eveny," Caleb says, struggling to his feet. "We have to get out of here before someone else from Main de Lumière arrives."

He scoops me up in his arms, wincing, and I'm vaguely aware of the blood flowing from the gaping wound on his shoulder. He begins stumbling back towards Bourbon Street, and as I strain to see behind him, the world begins to fade. "We just have to find Peregrine or Chloe, and they'll heal you," Caleb says, his voice sounding very far away, although I know I'm still nestled against his blood-soaked chest. "You just have to hold on…"

His voice disappears as I lose consciousness.

I come to for a moment, long enough to register that we're back in the mansion on Chartres Street, and that Caleb is leaning over me on the couch.

"Thank God you're awake," he sighs.

It's only then that I realize Caleb is crying. "Caleb," I say weakly, reaching up to touch his face, which only makes his tears fall faster. He wipes them away.

"I didn't mean to kill him," he says.

"Caleb." I struggle to sit up. He puts his strong arm on my back to support me, and I gaze into his eyes.

"He was coming at me with that knife, Eveny," he says. "I knew he'd come for you next…"

Before I can think what I'm doing, I silence him with a kiss, pressing my lips to his with as much force as I can muster. I feel a sob escape his mouth, and then he's kissing back, passionately, hungrily. "Eveny," he breathes. He pulls me closer, and I wince, suddenly all too aware of the knife wounds that have shredded my neck and chest.

"I'm so sorry," he gasps, lowering me slowly back down to the couch.

"You came back for me," I murmur. I look at him in awe as his eyes fill with tears again.

"Of course." He pushes a tendril of my hair out of my face and leans down to kiss me gently on the lips. "I came back because I love you."

It's the last thing I remember before the world once again fades to black.

Thirty-three

Drew's funeral is the following Wednesday in the Carrefour cemetery.

Peregrine and Chloe had healed me the night of Mardi Gras, and once I was conscious again, the three of us had joined hands and mended Caleb's wounds. Physically, we're no worse for the wear today as we stand beside Drew's grave and watch two cemetery workers from the Périphérie slide his simple oak casket into his family's mausoleum. Our whole sosyete is there, mourning him publicly.

I'm surprised to realize that the tears I'm crying are real. Even though Drew tried to kill me, I still feel a sense of loss over his death. He wasn't all evil.

"He made his own choices, Eveny," Peregrine whispers in my ear as if she knows what I'm thinking.

I nod and dry my eyes, but I'm wondering whether that's really true. Yes, we all have free will, but in a way, our fates have chosen us already. I've been given power and riches beyond my wildest dreams, and although I don't want either, I know I no longer have a choice. This is my destiny.

The official story of Drew's death — the conclusion the police have come to, anyhow — is that he was murdered by a random stranger during Mardi Gras. Probably someone drunk and confused, everyone is saying.

Aunt Bea, who sat stone-faced while I filled her in on the details of what happened in New Orleans last week, is at the funeral too, sitting beside Drew's mother, who's either entirely uninvolved in her son's deception or is a terribly good actress. Arelia is on Aunt Bea's other side, her eyes red from crying.

She'd called me yesterday to apologize for not being truthful from the start about Glory. "I thought everyone would judge me," she said miserably.

Aunt Bea turns and locks eyes with me as the cemetery workers walk away from the gravesite. I force a smile to let her know I'm okay. She's been buzzing around me since I returned from Mardi Gras, apologizing profusely for keeping me in the dark for so long and therefore putting me in danger.

"There's no excuse for how removed and distant I've

been these last few weeks," she'd said this morning as we walked to the funeral together. "I couldn't stand to feel like I'd lost another person I loved because I was complicit in all of this. I just wanted to forget that zandara existed. But that means I wasn't there for you. I'm so sorry."

"You don't owe me an apology," I'd told her honestly. "You've always done your best with me. It's up to me from here."

But although the words seemed to make her feel better, I knew they were a lie. Because while the threat of Drew is gone, I have the feeling Main de Lumière isn't going to stop. If anything, they'll be angrier. We've killed two of their own now, and I expect them to come after us with a vengeance. What if there's another sleeper in our midst, someone who's been here as long as – or longer than – Drew? And I still don't know who killed my mother. I don't trust anyone any more. Except Caleb.

I'd told him, two days after Mardi Gras, the truths Drew had revealed about my father and how powerful my lineage makes me. He'd listened sombrely while I spoke, then promised he hadn't known about any of it. "This means you may be in grave danger all the time," he'd said.

"Not if I learn how to use my powers to protect myself," I had replied. "Not if I use them to protect Carrefour."

"It's not up to you," Caleb had said. "It doesn't have to be."

"I don't have a choice," I had replied.

Now, as we begin to shuffle away from Drew's grave and into the pale morning light of the cemetery, I try to catch Caleb's eye across the gravesite, but he doesn't look at me. I know he's still carrying the burden of being the one who killed Drew. I know no one can take that pain away from him.

Liv, who hasn't taken any of my calls in the last week, brushes up against me on the way out of the cemetery.

"Liv," I say. "I'm so, so sorry about what happened to Drew."

I'm unprepared for the anger I see in her eyes as she looks up at me. "I know it's crazy," she says, her voice tight and controlled. "But I have to ask. Did you have anything to do with Drew's death?"

"What?"

Liv frowns. "I know you were in New Orleans too. Drew told me that night, before he left the ball, that he was coming to find you. He said he had to warn you about something. Did you see him?"

"No," I lie. "I didn't."

"Well, then, did something happen between the two of you that I should know about?" she demands. "Because he was talking about you after you said you'd had that fight with Caleb. Like he was obsessed."

"That's crazy," I say without meeting her eye. "He was totally into you."

Liv looks at me suspiciously and presses her lips tightly together. I know she's trying not to cry. "I don't believe you," she says.

My heart breaks a little as she walks away. I'll do what I can to make it up to her in the future, but right now I know she needs some time alone.

Peregrine and Chloe hurry over and flank me as we head back towards our mansions on the cemetery edge.

"How are you feeling?" Chloe asks, putting a hand on my arm.

"Physically, better," I say. I lower my voice and add, "Emotionally? I'm feeling terrible."

"You can't blame yourself," Peregrine says.

"I know. But that doesn't make it any easier."

I'm still mad at them for not telling me about my father. They swore up and down that their mothers had only told them the basics: that my father was involved with some sort of magical sect in Georgia, and that they weren't sure whether to trust him. But they've told me several times that it never occurred to them that his blood might have made Main de Lumière more interested in me.

"We don't actually know that you're any more powerful than we are," Peregrine had said snippily.

But as they walk across the cemetery now, Chloe nudges me gently and says, "When this blows over, we'll get everyone together and talk to your aunt and our mothers. You deserve to know everything they know about your dad and what it means for you. We'll figure out what to do."

They walk away to join Margaux and Arelia, who have already reached the sunshine near Peregrine's back fence.

A few minutes later, I feel someone fall into step beside me, and I know without looking up that it's Caleb. We walk a few steps in silence, and then he gently takes my hand.

"Are you okay?" I ask him.

"Getting there. So, can I take my job back?" he asks. "Officially? I want to be your protector again, Eveny. I almost missed the chance to save you in New Orleans because you broke the link between us. If I hadn't been faking being possessed so I could try to keep an eye on you…" He trails off and adds, "I don't want to think what could have happened. As it was, I was almost too late."

"I don't want to put you in a position where you're under any obligation to me. Or where your life is tied to mine."

He stops walking, and when I stop too and look at him, I read frustration across his perfect face. "It has nothing to do with obligation any more," he says. "Have you thought of the fact that maybe I *want* my life tied to yours?"

We look at each other for a long time, then we begin walking again.

"What if I was just a normal girl?" I ask. "Instead of the most powerful zandara queen in Louisiana?"

"I'd still want to protect you," he says right away. He pauses. "What if I was just a normal guy?"

"I'd still want you around all the time," I say.

We continue to walk in silence, our fingers threaded together, our breath heavy, until we reach my back wall. Caleb helps me over and follows a second later, landing with a soft thud beside me.

He moves closer and pulls me towards him. "If you were just a normal girl, and I was just a normal guy, I'd probably do this" – he kisses me softly – "all the time."

I kiss him back, hungrily, and after a pause, he responds with a hunger of his own. The garden, the woods, Carrefour itself all disappear as I fade into him. He holds me, caresses me, drinks me in like I'm the only thing anchoring him to earth.

When the kiss ends and we finally pull away, there are tears in his eyes. "But I let my guard down once. I let my feelings, my pride get in the way. And you almost died."

"I *didn't* die, though," I whisper. "You saved me."

He shakes his head. "Next time, we might not be so lucky."

He takes a deep breath. "Eveny, I love you. But this is why protectors are forbidden from having a relationship with their queens; I can't think straight and protect you when I feel like this."

"But—" I begin.

"I'm sorry," he says. "I'm so sorry. I can't do this. But I'll always be nearby, watching over you if you need me."

"Caleb," I say desperately. "I *do* need you. I need you now. I need you to be with me. I need you to forget all the things we're supposed to do and just follow your heart."

He smiles sadly. "I'm sorry, Eveny. But you know as well as I do that's not how this town works."

And then he's gone, back over the cemetery wall, before I can say anything else. I stare in the direction he disappeared for a very long time, tears streaming down my face, before I whisper, "I love you too."

I turn and walk slowly towards the back door of my house. The world feels like it's been upended again. I want to go after him, to beg him to stay, to plead with him to reconsider. But I saw the resolution in his eyes. I'll have to find another way.

I open the door. The first thing I realize once I'm standing inside is that something feels different. There's a heaviness in the air that puts me instantly on edge.

Before I can say anything, Boniface steps out from

the living room, his face creased with concern. "Honey, I didn't know—" he begins, but a voice behind him cuts him off.

"I'll take it from here," says the tall, handsome man who rounds the corner behind Boniface. His hair is sandy, his eyes a brilliant green. I recognize him instantly.

"Dad?" I ask in disbelief.

"Eveny," he says. He crosses the space between us swiftly and pulls me into a tight hug. I'm so shocked, I can barely hug back.

"What are you…?" My brain is suddenly a jumble of questions, and I can't find the words to ask him why he's here. "You left us," I finally manage to say, my voice breaking.

"I had to," he says. "I had to keep you safe. Staying would have put you in terrible danger."

"But…" I can hardly believe what I'm seeing. "You came back."

"You needed my help." He touches my cheek gently, and for a second, I'm not thinking about the present; I'm thinking about the moments like this that we missed, the times he should have been there to hold my hand, the instances I felt so abandoned by both of my parents when one of them was out there all along.

"But why now?" I manage. "After all this time?"

"What happened with Main de Lumière is only the

beginning, Eveny. You're going to be in danger until we figure out how to stop them for good."

I nod. He's right, of course.

"So the way I see it," he continues gravely, "we have two choices: you and I can run tonight, go somewhere they'll never be able to find us. Or we can stay and do our best to protect this town. It's up to you, Eveny. I'll stand by you, whatever decision you make."

My heart hammers, and my Stone of Carrefour grows hot against my chest. Magic is in my blood – it's who I'm destined to be. My mom believed I'd become the greatest queen the world has ever known, and I won't let her down. I take a deep breath and steel myself. "We'll stay."

"You're sure?" His eyes bore into mine. "You could die trying. You realize that's a risk, don't you? I'll do everything I can to protect you, but there's always a chance…"

"Mom lost her life trying to make things right," I say. "I have to stay – for her. Carrefour was her home. It's *my* home. Everything about this place, it's who I am. I can't run from that any more."

He stares at me for a minute. "Your mother would be so proud of the young woman you've grown up to be." He smiles sadly. "I'm with you. So let's win back Carrefour and avenge your mom's death. Whatever it takes."

"*Whatever* it takes," I agree, my heart hammering. I don't quite know what to make of my father's return after all these years, but my gut tells me the emotion in his eyes is real. So I push aside thoughts of Caleb, the Dolls, and everything else I'm responsible for, and for just a second, I let myself believe in a future that isn't fraught with complications and lies.

Outside, a mist begins to rise over the cemetery as the setting sun paints the sky a burning red. By the time morning comes, news of my father's return will have begun to spread. There will be no going back from the decision we're making tonight, the decision to stay and defend what's ours. We've chosen our path.

The only way through the fire is forward. I know that now. And I'm ready to fight.

Can Eveny trust her father?

Will Eveny and Caleb find a way to be together?

What's next for The Dolls?

Join the discussion online and unlock
the world of Carrefour:

#TheDolls
@Usborne @Sullivan_Kiki

www.thedollsbooks.co.uk

JOIN EVENY, PEREGRINE AND CHLOE
FOR THE SECOND, STUNNING
INSTALMENT...

Midnight
Dolls

COMING SOON

When Main de Lumière stages an attack against Eveny in her own garden, her father insists that she and her sister queens come to his island home. But Caouanne Island reveals more secrets from Eveny's past…and her future. Because her father is an andaba king – and Eveny discovers she is an andaba queen.

Now Eveny finds herself torn between two magical traditions – and two boys; her zandara protector, Caleb, and Bram, her fellow andaba king.

With Main de Lumière drawing ever closer, her father and sister queens, Chloe and Peregrine, want to do everything they can to keep her safe. But Eveny has other ideas. She's ready to fight, for the people and the town she loves – and for her life.

ACKNOWLEDGEMENTS

This book was the result of some pretty incredible teamwork, so I'd love to say a huge "thank you" to Holly Root (the world's best literary agent), Nick Harris (who provided the seed from which this book grew and who has been a huge advocate for the story), and Sara Sargent (whose patience, vision, keen editorial eye, and witty emails kept me sane – and made this book a thousand times better). Novelist Wendy Toliver – my longtime friend and the closest thing I have to a writing partner – also supported me every step of the way and speed-read drafts for me in record time. She's a rock star.

Thanks to Jerry Gandolfo of the New Orleans Historic Voodoo Museum for welcoming me into his world and helping me to understand the intricacies of a fascinating spiritual system in which herbs, dolls, spirits, and magic intersect. And of course thanks to the people of New

Orleans: your city's beautiful blend of history, culture, food, drink, architecture, excess, faith, and *bon temps* inspires me to no end.

Thanks to the other great folks of Waxman Leavell Literary Agency, The Story Foundation, and Balzer + Bray, especially Sam Howard, Taylor Haggerty, Julianna Wojcik, Alessandra Balzer, Donna Bray, Caroline Sun, Emilie Polster, Stefanie Hoffman, Alison Klapthor, Viana Siniscalchi, and Veronica Ambrose. A special thank you to literary agent Farley Chase (a foreign rights superhero) and the lovely Kate McLennan in London.

And thanks to all my family and friends whose patience I certainly tried while writing this novel! Special thanks to my very own Prince Charming, who listened to me babble endlessly about magic, brought me flowers when I was under tight deadlines, and took me out for Louisiana-style crawfish to celebrate the completion of drafts. I love you, Jas!

About the Author

Like her main character, Eveny Cheval, Kiki Sullivan used to live in New York and now calls the American South home. Unlike Eveny, she finds it impossible to keep her rose garden alive and has been singlehandedly responsible for the demise of countless herbs. She may or may not have hung out with queens of the dark arts, strolled through creepy New Orleans cemeteries at night, and written the first book of this series with a redheaded Louisiana voodoo doll beside her computer.

FIND OUT MORE AT WWW.KIKISULLIVAN.COM

Wilbur Smith is a global phenomenon: a distinguished author with an established readership built up over fifty-five years of writing with sales of over 130 million novels worldwide.

Born in Central Africa in 1933, Wilbur became a fulltime writer in 1964 following the success of *When the Lion Feeds*. He has since published over forty global bestsellers, including the Courtney Series, the Ballantyne Series, the Egyptian Series, the Hector Cross Series and many successful standalone novels, all meticulously researched on his numerous expeditions worldwide. His books have now been translated into twenty-six languages.

The establishment of the Wilbur & Niso Smith Foundation in 2015 cemented Wilbur's passion for empowering writers, promoting literacy and advancing adventure writing as a genre. The foundation's flagship programme is the Wilbur Smith Adventure Writing Prize.

For all the latest information on Wilbur visit www.wilbursmith books.com or facebook.com/WilburSmith

Also by Wilbur Smith

On Leopard Rock

The Courtney Series

When the Lion Feeds
The Sound of Thunder
A Sparrow Falls
The Burning Shore
Power of the Sword
Rage
A Time to Die
Golden Fox
Birds of Prey
Monsoon
Blue Horizon
The Triumph of the Sun
Assegai
Golden Lion
War Cry
The Tiger's Prey

The Ballantyne Series

A Falcon Flies
Men of Men
The Angels Weep
The Leopard Hunts in Darkness
The Triumph of the Sun

The Egyptian Series

River God
The Seventh Scroll
Warlock
The Quest
Desert God
Pharaoh

Hector Cross

Those in Peril
Vicious Circle
Predator

Standalones

The Dark of the Sun
Shout at the Devil
Gold Mine
The Diamond Hunters
The Sunbird
Eagle in the Sky
The Eye of the Tiger
Cry Wolf
Hungry as the Sea
Wild Justice
Elephant Song

WILBUR SMITH

THOSE IN PERIL

ZAFFRE

First published in Great Britain in 2011 by Macmillan

This edition published in 2018 by

ZAFFRE PUBLISHING
80–81 Wimpole St, London, W1G 9RE
www.zaffrebooks.co.uk

A CIP catalogue record for this book is available from the British Library.

ISBN: 978–1–78576–701–2

Also available as an ebook

1 3 5 7 9 10 8 6 4 2

Typeset by IDSUK (Data Connection) Ltd
Printed and bound by Clays Ltd, St Ives Plc

Zaffre Publishing is an imprint of Bonnier Zaffre,
a Bonnier Publishing company
www.bonnierzaffre.co.uk
www.bonnierpublishing.co.uk

This book is for my wife
MOKHINISO
who is the best thing
that has ever happened to me

GOLDEN GOOSE

BRIDGE →

GUN PLATFORM →

OWNER'S SUITE →

← CREW
← CREW
← CREW

HATCH DOWN TO SERVICE TUNNEL

T A N K S

④ ③ ② ①

COVERT AREA

TURBO GENERATOR

STEERING GEAR

PUMP ROOM

PROPULSION MOTOR

GAS EGRESS SHAFTS

Eternal Father, strong to save,
whose arm hath bound the restless wave,
who bidd'st the mighty ocean deep
its own appointed limits keep,
O hear us when we cry to thee
for those in peril on the sea.

THE KHAMSEEN had been blowing for five days now. The dust clouds rolled towards them across the brooding expanse of the desert. Hector Cross wore a striped keffiyeh wrapped around his neck and desert goggles over his eyes. His short dark beard protected most of his face, but the areas of exposed skin felt as though they had been scoured raw by the stinging grains of sand. Even above the growl of the wind he picked out the throbbing beat of the approaching helicopter. He was aware without looking at them that none of the men around him had heard it as yet. He would have been mortified if he had not been the first. Though he was ten years older than most of them, as their leader he had to be the sharpest and the quickest. Then Uthmann Waddah stirred slightly and glanced at him. Hector's nod of acknowledgement was barely perceptible. Uthmann was one of his most trusted operatives. Their friendship went back many years, to the day Uthmann had pulled Hector out of a burning vehicle under sniper fire in a Baghdad street. Even then Hector had been suspicious of the fact that he was a Sunni Muslim, but in time Uthmann had proved himself worthy. Now he was indispensable. Among his other virtues he had coached Hector until his spoken Arabic was almost perfect. It would take a skilled interrogator to discern that Hector was not a native-born speaker.

By some trick of the sunlight high above, the monstrously distorted shadow of the helicopter was thrown against the cloud banks like a magic lantern show, so that when the big Russian MIL-26 painted in the crimson and white colours of Bannock Oil broke through into the clear it seemed insignificant in comparison. It wasn't until it was three hundred feet above the landing pad that it was visible. In view of the importance of the single passenger, Hector had radioed the pilot while he was still on the ground at Sidi el Razig, the company base on the coast where the oil pipeline terminated, and ordered him not to fly in these conditions. The woman had countermanded his order, and Hector was not accustomed to being gainsaid.

Although they had not yet met, the relationship between Hector and the woman was a delicate one. Strictly speaking he was not her employee. He was the sole owner of 'Cross Bow Security Limited'. However, the company was contracted to Bannock Oil to guard its installations and its personnel. Old Henry Bannock had hand-picked Hector from amongst the many security firms eager to provide him with their services.

The helicopter settled delicately on the landing pad, and as the door in the fuselage slid open, Hector strode forward to meet the woman for the first time. She appeared in the door-way, and paused there looking about her. Hector was reminded of a leopard balancing on the high bough of a Marula tree surveying its prey before it sprang. Though he thought that he knew her well enough by repute, in the flesh she was charged with such power and grace that it took him by surprise. As part of his research he had studied hundreds of photographs of her, read reams of script and watched hours of video footage. The earlier images of her were on the Centre Court of Wimbledon being beaten in a hard-fought quarterfinal match by Navratilova, or three years later accepting the trophy for the women's singles at the Australian Open in Sydney. Then a year later came her marriage to Henry Bannock, the head of Bannock Oil, a flamboyant billionaire tycoon thirty-one years her senior. After that came images of her and her husband chatting and laughing with heads of state, or with film stars and other show-business personalities, shooting pheasant at Sandringham as the guests of Her Majesty and Prince Philip or holidaying in the Caribbean on their yacht the *Amorous Dolphin*. Then there were clips of her sitting beside her husband on the podium at the annual general meeting of the company; other clips of her fencing skilfully with Larry King on his talk show. Much later she was wearing widow's weeds and holding the hand of her lovely young daughter as they watched Henry

Bannock's sarcophagus being installed in the mausoleum on his ranch in the Colorado mountains.

After that her battle with the shareholders and banks and her particularly venomous stepson was gleefully chronicled by business media around the world. When at last she succeeded in wresting the rights that she had inherited from Henry out of the grasping fingers of her stepson and she took her husband's place at the head of the board of Bannock Oil, the price of Bannock shares plummeted steeply. The investors evaporated, the bank loans dried up. Nobody wanted to bet on a sometime tennis player cum society glamour girl turned oil baroness. But they had not taken into account her innate business acumen or the years of her tutelage under Henry Bannock which were worth a hundred MBA degrees. Like the crowds at the Roman circus her detractors and critics waited in grisly anticipation for her to be devoured by the lions. Then to the chagrin of all she brought in the Zara Number Eight.

Forbes magazine blazoned the image of Hazel in white tennis kit, holding a racquet in her right hand, on its front cover. The headline read: 'Hazel Bannock aces the opposition. The richest oil strike for the last sixty years. She takes on the mantle of her husband, Henry the Great.' The main article began:

In the bleak hinterland of a godforsaken and impoverished little Emirate named Abu Zara lies an oil concession once owned by Shell. The field had been pumped dry and abandoned in the period directly after WWII. For almost sixty years it had lain forgotten. That was until Mrs Hazel Bannock came on the scene. She picked up the concession for a few paltry millions of dollars and the pundits nudged each other and smirked. Ignoring the protests of her advisors she spent many millions more in sinking a rotary cone drill into a tiny subterranean anomaly at the northern extremity of the field; an anomaly which, with the primitive exploration techniques of sixty years previously, had been reckoned to be an ancillary of the main reservoir. The geologists of that time had agreed that any oil contained in this area had long ago drained into the main reservoir and been pumped to the surface leaving the entire field dry and worthless.

However when Mrs Bannock's drill pierced the impervious salt dome of the diapir, a vast subterranean chamber in which the oil deposits had been trapped, the gas overpressure roared up through the drill hole with such force that it ejected almost 8 kilometres of steel drill string like toothpaste from the tube, and the hole blew out. High-grade crude oil spurted hundreds of feet into the air. At last it became evident that the old Zara Nos. 1 to 7 fields which had been abandoned by Shell were only a fraction of the total reserves. The new reservoir lay at a depth of 21,866 feet and held estimated reserves of 5 billion barrels of sweet and light crude.

As the helicopter touched down the flight engineer dropped the landing ladder and dismounted, then reached up to his illustrious passenger. She ignored his proffered hand and jumped the four feet to the ground, landing as lightly as the leopard that she so much resembled. She wore a sleekly tailored khaki safari suit with suede desert boots and a bright Hermès scarf at her throat. The thick golden hair, which was her trademark, was unfettered and it rippled in the Khamseen. How old was she? Hector wondered. Nobody seemed to know for sure. She looked thirtyish, but she had to be forty at the very least. Briefly she took the hand that Hector proffered, her grip honed by hundreds of hours on the tennis court.

'Welcome to your Zara No. 8, ma'am,' he said. She spared him only a glance. Her eyes were a shade of blue that reminded him of sunlight radiating through the walls of an ice cave in a high mountain crevasse. She was far more comely than he had been led to believe by her photographs.

'Major Cross.' She acknowledged him coolly. Once again she surprised him by the fact that she knew his name, then he recalled that she had the reputation of leaving nothing to chance. She must have researched every one of the dozens of her senior employees that she was likely to meet on this first visit to her new oilfield.

If that's the case, she should have known that I don't use my military rank any longer, he thought, then it occurred to him that she probably did know and she was deliberately riling him. He suppressed the grim smile that rose to his lips.

For some reason she doesn't like me and she makes no effort to hide the fact, he thought. *This lady is built like one of her oil drills, all steel and diamonds.* But she had already turned away from him to meet the three men who tumbled out of the big sand-coloured Hummvee that braked to a halt beside her and formed an obsequious welcoming line, grinning and wriggling like puppies. She shook hands with Bert Simpson, her general manager.

'I am sorry it took me so long to visit you, Mr Simpson, however I have been rather tied up at the office.' She gave him a quick, brilliant smile, but did not wait for his reply. She moved on and in rapid succession greeted her chief engineer and senior geologist.

'Thank you, gentlemen. Now let us get out of this nasty wind. We will have time to become better acquainted later.' Her voice was soft, almost lilting, but the inflexion was sharp and clearly Southern African. Hector knew that she had been born in Cape Town and had only taken up US citizenship after she married Henry Bannock. Bert Simpson opened the passenger door of the Hummvee and she slipped into the seat. By the time Bert had taken his place at the wheel, Hector was in an escort position in the second Hummvee close behind him. A third Hummvee was in the lead. All the vehicles had the logo of a medieval crossbow painted on the doors. Uthmann was in the first, and he led the little convoy out onto the service track which ran alongside the great silver python of the pipeline that carried the precious muck a hundred miles down to the waiting tankers. As they drove on the oil rigs appeared out of the yellow haze on each side, rank upon rank like the skeletons of a lost legion of warriors. Before they reached the dried-out wadi Uthmann turned off the track and they climbed a ridge of gaunt rock, sooty black as though scorched by fire. The main building complex was perched on the highest point.

Two Cross Bow sentries in battle fatigues swung the gates open and the three Hummvees raced through. Immediately the vehicle carrying Hazel Bannock peeled off from the formation and crossed the interior compound to stop before the heavy doors that led into the air-conditioned luxury of the executive suites. Hazel was whisked through them by Bert Simpson and half a dozen uniformed servants. The doors closed ponderously. It seemed to Hector that something was lacking once she had gone – even the Khamseen wind howled with less fury – and as he paused at the doorway to Cross Bow headquarters and looked up at the sky he saw that the dust clouds were indeed breaking up and subsiding on themselves.

In his private quarters he removed the goggles and unwound the keffiyeh from his throat. Then he washed the grime from his face and hands, squirted soothing drops into his bloodshot eyes and examined his face in the wall mirror. The short stubble of dark beard gave him a piratical air. The skin above it was darkly tanned by the desert sun, except for the silver scar above his right eye where years ago a bayonet thrust had exposed the bone of his skull. His nose was large and imperial. His eyes were a cool and steady green. His teeth were very white like those of predator.

'It is the only face you are ever going to get, Hector my lad. But that doesn't mean you have to love it,' he murmured, then he answered himself, 'But, thank the Lord for all those ladies of less fastidious tastes out there.' He laughed softly and went through into the situation room. The hum of the men's conversation died away as he entered. Hector stood on the dais and looked them over. These ten were his squad leaders. Each of them commanded a stick of ten men, and he felt a small prickle of pride. They were the tried and true, hardened warriors who had learned their trade in the Congo and Afghanistan, in Pakistan and Iraq and in other bloody fields around the wicked old world. It had taken a long time for him to assemble them, and they were a totally reprehensible bunch of reprobates and hardened killers, and he loved them like his brothers.

'Where are the scratches and teeth bites, boss? Don't tell us you got away from her scot free,' one of them called. Hector smiled tolerantly and gave them a minute to deliver their heavy humour and to settle down. Then he held up his hand.

'Gentlemen, and I use the term loosely, gentlemen, we have in our care a lady who will attract the ardent attention of every thug from Kinshasa to Baghdad, from Kabul to Mogadishu. If anything nasty befalls her I will personally cut the balls off the man who let it happen. I give you my solemn oath on that.' They knew this was not an idle threat. The laughter subsided and they dropped their eyes as he stared at them expressionlessly for a few seconds after silence had fallen. At last he picked up the pointer from the desk in front of him and turned to the huge aerial blow-up of the concession on the wall behind him and began his final briefing. He delegated their duties to them and reinforced his previous orders. He did not want any carelessness on this job. Half an hour later he turned back to face them.

'Questions?' There were none and he dismissed them with the curt order, 'When in doubt shoot first and make damned sure you don't miss.' He took the helicopter and had Hans Lategan, the pilot, fly him along the pipeline as far as the terminal on the shore of the Gulf. They flew at very low level. Hector was in the front seat beside Hans, searching the track for any sign of unexplained activity; alien human footprints or wheel tracks made by any vehicle other than his own GM patrol trucks or the engineering teams servicing the pipeline. All his Cross Bow operatives wore boots with a distinctive arrowhead tread on the soles, so even from this height Hector could tell friendly tracks from those of a potential thug.

During Hector's tenure as head of security there had already been three vicious sabotage attempts on the Bannock

Oil installations in Abu Zara. No terrorist group had as yet claimed responsibility for these acts, probably because none of the attacks had succeeded.

The Emir of Abu Zara, Prince Farid al Mazra, was a staunch ally of Bannock Oil. The oil royalties that accrued to him from the company amounted to hundreds of millions of dollars a year. Hector had forged a strong alliance with the head of the Abu Zara police force, Prince Mohammed, who was a brother-in-law of the Emir. Prince Mohammed's intelligence was strong and three years previously he had alerted Hector to an impending seaborne attack. Hector and Ronnie Wells, his area commander at the terminal, had been able to intercept the raiders at sea with the Bannock patrol boat, which was an ex-Israeli motor torpedo boat, with a good turn of speed and twin .50-calibre Browning machine guns mounted in the bows. There were eight terrorists on board the attacking dhow, together with several hundred pounds of Semtex plastic explosive. Ronnie Wells was a former Royal Marine sergeant-major, a seaman of vast experience and an expert handler of small attack craft. He came out of the darkness astern of the dhow, and took the crew by complete surprise. When Hector called on them to surrender over the loud-hailer they replied with a fusillade of automatic fire. The first burst from the Brownings touched off the cargo of Semtex in the hold of the dhow. All eight terrorists on board had simultaneously departed for the Gardens of Paradise, leaving behind them very little trace of their previous existence on this earth. The Emir and Prince Mohammed had been delighted with the outcome. They ensured that the international media were given not even a sniff of the incident. Abu Zara was proud of its reputation as a stable, progressive and peace-loving country.

Hector landed at the terminal at Sidi el Razig and spent a few hours with Ronnie Wells. As always Ronnie had everything shipshape, renewing Hector's faith in him. After their meeting they walked out together to where Hans was waiting in the helicopter. Ronnie glanced obliquely at him, and Hector knew exactly what was worrying him. In three months' time Ronnie would be sixty-five. His children had long ago lost interest in him and he had no home outside Cross Bow, except possibly the Royal Hospital, Chelsea, if they would accept him as a pensioner. His contract with Cross Bow would come up for renewal a few weeks before his birthday.

'Oh, by the way, Ronnie,' Hector said, 'I have got your new contract on my desk. I should have brought it with me for you to sign.'

'Thanks, Hector.' Ronnie grinned, his bald head glowing. 'But you do know I will be sixty-five in October?'

'You old bastard!' Hector grinned back at him. 'Here I have been thinking you were twenty-five for the last ten years.' He swung up into the helicopter and they flew back just above the sandy surface of the track alongside the pipeline. The Khamseen wind had swept the surface like an industrious housemaid so that even the tracks of the desert bustards and oryx were clearly printed on it. Twice they landed for Hector to examine any sign that was less self-evident and might have been made by unwelcome strangers. These proved innocuous. They had been made by wandering Bedouin probably searching for lost camels.

They landed again for the last time at the site where three years previously an ambush had been laid by six persons unknown who had infiltrated the concession from the south. They had covered sixty miles on foot through the desert to reach the pipeline. When they arrived the intruders made the unfortunate choice of attacking the patrol truck in which Hector was riding in the front seat. Hector spotted something suspicious halfway up the dune that ran beside the track as they drove along it.

'Stop!' he yelled at his driver, and he scrambled onto the roof of the truck. He stared up at the object that had caught his attention. It moved again, a tiny slithering movement like a crawling red snake. That movement was what had first caught his attention. But there were no red snakes in this desert. One end of the snake protruded from the sand and the other end disappeared under the scrawny hanging branches of a thorn-bush. He studied it carefully. The bush was sufficiently dense to hide a man lying behind it. The red object was like nothing in nature that he knew of. Then it twitched again and he made up his mind. He mounted his assault rifle to his shoulder and fired a three-shot burst into the thornbush. The man who had been lying behind it leaped to his feet. He was turbaned and cloaked with his AK-47 slung over his shoulder and a small black box in his hands, from which dangled the thin red insulated cable.

'Bomb!' Hector screamed. 'Heads down!' The man on the dune detonated the bomb, and with a thunderous explosion the track 150 metres ahead of the truck erupted in a towering col-umn of dust and fire. The shock wave almost knocked Hector off the roof of the truck, but he braced himself and kept his balance.

The bomber was almost at the top of the dune, running like a desert gazelle. Hector was still unsighted by the blast, and his first burst churned up the sand around the Arab's feet, but he kept running. Hector caught his breath and steadied himself. He saw his next burst catch the Arab across his back, dust flying from his robe as the bullets struck. The man pirou-etted like a ballet dancer and went down. Then Hector saw his five companions leap up out of cover amongst the scrub. They crossed the skyline and disappeared before he could take them under fire.

Hector swept a glance along the face of the dune. It extended for three or four miles both forward and aft of their present position. Along its whole length it was too steep and soft for the truck to climb. It would have to be a foot chase, he decided.

'Phase Two!' Hector shouted at his men, 'Hot pursuit! Go! Go! Go!' He leapt from the truck and led the four of them up the dune face at a run. When they reached the top the five insurgents were still in a loose group running across the flat salt-pan almost half a mile away. They had established that lead while Hector and his stick were forced to struggle up the face of the dune. Looking after them, Hector smiled grimly.

'Big mistake, my beauties! You should have bomb-shelled, each of you should have taken a different direction! Now we have you nicely grouped.' Hector knew with absolute certainty that in a straight chase there was no Arab born who could run away from these men of his.

'Come along, boys. Don't dawdle. We have to bag these bastards before sundown.' It took four hours; 'these bastards' were just a wee bit tougher than Hector had reckoned. But then they made their final mistake. They stood to fight it out. They picked a likely depression, a natural strong point with a clear field of fire in all directions, and went to ground. Hector looked up at the sun. It was twenty degrees above the horizon. They had to finish this thing quickly. While his men kept the terrorists' heads down, Hector wriggled forward to where he could have a better view of the field of play. Immediately he saw that they could not take the Arab position head-on. He would lose most if not all of his men. For ten minutes more he studied the terrain, and then with a soldier's eye he picked out the weak spot. Running past the rear of the Arab position was a very shallow fold of ground; too shallow to deserve the name of wadi or donga but it might conceal a man crawling on his belly. He squinted his eyes against the low sun and judged that the fold crossed forty paces behind the enemy's redoubt. He nodded with satisfaction and wriggled back to where his men lay.

'I am going to get around behind them and toss in a grenade. Charge as soon as it blows.' Hector had to take a wide detour around the enemy to keep out of their sight, and once he was into the donga he could only move very slowly so as not to raise the dust and warn them of his approach. His men made the Arabs keep their heads well down, shooting at any movement above the rim of the depression. However, by the time Hector reached the nearest point to the depression there was probably only another ten minutes of shooting light before the sun went down below the horizon. He rolled onto his knees and with his teeth pulled the pin on the grenade he was holding in his right hand. Then he sprang upright and judged the distance.

It was at extreme range. Forty or maybe fifty metres to lob the heavy fragmentation grenade. He put his shoulder and all his strength behind the throw and sent it up on a high looping trajectory. Though it was a good throw, one of his very best, it struck the rim of the redoubt and for an instant seemed as if it would stick there. But then it rolled forward and dropped in amongst the crouching Arabs. Hector heard the screams as they realized what it was. He leapt to his feet and drew his pistol as he raced forward. The grenade exploded just before he reached the redoubt. He paused on the edge and looked down on the carnage. Four of the thugs had been torn into bloody rags. The last one had been partially shielded by the bodies of his comrades. Nonetheless shrapnel had ripped through his chest into his lungs.

He was coughing up gouts of frothing blood and struggling to catch his last breath as Hector stood over him. He looked up and to Hector's astonishment recognized him. The man spoke through bubbling blood and his voice was faint and slurred, but Hector understood what he was saying.

'My name is Anwar. Remember it, Cross, you pig of the great pig. The debt has not been settled. The Blood Feud continues. Others will come.'

Now, three years later Hector stood on the same spot, and once again puzzled over those words. He could still make no sense of them. Who was the dying man? How had he known Hector? At last he shook his head, then turned and walked back to where the helicopter stood with its rotors turning idly. He climbed aboard and they flew on. The day melted away swiftly in the desert heat and when they got back to the compound at No. 8 there was only an hour before sunset. Hector took advantage of what remained of the light to go out to the range and fire a hundred rounds each from both his Beretta M9 9mm pistol and his SC 70/90 automatic assault rifle. All his men were expected to fire at least 500 rounds a week and turn in their targets to the armourer. Hector regularly checked all of them. His men were all deadly shots, but he did not want any complacency or sloppiness to creep in. They were good but they had to stay that way.

When he got back to the compound from the range the sun had gone and in the brief desert twilight the night came swiftly. He went to the well-equipped gym and ran for an hour on a treadmill and finished with half an hour of weights. He took a steaming hot shower in his private quarters and changed his dusty camouflage fatigues for a freshly washed and ironed pair, and at last went down to the mess. Bert Simpson and the other senior executives were at the private bar. They all looked tired and drawn.

'Join us for a drink?' Bert offered.

'Decent of you,' Hector told him and he nodded to the barman who poured him a double tot of the Oban eighteen-year-old single malt. Hector saluted Bert with the glass and they both drank.

'So, how is our lady boss?' Hector asked.

Bert rolled his eyes. 'You don't want to know.'

'Try me.'

'She is not human.'

'She looked more than just a touch human to me,' Hector commented.

'It's an illusion, old boy. Done with bloody mirrors or something. I will say no more. You can find out for yourself.'

'What does that mean?' Hector demanded.

'You are taking her for a run, matey.'

'When?'

'First thing in the morning, day after tomorrow. Meet 0530 hours sharp at the main gates. Ten miles, she stipulated. I would hazard a guess that the pace she sets will be somewhat faster than a stroll. Don't let her lose you.'

• • •

For Hazel Bannock too it had been a long and demanding day, but nothing that she couldn't wash away in a hot bubble bath. Afterwards she shampooed her hair and used the electric dryer to style the blonde wave above her right eye. Then she put on a blue satin robe that matched her eyes. All her luggage had been sent on ahead of her days before. Her matched set of croc-skin cases had been unpacked by the servants and her clothes were freshly pressed and hanging in the commodious cupboards of her dressing room. Her toiletries and cosmetics were arranged in neat ranks on the glass shelves above the wash basins in her bathroom. She dabbed Chanel perfume behind her ears, then she went through into her sitting room. The drinks cabinet contained every item that her personal assistant, Agatha, had stipulated in the email she had sent Bert Simpson. Hazel filled a long glass with crushed ice and freshly squeezed lime juice and added a very small amount of Dovgan vodka. She carried it next door into her private communications centre. There were six large plasma screens on the facing wall so she was able to watch simultaneously the stock prices and commodity prices on all the major bourses; the other screens displayed the news channels and the sports results. At the moment she was particularly interested in the Prix de l'Arc de Triomphe at Longchamps in which she had a horse running. She grimaced with disgust when she saw that it had run a disappointing third. This confirmed her decision to fire her trainer, and take on the young Irishman. She switched her attention to the tennis. She liked to follow the efforts of the young Russian and Eastern European girls. They reminded her of those days when she was eighteen and hungry as a she-wolf. She sat at her computer and sipped the vodka which tasted like a fairy potion while she opened her emails. Agatha in Houston had screened them for her so there were fewer than fifty for her personal attention. She went through them rapidly. Although it was 0300 hours in Houston Agatha slept with the telephone on her bedside table always ready for her call. Hazel raised her on the Skype connection. Agatha's image appeared on the screen. She wore a nightgown with embroidered roses around the collar and her grey hair was in curlers and sleep filled her eyes. Hazel dictated to her the replies to the mail. Finally she asked,

'How is your cold, Agatha? You don't sound as croaky as you were yesterday.'

'It's so much better, Mrs Bannock. And thank you ever so much for asking.' That was why her employees loved her, their caring employer, until they slipped up and then she fired them into orbit. She cut the connection to Agatha and checked her wristwatch against the digital clock on the wall. It would be the same time aboard the *Amorous Dolphin*. Hazel disliked the name that Henry had christened the yacht and always referred to it as simply the *Dolphin*. Out of respect to the memory of her husband she could not bring herself to change it, besides which Henry had assured her that it was the worst possible luck to do so. The name was the only thing Hazel disliked about the vessel, which was 125 metres of pure Sybaritic luxury, with twelve double guest cabins and a palatial owner's stateroom. Her dining salon and other spacious entertainment areas were decorated with colourful murals by sought-after modern artists. Her four powerful diesel engines could drive her across the Atlantic Ocean in under six days. She was equipped with state-of-the-art navigation and communications electronics, and she could deploy all her expensive toys and gadgets for the amusement of even the most spoilt and sophisticated guests on board. Hazel dialled up the contact number of the *Dolphin*'s bridge and it was answered before it rang twice.

'*Amorous Dolphin*. Bridge.' She recognized the Californian accent.

'Mr Jetson?' He was the first officer, and the tone of his voice became awed as he realized who was calling.

'Good evening, Mrs Bannock.'

'Is Captain Franklin available?'

'Of course, Mrs Bannock. He is here beside me. I will hand you over to him.'

Jack Franklin greeted her and Hazel asked at once, 'Is all well, Captain?'

'Very well indeed, Mrs Bannock,' he assured her.

'What is your present position?'

Franklin reeled off the coordinates from the satnav screen, then quickly translated them into more intelligible form. 'We are 146 nautical miles south-east of Madagascar on course for Mahe Island in the Seychelles. Our ETA at Mahe is noon Thursday.'

'You have indeed made good progress, Captain Franklin,' Hazel told him. 'Is my daughter on the bridge with you?'

'I am afraid not, Mrs Bannock. I understand that Miss Bannock has retired early and has ordered her dinner served in your stateroom. I beg your pardon, I meant in *her* stateroom.'

The daughter was allowed to occupy the owner's stateroom when Mrs Bannock was not aboard. Franklin had always thought that the Gauguin and Monet oils, and the Lalique chandelier were rather wasted on an unbridled teenager who considered herself every bit as important as her illustrious parent. However, he knew better than to even hint at the child's defects to the mother. This pretty but unpleasant little bitch was Hazel Bannock's only blind spot.

'Please put me through to her there,' said Hazel Bannock.

'Certainly, Mrs Bannock.' She heard him speak to the radio operator. The line clicked dead and then came to life again with the ringing tone. She waited for twelve rings and she was becoming restless before the receiver was lifted. Then she recognized her daughter's voice.

'Who is that? I left orders that I was not to be disturbed.'

'Cayla baby!'

'Oh, Mummy, so lovely to hear your voice. I have been waiting for you to call all day. I was beginning to think you didn't love me any more.' Her delight was evident, and Hazel's heart swelled with maternal joy to hear it.

'I have been awfully busy, darling. So much is happening here.' Cayla, the pure one: the name she had chosen for her daughter was so appropriate. The image of the girl's face appeared in her mind's eye. Cayla's skin always seemed to Hazel to be fashioned from translucent jade beneath which the young blood pulsed and glowed. Her eyes were a lighter, more ethereal blue than Hazel's own. Purity of mind and spirit seemed to shine from them. At nineteen years of age she was a woman trembling on the brink, but still untouched, virginal, perfect. Hazel felt tears shimmer in her eyes as the strength of her love overwhelmed her. This child was the most important element in her life, this was what all the sacrifice and striving was for.

'That's my darling mummy. Only one speed. Full throttle!' Cayla laughed sweetly, and slowly rolled off the masculine figure on the bed beneath her. Their naked bellies were stuck together with their sweat and they came apart with sucking reluctance. She felt his penis slither out of her followed by a warm gush of her own vaginal fluid. She felt empty without him deep inside her.

'Tell me what you have been doing today,' Hazel demanded. 'Have you been studying?' This was the reason why she had left the child on the *Dolphin*. Cayla's term results had been abysmal. Her professor had threatened that without considerable improvement she would be sent down at the end of the year. Up to now only her mother's large donations to the university coffers had saved Cayla from that fate.

'I have to admit that I have been terribly lazy today, Mummy darling. I did not get out of bed until almost 9.30,' and she smiled with a wicked slant of those innocent blue eyes and thought to herself, *and not until Rogier had given me two monumental orgasms*. She sat up on the white sheets and wriggled closer to his beautifully sleek and muscled body. His skin was glossy with sweat like melting chocolate. They were still touching and she drew her knees up to her chin and turned slightly so he could have an uninterrupted view of the nest of fine blonde hair nestling between the backs of her thighs. He reached out and parted her thighs gently and she shuddered as he spread the swollen lips of her vulva and his forefinger sought out the pink rosebud between them. She held the telephone receiver to her ear with her left hand and with the right reached down to his penis. He was still fully tumescent. Cayla had come to think of this organ as a separate entity with a life force of its very own. She even had a pet name for it. Blaise, the master of Merlin the magician. Blaise had bewitched her. He was stretched to his full majestic length, hard and glistening with her own sweet essence with which she had anointed him. She encircled his girth with her thumb and forefinger and began to milk him with slow voluptuous strokes.

'Oh baby, you promised you would apply yourself to your studies. You are a clever girl, and with only a little effort I know you can do so much better.'

'Today was an exception, Mummy. I have been working very hard all the other days. Today I started my monthly thing. I have had a terrible tummy ache.'

'Oh, poor Cayla. I hope you are feeling better now?'

'Yes, Mummy. I am much better. I will be fine again tomorrow.'

'I wish I was there to look after you. It's only a week since I left you in Cape Town,' Hazel said, 'but it seems an eternity. I miss you so, baby.'

'I miss you too, Mummy,' Cayla assured her. Then she had no further need to reply as now her mother went on talking about the running of her grotty old oilfields and the problems she had with the coarse unwashed oafs who ran them for her. At intervals Cayla made small noises of agreement, but she was studying Blaise with a little frown of concentration. He was circumcised. The others she had known before him had all had that untidy hood of skin dangling from the tip. Only after meeting Rogier had she come to realize how ugly they were in comparison to this beautiful shaft of flesh she now held reverently between finger and thumb. Blaise was dark blue-black, smooth and glossy as a rifle barrel. A clear droplet oozed slowly from the slit in his head. It trembled there like a drop of dew. It was so exciting to watch that it made her shiver with delight and goose bumps rose on the unblemished skin of her forearms. Quickly she dipped her head over him. She took the droplet on the tip of her tongue. She savoured the taste of him. She wanted more, much more. She began to milk him more urgently, her long delicate fingers flying up and down his shaft like a shuttle in a loom. He thrust his hips forward to meet her. She saw the muscles in his belly contracting. She could feel Blaise swelling, hard and thick as a tennis racquet handle in her grip. Rogier's features contorted. He threw back his marvellous dark head and his mouth opened. She saw that he was about to groan or cry out. Quickly she released his penis and clapped her hand over his mouth to silence him, but at the same time she leaned forward and took as much of Blaise's length as she could into her own mouth. She could engulf less than half of him and the tip of his swollen head pressed against the back of her throat starting her gagging reflex. But she had learned to control that. She risked taking her hand away from over his mouth. She wanted to feel the building up of his seed deep inside him. She slipped her hand down between his thighs and grasped the root of his scrotum. Still sucking and bobbing her head up and down she felt his ejaculation begin, pulsing and pumping in her hand, and his testicles were drawn up tightly against the base of his belly.

Even though she was prepared for it, the force and volume took her by surprise every time. She gasped and swallowed as rapidly as she could but she could not take it all and the excess overflowed and drooled down her chin. She wanted to suck every last drop out of him. She went on drinking it down and now despite herself she was moaning softly. Her mother's voice roused her from her daze of ecstasy.

'Cayla! What's happening? Are you all right? What is happening? Speak to me!' Cayla had dropped the telephone receiver and it lay squawking on the bed beside her. She snatched it up, and gathered her wits.

'Oh! I spilled the coffee all over myself and the bed. It was hot and it gave me a start.' She laughed breathlessly.

'You didn't scald yourself, did you?'

'Oh, no! But the duvet is a mess,' she said and ran her fingertips through the slippery outpourings that were splattered over the silk coverlet. It was still warm from his body. She wiped her fingers on his chest and he grinned up at her. She thought he was the most beautiful man she had ever laid eyes upon. Her mother changed the subject and began to reminisce about their recent visit to Cape Town where the *Dolphin* had stopped over for two weeks. Cayla's grandmother lived in a magnificent old Herbert Baker-designed mansion amongst the vineyards just outside the city. Hazel had purchased the wine estate with the idea of retiring there one day in the far distant future. In the meantime it made a perfect home for her beloved mother, who had scrimped and saved every penny to enable her daughter to follow her quest to the great tennis tournaments of the world. Now the old lady had a magnificent home, filled with servants, and a uniformed chauffeur to drive her to the village in the Mercedes Maybach every Saturday, to do her shopping and to drink tea with her cronies.

Rogier stood up from the bed and made a sign to Cayla. Then he sauntered naked to the bathroom. His muscled buttocks oscillated tantalizingly. Cayla jumped up from the bed and followed him, with the telephone receiver still held to her ear. Rogier stood at the urinal and she leaned against the bulkhead beside him and watched with complete fascination.

She had met Rogier in Paris where she was studying the art of the French Impressionists at the Université des Beaux-Arts. She knew that her mother would never approve of her relationship with him. Her mother was only a lip-service liberal. She had probably never been brought to bed by any man with darker skin pigmentation than orange skin pith. However, on first sight Cayla had been enthralled by Rogier's exoticism: the glossy iron blue patina of his skin, his fine nilotic features, his tall willowy body and his intriguing accent. She had also been titillated by the accounts of the girlfriends of her own age, those with more experience than her, when they described in prurient detail how men of colour were so much more abundantly endowed with masculine apparatus than those of any other race. She recalled vividly that when she had first seen Blaise in his full imperial tumescence she had been terrified. It seemed impossible that she would be able to accommodate all of him inside herself. The task had not proved as difficult as she had at first imagined. She giggled at the memory.

'What are you laughing at, baby?' her mother asked.

'I was just remembering Grandma's story about the wild baboon that got into her kitchen.'

'Granny can be very funny,' her mother agreed and she went on talking about their impending reunion at Ten League Island in the Seychelles. Hazel owned the entire 1,750-acre island and the big sprawling beach-side bungalow where she planned to pass the Christmas holidays with the family, just as she did every year. She would send the jet to Cape Town to fetch her mother and Uncle John. Cayla put the thought aside. She did not wish to be reminded of her coming separation from Rogier. She reached down and took a firm hold of Blaise and led Rogier back to the bed. Her mother ended the conversation at last.

'I must go now, baby. I have a very early start tomorrow. I will call you again the same time tomorrow. I love you, my little one.'

'I love you a zillion times plus one, Mummy.' She knew the effect that her baby talk had on her mother. She broke the connection and tossed the telephone onto the antique silk carpet on the deck beside the bed. She kissed Rogier and slipped her tongue into his mouth then she drew back and told him in a peremptory tone,

'I want you to stay with me tonight.'

'I cannot do that. You know I can't, Cayla.'

'Why not?' she demanded.

'If the captain finds out about us he will wrap an anchor chain around my neck and drop me overboard.'

'Don't be utterly wretched. He won't find out. I have Georgie Porgie under my thumb. He will cover for us. If I smile at him he will do anything for me.' She was referring to the ship's purser.

'Anything for your smile and a couple of hundred-dollar bills.' Rogier switched into his native French with a chuckle. 'But he is not the captain.' He stood up and went to where his uniform was thrown over the back of an easy chair. 'We cannot afford to take that chance, we're taking enough chances as it is. I'll come to see you again tomorrow at the same time. Leave the door unlocked.'

'I am ordering you to stay.' Her voice rose. She was also speaking French now, but a more rudimentary form of the language. He grinned infuriatingly.

'You can't order me to do anything. You are not the captain of this ship.' He was fastening the brass buttons of the white jacket of his steward's uniform.

Captain Franklin was right. Cayla didn't give a damn for the French Impressionists, or, for that matter, any other Impressionists. It had been at her mother's insistence that she had gone to the Université des Beaux-Arts in Paris. Her mother was besotted with paintings of water lilies or of half-naked Tahitian girls, just like the one hanging on the bulkhead facing her bed, painted by a syphilitic, drug-blowing, alcoholic Frenchman. She had a crazy idea of setting Cayla up as an art dealer once she had graduated, when the only thing that Cayla really cared about was horses, but there was no point in arguing with Mummy, because Mummy always got her way.

'You belong to me,' she told Rogier. 'You will do what I say.' With her Black Amex card she had paid for his first-class ticket from London to Cape Town, and she had arranged his job as a ship's steward, greasing Georgie Porgie with a peck on the cheek and a sheaf of green bills. She owned Rogier just as she owned her Bugatti Veyron sports car and her string of show-jumping horses, the true loves of her life.

'I'll come tomorrow night at the same time.' He gave her that infuriating grin again and slipped out of the cabin, closing the door softly behind him.

'You will find the bloody door locked!' she screamed after him, and scooping up the telephone from the deck she hurled it with all her strength at the glowing Gauguin nude. The telephone receiver bounced off the taut canvas and slithered across the deck. Cayla threw herself back on the bed and sobbed into the pillow with fury and frustration. When Rogier refused to obey her was when she wanted him most.

• • •

Rogier checked the stock in the cocktail bar in the main salon. Georgie Porgie trusted him to do this. He retrieved his knife from where he had hidden it under the counter before going to his assignation with Cayla. The blade was of Damask steel made by Kia, the same Japanese firm who had once crafted Samurai swords. It was as sharp as a surgeon's scalpel. Rogier lifted the cuff of his trouser leg and strapped the sheath to his calf. His life was dangerous and the weapon gave him security. He locked up the bar for the night, and then ran lightly down the companionway to the working deck. Before he reached the crew's mess he smelt the roasting pork. The greasy odour sickened him. He might have to go hungry tonight, unless he could work his charms on the chef. The chef was as gay as a lark on a spring morning, and Rogier was beautiful with thick dark crinkly hair and smouldering eyes. His smile matched his outwardly sunny personality. He took his seat at the crew's long dining table and waited until the chef looked through the hatch from his kitchen. Rogier smiled at him then gestured at the thick slice of pork on the plate of the stoker beside him and rolled his eyes in an eloquent gesture of disgust. The chef smiled back at him and five minutes later he sent a thick middle cut of kingklip through the hatch to him. One of the finest eating fish in the seas, it was cooked to flaking white perfection and slathered with the chef's famous sauce. It had been destined for the captain's table before it was diverted.

The stoker glanced at Rogier's plate and muttered, 'Bloody bum boy!'

Rogier kept smiling but he leaned forward and lifted the cuff of his trouser leg. The thin stiletto blade appeared in his hand below the table top.

'You really should not say that again,' Rogier advised him and the stoker glanced down. The point of the stiletto was aimed at his crotch. The colour drained from his face and he stood up hastily, abandoned his pork cutlet and hurried out of the mess. Rogier ate his fish with genteel relish. His elegant manners seemed out of place in these surroundings.

Before leaving he paused at the hatch and waved his thanks to the chef. Then he went up on the stern deck where the crew were permitted to exercise or to relax in their off-duty periods. He looked up at the sickle moon. He felt a deep longing to pray here under this symbol of his faith. He wanted to expunge the memory of the Christian whore and make atonement for the sacrilege he had been forced to commit with her by his grandfather's orders. But he could not pray out here. There was too great a danger of being observed. He had let it be known on board that he was a Roman Catholic from Marseille. This explained his North African complexion.

Before he went below he looked to the northern horizon and was able to fix the direction of Mecca in his memory. He went down to his tiny cabin, collected his wash bag and towel, and went along the passage to the shower and toilet that were shared by all the lower deck crew. He washed his face and body carefully, brushed his teeth and rinsed his mouth in ritual purification. When he had dried himself he knotted the towel around his waist, returned to his cabin and bolted the door. He took his kitbag down from the rack above his bunk and unpacked his silk prayer mat and his spotless white prayer caftan. He spread the mat on the deck facing Mecca, whose direction he had calculated from the yacht's heading. There was barely enough space on the deck for the mat. He slipped the caftan over his head and let the hem fall to his ankles. He stood at the foot of the rug and whispered a short introductory prayer in Arabic. He did not wish to chance being overheard by any of his shipmates as they passed his cabin door:

'In the sight of Allah the Merciful and of his prophet I declare that I am Adam Abdul Tippoo Tip and that from the day of my birth I have embraced Islam and I am now and have always been a true believer. I confess my sins in that I have cohabited with the infidel and have taken unto myself the infidel name of Rogier Marcel Moreau. I pray your pardon for these deeds; which I have committed only in the service of Islam and of Allah the Most Merciful and not by my own wishes or desires.'

Long before Rogier's birth his sainted grandfather had taken the precaution of sending his pregnant wives and the wives of his sons and grandsons to give birth to their offspring on the tiny island of Réunion in the south-eastern corner of the Indian Ocean. By a happy chance his grandfather had himself been born on the island and so he knew just how convenient this birthplace was. Réunion Island was a directorate of Greater France and thus any person born on its rugged black volcanic slopes was a citizen of France and entitled to all the rights and privileges which that entailed. Two years previously at the beginning of the present operation, and at the insistence of his grandfather, Adam had formally changed his name by deed poll in the directorate of Auvergne in France and had been issued with a new French passport. As soon as he had delivered his personal appeal to Allah, Rogier began the evening prayer with the Arabic salutation:

'I intend to offer four Rakats of the Isha prayer and face the Qibla, the direction of Mecca, for the sake of Allah and Allah alone.' He commenced the complicated series of bowing, kneeling and prostrating as he whispered the required prayers. When he had finished he felt enlivened and powerful in body and in faith. It was time for the next move against the infidel and the blasphemer. He removed his prayer robe and rolled it into the silk rug, and returned both items to the bottom of the large kitbag. Then he dressed in a pair of denim jeans, a dark shirt and black windcheater. Next he brought down his rucksack from the luggage rack above his bunk, and opened the side flap of one of the pockets. He took out a black Nokia mobile phone. It was an identical model to the one he used for ordinary communications. However, this device had been modified by one of his grandfather's technicians. He switched it on and checked that the battery was full. It had sufficient power for at least a week of operation before he had to recharge it. Ever since sailing from Cape Town he had surreptitiously searched the superstructure of the yacht for the most suitable place in which to plant the device, and had finally decided on the small locker on the aft deck in which the deck-chairs and cleaning equipment were stored. Its door was never locked, and between the door lintel and the low roof was a narrow ledge which was ideally suited to his requirements. From the pocket of his rucksack he took a roll of double-sided adhesive tape and a small Maglite. He cut two pieces of the tape and stuck them to the back of the mobile phone. He zipped the mobile phone and the Maglite into the pocket of his windcheater, left the cabin and went up the companionway to the aft deck. He leaned his elbows on the rail and looked down on the vessel's wake. It was creamy with the phosphorescence emitted by the tiny marine creatures being churned up by the propellers. Then he looked up at the sickle moon which was now well clear of the dark horizon. The Moon of Islam; he smiled, it was a propitious sign. He straightened up from the rail and looked about him casually to make certain he was not being observed. He had made it his habit to come on deck every evening after his bar duties were finished, so that there was nothing suspicious about his presence here on this occasion. The door of the storage locker was in the shadow of the superstructure. In his dark clothing Rogier was almost invisible as he moved towards it. The latch on the door opened easily. He let himself in and closed the door. He switched on the Maglite, but shaded the powerful beam with his hand and shone it into the recess above the lintel. This was above the eyeline of even a tall man entering the locker. With his free hand he took the mobile phone from his pocket and decided on the exact spot in which to place the device. He reached up and pressed the adhesive strips against the bulkhead. He tried it carefully and found the device was firmly attached; it would take considerable force to remove it.

He pressed the 'Power' button and the small red light glowed immediately, emitting an almost inaudible electronic tone. The transponder was transmitting. Rogier grunted with satisfaction and pressed the mute button. The tone was silenced but the red light continued pulsing softly. Only a receiver that was tuned to the precise wavelength of the transponder and that was correctly encoded would be able to read the transmissions. The squawk code was 1351. This was the Islamic equivalent of 1933 in the Gregorian calendar, the year of his grandfather's birth. Rogier switched off the torch and slipped out of the locker, shutting the door quietly behind him. He went down to his cabin.

• • •

One hundred and eight nautical miles north of Madagascar and five hundred and sixteen miles east of the port of Dar es Salaam on the African mainland lay a tiny scattering of uninhabited coral atolls. In the lee of one of these a 170-foot lateen-rigged Arab dhow lay at anchor in six fathoms of water with her grubby canvas sail furled around the long boom. She had been lying there for eleven days, indistinguishable from any other coastal Arab trader or fishing boat. Her hull had not been painted for many years, and it was zebra-striped by the human faeces which the crew had voided as they hung their buttocks over the ship's rail. The only oddity that might have caught the attention of a casual observer was the three much smaller craft that were moored to the side of the dhow. Twenty-eight feet long, their low hulls, with sharply streamlined prows, were of modern fibreglass construction, and painted a nondescript matt colour which would merge into the watery wastes of the open ocean. On the stern of each boat were bolted two massive outboard motors. The engine maker's original flamboyant paintwork was covered by a blotchy coating of the same colour as the hulls. However, they were finely tuned and capable of pushing the light craft at speeds of over forty knots, even when fully laden.

The long boats were empty at the moment. The crews were all assembled on the deck of the big dhow, where they had just completed the evening prayers. They were moving about the deck, embracing each other and repeating the traditional invocation,

'May Allah hear our prayers.'

Above the hubbub of their voices the radio operator's trained ear picked up the soft electronic beeping coming from the deck house forward of the single mast. He broke away from the group and hurried to attend to his equipment. As soon as he entered the deck house he saw the red light blinking on the front panel of the radio receiver and his heart beat faster.

'In the name of Allah the All Merciful, may his glorious name be exalted for ever!' He squatted cross-legged on the deck before the radio set. Ever since they had reached the atoll and dropped the lump of coral which served the dhow as anchor the radio had been tuned to the correct frequency. In Morse he tapped out the squawk code: 1351. Immediately the transponder in the locker on the aft deck of the *Amorous Dolphin* changed from broadcast to passive mode, waiting to respond to interrogation. The radio operator sprang to his feet and rushed to the doorway. He shrieked excitedly,

'Master! Come swiftly!' The dhow's captain came over with long strides. The deck was lit with kerosene lanterns hanging from the boom of the mast. In their light the captain was a tall lean figure dressed in a checked red and white shumag head cloth and a long white dishdashah robe. His full beard was still dark although he was past fifty years of age. He ducked into the radio shack and replied to the operator expectantly,

'Yes?'

'By the grace of Allah and his Prophet may they be praised eternally.' The operator affirmed the contact and moved aside in the cramped shack to allow the captain a clear view of the radio and the steady red light glowing on the front panel. Wordlessly the captain squatted in front of the equipment and began to interrogate the transponder. First he asked it for its present position and speed over the ground. It replied at once. The captain repeated these details of longitude and latitude to the operator and he scribbled them on his pad. They knew these were accurate to within a few metres.

Despite the dhow's biblical rigging and archaic appearance the satellite navigation with which it was equipped was the most modern commercially available. When the captain had ascertained from the transponder the *Dolphin*'s heading and speed, he spread the chart of the Indian Ocean on the deck and pored over it. The dhow's present position was marked with a discreet red cross. He determined the position of the infidel yacht and marked that on the chart also. Then he began a calculation of the course and time for interception. He did not want to waste time and fuel by reaching the point too far ahead of the yacht, but more important he must not let the other vessel get ahead of him. While towing the long boats the dhow had a top speed of only fourteen knots and in a stern chase would be left floundering far behind. Once the captain was satisfied with his calculations he went out onto the open deck.

Thirty-nine men were crowded there, squatting silently and expectantly. The modern automatic weapons they all carried seemed incongruous in this setting. There were eleven men to crew each of the long boats and the others were the crew of the dhow itself. The captain moved with stately tread to his place at the tiller, from where he addressed them.

'The gazelle is in the jaws of the cheetah.' His first words brought forth a fierce hum of comment from the men. The captain raised a hand and they were immediately silent, concentrating all their attention upon him.

'The infidel is still far to the south-east but moving swiftly towards us. Tomorrow morning before it is light we will weigh anchor. It will take seven hours of sailing for us to reach the ambush position. I expect the infidel ship to pass us tomorrow afternoon two hours before sunset at a range of two miles to the east; too great a distance to make out more than our sail. She will take us for a harmless island trader—' Speaking slowly but emphatically he went over the attack plan once again. These were simple men, most of them illiterate and not overly intelligent, but when they smelt blood in the water they were as fearsome as barracuda. When he had finished he reminded them, 'We will sail before first light tomorrow morning and may Allah and his Prophet smile upon our enterprise.'

• • •

When she saw the door handle of her stateroom turn stealthily Cayla was ready for it. She had been waiting for him nearly an hour and her anticipation was feverish. She had rehearsed every biting and insulting word in her mind, and then the manner in which she would force him to submit to her in cringing apology. Now she leapt from the bed and raced silently to the door on bare feet. She placed her lips close to the panel and spoke just loudly enough for her voice to carry to him on the far side,

'Go away! I never want to see you again. I hate you. Do you hear me, I hate you.' She waited for his reply, but there was silence for half a minute, which seemed to her much longer. She wanted to call out again, just to make certain that he was still there. Then he spoke and his voice was level and cold.

'Yes, I hear you. I am leaving immediately as you request.' She heard his footsteps retreat along the passageway. This was not going as she had envisaged it. He was supposed to beg her forgiveness. Quickly she shot back the bolt and jerked the door open.

'How dare you insult and defy me. Come back here at once. I want you to know how much I hate you!' He turned back to face her and he smiled, that smile of his that thrilled and infuriated her. She stamped her foot, and she could hardly believe that she had made such a childish gesture.

'Come back here immediately. Don't stand there with that stupid grin on your face. Come here.'

He shrugged and sauntered back to where she was holding the door half-open. She gathered the most scathing insults she could think of, but before she could deliver one of them he had reached the door. He was still smiling, but his next action took her completely by surprise. He put his shoulder to the door and forced it fully open. She recoiled in astonishment.

'You bastard!' she said shakily. 'How dare you, you uncouth peasant!' He closed the door behind him and shot the deadlock. Then he advanced on her unhurriedly and she was forced to retreat.

'Get away from me. Don't you dare touch me. *Vous êtes une merde noire.*' She sprang at him with a clenched fist and launched a savage round-arm blow at his head. He caught her wrist and slowly forced her to her knees in front of him.

'You can't do this to me! I will tell my mother.'

'So, now Cayla is not a big fierce girl any more. She is a spoilt little baby crying for her mummy.'

'Don't you talk to me like that. I'll kill you—' She broke off in astonishment as she realized that he was unzipping his trouser fly and bringing out his penis only inches from her face. Blaise was already in full erection. She realized that her violence had aroused him.

'You can't do this to me,' she whispered. 'You're hurting me.' He had twisted up her arm painfully but he was still smiling. Despite the pain she was suddenly as aroused as he was. She could feel her vaginal lubricant seeping through her silk panties. His penis was touching her lips.

'Open your mouth!' he ordered her. Slowly she parted her lips and he forced the head deep inside. Now she abandoned any show of reluctance and her head nodded in rhythm to his thrusts. Suddenly she froze with horror, and then jerked her head back coughing and spitting.

'You bastard!' she sobbed with disgust. 'You pissed in my mouth. *Vous êtes un cochon dégoûtant!*' He let go of her wrist, but immediately grabbed a handful of her blonde hair and twisted her face up towards his.

'Never, never call me a pig again,' he said with deadly calm. 'And this is just to remind you.' Open-handed he struck her across the face, knocking her head to one side. She looked up at him with astonishment and awe, tears of pain from her stinging cheek flooding her eyes, but she could not speak from the shock rather than the pain.

'Now, open your mouth again,' he ordered, but she mumbled an incoherent refusal, and tried to turn her head away. He tightened his grip on the handful of her hair, until it felt to her as if he was going to rip it off her scalp. She lifted her face towards him, her cheek glowing pinkly where the blow had landed.

'Please, Rogier, don't hurt me again. I did not mean what I said. I love you so much. You will never know how much. Forgive me, please.'

'Prove it to me,' he said. 'Open your mouth again.' She had never felt so overpowered and helpless. It was as though she knelt not at the feet of a human being, but of a god. She longed for him to possess her completely, to subjugate her, to violate and demean her. Slowly she opened her mouth as he had ordered her and he thrust so hard into her that the hinges of her jaws ached. As the pungent warm flood spurted into her mouth again it swamped her senses. She knew then that she belonged to him, to him alone and to no other, not even to herself.

Two hours later he left her lying exhausted on the rumpled sheets. Her lips were swollen and inflamed with his rough kisses and the stubble of his new beard, her mascara had run leaving her eyes like those of a tragic clown, her alabaster skin was deathly pale except for the one vivid pink cheek where he had slapped her. Her hair was tousled and darkened with her sweat. She struggled up on one elbow as she heard him at the door. But she could not find the words to plead with him to stay with her. Then it was too late and he had gone. Broken and ravaged, she was too tired to weep. She lowered her head to the pillow and within minutes she was asleep.

• • •

Rogier went up on deck after evening prayers and leaned on the rail as was his established habit. Once he was sure that he was unobserved he slipped into the locker and one glance at the transponder in its hiding place assured him that it had been interrogated by another station. A second bulb had lit up above the first. He typed in the squawk code and the tiny screen came alive. It gave him the date and time of the last contact. This had taken place only a few hours previously. He felt a lift of excitement. Everything was going exactly as it had been planned many months before. There had been so much that could have gone wrong, and had almost done so.

Originally his grandfather's plan had been to make the Bannock woman herself the target. But it soon became apparent that this was not feasible. Even the most elementary research had made it clear that the woman was much too worldly-wise and canny to be lured into such an obvious honey trap. Although it seemed she had dallied once or twice since her husband's death, it had always been on her own terms with mature and powerful men of similar status to her own. She would certainly be proof against Rogier's more obvious and boyish charms and wiles. However, her daughter was an innocent lamb; alone in Paris and eager to experience life and all its excitements. Rogier's grandfather had sent him to Paris, and the meeting with and ensnarement of the girl had been pathetically simple.

All that was required now was for the mother to make her annual Christmas visit to the Seychelles on board her yacht and of course take her daughter with her, but this seemed to be beyond reasonable doubt. The unexpected twist had been when the mother had left the yacht in Cape Town, leaving her daughter on board to sail to the island accompanied only by the crew, of which Rogier was now a member. His grandfather had been pleased with this unexpected turn of events. Rogier had telephoned him from a dockside call box at the Cape Town waterfront and the old man had chuckled when he heard the news.

'Allah has been magnanimous, exalted be his name. I could not have arranged it better myself. The girl will be more vulnerable and malleable without her mother to protect her, and once she is in our power the mother will be helpless to resist us. Take the cub and the lioness must follow.'

Rogier was about to leave the locker when the transponder beeped softly. The tiny green screen had come alive and Rogier scanned the Arabic text message on it. It was from his uncle Kamal, his grandfather's youngest son, who was the commodore of the fleet of pirate craft with which Tippoo Tip ravaged the Indian Ocean shipping. For this important operation Kamal had personally taken command of the dhow. He was giving Rogier the estimated time the following day when he expected that his vessel would be within visual range of the *Dolphin*.

• • •

At precisely 0530 hours the doors to the executive suite opened and Hazel Bannock stepped into the dark courtyard. She wore a black leotard which seemed moulded to her long athletic torso and legs. Over it she wore a pair of wide-legged silk shorts that were meant to modestly conceal the shape of her buttocks. They had the opposite effect of enhancing their perfection. On her feet was a pair of white running shoes. The famous golden hair was gathered back severely by a black band behind her head.

'Good morning, Major. Are you happy to run in your full warlike paraphernalia?' Her tone was mildly mocking. He wore combat boots and a webbing belt over his camouflage fatigues. There was a pistol in a holster on his hip.

'I do everything in this gear, Ma'am.' Though his expression was deadpan they were both aware of the double entendre. And she frowned with quick annoyance at the liberty.

'Then let's run,' she said curtly. 'Lead the way, Major.' They left the compound, and he took her up the path that climbed to the highest point of the ridge. He set a moderate pace for the first mile until he could judge her capability. He could hear her close behind him on the path and when they crested the slope she spoke in an easy tone with no hint of exertion.

'When you have finished admiring the view, Major, we might try at least a jog trot.' Hector grinned. The sun was still just below the horizon but its spreading rays were perfectly traced across the heavens by the fine dust of the Khamseen. The sky was ablaze with a flaming glory.

'You must admit, Ma'am, that it's worth more than a passing glance,' he said, but she did not reply and he lengthened his stride. They traversed the ridge, and finally he reckoned they were five miles out from the compound. The sun was up now and the heat was mounting swiftly. Far below them the oil rigs emerged from the dense shadow cast by the ridge, and he could make out the shining silver pipeline running across the dreary desert wastes down towards the coast.

'There is a narrow path down the ridge just ahead. The footing is treacherous, but if we take it we can meet the patrol road along the pipeline for the home run, Mrs Bannock. It would be another five miles from there to the compound. Do you want me to take that route?'

'Go ahead, Major.' When they reached the patrol road she moved up easily and took over the lead. She ran lightly, gracefully, but very fast. He had to stretch out to just below his own top speed to hold her. Now he could see that at last she was perspiring through her leotard in a darker line down her spine, and the golden hair at the nape of her neck was damp. Under the baggy silk shorts he could make out the shape of her buttocks bouncing with each stride. He stared at them.

Tennis balls? he asked himself, and felt a sharp stab of lust in his groin. *Son of a gun, she can give me a hard-on even at this speed. Not half bad!* he thought, and grunted with suppressed laughter.

'Share the joke, Major,' she invited him, still speaking in conversational levels, showing no signs of tiring.

Bloody woman, he thought, *she is just too bloody good to be true. I wonder what her weakness is.*

'Schoolboy humour. You would not find it entertaining, Ma'am.'

'Come up alongside, Major. We can talk.' He moved up and ran at her shoulder, but she was quiet, forcing him to speak first.

'With all due respect, Ma'am, I am no longer a Major. I would much prefer it if you simply called me Cross.'

'With the utmost respect, Cross,' she replied, 'I am not the Queen of England. You can drop the ma'am business.'

'Certainly, Mrs Bannock.'

'I am fully aware why you eschew the military rank, Cross. It reminds you of the reason why you were thrown out of your regiment. You shot three helpless prisoners of war, did you not?'

'If I may correct you, I was not thrown out of the regiment. I was found not guilty by the court martial. Subsequently I requested and was granted an honourable discharge.'

'But your prisoners were still very dead after you had finished with them, were they not?'

'They had just blown up six of my comrades with a road-side bomb. Though they had their hands in the air at the time of their departure from this mortal coil they were still active hostiles. When one of them reached for what I thought was a suicide belt under his robe I had no time to be selective. I had a squad of my men within range of any blast. We were all in peril. I had no option but to cull all three of them.'

'When the corpses were examined none of them were found to be wearing a belt. That was the evidence at your court martial. Was it incorrect?'

'I was not afforded the luxury of making a prior body search of the prisoners. I had about one hundredth of a second to make the decision.'

'Cull is a euphemism that usually applies to the killing of animals.' She changed tack.

'In the military it has another usage.'

They ran on in silence for another ten minutes. Then she said,

'Since entering the service of Bannock Oil there have been a number of further fatal incidents in which you were involved.'

'Three to be exact, Mrs Bannock.'

'During these three incidents another two dozen men were killed by you and your men. All the victims were Arabs?'

'Nineteen of them to be exact, Mrs Bannock.'

'I was close enough,' she said.

'Before we continue may I point out, Mrs Bannock, that those nineteen insurgents were all intent on blowing the hell out of Bannock Oil installations.'

'It did not occur to you to arrest them and hold them for questioning to make certain they were truly terrorists?' she asked.

'The idea did cross my mind, Mrs Bannock, but at the time they were all shooting at me and they did not seem amenable to polite conversation,' Hector said and this time he let a small sneer twist his lips. He had learned enough about her to know that would infuriate her. She ran on in silence for a while as she regrouped her attack. Then she went on,

'Tell me truly, Cross. How do you feel about people of a darker complexion than your own lily white?'

'Truly, Mrs Bannock, I don't give a good stuff. I am as strongly antagonistic to bad-arsed lily-whites as I am to bad-arsed coal blacks. But I hold for both good lily-whites and good blacks alike a deep and abiding affection.'

'Please moderate your language, Cross.'

'Okay, Mrs Bannock, just as soon as you cut out the clever innuendo.'

'Very well, Cross. I will come straight out with it. I think you are a blood-thirsty racist, and I don't particularly like you for it.'

'Mr Bannock did not think the same thing about me when he signed my contract with Bannock Oil.'

'I know my husband had a higher regard for you and your abilities than I do, but then my husband also voted for the Bushes, father and son. Henry Bannock was almost but not entirely perfect.'

'Of course, you voted for Mr Clinton and Mr Gore?'

She ignored the question, and went on, 'I note your subtle reference to your contract with Bannock Oil, Cross. I have read that document through, every word of it.'

'Then you know it will be an expensive one to break.'

'At this stage no one is talking about breaking any contracts, especially one that was authorized by my husband. But I will have my eye on you.' At the completion of their run she turned away from him with a curt 'Thank you, Cross,' and started into the building, glancing at her wristwatch.

'Mrs Bannock!' He made her pause and look back. 'Like me or loathe me, if you ever need me you will need me badly, and I will be here, if for no other reason than that your husband was one of the good guys. They didn't come any better than Henry Bannock.'

'Let's hope I never need your services that badly.' She dismissed him. In twenty minutes she had a final meeting with Simpson before she helicoptered back to the oil terminal at Sidi el Razig. The jet was waiting for her on the runway there to take her down to Mahe Island in the Seychelles to be with her beloved family. She showered quickly and used a moisturizing sun cream, but no makeup. She went through to her communications room. There was a string of emails from Agatha, but she did not have time to deal with those now. She would run through them once she was on the jet. She started for the door on her way to the meeting with Simpson. At that moment she heard her BlackBerry buzz in the outside pocket of her crocodile skin handbag that stood on her bedside table. She turned back. Very few people had that number. She took the mobile phone from the pocket of her handbag and switched it on. The legend on the screen read, 'You have 2 missed calls and 1 message. Do you wish to view your messages?' She pressed 'Show'.

'I wonder what my little monkey wants now,' she said to herself fondly and the text appeared. It was chillingly short and simple:

Terrible things happening. Strange men with guns . . .

It broke off as if Cayla had been interrupted in mid-sentence. Hazel felt a dark shutter flicker over her vision. She swayed on

her feet. Then her vision cleared and she stared at the message
blankly, deliberately refusing to face up to the enormity of it.
Then it dawned upon her and she felt an ice-cold hand clutch
her heart and start squeezing the life out of her. With shaking hands and short asthmatic breaths she punched the reply
button on her BlackBerry and listened to the endless ringing
tone at Cayla's end of the line. It was interrupted at last by an
impersonal voice:

'The person you have dialled is not available at present.
Please leave a message after the tone.'

'Darling! Darling! I am going mad. Please call me back as
soon as you can.' She spoke into the BlackBerry then darted
through to her communications room. She punched the contact number for the *Dolphin*'s bridge. For the security of the ship
and the passengers most of her crew were combat-trained and
well armed. *Surely they would have defended Cayla*, she thought
desperately. But the phone rang interminably. Her mouth was
dry and her eyes blurred.

'Please!' she begged. 'Please somebody answer me.' Then
the ringing tone switched off, and the ready signal buzzed
infuriatingly in her ear. She slammed down the receiver and
dialled Agatha. Her heart bounded at the sound of the prim
old-maidish voice.

'Agatha, I have had a terrifying text message from Cayla,
something about strange men with guns on board the *Dolphin*.
I cannot contact her. I cannot contact the ship. The last position I have for her was yesterday evening. Write down these
coordinates, Agatha.' From memory she recited the longitude
and latitude that Franklin had given her. 'Now it seems that she
has disappeared with Cayla on board. You must phone Chris
Bessell at home. Get him out of bed—' Chris was her senior
executive vice-president in Houston. 'He must get everybody
he can onto this. He must use all his contacts at the Pentagon
and the White House. Request an urgent over-fly of the area
from the nearest military satellite. Find out if there is a US
warship in the immediate area. Ask them to send it in at its best

speed. Ask for a reconnaissance aircraft to fly out of the airforce base on Diego Garcia to widen the search. Keep trying to contact the ship directly. I am flying back home as fast as I can. Try and arrange for me to see the President personally as soon as I arrive in Washington. You and Chris must pull all the strings and press all the buttons.' She was panting as though she had just run a marathon. 'Agatha, this is Cayla, my baby! I am relying on you. You cannot let me down.'

'You know I won't, Mrs Bannock.'

Hazel broke the connection and rang Simpson's number on the internal line of the compound. He answered almost immediately.

'Good morning, Mrs Bannock. We are waiting for you in the boardroom—'

She interrupted him brusquely. 'Have the helicopter ready for me in five minutes. Radio ahead to have my jet standing on the runway at Sidi el Razig. Order my chief pilot to have her fully refuelled with engines running, ready for immediate takeoff the minute I arrive. Tell my pilot to file a flight plan direct to Farnborough airport in England. We will refuel there before flying on across the Atlantic to Washington DC. We must not waste a single moment.'

She opened her safe and snatched out the satchel which contained her passport, emergency cash and credit cards, then she burst out of her suite and raced down the long passage towards the front doors. Bert Simpson, two of his underlings and Hector were standing there. They had been waiting there since her call to Simpson.

'What the hell is going on, Bert?' Hector asked quietly.

'Damned if I know. But it must be a major catastrophe. She was in a terrible state when I spoke to her—' He broke off as Hazel Bannock came running down the passage towards them.

She called out urgently, 'Is the helicopter here?'

'It has just this moment landed,' Bert assured her as she strode past him towards the door. Then she saw that Hector Cross was with the other men. He was the only one whose expression was calm. He spoke quietly, holding her attention with that penetrating green gaze.

'Please remember, Mrs Bannock,' he said, 'if you need me, one word will be enough.'

It was then that she realized for the first time that she was weeping openly and that the tears were pouring down her face and dripping from her chin. She dashed them away with the back of her hand, but she wished desperately that Cross had not been there to witness her condition. She had never in all her life experienced such a seething witch's brew of emotions. She knew she was close to snapping point, and the knowledge frightened her. Hector Cross was the nearest target for her terror and confusion. She rounded on him with the face of a Fury.

'Don't you dare mock me, you arrogant bastard, Cross. You know nothing, so what can you do? What can anybody do?' She turned away and stumbled slightly as she went down the front steps. Hector was gripped by a strange and alien sensation. It was a long, long time since he had last experienced it, so it took him a moment to recognize it. It was compassion. Maybe Hazel Bannock was all too human under that polished veneer. He no longer believed in love. What had remained of that he left on the floor of a divorce court somewhere. Yet this feeling of compassion felt very much like the other thing. It was disturbing.

You are not going to make a total arsehole of yourself again, are you, Cross? he asked himself as he watched her run to the helicopter that waited in the middle of the courtyard with its rotors turning slowly. She scrambled up the ladder and the engine of the big machine roared as it rose into the air and swivelled around to face the coast. It lowered its nose and bore away swiftly.

You haven't answered the question, Cross, the little voice inside him whispered. He grinned without humour and replied to himself, *No! But it will be interesting to find out if she is human.*

· · ·

Rogier carried the tray containing Mr Jetson's dinner up to the bridge. On a spotlessly white linen cloth he laid out the dishes and silver on the small table against the stern bulkhead. Then he stood by attentively as Jetson ate quickly, not seating himself to savour the meal but continuing to pace back and forth as he chewed. His eyes continually swept the darkening horizon ahead and then darted to the radar repeater. There was a tiny contact glowing on the screen. The bearing was 268 degrees. The range was showing as 3.8 nautical miles.

'Helmsman, keep a sharp eye on that vessel.'

'Very well, Mr Jetson.'

'What do you make of her, Stevens?'

The helmsman squinted at the horizon. 'Looks like one of them Arab dhows. Plenty of them in these waters, sir. They do say that they use the trade winds to cross the ocean clean as far as India. Been doing that since the time of Christ, or so they say.'

Rogier had been following the conversation without seeming to do so. He turned his head to gaze out of the window on the port wing of the bridge and he narrowed his eyes and studied the gunmetal-grey, choppy surface of the sea to the east. The setting sun was at their backs, but it still took him a few moments to pick out the tiny grey pyramid of canvas that was surely the sail of his uncle Kamal's dhow. Even from the height of the bridge it was hull down, and it seemed to be on a parallel course to their own. Then Rogier saw the distant lateen sail spill its wind as the dhow briefly hove to.

Uncle Kamal is launching his attack boats at last, he told himself. Then the sail filled once more and the dhow went on the other tack and pointed down into the south. It began to merge into the dusk until at last it disappeared from their view.

Jetson walked back to the radar screen. 'They have altered course thirty degrees into the south. I doubt they are making more than fourteen knots and at that speed and heading they are shaping to pass us twenty miles astern.' Then he glanced at

Rogier. 'Thank you, steward,' said Jetson. 'You can clear away the dinner dishes now.'

Rogier stacked the dishes and carried them down to the scullery. When he had finished washing up he called across to the chef, 'All done, Cookie. Can I knock off now?' The chef was sitting at his own small table next to his pantry with a crystal wine glass and an open green bottle placed in front of him.

'What's the big hurry, Rogier? Come and drink a glass of this excellent Château Neuf with me.'

'Not tonight, Cookie. I am beat. I can hardly keep my eyes open.' He left quickly, before the chef could prevail on him further.

In his cabin he made an apology to Allah and the Prophet. 'You know that there are desperate matters afoot. Please forgive me that I will miss the evening prayer. After I have obeyed your call to jihad I will make full recompense tomorrow evening.' Then he dressed in his casual dark clothing and went up to the aft deck. He stood at the rail and stared back along the ship's wake. He could see nothing but the black swells running away into the darkness. The chase boats were designed to sit low in the water. Hidden in the clutter of the wave crests, they would be under the *Dolphin*'s radar. In any case this was not a warship and the watch was more relaxed. As he had witnessed, all their attention was focused ahead. They did not expect any other vessel would have the speed to come up on their stern. However, Rogier knew the boats were out there. Uncle Kamal had given a contact time on the transponder for 2300 hours. That was when most of the crew would be settling down for the night, and entirely off their guard.

Rogier waited an hour and then another. At intervals he checked the luminous dial of his cheap Japanese wristwatch. The *Dolphin* was running with all her lights burning. She was lit up as brightly as a fairground. The attack boats would be able to pick her up from twenty kilometres out, but he knew they were already much closer, probably tailing the *Dolphin* by only a few hundred metres. It was minutes before 2300 and he knew Kamal would be punctual. Rogier stared down the wake and suddenly there was a tiny pinprick of light on the dark sea. It flashed three times far beyond the foam. Rogier aimed his Maglite over the stern and flashed three times in reply. Then he waited impatiently. The long boats were not a great deal faster than the *Dolphin*, so it was almost ten minutes before he picked out the first sharklike hull emerging from out of the darkness astern. As it came closer he made out the shapes of the crew crouching low under the gunwales. Of course they were all dressed in dark clothing rather than the traditional white dishdashahs, and their faces were swathed in black head cloths. They were being careful not to let their weapons show above the boat's gunwales. The other two attack boats appeared out of the gloom behind the leader.

A single figure stood up in the bow of the leading boat as it sheered out alongside the *Dolphin's* port quarter, and then edged in close alongside.

Despite the head cloth Rogier recognized his uncle Kamal's tall lean frame. He was leading the raid personally. Rogier flashed the Maglite down to confirm that he was ready to take the line on board. Kamal stooped and picked up something from the deck, then stood again holding a small Lyle gun like a rifle. He raised the butt to his shoulder, and aimed up at where Rogier stood. There was a muted pop of the discharge and a puff of white smoke as he fired. Rogier ducked as the white line snaked upwards and arced over his head. The small grappling iron on the end of the line clattered on the deck behind him and Rogier darted forward to catch the line before it was carried overboard by the drag through the water. He took three quick loops of the line around the mooring stanchion on the deck and tied it off with a bowline knot. He waved down at his uncle and immediately one of the crew, a small wiry man of ape-like strength and agility, swarmed up the rope and landed barefoot on the deck at Rogier's side. Tied around his waist was a heavier line that could support any number of climbers. The rest of the boarders came up it in quick succession. One of them handed Rogier a holstered Tokarev pistol and he strapped it around his waist under his windcheater. Five of them had already been delegated to secure the bridge. At a single word from Rogier their breech blocks snicked as each man locked and loaded the automatic assault rifle he carried. They followed Rogier on the run.

As Rogier entered the companionway that led to the upper deck he came face to face with the chef coming down the stairs. The chef stared at him and the armed men that followed him in blank incomprehension, then opened his mouth to scream. Rogier smashed the butt of the pistol into his temple and heard the bone of his skull crack. The chef dropped without a sound. Rogier stooped over his limp body and with another three blows crushed in the back of his head, making certain of the kill. Then he jumped over the corpse and raced on upwards. At the entrance to the bridge he paused to let the men that followed him regroup. Then he stepped through onto the bridge. Jetson was standing beside the instrument panel and discussing something with the helmsman. The radio operator was in his shack at the back of the bridge. He was leaning back in his swivel chair with his full attention on the paperback novel he was reading. But if he were alarmed it would take him only an instant to reach out and punch the red alarm button on the bulkhead beside him. That would begin a series of electronic measures which would automatically sound the ship's alarm bells and broadcast a distress radio call which would be picked up by every marine listening station from Perth to Cape Town, and from Mauritius to Bombay. Rogier held the Tokarev behind his back as he walked into the radio shack.

'Hi, Tim!' He smiled at the operator as he looked up from his book.

'Rogier, what the hell are you doing up here? You know this station is out of bounds.'

Rogier pointed past his shoulder. 'Why is that red light flashing, Tim?' he asked and Tim swivelled his chair quickly.

'What red light?' he demanded, and Rogier brought the pistol out from behind his back and shot Tim at the point where his top vertebrae joined his skull. The bullet blew out between his eyes in a bright burst of blood and brain matter which splattered over the radio panel. Tim toppled out of the chair and slid to the deck. Rogier turned swiftly and found that his men already had their guns on Jetson and the helmsman.

'By Christ, Moreau. You have murdered that man—' Jetson's voice shook with shock and outrage. He started towards Rogier. Rogier lifted the pistol and shot him in the centre of his chest. Jetson clasped the wound with both hands and stood swaying slightly.

'Are you mad?' he whispered, shaking his head in awed disbelief.

'You must kill the officers immediately. They are the ones who will organize any resistance,' Rogier's grandfather had ordered him, so Rogier shot Jetson twice more in the chest and then watched with professional interest as he staggered backwards into the control panel and collapsed in a huddle.

'Secure the crew. They can be useful later as bargaining chips,' his grandfather had ordered. Rogier nodded to his men and they pinioned the helmsman's arms behind his back and bound his wrists together with a heavy-duty nylon cable tie. Rogier went past him to the control panel of the yacht and moved the engine telegraphs to the 'Stop' position. The vibration of the engines through the deck under his feet died away and he felt the subtle change in her motion as the *Amorous Dolphin* lost her forward way.

'Sit down.' Rogier turned to the helmsman. 'Don't move until you are told to do so.'

'For Christ's sake, Rogier—' the helmsman pleaded, but Rogier shoved the pistol into his ribs and with his arms still pinioned the helmsman dropped hurriedly to the deck and sat in the spreading puddle of Jetson's blood. It soaked into his breeches.

Rogier left one of his men on guard and led the rest of them to the lower deck. He stopped outside the door to the captain's suite. In his capacity as a ship's steward he had his pass key to let himself into any cabin which was not doubled-locked. Rogier had brought Franklin his coffee at 6 a.m. daily, so he knew from experience that the captain never double-locked. The door slid open quietly and Rogier stepped into the sitting room of the suite. He switched on the desk light and saw that the door to the bedroom was open a crack. There was the sound of heavy snoring from the cabin beyond. He crossed the sitting room and looked through into the bedroom. Franklin lay on his back on his bunk, on top of the bedclothes. He wore only a pair of boxer shorts. His paunch was protuberant, pale and covered with grey and straggly hair. His mouth hung open and the regular snores sawed up his throat. Rogier went to him and held the muzzle of the Tokarev half an inch from his ear. He fired a single shot. Franklin gulped noisily and cut off halfway through the next exhalation, but after that he made no further sound or movement. Rogier fired a second shot into his brain. Then he reloaded the magazine of the pistol, and led his men out of the cabin and down to the main salon.

Uncle Kamal came to embrace him as soon as he entered. 'May Allah hold you to his bosom. You have done God's work this day, Adam.' He made a gesture to indicate the row of other prisoners squatting on the deck with their hands pinioned behind their backs. 'Are these all of them? Is anyone missing?'

Rogier counted the heads of the squatting crew members swiftly. 'Yes, they are all here. The captain, the first officer, the cook and the radio operator are in the cruel clutches of Iblis, the Devil, where they belong. The other missing crewman is the helmsman who is under guard on the bridge.' He pointed out Georgie Porgie, the purser. 'Keep that one here,' he ordered, 'I will deal with him later.' Then he singled out the two junior officers and the chief engineer. 'Those are officers. Take them to the stern and shoot them. Throw the bodies overboard.' He was speaking in Arabic so his victims were unaware of their fate as they were hoisted to their feet and led away.

Rogier waited for the sound of gunfire before he went on. 'That accounts for every infidel aboard except the girl. She will still be asleep in her cabin.' He smiled bleakly as he recalled the exhausted state in which he had left Cayla, utterly worn out by his copulatory expertise. 'I will go down and fetch her now. Meanwhile, Uncle Kamal, you must go up to the bridge and get the ship under way again.'

• • •

Cayla was not certain what had awakened her. She thought she must have heard something. She sat up sleepily on the rumpled bed and listened with her head on one side. The sound was not repeated but something else had changed. Sleep slowed her mind so it took another few seconds for her to realize that the ship's engines had stopped, and she was rolling ponderously to the scend of the sea.

'That's strange.' She was unconcerned. 'We cannot possibly have reached port yet.' Then she realized that her bladder was uncomfortably full. She threw her legs over the side of the bed and stood up. She braced herself to the unusual motion of the yacht and then staggered to the bathroom. She perched on the toilet and sighed with relief as she emptied her bladder. She stood up and started back towards the bed. Moonlight was pouring in through the porthole that looked out over the owner's private deck and swimming pool. She was awake now and she paused at the porthole to look out at the starry sky and the dark sea. There was no wake pouring back behind the stern and she realized that her first impression was correct. The *Dolphin* had stopped. She thought that she would telephone the bridge and find out from the officer of the watch what was happening, but at that moment a shadow passed the porthole, and she realized that there was somebody out there on the private deck. Immediately she was angry. That area was strictly out of bounds to the crew.

She and her mother used it for nude sunbathing and swimming. Now she would certainly call the bridge and have the trespasser castigated. But before she turned away another figure came into her line of sight. He was dressed in dark clothing and had a black Arab shawl wound around his head to cover his face, leaving only his eyes showing. They glinted as he turned towards her. He paused in front of the porthole and peered in. She shrank back in alarm. The man put his face against the glass and raised one hand to shade his eyes, and she realized that the moonlight was insufficient to enable him to see into the darkened cabin. His demeanour was furtive but at the same time menacing. She held her breath and stood frozen with terror. He seemed to be staring into her eyes, but after a few seconds he stepped back from the porthole. With another pang of fear she saw that he had an automatic rifle slung over his shoulder. He vanished from her view but immediately three more dark figures filed swiftly and silently past the porthole. All of them carried automatic weapons.

Now she realized that it must have been the sound of rifle fire that had woken her. She had to get help. She was terrified and shaking. She ran back into her cabin and snatched the satellite telephone from the bedside table. Frantically she dialled the bridge. There was no reply but she let it ring while she tried to think what to do next. There was only one other person she could appeal to. She dialled her mother's private line. Hazel's recorded voice instructed her to leave a message. She rang off and immediately dialled again with the same result.

'Oh, Mummy! Mummy! Please help me.' She whimpered and began to compose a text message on her mobile phone, her thumbs flying over the keys as she typed.

Terrible things happening. Strange men with guns . . .

She stopped in mid-sentence. There was somebody at the door of her cabin. Somebody was opening the lock with a pass key. She punched the send button on her mobile phone and threw the device into the drawer of her beside table and slammed it shut. In almost the same movement she sprang from the bed. She rushed to the door and threw her weight against it as it began to open.

'Go away. Get away from me, whoever you are,' she screamed hysterically. 'Leave me alone!'

'Cayla! It's me, Rogier. Let me in, Cayla. It's all right. Everything is going to be all right.'

'Rogier! Oh, thank the sweet Lord. Is it really you?' She jerked the door open and for a moment stared at him in disbelief, pale-faced and wide-eyed, and then she sobbed with relief. 'Rogier! Oh, Rogier.' She flung herself against his chest and clung to him with desperate strength. He held her with one arm and stroked her hair with the other hand.

'Don't be afraid. It's all going to be just fine.'

She shook her head wildly and blurted, 'No! You don't understand. There were men here. One of them looked into the cabin. There were others with him! Men! Horrible men. They all had guns. And I heard shooting—'

'Listen to me, my darling. It's all going to be all right. I will explain to you later. But nobody is going to hurt you. You must be brave. I want you to get dressed. We have to leave here. Dress warmly, Cayla. Wear your waterproof coat. It will be cold outside.' He reached over her shoulder and switched on the main cabin lights. 'You must hurry, Cayla.'

'Where are we going, Rogier?' She pulled back and stared into his face. Then her eyes went down to his chest. 'You are bleeding, Rogier. There is blood all over you.'

'Just do as I tell you, damn it. We haven't got much time. Get dressed.' He took her arm and led her forcibly towards her spacious walk-in cupboard. He shoved her through the door. The shelves on both sides were crammed with clothing, and more dresses and trousers were strewn carelessly over the couches and chairs and even the deck in untidy profusion. On her makeup table stood dozens of pots and jars and bottles of creams and unguents and perfumes, many of them without their tops screwed back.

'You're hurting me,' she protested. 'Let go of my arm.' He ignored the plea, picking up a pair of strawberry-pink corduroy jeans from a chair and thrusting them at her.

'Here, put those on. Hurry!' But she stood frozen and staring at the pistol in the holster at his side.

'That's a gun! Where did you get it from, Rogier? I don't understand. You're all splashed with blood, but it's not yours, is it? And you have got a gun.' She started to back away from him. 'Who are you? What are you, tell me that.'

'I do not want to hurt you, Cayla, but you must do exactly as I tell you.'

She shook her head wildly. 'No! Leave me alone. You can't do this to me.'

He caught her wrist and twisted her arm up behind her back. Then he began to lift her slowly by the wrist alone. Her cries of defiance became squeals of agony, but he kept on lifting her until she was standing on the tips of her toes. Her squeals became louder and sharper, until she capitulated.

'Stop, please stop, Rogier,' she blubbered. 'I will do anything you want, only don't hurt me any more.' He was pleased with how little it took to break her resolve. There had been others who had died still resisting him. This way he was spared so much time and effort. She dressed herself without looking at his face again, her head hanging and an occasional sob bursting past her lips. When she had finished he took her by the elbow and led her into the bedroom.

'Where is your mobile phone, Cayla?' he demanded. She shook her head sullenly, but could not prevent herself glancing at the drawer of the bedside table.

'Thank you.'

He yanked the drawer open and took out the phone. He opened the 'Sent Messages' list and read aloud the words she had sent to her mother only minutes before: '"Terrible things happening. Strange men with guns"—I wish you had not done that, Cayla. You have only made it more difficult for yourself,' he said in a mild tone, and then struck her another vicious open-handed blow across the face that snapped her head to one side and sent her sprawling to the deck. 'No more tricks like that, please. I don't enjoy punishing you, but I will if you force me to it.'

He opened the back cover of the device and took the Sim card from its slot, slipped it into the side pocket of his wind-cheater and zipped it closed. Then he tossed the phone aside. He stooped and grabbed her elbow again and hauled her to her feet. Gripping her arm he marched her out of the cabin and down the companionway to the main salon. She gasped with shock and pulled back against Rogier's grip when she saw the crew squatting on the deck with bound arms and the masked men standing over them with levelled rifles.

He shook her arm roughly. 'No more of that nonsense now!' He led her to the far end of the salon and forced her to sit. Then he beckoned one of the masked men to come to him. Cayla looked up in astonishment when he spoke to the man in Arabic.

'I do not want any harm to come to this woman. She is more valuable than your own miserable life. Do you understand what I am saying to you?'

'I understand, Lord.' The man touched his own breast in a gesture of respect.

'Why are you speaking in that language, Rogier? Who are you? Who are these people? Where is Captain Franklin? I want to speak to him,' Cayla pleaded.

'That will be difficult to arrange. The captain has two bullets in his brain.' He tapped the pistol at his side. 'That is enough questions from you. You just wait there quietly. I will return later. I think you are beginning to learn that I must have your complete obedience.'

When Rogier entered the bridge he found his uncle had the helm. Kamal was a skilled seaman who had spent his life on the oceans on everything from tiny dhows to giant oil tankers. Rogier glanced at the compass heading and saw that the *Dolphin* was on the reciprocal course to the one that Franklin had set. They were heading back the way they had come. He went to the wing of the bridge and looked back. The three attack boats were being towed along in their wake, which explained the reduced speed. Kamal was being careful not to swamp them with the *Dolphin*'s wake. Rogier went to stand beside his uncle.

'Have you made contact with the dhow yet?'

Kamal slitted his eyes against the smoke from the hand-rolled Turkish tobacco cigarette between his lips as it spiralled upwards.

'Not yet, but soon!' he said.

'The girl managed to send a message to her mother. The entire American navy and airforce will be searching for us as soon as it is light. The girl's mother is very powerful.'

'Everything will be taken care of before sunrise,' Kamal assured him, and then he smiled and pointed over the bows. On the horizon dead ahead a red distress flare burst suddenly into flame, its ruddy reflection dancing along the crests of the swells. 'There shc is,' he said with satisfaction.

The two ships came together swiftly, and when they were only a few hundred metres apart Kamal throttled back and laid the *Dolphin* across the wind and the sea, forming a breakwater for the dhow. The ancient vessel came alongside in the *Dolphin*'s lee and mooring ropes were thrown down to the men on the deck. Once she was moored securely the prisoners were transferred into her, and hustled down into the forward hold. Only Cayla was dragged struggling and weeping to Kamal's quarters in the dhow's deckhouse and locked in with a guard at the door.

Working swiftly a party of Arab seamen knocked open the hatch on the dhow's stern hold. From the hold they winched up to the *Dolphin*'s deck five cargo pallets. Once they were on board the yacht the heavy canvas covers were pulled back to reveal a stack of a dozen large packages on each pallet. These were wrapped in bright yellow plastic sheeting and painted with black Chinese characters. It took three men to manhandle each crate below decks. The handlers worked gingerly, treating them with elaborate respect. The contents of each crate were thirty kilograms of Semtex H plastic explosive.

'Hurry it up there!' Rogier bellowed at them. 'The detonators have not been primed. It's quite safe to handle.' He and Kamal followed the working party below deck, down to the *Dolphin*'s bilges, and supervised the yellow crates being packed along the length of the keel under the engine room. Rogier left Kamal to set the charges and arm the delay device, and went up to the purser's office. Georgie Porgie was sitting on the deck with the guard standing over him.

'Untie him!' Rogier ordered the guard, who obediently forced the point of the bayonet on his rifle between Georgie's wrists and cut away the nylon cable tie. The blade nicked his chubby arm.

'The brute has cut me,' Georgie whimpered. 'Look! I am bleeding!'

'Open the safe!' Rogier ignored his complaints, and Georgie Porgie began to protest more vehemently. Rogier drew the pistol from its holster, and shot him in the leg. The bullet shattered his knee cap. The purser squealed shrilly. 'Open the safe,' Rogier repeated, and pointed the Tokarev at his other leg.

'Don't shoot me again,' Georgie whined and dragged himself to the steel safe set into the bulkhead behind the desk. His wounded leg dragged behind him, leaving a trail of wet blood across the planking. Moaning with the pain, Georgie fiddled with the combination lock, spinning the dial back and forth. There was a click and he turned the locking handle. The safe door swung open.

'Thank you!' said Rogier and shot him in the head. Georgie Porgie was knocked forward onto his face and his good leg drummed spasmodically on the deck. At Rogier's nod the guard grabbed the leg before it stopped kicking and dragged Georgie Porgie's corpse aside. Rogier knelt in front of the open safe and sifted swiftly through the contents.

He discarded the ship's working documents, amongst them her bills of lading and Grand Cayman registration certificate. But he selected the thick wad of the crew's passports. His grandfather would have good use for the genuine green US and maroon EU booklets. Under the desk there was a canvas briefcase which he had noted every time he had previously been in the purser's office. Rogier stuffed the passports into this. There were also about fifty thousand US dollars in bills of various denominations; without counting them he placed them with the passports. On the steel shelf below the cash were five blue jewellery boxes. The lid of the first one he picked up was lettered in gold: 'Graff. London'. He snapped open the lid. The diamonds that made up the heavy necklace nestling on the white satin lining were as big as quail's eggs and bright as sunlight on a mountain stream. Rogier knew they had once belonged to the American heiress to the Woolworths fortune. These were what had really interested him.

'Thank you, Mrs Hazel Bannock,' he said with a smile. 'However, I doubt that the Flowers of Islam will see fit to send you a formal receipt.' He knew what the other jewellery boxes contained, so he did not waste time opening them but dropped them all into the briefcase. He nodded to the Arab guard and they went up the companionway to the main deck at a run. His uncle Kamal was waiting for him by the rail. Rogier handed him the briefcase. 'Take good care of this, my honoured uncle.'

'Where are you going?' Kamal demanded as he turned back to the companionway.

'There is one more thing I have to do before we leave.'

'You have very little time. The delay on the fuses has only an hour and forty-five minutes to run,' Kamal warned him.

'Time enough,' Rogier replied. He leaned over the rail and whistled shrilly. Three of his men whom he had delegated to the duty looked up at him. Each of them carried a specially constructed packing case which Rogier had asked his grandfather to send to him. He beckoned to the men and they came up the side of the *Dolphin* with the cases. Rogier led them down to Cayla's deserted suite. He moved quickly into the main cabin and stood in front of the large Gauguin oil painting. As always he found the bright colours pleasing but the depiction of a naked female body offended his pious sensibilities. Nonetheless he lifted the painting down from its hooks and laid it face down on the bed. He had brought a folding knife with him expressly for this purpose and he used the blade to lever loose the ornate gold-leaf frame. He discarded the frame and left the painting lying face upwards on the bed. He hurried through into the owner's private dining room, took Monet's water lilies painting down from the facing bulkhead, and laid it on the dining table to remove the frame. As he worked he mulled over the fact that the previous year a similar picture had sold at auction for £98.5 million sterling. Then he went to Van Gogh's *The River at Arles* that hung on the side bulkhead. He took it down and then laid it beside the Monet. He prised off the frame, and wasted a few moments admiring these two marvellous works. His grandfather was no connoisseur of the arts, but when Rogier told him the value of these three pieces he would be flabbergasted and delighted by this unexpected addition to his war chest. All this time the men with the packing cases had been watching him with expressions of complete mystification.

Each packing case had been made to the exact size of a particular painting. Rogier had downloaded the dimensions from an arts catalogue on the internet. He packed the Gauguin into its case, and with relief found that his grandfather's carpenters had done a good job, for it fitted precisely. The other two paintings were equally snug in their own containers. He closed all three and ordered his men to take them up to the main deck. By the time Rogier got back up there Kamal was acutely agitated.

'What took you so long, Adam? The timer on the detonator cannot be cancelled or reset. We must hurry!' They swung down into the dhow and as Kamal gave the order to cast off, Rogier supervised the stowage of the three cases in the forward hold. Kamal put the dhow on an easterly heading and bore away at her best speed. Rogier stood with his uncle beside the massive wooden tiller and stared back over the stern.

'It is a great pity that we could not have taken the vessel as well as the girl. Its value is enormous,' Rogier mused.

'What is the value of fifty years in an American prison?' Kamal asked. 'That's all the payment you would get if you were stupid enough to try to keep it.' He looked at his wristwatch. 'Another seven minutes,' he said. When it came it was a single tremendous blast, the night sky lit as though by the sunrise. Seconds later the shock wave from the explosion swept over the dhow, flapping the canvas of her sail and pressing in against Rogier's eardrums for a painful instant. Then the glow faded away and the darkness descended once again.

'Let the infidel try to find her now,' Kamal said with satisfaction.

'How many days' sailing to Ras el Mandeb?' Rogier asked. 'Six, is it?'

'Longer,' said Kamal. 'We cannot set a direct course. We must get well inshore of the Kenyan coast, and merge with the other small shipping.'

• • •

Deep snow on the Farnborough runway in England had delayed her for thirty-six hours, so it had taken Hazel almost four days to return from Abu Zara to the States, but even then she had not headed for her principal home in Houston. She had come directly to Washington DC.

Henry Bannock had always maintained a large, old-fashioned apartment on East Capitol Street overlooking Lincoln Park. It was not the most salubrious section of the city but Henry had liked to be close to the seat of power whenever the Senate was in session. For the same reason Hazel had kept the apartment after his death, but she had renovated it entirely. It was an ideal position from which she could launch an assault on the Administration. Ever since her arrival she had bullied and pestered Senator Reynolds from Texas and the staff at the White House. She had already been granted a short meeting with the President, who had promised her that he would take a personal interest in the search for the *Dolphin* and her daughter. Bannock Oil had been a major contributor to his campaign funds. Despite her left-wing leanings Hazel always believed in two-way bets, so she made large contributions to both Republicans and Democrats for just such an eventuality, and now Hazel was calling in all her markers.

An Airforce Colonel Peter Roberts from the Presidential staff was unofficially assigned to be her liaison officer during the crisis, and even Hazel had to admit that he had performed sterling service in difficult circumstances.

Already a US military observation satellite had been diverted to make two reconnaissances, overflying the area of the *Dolphin*'s last contact at heights of 47.5 kilometres and 39.8 kilometres at orbital velocities of almost 7,000 mph. Unfortunately, it had not been able to record a significant contact. There were three very large container ships and numerous much smaller vessels in the area, but nothing that could possibly be the *Dolphin*.

In addition the USS *Manila Bay*, a guided missile destroyer, had been diverted southwards by Presidential orders from its patrol station in the Gulf of Aden off the Yemeni coast. However, it had over 1,200 miles to sail and it had not yet reached the area.

Colonel Roberts had urgently contacted all the American embassies in the Middle East and African mainland. Using the President's authorization, he had initiated delicate enquiries with all the governments, both friendly and antagonistic. None had offered any encouragement. Apart from Cayla's truncated text message there had been no other trace of her or the *Dolphin*.

The days were wasting away and Hazel Bannock was nearing her wits' end. The telephone on her desk in the East Capitol Street apartment rang. She had been hovering over it and she pounced on it before it could ring a second time.

'Bannock,' she said. 'Who is this?'

'Peter Roberts, Mrs Bannock.' She did not let him continue, but cut in brusquely,

'Good morning, Colonel. Do you have any news for me?'

'Yes, I have some news.' The tone of his voice made her take a sharp breath. It was not encouraging.

'Have they found the *Dolphin*?' she demanded, but he avoided the question.

'I would prefer not to talk on this line. I would like to come to see you immediately, Mrs Bannock.'

'How long will it take you to get here?' she demanded.

'The traffic is terrible this morning, but I should be with you in twenty minutes or less.' She hung up and then phoned the concierge in the lobby.

'I am expecting Colonel Roberts to call. You know him. He has been here often over the last few days. Send him right up when he comes.' It took Roberts twenty-three minutes, and she opened the door on his first ring.

'Come in, Colonel.' She was studying his face, trying to read what he had in store for her before he spoke. He gave his coat to the Mexican maid and followed Hazel through into the sitting room, where she rounded on him, no longer able to contain herself.

'What do you have for me?'

'You know that the US Navy sent a destroyer to the last known position of the *Dolphin*. It reached there a few hours ago.'

She caught his sleeve. 'Please don't keep me in suspense, Colonel. What have they found?' He made an embarrassed gesture of running his hands over his thick iron-grey hair.

'Only an area of floating wreckage.'

She stared at him. Her expression was blank.

'So?' she said at last. 'What does that tell us? How do we know this has anything to do with my yacht, or my daughter?'

'There was a lifejacket in the wreckage. It was from your yacht. The name was painted on the jacket.'

'That proves nothing,' she said and then saw his expression of pity.

'The *Manila Bay* has been ordered to return to its patrol station,' he said.

'No!' she exclaimed, her voice rising sharply. 'No! I won't believe it. They are not calling off the search.'

'Mrs Bannock, they've searched the area by ship, plane and satellite. The *Dolphin* is a large vessel. It could not possibly have been overlooked, if it was on the surface.'

'You think she's been sunk,' she demanded, 'and that my daughter has gone with her? My Cayla dead? Is that what you're saying? Then how do you explain Cayla's text message to me that there were strange men on the ship?'

'With all due respect, Mrs Bannock, you're the only one who has seen this message. And we have the evidence of the floating wreckage,' he said gently. 'I think we will now have to make an announcement to the press that the *Dolphin* has disappeared—'

'No!' she cut him off. 'That would be an acceptance of the fact that Cayla is dead.' She went to the window and looked down over the park, struggling to regain her composure. Then she turned back to him. 'My daughter is still alive,' she said firmly. 'I know this with a mother's instinct. My baby is alive!'

'We all hope that is the case, but with every day that passes that hope fades a little.'

'I am not giving up!' she shouted at him. 'Nor should they.'

'No, of course not. However, we have to think of other possibilities.'

'Such as what?' She was very angry and very frightened.

'That part of the Indian Ocean is an area of intense seismic activity on the seabed. A number of tsunami have been recorded recently—'

She cut him off again. 'Tidal wave. You think the *Dolphin* was sunk by a tidal wave? You think my daughter has been drowned?'

'Believe me, Mrs Bannock, we all sympathize with you—'

She jerked her arm away. 'I don't want your bloody sympathy. I want you to find my daughter.'

• • •

Hazel sat alone in her beautiful bedroom in her beautiful apartment looking out over the most powerful city on the globe, and she was truly alone as she had never been in her life before. The desolation swept over her in regular waves. Every time it took her longer to rise to the surface again. She was being drowned by her loneliness. Even the most powerful man in the world was unable to help her. There was nobody. She paused at the thought.

Perhaps there is one last resort. She sensed a tiny spark of hope in the suffocating darkness. She remembered his voice, the last thing he had said to her: 'If you need me, one word will be enough.' Her pride rose up her throat and almost choked her. She had called him an arrogant bastard, and of course that was what he was. A tough, callous, overbearing bastard.

Exactly the kind of man I need now, she told herself. She forced back her pride and reached for the telephone. She rang Agatha in Houston.

'Have we heard anything, Mrs Bannock?' Agatha loved Cayla almost as much as she did.

'Yes, they have found traces of the *Dolphin*.'

'And Cayla, have we any news of Cayla?'

'Not yet, but soon,' she promised, and then went on quickly to forestall the next question. 'Do we have an emergency number for Hector Cross at Cross Bow Security?'

'One moment, Mrs Bannock,' Agatha said and came back to her almost at once. 'It's his satphone. Twenty-four-hour contact—' She reeled off the number, then went on, 'We have to be brave, Mrs Bannock. We have to be strong for Cayla's sake.'

'I love you, Agatha,' Hazel said and left her gasping with shock and delight. Nobody had said that to Agatha Reynolds in a very long time.

Hazel knew it was well after midnight in Abu Zara, but Hector answered the call on the third ring and his tone was sharp as a rapier.

'Hector Cross.'

'I need you badly, Cross,' she said. 'Just as you said I would.'

'Tell me what it is,' Hector demanded.

'My yacht has disappeared at sea with my daughter on board. But she sent me a text to say there were men with guns on board the yacht. The people here in Washington seem to be ignoring this. Unfortunately I was so distressed that I deleted the message from my phone by mistake, so I can't prove it to them. Perhaps they think I am fantasizing. That it is just my wishful thinking.' She tried to keep her voice from wavering. 'They have found wreckage. That's what they are fixed on. They are trying to tell me that she is dead.'

I knew it was bad, Hector thought, *but not as bad as this*. He kept his tone totally non-committal.

'Where?' he asked and she repeated the position that Roberts had given her. Should she be angry at his lack of sympathy? Shouldn't he at least have acknowledged her loss with a kind word? No, he was a tough, callous, overbearing bastard, she reminded herself.

'When?' he asked and she told him. He was silent, and she waited until she could bear it no more.

'Hello. Are you still there?'

'I'm thinking,' he said.

'The brass here believe the *Dolphin* was sunk by a tidal wave.' She could not remain silent.

'Bullshit!' he drawled and her heart danced with joy at the coarse expression. That was exactly what she wanted to hear. It was just what Henry Bannock would have said.

'Why do you think that?' she asked, longing for more reassurance.

'No tidal waves in deep water. Only when it hits the land does the tsunami rear up.' He went quiet again for nearly a minute. Then he asked, 'No ransom demand yet?'

'No. Nothing. They want to send out an appeal to anybody who knows—' she started, but he cut her off.

'For God's sake, we can't let them do that.' She rejoiced to hear him say 'we'. He was firmly on her team now. He went silent again, and she bore it with difficulty.

'Okay. I'm starting to pick up a faint scent.'

'Tell me!' She felt hope surge in her chest, but he answered obliquely.

'How long will it take you to get back to the Zara No. 8?'

'Forty hours max.'

'This is where it's all going to happen. Come!' he ordered. 'I want you here when it breaks cover.'

'Who? What will break cover?' she demanded.

'The Beast,' he said.

• • •

Thirty-five hours later he was waiting at Sidi el Razig airport when the jet touched down. 'You made good time,' he said as he met her at the foot of the steps of the G5 Gulfstream.

'We only stopped over for forty minutes at Farnborough to refuel and we had a fifty-knot following wind across most of Europe and the Med.' They shook hands. 'Have you made any progress?' The first thing she noticed was that he had recently shaved. The second thing she noticed was that in an ugly sort of way it made him look quite attractive. Immediately she was struck by guilt that she should notice his looks at a time like this. It was a betrayal of her lovely daughter.

Down, Hazel girl! He's not your style at all, she told herself sternly. *He is just a service man and in slightly different circumstances could be cleaning your swimming pool.*

'Come!' He took her arm above the elbow, and she was surprised that she did not pull away. 'I have moved our base of operations from Number Eight to the terminal here. Much closer to the epicentre.' When they reached the administration building he told her, 'I have had them prepare a room for you. It's pretty utilitarian but at least it has air conditioning and its own bathroom. I have brought down all the luggage that you left at Number Eight.' He led her to the room from which the flow of oil through the pipelines was controlled. It was large, well equipped with electronics. The station manager's office was raised above the main floor and was sealed off by a wall of sound-proofed glass. He led her to this private and secure area. At a word the overseer stood up, excused himself and left. Hector indicated the chair he had vacated and Hazel slumped down on it. She was on the edge of exhaustion. Hector called the mess and almost immediately a steward carried through a tray covered by a fine muslin cloth. He placed it on the desk in front of her, and suddenly she realized that she had eaten almost nothing since leaving Washington.

'I brought the chef down from Number Eight,' Hector said as he dismissed the steward. On the Wedgwood platter was laid out a cold collation of fillets of red Gulf snapper and salads.

'I know that you don't take wine before sunset,' he said as he screwed the top off a bottle of San Pellegrino, and poured the sparkling water into her glass. The fish was delicious. She tried not to gobble it down in front of him, but he had tactfully turned his attention to the computer screen. He let her finish and then swivelled his chair to face her.

'Very well. This will be our situation room for the duration of this operation. We will try not to discuss any vital information outside of it. Now, tell me everything you know!' he ordered her. 'Try not to leave out any detail, no matter how insignificant you think it may be.' She spoke quietly but lucidly. By the end of the recitation her hands were shaking and she was deathly pale.

'Pace yourself, Mrs Bannock. This might take a long time. Eat and rest to conserve your strength.' He saw her impatience and suppressed his smile. 'Okay. No more lectures from me. You're a big girl now.'

'I have told you all I know. What have you got to tell me?'

'Nothing concrete yet, but now with what I have heard from you I have a much better idea of what we're up against.' He turned to the map projection on the large screen on the wall opposite their desks. From the keyboard of his computer he was able to move the electronic pointer around the map.

'Let's look at the location. Is it entirely blind chance that the *Dolphin* disappeared on the front doorsteps of all the most important Al-Qaeda strongholds west of Pakistan?' Hector moved the marker from the northern end of the Indian Ocean to the eastern coast of the Gulf of Aden.

'Yemen! The number-one terror capital of the world.' Then he moved the marker a short distance across the Strait of Bab el Mandeb to the African mainland. 'The cosy neighbours of Yemen just across the Red Sea or the Gulf of Aden are Puntland in Somalia, Eritrea and Ethiopia. Here we have Satan's Circle,' he said. 'A seething nest of fanatical Islamic killers.' He moved the marker down the map to a position a relatively short distance to the south. 'Here is where your *Dolphin* was, sailing right into their jaws.' He stood up from his desk, crossed to the window and stood with his hands clasped behind his back, staring across the blue waters of the Gulf. Then he wheeled around and thrust out his jaw at her. 'And they knew she was coming.'

'How did they know that?' she asked sharply.

'Because you sail exactly the same route every year at the same time, don't you?' She inclined her head to acknowledge that the point was well taken.

'But how did you know that?'

'Mrs Bannock, you are my boss. I make it my business to know as much as I can about you. I even know what school you went to.'

'Do you just!' she challenged him.

'Herschel Girls High in Cape Town.' He didn't wait for her confirmation but went on, 'Every year the *Dolphin* stops over in Cape Town to enable you to visit your mother who lives on your wine estate there. I know that and they know that.'

'Very obvious of me.' She looked abashed.

'They probably put somebody on board the *Dolphin* in the Cape.' She arched one perfectly groomed eyebrow at him. Those bloody marvellous eyes, he thought, how I hate them. He looked up at the map on the wall. 'How do I know that?' He asked the question for her.

'Well?' she demanded. 'How do you?'

'Because of what happened after the yacht left Cape Town. They were in an ambush, but the *Amorous Dolphin* is a fast boat and the ocean is a big place. Somebody was vectoring them in. But this is guesswork. Can we check if the ship took any crew on board in the Cape?' She nodded.

'That should be fairly simple,' she said. 'The *Dolphin* is owned by a private company in Basle, Switzerland. All the administration is done from there.'

'Including all the hiring and firing?'

'Including that, yes.' Hector glanced at the clock on the wall, which showed the time in all the main capitals around the globe.

'It's 1400 hours in Zurich. Can you phone your man there?'

She nodded and dialled the number from memory. 'Please put me through to Herr Ludwig Grubber. This is Mrs Hazel Bannock calling.' Hector was mildly amused by the alacrity with which Ludwig came on the line. 'Mr Grubber? Can you please tell me if the *Dolphin* took on any crew in Cape Town? Yes, I'll hold.' She did not have to hold too long before he came back on the line. 'Yes, you can scan it and send it to my usual email address. Thank you, Mr Grubber. Please give my warmest regards to your father.' She hung up, and looked across at Hector. 'The *Dolphin* took on a temporary third steward in Cape Town.'

'Of course, he had excellent references, or he would never have been allowed aboard?' Hector was stating a fact, and she nodded reluctantly and then gathered her courage.

'Apparently he was a friend of my daughter's. She vouched for him.'

'But she never told you about this before you left Cape Town to come here?' She shook her head and looked away. Hector hated to watch her come to terms with the possibility that her beloved daughter might be less than a vestal virgin.

He's such an awful know-it-all, she thought angrily, *and he is insinuating things about Cayla.* Hazel didn't want to look at him just yet. She remembered what Henry had said of him the only time they had discussed him. 'Young Heck is a heck of a guy. He flies by the seat of his pants and shoots out of hand but more often than not he hits the bull slap bang on the nose.'

'What is the friend's name?' Hector's probing was gentle. He knew she was seething. She glanced at the notepad.

'Rogier Marcel Moreau.'

'Sounds like a nice young Frenchman. Do we have a copy of his passport?'

'Basle is scanning it to me.' Fifteen minutes later the scan came through on Hazel's laptop. Hector read it off.

'Date of birth 3 October 1973. His place of birth is Réunion Island in the Indian Ocean. Pretty close to home?' He took the phone from its cradle.

'Who are you calling?'

'Just a friend in Paris. He is a Chief Inspector in French Interpol.' He began to speak in rapid-fire French that Hazel could not follow very well. He was obviously being transferred up the chain of command. At last he seemed to reach his final destination for there were many cries of '*Allons, mon brave!*' and '*Courage!*' and '*Formidable!*' before he hung up and looked across at Hazel. 'My bosom buddy, Pierre Jacques, has promised a copy of Rogier's birth certificate within the hour. Sometimes I just love computers and jovial French coppers, don't you?' For the first time he smiled at her. It was strange how the shape of his face changed and softened when he did so.

'Shall we continue our little fantasy?' he suggested. 'Now they have their man on board the *Dolphin*, and he has some kind of electronic transmitter, probably a transponder. Through him they will know the exact position of the yacht. Their ambush boat starts to move into position, but then panic! Mrs Bannock, who is their target, leaves the ship at Cape Town. This is totally unexpected. Then suddenly the panic is over. Miss Cayla Bannock remains on board, and she and Rogier are good friends. She trusts him. This is almost as good as having her mother in their clutches. The plan can go ahead.' Hazel hugged herself and shivered violently.

'This is terrible.'

'It gets better. There is hope,' he promised her. 'Now everything goes exactly as planned. The *Dolphin* sails into the trap. Rogier is able to assist the boarding and get the pirates into the fast-moving ship. Smart lad, our Rogier. The crew is taken into custody. There is only one small bleep on the screen. Cayla Bannock is a bright brave girl. She manages even in these terrifying moments of her capture to get off a text message to her mother.' Hector paused and glanced at his computer screen. 'Excuse me. It seems I have mail.' He tapped the keyboard opening the attachments to the message and then he swore bitterly, but immediately excused himself.

'Go ahead. I am becoming accustomed to it,' she said. 'What have you got?'

'Our junior ship's steward was born Adam Abdul Tippoo Tip on Réunion. In 2008 Adam changed his name to Rogier Marcel Moreau by deed poll in Auvergne in the south of France.' He was silent for a moment as he studied the copy of the birth certificate.

Hazel burst out impatiently, 'Does that name mean anything to you?'

He shook his head. 'Nothing at all,' he admitted. 'However, the good news is that your daughter is almost certainly alive.'

'Where is she then?' Hazel pleaded.

'Even money that Cayla is a captive on the Arab ambush vessel. She is priceless goods. They would never harm her.'

'And the *Dolphin*?' She shook her head in bewilderment.

'Oh, they scuttled her. She was too obvious a target. The US airforce would have picked her up within a few hours of her being reported missing. My guess is they blew the bottom out of her. She is probably lying in a few thousand feet of water at the bottom of the Mascarene Basin off Madagascar. I feel certain you have insurance cover on her, with a piracy clause.'

'The money is not important,' she said.

'In my limited experience the money is always important. How much is she insured for?'

'One hundred and fifty-two million euros. God, Cross, don't you have any concern for other people's feelings?'

'Very little,' he admitted. 'Only one thing concerns me at the moment, and that is finding and rescuing your daughter. But in the meantime the sun is setting.' He stood up and stretched. 'I would like to make you a drink. Both our nerves are on edge but we don't need to fight each other. There are lots of other lovely people out there for us to fight. Vodka and fresh lime juice with ice, is it not?'

'Yes, and you were right. I did attend Herschel Girls High.' He knew it was a peace offering. He poured the clear spirit over the crackling ice in the long glass, then filled it with juice. She thanked him with a smile. When he had poured Scotch into his own glass they saluted each other. After they had both sipped and murmured approval, she sat back and studied his face.

'My husband told me once that you fly by the seat of your pants. Are you right about this one, Cross?' she asked him. He touched the side of his nose.

'It smells good to me. It's better than a hunch. It's a reasoned scenario that all hangs together.'

'Then where is my daughter? If this is a hostage taking, why haven't they come through with a ransom demand? It's been almost ten days since the *Dolphin* disappeared.'

'They are giving themselves time to get well clear. Their vessel is probably a slow and nondescript sailing dhow. They want to be in their own territorial waters where they are safe from the warships of the civilized Western powers before they break cover. Also they want you to soften up and start breaking down with the suspense and the uncertainty.'

'How much longer?'

'Say they can make fourteen knots, and they are heading for Yemen or Puntland in Somalia, then they will almost have reached their destination by now,' he said. 'Not more than two or three days more.'

'You have mentioned Puntland before. I've never heard of it until now.'

'It's in north-eastern Somalia and comprises the Great Horn of Africa. It is an inhospitable semi-desert, rugged and arid, three times larger than New Mexico. It is virtually cut off from the rest of Africa by the high mountain range on the west side of the Great Rift Valley. These mountains also block the prevailing westerly winds which drop all their rain on the slopes. The vegetation of Puntland is coarse acacia, thorny shrub bush and sparse rank grass. However, the country is very strategically positioned on the coast of the Gulf of Aden guarding the approaches to the Red Sea. Puntland broke away from the rest of Somalia at the end of the civil war and declared itself autonomous. It named itself after the Land of Punt in ancient Egyptian historical lore. It is believed to be the country to which Queen Hatshepsut sent her famous expedition in 1550 BC. Now it is governed by a loose-knit gang of independent warlords who answer to nobody and keep their own particular brand of law and justice.'

He changed the subject with disconcerting suddenness. 'Will you take your dinner in your room where you will be able to mope in private? Not recommended. Or will you dine with me in the mess? Chef has some superb Japanese Wagyu rib eye beef. Food, wine and company most highly recommended on page one hundred of the latest edition of the Michelin guide.' She had sat alone all these last dreadful nights, and at least he was not boring. Infuriating? Yes definitely, but not boring. She smiled and capitulated.

During the meal he kept the conversation away from the subject of her missing daughter and yacht, instead he spoke about the political structure of Abu Zara and the operations of Bannock Oil in the Emirate, then he moved on to the subjects of horses and horse racing which he knew interested her.

'My father kept a few horses in training on the ranch,' he explained when she looked askance at his obvious knowledge of the subject. 'As a skinny kid I was his head groom and jockey. Once a month we attended the race meetings in Nairobi. It was all knock-about and amateur stuff but we took it extremely seriously.'

He was informed and articulate, with a wry and quirky sense of humour which diverted her just a trifle from her worry over Cayla. She relaxed and let herself enjoy listening to him. She had drunk only an inch or so out of the wine glass but he lifted the bottle to top it up. The wine was a lovely ten-year-old Romanée-Conti. It amused her that he had researched her tastes so accurately. It seemed a shame to refuse him so she pushed her glass towards him, but at that moment one of his men hurried into the mess and stooped to whisper urgently in Hector's ear. Hector slammed down the bottle, splashing red wine on the table cloth. He seized her arm and hauled her to her feet.

'Come on!' he almost shouted. He ran with her into the long passageway that led to the situation room.

'What is it?' she gasped. 'What's happening?'

'The Beast has broken cover!' he said and pulled her through the doorway. Four of his men were gathered in front of one of the TV screens. The man who had come to summon him was there. Hector had introduced him to her as Uthmann, one of his senior operatives. He was an Arab and a Muslim but Hector trusted him implicitly.

'One of the good guys,' he'd said of him.

'What channel is it on, Uthmann?' Hector demanded now.

'Al Jazeera Arabic TV broadcasting from Doha. They listed it in the headlines at the beginning of their world news. I just caught the tail end of it, but they will repeat it at the end of the bulletin.'

'Get a chair for Mrs Bannock,' Hector ordered. They sat tense and silent through coverage of the visit of the King of Jordan to Iran, a suicide bombing in Baghdad and other items of Middle Eastern importance. Then suddenly an image of a sleek white oceangoing yacht appeared on the screen and the TV news presenter spoke in Arabic. Hector simultaneously translated his words for Hazel.

'A group of fighters calling themselves the Flowers of Islam has claimed responsibility for the capture of a private yacht in the western Indian Ocean. The yacht named *Amorous Dolphin* is a 125-metre luxury pleasure vessel registered in the Cayman Islands but belonging to Mrs Hazel Bannock, president of Bannock Oil Corporation in Houston, Texas. Mrs Bannock is reputedly one of the richest women in the world.'

On the screen appeared the image of Hazel, splendid in a full-length ball gown with the legendary diamond necklace, which had once belonged to Barbara Hutton, at her throat. She was dancing with John McEnroe, a fellow tennis champion, at a Democratic Party fundraiser ball in Los Angeles. The presenter went on speaking, with Hector translating.

'According to the spokesman for the fighters the yacht has been scuttled at sea as a reprisal for the recent atrocities committed by American troops in Iraq. The passengers and crew have been taken into protective custody. Mrs Bannock was not on board the yacht at the time of its capture. Her daughter, Miss Cayla Bannock, was the only passenger. She is among those in custody.'

There was a photograph of Cayla in a wet swimsuit emerging from a swimming pool. Laughing, she was the popular image of a young, privileged and spoiled Western millionairess. The scanty costume she wore must certainly raise the ire and indignation of devout Muslims around the world.

'The fighters will demand an apology from the American government for its terrorist actions in Iraq, together with appropriate financial recompense for the release of the crew and of Cayla Bannock.'

The Arabic presenter switched to coverage of a football match in Cairo. Uthmann turned off the TV set.

Hazel's face was alight with joy. 'Oh God! She is alive. My baby is alive. You were right, Cross. She is alive.' Although Uthmann and the other three Cross Bow operatives were not looking in their direction they were all in attitudes of listening. Hector frowned her to silence and stood up.

'Come with me,' he said quietly and led her out of the building. The sun had set an hour ago. Neither of them spoke until they reached the beach on which a low surf was slapping lazily. There was an ancient wooden piling half-buried in the sand just above the high tide line. They sat on it side by side. Out in the Gulf two enormous tankers were moored at the offshore terminal taking on their cargoes of oil, their floodlights reflected off the surface of the water. By this light Hazel and Hector were able to see each other's faces quite clearly.

'I brought you out here so that we might talk without being overheard,' he explained, and she looked surprised.

'They are all your men. Don't you trust them?'

'Those four are probably the only people on this earth I do trust. However, no point in placing unnecessary strain on their loyalty. They don't have to know what you and I are discussing.'

She nodded. 'I understand.'

'I wonder if you really do. The people we will be dealing with from now onwards are the most ruthless and devious individuals in existence. They are sucking you into a world of smoke and mirrors, of subterfuge and lies. They call themselves the Flowers of Islam.' He leaned forward and with his finger drew a design in the sand between his feet. It was the sickle moon of Islam. 'A more appropriate name might be the Hemlock of Hell.' He straightened again and scuffed out the drawing under the heel of his boot. 'All right, enough of that. So let's try to map the way ahead.'

'I think I must contact my friends at the White House. Now we know where Cayla is they will be able to secure the terms of her release, either by negotiation or by force,' Hazel suggested.

'Wrong on the first count. We don't know where Cayla is. We know vaguely who has taken her, but we don't know where they are holding her. And wrong on the second count. Your friends won't do either of those things you mention,' he said. 'Firstly their declared policy is never to negotiate with terrorists. When it comes down to the use of force they have burned their fingers too often already. Remember the seizure of the US Embassy in Tehran, and *Black Hawk Down*, the film about the helicopter attack on the terror base in Mogadishu. They have learned bitter lessons. They won't negotiate and they cannot and will not use force. You can thank God for that. If the marines go storming in it will be the end of Cayla Bannock.'

'But they must do something. I am an American citizen; the President himself has promised to help me.' Despite herself she let out a smothered sob. He looked away from her at the tankers. Her distress was a private thing. He gave her time to steady herself.

'So what do we do?' she asked at last.

'You do what they expect you to do. You try to put pressure on your friends in Washington just as you suggested a moment ago. We string the Beast along. We pretend to negotiate with him, but at the same time you must understand the utter futility of doing so.'

She blinked and shook her head. 'I don't understand.'

'There is no offer or promise that you can make that will persuade them to meekly hand Cayla back to you. Give them a dollar and they will demand ten more. Agree to their terms and they will come up with a whole new set of demands.'

'Then what are we doing it for? Aren't we just wasting our time?'

'No, Mrs Bannock, we are buying time, not wasting it. Time to find out where they are holding Cayla.'

'Can you do that?'

'I hope so. Indeed, I think so.'

'If you succeed, then what? What happens when you do find out where she is?'

'I will go in and fetch her out.' His lips formed a thin smile which his eyes refuted.

'A moment ago you said—'

'I know what I said. But there is a difference between me and the Marine Corps. The marines would storm in like ten thousand butchers wielding meat axes. I will slip in like a heart surgeon with a scalpel.'

'Can you do it?' she demanded and he shrugged.

'It's one of the things I do. One of the things you pay me for. But as of now we can only wait for the ransom demand. That will give me something to work with.'

'How much time do we need to buy?' she asked and he shrugged.

'A month, six months, a year. As long as it takes.'

'A year! Are you out of your mind? I can't do it. Every day that goes by I die a hundred deaths. If it is that bad for me, what must it be like for my baby? No, I just cannot do it.'

'That outburst is not at all your style, Mrs Bannock. You can do it, and if you really love your daughter you will do it.'

• • •

When Kamal's dhow was still fifty miles offshore he broadcast a brief message on the shortwave radio.

'The fish are running on the ten-mile reef.' It was acknowledged at once. They had been listening out for him. Within the hour a thirty-five-foot fast motor launch left its moorings in the bay and raced out to meet the dhow. As the two vessels came together both crews ululated and waved their weapons on high.

'*Allahu Akbar!* God is great!' they shrieked, dancing on the narrow decks.

As the gap between the vessels narrowed they leaped across it and embraced wildly, stamping their bare feet on the deck. Cayla crouched in a corner of the deckhouse on the pile of rags which was her bed, listening in terror to the uproar. For eleven days she had not been allowed to bathe or change her clothes.

She had been fed on a single bowl of rice and fiery chilli fish stew a day, and the water she had been given was brackish and was redolent of the sewer. She had suffered gut-wrenching diarrhoea and vomiting, a combination of food poisoning and sea sickness. Her latrine was the filthy bucket which stood beside her on the deck. The only time she had been allowed out on the main deck was to empty its contents over the ship's side. Now the door of the deckhouse was flung open and Kamal was outlined against the brilliant sunlight behind him.

'Get up! Come!' he ordered in heavily accented English. Cayla had no resistance left in her. She tried to stand up but she was very weak and she swayed on her feet and clutched at the bulkhead beside her for support. He grabbed her arm and led her through the door and onto the open deck. She tried to shield her eyes from the fierce sunlight with her free hand, but Kamal dashed it away.

'Let them see your ugly white face!' He laughed at her. She was pale as a corpse and her eyes were sunken into their deep dark sockets. Her hair was matted with sweat, and her clothing was soiled and stinking with vomit and faeces. The crew of the launch pressed closely about her, shouting religious and political slogans in her face, plucking at her hair and clothing, laughing and jeering, stamping and singing. Cayla's senses reeled. She would have fallen but the press of men around her kept her on her feet.

'Please!' she whispered with the tears streaming down her pale cheeks. 'Please don't hurt me any more.' They did not understand her. They dragged her across to the motor launch, and like a sack of dried fish passed her over the gap between the two vessels, and shoved her into its main cabin. Rogier was waiting for her there. He came to her at once.

'I am sorry, Cayla. I cannot control them. You must not try to resist. I will do my best to protect you, but you must help me.'

'Oh, Rogier!' she sobbed. She had seen him at odd intervals since she had been taken aboard the dhow, but had not been able to speak to him. Now he embraced her. She clung to him. His kindly assurance and the tenderness in his expression overwhelmed her. In her terror and confusion he was the only thing she could believe in. Her mother's memory and the other safe and comfortable world from which she had been wrenched had faded into unreality. He was all she had left. She was totally dependent on him.

'Be brave, Cayla. It is nearly over. Very soon we will reach land and you will be safe. Once we are there I will be able to protect you and care for you.'

'I love you, Rogier. I love you so very much. You are so strong and good to me.' He led her to the wooden bunk at the rear of the cabin, and laid her upon it. He stroked her filthy hair and at last she fell into an exhausted sleep.

It was two hours before the land came up as a low dark line along the horizon ahead, and almost another hour before the launch ran into the bay. Gandanga Bay was formed by a headland that curved out from the mainland like a lion's claw to form an enclosed area of deep water, protected from the prevailing trade-winds which relentlessly scoured this coast. The launch rounded the point and the bay opened up ahead of her.

• • •

Cayla was awakened by the commotion on the deck and she sat up to find Rogier gone. She peered out through the forward windows of the cabin. She was taken aback by the extent of the bay ahead and the mass of shipping that was crowded into it. There were ships of many shapes and sizes anchored in the protective arms of the bay. Closest to the beach were clusters of fishing dhows, while further out in the deeper water were assembled the vessels of more modern design. The nearest of these was a medium-sized oil tanker, her sides streaked with red-brown rust. The name on her stern was illegible but her port of registry was Monrovia. A dozen Arab guards looked down from the rail as the launch ran past. They waved and fired a fusillade of shots in the air. Cayla could not know that this bay was the main pirate lair and the tanker had been anchored there for the past three years since her capture. She was in ballast, her tanks filled with seawater rather than the precious oil. The owners had been unable or unwilling to pay the ransom money demanded by Rogier's grandfather.

Anchored beyond the tanker were two container ships. They had been there less than six months. The steel containers stacked high on their decks were filled with a vast assortment of goods valued at tens of millions of dollars. The insurance companies would soon pay for their release. Lying between these container ships were numerous other craft which had been seized on the high seas. They varied from small sailing yachts to larger long-line fishing boats and a refrigerated ship with a cargo of frozen mutton from Australia rotting in her holds. The guards on all of these craft gave the launch a tumultuous welcome as it passed. Already they had heard the rumour of the priceless treasure she carried: an American princess whose family was the richest in that hated infidel country. The ransom that would be coerced from the grieving relatives for the return of the woman would be vast, and there would be a share for each one of them.

On the shore the town lined the water's edge, a jumbled conglomeration of shacks and hovels with thatched or corrugated-iron roofs and walls built of sun-dried clay bricks. They were painted in a motley array of colours, with paints that had been looted from the stores of the captured ships. When the launch ran aground on the sandy foreshore the crew leaped overboard and with their robes tucked up around their waists dragged her higher up the beach. Rogier waded ashore with Cayla in his arms. The beach swarmed with armed men, but their ranks parted to let Rogier carry Cayla through to where a column of battered and dusty Land Rovers and Toyotas was parked above the high-water mark. Rogier seated her in the rear of the leading vehicle and four of his men squashed in beside her, two on each side. They smelled of wood smoke, rancid mutton fat and hashish. Their sweating bodies pressed against her lewdly, and their heavy weapons dug into her body. One of them grinned at her, his face a few inches from hers. His teeth were black and rotten and his mouth smelled like a pit latrine.

Rogier climbed into the driver's seat and the gears clashed. They roared off along the unsurfaced road. The other Land Rovers followed in their dust. Cayla turned her face away from the man beside her and shielded her nose and mouth with her hand.

'Where are you taking me, Rogier?' she called above the racket of the engine. He turned his face to her and the Land Rover swerved wildly across the narrow track.

'You are now in my world. You must never call me that false name again. My true name is Adam.'

'Him Adam Tippoo Tip!' said her guard, 'Hot damn!' They crashed through a deep pothole and all of them were thrown upwards with such force that their heads cracked against the steel roof. Cayla was the only one of them who showed any distress.

'Where are you taking me, Rogier?' she begged him.

'That is not my name.'

'Please forgive me. Where are you taking me, Adam?'

'To my grandfather's house.'

'How far is it?'

'Three, maybe four hours,' he shouted back. 'Now stop asking questions.'

They halted only once. They were on a hot treeless plain. The ground was strewn with red agate pebbles, and the twin ruts of the track were the only feature in all that monotonous waste. Adam let her drink a few mouthfuls of warm water from an old wine bottle. The men carelessly relieved themselves in the open, but when Cayla went around the back of the Land Rover to do the same her guards followed her and, still pointing their rifles at her, formed an interested and appreciative audience. Cayla was past caring. They all mounted up again and went on. Eventually out of the shimmering heat mirage a range of blue hills rose up before them. As they drew closer Cayla saw that tucked away amongst the rugged foothills lay a startling green garden. There were groves of palms and orange trees. Beds of melons and maize were irrigated from furrows of running water. They drove past strings of camels which were hauling up leather buckets of water from the deep wells of the oasis and spilling it into the furrows.

'How lovely it is here. What is the name of this place?' Cayla asked, the first time she had spoken in an hour.

'We call it the Oasis of the Miracle,' Adam replied. 'The brother of the Prophet, may he be praised through eternity, slept here on his journey through the wilderness, and in the morning when he awoke the sweet water bubbled from the earth on which he had lain.'

'Is this the home of your grandfather?'

'Up there.' He pointed through the open window of the vehicle. She craned her head and looked up the steep hillside. She saw there were many stone buildings along the cliff face. Atop the largest of these was the distinctive cupola and minaret of a mosque, and adjoining this was a large shapeless building which sprawled down the slope, seemingly without design or purpose. Adam pointed it out to her. 'That is my grandfather's palace. Our family has lived there for three hundred years.'

'It seems to me to be more a fortress than a palace.'

'It is both,' he replied and parked the Land Rover halfway up the hillside. A party of servants in white robes ran down to meet them. They offered baskets of cool damp cloths for the travellers to refresh themselves, and pitchers of orange juice sherbet. Adam poured a glass for Cayla which she gulped down gratefully, spluttering and choking in her haste. As soon as she had finished the delicious drink, Adam took her arm and led her up the slope that was too steep and rocky even for the Land Rover. Twice Cayla had to slump to the ground to rest. But at Adam's urging she struggled back onto her feet and toiled on upwards. She felt no resentment of his dominance over her. She was numb with despair, and the only thing that mattered to her any longer was to please him and to avoid his anger. But every part of her body ached and the rocky path sent thrills of pain shooting up her legs into the base of her spine. She tried to think about her mother, but the image was unclear in her mind and soon faded completely. When she crumpled to the ground for a third time, Adam ordered two of the servants to carry her the last hundred metres, until they came to an ornately carved door in the side wall of the palace. Here they handed her over to four female slaves who were veiled and clad in full-length black Islamic habits.

The women led her into a warren of passages and dark rooms until they entered what was clearly the harem area. A crowd of women and young children materialized out of the gloom and pressed around her, laughing and exclaiming and tugging at her clothing or reaching out to touch her bedraggled blonde hair. Most of them had never seen hair of that colour before, and it fascinated them. They followed her into a tiny courtyard that was open to the sky.

The slave women stood her in the centre and, despite her protests, stripped off her filthy clothing. The women and children crowded closer to prod her white flesh. One of them tried to pluck a hair from the blonde bush at the base of her belly as a trophy, but Cayla lashed out at her with her fists and she squealed and recoiled, to the hilarious delight of the others.

From clay pitchers the slave women poured cool well water over Cayla's head and shoulders. One of them handed her a bar of blue mottled carbolic soap and she scrubbed herself from the top of her head down to the soles of her feet. The harsh suds streamed down from her hair and stung her eyes, but she hardly noticed it in the joy of at last being clean again. When she had dried herself, the slaves helped her don a shapeless black robe like those they were wearing. The wide sleeves covered her arms down to her wrists and the skirts swept the floor. Chattering amongst themselves, they demonstrated to her how to wear the long black headscarf, so that it covered her hair and face, leaving only her eyes exposed. They placed a pair of goatskin sandals on her feet.

The alien attire gave her a strange sense of privacy, the first she had experienced since the taking of the *Dolphin*, and she held the scarf closer to her face and mouth, hiding from them and from the nameless terrors and dangers that she knew surrounded her. They would not let her rest and led her back through the maze of the building. As they went on the rooms they passed through became progressively more spacious and richly furnished with colourful rugs and piles of cushions on the floors and painted tiles on the walls. The tiles were decorated with texts from the Koran in swirling Arabic script.

Finally they came to the end of a passage that was closed off by a pair of sturdy doors. These were guarded by two men armed with AK-47 rifles. The slave women left her there, and once they were gone the guards swung the heavy doors open and signed for Cayla to go through into the large room beyond. She paused at the entrance and looked around quickly. She realized that this was part of the mosque. There was a row of robed men seated on cushions on the tiled floor. They were facing the pulpit at the far end of the hall. Adam was in the middle of the row. He turned to look back at her and beckoned her to come to him. She scurried to do his bidding, dropping to her knees beside him.

'Adam!' she started to speak but he silenced her.

'Be quiet, woman. Go forward five paces and kneel facing the pulpit. Wait there in silence. When my grandfather comes through the door behind the pulpit you will place your forehead on the tiles and keep silent. You will speak only when you are spoken to. You will not look into his face at any time. He is a mighty lord and a descendant of the Prophet. You will show him total respect. Go now! Do as I have told you!' She went forward and sank to her knees. She waited and she could hear the small sounds of the men behind her; one of them coughed and another shifted his position. Then she heard the door in front of her begin to open and she looked up, but Adam's sharp command stopped her. 'Down!'

She pressed her forehead to the floor and so saw nothing of what was happening around her. The door opened fully and a portly but stately figure strode through. He did not shuffle like an old man despite his snowy beard, the tips of which were dyed with henna in tribute to the Prophet whose beard had been red. His face was deeply wrinkled and his eyebrows were white and bushy. On his head was an ornately wrapped turban, and he wore a gold-coloured gown whose skirts swept the tiles. Over that was a waistcoat that came down to his knees. It was thickly encrusted with gold and silver filigree. His sandals had exaggeratedly pointed toes and were also embroidered with designs in delicate gold wire and polished semi-precious stones. As a symbol of his power he carried in his right hand a long hippo-hide whip with a handle of beaten gold. He looked over the row of prostrate figures and singled out Adam.

'Come greet your grandfather, son of my son!' he ordered. Adam sprang up and went to him with head bowed and eyes averted. He went down on his knees again before the old man and lifted his right foot, and placed the sole of his grandfather's bejewelled sandal on his own head.

'Stand before me, my grandson. Let me see your face. Let me embrace you.' He lifted Adam to his feet, and stared into his eyes. 'Through me and my son the blood of the Prophet runs in your veins. What I see in you is good and growing stronger with each day that passes.' Adam was awed by the words, for his grandfather was Hadji Sheikh Mohammed Khan Tippoo Tip, one of the great warriors of Allah. The titles *Hadji* and *Sheikh* were honorifics acknowledging the facts that he had made the pilgrimage to Mecca and that he was the leader of a great clan. For five generations the eldest son of the family had borne the name Tippoo Tip. All of them had been legendary warriors, fearsome man-takers and relentless hunters of the elephant. Legend related that between them they had gathered up over a million souls from the interior of Africa and marched them down to their slave-trading stations on the coast. The number of elephant that they had killed was beyond counting, more numerous than the swarms of locusts that darkened the African sky in the time of the rains. Down the centuries fleets of Tippoo Tip dhows had plied the oceans carrying the ivory and slaves from Africa to Arabia and India, and beyond to China.

Allah curse the devil-worshipping infidels, the English and the Americans, who have outlawed the taking of men and the killing of the elephant and driven my great family into decline and obscurity, Adam thought. *But the wheel has turned. Just as the sun goes through the night to emerge again at dawn in its full power and glory, my family will regain its power. Men will learn to fear us once more as we gather up the ships and citizens of the infidel with impunity.* At this very moment scores of captured ships lay in Gandanga Bay, and hundreds of prisoners filled the slave compounds awaiting ransom. Now he had brought his venerated grandfather a diamond beyond price, the richest prize the family had ever taken. With this deed Adam had become a fearsome man-taker like his ancestors. Adam and his grandfather embraced, and then Sheikh Khan turned to look down at the woman who still knelt in obeisance before him.

'Tell this female to rise,' he commanded and Adam spoke quietly to Cayla.

'Stand up! My grandfather wants to look at you.' Cayla rose to her feet and stood with her head hanging submissively.

'Tell her to remove the veil. I wish to see her face,' Sheikh Khan ordered. Adam passed on the command and Cayla drew the head shawl off her hair and face. She stood quietly until the old man seized her chin and lifted her head to stare into her face. At a loss for how to behave, Cayla looked directly into his eyes and smiled. It was an uncertain but winning smile that must have charmed any other male. Sheikh Khan stepped back and slashed her across the face with the hippo-hide whip. Cayla shrieked with the agony of the stroke.

'Infidel whore!' he shouted at her. 'How dare you gaze upon my countenance with your devil's eyes? I am proof to your evil spells.' Cayla covered with both hands the raised crimson weal which the whip had left across her face, and she sobbed out an apology.

'I am sorry. Please forgive me. I did not mean to give offence.' But Sheikh Khan had turned away to command Adam.

'Bring her through to my sanctuary.' He strode back through the doorway, and Adam seized Cayla's arm and pulled her after him.

'You fool,' he hissed at her, 'I warned you.'

In the room beyond the doorway a grim tableau had been laid out. The far wall was draped with a large flag. The central emblem was the black silhouette of an AK-47 automatic rifle on a green field. Above this was written in Arabic script:

'*The Flowers of Islam. Death to the infidel. Death to all the enemies of Allah. God is great.*'

A wooden stool had been placed in front of the flag. On each side of the stool was a uniformed warrior in camouflage battle-dress. Their faces were hidden behind black headscarves. Only their eyes were visible. The men were armed with assault rifles and their masks gave them an ominous satanic appearance.

Adam led Cayla to the stool and made her sit facing the photographer who had been waiting for them. His camera was mounted on a tripod and he focused it on the scene. One of his assistants brought Adam a rolled sheet of heavy white paper, which Adam unrolled and took to Cayla.

'Hold this so we can read the date on it,' he told her.

'What is it?'

'It's the front page of today's *International Herald Tribune* newspaper, downloaded from the internet. It is merely to establish the date on which your portrait was taken.' He stepped back and gave a curt order to the men on each side of the stool. They raised their clenched fists in a warlike gesture. Adam nodded to the cameraman. The photographic flash lit the scene briefly. It caught Cayla staring into the camera lens with an expression of utter despair.

· · ·

Hector and four of his senior field operatives were gathered around the central desk in the situation room of the Sidi el Razig terminal. They were in deep discussion. Hazel Bannock sat to one side. She was trying to follow their discourse but a great deal of it was in Arabic. She gave up and occupied herself with studying the men Hector had chosen to work for him. These were some of those who would attempt to rescue Cayla for her. She prided herself on being a good judge of character and ability and she had discussed each of them with Hector, and finally admitted that he had chosen well.

Two of his men were of European extraction. The first of these was David Imbiss. He was young, fresh-faced and gave the illusion of plumpness. However, this was not fat but muscle. Hector had introduced him to her as an ex-captain of US infantry who had done his time in Afghanistan as a liaison officer seconded to the brigade that Hector commanded. At the end of his tour he left the army with a Bronze Star and a few scars. Hector had told Hazel that when David returned home to California he found that his wife had taken the baby and gone off with an orange grower she had known at college. David's boyish and ingenuous countenance was deceptive, for behind it he was tough, bright and savvy. With his training in the military he was a computer and electronics expert, a skill that Hector valued highly.

Leaning over the desk on Hector's righthand side was Paddy O'Quinn. He was much younger than Hector, and had served under him in the SAS. He was tall, lean and muscled with a quick temper and even quicker mind. He had been a career soldier until he had made one small error of judgement. On the battlefield he had struck a junior officer with sufficient force to break his jaw.

'The man was a prick,' was how he had explained this lapse of judgement to Hector. 'He had just had half his platoon mown down thanks to his stupidity, and then he started to argue with me.' Paddy would probably have been a senior officer by now, without that single mistimed punch. The army's loss was Hector's and Cross Bow's gain. The other two men facing Hector across the desk were both Arabs. This had at first surprised Hazel; after all, Hector Cross was a renowned racist, was he not?

'I would rather have one of those gentlemen covering my backside in a hard fight than most other men I know,' Hector had told her when she remarked on his choice. 'Like most of their race they are hard warriors and cunning as hell. Of course, they are able to think like thugs, talk like thugs and pass as thugs. Set a fox to catch a fox, as someone once said. Together we make a good team; when things get really tough I can pray to Jesus Christ while they can pray to Allah. That way we have all our bets covered.'

Tariq Hakam had been attached to Hector's unit in Iraq as his interpreter and local guide. He and Hector had taken to each other from the first day when they ran into an ambush and had to fight their way out. He had been at Hector's side on the dreadful day of the roadside bomb. When Hector had opened up on the three Arab insurgents who had laid the bomb and seemed to be about to deploy a suicide device, Tariq had backed Hector's fire and taken down one of the enemy. When Hector had resigned his commission Tariq had come to him and said, 'You are my father. Where you go I will go also.'

'Can't argue with that,' Hector had agreed. 'Not sure where I'm headed, but pack your kit and come along.'

The other Arab facing Hector across the desk was Uthmann Waddah. 'Uthmann is Uthmann,' Hector had told Hazel. 'No one can replace him. I trust him as I trust myself.'

Hazel smiled at the memory of Hector's simple explanations of his relationship with the four men. She had taken much of it as gross hyperbole at the time, but watching them now as they debated their options around the situation room desk she was revising that opinion.

We few, we happy few! she thought and in a strange way she felt envious of Hector. It must be wonderful to belong to such a tight-knit band; to spend your days in the company of brothers with whom you could trust your life. Never to know loneliness. Henry had been gone many years now. Even in the midst of the throng loneliness was her austere and constant companion.

Her laptop beeped, alerting her to an incoming message. It would be Agatha. Hazel quickly turned to it. She stared at the screen in disbelief, and then let out a choking cry.

'Oh, my dear God! This cannot be happening!'

'What is it?' Hector demanded.

'Cayla has sent me a message!'

'Don't open it! It's not Cayla,' Hector shouted, but he was on the opposite side of the desk and couldn't reach her in time to stop her. Her fingers flew over the keys. There was an alert that there was an attachment. She pressed the 'Download' button and then stared at the screen. The blood drained from her face. She opened her mouth as if to speak but the sound that burst past her lips was a high keening cry of mourning. Hector thought she might fall for she reeled in her chair. He caught her shoulders and shook her.

'What is it? Pull yourself together! For God's sake, woman. What is it?' She closed her mouth and stared at him as if she had never seen him before. Then she straightened in the chair and drew a deep breath, fighting for control of her emotions. She still could not speak, but handed him the laptop. He looked down at the image on the screen. It was of a pretty young white girl in Muslim dress, but with her face and hair exposed. Her expression was haunted and forlorn. She held a copy of a newspaper so he could read the date under the headline. On each side of the girl stood armed and masked men. On the wall behind her was a banner with messages of militant and radical religious cant printed over it in black Arabic script.

'Is it her?' he asked, and when she could not reply he shook her gently. 'Is this Cayla?'

She gasped to catch her breath and then she whispered, 'Yes, it's Cayla. It's my baby.' She shivered. 'But why should she send me this terrifying picture of herself?'

'She did not send that,' Hector said harshly. 'It was sent by her captors. They are opening a line of contact with us. The picture was just to intimidate you, but they are ready to negotiate at last.'

'But it's from Cayla's mobile phone.'

'They have taken it from her, or at least they have taken the Sim card out of her phone.' He turned her to face him. 'Listen to me. This is to the good. We know now with certainty that Cayla was alive three days ago. That is the date on the newspaper she is holding.' Hazel nodded. 'Now we have a direct line to her captors. We can negotiate with them. We might even be able to trace the origin of the message by the network that sent it.' He handed the laptop across the desk to David Imbiss. 'You're the geek, Dave. Tell us what you can about this transmission. Can we tell which country it was sent from?'

'Sure, Heck.' Imbiss examined the laptop. 'Might take time, but with a court order the company which is the server might be forced to tell us which of their networks sent it.' He handed the computer back to Hector. 'But it would be a sweet waste of time.'

'How's that, Dave?'

'The photograph was taken three days ago. Suppose it was taken in Cairo. There was plenty of time to courier the Sim card to an accomplice in, say, Rome. He or she transmits the message to us and then returns the Sim card to the main man by the same route that it came.'

'Shit!' Hector said.

'Shit indeed,' Dave agreed. 'If we are going to have ongoing correspondence with these people you can be certain every message from them will be sent from a different country. Today Italy, next week Venezuela.' Hector thought about this and then turned back to Hazel.

'What is the balance on Cayla's BlackBerry account, do you have any idea? The Beast will not top up the account if it goes dry, it would be too dangerous for them. We don't want the trail to break off for lack of a few dollars.'

'I put two thousand dollars into Cayla's account while we were in Cape Town.'

'You could talk for a year on that,' Hector opined. *With this lady nothing is ever done by halves*, he thought and smiled inwardly.

'I didn't want her to have any excuse not to call me,' said Hazel, justifying herself.

'Excellent! So we want to make sure that they keep on using this number.' He told her, 'What you must do right away is reply to them. Make sure that they know we will be listening in for them. Do it now, please, Mrs Bannock.' She nodded and then typed in a message on the keyboard. When she had finished she turned it towards him to read.

Gentlemen, I will be waiting to receive
your further messages. In the meantime
please do not hurt her.

'No!' Hector said sharply. 'Leave out the salutation. Gentlemen they are not, and it serves no purpose. Then cut out the appeal not to hurt her. Just leave the bare bones. *I am waiting.* That's all.' She nodded, made the amendment and showed Hector the result.

'Good. Send it!' he said. Then he looked up at his men. 'Everyone out, please. From now on it's "need to know" only.' They understood. If one of them were to be captured and tortured they could not divulge information they did not have. They began to file out of the room.

'Tariq. Uthmann. Stay behind, please.' The two Arabs turned back to their chairs at the table. Hazel could contain herself no longer.

'Cross,' she blurted, 'is there nothing more we can do? Oh God, how do we find where they are holding her?'

'That's what we have been discussing for the past hour,' Hector reminded her. 'If there is one weakness the Beast has it is that it loves to talk, it loves to boast of its victories.'

Hazel shook her head. 'I don't understand.'

'If you know where to listen you may be able to pick up the echoes of its gloating.'

'Do you know where to listen?' she asked.

'No, but Uthmann and Tariq do,' he replied. 'I'm sending them into deep cover. I'm putting them into the countries in which they were born and where their links to the local populace will be strongest. Tariq will go to Puntland and Uthmann to Iraq. They will sniff around until they pick up the scent. Even if they are holding Cayla somewhere else, these two will find out where she is.'

'That will be terribly dangerous for them, won't it? They'll be on their own entirely and you won't be able to protect them.'

'You are greatly understating the case, Mrs Bannock. They will be at deadly risk. But they are hard to kill. They have survived so far against all odds.' Hazel looked across at the two Arabs.

'I can never thank you enough. You are risking your life for my daughter. You are very, very brave men.'

'Not too much praise!' Hector protested. 'They already have highly inflated opinions of their own worth. Next thing they will be asking me for a raise, or something equally ridiculous.' Everyone, except Hazel, laughed and it eased the tension a little.

'Until they come up with a definite lead we will keep the ball in play here. At the same time we will make every possible preparation for the moment when we are certain where they are holding Cayla, and we can go in to bring her out.'

• • •

There was a daily flight on Zara Airlines' Fokker F-27 Friendship twin turbojet passenger plane from the airstrip at Sidi el Razig to Ash-Alman, the capital of Abu Zara. The next morning Tariq and Uthmann quietly joined the crowd of oil rig workers and labourers in the small airline check-in area. Dressed in traditional garb, with their faces half-covered by their shumag, they blended into the crowd. Once they reached the capital they separated. Tariq boarded the aircraft to Mogadishu in Somalia and an hour later Uthmann took the flight to Baghdad. They had vanished amongst the faceless Arab multitudes.

• • •

The next morning Hector sought out Hazel and found her at breakfast in the tiny company mess. As he stood over her he glanced down at the bowl of cereal and the cup of black coffee on the table in front of her. No wonder she is in this kind of shape, he thought.

'Good morning, Mrs Bannock. I hope you slept well.'

'An attempt at a light witticism is it, Cross? Of course I did not sleep well.'

'It's going to be a long day. Nothing is likely to break just yet. I'm taking a few of my lads out for some parachute practice prior to the big show. Some of them have not jumped for over a year. They need polishing.'

'Have you got a chute for me?' she asked. He blinked. He had thought that she might want to watch them to distract herself from her own worries. He hadn't contemplated that she would want to join in. He wondered what experience she had.

'You have done some para before?' he asked tactfully.

'My husband loved it, and he used to drag me along. We did quite a bit of base jumping together in the Norwegian fjords at Trollstigen.' Hector gaped at her for a moment before he found his voice again.

'That's the end of the road,' he conceded. 'They don't come more extreme than jumping off a mountain into a two-thousand-foot abyss.'

'Oh! Have you done the fjords?' she asked with quick interest.

'I am brave, but not crazy.' He shook his head. 'Mrs Bannock you have my admiration and I would be honoured to have you jump with us this morning.'

Hector had assembled fifteen of his best men, including Dave Imbiss and Paddy O'Quinn. They made three jumps from the helicopter. The first was from 10,000 feet and the third and last was low level from 400 feet; just enough air left for the parachute to flare before their feet hit the ground. This technique would give an enemy firing from below little chance of hitting them while they were dropping and vulnerable. After the third jump all the men were in obvious awe of Hazel. Even Paddy O'Quinn could barely conceal his admiration.

They ate their ham and cheese sandwiches and drank black coffee from a flask while sitting on the side of a sand dune. Afterwards Hector rolled an old truck tyre from the top of the dune, and as it bounced and bounded down the steep slope they took turns firing their Beretta SC 70/90 automatic assault rifles at the cardboard target that Hector had fixed inside the tyre. Hazel was the last to shoot. She borrowed Hector's weapon and checked the loading and balance with a quick and competent air. Then she stepped up to the firing mark and took on the target in elegant style, swinging smoothly out ahead of the tyre like a 12-bore shooter lining up on a high-flying pheasant. Dave retrieved the tyre from the bottom of the dune, they all gathered around it and regarded the bullet holes punched through the cardboard target. Nobody said much.

'Why are we all so surprised?' Hector mused. 'She is a world-class athlete. Of course she is as competitive as hell, and has the hand-to-eye coordination of a leopard.' Then he said ingenuously, 'Let me guess, Mrs Bannock. Your husband liked to shoot and he dragged you along with him. That's it, isn't it?' The laughter was spontaneous and infectious, and after a few moments Hazel was forced to join in. It was the first time she had laughed since she had lost Cayla. It was cathartic. She felt some of the debilitating grief being purged from her soul.

Before the laughter ceased Hector clapped his hands and called out, 'Righty-oh, boys and girls! It's just under seven miles back to the terminal. Last one home buys the drinks.'

The sandy soil made heavy going. When they streamed in through the gate in the barbed-wire perimeter fencing of the terminal Hector was a few paces behind Hazel. She was running strongly and smoothly but the back of her shirt was dark with sweat. Hector grinned.

I doubt that Madam will have too much trouble getting to sleep tonight, he thought.

• • •

Uthmann heard the explosion and saw the pillar of black smoke rising above the roofs of the buildings ahead of him. He knew at once that it was a car bomb and he burst into a swift run to his brother's house, which was somewhere close to the explosion. He turned the corner and looked down the narrow winding street. Even for a hardened veteran like Uthmann the carnage was horrific. One man was running towards him with a child's blood-soaked body clutched to his chest. His blank staring eyes did not even focus on Uthmann as he ran on past. The front had been blown off three buildings. The rooms inside were opened up like a doll's house. Furniture and personal possessions hung out of the open rooms or cascaded down into the street. In the middle of the roadway stood the blackened and twisted wreckage of the car that had carried the bomb.

'You are no martyr,' Uthmann shouted at the smoking wreckage and vaporized remains of the driver as he ran past it. 'You are a Shi'ite murderer!' Then he saw that his brother Ali's house was further down the street and that it was intact. Ali's wife met him at the door. She was weeping and cradling two of the children. 'Where is Ali?' he yelled at her.

'He has gone to work at the hotel,' she sobbed.

'Are all the children with you?' She nodded through her tears.

'May the name of Allah be praised!' Uthmann cried and led her back into the house.

Uthmann's own wife and three children had not been as fortunate as his brother's family. Three years before Lailah had been in the market place with the boys when a bomb had blown up within thirty paces of them. Now Uthmann picked the little boy out of the arms of his sister-in-law and rocked him until he stopped blubbering. He remembered the feel of his son's warm little body and tears welled up in his eyes. He turned away so she could not see them.

His brother Ali came back from work an hour later. Because of the bomb the general manager of the hotel had given him permission to leave early. His relief when he saw all his family safe was heartrending for Uthmann to watch. It was only the following day that Uthmann was able to hold a serious discussion with him. To begin with Uthmann broached the subject of the taking of the American yacht and the capture of the young heiress to the Bannock Oil fortune.

'This is the most exciting news that we have had for years,' Ali responded at once. 'All the Muslim world is agog with it since the day the comrades announced it on Al Jazeera. What dedicated planning and duty it took to bring such an operation to its flowering. It is one of our greatest victories since the attacks on New York City. The Americans are reeling. Their prestige has taken another deadly assault.' Ali was jubilant. In everyday existence he was a floor manager at the Airport Hotel, but in reality his main occupation was as a coordinator for the Sunni Fighters who were pursuing the jihad against the Great Satan. It was clear to both brothers that Ali had been the main target of the Shi'ite bomb that had caused such devastation in the street outside the house in which they sat.

'I am sure our leaders will demand an enormous ransom for the captured American princess,' Ali said seriously. 'Enough to finance the jihad against America for another ten years or more.'

'So which of our groups were responsible for this achievement?' Uthmann asked. 'I have never heard of these "Flowers of Islam" until the name was used on Al Jazeera.'

'Brother, you know better than to ask me that. Even though you have proved your loyalty a hundred times over I could never answer that question even if I knew the answer, which I do not.' Ali hesitated, and then went on, 'But I can tell you that soon you may be one of those with a need to know.'

'My connection with Bannock Oil?' Uthmann smiled at him, but Ali waved his hands in denial.

'Enough, I can say no more.'

'Then I will leave tomorrow, and return to Abu Zara—'

'No!' Ali cut him off. 'It is the hand of Allah that brought you here today. Stay with me another month at least. *Inshallah!* I may have something to tell you then.'

Uthmann nodded. '*Mashallah!* I shall stay, brother.'

'And you are welcome at my board, brother.'

• • •

In the palace on the hillside above the Oasis of the Miracle another group of men were drinking coffee from tiny silver cups and talking quietly and seriously. They were seated in a circle around a table that was inlaid with ivory and mother of pearl. The only item on the table was the silver coffee kettle. There were no writing materials anywhere in the room. Nothing was written down. All decisions were announced by Sheikh Khan Tippoo Tip in person, and memorized by his listeners.

'So this is my decision.' He was speaking in the deep measured tones in which he conducted all momentous business.

'My grandson Adam will send the first ransom demand.' He looked at Adam who, still sitting on the silk cushion, bowed until his forehead touched the tiles.

'To hear your command is to obey it,' he murmured.

Sheikh Khan mused, 'The amount of our demand will be so large that even in the sick and accursed land of the Great Satan there will be none so rich as can pay it.' When he smiled his eyes disappeared behind the wrinkled lids. 'No amount of money can settle the blood feud I have with this man Cross. Only blood can pay for blood.' They sipped from the silver cups in silence, waiting for the Sheikh to continue speaking.

'This perfidious infidel has killed three of my sons.' He held up one finger twisted with arthritis. 'The first was my son and the father of my grandson, Saladin Gamel.' Adam bowed again, and Sheikh Khan went on, 'He was a true warrior of Allah. Cross shot him dead on a street in Baghdad seven years ago.'

'May Allah welcome him into the Gardens of Paradise,' the other men in the circle murmured.

'The second blood debt is my son, Gafour. He was sent to honour the blood feud of his elder brother Saladin, but Cross killed him also when he attacked the dhow in which Gafour was sailing to Abu Zara to carry out the task I had set for him.'

'May Allah welcome him into the Gardens of Paradise,' the others intoned again.

'The third of my sons to die at the hands of this Christ-worshipping infidel was Anwar. I sent him also on a mission of honour, but Cross murdered him.'

'May Allah welcome him into the Gardens of Paradise,' they chorused for the third time.

'The blood feud has become a heavy toll on my conscience. The lives of three of my fine sons have been taken by this foul idolater, servant of a false God. It is no longer sufficient for me to take his life. One life cannot repay me for three. I must capture him and hand him over alive to the mothers and wives of the men he has killed. The women are highly skilled in these matters. Under their hands and the sharp blades of their skinning knives he shall endure many days in torment before he passes into the belly of hell and the arms of Satan.'

'As you command, mighty Khan, so shall it be,' they murmured agreement.

'Are you listening to me, my grandson?' Sheikh Khan demanded. Adam bowed again, deeply, reverently.

'I am listening, revered grandfather.'

'I place the debt of the blood feud squarely on your shoulders. You must collect payment for your two uncles and for your own father. May you know no rest or peace until the debt is paid in full.'

'I hear you, my grandfather. It is a sacred trust.'

'When you bring this infidel pig of a pig to me alive I will raise you up higher than any man in our tribe. You will take a place in my heart alongside the memory of your murdered father and uncles. When I die you will take my place as leader of our clan.'

'I acknowledge this as my sacred duty, my grandfather. I shall deliver the man and the woman to face your judgment and wrath, even as you command.'

• • •

The waiting is always the hardest part, Hector Cross had told her at the beginning. Gradually she learned just how right he was. Each day she spent many hours on Skype conference calls conducting the business of the company with the senior executives of Bannock Oil around the world. The rest of the time she trained with Hector's men, running, jumping and shooting until she was as physically fit and mentally focused as she had been when she walked on court at Flinders Park on that day of glory so long ago.

But the nights, those terrible nights, passed in spiritual agony. She slept little but when she did she dreamed of Cayla; Cayla galloping beside her on her palomino through the high meadows of the ranch. Cayla squealing with excitement as she opened the extravagant present that Hazel had given her on her eighteenth birthday. Cayla falling asleep with her head on Hazel's shoulder as they watched old movies on late-night cable TV together. Then in her dreams there were men, masked men with guns in their hands, and her terror was infinite. Cayla! Cayla! The name rang incessantly in her head, tormenting her and driving her to the very edge of madness.

Every day she spoke with Chris Bessell and Colonel Roberts in the States, but they had little for her comfort. Every night alone in her room she prayed as she had as a small girl, on her knees and weeping. But the trail had gone cold. Neither all the power of her prayers nor the might of the CIA was able to turn up any trace of Cayla or of the Flowers of Islam. She spent many hours each day with Hector Cross, drawing strength from his companionship.

'But we've heard nothing in almost a month, Cross!' She said that at least once every day.

'They play the game of cat and mouse with infinite skill. They have had years of practice at it,' he replied. 'They're in no hurry. We must wait them out. But remember that Cayla is still alive. Hold that thought close to your heart.'

'But what about Tariq and Uthmann? Surely they must have found out something by now.'

'It's a deadly slow game,' he emphasized. 'If Tariq and Uthmann make a single slip, they will die an unenviable death. They're in very deep cover, living, eating and sleeping with the Beast. We cannot hurry them, indeed I cannot even contact them. To try to do so would give the same result as a bullet through the head.'

'I just wish there was something we could do,' she lamented.

'There is one thing you could do, Mrs Bannock.'

'What is it, Cross?' she asked eagerly. 'I will do anything you suggest.'

'Then I suggest you stop sending mail on Cayla's mobile phone to the Beast.'

'How—?' Her voice trailed off, then she shook her head and admitted, 'I was only repeating the message you made me send to them before. Just that we are waiting. But how did you—' She broke off again.

'How did I know what you were up to?' He finished the question for her. 'Sometimes you're not as smart as you think you are, Hazel Bannock.'

'As for you, Hector Cross, you think you're just the cleverest Dick in the whole wide bloody world,' she flared at him.

'Feels good to let fly like that occasionally, doesn't it, Hazel?'

'Don't you dare call me Hazel, you bloody arrogant bastard!'

'Good, Mrs Bannock! Your choice of language improves all the time. Soon you will be up to my high standards.'

'I hate you, Hector Cross! I really do.'

'No, you really don't. You are much too astute for that. Save your hatred for where it will do the most good.' He laughed. It was a gentle infectious laugh, mild and understanding, and despite herself she laughed with him, but her laughter had a hysterical edge.

'You are incorrigible!' she said through her laughter.

'Now that you understand me, you may call me Hector or even Heck, if you so choose.'

'Thank you.' She tried to stem her laughter. 'But I do not so bloody choose, Cross.'

• • •

'What will force them to come and try to free the girl?' Sheikh Khan stared at his grandson, waiting for him to answer.

Adam thought carefully before he answered. 'First they must know where we are holding her.'

His grandfather nodded. 'Then they will call for help from their friends in Washington. We know the mother is a friend of the American President. He will send his crusaders in their multitudes to overwhelm us.' Sheikh Khan combed his fingers through his beard, watching his grandson's eyes, waiting for the moment that the boy would see the way ahead as clearly as Sheikh Khan himself saw it. 'It will take the Americans many weeks or even months to prepare to strike at us. We can move out of this place within hours and be gone into the desert. Hector Cross, the murderer of my sons, will know that. Will he and the mother of the girl be willing to wait for the US Army to move?'

'Yes!' said Adam with certainty. 'Unless—' Sheikh Khan saw the solution dawn in his grandson's eyes and his heart swelled with pride.

'Yes, Adam?' He encouraged his grandson to speak.

'Unless we can convince them that the girl is in dire danger of death, or of a danger worse than death itself,' said Adam, and his grandfather smiled until his eyes almost disappeared in the deep creases of his skin. 'Then they will come for us; without hesitation or fear they *will* come for us.'

'Where shall we do it?' Sheikh Khan whispered gleefully. Adam replied at once.

'Not here in a stone cell of the fortress. It should be in a place where the beauty of the scenery contrasts with the horror of the deed.' He thought for a moment and then said, 'The pool of the water lilies, in the Oasis of the Miracle!'

'Do we show them the danger first, and then allow them to learn where we are? Or should they know the location first and then witness the deed?' Sheikh Khan pretended to ponder the question, but Adam spoke again.

'First they must see what the girl is suffering so when at last they learn the location they will rush in without hesitation or pause for thought.'

'I am proud of you,' said Sheikh Khan. 'You will make a great general and a ruthless warrior of Allah.' Adam bowed to acknowledge the compliment. Then he beckoned to one of the trusted guards who stood at the door with folded arms. The guard came swiftly to his side and went down on one knee to receive his orders.

'Send word to the photographer,' Adam said softly. 'Tell him he must be waiting tomorrow at the main gates of the palace after the morning prayers. He must bring his video camera with him.'

• • •

The slave women came to fetch Cayla from the cramped cell in which she had been kept since she had been brought to the Oasis of the Miracle. Again they bathed her from pitchers of water and then dressed her in fresh clothing, a full-length black abaya gown, and wrapped a black shawl modestly around her face and over her hair. Then they led her to the main doors of the palace where four men with automatic rifles were waiting to escort her down the mountainside to the oasis.

After the musty cell of her confinement the desert air was clean and warm. She breathed it with relief. She had long ago lost any interest in what would happen to her next. She had retreated into a state of dull resignation. Halfway down the mountain track she became aware of the crowd that was gathered beside one of the pools in the lush green gardens below her. They appeared to be drawn up in some sort of order, a half-circle. All of them were men. As she came closer she saw that in the open centre of the circle a man sat cross-legged on a spread of woollen rugs. He wore traditional white baggy trousers, black waistcoat and turban, but even though a keffiyeh covered his face she recognized Adam. She felt a lift of her spirits. She had not seen him since the day almost a month ago when she had been photographed while she held up a copy of the *International Herald Tribune*. She wanted to run to him. In all this cruel and savage mob he was the only one she could trust. She knew he was her protector. He was the light in the darkness of her despair. She began to press forward eagerly but the men on each side restrained her, and they went on down the hill at the same easy pace. Suddenly another man appeared in front of her. He walked backwards with a large black professional video camera focused on her face.

'Smile please, Missy,' he entreated her. 'Watch the birdie please, Missy.' His English was almost unintelligible.

'Go away!' she shouted at him with the last flicker of her once fiery spirit. 'Leave me alone.' She made a lunge at him, but he skipped away, keeping just out of her reach. The guards seized her arms and jerked her back. The cameraman kept on filming. They entered the semi-circle of armed and masked men, and Cayla called pathetically to Adam, 'Please! Oh, please, Adam! Stop them tormenting me.'

Adam gave an order. Her guards hustled her forward and forced her to sit beside him on the brightly coloured and patterned carpet. Now the cameraman came and knelt in front of them. He had screwed his camera onto a tripod. He bent over it to focus on Adam's face and the camera purred softly. Adam removed the keffiyeh that covered his face and looked directly into the camera lens.

'Cayla,' Adam said in his almost perfect English, only lightly tinged by his French accent, 'they are taking this footage to send to your mother, to show her that you are being well cared for. You can send her any message you like. Speak into the camera. Tell her that they will soon send her a ransom demand. You must ask her to pay it at once. Once they receive the money all this unpleasantness will be over. You will be released and sent back home to your mother again. Do you understand?' She nodded dumbly.

'Remove the veil,' Adam ordered her gently. 'Let your mother see your face.' Slowly, as if in a trance, Cayla lifted the headscarf and let it drop over her shoulders. 'Now, look into the camera. Good, that's it. Now, speak to your mother. Tell her what is in your heart.'

Cayla drew a long shaky breath and said, 'Hello, Mummy. It's me, Cayla.' She stopped and shook her head. 'I am sorry. That's a stupid thing to say. Of course you know who I am.' She gathered her wits again. 'These people are holding me in this horrible place. I am so afraid. I know that something terrible is going to happen to me. They want you to send them some money. They promise they will let me go when you do. Oh, Mummy, please help me. Don't let them do this to me.' She began to sob and lowered her face into her cupped hands, her voice muffled by her fingers and the force of her terror and grief. 'Please, my darling mother. You are the only one in the world who can save me.' Her sobbing became wilder, and her words lost any form or sense. Adam reached across and stroked her hair tenderly. Then he looked directly into the camera.

'Mrs Bannock, I want to tell you how sorry I am that this is happening to your daughter. Cayla is a lovely young girl. It is a tragedy that she has been caught up in this. I am truly sorry. I wish there was something I could do. However, I am not responsible for the actions of these men. They are a law unto themselves. You are the only one who can put an end to this horror. Do as Cayla has requested you. Pay the ransom money and your beautiful daughter will immediately be returned to you.'

He stood up and moved out of camera shot. His place was taken by four of the masked men. They had laid aside their firearms. They lifted Cayla to her feet and turned her to face the camera. One of them took a handful of her blonde hair from behind and hauled her head back. Another masked man entered the shot from the right, and he drew a dagger with a rhino-horn handle and a curved ten-inch blade from his belt. The blade was inlaid with gold Arabic script. He held the point of the blade under Cayla's chin, almost touching the velvety skin of her throat.

'No! Please!' she gabbled. The group stood for a full minute without moving. Then he lowered the blade slowly until it pointed at her left breast, the outline of it showing through the black cotton of her abaya. Then the man moved his free hand up over her right breast. He cupped it in his hand and joggled it almost playfully. Cayla redoubled her struggles, and the men holding her laughed under their masks. The sound was like the cackling of hyenas that had picked up the scent of blood on the wind.

The dagger man hooked his finger into the collar of the abaya and held it open. Then he ran the blade into the space between the black cloth and Cayla's skin. She felt the cold metal and she froze and looked down as he moved the knife blade down between her breasts. The cloth split open and one of her breasts bulged out. The skin was pale as cream but the nipple was red as a ruby. The man sheathed the dagger and then reached into the open gown. He brought out both her breasts, one in each hand, and squeezed them so brutally that their delicate nipples stood out and Cayla screamed with pain. He released her breasts and hooked his forefinger into the slit in the thin cloth and ripped it down to her ankles. Under the abaya she was naked. The photographer panned the camera in and lingeringly recorded every detail of her body, dwelling on her bosom and then moving down to the soft golden fur of her pubes.

Cayla stood docilely. She offered no further resistance when the four men holding her lowered her onto her back and held her spreadeagled on the carpet. There was one of them on each of her arms, holding her by the wrists. The other two grasped her ankles. They pulled her legs wide apart. The photographer altered the focus of his lens, moving into a close-up and high-definition shot of the pink lips of her genitalia. Cayla rolled her head from side to side.

'Please don't do this!' she whimpered. 'Please—'

The man who stood over her undid his belt and let his baggy white trousers drop around his ankles. He stared down at Cayla's sex and spat on the palm of his right hand. He spread the spittle over the head of his penis to lubricate it. The camera followed each of his movements. His penis stiffened and extended out of the mass of jet-black pubic hair. It was enormous. Thick blue veins twisted around the shaft like some loathsome climbing vine. Cayla stared up at it, wide-eyed and speechless with fright. He knelt between her knees, and lowered himself onto her. She tried to kick him off, but the men held her legs apart. The buttocks of the man on top of her were muscular and covered with dense black hair like those of an animal. They clenched and drove downwards. Cayla screamed shrilly and her whole body convulsed. While he pounded down on her, the other men from the watching circle laid aside their weapons and came forward to form a line, lowering their trousers and with their hands working themselves up into a state of readiness for their turn.

As one finished and stood up, another took his place immediately. After the fourth rape Cayla lay quiescent, no longer screaming or struggling. After the sixth there was blood, much blood, bright against her pale thighs. When the tenth man stood up grinning and hoisting his breeches, the camera pulled away to focus on the face of Adam, as he watched emotionlessly. He turned to look into the lens.

'I am very sorry you had to witness this, Mrs Bannock,' he said softly. 'I do not think that your daughter can stand much more of it. You and I can put a stop to it at once. All you have to do is to order a wire transfer to a bank in Hong Kong for the amount of ten billion United States dollars. You know how to contact the people who are doing this to Cayla. You will be given the bank details when you let them know that you are ready to send the money.'

During the day Hazel carried the BlackBerry under her blouse, suspended on a cord around her neck. She had strapped it to the skin between her breasts with a strip of adhesive tape so that, even when she was running, parachuting and training with the men she could reach it before it rang twice. At night she kept it under her pillow and often woke to find she was holding it in her hand. It was as close as she could get to Cayla.

When at last it did ring she was sitting at the situation room table with Hector Cross while he gave his senior operatives their daily briefing. The security duties of Cross Bow had to continue with their full efficiency. Hector was very much aware that the enemy might take advantage of the disarray caused by Cayla's abduction and that they could spring another surprise attack at any time. The meeting ended and Hector looked around the table.

'Any questions? Good! I will detain you no longer—' He broke off as the BlackBerry under Hazel's khaki safari shirt rang.

'Oh, God!' she whispered and ripping open the buttons, she reached under her shirt and brought out the device.

'Leave us!' Hector snapped at his men. 'Get out! Now!' They obeyed instantly, and Paddy O'Quinn led them out and closed the door behind them. Hazel already had the phone to her ear and was shouting into the mouthpiece,

'Hello! Who is this? Speak to me. Please, speak to me!' Hector reached out and took her shoulder. He shook it gently.

'Hazel, it's not a voice call. It's a text message or an attachment.' In her agitation she had not recognized the difference in the ringtones. Working in desperate haste, she located the body of the message.

'You're right,' she blurted. 'It's an attachment. It seems to be a photograph or a video. Yes, it's a video! A long one . . . twelve megabytes.'

'Wait! Don't open it yet!' Hector tried to stop her. He had a presentiment of the evil to come. He wanted to prepare her for it. But she seemed not even to hear him. She was already running the video directly onto the small screen of the device.

'It's Cayla!' she exclaimed joyfully. 'She's still alive. Oh, thank God! Come and watch her, Cross!' He came around to her side of the desk.

'My poor baby, she looks so beautiful but so tragic.' On the screen Cayla was walking towards the man seated on the carpet in the circle of masked and armed Arabs. The man's face was also masked with a head shawl. But the camera closed in on him until only his head and shoulders were framed in the shot. The man removed the shawl that concealed his features.

'Who is that man, Cross? Do you know him?' Hazel asked with agitation.

'No, I have never seen him before. But now I shall never forget him,' Hector said quietly. Adam made his short speech and they both listened in silence staring at the screen as though it were a venomous reptile.

'—Pay the ransom money and your beautiful daughter will immediately be returned to you,' Adam ended quietly.

'I'll pay it,' Hazel whispered, 'I'll pay anything to have her back.'

'I am sorry, Mrs Bannock,' Hector said gently, 'but he's lying to you. Everything he says is a lie. This is the Beast and he is the master of the lie.' The image on the screen changed, the Arab with the knife advanced on Cayla.

'He isn't going to hurt her. No, he mustn't hurt her. I will pay anything. Anything to stop them hurting my baby!' Her voice was rising hysterically.

'Be brave! For Cayla's sake, be brave.'

'Surely these people are human beings, not animals,' she said. 'They won't hurt an innocent young girl who has done them no harm.'

'No, they are not animals. The most savage animals are good and noble compared to these creatures.' The Arab on the screen stood over Cayla and exposed his grotesque sex. Hazel sobbed and reached for Hector's hand. Then she was silent as the full horror began to unfold. But she was shaking as though in high fever.

'Turn it off!' Hector ordered her, but she shook her head and her grip on Hector's hand was like a steel vice. He could hardly believe the power of it. He made no effort to remove her hand; although the pain made his eyes water he could not deny her any comfort he was capable of giving to her. It seemed to both of them that the multiple rapes of her daughter went on endlessly. Hector felt a rage rising in him such as he had never experienced before. When the image of Adam appeared again on the screen, Hector had a focus for his hatred. He stared at the face as though trying to engrave the features indelibly on his mind. At last the video had run its dreadful course and the screen went blank. Neither of them moved or spoke for a long time. They went on staring at the empty screen.

'I would pay them if I could,' Hazel whispered.

'You don't have the amount they are asking. Ten billion dollars,' Hector said, and it was a statement rather than a question. She shook her head, and released her grip on his hand.

'Bannock Oil does not belong to me. It belongs to the shareholders. Seventy-three per cent of the issued share capital is owned by Henry's trust. I have the power of attorney to vote those shares, but I certainly cannot dispose of them. I have only about two and a half per cent of the total paid-up share capital of the company registered in my own name. If I sold those shares and all the other assets I have, I might be able to scrape together five billion or perhaps five and a half. Perhaps I could negotiate with them.'

'Don't even think of it!' Hector said. 'If you had twenty billion it would still not be enough. They want something else from you.'

'What else can we do?'

'We have got to stall them, until Uthmann and Tariq get back. Tell them you are raising the money, but that it will take time. Tell them anything. Meet their lies with our own.'

'Then what?'

'I don't know,' he admitted. 'At this stage there is only one thing I know with any certainty.' Hazel turned to look at him for the first time since the video had started playing. It was as though she had never seen him before. His face seemed sculpted from a pale adamantine marble. It had been purged of any trace of human emotion, except hatred. His eyes burned green. This face was the mask of Nemesis.

'What are you certain of?'

'That I am going in to get that child out of there, and I will kill anybody who tries to stop me.' She felt a strange emotion rising in her like an incoming spring tide. Here was a man, the first real man she had known since Henry Bannock had been taken from her. This is the one I have waited for. I want him, she thought, I need him. Cayla and I both need him. Oh God, how we need him.

• • •

'We have received a ransom demand, at last,' Hector told the men that he had assembled in the communications room. They watched his face intently.

'How much?' Paddy O'Quinn asked quietly.

'It doesn't matter how much,' Hector replied. 'We can't pay it. We won't pay it.'

Paddy nodded. 'You'd be bloody mad to do so. But what are you going to do?'

'Hot extraction,' Hector said. 'We are going in to pull the girl out.'

'Do you know where they are holding her?' They all leaned forward eagerly as hounds given a whiff of the scent.

'No!' They sat back in their seats, and made no effort to hide their disappointment. Paddy spoke for all of them.

'Then it seems to me that we have a small problem.'

'Tariq and Uthmann will be back soon. They will have found out where they are holding her.'

'Are you sure of that?' Paddy asked.

'Have they ever failed yet?'

No one replied for a few moments, then Paddy remarked, 'Always a first time.'

'Listen, you dismal Johnnie, I'll give you odds of ten to one, if you put a hundred pounds on it. Put up or shut up.'

'Where am I going to find that sort of money with what you pay me?'

'Right! When Tariq and Uthmann do get back we must be ready to go immediately. Wherever we are going, there is only one way in. We jump at night from high altitude.' There were nods of assent. 'Not too many of us, a stick of ten men. All our Arabic speakers who can pass for locals.'

'Instead of parachuting in, why can't you use the company helicopter?' Hazel asked.

'They would hear us coming. Then a night landing, even in a chopper? No thanks.' Hector turned her down brusquely, but she showed no resentment.

'Okay, you can use my jet.'

'I have never jumped from a Gulfstream before.' Hector glanced around the room. 'Anyone here done it?' They shook their heads, and Hector looked back at Hazel. 'I don't think it's a good idea. There is the problem of the pressurized hull, and the location of the hatch forward of the wing. The wing could slice your head off as you jump. Then the speed of the plane—No, I think we will have to go for something not quite so exotic.'

'How about Bernie Vosloo?' Paddy suggested.

'Just what I was thinking.' Hector nodded and turned to Hazel. 'Bernie is an ex-South African Airforce pilot. He and his wife operate an ancient C-130 Hercules transport, hauling heavy loads around Africa and the Middle East. They aren't too fussy about the nature of the cargo and they know how to keep their mouths tight shut. I have used them a number of times in the past. Their Hercules has a partly pressurized hull, and they can get up to 21,000 feet if they give it a kick in the arse. At that altitude, to a listener on the ground they will not be making much more noise than a cat pissing on a sheet of velvet.' Hazel had never heard the expression before and she kept an elaborately straight face as she tried to suppress a smile, but her eyes twinkled blue as fairy lights. Bloody marvellous eyes, Hector thought, but distracting. He looked away from her to the men.

'However, we don't want to jump from 20,000 feet, so Bernie will throttle well back to keep the noise level low and he will descend to 10,000. At which level he can depressurize the cabin and we can bail out. As always we keep close contact during the drop, so that we hit the ground in a formation and we will be fully wired to deal with an unfriendly reception committee.'

'After that what happens?' Dave Imbiss asked.

'Don't worry about it, David old son. You won't be there, you and your baby-pink face,' Hector told him and then went on, 'That's the easy part. The difficult part will be the return journey. As usual there are three possible ways out: land, sea and air. The first-class return ticket would be by company helicopter.' He nodded at Hans Lategan who was sitting in the back row. 'We will have Hans in his chopper standing by on the border of the nearest civilized state, ready to pick up our call sign and come in to fetch us. That should do it – ' he paused – 'but we are all aware of what can happen to the best laid plans of mice and men, so we will cover the other two exit routes. I'm pretty certain that they are holding Miss Bannock in either Puntland or Yemen. These lads are pirates so they will probably never be too far from the coast.' Hector pulled up the map projection on the wall screen and moved the marker over the area to demonstrate his point. 'Whatever happens we will have Ronnie Wells waiting offshore in his MTB.' He looked at Ronnie in the back row, sitting next to Hans. 'What's your range in that old tub of yours?'

'With my new auxiliary deck tanks, it is well over a thousand nautical miles,' Ronnie replied, 'And I'll thank you for remembering that she is no *old tub*. She can touch forty knots if I open her up.'

'I apologize for the unfortunate choice of words, Ronnie,' said Hector with a smile. 'So Ronnie will be waiting to give any of you who make it to the beach a free pleasure cruise of the Red Sea on your way home.'

'And if neither Hans nor Ronnie is able to keep the appointment, what happens then?' Paddy asked.

'Ah! That's where you come in, Paddy. You will be waiting on the nearest land border with a column of trucks. If the target turns out to be in Yemen you will be on the border of either Saudi or Oman. If the target turns out to be Puntland then you will be waiting in Ethiopia to come in and fetch us. Bernie Vosloo and his good wife can fly you and your trucks into position once we know where we are heading. By the way, you'd better make damned sure you have the doctor with you. Somebody is sure to be hurt if we are forced to take the Ethiopian route.' Hector looked around the circle of their faces. 'So all of you have some work to do. I want to be ready to go within twenty-four hours of acquiring our target, and that could be any day now. Let's move arse!' As soon as the others had left the room, Hector called Bernie Vosloo on the satellite phone. Hazel was listening in on the extension.

'Bernie, it's Hector Cross. Whereabouts are you and your lovely missus?'

'Hi, Heck. I am in Nairobi, but not for much longer. Are you still alive? Those darkies are really poor shots, aren't they?'

'Their aim is just fine, but I have learned to dodge. Listen, Bernie, I have a job for you.'

Bernie chuckled. 'So has everybody else in Africa, Heck. Nella and I are flying our cute little bums off day and night. Tomorrow we light out for the Democratic Republic of the Congo, that ironically named little cesspit of a country.'

'Come to Abu Zara. The weather and the beer are great here.'

'Sorry, Heck. I have a contract to fulfil. A big client. I cannot let him down.'

'How much is the contract worth?'

'Fifty thousand.' Hector covered the mouthpiece with his hand and looked across at Hazel.

'How far can I go?' he whispered.

'Who is that you are talking to?' Bernie demanded sharply.

'The lovely lady I work for. Hold on, Bernie.'

'As much as it takes to get him,' Hazel whispered back, and she scrawled on the pad in front of her '$1,000,000?' and turned it towards him so he could see.

'That's crazy!' Hector shook his head, and said into the receiver, 'We will go to quarter of a million.'

Bernie went very quiet for a while then he said, 'I would really love to help you. Sorry, Heck. But it's my reputation on the line.'

'Is Nella there?' Hector asked.

'Yes, but—'

'But nothing! Put her on.' Nella came on the line with her thick Afrikaans accent.

'Ja, Hector Cross. What's your latest bullshit story, man?'

'I just called to say I love you.'

'Kiss my butt, Cross!'

'Nothing would give me greater pleasure, Nella. But you have to divorce that stupid husband of yours first. You know what he has just done? He turned down my offer for half a million, for ten days' work.'

'How much?' Nella asked thoughtfully.

'Half a million.'

'Dollars? Not African Monopoly money?'

'Dollars,' he confirmed, 'lovely US greenbacks.'

'Where are you?'

'Sidi el Razig in Abu Zara.'

'We'll be there the day after tomorrow for breakfast. And I love you back, Hector Cross.'

• • •

Hector and Hazel and four of the Cross Bow operatives were waiting on the airstrip as the monstrous four-engine transport aircraft circled and then banked steeply onto its approach run.

'Nella is at the controls,' Hector said with certainty.

'How do you know?' Hazel demanded.

'Bernie flies like an old maid. Nella is the original rodeo cowgirl from Germiston, the city they would have to put the tube in if they wanted to give the world an enema.'

'Don't be rude. My paternal grandfather was born in Germiston.'

'I bet that in every other respect he was a splendid fellow.'

The C-130 Hercules touched down, trundled down the airstrip and swung off to park close to where they were standing, its four huge contra-rotating propellers sending a stinging cloud of sand over them. Nella cut the engines and dropped the roll-on-roll-off ramp at the rear of the fuselage. She and Bernie came down the ramp. Nella was a brawny blonde with a baby-doll face. She was dressed in camouflage overalls. The sleeves were cut off and showed a tattoo of a flying angel on her beefy right arm. She towered over her husband.

'Okay, Heck, what do you want us to do for half a mill? Knowing you, I bet it's not going to be easy,' she said as they shook hands.

'You've got me all wrong, like you always did.'

'Introduce us to your girlfriend.' Nella looked Hazel over with a penetrating eye, trying not to let her jealousy seem too obvious.

'You figure the relationship slightly wrong, Nella my love. This is Mrs Hazel Bannock – my boss and yours. So a little respect might be in order. Come on, let's go up to the terminal where we can talk.' They all piled into the two Hummvee trucks. In the situation room they sat at the long table and Hector explained their predicament to the Vosloos. When he had finished they were all silent for a while and then Nella looked at Hazel.

'I also have a daughter. Thank the Lord, she's found herself a good man in Australia. But I know how you must feel.' She reached across the table and covered Hazel's silken hand with her own huge paw which was ingrained with engine oil and grime. The nails were torn and broken off short. 'I would fly you for free if you asked me, Mrs Bannock.'

'Thank you, Nella. You are a good person. It shines out.'

'For God's sake, ladies. Cut it out. You will have me in tears if you don't stop,' Hector interrupted. 'There's only one problem. We're not sure where we are going or when. But it will be close and it will be soon.'

'How soon?' Bernie Vosloo asked. 'We can't wait around here for weeks. Every day we spend sat on the ground costs us money.'

'You hold your mouth, Bernie Vosloo!' Nella rounded on him. 'Didn't you hear me give the lady my word?'

'He's right!' Hazel said. 'Of course, I will pay your down time. Twenty thousand dollars for the first day, increasing by another ten thousand every day longer that you sit on the ground.'

'You don't have to do that, Mrs Bannock.' Nella looked abashed.

'Yes I do,' Hazel replied. 'Now let's listen to Mr Cross.'

• • •

It took four days but by then they were all on the starting blocks. Ronnie Wells and three of his men had taken the MTB down the Gulf and around to Ras el Mandeb. He was anchored in a deserted cove on the Saudi coast just north of the border with Yemen and across the strait from Puntland. His fuel tanks were topped up from the canisters he carried on deck, and he was in full and constant radio contact with Sidi el Razig.

The Hercules stood on the fringe of the airstrip beyond the tiny airport building. She had three of the Cross Bow long-range GM trucks lashed down in the hold, and a small 750-gallon two-wheel gasoline tanker which could be towed behind one of the trucks. The trucks were packed with equipment and each of them carried a pair of 50 calibre Browning heavy machine guns concealed under the tarpaulins. They could be mounted in minutes, and their fire power was devastating.

Hector had rehearsed the drop procedure with Bernie and Nella. As soon as they had acquired the target they would take off at nightfall and overfly it. Bernie and Nella had carried out dozens of parachute drops. They were experts. Hector's stick would jump, and the Hercules would fly on to the selected border airfield. There it would land and Paddy and Dave would unload the trucks and take up a listening and waiting position as close to the enemy base as was safe and feasible. At the radio summons from Hector they would race across the border and head for a pre-arranged rendezvous.

Those were the two least desirable extraction vehicles. Hector was really relying heavily on Hans Lategan in Bannock Oil's big Russian MIL-26 helicopter getting through to them for a quick and neat extraction. The crimson and white paintwork, in the colours of Bannock Oil, had already been sprayed over with mottled brown and dark green camouflage. It would be waiting on the nearest border, fully fuelled.

Hazel had sent a reply to the ransom demand, assuring the Beast that she was doing all in her power to raise the money that they demanded, but stating that considering the amount involved this would take time. She hoped that she would have the full amount ready to send to their instructions within twenty days. She received no acknowledgement, and she fretted incessantly. There was nothing left to do but wait, and Hazel Bannock was not good at waiting. After she had finished her daily conference call to her people in Houston and checked with Colonel Roberts at the Pentagon there were still eighteen hours of each day to fill.

Every morning Hector took her with him to meet the local passenger flight from Ash-Alman, the capital of Abu Zara. They scanned the faces of everybody disembarking, but Uthmann and Tariq were never amongst them. There was a limit to even Hazel's athletic endurance, so they could not pass more than seven or eight hours a day running in the dunes or skin diving in the coral paradise offshore. Fortunately she was very easy to talk to once she began to trust Hector a little and to lower her defences a few inches. When they argued politics he began to detect a swing to the right in her original stance. However, she was vehemently opposed to capital punishment, and she still believed in the sanctity of human life.

'You're telling me that there is not a single ugly thug in this world, no matter how evil he is, who does not deserve to die?' Hector demanded.

'That decision remains with God. Not with us.'

'The old man upstairs has whispered in my ear often enough when I have one of the thugs in my sights, *Take him down, Hector my lad!* When the Lord calls then Hector Cross obeys.'

'You are a total heathen.' She could scarcely hide her smile. He found that she was an old-fashioned believer, sublimely certain of the omnipresence and omnipotence of Jesus Christ.

'So you think that every time you get down on your knees J.C. is tuned in on your call sign?' he asked.

'You just wait and see, Cross. You just wait and see.'

'You've been chatting to him recently, I can tell,' he accused, and she smiled like the Sphinx. These discussions, and others like them, were good for passing the hours. Then after dinner one evening she spotted a cheap wooden chess set on a shelf behind the bar in the mess and challenged him to a game. He had not played since leaving university. They sat facing each other across the board, and he swiftly learned that she cared very little for defence, and relied on a fiery queen attack. Once she united her rooks she was well nigh impossible to contain. However, twice he was able to sucker her into a royal knight fork on her king and queen. They came out about equal over a dozen hard-fought games.

Then on the fifth day after the arrival of Bernie and Nella at Sidi el Razig, Hector told her, 'Mrs Bannock, I am taking you out to dinner tonight, whether you like it or not.'

'Keep going, and you might be able to talk me into it,' she said. 'Should I dress up?'

'You look good to me just like that.' He drove her out to a stretch of beach three miles up the coast. She watched him expertly setting up the barbecue.

'Okay, you are a regular boy scout at fire-making, but what's to cook?'

'Come on, we have to go shopping.' There was only an hour until sundown, but they swam out a few hundred metres to his secret coral reef. With three dives he collected a six-pound strawberry-coloured rock cod and two big rock lobsters. She sat on a picnic rug with her long bare legs curled up under her and a glass of red Burgundy in her hand while she watched him cook.

'Dinner is served,' he announced at last and they ate with their fingers, picking the succulent white meat off the rock cod's bones and sucking the flesh out of the armoured crayfish legs. They threw the scraps in the fire and watched them blacken and burn. Then Hazel stood up.

'Where are you going?' he asked lazily.

'Swim,' she answered. 'You can come along, if you have a mind.' She reached behind her back with both hands and popped the clasp of her bikini top. Then she placed her thumbs inside the elastic of the pants bottoms and wriggled them down over her hips until they fell to her ankles. She kicked the wisp of pretty cloth high in the air and stood for just a moment facing him. He caught his breath with the shock of delight. She had the body of a woman in her magnificent prime: tight and high-breasted, her belly flat and hard, with hips swelling out proudly from her narrow waist into the perfect lines of an Etruscan vase. This was a natural woman, not shaven in the modern fashion like a pornographic starlet. She laughed in his face, provocatively and wantonly, then spun around and raced down the beach to dive into the low surf and swim out into deeper water with a powerful over-arm crawl. There she trod water and, laughing still, watched him hopping around on one leg in the sand before he could kick off his swimming trunks.

'I am coming after you, you little vixen!' he shouted in warning and charged down the beach. She shrieked with delicious terror and churned the water foamy as she swam away from him. He caught her and turned her to face him while he reached for her mouth with his own. She placed her hands on his shoulders submissively until his lips were an inch from hers. Then she rose high above him and placed her entire weight on his shoulders, driving him deep below the surface. By the time he came up spluttering she was ten metres away. He bulled his way after her but as he reached out to grab her, she flicked both legs high in the air, jack-knifed her body and duck-dived deep into the dark water. He lost sight of her and trod water, turning slowly and watching for her to surface again. She came up nearer the beach and he charged after her, swinging his arms and kicking the water to foam behind him. She ducked down again like a cormorant after a fish. She was slowly and disingenuously working him back into shallow water.

Suddenly she stood up, only waist deep. She waited for him to come and then ran to meet him. They locked together, breath and belly. She felt him against her, huge and hard, as ready for her as she was for him. She flung her arms round his neck and clamped both her thighs around his hips. It took a moment of frantic manoeuvring by both of them before they could get themselves perfectly aligned and then he glided up deeply into her belly. It seemed to her that he might touch her very heart.

'Oh, sweet God. This is the one I have waited for, for so very long,' she breathed, and gave herself to him without check or reservation.

• • •

It was after midnight when they arrived back at the terminal buildings. He saw her to her room and would have left her at the door with a single lingering kiss.

'Don't be daft,' she said, and held the door open. 'Come on in.'

'What will people think?'

'To use your own lyrical terminology, I don't give a good stuff!' Hazel replied.

'What a grand idea! Let's do it.' He chuckled and followed her through the door and locked it behind them. They showered together, openly and lingeringly gloating over each other's bodies as they washed off the beach sand and sea salt. Then they went to the bed.

'Hemingway called his bed the Fatherland,' Hector remarked as they slid between the sheets.

'Old Ernie has my vote,' she laughed as she came in from the other side and they met in the middle. They made love joyously and tenderly, but always the shadow of tragedy coloured their happiness. When they had exhausted each other for the moment, she lay in his arms and pressing her face to his naked chest she wept softly but bitterly. He stroked her hair and shared her agony.

'I am going to come with you when you go in to fetch Cayla,' she said. 'I cannot stay here alone. I have only endured this long because of you. I am as tough as any of your men. I can handle myself in a crisis, you know that. You must take me in with you.'

'Do you know that you have the bluest and most beautiful eyes in all the world?' he said. She sat up and stared at him angrily.

'Are you cracking your stupid jokes at a time like this?'

'No, my darling. I am telling you why you cannot come with me.' She shook her head in incomprehension, and he went on, 'Things might not go as we planned them. We might become stranded and have to try and blend into the local populace and worm our way out. The Arabs call eyes like yours devil's eyes. The first of the enemy who looked into your face would know what you are. If I took you with me it would halve the chances of getting Cayla out safely.' She looked at him steadily for a long while, then her shoulders slumped and she hid her face against his chest again.

'That is the only reason why I would stay,' she whispered. 'I would not do anything that reduced the chances for her. You will get her out, Hector? You will bring her back to me?'

'Yes, I will.'

'And you? Will you come back to me? I have only just found you. I cannot lose you now.'

'I will be back, I promise you, with Cayla beside me.'

'And I believe you,' she said. She slept holding on to him. He could barely hear her breathing. He was careful not to move and disturb her. She woke as the dawn light filtered through the curtains.

'That's the first night I have slept straight through since Cayla—' She didn't finish the sentence. 'I'm starving. Take me to breakfast.'

Big Nella was in the mess before them with a huge platter of scrambled eggs, bacon and sausage in front of her. She looked up at Hazel, and a flash of intuitive understanding passed between them. Nella looked down at her plate and grinned.

'*Mazel tov!*' she said to her eggs, and Hazel blushed. Hector would never have believed that she was capable of such a thing, and he stared at the phenomenon with astonishment; for him it was more lovely than the sunrise. After they had eaten he took Hazel out to the Hummvee. She sat beside him in the front seat and every time he changed gear he touched her leg, and she smiled demurely. Hector parked the Hummvee in the shade under the wing of the Hercules, for even at this hour the sun was already uncomfortably warm. Now they could hold hands. The Fokker F-27 Friendship was only half an hour behind schedule.

'For Abu Zara Airways that is almost early,' Hector told her, as they watched it taxi up to park in front of the terminal building and shut down its engines. The twenty or so passengers began to disembark and Hector watched them without any real expectations. They were nearly all Arabs in traditional dress carrying bundles and parcels of their possessions. Suddenly Hector stiffened and squeezed her hand hard.

'Son of a gun! It's them!' He swore softly.

'Which ones?' Hazel sat upright. 'They all look the same to me.'

'The last two. I could tell them from a mile off by the way they walk.' He blew a single short blast on the horn and started the engine of the Hummvee. The two Arabs looked across at them, and then headed towards them. They climbed into the back seat.

'Peace be on you!' Hector greeted them.

'On you, peace.' They responded in unison. Hector drove a mile along the track above the beach before he parked. Hazel swivelled in her seat to look back at the two men behind her.

'This is driving me screaming mad,' she blurted out. 'I have to know! Have you found where my daughter is, Uthmann?'

'Yes, Mrs Bannock. We have found her. I have been staying with my brother Ali in Baghdad. He is different to me. He believes the only way forward for our nation is the road of jihad. He is a mujahid and is allied strongly with Al-Qaeda. He knows that I do not support his views, but we are brothers and bound together by our blood. He would never divulge any of his jihadist affairs to me, but after I had spent these last weeks in his home he became relaxed and less secretive. Usually he uses a mobile phone and he never makes business calls from his home. A few days ago he mistakenly believed that I had gone out with his wife to visit friends of ours, but I was in the upper floor of the house when Ali used the land line to speak to one of his Al-Qaeda associates. I listened to the conversation on the extension. They were discussing the capture and the imprisonment of your daughter, and one of them mentioned that she was taken by members of the clan of Sheikh Khan Tippoo Tip.'

'Tippoo Tip! That is the same name as the steward that got on board the *Dolphin*. But who is this sheikh?' Hazel demanded, and Uthmann answered her.

'He is a warlord, and the head of one of the most powerful clans in Puntland.'

Hector touched his shoulder. 'As always, you have proved your worth, old friend,' he told him.

'Wait! I have more to tell you.' Uthmann shook his head sadly. 'Do you remember the men you shot and killed in Baghdad many years ago?'

Hector nodded. 'The three jihadists that had detonated the roadside bomb.' He glanced sideways at Tariq. 'Of course Tariq and I remember them.'

'Do you know what their names were?'

'No,' Hector admitted, 'apparently they were all using code names. Even Military Intelligence could not identify them. What have you discovered, Uthmann?'

'The man you killed was named Saladin Gamel Tippoo Tip. He was the son of Sheikh Khan Tippoo Tip and the father of Adam Tippoo Tip. The sheikh declared a blood feud with you.' Hector stared at him speechlessly, and Uthmann went on, 'The dhow that you and Ronnie Wells destroyed had six men on board. They had been sent by Sheikh Khan to avenge his eldest son. Amongst those who died was Gafour Tippoo Tip, the sheikh's fifth son. The blood debt then stood at two. The Sheikh sent a third son to find you and avenge his brothers—'

'The one called Anwar!' Hector exclaimed. 'My God! I will never forget him. With his last breath he mocked me:

My name is Anwar. Remember it, Cross, you pig of the great pig. The debt has not been settled. The Blood Feud continues. Others will come.'

Tariq nodded. 'It is even as you say, Hector.'

'Where can we find this creature, Sheikh Tippoo Tip?' Hector demanded.

Tariq cut in sharply. 'I know him. His stronghold is in Puntland.'

'Puntland! That name keeps cropping up,' Hazel interjected.

'It's a rebel province of Somalia. Puntland is Tariq's home turf,' Hector explained, and looked back at Tariq. 'This is what we've been waiting for. What can you tell us about this thug?'

'Only what everybody else in Puntland knows: Tippoo Tip has his stronghold in the north-western part of the country at a place called the Oasis of the Miracle. It's south of the main road in the province, near the small village of Ameera.'

'Do you know the area?' Hector demanded, but Tariq shook his head. Hector knew him so well that he had no doubt that he was lying, or at least skirting the truth.

'Okay.' Hector needed no further confirmation. 'We need to find out all we can about Tippoo Tip and his fortress. We need maps of the area. I must get back to the terminal and get everybody working on this.'

When they were all assembled around the long table again Hector looked them over, before he spoke.

'Well, we now know where we are going. Does anybody here, apart from Tariq, know of a place in Puntland called the Oasis of the Miracle, or the village of Ameera? Those are our targets.' They all looked mystified. Hector singled out Dave Imbiss.

'Dave, can you get on to the website of Google Earth. Tariq will point out the targets on the map. I want copies of the satellite photographs of the area. I want to know the distance to fly. I want to know which is the closest airstrip in Ethiopia, and the distance by road from there to our target.' Then he paused and looked across at Bernie and Nella. 'Or do you two have any ideas on that? Do you know of a landing strip which fits the bill?'

'Jig Jig!' said Nella, and then screamed with laughter and gave Bernie a nudge in his ribs with her elbow that doubled him over.

'A landing ground with a name like that?' Hector raised an eyebrow. 'Interesting!'

'Nella gave it that name, not me,' Bernie protested as he straightened up rubbing his ribs. 'I don't know what its real name is, probably doesn't have one. It's an old deserted Italian military strip from World War Two. It's in shocking condition, but the Hercules doesn't mind rough ground.'

'We made an emergency landing there once.' Nella was still bubbling with laughter. 'I was taken short with an acute case of the hots and we landed there for Bernie to bonk me. It was terrific! One of his very best efforts, ever. Never forget it.' Bernie maintained his sober mien despite the hoots of laughter and general levity.

'It's perfectly situated, less than thirty miles from the Puntland border but, best of all, there is no official presence, no police and no immigration,' Bernie said.

'Sounds as though it was made for us. Show Dave where it is on the map. Nella, do you think you can restrain yourself when you land there again? No more indiscriminate bonking!' He turned to Paddy. 'Paddy, get on the radio to Ronnie Wells and tell him to move his MTB across to the Puntland coast and find a safe anchorage as close to the target as he can get. Let us know when he gets there.' All the time he was giving his orders he was aware that Tariq was watching him covertly. At last he glanced at him directly and Tariq jerked his head almost imperceptibly and then stood up and left the room. Hector gave him a minute, and then he said to Paddy O'Quinn, 'Carry on here. I won't be away too long.'

He went out to search for Tariq and after a few minutes spotted him behind one of the parked trucks. He was smoking a cigarette in blithe contempt of the no smoking sign on the side of the truck. When he saw Hector approaching he ground out the cigarette under his heel and walked off along the pipeline. Hector followed him, and found him squatting behind one of the pump stations.

'Speak to me, oh beloved of the Prophet,' Hector invited as he squatted beside him.

'I could not speak in front of the others,' Tariq explained.

'Not even Uthmann?'

Tariq shrugged. 'Did it not seem to you that Uthmann was able to gather a great deal of information about the Tippoo Tip clan by simply eavesdropping on his brother's telephone? It's the safety of my family I fear for, Effendi. I can take no chances.'

'There is truth in what you say, Tariq.' Hector nodded thoughtfully. Despite his deep affection for Uthmann he felt the worms of treachery stirring in his bowels.

Tariq drew a breath and then said, 'My aunt married a man from the village of Ameera, very close to the Oasis of the Miracle. When I was a child I spent many months there every year. I herded the camels with my cousins. I saw the fortress of Tippoo Tip many times, but only from a distance. My aunt was a servant to the Khan in the fortress. But that was long ago and perhaps my aunt is dead by now.'

'Then again, perhaps she is not dead. Perhaps she still works in the fortress. Perhaps she knows where they are keeping the girl. Perhaps she still loves you enough to show you how to get into the fortress and where to find the girl.'

'Perhaps.' Tariq grinned and stroked his beard. 'Perhaps all those things.'

'Perhaps you will visit your aunt and find out.'

'Perhaps.' Tariq nodded.

'Perhaps you will go tonight. We will drop you from the Hercules close to Ameera. I will give you one of the satellite phones. You will call me as soon as you make contact with your family. And that is not perhaps.'

'As always, to hear you is to obey you, Hector.' Tariq nodded and his grin grew wider. Hector punched his shoulder and started to rise to his feet, but Tariq laid a hand on his arm.

'Wait, I have something else to tell you.' Hector squatted beside him again. 'If we get the girl out of the fortress we will be hunted by many men. They will be in four-wheel-drive trucks. We will be on foot with the girl. She may be sick and weak after what they have done to her. We may have to carry her.'

'Tell me what you suggest.'

'To the north of the fortress there is a deep and rocky ravine. It runs for seventy miles east to west. We can cross it on foot, but even a four-wheel-drive vehicle will not be able to follow us. They will have to go around thirty or forty miles east to cross the wadi. Once we get across the wadi, it will give us a start of at least two or three hours, if not much longer.'

'You deserve to be rewarded with a hundred virgins!' said Hector smiling.

'I will be happy with one,' said Tariq, returning his smile, 'but a good one.' Hector left him squatting in the shade of the pump house rolling himself another cigarette.

As Hector walked into the situation room Dave called across. 'These are the Google Earth satellite pics of the area, boss.' He tapped the sheets spread on the table in front of him. 'The village of Ameera is tagged but I can't find anything about the Oasis of the Miracle.'

'Let's have a look.' Hector studied the high-resolution photograph then stabbed his forefinger down on it. 'There it is!' he exclaimed. '*Mo'jiza*. The miracle. Let me have the coordinates, Dave.' While Dave worked them out, Hector continued scanning the map. Now he knew what to look for and where, he picked out the wadi immediately. He took Dave's magnifying glass and examined the wadi carefully. The information that Tariq had given him seemed to be confirmed: no roads or tracks traversed the wadi.

He straightened up and went to where Bernie and Nella were standing outside the door, puffing on their cigarettes. Hector spoke quietly to them. 'Tonight I want you to drop Tariq as close as you can to the village of Ameera. I am inserting him to make a reconnaissance of the area. After you have dropped him you will carry straight on to the Jig Jig landing strip with Paddy and his gang who will be on board. You will disembark them there with the trucks, and then come back here to Sidi el Razig.' He glanced through the door at Hazel, who had followed him out of the situation room. He knew it was neither wise nor kind to let her sit alone in Sidi el Razig, with nothing to keep her fully occupied.

'Mrs Bannock and I will come along with you for the ride to Ameera and Jig Jig.' Hazel nodded her agreement, and Hector turned back to Bernie.

'Work out your flying time for each stage of the flight. We must arrive at Jig Jig when it's light enough to make a landing. We don't want to attract any attention by circling around the area too long. Do you think you can find the strip straight off?'

'Stupid question,' Nella replied. 'We've been there before, if you remember.' She placed a pair of reading glasses with bright-orange plastic frames on her nose and she and Bernie went to work with a hand-held calculator. Nella looked up after only a few minutes. 'Okay, takeoff from here will be at 2000 hours sharp. Anybody not on board gets left behind.'

• • •

Hector and Hazel stood together at the back of the flight deck of the Hercules, and over the heads of the pilots they watched the African nightfall. Hazel leaned lightly against him. The last rays of the sun lit the crests of the mountains ahead, turning them the colours of bronze and freshly minted gold. At the same time the land directly beneath them had already been blotted out by the darkness, and only the tiny pinpricks of light marked the positions of the widely scattered hamlets and villages of Puntland.

'It's so beautiful,' Hazel whispered, 'but I cannot see the beauty for the hideousness. Cayla is down there somewhere.' The night closed its grip on them and the stars spread in splendour above them. Nella turned in her seat and lifted her headphones from her ears.

'I'm beginning the descent now. Twenty minutes to the drop zone, Hector. Get your man kitted up and ready to go.' Hector went back into the main cabin. Most of Paddy's men had climbed into the trucks and found themselves comfortable places to sleep.

But Tariq was waiting for Hector near the tail gate. He was dressed like a Somalian peasant with his possessions in a goatskin satchel tied around his waist, and rawhide sandals on his feet. While Hector helped him to buckle on his parachute, he went quickly over the pre-arranged contact and recognition signals.

'Ten minutes to drop zone!' Nella's voice came over the tannoy. Hazel came back to shake Tariq's hand.

'This is not the first time you have risked your life for me, Tariq. I will find a way to repay you.'

'I ask no payment, Mrs Bannock.'

'Then I pray for Allah's blessing and protection over you,' she said, and at that Nella's voice came over the tannoy again.

'Five minutes to drop zone. I am opening the tail gate now. Make sure your safety harnesses are hooked on.' The ramp lowered ponderously and the cool night air whipped around their heads and tugged at their clothing.

'I can see the lights of Ameera dead ahead,' Nella sang out. 'One minute to jump.' Then she began to count down the seconds: 'Five, four, three, two and Go! Go! Go!'

Tariq ran forward and sprang head first over the edge of the ramp. The slipstream snapped him away instantly into the darkness. Nella closed the tail ramp and gradually increased the power on her engines. They climbed away on course for Jig Jig.

They circled the airstrip in the dawn. There were the ruins of a building, roofless and with the remaining walls crumbling. Even after eighty years the abandoned runway was still marked by small cairns of whitewashed rocks. The only sign of life was on the hillside above the strip, where a small boy in a red blanket warmed himself at a smoky little fire while his herd of goats grazed around him. The smoke from the fire gave Nella the wind direction. As the Hercules thundered low over them the boy and the goats scattered in panic. Nella touched down the big machine as lightly as a butterfly landing on a rose. Then it bumped and jarred over the rutted ground and pulled up long before it had run out of track. Nella dropped the tail gate, and Paddy led the little convoy of three trucks down off the tail ramp, and with a last wave of his gloved hand roared off back towards the Somali border. Nella used the engines to gun the Hercules around in a 180-degree turn and they were airborne again within five minutes of touch down.

'Five and a half hours' flying time home,' Hector said as he slipped his arm around Hazel's shoulders. 'I have no idea how we are going to pass the time.'

'We have this cargo hold completely to ourselves,' Hazel pointed out. 'May I make a suggestion?'

'I read your mind and find it to be an excellent suggestion. Mrs Bannock, you are a genius.'

• • •

Tariq found an aardvark hole and stuffed his parachute and his para helmet down it. He wound his turban around his head, and slung the goatskin satchel over his shoulder. During his descent he had carefully marked the direction of the village. There were only two or three dim lights showing and he was amazed by the acuity of Nella Vosloo's eyesight that had enabled her to pick them out from 10,000 feet. He set off for Ameera and within half a mile he smelt the woodsmoke of the cooking fires and the strong odour of goats and men. As he approached the village a dog barked, and another joined in, but the village slept on. It had been ten years since his last visit, but there was a gibbous moon to give him sufficient light to orient himself as he moved quietly among the thatched huts. His aunt's was the third after the well. He tapped on the door, and after a while a woman's voice spoke softly from behind it.

'Who is it? What do you want so late at night? I am a decent woman. Go away!'

'I am Tariq Hakam, I am looking for my mother's sister, Taheera.'

'Wait!' called the unseen woman. He heard her moving around in the hut and then there was the strike and flare of a match. The soft yellow light of a kerosene lamp showed through the chinks in the mud wall. At last the door scraped open, and the woman stood looking out at him.

'Is it truly you, Tariq Hakam?' she asked and held the lamp so that the light fell on his face. 'Yes,' she whispered shyly, 'it is indeed you.' Artlessly she let her veil fall open.

'Who are you?' He stared at her face. She was young and very pretty. Her features were vaguely familiar.

'I am sad that you do not know me, Tariq. I am your cousin Daliyah.'

'Daliyah! But you have grown so big!' She giggled coyly and pulled the veil over her mouth and nose again. Only ten years before she had been an urchin who had trailed around behind him in a most irritating manner in her grubby short skirts with unkempt hair and flies crawling on the dried snot under her nostrils.

'So have you grown big,' she said. 'I thought I would never see you again. I have often wondered where you had gone and what you were doing.' She stood aside and held the door open. He stooped under the lintel and brushed past her. The light contact made his breath come a little shorter.

'Is my aunt here, Daliyah?'

'My mother is dead, Tariq, may Allah preserve her soul. I have returned to Ameera to mourn for her.'

'May she find happiness in paradise,' he said quietly. 'I did not know of her death.'

'She was very sick for a long time.'

'What of you, Daliyah? Is there someone to protect you? Your father, your brothers?'

'My father has been dead these five years past. My brothers have gone away. They have gone to Mogadishu to become fighters in the army of Allah. I am alone here.' She paused then went on, 'There are men here, coarse rough men. I am afraid. That is why I hesitated to open the door for you.'

'What will become of you?'

'Before she died my mother arranged for me to work as a servant at the fortress at the Oasis of the Miracle. I have come back here only to bury my mother and to mourn her. Now the days of mourning are spent I will return to my work at the fortress.' She had led him through to the small lean-to kitchen at the rear of the hut. She set the lantern down and turned to him. 'Are you hungry, cousin? I have some dates and unleavened bread. I have curdled goat's milk also.' She was eager to please him.

'Thank you, Daliyah. I have some food with me. We can share it.' He opened his leather satchel and brought out a pack of military rations. Her eyes lit up when she saw it. He guessed that she had eaten little for some while. They sat cross-legged on the dry mud floor facing each other with the small enamelled bowls between them, and he watched her eat with pleasure. She knew he was watching her and she kept her eyes modestly down-cast, but now and then smiled a little to herself. When they had finished she rinsed out the bowls and came back to sit across from him again.

'You say that you work at the fortress?' he asked, and she nodded confirmation.

'I have business there, in the fortress,' he said, and she looked at him with quick interest.

'Is that what brings you here?' He inclined his head and she went on, 'What is it you seek, cousin?'

'A girl. A young white girl with pale hair.' Daliyah gasped and covered her mouth with her hand. Her eyes were dark with shock and fear. 'You know her!' he said with certainty. She did not reply but hung her head and looked at the ground between them.

'I have come to take her back to her family.'

She shook her head sadly. 'Beware, Tariq Hakam. It is dangerous to talk loosely like this. I fear for you.'

They were silent for a long time, and he saw her shiver.

'Will you help me, Daliyah?'

'I know this girl; she is young, as I am. Yet they have given her to the men to sport with.' Her voice was almost inaudible. 'She is sick. She is sick with the injuries they have inflicted on her. She is sick with loneliness and fear.'

'Take me to her, Daliyah. Or at least show me the way.'

She did not answer for a while, then she said, 'If I do as you ask, they will know that it was me that led you to her. They will do to me what they have done to her. If I lead you to her, I cannot remain in this place. Will you take me away with you when you go, Tariq? Will you shield me from their wrath?'

'Yes, Daliyah. I will take you away with me, and gladly.'

'Then I will do it, Tariq Hakam, my cousin.' She smiled shyly and her dark eyes shone in the lantern light.

• • •

Tariq crouched under a ledge of rock facing the east. He had been there since an hour after nightfall. He was thinking about his cousin Daliyah. He was still wondering at her transformation from child to woman. Thinking about her made him feel happy. That morning before she left him to walk the four miles to the Oasis of the Miracle she had touched his arm and said, 'I will be waiting when you come.' He rubbed his arm where she had touched him, and smiled.

His thoughts were distracted by a soft tremble of sound in the sky. He looked up, but there was nothing to see but the stars. He cocked his head and listened. The sound grew stronger. He stood and picked up the old kerosene can with its lid cut off that Daliyah had given him and carried it into the open. He stacked the stones that he had collected earlier around the sides of the can to hold it securely. He listened again; now there were no doubts. The throb of multiple aircraft engines was unmistakable. From his satchel he brought out the naval distress flare and pulled the ignition tape, then dropped the flare into the can. He stepped back. It burst into flame and sulphurous smoke boiled from the can. The ruddy brilliance was reflected upwards. The sound of the engines increased until it was almost overhead.

• • •

Nella's voice boomed over the tannoy. 'I have the red marker flare visual. Two minutes to drop zone. I am opening the tail gate now.' Hector had divided his men into two sticks of five. He would jump first with his stick, and Uthmann would follow him immediately with his four men. They were all dressed in traditional clothing with black scarves covering most of their faces, but over that they wore flak jackets and battle helmets, and they carried survival packs and ten clips of ammo for the assault rifles on their webbing belts and a sheathed trench knife. The Cross Bow armourer had sharpened the blades until they were keen enough to shave with.

'First stick on your feet!' Hector ordered and they stood and shuffled towards the open tail gate. 'Switch on your marker lights!' Each of them had a tiny fluorescent light fixed to the front of his helmet with an elastic strap. They reached up and switched them on. The bulbs were coloured blue and the light they threw was so feeble that it was unlikely to be picked up by a hostile watcher at ground level, but the pinpricks of light would orient them to each other during the free fall. Hazel had been sitting on the bench beside Hector, and now she stood up and wrapped her arms around his neck.

'I love you!' she whispered and he was the first man she had said that to for a very long time. 'Come back. Come back to me.' Over the tannoy Nella's voice had begun the final count-down to the drop.

'I love you beyond the telling of it,' he said, and kissed her, leaving a smudge of cammo paint across her cheek. He rubbed it off tenderly with his thumb. 'When I come back, I'll have Cayla with me.' She turned away quickly from him and ran forward towards the doorway onto the flight deck. She did not want him to see her cry. Before she reached the flight deck Nella gave the jump command over the tannoy.

'Number one stick! Go! Go! Go!' Hazel turned swiftly for a last glimpse of him, but he had been sucked down into the dark maw of the night.

In the rush of the wind Hector stabilized his fall in the belly-down star position, and looked firstly for Tariq's red distress flare. He spotted it ten thousand feet below, at a down angle of approximately 45 degrees. Then he checked the space around him for the blue assembly lights of his men. Once he had located all of them he steered with subtle movements of his limbs and body to place himself at the head of their formation. His four companions were within touching distance as they dropped towards the red flare. He checked his altimeter and stopwatch. The time to fall was a little over a minute. Already they had reached their terminal velocity, and the earth was coming up to meet them rapidly. They were less than four hundred and fifty metres above ground level when he gave the hand signal to deploy their chutes and flare out. Now it was easier to steer and they slipped across the small breeze to settle like a flock of cranes within twenty paces of the burning red flare, landing almost simultaneously and staying on their feet as they spilled the air out of their parachutes. Immediately they formed a defensive circle with their weapons aimed outwards.

'Tariq!' Hector called softly. 'Show yourself!'

'It is me, Tariq Hakam.' He stood up from behind a pile of broken rock. 'Don't shoot!' He ran to meet Hector and they shook hands quickly, using the double grip.

'Is all well?' Hector demanded. 'Where is this girl, your cousin?' Tariq had spoken briefly of her this morning over the satellite phone.

'She is inside the fortress. She will lead us to where they are keeping the Bannock girl.'

'Can you trust her?' Hector demanded. Having someone inside the fortress was an amazing stroke of luck, and he was always wary of too much luck.

'She is of my blood,' Tariq replied, and almost added, 'and of my heart.' But he did not want to tempt Iblis, the Devil.

'Okay, I'll accept that.' Hector handed Tariq the spare rifle and pack he was carrying. At that moment Uthmann and his four men dropped out of the dark sky and landed close beside them. Tariq kicked over the can and piled rocks on top of the burning flare. The others were bundling and burying the parachutes.

Within minutes they had regrouped and Hector gave the order, 'Tariq, take the point. Move out at the double.'

They followed Tariq at carefully maintained intervals. With weapons at the ready, they trotted at a ground-consuming pace along a rugged path made by grazing goats. They reached the first palm trees of the oasis in forty-four minutes and went into a defensive circle again, lying belly down and heads up. Tariq signalled that the ground ahead was clear and Hector waved him forward. Tariq slipped away amongst the trees. Uthmann crawled up alongside Hector.

'Where is he going?' he whispered. 'Why are we stopping here?'

'Tariq has someone inside the fortress. He has gone to make contact, and then he will lead us through one of the side gates.'

'I did not know of this. Who is this informer? Is it a man or a woman? One of Tariq's relations?'

'What does it matter?' Hector felt a tiny flutter of ill ease. Uthmann was too insistent.

'You did not tell me of this, Hector.'

'You did not need to know until now,' Hector replied and Uthmann looked away. The set of his head and body was angry. Was he displaying his resentment that Hector had not trusted him? This was not Uthmann's usual style. Hector wondered if he was getting too old for the game. Was he losing his nerve? Hector could not face any darker possibility. Suddenly he made a decision, and he touched Uthmann's arm, forcing him to look into his face.

'Uthmann, you are to remain here with your stick as a fall-back for us. If we run into trouble inside the fortress we will come out in a hurry. I want you here to cover us. Do you understand?'

'I have always been at your side,' Uthmann said bitterly. His surly behaviour was excessive, and it reinforced Hector's decision not to take the man with him into the lair of the Beast.

'Not this time, old friend,' he said, and without another word Uthmann turned his face away and crawled back to his position with the second stick. Hector put him out of mind and stared into the trees of the oasis. He saw a moving shadow like a flitting moth, and he gave the soft two-tone recognition whistle. The reply came at once and Tariq materialized silently out of the trees. He had someone with him, a slim figure dressed in a long black abaya.

'This is my cousin Daliyah,' he said as the two of them dropped down beside Hector. 'Her news is disturbing. She says that there has been much excitement amongst the Khan's men. Nearly every man in the garrison has been sent to the north section beyond the mosque.'

'Why?' Hector demanded of the girl.

'I do not know.' Her voice was very soft.

Hector pondered a moment. 'Is there a gate there in the north section where the men have been sent?' he asked.

'There is a gate,' Daliyah confirmed, 'but it is not the main gate.'

'Did you intend to lead us into the fortress through that gate?'

'No!' She shook her head. 'In the east wall behind the kitchens there is another entrance. It is a very small opening through which only one man can pass at a time. It is almost never used and few people even know that it exists. That is the way I planned to guide you.'

'It is locked?'

'It is locked, but I have one of the keys. This morning I took it from the pocket of the head cook. He has not missed it.'

'Guards? Is this gate guarded?'

'I have never seen guards there. I came out that way tonight. The way was open and the place was deserted.'

'Tariq, it seems that your cousin is a brave and intelligent woman.' Hector peered at her but could make out nothing behind the veil.

'This I know,' Tariq said gravely.

'Is she married?'

'Not yet,' Tariq replied, 'but perhaps soon.' Daliyah hung her head modestly, but said nothing. 'She advises us to wait here for a while before we go up to the fortress. Give time for the disturbance in the fortress to settle.'

'How long does she think we should wait here?' Hector asked, and Tariq pointed out the moon that was rising beyond the palm grove. It was five days from full.

'We should wait until it is level with the tallest palm. By that time the guards will have relaxed and some of them might even be sleeping.'

'About an hour and a half,' Hector estimated and he checked his wristwatch. He crawled across to where Uthmann lay, and in a few terse words he explained his intentions. Then he crawled back to the head of his own stick. They lay silent and unmoving while the luminous minute hand crawled around the dial of his wrist-watch. Suddenly the heavy silence was broken by the howling and squealing of a pair of jackals under the walls of the fortress. This was challenged immediately by the clamorous baying of a pack of hounds within the walls.

'My God, how many dogs is the Khan keeping in there, Daliyah?'

'He has many. He likes to hunt with them.'

'What does he hunt . . . gazelle, oryx, jackals?'

'All those animals, yes,' Daliyah replied, 'but mostly he likes to hunt people.'

'People?' Even Hector was shocked. 'Do you mean, human beings?' She nodded and the starlight caught the sheen of tears in her eyes through the slit in her veil.

'Even so. Men or women who have angered him. Some of them my relations or good friends. His men take them out into the desert and release them. Then the Khan and his sons run them with the dogs. They glory in this sport and laugh as the hounds tear their victims to pieces. They allow the dogs to feed on the meat that they kill. The Khan believes it makes the dogs fiercer.'

'What a charming old chap he must be. I look forward to our first meeting,' Hector murmured. They waited while the baying of the pack died away into silence, and the moon came up from behind the palms. Only then did he stir again.

'Time to go, Tariq. Tell Daliyah to take the lead. We will keep well back behind her. If she meets anybody from the fortress she must try to divert them and give us a chance to deal with them before they kick up a fuss. You follow her and I will bring up the rear with the rest of the stick.' The girl moved off quickly and with confidence. They followed her out of the trees and onto the hillside. Now Hector had his first clear view of the fortress. It loomed above them, massive and black. No lights showed and it seemed as lifeless as the moon that was rising behind it. The path climbed up towards it steeply. The girl did not slow her pace. Now the stone walls towered over them, as implacably malevolent as an antediluvian monster lying in ambush for its prey. Suddenly Daliyah turned off the main pathway and took a less clearly defined track which ran below the battlements. They skirted stinking piles of refuse that had been thrown down from the tops of the walls. Jackals were scavenging among the rubbish, and they fled at the approach of the men. At last Daliyah paused beside a ditch that emerged from a low arched opening in the stonework. The opening was barred with a lattice of rusting iron bars. Human waste trickled from the archway into the ditch, and the stench assaulted the senses. Daliyah stepped over the ditch and turned abruptly into another narrow defile in the stonework, just wide enough to admit one man at a time. She disappeared and in single file they followed her into the opening. They climbed up a series of roughly hewn steps and Daliyah was waiting for them at the top, outside a low and sturdy wooden door that was studded and banded with iron.

'From here we must stay close together. It is very easy to lose your way once you are inside,' she whispered, and drew a heavy iron key of ancient design from under her gown. She fitted it into the lock and with an effort turned it. She put her shoulder to the door and it creaked open. She had to duck low to pass under the stone lintel. They followed her. She closed the door behind the last man.

'Don't lock it. We will be in a hurry when we return,' Hector told her softly. The darkness was so complete that it seemed like a crushing weight on their shoulders. Hector switched on the fluorescent headlight of his helmet, and the others followed his example. Daliyah led them on into a warren of twisting passages and interlinking rooms. There were small sounds: women were talking and laughing in one of the rooms they passed, and in another a man snored loudly. At last Daliyah motioned them to stop.

'Wait here,' she whispered to Tariq. 'Put out your lights and remain quietly. I will go to make sure it is safe.' She slipped away down the narrow corridor. The men squatted to rest, but they kept their weapons in their hands. Before long Daliyah came back, moving silently and swiftly.

'There are two men guarding the door to the girl's chamber. This is unusual. Usually there are five or six of them. Tonight the others must have been ordered to the north gate. One of the remaining guards will have the key to the girl's cell. Make no noise. Follow me.' Hector and Tariq moved up close on each side of her. After a short distance she stopped again and pointed ahead. The passage opened out suddenly and turned at right angles. They could hear men's voices coming from beyond the bend, and yellow lamplight was thrown against the angle of the side wall and the ceiling. Hector listened intently and realized that there were at least two men droning out a passage from the 'esha prayers. Then he saw their shadows on the side wall as they knelt and sat upright again. Hector held up two fingers and Tariq nodded. Hector tapped his chest and showed one finger, and then tapped his own chest and held up another finger

'One for each of us!' Tariq nodded. They handed their rifles to the men behind them, and each of them unrolled the piano wire garotte he carried in his button-down pocket, and tested it between his hands. Hector crept up to the corner. Tariq followed him. They waited there until the two warders knelt with their foreheads pressed to the paving slabs. Then he and Tariq moved out behind them, and as they rose again into the sitting position Hector and Tariq dropped the wire nooses over their heads and whipped them up tightly under the chins. The Arabs struggled, kicking and flailing their legs and arms. But they uttered not a sound. Hector placed his knee between his victim's shoulder blades and applied the power of both his hands. The man stiffened and kicked convulsively one last time as his bowels voided with a spluttering sound. Then he was still. Hector rolled him over quickly and patted down his robe. He felt the big iron key under the cloth and pulled it out. Daliyah was standing at the corner. Her eyes behind the veil were huge and bright with horror; perhaps she had not expected this killing.

'Which door?' Hector asked – there were three in the facing wall – but Daliyah was still too distressed to answer. Tariq sprang up and seized her shoulders. He shook her roughly.

'Which door?' She gathered her wits and pointed at the one in the centre.

'Back me up,' Hector told Tariq and went to the door. He unlocked it with the key he had taken from the warder and opened it slowly and stealthily. The cell was unlit, but he turned on his headlight. By its beam he saw how small the cell was. It was without any windows or ventilation. In the one corner stood a toilet bucket and a clay water pitcher. The bucket emitted a powerful odour. In the middle of the floor a small child-like figure was curled on a straw-filled pallet. She wore only a dirty shift that came down as far as her waist, so that there was no mistaking that she was female. He knelt over her and gently turned her so he could see the face. It was the face of the girl in the brutal video, the girl whose photograph Hazel had showed him. It was Cayla, but so pale and thin that her skin seemed transparent.

'Cayla!' he whispered in her ear and she stirred. 'Wake up, Cayla.' She opened her eyes but for a moment could not focus them. 'Wake up, Cayla. I have come to take you home.' Suddenly her eyes flew wide open. They seemed to fill her whole face. They were brimming with the shadows of terrible memories. She opened her mouth to scream but he whipped his hand across it, and whispered urgently,

'Don't be afraid. I am your friend. Your mother has sent me to take you home.'

She was deafened by her fear, not understanding the words, fighting him with all her meagre strength. 'Your mother told me you have a Bugatti Veyron which you call Mister Tortoise. Your mother is Hazel Bannock. She loves you, Cayla. Do you remember the filly she gave you for your last birthday? You named her Milk Chocolate.' She stopped struggling and stared at him with huge eyes. 'I am going to take my hand off your mouth now. Promise not to scream.' She nodded and he took his hand away.

'Not Milk Chocolate,' she whispered, 'Chocolate, just plain Chocolate.' She began to weep, silent sobs that racked her entire body. Hector picked her up in his arms. She was light as a bird, but burning up with fever.

'Come on, Cayla. I'm taking you home. Your mother is waiting for you.' Tariq was in the doorway covering him. Hector nodded towards the corpses of the two Arabs. 'Lock them in the cell.' They dragged them feet first with their heads bumping and rolling on the paving, and dumped them in the middle of the cell. Hector locked the door and pocketed the key. 'Now! Tell your cousin to get us out of this stinking place, Tariq.'

Daliyah led them back the way they had come. At every turn Hector anticipated a challenge or a burst of gunfire. 'This is too easy. It was never meant to be this easy. There is a shit-storm brewing. I can feel it in my guts,' he told himself grimly. But at last he stepped out through the little door into the narrow defile and he tasted the night air from the desert. 'Sweet as a virgin's kiss,' he murmured and filled his lungs with it. Cayla shivered in his arms. He carried her down to the opening of the defile where there was a clear escape route down the mountainside. He sat her down gently on the stony ground and knelt over her. Hazel had packed clean camouflage coveralls for her, a pair of canvas sneakers in her size and a pair of panties. Hector dug them out of the side pocket of his pack and, as though she were a baby, dressed her in them. He averted his eyes as he pulled up her knickers. He felt a strange paternal affection for her. But at first he had difficulty recognizing the emotion. He had never had kids of his own; he had never wanted any. His life was too full with other things. There was no space in it for kids. Now he thought this is what it must be like to have one. This was Hazel's baby, therefore in a strange way she was also his. This sick little creature tugged at feelings deep inside him that he had never suspected existed. He found the plastic bottle in his pack, and forced her to swallow three broad-spectrum antibiotic tablets and wash them down with a swig of water from the bottle he held to her lips.

'Can you walk?' he asked her tenderly.

'Yes, of course!' She stood up, took two shaky steps and collapsed.

'Good try,' he said, 'but you still need a little practice.' He swept her up in his arms again and ran with her. Tariq and Daliyah were on point, and the rest of the stick backed him. On the rough track they skirted the walls until they joined the main pathway and turned directly down the hillside. The night was as quiet as though all of creation held its breath. They slowed as they entered the oasis, and moved through the palms towards where they had left Uthmann and his stick.

Too quiet, Hector thought. Too bloody quiet. The whole place reeks with the stink of the Beast. Suddenly Tariq and Daliyah ahead of him went to ground. Tariq pulled her down with him and they dropped out of Hector's sight as though through the trap of a scaffold. Hector went down in almost the same instant, cradling Cayla to protect her from the impact as they hit the earth.

She whimpered and he whispered, 'Quiet, sweetheart, quiet!' and stared ahead as he cautiously slipped the rifle sling from his shoulder. He stared through the night scope but could make out nothing that might have alarmed Tariq. Then he saw Tariq raise his head cautiously. After a full five minutes he gave the soft fluting recognition whistle. There was no response. He turned slowly and looked back at Hector, waiting for an order.

'Stay here and don't move!' Hector told the girl.

'I'm afraid. Please don't leave me.'

'I'll be back. I promise you.' Then he was on his feet and running. He dropped beside Tariq, and rolled twice to throw off the aim of an enemy. The silence was heavy and fraught.

'Where?' he asked.

'Beyond that palm. There is a man lying there, but he does not move.' Hector picked up the dark shape, and watched it for minute. The shape remained still.

'Cover me.' He darted forward again. Even his flak jacket would not stop a rifle bullet at this range. He reached the dark human shape and dropped beside him. His face was turned towards Hector, and he saw it was Khaleel, one of his really good men.

'Khaleel!' he breathed but there was no response. He reached across to check his carotid artery. Khaleel's skin was warm but there was no pulse. Then Hector felt the wetness on his fingertips. He knew what it was; in his life he had probably seen as much blood as any surgeon. With his fingertips he searched for the wound. He found it exactly where he had expected it to be, at the back of the jawbone just under the earhole. A tiny puncture; a thin very sharp blade, through the earhole and into the brain. Hector felt sick to the guts. He did not want this to be true. There was only one man he knew who could kill with such precision. He called Tariq to his side with a hand signal. He darted forward to join Hector. At a glance he spotted the blood on Hector's fingers. Then he turned to Khaleel's corpse and touched the wound behind his ear. He said nothing.

'Find the others,' Hector ordered. Three corpses were lying in a defensive circle looking outwards. They must have trusted their killer to let him come in so close. Each of them would have died instantly. All of them had an almost identical wound.

'Where is Uthmann?' The question was redundant, but Hector had to ask it.

'He is not here. He has gone to where his heart belongs.' Tariq looked up at the dark massif of the fortress.

'You knew, Tariq. Why did you not warn me about him?'

'I knew with my heart, but I did not know with my head. Would you have believed me?' Tariq asked. Hector grimaced.

'Uthmann was my brother. How could I believe you?' Hector said, but Tariq looked away.

'And now we must leave this place, before your beloved brother returns,' Tariq said. 'With his other brothers, the ones he truly loves but who do not love you, Hector Cross.'

• • •

Uthmann watched Hector and Tariq move away through the palms with the woman, Daliyah, and the rest of his stick. He was angry and frustrated. Hector Cross had thrown all his carefully laid plans into turmoil. Now he had to re-evaluate his position very quickly. Sheikh Tippoo Tip and his grandson Adam were waiting for him with most of their men at the North Gate. Uthmann had promised Adam that he would deliver Hector Cross to him there. Firstly and most importantly he had to get a message to Adam, to let him know that Hector would not be walking into the trap, as they had planned, but that he had entered through another gate. They would have to close all the gates, and scour the fortress for him. Find him before he could wriggle his way out and escape into the open desert. There was only one way he could get a warning to Adam. He must take it himself. But first he must deal with the four men of his stick.

He checked the dagger in its sheath strapped to his left fore-arm. He had made the blade from the steel of the front spring of a GM truck. It had taken many hours of filing and sanding, of heating and forging and annealing and shaping to achieve this perfection. The handle was bound with a strip of oryx hide to fit his hand. Its balance was exquisite. Its edge was sharp enough to cut down to bone with the lightest stroke, and its point could slip through living flesh under its own weight. He gave Hec-tor's group ten minutes to get well clear, then he crawled to the nearest of his men.

'Khaleel, is all quiet here?' he asked. 'No, don't look at me. Keep looking ahead.' Khaleel turned his head obediently. The lobe of his right ear showed beneath the rim of his helmet. Uth-mann ran the point of his blade into his ear canal and through to his brain. Khaleel sighed softly and dropped his head onto the butt of his rifle. Uthmann meticulously wiped the blade on Khaleel's sleeve, before he crawled on to the next of his men in the circle.

'Keep good watch, Faisil,' he whispered as he reached the man's side, and then he killed him, swiftly and quietly. The other men were lying less than thirty paces away and they heard nothing. Uthmann crawled towards them. When all four were dead Uthmann stood up and turned towards the for-tress. He started to run. He climbed the path up the hillside. He had only been this way once before, but he took the left turn under the wall and ran close beside it to the North Gate. When he was still a hundred paces from the gate he began to shout a warning to the men who he knew were waiting on top of the walls.

'Do not shoot! It is me, Uthmann. I am the Khan's man. I must speak to Adam.' There was no response and he ran on towards the gate, shouting the same warning. When he was fifty metres from the gate a blinding white light suddenly burned down catching him full in its beam. He stopped and threw up his hands to shield his eyes. A voice called down to him from the battlements.

'Throw down your weapon! Raise your hands! Walk towards the gate slowly. We will shoot you if you try to escape.' Uthmann approached the gate and it opened just before he reached it, but he was still dazzled by the beam of light and could see nothing in the darkness beyond the opening. He hesitated when he reached the threshold, but the voice called down to him, 'Keep walking. Do not stop!' He entered the gateway and immediately a mob of men rushed out of the darkness and beat him to his knees.

'I am one of the Khan's men.' Uthmann covered his head with both arms. 'I have a vital message for him. You must take me to him.' They would have continued the beating, but at that moment an authoritative command froze them.

'Leave him be! I know this man. He is one of our trusted agents.' Uthmann climbed to his feet and made a deep obeisance to the man who strode towards him out of the shadows.

'Peace be on you, Adam. Blessing and peace on your illustrious grandfather, Sheikh Khan Tippoo Tip!'

'What is amiss, Uthmann? The plan was that you lead the infidel here. Where is Cross, the blaspheming assassin?'

'Cross has a wild animal's instinct for survival. At the very last moment he would not follow me. He has found a woman who knows the fortress well. He commanded me to remain without, while he went with her through a secret way to enter the walls.' Adam stared at him.

'Where is Cross now?'

'Doubtless he is already within the fortress.'

'Why did you not warn us before?' Adam's voice rose in agitation.

'Because I did not know myself until a short while ago,' Uthmann replied. 'You must waste no time closing all the gates, then send more men to stand guard at the prisoner's cell and others to search the citadel to find Cross.'

'Come with me!' Adam snarled at him. 'We will go to my grandfather. However, if you have let the infidel escape with our hostage it will go hard with you, this I warn you.' Adam lifted his robe and ran, but by the time they reached his grandfather's council chamber he was panting wildly.

This descendant of the Prophet is as soft as the withered dugs of an old woman, Uthmann thought contemptuously as he followed Adam into the chamber and prostrated himself at the feet of the Khan, and gabbled out his extravagant praises and wishes of eternal life for the old man.

'Enough!' Sheikh Khan rose from his cushions and towered over Uthmann. 'Why do you tremble? Do you have a fever? Or is it that you have broken faith with me? Have you brought mine enemy to me that I may pay off the debt of blood and go peacefully to my grave, or have you allowed him to escape my vengeance? Answer me, you stinking puddle of diseased pig dung. Is the son of a Christian whore your prisoner? Or is he not?'

'Mighty scourge of the infidels, I know not—'

'You know not? Then I will make you know.' He lashed the hippo-hide whip across Uthmann's back. His flak jacket absorbed the blow, but Uthmann squealed and writhed as he blurted out his report. After half a dozen strokes the Khan's ancient arm tired and he stood back. 'Send men immediately to the cell of the Christian whore. Bring her to me. I will have her chained at my side where I can guard her myself. Go! Swiftly!' The men he sent to fetch Cayla returned within a short space of time and cast themselves at his feet. They were gibbering with terror and the Khan's hearing was dull, but at last he understood what they were telling him.

'The infidel sow has disappeared and her guards are strangled? Are these the ravings of apes and lunatics?' He was panting with rage and his wrinkled features had swollen and turned puce.

'We should lock the gates to prevent them from escaping, and we must search the palace and find the girl and these infidels who have violated your stronghold.' Adam had also prostrated himself. He knew well how to deflect his grandfather's rage.

'Shut the gates!' roared the Khan. 'Search every room in the palace. Find them and bring them to me.' Then he turned to Adam. 'You cannot let him escape now.'

'We are wasting time here, Grandfather. Cross is not in the palace. Every minute you delay he is getting further beyond our reach. Cross has only five men with him. Uthmann killed the others. Give me your dogs, enough men and trucks and I will bring him to you.'

'There is only one truck here, but it has two punctured tyres that have not yet been repaired. I have sent the other trucks and most of the men to your uncle Kamal at Gandanga Bay to man the attack boats.'

The Khan went on, 'But we can take my personal hunting truck. As soon as the tyres of the big truck are repaired it will follow us with the rest of the men. We will take my dogs also, and I will ride with you. I want to be in at the death when you run them down. I want to see them bleed and listen to their death squeals.'

• • •

'Before we leave this oasis I must call in Hans Lategan in the helicopter to pick us up,' Hector told Tariq, and pulled the satellite phone out of his pack. He extended the aerial and switched on the handset. Hans answered on the first ring. Hector smiled. He must have been waiting with his thumb on the button.

'This is Kudu.' Hans gave his call sign.

'Stilton cheese!' Hector replied. This was the arranged code that they had exited the fortress with Cayla and were heading for the pick-up rendezvous. Hector had considered having the helicopter hovering nearby. But the sound of the engines would have alerted the enemy to their presence.

'Roger that! The Duchess is ecstatic.' Damn Hans for that additional piece of chit-chat, Hector thought angrily. Duchess was Hazel Bannock's code name. She was waiting at Sidi el Razig; how could she know already that Cayla had been rescued from the fortress? He dismissed the thought. The arranged pick-up point was on the far side of the northern ravine. Hans would come in from the Jig Jig airstrip and fly up the ravine until he spotted their recognition signal: another red distress flare. Hans had calculated that it would take about two hours and ten minutes to fly from Jig Jig. Hector reckoned it was approximately four miles to the southern bank of the deep ravine, or maybe a little less. Their pursuers would be riding in four-wheel-drive trucks. Although the terrain was rugged and criss-crossed with rocky outcrops and wadis, the trucks should be able to travel at least twice as fast as his small party. In her sick and starved condition Cayla weighed around one hundred pounds. He knew that under ideal conditions his men could probably reach the ravine in approximately an hour and fifty minutes. But not in darkness, not over this type of terrain, not with him having to carry Cayla. *What if they unleash the dogs?* He posed the question to himself, and then answered it: *To hell with the dogs!*

Tariq was watching his face, and Hector spoke aloud.

'I know what you want to ask me: did I tell Uthmann that we would head north for the ravine? The answer is, no I did not. Even though he knows our exact starting point, he does not know in which direction we will run. In the dark he will not find it easy to track us down.' He did not want to even mention the dogs. 'So, we will waste no further time.' He stood up. 'All of you drink as much as you can now. We will not stop again until we hear the helicopter on its way.' While they had been talking Hector had buckled three of the webbing belts together to make a carrying sling for Cayla. He lifted her to her feet.

'Heck's Transport and Removals Service at your command, Miss Bannock.'

'Is that your real name? Heck?' Her voice was weak and breathy.

'Absolutely.' He helped her to wriggle into the improvised sling seat, and lifted her until she was on his hips with both her legs dangling backwards. 'Put your arms around my neck and hold fast.' She obeyed him meekly and he ran with her, starting at less than his top speed, pacing himself to last the distance. Tariq sent two of his men ahead to find the easiest route and the other two to follow up and try to sweep out any obvious sign that they had left on the desert sand. They covered the first mile and Hector found his second wind. He lengthened his stride.

'You said your name was Heck. Is that short for Hector? My mother has spoken about you. You must be Hector Cross.'

'I hope she had good things to say about me.'

'Not really. She said you were arrogant and bumptious and she was going to fire you come the first opportunity. But don't worry, I'll talk to her.'

'Cayla Bannock, my protector.'

'You may call me Cay. All my friends call me that.' He grinned as she tightened her grip around his neck. He had always thought that when the time came it would be a son. *The hell with it, a daughter will do me just fine*, he decided. They ran on for another forty minutes before he stopped and looked back. He thought he had heard something. Now he was sure. It was faint but unmistakable.

'What is it, Heck?' Cayla was trembling again, and her voice was panicky. 'I think I can hear dogs barking.'

'Oh, it's nothing to worry about. Lots of stray dogs out here.' Then he called to Tariq, 'You hear it?'

'I hear it. They have the dogs and at least one truck. They will catch us before we reach the ravine.'

'No they won't,' Hector retorted. 'Now we are really going to start running.'

'What are you two talking about? I don't understand.' They were speaking Arabic, and Cayla was becoming more agitated. 'I am afraid, Heck.'

'Nothing to be afraid of. You take care of me and I will look after you. Is it a deal?' He fixed his attention on the north star which was showing just above the horizon, and he ran. He ran with every breath in his lungs and the beat of his own heart sounding in his ears like a war drum. When his legs began to wobble under him he dropped his pack and his rifle and ran on. His legs steadied and he found reserves of strength that he had never known about. He ran another mile, and then another. Now, at last he was sure he was finished, he couldn't take another step. But his legs kept pumping under him. Tariq and Daliyah ran beside him. Daliyah was carrying the rifle that Hector had dropped and Tariq had his pack.

'Let me take the girl from you,' Tariq pleaded with him. Hector shook his head. Tariq was a wiry little man, but he did not have the bull muscle for this load. Hector knew if he stopped running for even a second he would not be able to start again. He covered another mile and now he knew it was over, well and truly over.

This is where I die, he thought, *and I don't even have a rifle. Life is a bastard*. He stopped and lowered Cayla to the ground. He was reeling on his feet. The sound of the dogs was closer, louder. He still had his pistol on his belt.

I cannot let them take Cayla. I cannot let her fall into their clutches again. At the very end I will share the pistol with her, a bullet for each of us. It was the hardest and saddest decision of his life. It numbed his mind so when he heard men shouting his name he could not understand what they were saying. All he could hear were the dogs. *In the desert noise carries a long way*, he reassured himself, *they are not as close as they sound*.

'We have reached the ravine, Hector.' Tariq was shouting at him, and at last the words penetrated his exhaustion and his sadness. 'Come on, Hector. You have made it. The lip of the ravine is only twenty metres ahead. Come on, my friend!' Hector was past logical thought. His brain told him that he was finished and he could not go on. But he picked Cayla up in his arms and he ran. He only stopped when the earth disappeared from under his feet and he fell, sliding and rolling down the first steep pitch of the ravine. He was laughing and Cayla sat up beside him. She was powdered with dust and her elbow and one cheek were grazed. She stared at him in aston-ishment, and then she started to giggle.

'You should see a doctor, Heck. You're crazy, man. I mean, you're bouncing off the walls crazy. But on you craziness looks good.' Still laughing, Hector used the wall of the ravine to drag himself upright.

'Tariq!' he yelled. 'We cannot let the dogs catch us here. We have to get to the north side of this canyon where Hans can reach us for the pick-up. Get your lads together.' Then he turned to Cayla. 'Come on, Cay. Not far to go now.'

'You make me feel that anything is possible. I am on my own two feet from here on.' She set off down the slope. She stum-bled and almost fell, but then steadied herself and kept going. Hector caught up with her and with a hand on her shoulder steered her, slipping and sliding, down the slope.

'You'll do!' he said to encourage her. 'You've got good genes, Cay Bannock.' Tariq came slithering down the slope behind them, staying on his feet like a downhill racer. His men fol-lowed him. When he reached Hector's side he handed him his rifle and pack.

'You dropped these, Hector.'

'Careless of me.' Hector slung them on his back, and led them down into the gut of the ravine. They reached the bot-tom and faced the northern wall. Cayla was panting so that she could not talk but he could not allow her to rest. He grabbed her hand and dragged her up the far side of the ravine. It was steep and heavy going but at last they staggered over the rim onto level ground. He stared back at the far side of the ravine. First light was breaking from the east. There was no glimpse of the enemy, but he could hear the clamour of the dog pack very clearly.

'Tariq, we have to find a place to make a stand until the heli-copter comes.' He looked ahead with a soldier's eye, and picked the spot. 'Do you see that rocky outcrop, there on the left? That looks like a good spot. Come along, Cay.' They ran into the rocks. Hector's instinct had been right. This was a place where they would have a small advantage. There was good killing ground back to the lip of the ravine which the dogs and Uthmann would have to cross to come at them, but it was scattered with large boulders. He knew the dogs were trained to hunt men. They would work in a pack. But they would be broken up as they wove through the obstacles, and they would not be able to rush the men in a single concerted charge. Hector ordered Cayla to crawl in under the shelter of the largest rock and to sit with her back against the stone wall. He set down his pack beside her, and handed her the pistol.

'Can you shoot?' Cayla nodded. Stupid question, Cross, he smiled to himself. She is Henry and Hazel Bannock's daughter. Of course she can shoot. 'There is a bullet up the spout. No safety catch. I don't ask much of you. Just kill those bloody animals if they come at you.' He went to take his position beside Tariq. They both looked up at the sky. Full dawn was on its way.

'I have left a man on the lip of the ravine.' Tariq pointed ahead. The man squatted behind a boulder on the skyline. 'He will warn us when the dogs come into sight.'

'Good. Sunrise in ten minutes or so,' said Hector. 'Hans should arrive about the same time. We have only to hold them off until the helicopter gets to us.' They waited and the light strengthened. Then the lookout shouted in Arabic,

'Dogs coming. Many dogs.' He left his position and bolted back towards them.

'Did you see any men following?' Hector shouted.

'No, just the dogs. Many, many dogs.' The man took his place with them. The hunting chorus of the dog pack changed its intensity, becoming a ferocious baying.

Uthmann was at the wheel of the big Mercedes truck. Adam was on the bench seat beside him, and Sheikh Khan sat on the raised hunting seat behind them. He had one of his bodyguards on each side of him to steady him and prevent him from being thrown about violently as the truck bounded and crashed through the darkness over the broken ground. Four other armed men were crowded into the open truck bed in the rear. Uthmann was driving fast. They had long ago lost sight of the pack of hounds, but he followed their hunting chorus.

'They are heading for the northern wadi. How did they know about that?' Adam yelled above the roaring truck engine. 'Did you tell them, Uthmann?'

'No, but one of Cross's men knows this district well. He has family here,' Uthmann replied.

'If they reach it we will not be able to follow them through. We will have to go around. That is a detour of over fifty miles. They will get clear away,' the old Sheikh lamented. 'You cannot allow that to happen, my grandson.'

'They have a helicopter flying in to pick them up,' Uthmann told him.

'Are you sure of that?'

'I was sitting in on their planning sessions, indeed I am sure, Great Sheikh.' Now the dogs were so far ahead that before they could be certain they were still on the right track Uthmann had to stop the truck and switch off the engine and listen for them. Then he restarted the engine, and they tore on into the darkness.

'How will the helicopter find them?' Adam insisted.

'They will call it in on their satellite phone, and lay down flares to mark their exact position.' Suddenly Uthmann hit the brakes and the truck skidded to a halt. Adam's head cracked against the folded-down windscreen and the men standing in the truck bed were hurled overboard.

'Why did you do that?' Adam shouted angrily, holding the tail of his headscarf to the wound in his forehead to stem the bleeding. 'You nearly killed us all.' In answer Uthmann pointed ahead.

'We have reached the southern wall of the wadi. Another few metres and we would have crashed over the edge and all been killed.' Uthmann jumped out of the driver's seat and ran to the lip of the precipitous drop. He stood for a minute listening, then ran back to the truck. 'The dogs are still on the scent. I can hear them clearly now. We have to leave the truck here and follow them on foot.' He ran to the men who had been thrown from the truck and kicked their sprawling bodies. One of them was probably dead, his head lolling on its broken neck. Two of the others were out of the game, one with a shattered right elbow and the other with both his legs fractured. The fourth man clambered uncertainly to his feet, but he was dazed and concussed.

'None of these pigs is of any use to me,' Uthmann snarled. He pointed at the men sitting on either side of the Sheikh. 'You two, get down and follow me!'

'No!' Adam shouted back at him. 'They are my grandfather's bodyguards. They stay with him at all times. We cannot leave him here unprotected. There are thirty men from the fortress following us on foot. We can wait for them to arrive before we go on in force.'

'By the time they arrive Cross and the girl will be in the helicopter and out of our reach. If you do not now have the stomach to come with me, then wait here as long as you wish.'

'My grandson is immaculate in courage and honour. He will go with you, and show you the way,' Sheikh Khan intervened. Adam scrambled down to the ground, still clutching the bloodied cloth to his forehead.

'Are you ready for a fight?' Uthmann asked him.

'More ready than you will ever be,' Adam snarled at him and grabbed his rifle from the rack behind the seat.

'You must thank Allah that he gave you a head of stone.' Uthmann laughed at him as he ran to the back of the truck.

From the pile of weapons and equipment that had been thrown into confusion by the emergency braking, he selected an RPG of Russian construction and a canvas pouch containing two bombs for the weapon. He slung these on his back and came around the front of the truck. He looked up at Sheikh Khan in the high seat.

'Where will we meet, Lord Khan?' he asked the old man.

'I will take the truck along the rim of the wadi until we find the road that crosses it. Once we have crossed we will turn back this way again and look for you on the far side.' The Sheikh pointed out across the dark expanse of land to the north. 'By that time the sun will be up, and we will be able to search for your tracks or hear the sound of the dogs.'

'When we meet again I shall lay the head of the infidel that killed my father and my uncles at your feet,' Adam told him. 'Now I pray your blessing, Grandfather.'

'You have my blessing, Adam. Go with Allah, and keep this jihad fierce in your heart.'

Adam had to run to catch up with Uthmann before he disappeared down into the ravine. They went down the almost sheer incline, slipping and sliding on shale and loose rocks. Adam steadily lost ground to Uthmann.

'Wait for me.' He panted. His shirt was already soaked with sweat.

'Hurry! The helicopter will already be on its way to pick them up,' Uthmann shouted back at him without stopping. 'The infidel will escape the rightful wrath of Allah and your grandfather.' Adam's legs were turning to butter under him. He slipped and sprawled on his belly. He hauled himself to his feet and stood gasping and coughing in the dust he had raised. Then he started down again, but now he was reeling and staggering. Uthmann reached the bottom and paused for the first time to look back.

Soft piglet! Good only at raping women and slaughtering captives, Uthmann thought but did not let his contempt show.

'You are doing well. Not much further,' he called, but Adam lost his footing again. This time he fell forward and struck the rocky ground heavily. He rolled the last twenty feet to the bottom of the gorge. He tried to regain his feet, but his right ankle was injured and could not support him. He dropped back on his knees.

'Help me!' he cried. Uthmann turned back and hoisted him to his feet. Adam hobbled a few paces and then stopped.

'My ankle! I cannot put my weight on it.'

'You must have sprained it. There is nothing I can do to help you,' Uthmann told him. 'Come on after me at your best speed.' He left Adam and started up the far wall of the wadi.

'You cannot leave me here!' Adam shouted after him, but Uthmann did not look back.

• • •

'Listen to the dogs. They have our scent, hot and sweet,' Hector called out. 'Lock and load!'

The breech bolts of the rifles clattered. Six rifles, each with thirty rounds in the magazine. They could lay down an almost solid wall of fire. They had a clear one hundred yards of forward vision. His men were all skilled marksmen. None of the dogs was going to reach them. But if they did they would take the bayonets to them.

'Fix bayonets!' Hector ordered, and the men reached forward and unfolded the bayonets from under the rifle muzzles. 'Tariq! Light the signal flares for the helicopter now!' The flares would burn for twenty minutes, and by that time Hans would certainly arrive and be guided to their position. Each of the men carried a flare in his pack. Tariq shouted the order and they ignited the flares and threw them out. Hector realized too late that he should have made it clear to them that they must throw the flares back, not dead ahead of their position. The dawn breeze was into their faces and it rolled the dense smoke cloud back over them, almost completely blotting out their vision. Before Hector could send a man to move the flares, the dogs came out of the smoke. They were only fifty feet ahead of the line of men when they became visible. They rushed straight in at full run. Too many for Hector to count. Dark wolfish shapes through the smoke, clamouring for blood. They had run hard and froth streamed from their open jaws and splattered over their flanks.

'Shoot!' Hector bellowed. 'Shoot!' He got off only three shots, killing an animal with each bullet. The men on each side of him were firing as fast as he was. Dogs were screaming and going down, but others charged in through the swirling smoke. At Hector's side Tariq was knocked over backwards by the weight of a huge black hound smashing into his chest. Hector spun around and before it could lock its fangs into Tariq's throat he thrust his bayonet full length into the animal's neck. It howled and flopped over with its hind legs kicking. But at that moment another dog crashed into Hector from behind, catching him off balance and sending him sprawling to the ground. The hound was on top of him. The rifle was of no use in this close-quarter mêlée. Hector dropped it and caught the dog by the throat with his left hand; with his right he reached down for the trench knife on his webbing belt. Before he could bring the knife up two more hounds were on top of him. Snarling and snapping they fought to sink their fangs into him. One got a grip on the shoulder of his flak jacket and, bracing its front legs, it held him pinned down on his back. The third dog clamped his knife arm at the elbow and worried it with powerful shakes of its head. The first animal was still on top of him, its gaping jaws inches from his eyes, frothing saliva blown by its stinking breath into his face. It was twisting and heaving in his grip so violently that he could not hold it off much longer.

A pistol shot went off only a foot from his right ear and the muzzle blast half-deafened him. The dog on top of him loosed its grip and collapsed on top of him with blood squirting from the wound in its head. Two more shots cracked in quick succession and the other dogs that were attacking him fell away. Hector sat up and wiped the animal's blood out of his eyes with his sleeve and spat it from his mouth. As his vision cleared he stared in astonishment at Cayla. She had crawled out of her safe retreat under the rock and now knelt beside him, holding the pistol in a professional double-handed grip with her right arm fully extended, weaving it from side to side as she sought the next target.

'You beauty!' he panted. 'You bloody little beauty. You are your mother's daughter, all right!' He snatched up his rifle and sprang to his feet, but the dog fight was almost over. The field was littered with canine corpses and the men were finishing off the few wounded animals that were still milling about in pain and terror. Then he looked up at the horizon and saw less than a mile away the big Russian MIL-26 helicopter skimming over the ridge towards them.

'Here comes Hans.' He burst out laughing. 'It's all over. Steak and a bottle of Richebourg for dinner in Sidi el Razig tonight.' He pulled Cayla to her feet and placed a paternal arm around her shoulders. They watched the big machine racing towards them. Every so often it was hidden by the clouds of smoke from the flares, but each time the breeze blew the smoke aside the helicopter was closer and the sound of its engines was louder. At last it hovered in front of them only fifty feet from the ground and they could see Hans behind the canopy peering down at them. He grinned and saluted them then rotated the helicopter until it was broadside to them. The main hatch in the fuselage was open and two figures stood in the opening. One was the flight engineer but Hector gaped at the other.

'Crazy mad woman!' he whispered. He had ordered her to return to Sidi el Razig after the trip to Jig Jig, but he should have known all along that Hazel Bannock was not very good at taking orders. Giving them, yes, but not taking them.

'Mummy! Mummy!' Cayla screeched wildly. She hopped up and down and waved the pistol above her head. In the hatchway Hazel waved back just as energetically. Hans lowered the MIL-26 to earth and the instant the landing gear touched the ground Hazel jumped down from the hatch, landed neatly and broke into a dead run towards her daughter. Cayla pulled out from Hector's protective arm and stumbled unsteadily to meet her mother.

'Now that's what I call a fine sight!' said Hector with a smile as he watched the two women race into each other's arms, shrieking and weeping with joy. He felt the tears sting his own eyes, and he shook his head.

'Bawling like a baby. You're getting soft, Cross.' Hazel looked at him over Cayla's shoulder as she hugged her daughter. Tears were streaming down her cheeks and dripping from her chin. She made no effort to wipe them away. She didn't have to say anything, the way she looked at him was eloquence enough.

'And I love you too, Hazel Bannock!' he shouted for the entire world to hear. Then he forced his mind back to the business in hand, and he waved Daliyah and the men of his stick forward to board the helicopter. They jumped up and charged in a bunch across the open ground.

'Hazel! Get Cayla on board.' He started towards the women. Hazel heard him and grabbed Cayla by the wrist and started dragging her towards the machine. Then another voice rang out in a tone that cut through Hector's exultant joy like a slash from a sabre.

'On the rim of the ravine, Hector!' It was Tariq. He was pointing beyond the helicopter, and Hector's gaze swivelled in that direction. There was a man there, and though he was almost two hundred yards away and only his head was showing above the lip of the ravine, Hector recognized him instantly.

'Uthmann Waddah!' The shock stalled his mind. Tariq did not have a clear shot at his former comrade from where he stood. The men of his stick and the two running women blocked him. Only Hector was in position to deal with the traitor. But for a few vital fractions of a second he was paralysed. Any other person than Uthmann, any other time and his reaction would have been instantaneous, but Hazel and Cayla had usurped all his attention. He moved at last, but it was as though he were trying to swim through a bath of clinging honey. He watched Uthmann jump out of the ravine, run forward three paces and drop to one knee. He saw him lift a long metal tube and place it across his right shoulder.

'RPG!' Even at this distance Hector knew exactly what it was. The rocket-propelled grenade, the insurgent's weapon of choice, could pop open the armour of a battle tank as though it were a cheap condom. Uthmann was taking a steady and deliberate aim at the helicopter.

By now Hector had his Beretta assault rifle to his shoulder. Subconsciously he noted that Uthmann was still wearing his flak jacket. It was Bannock issue and top of the range, made of Kevlar with ceramic plate inserts. At this range Hector's light 5.56mm NATO bullet had a notoriously poor performance against this grade of body armour. Originally designed to shoot squirrels and prairie dogs, not men, the bullet would probably tumble on impact and not penetrate flesh, but it would be enough to knock Uthmann flat. He fired and he knew his aim was true. The instant before Hector fired Uthmann let fly with the RPG.

Hector saw the blast of blow-back from the rocket billow out behind Uthmann, and the smoke trail of the grenade as it lanced towards the MIL-26. Before it reached the target Uthmann was spun around as Hector's bullet exploded against the front panel of his flak jacket and he was hurled to the rocky ground with brutal force. Before Uthmann hit the ground the grenade struck the front of the helicopter and exploded. Hector staggered as the blast wave blew over him, but he kept his feet. Just short of the big machine, Hazel and Cayla were knocked down in a heap together. Daliyah and the men with her were closer to the explosion. They all went down and Hector knew that some of them had probably been seriously wounded or even killed. The flight engineer standing in the hatchway was shredded. Hector saw his severed head and one arm spinning in the air.

The nose and front section of the helicopter's fuselage were torn away. The cockpit and its canopy were gone leaving a gaping hole, and there was nothing left that was recognizable as

Hans Lategan's body. He had borne the brunt of the explosion. Out of control, the gigantic machine toppled onto its side and the whirling rotors flogged into the hard-baked earth and rocks, twisting themselves into fantastic shapes before the engines stalled and a heavy pall of dust and smoke hung over the wreckage.

For a moment there was silence. Then Tariq yelled, 'Uthmann is up. Shoot him, Hector. In Allah's name, shoot him again!' By now Hector's vision was partially obscured by the smoke and dust, but he fired at the hazy figure stumbling back towards the lip of the ravine. Hector was not certain if he had hit him or if Uthmann had simply fallen over the edge. Tariq sprinted after him.

'Come back, Tariq!' Hector yelled at him, 'Leave him! His men are probably following close behind him. We have to get out of here. See to the others. See to Daliyah.' Tariq turned back, and Hector ran out to where Hazel and Cayla were lying. He was desperate with fear and concern for both of them. They had been well inside the danger zone, and could very easily have been hit by grenade shrapnel or flying slivers of metal from the fuselage. He dropped to his knees beside them. Hazel was on top of Cayla spreading her arms over her daughter to protect her. Afraid that he would see blood on them, Hector reached down and touched Hazel's hand. She rolled her head to look up at him with a dazed expression and then sat up quickly and reached for him with both arms.

'Hector!' She kissed him with an open mouth, then both of them turned their full attention back to Cayla. Between them they lifted her to her feet.

'Are you hurt, baby?' Hazel demanded anxiously.

'No, Mummy. Don't worry about me, I'm just fine.'

'That's great news,' Hector said, 'because we have to move immediately. Hazel, this daughter of yours is weak as a newborn, but fiery as Tabasco. She just does not give up. I will send someone to help you keep her on her feet.' He ran to where Daliyah and the others were reassembling. Some of them had been hit by flying fragments from the explosion, but though they had cuts and bruises none of them was unable to go on. Daliyah seemed untouched.

'The girl needs your help,' Hector told her and she hurried to Hazel and Cayla. He turned to his men and ordered, 'Get your gear sorted out, we will be moving out right now.'

'Which direction are we heading in, Hector?' Tariq asked.

'Back across the ravine.' They all stared at him in astonishment, and quickly he went on to explain, 'If we keep heading east we will find very little except desert and more bloody desert. Now that they have lost their dogs the enemy won't know for sure which route we have taken; but they'll probably expect us to keep heading east towards the coast.' He turned and pointed back the way they had come. 'However, the main north–south highway passes close to the Oasis of the Miracle and the fortress. Isn't that correct, Tariq?'

'That's right, it runs about ten miles west of the fortress. A lot of traffic uses it,' Tariq confirmed.

'If we can get there, we will commandeer the first likely truck or bus that comes along.' The men began to perk up immediately. The downing of the helicopter had left them numbed with despair, but Hector had given them a plan and with it a glimmer of hope. Within minutes they were ready to move out.

They made up an odd little caravan; the three women of different ages and colours, and six men in ripped and bloodied camouflage. All of them coated with dirt and dust. Hector took the point and Tariq brought up the rear, with two of the men to help him sweep the tracks left by the column. Cayla was in the centre of the line with her mother on one side of her and Daliyah on the other to support her. They filed over the lip of the ravine and began the long climb down to the bottom. By the time they began to climb the far wall most of them were close to exhaustion, and the pace slowed inexorably. Hector moved up and down the line, jollying them along, trying to keep them moving with false assurances and bawdy humour that Hazel and Cayla were fortunate not to understand. Those men who had been injured by the explosion of the RPG bomb were now suffering badly and Cayla's legs were once again beginning to give out on her. Hector carried her piggyback up the last steep pitch to the top of the wadi. As the others reached the top they threw themselves down in what little shade they could find, and lay panting like dogs. The water bottles were almost dry.

Hector sat with Hazel and Cayla and made them share the last few mouthfuls that were left in his bottle. He gave Cayla another antibiotic tablet to swallow. He was sure the medication was having a beneficial effect. She had a better colour and her spirit was stronger. He touched her forehead and judged that her temperature was close to normal.

'Show me your tongue!' he ordered.

'With the greatest pleasure.' She tried to look cocky and stuck it out at him as far as it would go. The white fur on it was dissipating. He leaned closer and smelled her breath. It no longer reeked of the infection.

'Put it back,' he said. 'You don't want to leave that thing lying around for people to trip over.' Cayla stretched out on her back and closed her eyes. Hazel sighed and leaned against Hector's shoulder. He caressed her sweat-soaked hair lightly, sweeping it back from her eyes as he murmured encouragement and endearments.

They were so engrossed with each other that they were unaware that Cayla was watching them through her lashes, until she opened her eyes wide and asked, 'So, we have changed our minds about firing Heck, haven't we, Mummy?'

Hazel looked startled for a moment, then sat up straight upright and without looking at Hector she blushed scarlet. Hector watched her with delight.

God, I love it when she does that, he thought.

'It's okay, Mummy. I was already puzzling how I could get you two guys together. Seems I didn't have to worry so much.'

'All right, ladies, on your feet! It's time to move out.'

Hector gave Hazel a chance to recover her poise and stood up. He looked ahead. In the early morning sunlight the desert was endowed with an austere splendour. There was not the faintest touch of green, but the sand sparkled like a trove of diamonds when the sun caught the grains of silica in it; the rocky hillocks were as majestic as Rodin sculptures. He could feel the heat rising. He had given the last of his water to the women. His mouth was dry, and when he touched his lips they were rough as sandpaper. He had passed many years of his life in desert places, so as he led them on he was looking for the signs of surface water as assiduously as he was searching out hidden enemies. Soon they were all struggling as dehydration began eroding their last reserves of strength, and he had to let them rest again. He had picked up a couple of quartz pebbles and now he gave Hazel and Cayla one each.

'Suck it!' he instructed. 'It will help keep your mouth from drying out completely. Breathe through your nose and speak only if necessary. You have to save body fluids.' He looked from them to the men. One was huddled with an agonized expression, fighting cramp. The rest of them did not look as if they would be much good in a fight. A small cloud passed over the brilliance of the sun, and the relief was immediate if temporary. He glanced up and saw birds, dark against the grey cloud. There were five of them, large and swift on quick wingbeats. He stood up and shaded his eyes. The women were both watching him.

'What have you seen?' Cayla demanded.

'*Columba guinea* to the ornithologist,' he replied, 'but to you and me they are plain old rock pigeons.'

'Oh!' Cayla did not try to hide her disappointment. 'I cannot tell you just how non-fascinating that is, Heck.' The flock of pigeons began to drop and as they wheeled in the sunlight they appeared a lovely shade of blue with wine-coloured necks, and white rims around their eyes.

'When they flock up like that at this time of day they are heading for water.'

'Water?' the two women asked together.

'When they descend like that they have found it,' he said. 'Isn't that just so non-fascinating, Cay?'

'Sometimes you make me feel like a retard,' she replied contritely.

'Rest assured, Cay, you act like one only on occasion. On your feet, ladies, let's go take a look-see.' He had marked the spot where the flock had gone on to settle a quarter of a mile ahead. As they approached it the geological features became clearer. There was another smaller wadi across their track, an offshoot of the main gorge. It cut through several strata of rock formations. The band of water-bearing limestone showed clearly, overlain by bright orange schist. Suddenly the pigeon flock rose from the wadi wall on clattering wings. They had been hidden in a horizontal fissure formed by the erosion of the softer limestone under the impervious rimrock.

'Jackpot!' cried Hector with a smile as he led them to the foot of the wadi wall. While they collapsed thankfully in its shade he scaled it until he reached the fissure beneath the limestone layer. When he peered into the dark opening he could smell the water. The cleft was just wide enough for him to crawl into on his belly and elbows. The water lay in a shallow puddle far back in the low cave. He scooped a cupped handful and tasted it.

'Shit!' he said. 'Literally! Pigeon shit! But what doesn't kill you makes you fat.' He shouted down to Tariq to bring up the water bottles. He strained the water through his shirt, and despite the foul taste they drank the bottles dry and Hector filled them again. At last all of them had quenched their thirst and Hector filled the bottles for the third time. When he descended the wall he looked the little group over. The change was almost magical. The men were smiling and chatting quietly. Hazel was sitting behind her daughter, humming softly as she combed and braided her hair.

'Women!' Hector murmured, shaking his head fondly. 'Where the hell did she find a comb?' Then he called, 'Don't get too comfortable, people, we are moving out right this minute.'

They fell into formation again and climbed out of the wadi. Hector kept to the higher ground as much as was possible as he headed west, maintaining a strict watch over the surrounding territory. Within the hour he had good reason to be pleased with his vigilance. A couple of miles to the south he spotted a tiny feather of pale dust rising into the brazen and burning sky. He stopped the column and squatted to study the dust for a few minutes. It was moving slowly in their direction, and he wished he had brought his binoculars, but he had been concerned to cut the weight of the packs to a minimum. After only a short observation it was apparent that the dust was being kicked up by a slow-moving vehicle of some kind.

'Whatever it is, it's good enough for me.' He stood up and called Tariq to him. Quickly he gave orders to leave two of the men to watch over the women, while he and the rest of them ran to meet the oncoming vehicle. It soon became evident that it was keeping to a sandy, dry riverbed that ran along the bottom of a shallow valley where the ground was not as broken and rugged. When it reached a point in the river where the banks were shallower Hector got his first clear view of it. He recognized it at once as a medium-sized four-wheel-drive Mercedes truck. The windscreen was folded down and there was a driver with three other men sitting on a raised bench seat behind him. All four men were armed and wearing traditional tunics and turbans. Hector waited until the truck was hidden again by the bank of the riverbed.

'Follow me!' Hector jumped to his feet and with his men close behind him raced down the hillside until they could drop flat on the lip of the riverbank ahead of the truck. The Mercedes appeared around the bend two hundred yards beyond them. Hector let it come on until it was almost level with their position, then he and Tariq dropped down into the riverbed and blocked the way with their rifles levelled at the occupants.

'Don't touch your weapons or we will kill you,' Hector shouted in Arabic. 'Switch off the engine. Raise your hands above your heads.' The driver and two of the men behind him obeyed with alacrity, but the third man who was sitting nearest the back of the vehicle rose to his feet. He was very tall but also very old. His face was impossibly wrinkled with a long white beard tipped with henna. In his left hand he held an AK-47 assault rifle. He glared at Hector with the wild hypnotic eye of a biblical prophet and raised his right hand to point at him with a clawlike arthritic finger.

'You are the murderer of my three sons. You are Cross, the foul infidel swine with whom I have declared a blood feud. I curse you with all the might of Allah. May you never know peace even after I have slain you.'

'It is the Sheikh Tippoo Tip,' Tariq shouted in warning. Hector held his aim in the centre of the Sheikh's chest.

'Put down that rifle!' he called harshly. 'Get down off the truck, old man! Do not force me to kill you.' The Sheikh was like a deaf man. Without taking his eyes from Hector's he began to raise the AK-47. His twisted hands were shaking with the force of his hatred.

'Don't do it!' Hector warned him but the Sheikh ignored the menace of the rifle pointed at his chest. He placed the butt of the AK-47 into his shoulder and took his aim over the wavering barrel.

'God forgive me!' Hector whispered and shot him in the centre of his chest. Tippoo Tip dropped the rifle but remained on his feet by clutching the grab rail for support.

'I curse you and all your descendants. I curse you with the fires of Hell and the claws and fangs of the black angels—' Before Hector could prevent it, Tariq shot him once more, this time in the head. The Sheikh was thrown backwards off the truck into the sand of the riverbed. His two bodyguards roared with fury and grabbed their weapons, but before they could get off a single round Hector fired short taps of three rounds at each of them. The guards were knocked out of their seats. Tariq fired a burst at the driver behind the wheel as he drew his pistol, killing him instantly. Then he went to the truck and heaved the driver out of his seat into the wadi. Standing over the bodies he delivered the coup de grâce to each of them at close range. However, when he went to the corpse of the Sheikh Hector stopped him.

'No, Tariq! That's enough. Let the old bastard lie.' Tariq looked at him with mild surprise, and Hector could not really understand his own squeamishness, except that the man was old. He knew that Tippoo Tip was a monster of cruelty and vice, but he was old. It had been unavoidable, but still it left a bitter taste. Thank God that Hazel hadn't had to witness it.

He went to the truck and climbed into the driver's seat. He hit the starter and the engine fired and caught.

'Sounds sweet enough.' Hector checked the fuel gauge. 'Just over three-quarters of a tank.' But he saw there were long-range fuel tanks fitted on each side of the body. 'A hundred gallons each,' he estimated with satisfaction. 'We're good for a thousand miles or more.' There was also a drinking water tank wedged in behind the front seats and he rapped the side of it with his knuckles. 'Full!' he said, but one of their bullets had punctured it and water was pouring from the hole. Hector tore a strip from the tail of his head cloth and plugged the leak. Then he nodded to his men and while they clambered up into the vehicle Hector rummaged in the locker between the seats. He pulled out a large-scale map of the area with all the roads and villages marked and named. This was a prize but best of all was the pair of powerful Nikon binoculars still in their green canvas carry pouch.

'I'm like a kid on Christmas morning!' he chortled. He hung the binoculars around his neck, checked that his men were all aboard and drove to where he had left the rest of his party hiding amongst the rocks with weapons ready. Then Hazel recognized him and ran down to meet the truck.

'Are you all right? We heard shooting.'

'As you can see, it was us doing the shooting. Now we can move out again in comfort. Hazel, you ride beside me in front.'

Then he jerked his thumb back. 'Cay, I want you in the truck bed, keeping your head well down in case we run into more flak.' Cayla clambered over the steel side of the truck and then paused in disgust.

'Oh, gross! There is blood all over the place. I am not going in there. I want to sit next to my mother in the front seat.'

'Cayla Bannock, stop playing the grand lady with me. Behave yourself. Get your fundament into this truck right now!'

'But I don't want—'

'Listen to me, little girl. People are bleeding and dying because of you. From now on you will do as you are told.'

'I never did anything wrong—' she started again.

'Oh, yes you did. You invited Rogier Marcel Moreau alias Adam Tippoo Tip onto your mother's yacht.'

'How did you know that?' She stared at him with a stricken expression.

'If you don't know you must truly be a retard. Now get in the bloody truck!' Without another word Cayla scrambled over the side and sat beside Daliyah in the truck bed.

Hector let out the clutch and they pulled away. Beside him Hazel sat very still and silent. He did not want to look at her, but he could feel her anger. He knew how protective she was of Cayla. He drove on fast, descending again into the riverbed. The sandy bottom made for heavy going, but it was a faster and smoother ride than over the rocky broken ground and ridges. They had been going for only a short while when suddenly he felt a hand on his thigh and he started with surprise. He glanced sideways at Hazel, and her eyes were sparkling. She leaned towards him until her lips were an inch from his ear.

'You have a wonderful way with kids, don't you, Hector Cross?' she whispered, brushing his bristly cheek with her lips. 'You will never know how many times I have wanted to do just that. When Mademoiselle Cayla starts acting up she can be a total little bitch.'

The admission astonished Hector. He covered the hand on his leg with his own much larger paw and squeezed it.

'I expect it's a sign she is getting her strength back. But I understand your predicament, Hazel. Cay hasn't had a father for a long time and you feel that you can't be too tough on her.' It was her turn to be startled by his perception. Then she recovered herself.

'I do have somebody in mind to take over the paternal role,' she said softly.

'Lucky somebody.' He grinned and they drove on.

Within the hour they left the riverbed and crested a rise of higher ground. Hector braked to a halt and cut the engine.

'What now?' Hazel asked anxiously.

'I want to make a couple of satphone calls. We should have good reception up here.' He climbed down and while he spread his newly acquired map on the engine bonnet and switched on the satphone, he told Tariq, 'Give everybody a full mug to drink. Let them get out to stretch their legs and water the roses.' He extended the phone aerial and nodded at Hazel. 'Good contact! There must be a satellite almost overhead.'

'Who are you calling?'

'Ronnie Wells on the MTB.' He dialled in the number and after a few ringtones Ronnie came on the line.

'Where are you?' Hector demanded.

'I'm anchored in a small cove of a rocky islet about five miles off the coast . . .' He gave the coordinates and Hector checked them on the map.

'Okay. I've got your position. Stay there until I call you again. Hans Lategan didn't make it. The helicopter is down. We're on the run, but we have acquired a vehicle. Depending on what lies ahead of us, it's going to take us eight hours or more to reach the shoreline opposite your position.'

'Good luck, Heck! I will be waiting for you.' They both rang off.

'Why don't we meet up with Paddy and his land column, rather than the MTB?' Hazel asked.

'Good question.' He nodded in acknowledgement. 'It's a judgement call. It's over a hundred miles further to the Ethiopian border where Paddy O'Quinn is waiting than it is to the coast where Ronnie is.'

'But will there not be better roads? If we head east towards the sea we will be travelling cross country.'

'Exactly,' he agreed, punching more numbers into the phone. 'The country in the uplands of the interior is much more fertile and heavily populated and by now it will be a hornets' nest, swarming with Tippoo Tip's militia. There will almost certainly be roadblocks at every junction. But I am calling Paddy now to let him know what we intend. He will be our last chance if we can't meet up with Ronnie.'

Paddy answered his call almost immediately. 'Where are you?' Hector asked.

'I am sitting on a mountain top on the Ethiopian border admiring the view over the picturesque Somalian hinterland. Where the hell are you?'

'We are about twenty miles east of the oasis. Uthmann Waddah is a traitor. He is firmly in the other camp.'

'Son of a gun! Uthmann a traitor? I can't believe it.'

'He blew the whistle. They were expecting us. Uthmann himself hit Hans Lategan's helicopter with an RPG. Hans is dead and the MIL is wrecked. I managed to commandeer a vehicle and we are on the run for the coast to meet up with Ronnie.'

Paddy whistled softly. 'Did you kill that black-hearted bastard Uthmann?'

'I had a shot at him, but he was still wearing his flak jacket. I hit him, but I don't think he is dead. His body armour probably fielded my bullet.'

'Big pity!' Paddy growled. 'I knew something must be up. From where I am sitting I can see that every road on your side of the border is swarming with vehicles. I have my binoculars on one of the enemy trucks right now. There must be twenty men in the back of it. All of them are heavily armed.'

'Okay, Paddy. Hold your position and wait for my next call. If we can't join up with Ronnie, we may be forced to come to you. Be ready to come in across the border and fetch us out.' He cut the connection and looked at Hazel.

'Did you hear what he said?'

She nodded. 'You were right. It's only our last option. But will it really take us eight hours to reach the coast?'

'If we're lucky,' he replied, and he saw her eyeline shift. He glanced around and found that Cayla had quietly come up beside him.

'I came to tell you sorry, Heck,' she said meekly. 'Sometimes there is a devil gets into me and I just can't help myself. Can we be friends again?' She held out her hand and he took it.

'We have never stopped being friends, Cay. And I hope we never will. But you owe your mother an apology more than you do me.'

Cayla turned to Hazel. 'I am so sorry, Mummy. Hector was right. I invited Rogier on board the *Dolphin*, and I bribed Georgie Porgie to give him a job.'

Hazel winced. Up until this moment she had tried not to believe it, but now she had to face the fact. Her baby was a baby no more. Then she reminded herself that Cayla was nineteen years of age, rather older than Hazel herself had been that momentous night on the back seat of her tennis coach's old Ford when she had also become a woman. She rallied and held out her arms to Cayla.

'We all make mistakes, baby. The trick is to never make the same mistake twice.'

Cayla looked back to Hector. 'What is this fundament thing you keep telling me to put somewhere?'

'It's upper-class Limey speak for your butt,' Hazel explained, and Cayla giggled.

'Well, okay! I'll buy that. Fundament is a pretty classy-sounding word. Much better than the other one.'

• • •

Uthmann struggled down the steep northern bank of the wadi. Every step was difficult and every breath was agony. He had abandoned the RPG and he clutched at his chest with both hands where Hector's bullet had slammed into the front panel of his flak jacket. At first he expected to hear Hector and his men following him, but after a while he realized that they must be trying to regroup after the destruction of their helicopter. He stopped for a few minutes to discard the heavy flak jacket and examine his injury. Even though the bullet had not penetrated, the bruising and swelling at the point of impact was massive. Carefully he probed the area and felt the sharp spike of a broken rib beneath the skin. He worried that it might have punctured his lung. Although the pain was hardly bearable he took a deep breath. It seemed as though his lungs were uninjured and he hugged himself and staggered on down to where he had left Adam in the bottom of the wadi. He was no longer there. He must have climbed back to the rim of the bank where they had left the Sheikh and his men. Uthmann climbed the same route and found Adam at the top of the wadi, sitting on a rock and binding up his ankle with strips of cloth torn from his shirt.

'What has happened?' he demanded as soon as he saw Uthmann. 'I heard shooting and a loud explosion.'

Between careful breaths Uthmann described what he had done, and Adam was elated.

'So they have not escaped! Now they are stranded and I have them in the palm of my hand.'

'Yes, we have them trapped for the moment. But as I explained to you and your grandfather, Cross has made contingency plans for other escape routes. Now he will probably head down towards the coast where he has a boat waiting to take them across to Saudi. Where is your grandfather? We need his truck to follow them up.'

'He must have gone on to cross the wadi further down just as we arranged with him.'

'Both of us are hurt. We can never catch up with either your grandfather or Cross on foot. We must wait for the other truck from the fortress to arrive. They should have been here long ago.'

'Probably they have lost our tracks in the darkness,' Adam said with a frown. 'Or else they have had another breakdown.'

It was another hour before they heard the engine of the vehicle approaching, and finally it came into view over the ridge. There were two men in the cab and another dozen in the rear. Uthmann took a few minutes to strap Adam's ankle and his own chest with bandages from the truck's first aid kit, and then they mounted up and followed the tracks of the Sheikh's hunting vehicle. From a distance of a mile they saw buzzards circling in the sky ahead of them, and Adam urged the driver of the truck on until they came on the scene where his grandfather had been murdered. His corpse lay in the sand of the dry riverbed. Half the old man's face had been torn off and devoured by the birds, but his beard was untouched. Adam climbed down painfully into the sand and limped to kneel beside the corpse. Some other scavengers, probably a pack of jackals, had ripped open his belly and the entrails were already putrefying in the heat. The stench was nauseating.

Reverently Adam uttered the traditional prayers for the dead, but in his heart he was rejoicing. The years of his grandfather's tyranny had ended and he was now indisputably the Sheikh of the clan of Tippoo Tip. Only four days previously the old man had formally named him as his heir in the mosque, in the presence of the mullah and all his sons and grandsons. From now on nobody dare dispute Adam's claim to the chieftainship of the clan.

When he finished his prayers he rose to his feet and ordered the men to wrap his grandfather in a tarpaulin and lay him in the truck bed. He saw the new veneration towards himself in the eyes and bearing of the men as they hurried to do his bidding. Even Uthmann's attitude towards him had changed remarkably in acknowledgement of his elevation in rank and authority.

Uthmann had searched the area carefully while Adam prayed. He had found the tracks left by Hector and his ambush party. He went to where Adam stood and explained to him how the infidels must have come back across the wadi after the destruction of the helicopter, and by some evil chance had met the truck with the Sheikh aboard. They had murdered the old man and seized the vehicle.

'What are your orders, my Sheikh?' he asked. The sound of the title soothed Adam's soul like a pipe of hashish.

'We must follow my grandfather's stolen vehicle until we can be certain in which direction the infidels are heading. Only then can we decide what we must do.'

Uthmann ventured to repeat his opinion. 'As I have already explained to you, I know this man Cross well enough to guess accurately what he will do. Now he has the stolen hunting car he will surely try to reach the coast where his escape boat is waiting for him.'

'What will he do if he cannot escape by boat?' Adam demanded.

'Then the only escape route still open to him will be the border of Ethiopia.'

'Let us see if you are right. Get the men mounted up and follow them.' They left the corpses of the bodyguards lying for the jackals and the birds and they went on after the tracks of the smaller vehicle. Soon they found the place where Hector Cross had stopped. They saw the footprints of his party where they had disembarked. Despite his injured chest Uthmann climbed down to examine the tracks, and then went back to report to Adam.

'There are nine of them; six men and three women.'

'Three women?' Adam demanded. 'One is my escaped prisoner, but who are the other two?'

'I think one of them is the woman of Tariq who showed Cross how to enter the fortress. The third and last one arrived in the helicopter. I saw her for a few seconds only before I fired the RPG. My view of her was from a distance and partially obscured by the fuselage so I cannot be absolutely certain, but I think the third woman is the mother of your captive. I saw her many times at Sidi el Razig and I am almost certain it is her.'

'Hazel Bannock!' Adam stared at him while he struggled to come to terms with the full extent of his great good fortune.

Not only was he now the Sheikh of his clan but he had one of the richest women in the world almost within his grasp. Once he closed his fist on her she would make him one of the most powerful men in Arabia and Africa.

'Tens of billions of dollars and my own private army at my back! There is nothing I desire that I will not be able to have.' His imagination reeled at the magnitude of it. 'As soon as I have received the ransom money I will give Hazel Bannock and her daughter exquisite deaths. I will let every one of my men sport with them. They will take these two Christian whores in both their holes, a thousand times over from the front and from the back. If they cannot kill them with their pricks then they can use their bayonets in the same holes to finish the job. It will be fine sport to watch. We will share the pleasure of it with the assassin, Hector Cross. Then I will have to think of something original for Cross. In the end I will probably give him to the old women of the tribe with their little knives, but for a start many of my men will enjoy him from behind. They will stretch his anus wide enough to ride a horse through it. For a man like him the humiliation will be greater than any physical pain.' He rubbed his hands together gleefully. 'I will have the ransom and I will also have full settlement of my family's blood feud.' He called aloud to the truck driver, 'Turn back to the oasis!' Then to Uthmann he explained, 'I must bury my grandfather with all the respect he deserves. I will radio to my uncle Kamal to warn him that the fugitives will try to escape by boat. However, if Cross wriggles out of it again he must try to reach the Ethiopian border, and that is where we will be ready for him.'

• • •

All the remainder of the day they headed east. The going was hard. Three times Hector found they had run into a cul de sac of impassable ravines and they had to back-track several miles and search for an alternative route. When darkness fell Hector dared not switch on the headlights for fear of giving away their position to any pursuers. They had to wait for the rise of the moon before they could continue to grope their way eastwards.

Hector estimated that they were still twenty miles from the shores of the Gulf of Aden when their fortune seemed to have changed dramatically for the good. They reached a salt flat whose smooth surface stretched out before them to the limit of their visibility, smooth and gleaming in the moonlight. When Hector drove out onto it he was able to change into top gear for the first time since they had hijacked the Mercedes. They roared away with forty miles an hour registering on the speedometer towards the great silver disc of the moon which hung in the sky ahead of them. They had covered at least ten miles when without the least warning the crust of salt on which they were running gave way under them, and the truck was bogged down to its axles in the treacherous yellow mud of quicksands under the crust. It took almost three hours of heavy work for Hector to extricate them, using the truck's high-lift jack to raise the wheels enough to be able to stuff dry salt bush under them, then burying one of the spare wheels with the end of the tow line attached to it to act as an anchor on which they at last managed to winch the Mercedes out backwards from the clutches of the quicksands.

It was only on the dawn of the second day that they looked down upon the azure waters of the Gulf of Aden from the vantage point of the low hills above the shoreline. They were on the Great Horn of Africa looking almost due north towards Yemen. Below the ridge on which they parked there was a single-lane road running parallel to the sea. Below that was the narrow beach of red sand. The water was shallow and clear as glass and Hector could see that the coral reef formed a barrier a hundred yards offshore. They would have to wade out that far to meet the MTB. All that time they would be very vulnerable.

While they watched only a single vehicle passed along the beach road, and that was one of the ubiquitous African buses that cover every mile of the network of roads across the entire continent. The bus was so dusty that no glimpse of the original paintwork was visible. The mountainous luggage of the passengers, including baskets of live chickens and bunches of coconuts, was strapped to the roof. The racket of the engine, the clash of gears and the rattling and banging of the bodywork and chassis over the heavily rutted road carried clearly to them as they watched from the ridge. No other traffic followed it and Hector could find no evidence of enemy presence. He set up the satphone and called Ronnie Wells.

'We are in sight of the beach, opposite the coordinates you gave me. How far are you offshore?'

'According to my chart we are four point three nautical miles out from the beach.'

Hector used his new Nikon binoculars to search the open waters along the bearing that Ronnie had given him, and immediately he picked up the cluster of tiny islands, dark as a pod of whales, at approximately the correct bearing and range.

'Roger, Ronnie! I think I have you. I want you to put up a yellow smoke rocket to confirm that I am looking in the right place.'

'Okay, Heck. Hold on. It will take me a few minutes to rig the rocket.' When it went up it left a brief yellow trail against the horizon, which dissipated almost immediately on the wind. It was so shortlived that an observer would have had to be watching out for it. Hector knew he had taken that chance, but he had to be absolutely certain of Ronnie's position before he exposed his party.

'Roger, Ronnie! You are on a bearing of fifteen degrees from our position. Come into the beach on a reciprocal heading.'

'Can you spot any other traffic in my vicinity, Heck?'

'There are a few small local fishing boats dotted about inshore of you, but they all seem to be at anchor. Then I can make out a large container ship on the horizon several miles beyond you. Nothing unusual.'

'Okay, Heck. I will be coming in at full throttle. Be ready for a quick pick-up. We don't want to muck about on the beach.'

'One other thing that you should be warned about, Ronnie. We have had a traitor in our midst. Uthmann Waddah is an enemy agent. He knew about our rendezvous here. At the first sign of trouble you must abort and make a run for it.'

'Uthmann Waddah! It's a hard game, Heck. I know how you feel about him.'

'What I felt about him, Ronnie – past tense. I will kill him next time we meet. I tried once already, but next time I will make no mistake.'

'Roger that! See you on the beach.'

• • •

As soon as he had received the warning from Uthmann Waddah that Hector Cross might attempt to escape by sea, Kamal Tippoo Tip had taken all his attack boats out of the harbour at Gandanga and run northwards to station them in a line along the stretch of coast nearest to the Oasis of the Miracle and the fortress. This is where he could reasonably expect the infidel to attempt his escape from Puntland. The boats were anchored a mile offshore and every boat was in sight of the others on each side of it, so that they formed a chain of observation almost fifty miles long. Kamal had placed himself in the centre of the chain, and it was he who spotted the ephemeral yellow smoke trail against the eastern sky. Before the smoke had blown away he was on his shortwave radio calling his entire fleet of twenty-three attack boats to assemble on him.

In the sandy cove three nautical miles further offshore than Kamal's ambush, Ronnie ordered his crew to stand by to weigh the anchor at which they had been riding for the past seventy-two hours. He went forward to remove the tarpaulin cover from the twin 50 calibre Browning heavy machine guns mounted in the bows. He loaded both weapons and traversed them port and starboard to make certain the mountings were clear. Then he hurried back to the cockpit of the MTB and started the engines. They kicked in smoothly and he ran them up to 3,000 revs, then throttled back to idle and let the needle of the engine temperature gauge climb into the green arc. He gave a hand signal to the foredeck crew and the anchor winch whined, the chain clattered into the anchor well and the anchor itself came aboard, and was lashed down securely by the crew. Marcus, the bosun, gave a thumbs up and Ronnie engaged the reverse gear and manoeuvred the boat until it was bows-on to the entrance of the cove. Then he opened up both engines and they roared out into the open sea, and swung onto the heading for the distant beach. In the binoculars Hector picked up the gleaming wake of the Rolls-Royce motors heading directly towards him.

'Here comes Ronnie!' he told Hazel as soon as he was certain.

'Second time lucky,' she said, and he nodded.

'It's a racing certainty,' he agreed, but the words of the old saw rang a caution in his head. 'The first the worst, the second the same, the third the best of all the game.' He put the saying out of his mind, and called to Tariq to get everybody into the Mercedes. They ran to obey him and Hector climbed behind the wheel and started the engine. He took one last look out to sea to make sure that everything was developing smoothly, and what he saw struck ice into his soul. Hazel saw his expression change.

'What is it, Hector?' she asked in alarm.

'We tempted fate, and fate was listening,' he said softly so as not to alarm Cayla. With his chin he pointed out to sea. She saw it at once.

'Holy mother of God!' she whispered and grabbed his hand for comfort. What they had taken to be small fishing boats were nothing of the kind. The surface of the sea, which minutes before had been troubled only by a light onshore breeze, was now boiling like a pot of soup. The silver wakes of numerous fast-moving small craft were lacing the surface, criss-crossing each other from every direction, like the spokes of a great wheel converging on a point in their centre. Moving less swiftly but kicking up a greater propeller wash than all the rest, Ronnie Wells's MTB was the central point of all this violent activity. Hector switched off the engine of the Mercedes and grabbed the satphone. On the MTB the phone rang once and Ronnie Wells snatched it up.

'Hector?' he demanded.

'Ronnie! Abort! Abort!' Hector shouted at him. 'There are pirate boats coming at you from every direction. It's an ambush. Of course, Uthmann set you up. Get out of there. Do you hear me?'

'Roger! Stand by for my famous vanishing act.'

'Leave the sat connection open,' Hector ordered. Ronnie dropped the telephone receiver onto the chart table beside him without breaking the contact. Now Hector was able to hear everything that was happening on board the MTB.

'Hold on!' Ronnie shouted to his crew and put the wheel hard over. The big boat whipped viciously around in a 180-degree turn. One of his men was unprepared and he was hurled off-balance headfirst into the coaming of the hatchway. His skull cracked loudly and he went down as though from a head shot with a .44 Magnum revolver.

Ronnie ignored him and shouted to his bosun, 'Marcus, get forward and man the Brownings. As soon as we have a target I will turn you on to it. Shoot any other boat you see. They will all be bandits!'

Ronnie was staring back over their wake. He could see nothing, but he knew they were there, so low in the water that they were not visible in the swells unless they were closer than a few hundred yards. From the locker under the chart table he took out an Uzi submachine gun, and checked the magazine before he laid it on the seat at the level of his knees, then from the same locker he brought out four M.67 phosphorus grenades and placed them beside the Uzi SMG.

He glanced back over the stern and saw the head and shoulders of a man pop out above the swells. He could not see the hull of the boat under him, but knew it was the driver of the first attack boat standing at the controls while the rest of his crew crouched in the bilges. They were closing the gap between the two craft surprisingly swiftly. Ronnie picked up the satphone.

'I am not going to be able to run away from this one, Hector. They have got the legs on me,' he said. 'I have to turn back and fight. They won't be expecting that.'

'That's what you were built for, you old sea dog,' Hector answered lightly although his heart was a stone in his chest. 'Give them hell, Ron!'

'Sorry you couldn't be here to join the fun.' Ronnie dropped the phone again and Hector heard him shout to Marcus behind the twin heavy machine guns. 'Ready about!'

Marcus acknowledged with a pump of his right fist and Ronnie put the wheel hard over. The MTB spun on its axis and went roaring back under full power. The two boats rushed together at a combined speed of almost one hundred miles an hour. The Arab boat was taken completely by surprise. Before its crew could emerge from hiding under the gunwale the tracer fire from the MTB's heavy machine guns was chewing the hull into splinters and wood chips. Almost immediately the boat went out of control and nosedived into the next wave.

'That was so lovely to watch!' Ronnie laughed, but three more attack boats appeared from behind the swells and the crews were all blazing away at the MTB with their assault rifles as they closed the range. Most of their fire was screeching overhead or ploughing into the waves ahead of the hull. But some of it was tearing into the MTB. Ronnie's windshield shattered and flying glass cut his forehead and the blood ran into his eyes, but he turned to take on the closest boat bow to bow. Relying on his superior size he went to ram it, but the attack boat sheered away and they roared past each other with only a narrow strip of water separating them. As they passed Ronnie tossed a phosphorus grenade into the attack boat and ducked as it exploded in a blinding white sheet of flame. Two of the Arab crew were blown clean overboard and the man at the helm simply disappeared in the flash and the smoke.

Ronnie was consumed with battle madness, that sense of euphoria that could not be induced by any drug. He turned after the next boat and rammed it full on. The collision wrecked the MTB's bows, but he trampled the attack boat under him and spilled its crew into the sea where they floundered and drowned.

Now there were attack boats converging on him from every direction. The Arab crews were screeching, *'Allahu Akbar!'*, and sweeping the MTB with close-range automatic fire. Marcus was killed outright by a burst from an AK and he collapsed over his guns, the twin barrels spiralling aimlessly and tracer shells spraying into the sky. Another boat hurtled alongside, and a robed and bearded Arab hurled a grappling iron onto the MTB's deck and the hooks bit into the wooden gunwale. Within minutes others had followed his example, and Ronnie was dragging a mini-flotilla behind his own. He looked around him and found that he was the only one of his crew still alive, the bodies of his men lying in abandoned attitudes in puddles of their own blood. Miraculously in the storm of gunfire Ronnie stood untouched. When he looked back over the stern he saw that a gang of Arabs were using the grappling lines to pull their attack boats up to the stern of the MTB, and they were bracing themselves to scramble onto his afterdeck. He emptied the magazine of the Uzi into them, knocking down two. When the magazine was empty he dropped the weapon, and locking the wheel hard astarboard he snatched up a grenade in each hand. He pulled the pins from the grenades with his teeth as he started back to hurl them into the trailing attack boats. But he had taken only two paces before a bullet from an AK hit him low in the abdomen. It sliced through his guts and exited from his spine, shattering two of his lower vertebrae. His legs collapsed under him, and he sprawled on the deck. His legs were paralysed, but he used his elbows to drag his maimed body as far as the auxiliary fuel tank and he curled up against it, still clutching the grenades against his chest. He felt the thumps as the hulls of half a dozen attack boats struck the sides of the MTB, and then the slap of many bare feet on the decking as the pirate horde came pouring on board, screeching and ululating triumphantly, jostling and shoving each other to be the first to take possession of the prize. One of them spotted Ronnie curled up against the fuel tank. He ran to him, stood over him and pulled his head back to slash his throat with a curved Arabian dagger. It was a clumsy stroke and it missed the jugular but sliced open the windpipe. Before he could hack at his throat again Ronnie rolled over and held up the two grenades.

The rest of the pirates were crowding forward, laughing and shouting, but when they saw the grenades they drew back in consternation. Ronnie felt no pain, just a great surge of adrenalin that lifted him like a magic carpet. Vaguely he understood that this was what he had wanted all along: to die with a weapon in his hands and an enemy confronting him, and not in the infirmary of the Royal Hospital, Chelsea. He laughed at them and the air puffed from his severed windpipe in a fine pink mist. He wanted to shout some witticism about beating them to paradise and expropriating every one of their seventy virgins, but his vocal cords were severed and he could not enunciate the words. He opened his hands and let the handles fly from the grenades.

The rabble of pirates broke and ran, howling with terror, but none of them reached the boats alongside before the explosion consumed them in flame. Ronnie was still laughing as he was caught up in the double explosion, and a moment later the fuel tank against which he had been propping himself exploded and a pillar of flame and black smoke shot high into the sky.

Hector was watching through his binoculars and he felt the shock wave of the explosion ruffle his hair, and saw the tower of smoke and the brilliance of burning phosphorus, brighter than the sunlight on the waves. Simultaneously the satphone in his cargo pocket went dead. He went on staring through the lens for a few minutes longer while he gathered himself. Then he felt Hazel's hand on his arm.

'I am so sorry, my darling.' It was the first time she had used that term of endearment. He lowered the binoculars and turned to her.

'Thank you for your understanding. But it's what Ronnie would have wanted. This very moment he is probably jeering at the fates.' He gave his head a little shake, putting his sorrow aside for the moment, and shouted to Tariq, 'Get everybody mounted up again.' Then he turned back to Hazel. 'That smoke rocket was my mistake. Now they can be sure we are here, and that Ronnie was signalling us. We have to move out quickly.'

With the Mercedes loaded Hector turned onto the coastal road and drove fast along it in the opposite direction to the pirate lair at Gandanga Bay. They covered almost fifteen miles before Hector spotted the dust of a strange vehicle approaching from the north. Quickly he pulled off the road and parked behind a clump of windswept thornbushes. He ordered all of them to dismount and sit behind the truck which was camouflaged by its thick coating of dust and dried quicksand. He crouched down behind the trunk of one of the thorny trees and watched another passenger bus grinding southwards, effectively wiping out their own tracks with its wide double tyres. As soon as it was out of sight he and Tariq each cut themselves a tree branch from one of the trees and went back to the verge of the road where they had left it. They came back to the parked truck, walking backwards and carefully sweeping all the signs of their passing from the hard baked surface, and straightening the strands of coarse brown grass that had been flattened by the wheels of their truck.

Satisfied at last that they had done all they could to throw off any pursuit by the pirates who were bound to come looking for them along the road, he ordered everybody to take their allotted seat in the vehicle and then headed back into the wilderness the way they had come, in the direction of the Oasis of the Miracle and the Ethiopian border. When darkness fell and it was not safe to continue onwards for fear of hitting a rock or crashing into one of the wadis, Hector parked the Mercedes. They brewed coffee on a small carefully screened fire of brushwood and drank it black and unsweetened to wash down the dry army survival rations. Every one of them was exhausted, so Hector took the first turn of guard duty. All the others threw themselves down on the hard earth and slept almost immediately. Even Hazel who was one of the toughest and most determined of them all had at last succumbed. She lay with Cayla cuddled in her arms, both of them still and silent as statues. When the night air turned cooler Hector spread his jacket over them; neither of them so much as twitched.

He let them all sleep for an hour after the moon rose. When at last he roused them and chivvied them back into the truck, he handed over the driving to Tariq and let the rocking and swaying of the Mercedes over the rough terrain lull him to sleep. He slept sitting upright in the high hunting seat with the loaded rifle across his lap held by the strap, ready for an instant response to any threat. He was awakened by a change in the truck's motion. Suddenly it was much smoother and the engine note changed as Tariq engaged a higher gear. Hector opened his eyes and saw that they were moving faster on a roughly demarcated but beaten track. He glanced at the stars to orient himself. Orion was hunting the western sky with Sirius, his dog, running ahead of him. The moon was high. They were still heading west without headlights showing, relying on the moon and the glow of the Milky Way to light their route. He checked his wristwatch; he had been asleep for almost three hours. They must be getting close to the more fertile and populous areas of land along the main highway. He leaned forward and touched Tariq on the shoulder.

'Peepee pause,' he announced. Tariq braked and they all climbed down. The women went to the rear of the truck and the men to the front. Standing shoulder to shoulder with him, Hector spoke quietly to Tariq.

'We have to dump this vehicle. Every man, woman and child in Puntland will be looking for it. We will requisition another. Then we must find the right clothing to be able to blend in to the local populace. You and Daliyah are the only ones suitably dressed.' While they were talking Hazel and Cayla came from behind the truck to join them. They listened for a while to the Arabic conversation, until at last Hazel lost patience.

'What's this all about?'

'We need other transport. Tariq and I are plotting to hijack another truck and then find suitable disguises for you and Cayla in particular.'

'Hijack?' Hazel asked. 'That means killing more innocent bystanders?'

'If that's what it takes,' Hector agreed.

'Not really humane or discreet. Why don't you send Tariq and Daliyah into the nearest town to buy a truck and the right gear?'

'Good idea.' Hector smiled in the moonlight. 'Just hold on a minute while I rob a bank.'

'You can be rather obtuse at times, Hector Cross.'

'Last one who called me that was my mathematics teacher at high school.'

'He must have been very perceptive. Come with me.' She led him around the back of the truck and once they were unobserved she began to unbutton her shirt.

'Mrs Bannock, at any other time this would be a splendid idea.' Unperturbed Hazel untucked the tails of her shirt from her breeches and he stared at the money belt that was strapped around her waist, lying snugly against her flat belly. She ripped open the Velcro fastener and handed him the belt. He shone the flashlight into it, then took out one of the wads of green US banknotes and riffled through it.

'How much have you got here?' he asked in awed tones.

'About thirty thousand. Sometimes it comes in quite useful.'

'Hazel Bannock, you are a bloody marvel!'

'Oh, at last you've noticed. Perhaps you are not quite as obtuse as I suspected,' she said and he grabbed her and kissed her. 'And getting smarter all the time.' Her voice was husky. 'To be continued later, right?'

'Couldn't be righter,' he agreed.

They drove on, still without switching on the headlights, more cautiously as the daylight strengthened. At last they were running through cultivated fields of dried maize stalks and once they passed a few darkened hovels beside the track. There was no sign of life except the smoke from a cooking fire drifting from a hole in the roof of one of the huts. Shortly after that they crested a rise and saw in the distance ahead of them the lights of a large settlement. Some of the lights appeared to be powered by electricity rather than wood or kerosene which was a sign of at least rudimentary civilization. They stopped and Hector shaded his torch as he examined the map.

'There was only one town that this could possibly be.' He pointed it out to Tariq on the map. 'Lascanood. Ask Daliyah if she knows it.'

'I know it. I have been here before with my father. Some of his relatives live here,' Daliyah confirmed. 'It's the biggest town in Nugaal province.'

'How far is it from Ethiopia?' Hector asked, and she looked embarrassed. She was a simple country girl and the question was beyond her.

'All right. How far is it from your home – could you walk there in a day?'

'In two days, not one.' She said it with certainty. She had obviously made the journey.

'Do you know if there is a road from this town to Ethiopia?'

'I have heard people say there is a road, but nobody uses it now, not since the troubles with that country.'

'Thank you, Daliyah.' He turned to Hazel. 'She knows the town and she says that there is a road from there to the border although I don't see it marked on this map. Apparently it has fallen into disuse, which suits us just fine.'

'So what do we do now?' Hazel asked.

'We find a place to hide out during the day, and I will send Tariq and Daliyah into the town to buy a bus or lorry and the other things we need.' Hector turned back to Daliyah. 'Do you know if there is a wadi or some other place close by where we can hide this truck while you and Tariq go into the town?' She thought for a moment and then nodded.

'I know a place,' she agreed. She sat beside Tariq, obviously bursting with pride at having been selected by Hector as a guide, and she pointed out the way with an authoritative air. Just before sunrise they turned off the track and drove a short way to a clump of scraggly acacia thornbush. In the centre of it was a water-hole, a shallow depression which was now dry; the baked mud in the bottom of it cracked into rectangular tiles curling up at the edges. The thornbush screened them on all sides.

'This is where my father and I used to camp,' said Daliyah, pointing out the black ashes of a cooking fire on the edge of the clearing. They all disembarked, Tariq drove the truck under the trees and they cut branches to cover it, concealing it from casual observation. Hazel called Hector aside, while Tariq and Daliyah were preparing to walk into the town.

'Should I give the money to Tariq to buy what we need?'

'Give him a hundred dollars. That'll be enough for the local-style clothing and food. I'm sick of dry rations.'

'What about transport for us to reach the border?' Hazel asked. 'He will need a few thousand, won't he?'

'No. That's too much temptation.'

'Don't you trust him?'

'After the little trick that Uthmann pulled on me, I trust nobody. Tariq can find transport and even haggle a price with the seller, but I will pay over the cash.' Hector went back to Tariq and gave him the hundred dollars in bills of small denominations. Then Tariq and Daliyah set off in the direction of the town. Daliyah trailed twenty paces behind him, as a good Islamic wife was bound to do. Once they were out of sight the rest of the party settled down to wait under the sparse cover of the thorn trees. Hector set up the satphone and after two or three attempts at last made contact with Paddy O'Quinn.

'Ronnie didn't make it,' he told Paddy. 'They were waiting for him. He put up a good fight, but in the end he bought the farm.'

'I would like to get my hands on that swine Uthmann Waddah,' Paddy growled. This was no time for sentiment or mourning.

'Join the queue,' Hector agreed.

'Where are you now, Heck?'

'Coming your way. We're making progress, Paddy,' he told him. 'We're hiding out near a town called Lascanood. Do you have it on your map?' There was a short pause while Paddy checked.

'Okay. I have it. Looks as though it's about seventy or eighty miles beyond the border.'

'Can you see a marked road that would get you from where you are to our vicinity?' Hector asked.

'Hold on a jiffy. Okay, there is a track indicated by a dotted red line, which is not a good sign. It usually means that the existence of the road is the subject of conjecture rather than hard fact. According to this, it joins the main highway about ten or fifteen miles north of Lascanood.'

'Paddy, start moving in our direction pronto. Do not, I repeat do not call me back. I might be surrounded by the bad boys. I will call you again once we are in the clear this end.'

'Roger that,' Paddy agreed, and they broke the connection.

• • •

It was two hours before noon when Tariq and Daliyah returned from the town. Once again Daliyah was following him at a discreet distance, balancing an enormous bundle on her head. In the grove of thorns Tariq helped her to lower it to the ground, and they all crowded around to see what Daliyah had brought back with her.

Firstly and most importantly she had a large bunch of maize cobs and three scrawny chicken carcasses. These went onto the coals immediately. While they grilled, the men removed their Cross Bow uniforms and equipment and from the bundle they selected and donned the typical jihadist dress of baggy pants and black waistcoat over a grubby and wrinkled white shirt. Then they bound loose black turbans around their heads; even on Hector the change was immediate and convincing. He took Tariq aside and questioned him about what he had discovered in the village.

'It is Friday so there are very many people in the town to attend mosque and to watch the public punishment,' Tariq told him.

'Of course. I had forgotten what day it is. But that's not a bad thing. We will be far less noticeable in a large crowd.'

'I overheard a group of men discussing the death of the Sheikh and the fighting in the desert. The new Sheikh is Adam Tippoo Tip and he has placed a bounty of five thousand dollars on our heads.' Hector grunted. That was an enormous sum of money in this part of the world and he realized that there would be thousands of eyes looking out for them, hoping to earn it.

While they were talking, Daliyah took Hazel and Cayla behind the truck and showed them how to wear the black full-length abaya and burqa that covered them from head to foot. The wearer was completely veiled and she looked out upon the world through a mesh screen. Daliyah made Hazel and Cayla shed their unmistakably western footwear. Both of them slipped on the leather sandals which she had brought for them. The men were still squatting in a circle engrossed in deep discussion, so once they were fully dressed Daliyah showed them how to paint their hands and feet with red henna. This was in accordance with local custom and it would cover their pale skin. In the circle of men Hector asked Tariq if he had been able to find other transport.

'Yes, I have found a man who will sell us a bus which will seat forty passengers. He says it is in good running condition, but he wants five hundred dollars for it.'

'That's promising. If he had asked fifty dollars I would worry somewhat. Did he let you see it?' Tariq shook his head.

'Daliyah knows him and she thinks he is honest. He says his son will bring the bus to town this afternoon. He also has as many AK-47s as we want to buy and much ammo. He is asking fifty dollars each for them. I told him we needed six.' Tariq grinned. 'I think he will take three hundred dollars for the bus, and another two hundred for the guns and five hundred rounds of ammo. They are probably not Russian anyway, but locally made.'

'And the barrels skilfully crafted to burst with the first shot and blow the proud new owner's head off,' Hector said with a grunt. 'But we can't walk around toting state-of-the-art Beretta SC 70/90s, like these.' He tapped the butt of the rifle that lay across his lap. 'We will have to bury them as a fallback and abandon them and the Mercedes when we go.'

While the men were talking Daliyah gave the two women a crash course in correct female behaviour when in the presence of strangers, and Hector summed it up for them when he inspected Hazel and Cayla before they set off for the village.

'Walk at least ten paces behind your male escort. Keep your face covered and your eyes downcast. Don't speak. Pretend that you just don't exist.' He grinned at Cayla. 'The same way that you always behave, Miss Bannock.' She lifted the hood of her burqa and stuck her tongue out at him. Hazel marvelled at the relationship the two of them had established in such a short time. It was so obvious that Cayla was already looking on him as a father figure, and at the same time there was a real but easy friendship growing up between them.

I'll be damned if he is not going to be able to manage her as nobody else has ever been able to do before, she mused. *This man is a creature of many skills and virtues.* She watched them both fondly, until Hector turned his attention to her.

'Hazel, not many ladies in this neck of the woods wear gold Patek Philippe watches. Hide it please.'

'You're wearing a Rolex Submariner,' she challenged him.

'In this neck of the woods every buck worth his salt sports a genuine-fake Bangladesh-made Rolex selling for twenty-five dollars a pop in the nearest bazaar. Impossible to tell them from the original. As you have remarked, I conform to custom very nicely.'

When they set off for the town, Tariq took the lead and the other men came close behind him. Hector walked in the middle of the party so as not to draw undue attention to himself. He had used a stick of charcoal to darken his beard, but he still kept the lower half of his face covered. The three women followed them decorously. The outskirts of the village were almost deserted with just a few cur dogs lazing in the shade and naked brown toddlers playing in the rubbish heaps that choked the narrow lanes, but as they approached the centre the crowds coalesced around them until they were jostled and bumped at almost every step. Soon they found themselves being carried along with the throng, and Hector was worried that the women would be separated from him or from each other. He glanced back surreptitiously and was relieved to see that Hazel had made them hold hands to keep them together in a tight bunch. They reached the opening to a deserted side alley and Hector whispered to Tariq to take this route to get them out of the press. But when they tried to leave the stream of humanity their way was immediately blocked by rifle-wielding militia who shouted and pushed them back into the crowd.

'Public punishment in the square in front of the mosque. Everybody must be there to witness it.'

'I did not expect this.' Hector was appalled when he realized the effect this might have on Hazel and Cayla if they were forced to watch the horror of radical Sharia law in practice. 'I have to warn them.' He eased his way back through the throng until he was walking a few paces behind Hazel. He pitched his voice low, and hoped that the babble of Arabic all around them would cover the fact that he was speaking English.

'Don't look around at me, my love. Nod if you understand me.' She nodded. 'We are going to be forced to watch something so horrible that there are no words to describe it. You must be strong. Look after Cayla. She must try not to show any sign of distress. She must not cry out in protest, or in any other way draw attention to herself. Get her to close her eyes or cover her face with her veil, but she must remain still and silent. Do you understand?' Hazel nodded again but uncertainly. He wanted to hug her or at least squeeze her hand, but he left her and went back to join his men.

The crowd debouched onto a dusty square in front of a green-painted mosque, by far the grandest edifice in the town. As they entered the square the armed religious guardians separated the men from the women. The men squatted in the front ranks facing the sunbaked open ground in the centre. The women were directed to the very back rows where they knelt and carefully covered their faces. A big jihadist with a potbelly and a curling black beard strutted up and down in front of them and harangued them through a loudhailer. His voice boomed and echoed off the walls so that it was almost unintelligible. The red dust was stirred up by the shuffling sandalled feet, and the heat was trapped by the surrounding buildings. Large bluebottle flies swarmed over everything, crawling on the faces and trying to creep into the mouths and eyes of the crowd. A heavily pregnant woman who was waddling along just ahead of Hector staggered and collapsed in a dead faint. The guardians dragged her to the nearest wall and propped her against it amongst the women. They would not allow her distraught husband to enter the ranks of seated women to go to her succour.

Assembling the entire population of the town and the surrounding district in the segregated ranks took almost two hours; only then could the administering of punishment begin. At last, accompanied by four lesser clerics, the Mullah emerged from the mosque and took over the loudhailer from the chief jihadist, addressing the spectators in stentorian tones.

'In the name of Allah, Most Gracious, Most Merciful,' he declaimed, his amplified voice booming around the square. 'All praise and thanks are due to Allah, and peace and blessings be upon His Messenger. My brothers in Islam, we are gathered here to witness punishment carried out in the name of Allah and by the power of his holy Sharia laws. Let all the virtuous know of his mercy and justice, and let the wrongdoers beware.' The first criminal was dragged forward by two jihadists. He was a starveling about eight years of age wearing only a brief loincloth. His limbs were thin as dried maize stalks, and his ribs showed clearly through his dusty skin. He was sobbing and wriggling in the grip of his gaolers. Tears cut runnels through the dust and dirt that covered his face. The Mullah introduced him to the crowds.

'This miscreant stole a loaf of bread from a stall in the market place. The Koran has instructed us that the penalty for theft is the amputation of the arms.' The crowd showed their approval with cries of 'God is Great!' and 'There is no other God but God!'

The Mullah held up his hand to silence them, then continued with his diatribe. 'Allah, in his wisdom and compassion, has decreed that the punishment of amputation may be mitigated in certain circumstances. After learned debate with my fellows we have decided that in this case the arms shall not be severed entirely.' He shouted an order to the guardians of the mosque and after some delay one of them drove a four-ton dump-truck into the square. The vehicle was loaded high with quarried grey stones, each one about the size of a baseball. When he saw it the child wailed shrilly and with a loud spluttering sound he soiled his already grubby loincloth. The crowd roared with laughter when they saw the extent of his terror.

The guards laid the struggling child on his stomach, and two of them pinioned him while a third slipped a rawhide noose over his wrists and pulled both his arms straight out in front of him, stretching him along the ground. The Mullah gave a signal to the driver of the truck and he rolled the vehicle forward slowly towards the boy's prostrate form. Another jihadist guided the driver with hand signals until the offside front wheel was lined up with the elbows of the child's outstretched arms, then the driver inched forward.

The boy's entire body convulsed and he squealed like a piglet having its throat cut, but the sound of his agony could not blot out the sound of crackling bone as both his arms were crushed under the immense weight of the heavily laden truck's tyre. The guardians released him, but the child lay racked by convulsions that contorted his entire body. One of the men hoisted him to his feet and shoved him in the direction of a side alley. The child no longer had control of his mutilated arms and they swung loosely at his sides. As he tottered towards the alley the limbs elongated grotesquely as the muscles no longer held together by bone stretched, until the boy's fingers almost dragged upon the ground.

'Allah in his wisdom and mercy has spared the arms of the thief,' the Mullah intoned sonorously and the watchers shouted in chorus, 'Allah is merciful! Allah is great!'

The next criminals were led into the square with their arms bound behind them with rawhide ropes. They were two men, one of whom was middle-aged, but the second was a strikingly beautiful youth with a graceful and effeminate gait. An executioner walked behind each prisoner. They carried curved Arabian scimitars at the present position in front of them.

'These base creatures are guilty of the most perverse and unnatural crime against God, and against all devout believers,' bellowed the Mullah. 'They have committed the vile sin of Lot, coming upon each other as man does to woman, one with the other. Four sound and reliable witnesses have given evidence as to their guilt. The sentence of this Sharia Court is that they both be put to death by beheading.' The watching crowds shouted their approbation and praised Allah for his wisdom and protection from evil.

In the centre of the square the two prisoners were forced to kneel facing each other so that they could look into each other's face and see the guilt there. The crowd was still and tense with anticipation. Gazing into his lover's face, suddenly the youth cried aloud in a voice that rang around the square, 'My love for you surpasses my love for Allah!'

The Mullah bellowed like a wounded bull, 'Strike! Strike off the blasphemer's head!'

The executioner standing over him lifted the scimitar with both hands and swung it down in a glittering arc. The youth's head sprang from his shoulders and for a moment a scarlet fountain pumped from the stump of the neck. Then the head-less body fell forward. The older man wailed with grief, and threw himself forward onto his lover's corpse. Two of the guardians seized him by the shoulders and lifted him back onto his knees.

'Strike!' howled the Mullah. The executioner swung the blade, and the headless man fell forward on top of the first corpse, united with his lover in death. The watchers screamed with excitement and exalted the name of Allah and his Messen-ger. Some of the women succumbed to the heat and the thrill of blood, and fainted away where they sat. They were left to recover without succour or interference from any of the other members of the crowd. Hector glanced around and saw that Cayla was one of those who seemed overcome. He suspected that Hazel had ordered her to feign unconsciousness to spare her further exposure to the horrors.

The last person to enter the punishment ground was a woman. Because of the long abaya and the full black veil it was difficult to judge her age; however, under her robe she moved like a young girl, supple and willowy. She knelt before the Mullah and hung her head with an air of total resignation.

'This married woman is accused by her husband and four reli-able witnesses of the mortal sin of adultery. Her accomplice has admitted his guilt and has already received one hundred strokes with a heavy cane. This Sharia Court, in the infallible wisdom bestowed upon its members by Allah and his Messenger, has condemned the woman to death by stoning.'

The Mullah signalled to one of the mosque guardians and again the big dump-truck came forward. Slowly it drove along the perimeter of the square, halting four times to lift the cargo bed and deposit a pile of the quarry stones in front of the crowd. The stones had been carefully selected to conform to the dictates of the Sharia law. They must not be pebbles that could not inflict a serious injury, nor should they be so large that they would kill the guilty woman with a single throw to the head. From the front row of the crowd the men scrambled forward excitedly to select their missiles, juggling them in their hands to judge their weight and balance. By custom Hector was forced to join in but he tasted vomit at the back of his throat as he stooped to pick up a pair of stones. In the centre of the square a hole had already been dug that was wide enough to admit the woman's hips and deep enough to accommodate her body as far as her waist. The earth that had been removed from the hole was piled beside it. When all the preparations for the execution were completed the guardians forced the accused woman to lie face down on the earth. Then they brought a large bolt of white cotton cloth from the truck and, starting at her feet, they wrapped her in the cloth like a corpse in a winding sheet. When they had finished she was covered from the soles of her feet to the top of her head. Two of the guardians lifted her and carried her to the hole, then between them they lowered her feet-first into it. She was now standing upright with the upper half of her body exposed. The guardians seized the spades which were stuck blade-first into the pile of loose earth, and they shovelled earth into the hole around the lower half of her body, then stamped it down firmly. The woman was now almost completely immobilized. She could twist her upper body from side to side and bow her bandaged head forward but that was the limit of her movement.

While they waited for the signal from the Mullah the men fondled their quarry stones, laughing and chattering with their companions, wagering amongst themselves as to who would be first to hit the head of the condemned woman. The Mullah recited a short prayer asking Allah for his blessing on their enterprise, and again citing the proven guilt of the woman.

The woman's husband came forward to claim the honour of hurling the first rock at his helpless wife. The Mullah gave the man his blessing and commended him to the approval of Allah, and then he shouted through the loudhailer, 'Do your duty under the law.'

The husband set himself up and took deliberate aim with the rock in his right hand, then he hurled it with a full sweep of his arm and his whole body behind it. It struck the woman on her shoulder and she shrieked with anguish. The men behind him hooted and ululated with delight, and then each of them launched the stone he was holding ready and even before it struck or missed the target they had stooped to pick up the next stone from the pile. The air was filled with flying stones, and at first most of them missed the target. One or two struck the woman's body and she cried out at the shock and the pain and made blind and fruitless movements as though trying to dodge the sharp-edged missiles. Finally one struck her head. It hit her squarely in her forehead and the force of it whipped her head backwards. Almost immediately the bright blood welled up through the white cotton. The woman's head drooped forward on her neck like a wilting flower on its stalk. She was struck again in the temple and her head flopped over to the other side. Soon there was no further sign of life but the flying rocks continued to thud and slog into the woman's quiescent body.

At last the Mullah gave his thanks to Allah for guiding them in their holy duties, and he and the other clerics retired into the green mosque. The men threw the last stones they were still carrying and the crowd began to break up, and singly or in small groups drifted away still chattering animatedly. A few mischievous urchins gathered around the woman's half-buried corpse and at point-blank range threw more rocks at the shattered head, screaming with laughter whenever one of them managed a hit.

'We can go,' Hector told Tariq quietly and they stood up and joined the spectators who were straggling out of the square. Hector glanced back only once to make sure that Hazel and the other two women were following them. Tariq led them through the bazaar where the stall keepers were once more spreading out their wares upon the dusty earth. After the distraction of the punishment the town was returning to normal life as if nothing out of the ordinary had taken place. On the far side of the bazaar was the large open space which served as a depot for the passenger buses and transport lorries, as well as a caravanserai for the passengers and travellers. They were camped out in the open, gathered around dozens of smoky cooking fires or around the wells dug at its centre.

Tariq bought a bundle of firewood from one of the vendors, and a sheep's head and a few bloody shanks from another. Daliyah stood in line with other women waiting to draw water at the well. As soon as the fire was burning they gathered around it in a circle and watched the mutton bones grilling. As this was not a public but a family gathering, Hazel and Cayla could sit close behind Hector still wearing their burqas. They were silent and subdued by the gruesome performance they had been forced to witness. Hazel was the first to speak.

'I told Cayla not to watch. Thank God that some of the other women succumbed so she did not draw undue attention. I wish I hadn't watched it. It is something that I will never forget. These people are not human. Even in my worst nightmares I could never conjure up such terrible things as they have done to Cayla and those other poor wretches today. I thought Islam was a religion of peace and kindness, of love and forgiveness. Never this monstrous orgy of bigotry and brutality we witnessed today.'

'Medieval Christianity was every bit as savage and barbaric,' Hector pointed out. 'You have only to look to the Spanish

Inquisition and to the Crusades, or to the scores of other wars and persecutions waged in the name of Jesus Christ.'

'But it's not like that any more,' Hazel protested.

'Some Christian sects are still pretty raw in their thinking, but on the whole you're right. Modern Christianity in general has evolved into something far more gentle and humane, closer to Judaism, Buddhism and Shinto. Likewise most thinking Muslims have adapted and moderated their philosophy. As they stand now both Christianity and Islam are fine and noble religions.'

'Then how can such abominations as we witnessed today still be perpetrated?' Hector could see her eyes flooding and she blinked at the tears.

'If a handful of Roman Catholic priests use their power to sodomize small children, does that make Christianity evil?' he asked her. 'If a few blindly fanatical oafs like the Mullah who orchestrated today's butchery remain trapped in the brutal philosophy and teaching of the sixth century, does it make Islam evil? Of course not.'

'No, I have to agree with you. But those few extremists are able to influence the unsophisticated masses and create such a climate of hatred and brutality that the kind of horrors we saw today, and the kind of treatment that Cayla was subjected to, become commonplace.' Hazel's voice shook, and Hector cut in.

'Darling, not all Muslims are terrorists.'

'I know that. But I will oppose this extreme Sharia law with all my might and to the last drop of my blood.'

'As will I and all enlightened men and women of whatever race or religion, including Islam. But you do realize, my love, that you might have to revise part of the code and doctrine that you expressed during our first meeting?'

'You mean the part where I called you a blood-thirsty racist?' she asked, and he could tell by her tone that behind the veil and through her tears she was smiling, probably for the first time since they had entered the village.

'That would do for a start.' He smiled back at her.

'You are too late, Cross. That opinion was revised some time ago.'

At that moment Tariq returned and squatted beside Hector.

'The man we discussed has brought the bus and the guns for you to see.'

The bus was parked among a dozen others at the far end of the campground. It was a sturdy TATA, built in India many years before. At a glance it was obvious that it had lived a hard life. It was almost indistinguishable from any of the other buses parked around it, except only in that it was not heaped high with passenger goods and chattels. Tariq introduced Hector to the owner. After they had gone through the elaborate ritual of greeting, Hector walked around the bus. Three of the windows were cracked and one was missing completely. Hector knelt down to look under the engine. Black oil dripped from the sump, but not in copious amounts. The engine bonnet was held in place with baling wire. Hector opened it and checked the oil level with the dipstick. It was almost full, as was the water in the radiator – clearly recently replenished for his benefit. He climbed up into the driver's seat and disengaged the fuel cut-off plunger. Next he turned the starter key to heat and waited for the light to show on the panel, then he turned the key to ignition. The engine turned over sluggishly but did not fire. The owner had followed him into the cab.

'If you will permit me, Effendi?' Hector relinquished the seat to him. The owner began a practised routine with the throttle and starter key. At last the engine fired, backfired and farted before dying again. Unperturbed the owner repeated the procedure and at last the engine fired more convincingly, almost died, backfired again and then caught and ran up strongly. The owner beamed triumphantly. Hector congratulated him then walked around the vehicle again. Blue smoke blew from the exhaust and water dripped from the same pipe.

Cracked block, Hector thought, and when he opened the bonnet again there was loud knocking from one of the cylinders. *For an African bus it's in almost pristine condition. Should still be good for a few hundred miles, which is all I ask from it.*

Then he looked the owner in the eye and said, 'How much?'

'Five hundred Americani,' replied the man delicately.

'Two hundred and fifty,' Hector countered, and the man wailed and clutched his brow as though Hector had insulted both his mother and his father.

'Five hundred,' he insisted, and then allowed himself to be beaten down slowly to the figure of three hundred that both of them had fixed in their own minds from the outset. They spat on their palms and slapped hands to seal the contract. Then they climbed into the bus and went down the aisle between the seats to the wooden case in the rear. The owner threw back the lid, and with a flourish presented the contents: six AK-47 assault rifles and five hundred rounds of ammunition. The wooden butts of the rifles were chipped and scratched, the blueing had rubbed off on any high-spots on the metal and when Hector looked down the bore of one of the barrels he saw it was worn so badly that they would be inaccurate at any range over fifty yards. Hector and the man settled for twenty-five dollars each. Before they parted with sincere expressions of deepest respect the vendor handed over the papers of the bus and mentioned almost as an afterthought that the local jihadist militia were on the lookout for a gang of criminal infidels who had murdered the old Sheikh and stolen one of his vehicles. He gave the impression that he did not mourn the passing of the old Sheikh to any great extent. He went on to add that a few hours earlier the stolen vehicle had been found abandoned not far from the town. The new Sheikh, may Allah grant him long life and great wisdom, had declared a curfew and issued a warning that any traffic moving on the roads between sunset and sunrise or failing to halt at a roadblock would be fired upon.

'I thought I should warn you.' The man shrugged indifferently.

'Thank you, brother,' Hector said, and added a hundred-dollar bill to the wad of cash that changed hands. As soon as he was gone Hector turned back to Tariq.

'Now we need some passengers to fill her. If there is no luggage piled on the roof and just the nine of us sitting like first-class passengers inside her, nobody would believe for a moment that we are pilgrims on our way to Mecca.' By this time the sun had set and Tariq wandered off into the campground to tempt a full load of passengers on board the bus with offers of heavily discounted fares as far as Berbera on the coast. The three women and all the men of Hector's party climbed aboard to reserve their seats by sleeping in them. The other seats filled up rapidly, and an hour before dawn there was standing room only in the interior, with half a dozen late arrivals clinging precariously to the mountain of luggage strapped to the roof racks. The bus was well down on its suspension with the weight of the load. Hazel, Cayla and Daliyah were squeezed into the bench seat at the rear. Cayla had managed to claim her place nearest to the window from which the glass was missing. Daliyah sat between them to field any questions that might be fired at them when they reached the roadblocks.

Cayla leaned across Daliyah to whisper to her mother, 'At least I will get a little fresh air. The stink in here is eye-watering.'

Hazel was half-submerged under the spreading bulk of an extremely large lady who occupied the seat beside her, balancing on her abundant lap a basket of dried fish. The fish were only half-cured and their smell competed strongly with the body odour of the lady herself. Hector sat on the floor cross-legged in the middle of the aisle with a heap of luggage piled in front of him and his ancient AK rifle across his lap. Anyone attempting to get back to where the women sat would be forced to climb over both the luggage and Hector. Tariq was the driver. If questioned at one of the roadblocks his accent was authentically Puntlandian. The remaining four Cross Bow operatives had been strategically placed by Hector so that in an emergency they could cover and defend the whole interior of the vehicle.

As the new day dawned and the sun showed its red dome above the hills, the fourteen buses that had been forced by the curfew to pass the night in the campground started their engines and beeped their horns to assemble their passengers. They formed up in a long convoy, and with the occupants shouting prayers and supplications to Allah for a safe journey, they drove out onto the main highway heading northwards. Tariq had managed to push their bus into the middle of the line.

'We don't want to be the first or the last,' he suggested to Hector. 'Those are the ones who will receive the closest attention.' Within a mile of leaving the town they ran into the first roadblock, manned by ten jihadists. The convoy ground to a halt while the driver and passengers of the first bus were forced at gunpoint to dismount and unload all their luggage into the road. Hector went forward and crouched down behind Tariq's driving seat to watch the search procedure. It was almost half an hour before they allowed the first truck to pass. The second took half that time. Some of the men were made to dismount and one of them was, for no apparent reason, beaten unconscious with a rifle butt, and thrown into the rear of the lorry parked at the side of the road. By the time the fifth bus reached the roadblock the militia had very obviously lost real interest in the business. Three of the militia climbed aboard and the rest of them walked around the bus peering at the cowering passengers through the windows.

'That one is the leader.' Hector nodded in the direction of a tall man with a huge beard descending from the bus tucking something into his waist sash and then turning to wave the driver forward. 'How much, do you think?'

'Ten dollars?' Tariq guessed.

'That should be enough. Try him with it.' Tariq nodded and Hector returned to his seat on the floor behind the barrier of luggage. At last they were summoned forward by the jihadists with masterful brandishing of firearms and fearsome shouts. The chief of the search party was once again first on board and he leaned over Tariq. From where he sat Hector could smell the arak on his breath. The passing over of the ten-dollar bill by Tariq was done as neatly as a stage illusion, and the jihadist straightened up and came down to where Hector was blocking the aisle. He pointed his rifle at Hector's face.

'Who are you and where are you going?' he demanded

'I am Suleiman Baghdadi. I am going to Berbera to catch the ferry to Jeddah to make the pilgrimage to Mecca.'

'You speak like a Saudi pig.' The man insulted him gratuitously but without rancour, then he looked beyond him at the fat lady on the back seat. He shook his head and laughed at her for no good reason. Then he turned and marched back along the aisle to the door and jumped down into the road. He shouted at Tariq, who drove on. They were stopped twice more before they covered the fifteen miles to reach a tiny scattering of huts beside the road. On the road verge were a few old women squatting under a thatched lean-to and selling groundnuts and bunches of yams and plantains to the passing travellers. Tariq stopped the bus and most of the passengers climbed down to buy from the old women. Tariq bought a dish of roasted groundnuts and tipped the seller a dollar, which earned him her immediate affection. The two of them chatted animatedly for five minutes before Tariq returned to his seat and Hector made his way forward again and crouched behind him. Tariq proffered the bowl of nuts and Hector took a handful.

'Yes? What did you find out?' he asked as he chewed.

'The old road to the mountains is only a short way ahead, just beyond the first dry wadi we have to cross. The woman said that very few people know that it exists, only the old ones like herself. Nobody uses it any more. She does not even know if it is still passable.'

'Does she know if there are any more roadblocks ahead?'

'She does not think so.' Hector thought about this for only a few minutes and then reached his decision.

'All right, Tariq. This is where we say farewell to our passengers. You know what to tell them.' Tariq climbed down onto the road and ordered all his passengers to do the same. Then he gave them the bad news.

'There is a fuel leak in the engine and a great risk of fire which will burn you to death or at the least will destroy all your possessions. We cannot safely take you further.' There were cries of alarm and anger from his passengers, then the voice of the fat lady with the fish basket rose above the hubbub.

'What about the money that we paid you?' she demanded.

'I will give you back all the money you paid, and another ten dollars each to buy a seat on another bus.' The cries of indignation subsided instantly; they chatted delightedly amongst themselves until the fat lady spoke up again.

'Promises are easy to make. Show us your money or you will not need your fuel leak. We will burn your bus for you.' She drew back the niqab that covered her face to make her threat more convincing and she glared at him.

'You shall be the first to be paid, old mother,' Tariq assured her and counted out the cash into her chubby paw. All the fire went out of her. She cooed like a chubby baby being offered her mother's teat. The others crowded forward and as soon as they were paid they offloaded all their luggage onto the dusty ground. Then they cheerfully waved goodbye to the much lighter bus as it drove on. The remaining passengers were also in celebratory mood.

'I don't think I could have survived that stench much longer,' said Cayla, removing the hood of her burqa and thrusting her head out of the empty window. She inhaled deeply and fluffed out her sweaty hair to dry in the wind.

'We call it L'Eau d'Afrique,' said Hector sympathetically. 'If you bottled it and sold it in the Rue Faubourg Saint-Honoré it is unlikely you would make your fortune.' Cayla wrinkled her nose at the thought.

'I think that is the wadi we are looking for just ahead,' Tariq said, pointing through the dusty windscreen.

'Watch out, everybody!' Hector called out urgently. 'There are two more militia lorries parked on this side. Get your head in, Cayla, and cover it.' She obeyed at once and Hazel put her arm around her and they both hunkered down on the seat. The men lifted their headscarves to cover the lower halves of their faces. Tariq drove on at a steady speed.

There were several groups of men in jihadist uniform standing around the two parked trucks but they stopped chatting among themselves and turned their attention to the approaching bus. One of them stepped into the road, unslinging his rifle from his shoulder. He held up his hand and Tariq braked obediently. The man came around to the driver's window.

'Where are you going?'

'Berbera.'

'Why so few passengers?'

'We broke down in Lascanood. Most of them would not wait and left us,' Tariq explained and the man grunted.

'We are thirsty,' he said. Tariq reached under the seat and produced a bottle of arak which he had bought in Lascanood for just such a situation as this. The man pulled the cork with his teeth and sniffed the fiery contents of the bottle, then stepped back and waved them on. They all relaxed and Cayla removed the hood of her burqa and stuck her head out of the window again.

The bus ran down the near bank of the wadi, laboured through the loose sand in the dry riverbed and reluctantly climbed the far side. They came out unexpectedly on another vehicle parked on top of the bank. This one was an off-white Toyota Hilux. There was a man behind the wheel and two others standing in the back of the truck bed. They both had binoculars trained on the mountains of the Ethiopian border away to the west. One of the men lowered his binoculars and stared at the bus.

'Shit!' Hector said with a hiss. 'It's Uthmann Waddah. Keep your faces covered,' he warned his men. He glanced back at the women. Uthmann had never laid eyes on Daliyah or Cayla. Cayla had pulled her head in as soon as she saw the truck, but her hair and her face were uncovered. Quickly she pulled a fold of her robe over her hair and she turned away to hide her pale complexion. Hazel had not removed her burqa hood. The only ones Uthmann could possibly recognize were Hector or any other of his erstwhile companions in arms. As the bus drew level with the Hilux the second man in the back of it dropped his binoculars and let them dangle on the strap against his chest. He placed his hands on his hips and stared up at the faces in the windows of the bus. He was younger than Uthmann, and strikingly handsome. His features seemed to have been carved in polished ebony. He looked up into Hector's face. Suddenly Hector recognized him as the central character from the video of Cayla's violation. Before Hector could give the warning he saw the man's gaze switch towards the back windows of the bus. His aloof expression changed instantly, becoming wolfish and fierce. Cayla had not been able to resist the temptation to turn her head back for a quick peep. She looked straight into Adam's eyes.

'That's her! That's the infidel pig-sow whore!' Adam shouted in Arabic. At the same time Cayla screamed in wild terror.

'It's Adam!' She flung herself down on the floor of the bus, and covered her face with both hands. She was shivering as though with a violent attack of malaria. Hector slapped Tariq on the back.

'Drive! Go like hell. We have been blown wide open.' Tariq crashed the gears and pushed the bus to its top speed. Hector ran to the back window and with the butt of his AK smashed out the glass. 'Take care of Cayla,' he told Hazel without looking at her. 'Make her keep down. There is going to be some gun-play.'

Hector was staring out of the rear window. He saw that Uthmann remained standing in the back of the Hilux, but Adam had scrambled down into the cab and the truck pulled out into the road and roared in pursuit of the bus. With its flying start the bus had gained at least a hundred yards on the Hilux. But Hector knew the smaller vehicle was much faster than they were. Adam was leaning well out of the side window and levelling his rifle at them. The range was still too long. His first burst of fire flew so wide that Hector could not mark where the bullets had struck. Much more experienced, Uthmann was holding his fire. Even at this distance he and Hector were studying each other. They knew each other so well. Each of them knew that the other had no obvious weaknesses. They were both swift and deadly. With his right hand Uthmann was balancing himself with the grab-handle on the roof of the Toyota. He held his rifle easily in his left hand, but Hector knew that he was ambidextrous and could shoot fast and accurately off either shoulder. Hector saw that Uthmann was still carrying his new Bannock-issue Beretta, the finest infantry weapon ever made. Hector had the ancient and abused AK-47 that he had never fired before. Uthmann had wide-angle optical sights and off a steady platform he could shoot to within a half-inch of his point of aim at a range of two hundred yards. He was certainly one of the finest shots Hector had ever known.

Except for yours truly, of course, and the back of a racing truck is not a steady platform even for Uthmann, Hector consoled himself. *The steel of this old TATA should be able to turn the light 5.56mm NATO bullets.* On the other hand Hector had crude and heavy iron sights. The bore of his AK was badly worn and the bullets would probably rattle through the barrel when it was fired. The Good Lord alone knew where they would strike.

Better try it, he decided and aimed out of the window at the front tyre of the Toyota, so that he had a background on which to mark the strike of his bullets. He fired a three-round burst and saw his bullets kick dust from the surface of the road six feet left of the tyre he was aiming at. He imagined the smirk on Uthmann's face at the quality of this shooting. He looked back quickly and shouted at Hazel, 'Get up to the front and lie flat on the floor. We are going to be under fire any moment now.' She obeyed at once, dragging Cayla with her, and Daliyah followed them. His other four men crawled back and crouched on each side of Hector with their weapons ready.

'Don't shoot for the men,' he commanded them, 'shoot for the front tyres. They are the easiest target. Are you ready? A quick burst and then down again. You all know Uthmann. Don't give him a clean shot. He does not miss.' They clutched their weapons, still crouching below the sill of the rear window.

'Up and fire!' Hector shouted. They all jumped up and opened up with automatic fire. Bullets sprayed all over the road but he saw none of them hit either of the front wheels. In the back of the Toyota Uthmann brought up his Beretta in a relaxed and easy motion. He fired two single shots in such swift succession that the reports blended in a single blast of sound. His first bullet hit the man standing beside Hector in the head, killing him instantly. He cartwheeled over the back of the seat. Uthmann's second bullet jerked at the fold of Hector's turban and he felt the sting of it as it nicked his right earlobe. He ducked down and clapped his hand to his ear. When he saw the blood on his palm it made him very, very angry.

'Bastard!' he exclaimed. 'Treacherous bastard!' However, even in his anger he acknowledged that it was magical marksmanship. Two head shots with two shots. He popped his head up again and saw that the Toyota was much closer. He ducked down instantly and Uthmann's bullet fluted over his head. He had only just been quick enough. He changed position and came up again fast, fired a burst of three shots and went down an instant before Uthmann answered with a shot that was only a fraction right. The Toyota was now so close that he could clearly hear the sound of its racing engine over that of the TATA. The Cross Bow man standing furthest from Hector jumped up with his AK poised but Uthmann killed him before he could loose a single shot.

Using the brief window of time that he knew it would take Uthmann to realign himself after the kill, Hector sprang up again. He found the Toyota had raced up to within forty yards of the rear of the bus, point-blank range even for the lousy old AK. Hector fired again at the front wheel, allowing for the left deflection in the AK's iron sights. He knew it was a lucky fluke when he saw the front tyre explode. Out of control, the Toyota swung wildly across the road and crashed into the drainage ditch beside it. Uthmann had fired an instant after Hector but he had been thrown off by the skidding truck under him, and his bullet flew wide. The Toyota cartwheeled in a cloud of dust and pebbles. Hector could not see what had happened to any of the occupants, and he thought for a moment this was his one chance to turn back and kill Uthmann while he was still dazed or incapacitated. Then he saw the dust from the other two jihadist trucks coming up the road at high speed behind the wreck of the Toyota. They must have heard the gunfire and were rushing to join the fray.

'Don't stop!' Hector yelled at Tariq. 'Drive on as fast as you can.' He started back down the length of the bus, but paused beside Hazel and Cayla. Cayla was in a desperate state. She was deadly pale, shaking, shivering and weeping. She looked up at him.

'Did you kill him, Heck?'

'I am sorry, darling. But I don't think I did. I'll get him for you next time.'

Cayla burst into heartbroken sobs and buried her face against her mother's shoulder. She had been so strong and so convincingly brave and cheerful up until this time that Hector had believed, or rather he wanted to believe, that she had come through her ordeal with little psychological damage. But now he knew it was an illusion. The damage was so deep that it had shattered the very foundations of Cayla's being. It was going to be a long hard fight back. He knew that she would need all the love and care that he and Hazel were capable of giving her.

There will be a time for that, he told himself. *But my first duty is to get them out of the jaws of the Beast.* He left them and ran forward to Tariq.

'We must not miss the turn-off to the old road,' he said quietly but urgently.

'The old woman told me that the sign was gone, but that there was still the pole on which it had once hung. That must be it there.' He pointed at the piece of steel water pipe reddened with rust, sticking up out of a patch of weeds on the lefthand side of the road ahead of them. He hit the brakes and slowed for the turn. 'I can't see any road.'

'There! Between the two rocks. Those must be the original markers.' The bus bounced over the verge of the highway and tore on between the two large rocks with barely a check.

'There! Now you can see the old road tracks.' Hector guided Tariq into them and once they were clear of the roadside weeds the track became even clearer. Hector was keeping a look out for the dust of the pursuing trucks, but at the same time he directed Tariq towards a cluster of large rocks a short way ahead. Obviously, the jihadist trucks had stopped to give assistance to the overturned Toyota, for they were no longer in sight. It took a while longer for them to come roaring down the main highway. By that time Hector had the bus concealed behind the rocks. The pursuers raced past the turn-off and went on along the highway without any check or hesitation. Hector watched them through the binoculars and he recognized both Adam and Uthmann in the back of the leading vehicle. They had survived the crash, more was the pity.

As soon as they disappeared into the dust and distance Hector told Tariq, 'That's not going to fool them for too long. Get moving again quickly.'

They pulled back onto the rudimentary path and accelerated along it. In places the summer thunderstorms and flash floods had washed the tracks out dangerously and Tariq had to bounce over the rough ground and low scrub to get around the worst spots. The land rose gently under them and there was very little cover. Hector looked back anxiously. He knew that when Uthmann realized they had been side-stepped he would come racing back to find where the TATA had left the road. They would immediately spot the bus on the open hillside. Laboriously the bus climbed towards the crest of the rise and the blue mountains of Ethiopia lay directly ahead. As they neared the crest Hector ran back the length of the bus and peered through the rear window.

'Damn it to hell,' he muttered. He could make out the dust of the jihadist vehicles coming back along the highway from the north. He looked ahead and saw that they were still out on the open hillside and well short of the crest of the hill.

'We're not going to make it!' he muttered under his breath. There was no purpose in urging Tariq on; he was making the best possible speed over the broken ground. The pursuing trucks were now in full view. Suddenly the leading truck came to a halt. It was still too far for Hector to recognize the men on the back of it, but he had a mental image of Uthmann standing up and training his binoculars on the TATA. Then as abruptly as they had stopped the two trucks sped forward again. They reached the point where the TATA had left the main road and they slowed down to almost a walking speed and then both trucks turned onto the old road behind them.

'Here they come!' Hector lamented. 'And we have gained less than a mile.' He watched them climbing the hillside behind them. However, they were forced to negotiate the same dangerously rugged road as the bus. Their superior speed was no longer affording them much advantage. The TATA reached the top of the hill. Ahead the track dropped down into another shallow valley a mile or so across to where the route began the final climb up towards the foothills of the mountain range. The bus rattled down into the valley, losing sight of the pursuers. The ground was smoother across the valley bottom and they made better speed.

Hector peered over Tariq's shoulder at the lie of the land ahead. The solid bulwark of foothills that confronted them seemed impassable until he made out the mouth of the narrow pass between their frowning cliffs. He leaned out of the side window and looked back just in time to see the first enemy truck appear on the skyline behind them. It paused only briefly while Uthmann found his bearings and then started down into the valley after them. The second truck followed closely behind the first. Hector knew that they were now in a position to take greater advantage of the smooth ground of the valley bottom than they themselves could in the old bus. The odds had swung heavily back in Uthmann's favour. Hector looked ahead to the mouth of the pass. It was going to be a near-run thing to reach it before the two trucks could catch them. Hazel and Cayla were watching him, and he smiled reassuringly.

'I am going to raise Paddy O'Quinn on the satphone. He can't be very far ahead of us.' He could see by Hazel's expression that she knew it was a white lie. There were at least a dozen reasons why Paddy should not be just around the first bend in the pass, wearing his shining white armour, ready to rush to the rescue. However, Cayla brightened a little and wiped at the tears with the back of her hand. He could not look into her eyes and see the false hope shining there. Hector went back to the rear window and watched the oncoming trucks while he switched on the phone and waited for it to search out the nearest satellite passing overhead. He watched the little screen avidly, but it showed only a very tenuous contact which glowed briefly and then faded almost immediately.

'The mountains are blocking us,' he fretted. On the off-chance he dialled in Paddy's number and heard the weak and intermittent ringtone coming and going. Then suddenly he heard a faint and unintelligibly garbled voice that might have been Paddy's, or anyone else's for that matter.

'If that's you, Paddy, you're breaking up badly. If you can hear me, our situation is this. We're on the old road heading into the mountains but the thugs are hard on our tail. I don't think we can outrun them. We are going to be forced to stand and fight. We are heavily outnumbered and outgunned. Uthmann is leading them. You are our last hope. Come if you can.'

He repeated the same message slowly and clearly, and when he cut the connection he looked up and saw that both Hazel and Cayla had heard every word even above the racket of the engine. He could not meet their eyes and he looked back through the missing rear window. The trucks were bearing down on them. Already he was able to recognize Uthmann standing tall in the back of the leading truck, and could faintly hear the voices of the men around him shouting triumphantly as they brandished their weapons. He looked ahead and saw that the mouth of the pass was not too far away, the red-brown rock walls looming up on either side of the opening. He picked up the weapons and the bandoliers of the two men that Uthmann had shot to death and handed them to the women.

He knew that Hazel was an expert shot with the rifle, so he spoke to Cayla. 'I know you are hot stuff with a pistol, Miss Bannock. But can you shoot an AK worth a damn?' She was still too shaken and distressed to speak up, but she shook her head and gave him an uncertain smile. He pulled the Beretta pistol from under his tunic and handed it to her with the two extra clips of ammunition. 'Ask your mother to show you how to reload the magazines of the AK. You can keep us supplied when the brown stuff starts to hit the fan.' At the very least reloading the magazines was something to distract them from the menace that was creeping up behind them. He looked ahead at the rocky portals guarding the entrance to the pass.

'Well, ladies, we are going to make it into the pass, damned if we aren't,' he said cheerfully, and started back to keep the enemy under surveillance through the rear window. At that moment they all ducked as a burst of automatic fire twanged and rattled on the body of the TATA, and a single bullet came in through the rear window, traversed the length of the bus and then shattered the windscreen in front of Tariq.

'They're getting a little impatient,' Hector remarked with a reassuring smile at Cayla. He reached the rear window and peered out. The leading truck was just a few hundred yards behind them, and now he could hear clearly the shouts of the enemy, but they were still too far back for him to take them on with the old AK. Dust kicked up from the road behind them as the jihadists blazed away at them. Now he could see Uthmann leaning on the cab of the truck with his rifle ready, waiting his chance for another clean shot. He had a red graze down the side of his face and blood on his shirt, probably where he had hit the ground when he was thrown from the capsizing Hilux. It gave Hector pleasure to know that he had not survived the wreck unscathed.

Just before they reached the mouth of the pass another burst of automatic fire slashed across the back of the bus. It hit one of the rear wheels. The tyre exploded loudly and the bus wobbled its rear end like a fat woman doing a Hawaiian hula. A moment later they rumbled into the mouth of the pass. For the time being the rock walls protected them from more hostile fire.

Now Hector was forced to make a snap decision. The old bus was staggering along on its last legs. He could hear the ruined tyre slapping the ground with every revolution of the wheel and their speed was bleeding away rapidly. They could not run much further. He had to choose a spot at which to make a stand. The shape of the pass gave him a small prickle of hope. In these confined spaces Uthmann would have very little ground for encirclement or manoeuvre. He would have to come at them head-on. Hector stuck his head out of the side window and saw that the pass ahead was not very wide. Perhaps he could use the body of the bus to block it, and the steel chassis might serve as a strongpoint from behind which they could defend the way.

He looked up at the red rock walls that rose on either hand. From this angle it was not possible to judge their height. The walls had been carved out over the ages by flood waters, until they were smooth and concave. They overhung the floor of the pass on either hand like the roofs of facing verandas. Uthmann would have difficulty getting men up there to fire down into the pass. Of course they could simply lob a few hand grenades down instead. That would enliven the proceedings considerably, but what the hell! Nothing in life came without its own little problems.

He looked ahead and saw that there was a bend in the pass coming up. He glanced back. The enemy were still not in sight. The old bus reached the turn in the pass and clattered on around it. Hector stared ahead in dismay. Not far in front of them the way ahead was completely blocked. The righthand wall of the red rock cliff had collapsed into the pass, blocking it from side to side with an impassable barrier of tumbled rocks.

Some of the slabs were as big as or bigger than the bus itself. His mind raced as he surveyed this obstacle. Then suddenly he realized that instead of a death trap this might be their safe haven. If they could climb the wall and get to the top before Uthmann and Adam arrived, it would change everything. The pile of rocks would become a formidable redoubt. Adam and his thugs would be forced to abandon their trucks and climb up to reach them, exposing themselves for every step of the way.

'Tariq! Get us as close to those rocks as you can,' he shouted, then turned to the three women and spoke urgently, translating for Daliyah as he went. 'Now, the rest of you listen to me. Hazel! You and Daliyah go first, and take Cayla between you. Do you see on the left there is a low place between those two big chunks of fallen rock? You have to get through there. It's not too far. Don't stop before you reach the top. The rest of us will come up behind you. Every man carries his own weapon. I will carry the case of ammunition.' That was almost a hundred pounds deadweight and he was the only one of them who had the strength to manage it easily.

Tariq skidded the bus broadside to the foot of the wall, and they piled out and started to scramble up. The sound of the jihadist trucks coming fast behind them was magnified by the containing walls, reverberating in the close and heated air, growing louder every second. The increasing din spurred them onwards. Cayla fell when they were only just below the cleft between the two big rocks. She brought both Hazel and Daliyah down with her. Hector dropped the ammunition case, dragged Hazel back onto her feet and slung Cayla over his shoulder. He ran up with her and dropped her over the far side of the barrier of stone. Hazel and Daliyah followed her closely. Without a pause Hector turned and slid down the slope to where he had dropped the ammunition.

'No, no!' Hazel screamed after him. 'Leave it. Come back.' Hector ignored her and picked up the case. He was the only one of them still on the exposed revetment of the wall. He hoisted the case onto his shoulder and started upwards again. The bellow of the truck engines echoing off the walls was growing ever louder. He heard the shouts behind him and then the crack and whine of rifle fire. He felt a bullet slam into the wooden case on his shoulders. It knocked him off balance so that he tumbled over the top of the wall into Hazel's arms.

'Oh God, I thought I was going to lose you.' Her voice was a sob.

'Sorry.' He gave her a swift hug. 'It's not going to be that easy to get rid of me.' He turned swiftly to direct the defence. He saw that Uthmann's truck had been forced to stop so violently that it had slewed across the pass below them. The second truck had run into the back of the first. Jihadists were tumbling out of both vehicles and running forward, firing up at Hector and his men. But Uthmann had not yet regained firm control over them. Hector, Tariq and the two surviving Cross Bow men dropped flat on top of the wall and poured automatic fire down on them. Men dropped under their fusillade. Their attack broke up; they turned back in disarray. They left several of their number lying on the floor of the pass. At this range, even the decrepit AK-47s were effective.

Some of the survivors ducked behind the bodies of the two trucks. The rest of them sprinted back around the bend in the pass. Hurriedly the drivers of the trucks disentangled themselves and executed a series of three-point turns then roared back the way they had come, with bullets from the AKs smashing into their bodywork. When both trucks had disappeared, Hector counted six bodies that the enemy had left behind them. Two of these were still moving. One man was calling to his comrades for help and the other dragged himself back with both his legs slithering uselessly behind him. The men on the wall opened fire on them with gusto. Before Hector could stop them both the stricken jihadists were dead.

Not really cricket, but out here nobody has even heard of the game. He had not the least sympathy with the dead men. He knew he could expect as much kindness and compassion if the roles were reversed, which they very well might be in the very near future.

'Tariq, have one of the men collect the empty magazines and give them to the women to reload. Uthmann will be coming back very soon, depend on it.' Twice more within the next hour Uthmann tried to storm the rubble barrier. These were both expensive attempts and there were now fourteen corpses lying out in front of Hector's position.

The silence after the second attack had been repelled was abruptly shattered by the roar of many more trucks arriving at the mouth of the pass.

'Adam has radioed for reinforcements. Now he probably has a couple of hundred men down there,' Hector told Hazel. 'How much ammunition do we have left?'

'We have about three hundred rounds left in the case you carried up here. You have been using it up rather quickly.' After a pause she asked, 'Why do you keep looking up at the cliffs?'

'I'm trying to work out what Uthmann is going to do next, now that he has built up his forces.'

'What will he do?'

'He's going to send thirty or forty men up there from where they can fire down on us. Once they're in position they will keep our heads down, then Uthmann will launch another direct attack on the barrier. This time we won't be able to repel them.'

'So what do we do?' she asked.

'We get under the overhang of the cliff so the men above us can't fire directly down on us,' he explained. 'Then we build some sort of rock parapet behind which we can shelter from enfilading fire.'

The three women kept watch from the top of the barrier, while Hector and the rest of the men threw up a stone parapet under the overhang. They worked fast piling stones roughly on top of each other. When they had finished they came back to their original positions beside the women to wait for the next frontal attack.

Hazel reviewed their preparations in silence for a while, and then she said softly so that Cayla could not hear, 'This isn't going to work, is it?'

'No,' he admitted, 'not for very long, anyway.'

'What do we do after that?'

'How good are you at praying? I am completely out of practice.'

'You could try to contact Paddy O'Quinn again,' she suggested.

'That can't do much harm. At least it will pass the time,' he agreed and switched on the satphone. 'In the meantime I want you to take the other women down to shelter behind the parapet, before we come under fire from up there.' He watched them go while he moved up and down the barrier, trying to find a place from which the phone could see a satellite. In the end he gave up.

'It's like being at the bottom of a well,' he muttered to himself. He scrambled down to join the women behind the newly erected parapet and sat beside Hazel.

'The lull before the storm,' he told her quietly.

'Let's not waste a second of it. Put your arm around me.'

'That feels good,' he said.

'Yes, doesn't it just. But, you know, it's going to be such a terrible waste if it ends here, like this. I had so many marvellous plans.'

'So did I.'

'If you decided to kiss me now, you would meet very little resistance,' she admitted.

'Cayla is watching us.' They both smiled at Cayla, and she smiled back uncertainly.

'Do you mind if I kiss your mother, Miss Bannock?' Hector asked and this time Cayla shook her head and giggled.

'You two are so damned naughty!' She watched them kiss with interest. The kiss went on for some time, but was interrupted in the end by the sound of men's voices echoing down from the cliffs above them. All three of them looked up.

'Don't go away,' Hector whispered to Hazel. 'I'll be back to continue where we left off.'

He stood up and reached for his rifle. He saw that Tariq and the men were already watching the cliff tops above them for the first enemy to show himself. Hazel and Cayla crouched down at his feet behind the parapet, both of them gazing up at the cliff top in trepidation. Hazel had the AK resting on the top of the wall with the butt in her shoulder, and Cayla had the Beretta pistol in her lap, holding it with a two-handed grip. Daliyah squatted behind them.

'Can you shoot a gun, Daliyah?' Hector asked. She shook her head and lowered her eyes.

'Then look after Cayla,' he told her, and she nodded and smiled, still not looking at him. He left them and climbed to the top of the wall, squatting down beside Tariq. Now they could also hear the voices of the men assembling around the bend in the pass below them. The rock walls were acting as a sounding board so that Hector recognized Uthmann Waddah's voice as he harangued them, working them up to fighting pitch.

Hector knew that the men on the cliff above them would show themselves first, so he concentrated his attention there. He saw a furtive movement against the blue of the sky, and he waited. The movement was repeated and he raised the rifle and mounted the butt to his shoulder. He saw a man's head peering over the lip of the cliff and he fired a three-round tap. Chips of stone flew from the top of the cliff, and the head jerked back out of sight. Hector thought he had missed. He waited a few seconds, ready for the next target, then suddenly a disembodied rifle slid over the rock lip and dropped into the pass. It clattered on the rocks close to where Hector sat. Seconds later a lifeless human body slithered over the same place on the cliff. It fell with its white robes fluttering like a flag and landed on top of the rifle. The dead man lay on his back staring up at the sky with one eye and a startled expression. His other eye had been ripped out by Hector's bullet.

Hector went to the body and rolled it off the rifle. He picked up the weapon and weighed it in his hands with a surge of delight. It was a Beretta SC 70/90. For a moment he wondered where it had come from; then he remembered the Cross Bow men that Uthmann had murdered at the oasis. Clearly this was one of their weapons. The one-eyed corpse had a bandolier draped around its waist. Hector pulled it off. He checked the pouches and found there were five clips, each loaded with thirty rounds of ammunition. He slung the bandolier over his own shoulder.

Quickly he checked to see if the optical sight of the rifle had been damaged by the fall. Before he could decide if it was still intact there was another movement on the cliff above him. Instinctively he swung the rifle upwards and in the magnifying lens the image of an enemy head appeared before his eyes with the crosshairs perfectly aligned. He fired. The bullet struck exactly where he had aimed. The jihadist tumbled over the edge of the cliff and dropped lifelessly into the rocks at Hector's feet.

Hector's pleasure at having a real rifle in his hands again was shortlived. Almost immediately dozens of other turbaned heads began popping out over the edge of the cliff and bullets drummed like tropical rain on the rocks around them. The war cries of the enemy resounded off the walls. They were coming from the assault force that Uthmann Waddah was assembling lower down the pass.

'Come on,' Hector yelled at Tariq and the two surviving men. 'We can't stay here to be picked off like fleas on a dog's belly. We have to get under the overhang!' They jumped up and started down the reverse side of the barrier. Almost immediately one of his men was hit by the bullets from above. He went down with that peculiar rag-doll limpness which Hector knew was death. Nevertheless Hector stopped in the middle of the firestorm to make certain that the fallen man was beyond help. Then he jumped up again and started after the other two. Before they reached the bottom of the barrier and were under the rock overhang Tariq was hit, and he went down sprawling. Hector saw the blood spring brightly on the back of his tunic and a dark shadow seemed to pass before Hector's own eyes.

'Not Tariq. Please God, not him.' He changed his rifle to his left hand and with barely a check in his run he scooped Tariq up from where he had fallen. Tariq was not a heavily built man and

Hector carried him easily and dropped him behind the stone parapet.

'Do what you can for him,' he told Hazel. He was angry again, and he stood tall and swept the cliff face above him with a long burst of fire. Three of the enemy toppled over the lip and came thudding down into the rocks. The other enemy heads jerked back behind cover. Hazel and Daliyah were already attending to Tariq. He saw that Daliyah was weeping, and even in the extremity of the moment this came as a surprise.

'Why is she bawling?' he blurted out.

'Stupid question. She loves him, of course,' Hazel replied without lifting her head.

'My God! Everybody's doing it.' Hector grinned recklessly with the battle madness fizzing in his blood. 'How bad is he hit?' He fired twice at the heads showing on the far side of the pass, and killed another man.

'I don't know. It's in his back. But there are no bubbles in the blood, so maybe it hasn't pierced his lung.'

'Put pressure on the wound. Try to stem the bleeding. That's all we can do for now. But in the name of all that's holy keep your own head down. You too, Cayla. You can't take them on with that handgun.' He punctuated his speech with single rifle shots.

A burst of enemy bullets splashed across the parapet, showering them with stone chips and dust. Hector ducked down and spat out a chip of stone. Then he lifted his head to listen. There were shrill Islamic war cries coming from the direction of the mouth of the pass. Uthmann's men were scaling the far side of the rock barrier and reaching the top without being offered any resistance. Hector wriggled around on his belly under the parapet until he was in position to fire up at the top of the barrier, without having to expose his head to the men on the cliffs when he did so. He was ready when the first man raised his head above the top of the barrier, but he held his fire and waited for more of them to show themselves. The first head bobbed down again, and when there was no rifle fire it rose again cautiously.

Then others came up and went down again. Hector waited for them to become careless. Three of them stood up to their full height and chanted, '*Allahu Akbar!*'

Hector fired five aimed shots so swiftly that they sounded like a burst of automatic fire. Men fell or threw themselves down, shouting with surprise or squealing with pain. In the uproar it was impossible to be certain, but Hector thought that he might have got all three of them.

'Not too dusty,' he congratulated himself in an undertone. 'We haven't completely lost the touch.'

The rest of the enemy reacted violently and from the top of both the cliff and the barrier they poured a stream of automatic fire into the overhang. The bullets tore chunks out of the cliff, filling the air with a white mist of dust and then whining away in ricochets. Hector put one arm around Hazel and the other around Cayla and pushed them down on the stone floor. All their faces were powdered dead-white by the fine stone dust. Through the chaos of gunfire and the shouted war cries Hector made out the distant but mounting roar of many truck engines.

What trick is Uthmann pulling now? he asked himself. *He isn't going to be crazy enough to try and bring his vehicles over the barrier, much as I'd love to see that.* But the engine beat grew louder, almost drowning the jihadist shrieks. Abruptly Hector realized that the engine roar was not coming from the other side of the rock barrier, but was echoing down the open pass from behind their position. The Arab gunfire began to shrivel and dwindle. Hector rolled over and, still keeping the two women pinned to the ground, sheltering them with his own body, he peered back up the open pass to the bend in the rock walls to their rear.

At that moment a column of three huge GM trucks roared into his field of vision, coming straight down the pass towards them. On their sides was blazoned the Cross Bow logo, and in the front of each was mounted a pair of 50 calibre Browning heavy machine guns. Behind the guns on the leading truck stood Paddy O'Quinn. He was grinning happily as he gripped the firing handles and swivelled the twin barrels onto the jihadists who were still swarming over the rock barrier that blocked the pass. In the truck that followed him Dave Imbiss was leaning back and aiming his heavy Brownings up at the cliffs.

'Paddy O'Quinn and his rock and roll band will now play their famous signature tune for us,' said Hector, laughing and hugging the two women. The guns opened with a tumultuous thunder that filled the pass with sound. Paddy's tracer shells ripped the top off the rock barricade and filled the air with dust. Running Arabs trying to get to the top of the rock pile disappeared in the storm of shot, cut down before they reached it. In the second truck Dave swept the tops of the cliffs with his fire. Human bodies rained down into the pass, like overripe fruit shaken from the trees of an orchard by a gale of wind. Within seconds all the visible targets were destroyed and the guns fell silent. Paddy looked around and spotted them huddled behind the parapet under the overhang, and he waved cheerily.

'Top o' the mornin' to you, Hector. What a lovely surprise to find you still in such good form. May I offer you a lift home?'

'Enchanted, I am sure,' Hector shouted back. 'I never truly appreciated the sunshine of your smile until this very moment.' Gently he picked up Tariq. 'How are you, my brother?' he asked as he carried him to the leading truck.

'I will be with you for many more years. You and I still have to kill that son of Shaitan, Uthmann Waddah,' Tariq said. His voice was feeble but at least there was no blood in his mouth. Hector knew he was going to make it. He laid Tariq in the back of the truck, and the women climbed in beside him.

'Look after him well,' he told Hazel. It was more a plea than an order.

'Don't worry, Hector,' Hazel replied. 'Daliyah and I won't let anything happen to him.'

'Where are the others?' Paddy asked lightly as Hector climbed up beside him.

'What you see is what you get, Paddy,' said Hector sadly. 'There ain't no others, not no more.' Paddy stopped smiling and let his next flippant remark die before it reached his lips.

'God save their souls,' he said soberly.

'Amen to that.'

'But I see you managed to rescue the girl.'

'She's not rescued until we get her home. Let's go, Paddy!'

• • •

They drove back up the pass towards the Ethiopian border. It was soon apparent that Uthmann had not been able to get his vehicles over or around the barrier of collapsed rock, for there was no pursuit. They stopped once so that the Bannock Oil company doctor whom Paddy had brought with him could attend to Tariq. He set up a plasma drip, gave him shots of antibiotics and painkillers, and strapped up the wound. Then they drove on, making good progress even though in places the track had been washed away. Paddy's men had hastily repaired it as best they could on their way in. They reached the crests of the foothills and debouched into a maze of interconnected valleys and mountain passes, through which the old road threaded. They followed it westwards for the remainder of that day, climbing gradually into the highlands. So far there had been no sign of human habitation, so they risked using the headlights of the trucks and drove on after dark. Paddy was navigating with his truck's GPS. Four hours after nightfall he announced that they had crossed into Ethiopia. However, there was no indication of any kind to mark the border. They halted the convoy briefly to celebrate with a cup of hot tea. While the canteen brewed Hector warmed up the satphone. From this high ground the reception was crystal clear and he spoke to Nella Vosloo at Sidi el Razig as though she were sitting beside him.

'We will be at Jig Jig before first light. Come and fetch us, my darling.'

'Bernie and I will be there. Trust me!' Nella told him. They kept on driving through the night. Hector stood beside Paddy in the open gun mounting, both of them vigilant and unsleeping. But the dark mountains through which they were travelling were deserted. Two hours before dawn they reached the Jig Jig airstrip without having encountered a single living being along the way.

They went into a defensive laager on the edge of the airstrip, and the women prepared breakfast. In the lorry's tucker box Paddy had two dozen fresh eggs, a side of streaky bacon and four loaves of mouldy bread. They made toast over the coals and plastered it with canned New Zealand butter while it was still hot. With Daliyah's assistance even Tariq was able to sit up and, devout Muslim though he was, wolf down a bacon butty. They were still drinking steaming mugs of black tea when they heard the sound of Hercules' engines approaching. Paddy ordered a truck to park at each end of the strip, and switch on their headlights. Nella brought the colossal aircraft down smoothly on the strip between the trucks, and as soon as she lowered the rear loading ramp Paddy led all three trucks up into the cargo bay and strapped them securely. The Hercules was airborne again within twelve minutes of touching down.

The doctor re-dressed Tariq's wound and gave his opinion. 'He's lucky. Looks as though the bullet missed any vital parts. He is as tough as he is fit, and will be on his feet again in no time.' Daliyah wept helplessly when Hector translated this into Arabic for her. Then at Hazel's request the doctor turned his attention to Cayla. He took her into the tiny pilot's cabin behind the flight deck and examined her carefully. 'Physically she is doing well enough,' he pronounced. 'The antibiotics that Mr Cross administered seem to have taken care of the food poisoning. However, once you get her back to civilization you should immediately see to it that she is tested for any infection. Of course, she is still weak but after the ordeal she has been through that is only to be expected. Her psychological state seems much more precarious. Of course that is not my field; however, I can only urge you to get her to a top specialist as soon as you possibly can.'

'I plan to do exactly that,' Hazel agreed. 'My jet should be waiting at Sidi el Razig. Right now I am going to make certain she gets some sleep.' She turned to Hector. 'You too! You haven't slept for three days.'

'Don't fuss so,' he protested as she tucked him in to one of the sleeping bags that she found in the rack above the bunk.

'Fussing is one of the things I do best. You have been giving the orders up until now, Hector Cross. From here on I am giving you a taste of your own medicine. Stop arguing and go to sleep!' She switched out the light. Both Hector and Cayla were still dead asleep when Nella landed the Hercules at Sidi el Razig.

● ● ●

From the moment they landed Hector found himself shunted into the background. He did not see Hazel again for the rest of that day. She disappeared into the executive offices of the Bannock headquarters, where she was locked in meetings with Bert Simpson or in conference calls with her head office in Houston. Every time Hector glanced out of the window of his own office he was made acutely aware of the big Gulfstream jet waiting on the airfield with all her luggage already loaded aboard and her pilots and cabin crew ready at a moment's notice to whisk her and Cayla away to the other side of the world.

The emotions he was experiencing were unfamiliar. Over the years countless women had walked into and out of his life, but these entrances and exits had always been orchestrated by Hector himself. He had given them only a cursory thought after they had gone. Now he found himself in mortal dread. He realized how very little he knew about the real Hazel Bannock. He was fully aware that she was no ordinary woman. He knew she could be totally ruthless; if that were not the case she could never have climbed to the position of pre-eminence which she now occupied. There were multiple layers and hidden depths to her which he could still only guess at. Up to this moment he had been totally blinded to any flaws in those depths. Now he realized that he was more vulnerable than he had ever been before. He felt naked and defenceless. For the first time he was not in complete control of a relationship. He was hanging on the thread which Hazel Bannock held in her hand, and which she could snip as blithely as he had cut free those other women. The roles were reversed and he was not enjoying the sensation.

So this is what it feels like to be really in love, he thought bleakly. *Seems to me it's a highly overrated pastime*. Hazel did not reappear to take lunch in the company canteen. Instead Hector went to Cayla's room and invited her to join him. She tried to refuse, but he insisted. 'I am not going to let you lock yourself into this ghastly little room and fret.' They shared a table with Paddy O'Quinn, Dave Imbiss and the young company doctor. The three younger men had not seen a pretty white girl for months and they competed to try and impress her.

Hector dreaded having to spend the rest of the day in his own office, waiting for a summons from Hazel, or for some other sign that she remembered his presence on this earth. He left a message with Bert Simpson's secretary to give to Hazel when she was free. He changed his boots for a lighter pair, then went out into the desert and started to run. Four and a half hours later he returned to headquarters drenched in his own sweat. He had run the equivalent of a standard marathon, but he had not succeeded in leaving his demons out there in the sands. The secretary was watching for him from the windows of her office, and she hurried to meet him as he came in the front doors.

'Mrs Bannock has been asking for you. She wishes to see you in Mr Simpson's office at your earliest convenience, please, Mr Cross.' The phraseology of the message was not reassuring.

'Please tell Mrs Bannock that I will be with her at once.' Hector ran to his own suite. He stood under the cold shower for less than a minute, dried himself so quickly that the clean shirt he threw on had damp patches down the back. He combed his hair while it was still wet, scrubbed his teeth with extra paste on the brush. There was no time for a shave, so he set off immediately for Bert Simpson's office. He found himself hurrying and he forced himself to slow down to a more dignified pace. He knocked on the door to the office and her voice bade him enter. He drew an involuntary deeper breath as though poised to dive from the high board into cold water, and opened the door. She was alone in the room, seated behind the desk. She looked up from the sheaf of documents she was perusing. Her gaze was even but unreadable. She stood up without a smile.

'We can't go on like this,' she said. The earth shifted under his feet as though in a quake. It was as bad as he had feared. He knew he was about to be dumped into the recycle bin. With a huge effort he hardened his expression.

'I understand,' he replied.

'I don't think you do,' she said firmly. 'You know that I have to take Cayla back to Houston first thing tomorrow morning. She must have professional care immediately. I have not seen you all day. That was bad enough. But now I have to leave you here. It's going to be like ripping a chunk out of my soul. We can't go on like this. I have to have you by my side, night and day, for ever.'

Hector felt joy rising up to fill the cold and empty space within him. He could find no words that would not make him sound like an idiot. He held out his hands to her and she came to him. They embraced with a fervour not far short of desperation.

'Oh, Hector!' she whispered. 'How cruel of you to have left me to exist without you all these lonely years!'

'All that time I was searching for you, but you were so damned elusive,' Hector replied.

After a while she led him to the leather sofa under the windows. He placed his arm around her and she pressed herself against him.

'All right, now we have to be serious. We have to make plans before I am forced to leave you,' she said. 'I ought to leave right away, but I cannot deny us the joy of one more night together. Cayla and I will go early tomorrow morning. I considered asking you to come with us. But you have new arrangements to put in place here.' She broke off with a laugh. 'I am getting a little bit ahead of myself. I have a proposition for your consideration. Do you want to hear it?'

'I am hanging on your sweet lips,' he replied.

'I would very much like to buy Cross Bow Security. The price on the table is forty-five million dollars cash on signature. But that is negotiable,' she added and Hector laughed.

'Wow, you work fast. But why would you want to give me all that money?'

'I don't do paupers. I like my men to be able to afford to buy me a drink or take me out to dinner.'

He laughed again then insisted, 'You do know that Cross Bow is valued at thirty-five million. What would your share-holders say if you shelled out ten million over the going rate?'

'Firstly, I have done the maths. Thirty-five undervalues the company. It's worth every dollar of forty-five. Secondly, Hazel Bannock and not Bannock Oil is buying Cross Bow. Have we got a deal?' She offered her hand.

'We have indeed got a deal.' He shook his head in admiration, and took her hand.

'I want to put Paddy O'Quinn in your place to take over Cross Bow. I want you to hand over to him as soon as you can do so in an orderly manner. That's why I'm forced to leave you behind for the time being.' She did not mention that she also had to make plans for his reception and welcome to their new home in Houston.

'Have you considered that this will leave me out of a job and starving to death on your miserly forty-five mill?' he asked.

'I have indeed considered that. It just so happens that there is a job going at Bannock Oil for a senior executive vice-president. You might care to consider it. The salary would be in the region of five million plus perks and bonuses per annum.'

'Would I be working close to the CEO by any chance?'

'You would be working directly under her during the day, and directly on top of her at night,' she answered with a salacious slant of those blue eyes.

'Cayla is right. You are damned kinky.' He laughed but suddenly looked serious. 'But I'm not qualified for the job you're offering me.'

'You're a smart boy, and you'll have me to teach you. You'll learn quickly.'

'Again I have to ask what your shareholders will think of my promotion. Won't they kick up a fuss?' he insisted.

'I can vote well over seventy per cent of the company's paid-up shares in Bannock Oil. People tend to do what I tell them without kicking up a fuss. Do you want the job?'

'I am certainly not going to be the one who kicks up a fuss. I want the job.'

'Good! That's all settled then.' She took both his hands and looked deeply into his eyes. 'God made you and me for each other.'

'Hallelujah! At last I am a believer!'

'We're leaving all the horrors behind us. Cayla is going to be fine, and you and I are going to have fun, Hector Cross.'

'We are damn sure going to do just that, Hazel Bannock.'

• • •

The chef had arranged for dinner to be served to the two of them on the terrace looking out across the bay. The crescent moon and the stars were magnificent but Hector and Hazel barely glanced up from each other's eyes to admire them. The wine was excellent but they did no more than taste it. There was so much they had to say to each other that they left most of the delicious grilled desert quails on foie gras on their plates when they went to the bedroom long before midnight. The first time they made love with furious haste. It was wonderful but not as good as those times that followed. At last, locked in each other's embrace, they sank into a sleep so deep that the terrible piercing screams brought them back only slowly from faraway places. Hector came fully awake a few seconds before

Hazel. He sprang to his feet and grabbed the Beretta pistol from the bedside table.

'It's Cayla,' he said as he cycled a live round into the breech of the pistol and started for the door into the passage that divided the two bedrooms. Hazel followed close behind. Not wasting time turning the handle he put his shoulder to the door, ripping the lock out of the frame. He burst into Cayla's bedroom. Her anguished screams goaded him to even greater haste. With the pistol levelled and ready to engage any target, he made certain the room was clear before he switched on the ceiling light.

Cayla was curled up in the middle of the bed hugging her knees with both arms. But when she lifted her face towards him it was white as the sheets on which she lay. Her eyes were wild with terror. Her mouth was wide open. The screams that poured up from her throat were shrill like high-pressure steam escaping from a ruptured machine boiler. Hector darted to the windows and checked them swiftly to make sure that no intruder had entered that way. Then he threw open the wardrobe doors and looked under the bed. Hazel seized Cayla in her arms, trying to quieten and comfort her. But Cayla was struggling so violently that Hazel could not hold her, and she broke away. Gradually her screams became more coherent.

'No! No! Please don't let him hurt me again.' Hector dropped his pistol on the bedside table and took her by the shoulders. He shook her, and stared into her face.

'Wake up, Cayla. It's me, Heck. You are having a nightmare. Wake up!' Her eyes focused. She shuddered and her screams cut off abruptly.

'Heck! Oh, thank God. Is it really you?' Then she looked around her in terror. 'He's here. Adam is here.'

'No, Cayla. You were having a nightmare.'

'I tell you he *is* here. You must believe me. He was so close I could smell his breath. It was horrible.' It took both Hazel and Hector to calm her down. Then still holding her tightly Hazel slipped under the bedcovers with her and rocked her like an infant, crooning softly to her. Standing at the foot of the bed, Hector suddenly realized that he was stark naked and he backed away towards the door. Immediately Cayla shot upright and her voice rose again hysterically.

'You mustn't go. You are the only one who can protect us. Stay with us, Heck. He will come back if you go. Please don't leave us alone ever again.' He snatched up the sheet that Cayla had thrown aside and draped it over his nakedness like a Roman toga. Then he sat on the end of the bed. Cayla subsided slowly and closed her eyes. As soon as he thought she was asleep again he stood up to switch off the lights. Cayla jerked into a sitting position. 'No! Don't switch them off. He will come back if you do.'

'Don't worry, sweetheart,' he reassured her. 'The lights will stay on, and I will not be going anywhere.' Both Hazel and Cayla fell asleep at last, clinging to each other with their heads on the same pillow. Hector kept vigil over them for the rest of the night. He watched their two lovely faces and listened to their mingled breathing and it gave him a sense of fulfilment such as he had never known before.

In the dawn he walked with them to where the Gulfstream stood with its engines warming and the two pilots already sitting at the controls. He went up the steps with them.

'I wish you were coming with us, Heck,' Cayla said.

'I'll follow you pretty soon.'

'How soon?' she demanded, and Hector glanced at Hazel for the answer. She was ready with the reply.

'Heck will be with us before the end of next month.'

'Is that a promise, Mummy?'

'It's a promise, baby. Now why don't you go and talk to the pilots and find out our flying time to Houston,' she suggested, but Cayla rolled her eyes.

'It's not safe to leave you two little devils alone together. You are not to be trusted.'

'Go!' said Hazel.

'Keep your hair on! I'm going.'

Hector stood alone and watched the sleek aircraft taxi to the end of the airstrip then swing around and with the screech of its engines arrow back towards him and rise into the air over his head. Framed in one of the oval windows of the fuselage Cayla was waving a pink handkerchief at him, and in the window behind her Hazel blew a double-handed kiss. Then they were gone.

• • •

Hazel phoned him at every opportunity over the next few weeks. Her first call was four days after she left Sidi el Razig.

'Cayla and I have already seen Doctor Henderson together,' she told Hector. 'She is a lovely lady. The very best there is. She got me back on track after Henry died. She has taken Cayla into her sanatorium where she can see her as many times a day as is necessary. While she's there Cayla will have a full medical checkup and I will make time to spend at least a couple of hours with her every day. What have you been playing at, big boy?'

Each time they spoke to each other the news was better. Cayla was making a strong recovery, but there were things that Hazel would only tell him when they met. They had been apart for almost a month when Hector could stand it no longer. She phoned him that evening.

'Paddy and I came back from Ash-Alman this morning. We spent a couple of hours with the Emir and Prince Mohammed. They were worried about me leaving Cross Bow, but when they heard I would be going to Bannock Oil they cheered up. Of course, they know Paddy and like him. So we are all squared away in Abu Zara.'

'What will be your next port of call?'

'I wanted to discuss that with you. I am planning for Paddy and I to go on to the shipyards in Osaka. What do you think?'

The Sanoyasu shipyard in Osaka was building a new super-tanker for Bannock Cargoes Inc. It was an entirely revolutionary design and when launched would be the largest bulk carrier afloat. The whole project was running on a budget of almost a billion dollars. The construction was being carried out behind massive security precautions, for which Cross Bow was responsible.

'Good thinking, Hector.'

'I had another rare thought. What if you visited Osaka at the same time? Surely you could sneak away to nip across the Pacific for a few days?'

'You are the great tempter, Hector Cross.'

'How about it? I have been separated from you for months.'

'Weeks,' she corrected him.

'To me it seems like months.' She was silent for a while.

'Aren't you missing me?' he probed.

'Like I have lost both legs and both arms.'

'Then come!'

'I'm sure Cayla will be well looked after in the sanatorium. But I'll have to check with Doctor Henderson if it will be okay,' she mused aloud. 'I will have to let you know tomorrow.'

The following evening when she phoned her voice was singing. 'Doctor Henderson says it will be fine. Cayla says I should bring a big box full of her love to you in Osaka. I'll meet you there on Thursday.'

'Four more days to wait,' Hector lamented. 'I don't know if I will survive.'

They spent five days together in Osaka handing over the reins of Cross Bow's operation in Japan to Paddy, meeting with the design engineers and senior Sanoyasu executives and inspecting the mountainous hull of the new gas tanker on the slipway. The next day Hazel chartered a helicopter and they left Paddy to get on with it, while they slipped away together to fly up to a Shinto temple at the base of Mount Fujiyama to see the cherry trees in blossom. Wandering through the orchard they came across an ancient tree with a marvellously gnarled trunk. Hazel took Hector's hand and led him under the spreading branches. She leaned back against the trunk and glanced around quickly to make certain they were unobserved, then facing him she lifted her pleated white skirt above her waist and at the same time slipped the crotch of her lace panties to one side, to reveal her nest of bright golden curls. With two fingers she spread her bush apart and let the roseate lips of her sex pout through.

'This is what I have, big boy,' she said huskily. 'Now show us what you've got.' Then she stared. 'My God! He gets bigger every time I see him! What are you feeding him on?'

'At this very moment he is contemplating with the utmost relish his favourite snack.'

Fully dressed and standing up they made love, both of them titillated by the risk of being discovered in the act by one of the temple priests. The cherry tree shook as they rocked against the stem and white petals rained down on them like confetti, sticking in Hazel's blonde locks. Rapt in the ecstasy of her orgasm she made such a lovely picture that Hector knew he would remember every detail of it to the very last day of his life.

That evening they ate bluefin tuna sashimi and drank hot sake from ancient porcelain bowls in the quaint little guest house that was run by the lay priests in the grounds of the temple. Afterwards they retired to their private quarters where they made love on a silk futon, serenaded by the tinkle of the fountain in the courtyard. In the brief intervals between their bouts of lovemaking they talked. There was so much to tell each other and not enough time in which to say it all. Their most absorbing topic was the progress of Cayla's recovery.

'I didn't know how to tell you this before, it's so horrible. But my little girl was all torn up inside by those filthy swine. Do you know what a vaginal fistula is?' He was so shocked that he could not speak; instead he squeezed her hand and nodded. 'The doctors have repaired it surgically,' she went on, 'but while they were doing so they discovered that she was in the very early stages of pregnancy.'

'Oh, God! The poor little thing.'

'They fixed that also. Cayla was under total anaesthetic and she doesn't know anything about that part of it. We must never tell her.' He held her close, trying to comfort her with the contact. She sobbed softly against his chest and hugged him with all her strength. They were silent for a long time, and then she stirred and drew back a little.

'But it's going to be all right now. The first tests show that Cayla is not infected with HIV or any other sexually transmitted disease, and she is recovering well from the surgery. Thelma Henderson is working her special brand of miracle over her. Cayla trusts her. Apart from the terrible traumatic events that my baby has suffered, she is also consumed by guilt. According to Thelma, Cayla believes that she has betrayed both my trust and her father's memory. She thinks that it is entirely her fault that she allowed herself to be seduced by that horrible monster. However, Thelma has made significant progress with her. No more nightmares for a while. She says that Cayla will soon be fit enough to go up to the ranch in Colorado with us. It has always been her favourite place in all the world. Mine too. Cayla wants to visit Henry's mausoleum and of course all her horses are on the ranch.' She propped herself up on her elbow. Hector could sense her eyes close to his face in the darkness. 'I truly believe that it's very important for you to spend some time with her,' she went on. 'You know how good you are with her, and how she dotes on you. To a large extent you have filled the great gap that Henry left when he died. You've become a real father to her, darling. You see, both of us Bannock girls need you.'

'Of course, I could return with you to Houston right away, and leave Paddy to find his own way around the Cross Bow operations in Nigeria and Chile.'

'You know I could never agree to that.' She shook her head. 'The company's security arrangements are of paramount importance. No, I will return to the States on a commercial flight tomorrow, and leave the Gulfstream at your disposal to speed up the handover process with Paddy. I want you in Houston by the twenty-fifth of this month. Do you remember we promised that to Cayla? Apart from that the board is having an extraordinary general meeting the following Monday to ratify your appointment. I have a strange premonition that they are going to approve of you. You have friends at court.' She smiled for the first time. 'After that the three of us can fly up to the ranch together.'

Three weeks later both Hazel and Cayla were waiting to meet Hector when the Gulfstream landed at William P. Hobby airport in Houston.

'God! I missed you,' Hazel whispered as they embraced.

'Not as much as I did you.'

'When you have finished with him, Mummy, may I have a little bit of what is left?' Cayla asked sweetly. Hector looked at her for the first time.

'Wow! You are looking great, Cay.' He was lying. The truth was that she was still very frail and pale, but he kissed her on both cheeks. Then he took one of the women on each arm and they went out through the VIP entrance into the car park to where the uniformed chauffeur was holding open the door of the Cadillac for them.

Hector was expecting Hazel's Houston home to be palatial and pretentious. He was way off the mark. It was in the rural outskirts of the city on what was obviously still a working cattle ranch. To reach it they drove through lush paddocks of alfalfa in which grazed herds of white-faced cattle. Then they passed stables and outbuildings before they came to her home.

'Looks like JR's pad in *Dallas*,' Hector remarked.

'This is Houston, Heck,' Cayla reminded him. 'We don't like to mention second-rate cities around here. Just wait until you see the master bedroom suite. Mummy has had it completely redone, especially for you.'

'Cayla!' Hazel said sternly.

'Oops!' She put her fingers to her lips. 'I wasn't supposed to tell you.' She was blithely unrepentant, and winked at him in a conspiratorial manner.

'Anything you want to know around here, just ask your old pal, Cay Bannock.'

• • •

The board meeting was planned to last for an hour and a half. In the end Hector held the board members enthralled for almost four hours. Hazel had never heard him speak to an audience before and even she was taken by surprise. She found her heart warming with pride as she listened to him. He was so handsome and self-assured. His grasp of his subjects was firm and extensive. He presented his thoughts in a clear and logical manner, and yet his choice of words was riveting and thought-provoking. He fielded all their questions adroitly, and his replies had them all nodding their heads in agreement. Of course John Bigelow, the retired Democratic senator for Texas, tried to trip him up. But Hazel had warned Hector about him, and Hector turned the tables on Bigelow so neatly that the others burst into spontaneous applause. As Hazel had predicted Hector was elected to the board by a unanimous show of hands. They crowded around to congratulate him.

Without seeming to rush him, Hazel extricated him from the circle of his fellow directors and drove him back to the ranch in her Maserati.

'It's terrible!' she lamented as soon as they were on the highway. 'I just never seem to have you alone to talk to. I haven't even told you about my trip to Washington. I saw the President. I told him that I had paid a ransom for Cayla's release. He tut-tutted and gave me a lecture on dealing with terrorists. Then he told me how happy he was for me and Cayla. Obviously he was relieved to have me off his back.'

'Didn't he want to know who the villains were?'

'Of course. Roberts and a gang of heavyweights from the CIA grilled me. But I told them that the negotiations had been done by telephone. The payment was made electronically. I knew nothing.'

'Did they believe you?'

'Probably not. But they didn't torture me to get the truth.'

'They're brave, but not stupid. They know a tough cookie when they meet one,' Hector laughed.

When she parked in the underground garage she consulted her watch.

'You ran over time at the meeting. We have just an hour and forty minutes before we must leave for the country club,' she warned him. 'I want to introduce you to some of the people who really matter in Texas.'

'So, we have just enough time for a little bit of TLC. What do you think?' he asked her seriously.

'You are really terrible, Hector Cross,' she told him sternly. 'Well, okay then. I suppose we can always find time for a little bit of that.' She grabbed his hand and they ran to the private elevator that took them up to the bedroom wing. An hour later he was waiting for her in their sitting room when she emerged from her dressing room. They stood at opposite ends of the room and looked at each other in awe.

'Not bad.' She gave her opinion at last. 'Not bad at all.'

'Turn around!' he ordered and she pirouetted for him, the skirts of her ball gown billowing out around her long athletic legs. Her feet were clad in diamante-encrusted black velvet slippers.

'I am trying to find the words to describe your beauty,' he said, 'but it's ineffable. All I can say is that you are the loveliest woman on this earth.'

'I'll accept that,' she said, laughing.

'But hold on!' His expression changed. 'Aren't those the Barbara Hutton diamonds that you're wearing?' She nodded and laughed again.

'Of course, my darling. Only the very best for my man.' He looked mystified.

'But . . . but . . .' he protested, 'you lost that necklace when the *Amorous Dolphin* went down.' She shook her head, still smiling at his confusion.

'That necklace was a replica.'

'A replica?' He was stunned. 'What about the one you're wearing now. Is that the original?'

'Of course not. The original is in a bank vault in Switzerland. Do you have any idea what the insurance premiums would be on it if I wore the original on every odd occasion that I went shopping in the mall or dancing at the club?' His eyes left her face and darted to the Gauguin painting on the wall behind her. It was a magnificent Tahitian landscape, with naked island women in the foreground swimming in a blue river pool.

'What is the insurance premium on that one?' She turned to see what he was looking at, and she smiled again.

'Oh, it isn't worth insuring.'

'It's another fake?'

'Fake is too pejorative a word. Let's rather say it's a representation of the original, which is in a secure vault in London wherein the temperature, humidity and exposure to light are all strictly controlled.'

'What about those paintings that disappeared with the *Amorous Dolphin*—?'

'Yes, indeed. Those were also representations. Apart from the danger of theft, imagine the damage that a constantly changing maritime climate could wreak on such fragile pieces. All my copying is done for me by a gifted husband-and-wife team in Tel Aviv whose work is almost indistinguishable from the real thing. At the very first opportunity I intend to take you to view the originals. You will be the only one who has ever had that privilege, apart from Henry and me.'

He burst out in delighted laughter. 'You are a cunning vixen, Hazel my heart!'

'You don't know the half of it. However, that's enough chit-chat for now. Take me dancing, please.' She paused, and then went on diffidently, 'I thought we might take Cayla with us. I don't want to leave her alone yet.'

'What a splendid idea. I'll be escorting the two loveliest girls in Texas, no less.'

• • •

Saturday night and the club was full, every seat in the bar and every table in the dining room taken. Hazel knew everyone. At her side Hector moved easily through the throng, charming the ladies of all ages, and impressing the men with his forthright manner and his straight sensible talking. He and Hazel had never danced together before, but they were both natural athletes and they adjusted to each other effortlessly. Most eyes were upon them as they glided around the floor.

A little before midnight she led Hector out onto the terrace. 'Darling, Cayla has not danced all evening. Some of the nicest boys in all the state of Texas are here. She hasn't looked at one of them. I want to have a chat to Sarah Longworth. Be a darling and take Cayla onto the floor, won't you? Try to get her to enjoy herself.'

'Okay, I'll see what I can do.'

Cayla accepted his invitation to dance with alacrity. 'Thank you for saving my life again, Heck. I was shrivelling up with boredom.'

Once they were on the floor he discovered that she was as supple and light on her feet as her mother, but she was still so thin that her collarbones were standing out, and he could feel her ribs under the bodice of her Tom Ford gown. Even the professionally applied makeup could not disguise her pallor. He could see the blue shades of pain deep in her lovely eyes.

'There are some good-looking boys here tonight. I saw more than one of them trying to charm you into a dance. What's up?' he asked her.

'I am off boys. All except for you of course, Heck. For your ears only, I am seriously considering becoming a lesbian, only I don't know how to get started.'

'Don't look to me for guidance.' He laughed. 'It sounds like fun, but I have never tried it.'

'Aren't you shocked by the idea? I hoped you might be.'

'I know that's what you hoped. But it didn't work. I am getting to know your wicked ways well enough.'

'Then let's drop the subject of my sexual orientation, shall we? Did you know that Mummy has promised to take you and me up to the Colorado ranch this coming weekend?'

'I am looking forward to it.'

'I know you're going to love it there. We've got horses in the paddocks, moose and bear in the forest and enormous rainbow trout in the lake. Of course, best of all, that's where Daddy is.' She spoke of her father as though he were still alive. He wasn't sure if that was healthy, so he did not follow up on the remark.

'Tell me about the trout fishing. Is it catch and release?'

'Good Lordy, no!' She was shocked. 'We eat them. Mummy and I are true hunter gatherers.'

'But you catch them on the fly?'

'Of course we do, we're not total barbarians. I'm the family casting champion. How about you? Can you cast a fly?'

'I don't have much of a clue,' Hector admitted. 'You'll have to give me lessons.'

• • •

On the flight into Steam Boat Springs airport they diverted to overfly the Bannock Ranch. All three of them crowded together at one window to peer down at the magnificent wilderness of snow-clad mountains, green forests, sparkling rivers and lakes. Hazel pointed out the boundaries.

'The spread is four and a half thousand acres. That's Guitar Lake. You can see how its shape gave it the name. All of it is on our property, and that's the homestead at the top end of the guitar's neck.' It appeared to be a large rambling building with a roof of redwood tiles and many different planes and gables. Numerous stone chimneys rose above it, most of them oozing woodsmoke. There were half a dozen bass boats moored in front of the wide wooden deck and rows of stables and outbuildings along the forest edge.

'Look there, Heck, on top of Spyglass Mountain.' Excitedly Cayla pointed out the glistening white marble edifice perched on the brow of the hilltop overlooking the homestead. Its tall double doors were guarded on each side by Corinthian columns that supported the neo-classical pitched roof. 'That's Daddy's mausoleum. Isn't it magnificent? I hope that one day I'll be interred there next to him.'

'Don't be so morbid, baby,' Hazel admonished her. 'It's much too lovely a day, and you are too young and lovely to think about death and dying.'

When they landed Dickie Munro, the ranch manager, was at the airport to meet them with a Chevy Suburban to carry all the Bannock females' luggage. It was getting late by the time they reached the ranch. There was just an hour before sunset for the three of them to hurry down to the deck with the fly rods. Dickie had ground-baited the water and wherever they looked big trout were rising.

'As the guest of honour, you are invited to make the first cast, Heck.' Cayla gave him a pretty little curtsy. He stepped up to the edge of the deck, stripped thirty yards of fly line off the reel and then shot all of it out over the water in a tight loop that unfolded gently. The fly settled like gossamer on the surface. It lay there for only a few seconds before there was a powerful swirl under it and the split cane rod arched over almost double as a ten-pound trout crashed through the surface.

'Lordy! Lordy!' Hector cried. 'There seems to be something on the end of the line. What should I do to get it off, Cay?'

'You should tell the truth once in a while. I really believed you when you said you hadn't got a clue.' Cayla shook her head sadly.

At half-past five the next morning Cayla banged on their bedroom door and shouted through the keyhole. 'Come on you two lazy bones. I am taking you for a ride before breakfast. I'll meet you at the stables in twenty minutes. Don't be late.'

Hazel groaned as she sat up in the big bed and with a flick of her head tossed her hair out of her face.

'That horrid child! Won't you take her down to the lake and drown her?'

Beside her Hector rolled onto his back, yawned and rubbed the sleep out of his eyes. 'That's too easy a death for any little barbarian who violates the sanctity of the Fatherland.'

Cayla was already mounted up on her golden palomino stallion when, forty minutes later, Hector and Hazel followed the path up to the stables. She was taking the horse around the jumps in the main paddock. Although she appeared very small on the back of the great animal, she melded so perfectly with it that horse and rider seemed to move as a single entity. The expression on her face was enraptured, transported with an almost palpable ecstasy. Her cheeks were high in colour. Her hands on the reins were quick and strong. Her abused body seemed whole again.

'She is totally transformed,' Hector whispered. 'Look at her, Hazel; this is what will be her salvation.'

'I realize I have been blind. Now I am seeing her through your eyes for the first time,' Hazel said quietly. 'I had my vision of what was good for her, and I tried to force her into a mould that she did not fit.' At that moment Cayla looked across and saw them.

'Oh, you've crawled out of bed at last,' she called to them. 'Dickie has your horses saddled up. Let's go!' They rode together around the lake and Cayla told Hector, 'You have quite a good seat on a horse, but it's not as good as your fly-casting. Where did you learn all these things?'

'I was raised on a cattle ranch in Kenya. We did all our work from horseback and we had a trout stream in the mountains.'

They galloped back along the forest path, startling a big bull moose from his bed and sending him lumbering in panic up the mountain side.

'Heck, I am taking you to meet Daddy,' Cayla called to him. Without waiting for her mother to forbid it she led them at a gallop up the steep winding path. They came out of the forest suddenly. The mausoleum stood above them on the very top of the mountain with the early morning sun glittering on the marble walls. It was smaller than Hector had thought when he had first seen it from the air, but its elegant lines made it seem grand and imposing. There was an elderly black man with shining silver hair waiting for them in front of the tall double doors. He came forward to salute Hazel and Cayla and hold the horses' heads while they dismounted.

'This is Tom. He is a family stalwart,' Hazel told Hector. 'He was Henry's chauffeur, but now he is the guardian of his tomb. Look how beautifully he keeps everything.'

Beaming at the compliment, Tom swung the doors open and Cayla took their hands and led them into the interment hall. The floor was composed of chequered black-and-white marble slabs. In the centre of it was a raised marble platform and on this stood an enormous sarcophagus of red granite. Hector saw at once that it had been copied from the tomb of Napoleon Bonaparte in Les Invalides in Paris. Hazel went forward and knelt on the blue velvet cushions which Tom had placed at the foot of the sarcophagus. She bowed her head silently. Cayla and Hector waited just inside the door until she raised her head again and stood up. Then Cayla ran forward and scrambled up onto the lid of the sarcophagus. She spread her arms over it and kissed the polished granite.

'Hello, Daddy. I've missed you so much.' Then she sat up, and perched cross-legged on the top of the sarcophagus. She beckoned Hector to come forward. 'Daddy, I have brought somebody to visit you,' she said. 'This is Heck. He's the one I told you about that saved my life. I know you are going to like each other. Say hello to my father, Heck!' Unembarrassed, Hector stepped forward and placed his hand on the casket.

'Hello, Henry. We met before, as you will recall. You signed on my company Cross Bow. I am going to try to look after your girls for you as well as you did while you were here with them.'

'That's so sweet of you, Heck,' Cayla told him seriously. 'It's exactly what Daddy would want to know.'

They stayed at the tomb for nearly an hour. Tom brought bunches of fresh cut flowers and the girls helped him to arrange them in the silver vases at the head and the foot of the sarcophagus. At last Cayla and her mother said goodbye to Henry Bannock and Cayla promised him she would return soon. Then they went out onto the front steps and down onto the lawn. A shadow passed over them and all three of them instinctively looked up. A blue goose flew low over their heads. The wind whistled softly over its great wings as they beat the air. It honked once and Cayla danced and waved up at the bird.

'It's Daddy! He likes you. He has come to welcome you into our family.' When the goose dwindled to a distant speck against the clouds Hazel explained.

'Henry's family nickname was Goose. For twenty years he was president of the Texas Goose Hunters Club. So you see, that's where Cayla gets the notion. I have the sneaky feeling she may be right; that bird may well have been Henry's shade coming to check up on us.' They went to the stone bench set on the lawn looking down on the lake and the homestead. They sat quietly, reflectively, moved by all that they had experienced together. Cayla broke the silence at last.

'Mummy, this is probably not the right time to discuss this with you. I don't think there could ever be a right time. So I'll just blurt it out and hope for the best.' She drew a deep breath. 'I am not going back to the Beaux-Arts. I tried so hard but I never really liked the study of art and I wasn't much good at it – was I?' She did not wait for an answer but went on quickly. 'And after all that happened to me in that city, I hate Paris.' Hector sensed Hazel's deep disappointment and he squeezed her hand.

After a moment Hazel looked up at her daughter and smiled. 'It's your life, baby. I know that I interfered, and I'm sorry. Just tell me what you want to do, and I'll do everything I can to help you.'

'I have already enrolled at Colorado State University College of Veterinary Medicine, and later on I will specialize in large animals.'

'Horses?' asked Hector.

'What else is there?' She laughed. Hazel did not laugh with her.

'You have already enrolled and been accepted?' Hazel looked stunned. Hector had never seen her so completely taken aback. He squeezed her hand again as she opened her mouth to protest and she closed it. For a moment she looked forlorn and bereft, then she rallied and smiled shakily.

'Okay, darling. If they have already accepted you, we'd better fly down to Denver City first thing on Monday.'

'Mummy, you're not going to see the Dean, are you?'

'Of course I am.'

'But this is me, this is my thing. I'm not a baby any more. It's probably the first time in my life that I have done what I want. Don't you understand?' The two women stared at each other. Hector saw that this was a situation that was about to explode violently. He coughed softly, and they both looked at him.

'Tell her, Heck. She doesn't understand,' said Cayla.

'Of course she understands, Cay. Your mother is the most perceptive human being, man or woman, I've ever known. She knows what it's like to go out on your own, just as she once did when she was your age. As you want to do now, she left everything to follow her dream. She knows, Cay. Believe me, she knows.' Both women subsided visibly. He let them think about it for a while.

'You're the one who's made the decision, Cay,' he went on gently. 'You're damned right, you are not a baby any more. Your mother knows that, and now she is offering you her total support. You cannot be so cruel as to shut her out of your life completely, can you?' Cayla's expression became one of utter dismay. She jumped and ran to Hazel.

'My darling mother, that's not what I wanted at all.' She began to weep. 'That was so unkind of me. You will always be at the very centre of my life.'

'Thank you, my darling daughter.' Hazel choked off and they hugged each other fiercely, both of them sobbing bitterly.

Well! Hector told himself, trying to hide his grin. *At least it's no longer Mummy and her baby. I think we're off to a brave new start.*

They had forgotten his existence. He stood up and left them. He walked down to where the horses were hitched to the post. He leaned on the stallion's shoulder and patted his neck. He had seldom felt so pleased with himself. The two women followed him down half an hour later and they were walking hand in hand.

'We're all going down to Denver on Monday morning to tour my new college and meet the Dean,' Cayla cried happily. 'You too, Heck!' She ran to her horse and sprang into the saddle. She raced away down the forest path, letting out a succession of shrill cowboy yells.

Hazel came to Hector. She looked up at him and said quietly, 'You are a bloody genius, but I suspect you are well aware of that fact.'

'I am forced to admit that I did have an inkling,' he said, and she kissed him.

ayla went up to the Vet School in Denver at the beginning of the first semester of the new year, while Hector took on his new role at Bannock Oil as Hazel's vice-president. At first he played no active part in the company affairs. Instead he looked on and he listened. And he and Hazel sat up late most nights, studying and discussing together the mountains of information that covered the company's activities over the previous five years. His questions were perceptive and thought-provoking. Hazel found them so stimulating that she saw again through his eyes what she had done right, and where her judgement had been at fault. She came to understand that the years of being completely on her own, without a kindred soul to turn to for solace and counsel, had taken their toll. Without realizing it, she had been losing impetus. It had been a long lonely race for her and she was flagging. Now, once again, she had somebody whose judgement she could trust beside her and it was like a jolt of electricity. She no longer woke up in the morning dreading the day ahead. Once again she relished the prospect of conflict and challenge, of being stretched to the utmost.

'It's like that final set at the Aussie Open on the day I won the title. My God, it's all fun again.' To add to her joy of life, Hector was at last ready to go forward beside her. For months he had been sitting so quietly at the boardroom table that the other directors had almost forgotten his existence, but now he began to speak out. When they got over the initial shock, they began to listen to what he had to say.

'This fella of yours has the nose and the instinct,' John Bigelow told her with respect in his tone. 'He is just like Henry at the same age.'

Bannock Oil's affairs had been lagging of late but now they took an upward turn, not entirely because of the increasing price of oil. Hector flew to Abu Zara and after five days of discussion with the Emir he obtained the offshore drilling rights for the entire coastline of the Emirate abutting the Zara No. 8. They brought in the first productive gas well eleven months later. It was a storming success.

Hazel and Hector flew out to Abu Zara together to inaugurate the new well. Paddy O'Quinn and Bert Simpson and a dozen other senior Bannock Oil employees were at the Sidi el Razig airstrip to greet them. Both Hazel and Hector embraced Paddy and shook hands with the others. Then Hector looked around.

'Where's Tariq?' he demanded. Paddy gave him a strange sideways glance.

'He will be back in a couple of days.' There was something in his tone that set off alarm bells in Hector's head.

'What?' Hector demanded.

'Later!' Paddy side-stepped the question. They did not have chance to speak again until they reached the oil terminal building. As they climbed out of the vehicle Hector gave Hazel his hand to help her down, and at the same time he glared at Paddy.

'Okay, Paddy, now tell me what's happened to Tariq.' There were just the three of them standing together, screened from the others by the bulk of the Hummvee truck, but still Paddy dropped his voice.

'Tariq has gone up to Ash-Alman to bury his wife Daliyah and their child and to mourn for them.' Both Hector and Hazel stared at him open-mouthed. Hazel broke the shocked silence.

'Daliyah? Dead?' Hazel burst out. 'No! I cannot believe it.'

'Their house burned down. Daliyah and the baby were caught in the blaze. It was late at night and they didn't have a chance to escape.'

'Baby?' Hazel shook her head. 'Daliyah was married to Tariq? They had a baby?'

Paddy nodded. 'A son. He was born six months ago.'

'I never knew,' Hector said softly.

'Tariq told me he wrote to you.'

'Then I never received the letter. I never knew.' Paddy had never seen him so distraught. Beside him Hazel began to weep quietly.

'Oh, God!' she mumbled. 'Daliyah and her baby, dead. Oh, God. It's too cruel.' Hector put his arm around her and led her into the terminal.

The next morning when they walked into the terminal control centre Hazel was still pale and her eyes were red-rimmed. Hector was drawn and taciturn. Bert Simpson and Paddy stood up from their seats in front of the computer screens at the long system control table.

'Tariq is here,' Paddy said. 'He heard that you'd arrived, and he came back from Ash-Alman early this morning.'

'Call him in,' Hector said. Paddy reached for the intercom and relayed the order. Within a few moments there was a soft knock on the door.

'Come in!' Hector called, his voice harsh with emotion. Tariq stood in the open doorway. His expression was cold and remote. Hector went to him swiftly and embraced him.

'It is hard, old friend,' he said and his voice was still rough.

'Yes, it is hard,' Tariq agreed. They stepped back from each other, both of them embarrassed and at a loss for words. Hazel went to Tariq and touched his right shoulder.

'My heart goes out to you. Daliyah was a lovely woman. I owed her my life.'

'Yes,' Tariq said softly, 'she was a good wife.'

'And your son?'

'He was a good boy.'

'How did such a terrible thing happen?' Hazel demanded.

'You were her friends,' Tariq replied obliquely. 'Can we walk together and remember her?'

This is 'Need to Know Only', Hector told himself. *Tariq is playing this thing very close to his chest.* He took Hazel's arm and said gently, 'We will be honoured to walk with you, Tariq.' They went out into the bright Gulf sunshine. The sky was cloudless and the waters mirrored its brilliance. It seemed too beautiful for all this sorrow. Hazel walked along the beach between the two men in silence. At last she could contain herself no longer.

'Paddy told us there was a fire in your house?' She framed the statement as a question.

'Yes, Mrs Bannock. There was a fire.' He was silent again and they saw his eyes glisten in the sunlight with tears and with anger. 'I tried to hide them. I took a house in a village where we are not known. I used another name. I had her brother stay with her to protect her when I could not. Her brother died in the flames with them.'

'It wasn't an accident, then?' Hazel asked.

'It was no accident,' Tariq confirmed. He looked at Hector. 'You know who did this thing.'

Hector nodded. 'I know,' he said flatly. Hazel stared into his eyes, and then she knew also.

'It was Uthmann Waddah!' Hazel whispered. 'It was the Beast again. Wasn't it?' Hector nodded. 'But how did you know?' she demanded.

'Mrs Bannock, Hector knew with his heart, not with his head. As did I.' Tariq explained, 'He and I know Uthmann as we know a beloved brother, or a mortal enemy.'

'Do you know where Uthmann is now?' Hector asked.

'Yes. He is with Sheikh Adam Tippoo Tip at the fortress by the Oasis of the Miracle.'

'You know this for certain?' Hector demanded, and Tariq nodded.

'After the funeral of my wife and my son and her brother, after the three days of mourning, I left them and went again by bus to Gandanga Bay in beggar's rags to look for their murderer. I could not reach the fortress. It was too heavily guarded. But I waited at Gandanga Bay for twelve days. I saw many things. I saw the great new fleet of attack boats that Sheikh Adam has built since the death of his grandfather, and which his uncle Kamal commands. I saw the ships they have captured lying at anchor in the bay. I heard men talk of Uthmann Waddah.

I heard them say that he walks at Adam's right hand, and wields great power under his master.'

'Did you see them, Tariq?' Hector asked gently.

'I saw them both. On the twelfth day they came to Gandanga Bay in great state with many men. Adam is now a mighty man of power, and Uthmann is his general. I could not reach him. There were too many of their men and they were careful. I might have to wait years, but my time will come,' Tariq ended simply.

They were all silent for a while, and then Hazel asked, 'What will you do now, Tariq?'

'This is a thing of the knife,' Tariq answered. 'Blood calls for blood. It is a debt of honour. My wife and my son lie unquiet in their grave. I must give them rest.'

'Must you do this thing, Tariq? We have lost Daliyah, must we now risk you?'

'Tell her, please, Hector.'

'Tariq has no choice in the matter,' Hector told her. 'He has to do what duty and honour demand.' He turned back to Tariq. 'Go then, old friend. If there is anything I can do, you know you can get a message to me through Paddy O'Quinn.'

'It may take time . . . years even,' Tariq warned him.

'I know.' Hector nodded. 'You will be on the Cross Bow payroll for as long as it takes. Come back to us when it is done.'

'Thank you, Hector. Thank you, Mrs Bannock.' Tariq embraced Hector, and bowed deeply to Hazel. Then he turned and walked away along the pipeline in the direction of the airfield. He did not look back.

Hector and Hazel spoke of him often over the months that followed, but as they heard nothing from him his memory faded gradually into the background of their frenetic lifestyles. They did not forget him, but daily his memory was less poignant and pressing. Hazel voiced it nicely on the evening a full year after their last meeting with Tariq Hakam at Sidi el Razig. Cayla had spent the Easter weekend with them on the ranch and on the Monday had returned to Vet School. The two of them were drinking a flute of champagne before bedtime. Hazel raised her glass to him.

'Thank the Good Lord that Cayla is safe here in America, and that those horrors are so far away in distance and in time.'

• • •

At Hector's urging the Bannock management started to take seriously the exploitation of alternative energy. Hector acquired five patents from a young engineering savant that nobody else had ever heard of. The patents had such potential for cheaper and more efficient production of wind energy that both Shell and Exxon were soon bidding for a share in the venture. At the end of the second financial year since Hector had come on board, Bannock was able to declare an increase of seven and a half per cent on their dividend. The share price, which had been drifting in the doldrums for several years, shot up to $255.

Then to cap it all for both Hazel and Hector, Cayla's results came in at the end of her penultimate year of Vet School. She finished third out of a class of thirty-six. Thelma Henderson, her psychiatrist, pronounced that Cayla was completely healed. She had put on a little weight and the fresh healthy young blood gave her skin a glow again. Hazel's happiness was complete.

Another year sped away under them. Thanksgiving came around, and Cayla came down from Denver to celebrate with them at the Houston home. She brought a guest. He was in his final year at Colorado University College of Medicine. His name was Simon Cooper. Cayla sat beside him at the festive board, and looked up at him with shining eyes. Hazel reacted predictably.

'His father is an ironmonger,' she confided to Hector with horror.

'You are an awful snob, my darling.' He laughed at her. 'Actually he owns and operates a chain of over one hundred and thirty enormous hardware stores. In comparison I am a pauper.'

'Don't you dare compare any other man in the world to yourself.'

'This is Cayla's choice. If you oppose it, all you will do is harden her resolve. You've learned that already, haven't you?'

As Cayla helped Hector prepare the barbecue that evening she asked Simon to fetch another bag of charcoal and as soon as he was gone Hector asked her,

'What happened about your proposed foray into the Sapphic delights of lesbianism? Are you making any progress?'

'Oh that!' she replied airily. 'I got no encouragement from you, so I stopped work on the project.' She forked another chop off the coals and onto the serving platter and asked without looking at him, 'I saw you and Simon chatting. So what do you think of him?'

'To me Simon Cooper looks like a keeper. I think you should think twice before you throw him back in the lake.'

'I love you, Heck. You have such impeccable judgement of character. But what does my mother think of him?'

'You should ask her, not me.' Cayla nodded, and at that moment Simon reappeared with the bag of charcoal. Cayla picked up the platter of chops and carried it into the kitchen. Hector pulled the tabs on another pair of Budweisers and handed one to Simon. They chatted amiably while they waited for the ladies to reappear. Hector learned that he was twenty-six years old, and that he was not only likeable and good looking, but he was intelligent with interests in so many things other than medicine: from jazz music and history to football, fly-fishing and politics. Hazel and Cayla emerged at last from the kitchen bearing salvers of food. Cayla was a few paces behind her mother, and Hector shot her an enquiring glance. She beamed and winked back at him.

Simon left the next morning to be with his own family for the remainder of the holiday. Hazel gave the household staff the day off. It was just the three of them again. All that day Cayla was in a teasing and ebullient mood. They watched football on television and Cayla went into the kitchen and returned with a huge bowl of hot buttered popcorn, which they wolfed while the women rooted loudly for the Texas Longhorns. Hector pretended to understand nothing of the rules of the game.

'Good Lord!' he protested. 'That big gorilla in the red helmet is cheating. He's throwing the ball forward, and the referee's letting him get away with it!' The two women rounded on him merrily, and he grinned. He had stirred them up nicely.

'All I can say is, it's neither cricket nor even rugby.' He backed down, and they realized that he had been having them on. Cayla punched his arm with a full swing.

'That was not funny!' she insisted. In the end the Longhorns won and she forgave him his sacrilege. Peace was restored.

'So what would we like to do now?' Hazel asked.

'What I would like to do now, Mother, is talk to you and Heck very seriously,' Cayla answered. 'I guess this is a good time for it.'

'You have our attention,' said Hazel cautiously. Cayla turned to Hector.

'You, sir, are turning my mother into a scarlet woman. People are talking. Don't you think it's time you did the decent thing by her?' Hector blinked. Cayla was living dangerously; he didn't know how to avert the volcanic eruption that was surely coming. He glanced sideways at Hazel and to his astonishment found that she was blushing pinkly. The sight was so splendid that it stopped his breath for a moment, then Hazel smiled.

'Thank you, Cayla. You have expressed my sentiments exactly,' she said. They both turned to regard Hector with interest.

'Well? Let's hear it from the boy now,' Cayla suggested.

'You mean here and now, in public like this?'

'I'll have you know that this is not in public. It's very definitely en famille.'

'You mean on my knees? The full ritual?'

'See how clever he is, Cayla darling. He understands exactly what he has to do, with only a small shove and a push.' Hazel smiled again, but she was no longer blushing. Hector stood up and switched off the TV, then he fiddled with the gold signet ring on his right hand. 'It doesn't come off easily,' he explained. 'It was my father's signet ring. It's all he left me. The ranch went to my little brother.' He smiled ruefully. '"Teddy needs help," my old man told me, "you don't. You'll make it on your own."' He rubbed the ring between thumb and forefinger as he looked at Hazel. 'You are the only one I have loved in all my life more than I loved the Old Man. It's fitting that you take his ring over from me.' He went to where she sat on the sofa and knelt before her.

'Hazel Bannock,' he said, 'I love you as much as – more than – man has ever loved woman. You light up my soul.' Her expression softened and her eyes shone. 'Will you marry me, and stay at my side through all the long joyous years ahead of us?'

'Definitely and without the faintest shadow of a doubt or hesitation, I will!' she replied. He slipped the heavy gold ring onto the third finger of her left hand. It was man-sized and much too large. It slipped around loosely on her finger.

'This is just a stopgap. I'll buy you a real engagement ring later,' he promised.

'You will do no such thing!' She hugged the ring protectively to her bosom. 'This is the most beautiful ring I have ever seen. I love it! I love it!'

'Now you may kiss your betrothed,' Cayla invited. He reached out and took Hazel in his arms, and Cayla laughed as she watched them and she said, 'It wasn't easy but at last I've herded the two of you into the home corral and slammed the gate shut.'

• • •

'We have to go down to Cape Town to tell my mother,' Hazel said. 'Will you come with us, Cayla? Since you are our self-appointed matchmaker.'

'Oh, Mother dear, I dare not miss a day of school. I just have to beat Soapy Williams in the finals at the end of next year. You would never believe how he has been gloating over me.'

'How have the mighty fallen. You took every excuse to bunk off Art School when you were in Paris; even Edith Piaf's birthday was such an occasion. As I recall.' Cayla looked as vague as if Hazel was speaking Mongolian rather than English, and she changed the subject.

'Give my very best love to Granny Grace,' she said.

Granny Grace was waiting at Thunder City at Cape Town airport when the Gulfstream taxied in. Hazel rushed down the steps to embrace her. Hector gave them a minute or two before he followed her down to the tarmac.

'Hector, I want you to meet my mater, Grace Nelson. Mater, this is—'

'I know exactly who this is, Hazel,' Grace interrupted, turning eyes on him that were an identical blue to Hazel's and Cayla's. 'Welcome to Cape Town, Mr Hector Cross.'

'How did you know? Who told you?' Hazel demanded, then her expression cleared. 'Cayla!' she exclaimed. 'I will ring her tattle-tale neck when I get my hands on her.'

'You do my granddaughter an injustice. You must remember, I am not yet completely senile. I am still capable of reading the slush columns in the celebrity magazines. As you well know, I subscribe to most of them. You and Mr Cross have cut a wide swathe around the globe, young lady. However, I do admit that what information I was not able to garner from that source was emailed to me by Cayla. My granddaughter has a high opinion of you, Mr Cross. I hope it is justified.'

Grace Nelson was a tall slim woman in her late sixties with a daunting air. What must have been great youthful beauty had matured to a statuesque if formidable presence. Her skin was still smooth and almost unlined. Her hair was burnished silver and carefully coiffured. However, the right hand she held out to Hector, although shapely and manicured, was speckled with the liver spots of age. Hector took the hand and kissed the back of it. Grace smiled for the first time since he had come down the steps.

'It seems my granddaughter was in some degree correct; you have breeding, Mr Cross.'

'That's Mater's greatest compliment,' Hazel murmured barely audibly.

'You are very kind, Mrs Nelson. I would be honoured if you called me Hector.' Grace thought about that for a moment, then she smiled again.

'Well, seeing that you are to be my son-in-law, I suppose that is acceptable, Hector.'

Grace's chauffeur drove them out through the mountains and vineyards in the Maybach. They passed through the picturesque little village of Franschhoek and went on up the valley of the Hottentots Holland until they passed through the imposing whitewashed gates of the Dunkeld Estate, named after Grace's place of birth. Beyond the gates were hundreds of acres of immaculately pruned and groomed vines on low trellises. These were coming into full bearing with bunches of dark purple grapes dangling from the stems.

'Pinot noir?' Hector asked, and Grace gave him a questioning look, before she nodded.

'So you know something about grapes and wines, young man?'

'Hector knows just about everything about everything there is to know. Sometimes he can be a regular pain in the butt,' Hazel explained.

'Don't be vulgar, Hazel,' admonished Grace.

The house was Cape Dutch, designed by Herbert Baker in 1910. Grace's younger brother was waiting on the front porch to welcome them. He was a tall straight man in his early sixties, suntanned and with wide shoulders and flat belly from manual work on his beloved vines.

Hazel introduced them. 'This is Mater's little brother, my uncle John, and this is Hector. Uncle John is the winemaker for Dunkeld.'

'Welcome to Dunkeld. We have heard a great deal about you, Hector.'

'As I have about you, John. Thirty-two gold medals for your wines over the years, and a ninety-eight-point rating from Robert Parker on your latest Cabernet Sauvignon.'

'You like wine?' John looked immensely gratified.

'I love wine.'

'Perhaps we can go down to the cellars for a little tasting when the ladies allow you a few spare moments.' Hazel watched with barely contained amusement as Hector worked his special brand of charm on her family.

On the second day Grace took him down to her cycad garden. It was noted by the Royal Botanical Society at Kew Gardens as being one of the most extensive private collections in Africa. The two of them spent half the afternoon in the garden together and by the time they returned to Dunkeld House the two of them were firm friends, and Hector had been given permission to employ her Christian name.

On the last evening of their visit the entire family was served with dinner in John's wine cellar. They returned to the big house with sparkling eyes, warm cheeks and garrulous tongues. Grace was only the tiniest bit unsteady on her feet. However, she pleaded a little headache and retired early, but before she went she offered her cheek to Hector to be kissed. The next morning John and Grace drove them out to Thunder City to see them off.

'You will come to the wedding, won't you, Mater? And you too, Uncle John.'

'You have my solemn promise, Hazel my child. We will both be there,' Grace replied and then she allowed Hector to kiss her cheeks, both of them, and told him, 'Welcome to our family, Hector. For a very long time Hazel has needed a man like you around.'

'I will be good to her, Grace.'

'She'd better be good to you, or she'll hear about it from me.'

• • •

Hazel chose the first day of June for her wedding day, and she managed to whittle down the list of invited guests to a mere 2,460. Hector invited two: his younger brother Teddy and Paddy O'Quinn. Teddy declined the invitation. He had never forgiven Hector for being their father's favourite. Paddy accepted and in addition took on the job of best man. Uncle John gave the bride away, and Cayla was her mother's bridesmaid. In the wedding marquee a special armchair with velvet cushions was placed in the front row centre for Grace Nelson, who after a glass or two of Louis Roederer Cristal Champagne had been known to develop a slight list to port.

The board of Bannock Oil voted to retire Hazel's Gulfstream jet from service and replace it with a BBJ, a Boeing Business Jet. This reconfigured Boeing 737 could fly from LA to Paris non-stop at a speed of Mach .78. Its luxurious interior had been created by Gianni Versace. It boasted a full owner's bedroom and bathroom suite, and accommodation for twenty other passengers. It was the directors' little wedding gift to Hazel.

Hazel's wedding gift to Hector was a platinum and diamond Rolex Oyster Perpetual Day Date wrist watch engraved '*H. from H. with eternal love*', and accompanied by a handwritten message on a gold-embossed letter-head:

> *My dearly beloved,*
> *I promise to always walk ten paces behind you all my life.*
> *(Only kidding!)*
> *Your dutiful and submissive wife,*
> *Hazel*

Hector gave Hazel an artistic representation of his father's signet ring which differed from the original by being set with a five-carat D flawless diamond and by being internally engraved, '*To H. from H. For ever*'. The note that accompanied it read,

> *Empress of my Heart,*
> *Now you can keep the original ring in your notorious Swiss bank vault.*
> *All my love to the end of the road,*
> *Hector*

The wedding was a triumph, even by Texan standards. In defiance of custom the jollifications went on for three days. It was long after midnight on the third day when at last they bade an emotional farewell to uncle John, Grace and Cayla at the foot of the BBJ's steps.

'You are now legal. Even Granny Grace can disapprove no longer,' Cayla told them. 'Go to it with all your might and main, my children!'

'Cayla Bannock, you are not a fishwife. Kindly do not speak like one,' said Grace and burst into tears all over again. At last the bride and groom climbed up into the great jet, resplendent in its crimson and white livery, and it sped them across the Atlantic Ocean. When they landed at Farnborough airport in England a chauffeur-driven Bentley was waiting on the tarmac to take them into London. At the Dorchester hotel the general manager ushered them up to the Oliver Messel suite. They did not emerge again for two full days. They told each other that they must recover fully from jet-lag but they both knew that was a pathetic excuse. On the third evening they went to a Royal Shakespeare Company performance of *As You Like It* at the Globe. 'If we go on like this, doing nothing but eating and sleeping, we are going to turn into a pair of fat sloths,' she told him at breakfast on their private terrace the next morning.

'When you say it like that with a sweet smile on your face, I know there is a kicker to follow. What are you going to get me into next?'

'It's a honeymoon special surprise, darling. The Ramblers Marathon is being run this Sunday. And you and I are in it.'

'Twenty-six miles!' he exclaimed.

'Don't forget the three hundred and eighty-five yards,' she corrected him. 'Anyway, what are you griping about? You have three days in which to train.'

On Marathon Day it rained and there was a chilly northerly wind blowing, but they were holding hands when they crossed the finish line in the Mall outside Buckingham Palace in positions 2,112 and 2,113 out of a field of 30,000 runners.

'That's enough exercise for a few days,' Hazel told him that evening as they sat at her special table tucked discreetly in the corner of Mark's Club. 'Tomorrow is culture and arts day.'

Hazel had given the Storage Company the requisite week's notice that she wished to view her paintings that they were holding in their vaults. She and Hector sat side by side on a white sofa in a room whose walls were draped with plain beige curtains so that there was nothing to divert the viewer's attention from the paintings. These were carried in reverently one at a time by the company employees and placed on a white wooden easel before them. Then the men withdrew and left them to gaze enraptured at some of the loveliest tangible expressions of human genius in existence.

'When David Livingstone discovered the Victoria Falls he said, "Sights such as these must have been gazed upon by angels in their flight,"' Hector told her softly.

'I understand how he felt,' Hazel whispered back.

• • •

Two days later they drove down to Berkshire to attend all five days of Royal Ascot. Hazel was a member so they had full access to the Royal Enclosure. Between races Her Majesty the Queen and the Duke of Edinburgh circulated amongst the members in the parade ring. Hazel and Henry had often been guests of the Queen at Sandringham, so Her Majesty stopped for a moment to chat with Hazel and to congratulate her and Hector on their marriage. Prince Philip took Hector by the hand, and gave him one of his notorious piercing looks.

'You are an African, aren't you, Cross?' he asked and his eyes twinkled with mischief. 'How on earth did you get in here?'

Hector blinked once, but then he rallied quickly and shot back, 'Ruddy Africans and Greeks! They get in everywhere. Don't they, sir?'

Prince Philip snorted with huge delight. 'Third Battalion, the SAS, weren't you? I hear you're a good shot, Cross. We must have you up to Balmoral to give us a hand with our pheasants.' He glanced at his secretary.

'I'll see to it, sir,' the man murmured.

When they moved on, Hazel whispered to Hector, 'I am so proud of you! You gave the old devil just what he was asking for. But isn't the Queen just the cutest little lady you ever laid eyes on?'

On the fifth day Hazel's horse The Sandpiper won the Golden Jubilee Stakes, and Hazel decided not to fire her new trainer after all. She held a celebratory dinner for twenty at Annabel's. The US Ambassador was one of the guests, and in return he invited them to a reception at Winfield House, his official residence, the following week. Famously, the US government had acquired the house from Barbara Hutton in 1955 for a token payment of one dollar. Hazel decided that this was an appropriate occasion to retrieve the authentic Hutton diamonds from the bank vault in which they had been languishing.

The Norwegian Ambassador was one of the other guests. He and Hector got on famously, and when he heard that Hector and Hazel were fly-fishermen, he invited them to try their luck on the five miles of water he owned on the Namsen River in Norway, which was one of the most famous big-fish rivers in Europe. When Hazel told Cayla of the offer, she shrieked so piercingly that Hazel had to hold the telephone at arm's length.

'Oh, I do wish I could be there with you, my darling mother. I do love you so. I really do. Please! Pretty please!'

'What about your resolution to rub Soapy Williams's nose in the dirt at the end of the year?'

'That's ages away. If you let me come I will work twice as hard when I get back, and I will love you for the rest of my life.' Hazel sent the BBJ to fetch her.

The waters of the Namsen were deep and wide. On the last day Hector and Cayla were fishing both banks of the same pool. Cayla threw a long cast towards him with her double-handed thirteen-foot Spey rod, and she let the fly drift through. Hector saw the silver flash deep beneath her fly like an enormous mirror catching the sunlight.

'Steady!' he yelled wildly. 'There's a bloody monster salmon tracking you. Don't do anything. Let it swing through. When he takes don't for God's sake strike him. You'll pull the hook out of his mouth. Let him take it down then lift it into him.'

'I know! You told me a hundred times,' Cayla squealed back.

'Steady! Here he comes again.' He watched the tip of her rod. The huge silver flank flashed deep in the river. 'Steady, Cay. He's still there. Oh, hell, he has refused. Bring your fly in and change it. Work quickly, Cay, he's not going to hang around all day.' She was waist-deep in the cold water but she stripped her fly back and bit through the trace with her strong white teeth.

'What fly should I put on?'

'What's the smallest and darkest you have in your box?'

'I have a No. 14 Munro Killer. It's tiny!'

'Tie it on, and cast it in the same place as before.' In her haste the cast was clumsy and fell a little short.

'Shall I pull it out, Heck?'

'No. Let it fish through.' He waited tensely. There was no flash in the water, but abruptly the fly line stopped swinging. 'Wait!' he shouted. 'Don't do a thing.' He saw the tip of her rod jiggle and nod.

'He's playing with it. Don't strike him. Please don't strike him, Cay.' Then the rod tip dipped slowly but purposefully. 'Lift it into him! Now!' She leaned back slowly putting her weight into the fish, the rod arching like a longbow. Nothing moved for a long moment.

'I think I've hooked up on a rock on the bottom,' she cried.

'It's a fish, a monstrous brute. Wait for it. He hasn't realized that he's hooked yet.' Suddenly her reel screamed like a soul in purgatory, and the line hissed from it into the darkling waters.

'Take your bloody fingers off the line or he'll break you. He's going to jump!' The surface opened and the salmon came out in a burst of spray, like a silver projectile from a cannon's mouth.

Hector went cold when he saw the size of it. That skinny little girl of theirs was fighting way out of her class. She was hanging on grimly as the line raced out and the fish went greyhounding away down the river.

'Hold on, darling! I'm coming,' he shouted, ripping off his waders. Then barefoot and clad only in his long-johns he plunged into the current and tore through it with powerful over-arm strokes. He came out on her side of the pool and splashed up behind her. He put his hands on her shoulders to steady her on the boulder-strewn bottom.

'Don't touch my rod,' she warned him possessively. 'This is my fish, do you hear!' She knew that if he touched the rod it disqualified the catch. Hazel, who had been fishing the pool above them, was alerted by the commotion and she came running down the bank with her rod in one hand and the camera in the other.

'What's happening?' she called, but both of them were too busy to reply.

'You have to turn him, Cay,' Hector warned her. 'There's a waterfall around the bend. If he gets in there it's bye bye blackbird. Tighten up on him slowly. Don't jerk the line.' Now he had a hold on the belt of her waders to prevent her being dragged into the deep water. She laid the rod in the crook of her left arm and palmed the reel with her right hand to brake the run of the fish. He began to slow and at last when there were only a dozen turns of backing line left on the spool of her reel, the fish stopped. The rod jerked from side to side as the salmon shook his massive head. Suddenly he turned and came back towards her as fast as he had run away from her.

'Get that line out of the water,' Hector told her. 'Reel!'

'You don't have to scream in my ear,' Cayla protested. 'I'm doing it.'

'But not bloody fast enough. Don't argue. Reel, girlie, reel! If you give him a bight to pull against he will snap your leader like cotton.' At the same time Hazel was contributing her advice from the bank, and trying to get them to pose for her camera. 'Look at me, Cayla, and smile!'

'Don't you dare listen to that crazy mother of yours! Keep your eyes on the bloody fish!' Hector warned her. The fish set off upstream like a silver shooting star. Hector hooked one arm around her waist and dragged her along after him, splashing and stumbling over the boulders. Howling like a pair of escapees from the mad house they chased after the salmon. The fish turned again and they were forced to turn with him and chase him back downstream. Back he took them and then around again. Suddenly, after almost a full hour of mayhem, the fish stopped and they could see him at last, lying on the bottom in midstream shaking his head like a bulldog with a bone.

'You've broken him, Cay. He's almost ready to come to you now.'

'I don't care about him. He's almost bloody broken me,' she whimpered.

'If you swear again I am going to tell your granny on you, girlie.'

'Go ahead. After this I am afraid of nothing, not even Granny Grace.' Slowly and delicately she pumped the salmon closer to the bank, easing him a few inches off the bottom with each lift of the rod and then dropping the tip to wind in the slack line.

'When he sees us he is going to make his last run. Be ready for it. Let him take all the line he wants. Don't try to hold him.' But the fish was almost done. His last run was less than twenty yards and then she was able to turn his head and bring him back towards the bank. In the shallow water he suddenly rolled onto his back in exhausted submission, his gill covers opening and closing like a bellows as he hunted for oxygen. Hector waded forward and slipped two fingers into his gills and, careful not to tear the delicate membranes, lifted his head gently until he could take him in his arms like an infant. He carried the fish to the bank and Cayla sat beside him waist deep in the icy river.

'How much does he weigh?' she asked.

'Over thirty pounds, but less than forty,' he answered. 'But it doesn't matter. He's yours for ever. That's all that counts.' Hazel knelt in front of them and photographed them with the great salmon across their laps and their faces alight with happiness.

Hector and Cayla carried the fish between them into deeper water and turned him to face into the current so the water flowed through his gills. He recovered his balance and strength swiftly and started to wriggle to be free. Cayla stooped to kiss him on his cold slippery nose.

'Adieu!' She bade him farewell for ever. 'Go and make lots of little fish for me to catch.' Then Hector opened his arms and the fish's tail thumped from side to side and he shot away into the depths. They laughed and hugged each other for the sheer joy of it.

'Strange how good things always happen when you are with us, Heck,' Cayla said with sudden seriousness. Hazel recorded the moment with her Nikon. That was how she would always remember her daughter.

• • •

They flew on down to Paris and put Cayla on the commercial flight direct to Denver. There followed four long days of discussions with officials of the French Board of Trade, discussing import tariffs and the other problems of importing natural gas into France. Nevertheless they found time to spend an afternoon at the Musée d'Orsay admiring the Gauguins and another full day in the Musée de l'Orangerie with Monet's water lilies. Then they went on to Geneva to attend another art auction. There was one item in the sale that Hazel wanted desperately: a lovely Berthe Morisot of a Parisian flower seller. This time Hazel found herself in a grim bidding contest with a Saudi prince. In the end even she had to capitulate, but she was furious.

'You were right, Hector darling. These people are dangerous.'

'Naughty! Naughty!' he admonished her. 'That isn't at all PC.' Secretly he was not unhappy with the result. Surely there had to be a limit to her spending?

'I am not objecting to his skin colour. It's the size of his wallet that really galls me.' It took a little sweet talking and a lot of loving before she regained her good humour.

Russia was the next stop on their movable honeymoon feast. As always the Hermitage museum in St Petersburg enchanted them with its vast array of treasures that the Bolshevik revolutionaries had plundered from their own doomed aristocrats. However in Moscow things turned a little sour once more. For the past two years Bannock Oil had been involved in a courtship dance with the Russian oil giant Gazprom. The proposed project was a joint venture in deepwater exploration of gas deposits in the Gulf of Anadyr in the Bering Sea. Bannock had spent tens of millions on bringing this proposal to the bargaining table. Now it ran into the iceberg of Russian intransigence and sank without a trace.

'Insufferable Russkies! I have to punish them somehow,' Hazel fumed at Hector when they settled once more into the lulling luxury of the salon in the BBJ, and took off for Osaka. 'I think I am going to have to seriously boycott their caviar and vodka.'

'If you destroy the Russian economy that way, just think of those millions of cute little Russian babies who will starve to death because of you.'

'God! You are a bleeding heart, Mr Cross! Okay. I give in. I never did fancy the Bering Sea, anyway. I hear it's dreadfully cold up there.' Hector called the chief steward on the intercom.

'Please bring Mrs Cross her usual Dovgan vodka and lime juice.'

'Not bad!' Hazel gave her opinion as she tasted it. 'But isn't there anything for afters?' She glanced at the door to the Versace bedroom.

'I did have something in mind,' he admitted.

'Goody! Goody!' she said.

• • •

In the shipyards of Osaka the mighty tanker stood on the slipway ready for launching. The entire board of Bannock Oil and a number of other dignitaries, including the Prime Minister of Japan, the Emir of Abu Zara and the US Ambassador to Japan, were assembled to witness the event.

The interior of the ship was still unfinished. She would sail with a skeleton crew to Chi-Lung, the seaport of Taipei in Taiwan, where she would undergo the final fitting out and the installation of the revolutionary new cargo tanks. A lift took the guests to the top of the scaffold at the bows of the hull, where they were seated in the aerial auditorium. They applauded as Hazel went to the front edge of the platform to name and launch the great ship. From such a height she felt as though she were standing on the peak of a mountain with the world far below her. The substitute for champagne that she was to break against the steel hull was a magnum of Australian sparkling chardonnay.

When Hector had queried her choice of wine she told him seriously, 'We aren't going to drink it, darling. We're going to smash it to little bits. I don't want to get the reputation of being spendthrift.'

'Extremely abstemious of you, my love,' he agreed. Fifty photographers had their lenses focused on her as she made her speech from the front of the high platform. Her voice was magnified by the loudspeakers until it echoed and reverberated around the yard below her where thousands of workers were assembled.

'This ship is a monument to the genius of my deceased husband Henry Bannock. He created and controlled the Bannock Oil Corporation for forty years. His nickname was The Goose. Therefore I name this ship the *Golden Goose*. God bless and protect her and all who sail in her.' The *Golden Goose* slid broadside down the slipway and when she entered the water she raised a tidal wave that rocked every other vessel in the basin. They sounded their foghorns and all the spectators cheered and clapped. There were another three days of meetings and banquets before Hector and Hazel were able to escape again.

They flew up to the Shinto temple of auspicious memories below Mount Fujiyama. Their hectic itinerary had left both of them close to exhaustion, so after their obligatory visit to the sacred cherry tree in the temple orchard they returned to their suite and bathed together in the hot tub. As they lay there soaking in the almost scalding waters, Hazel reached out for her mobile phone and switched it on.

'Five missed messages from Dunkeld,' she murmured lazily as she wriggled her toes against his back. 'I wonder what Mater wants. She isn't usually so persistent. I wonder what the time difference is?'

'Cape Town is about seven hours behind us here. It's just after lunchtime there.'

'Okay, I'll try and return her calls.' Hazel punched in the number and it was answered within a dozen rings.

'Hello, Uncle John. It's Hazel,' she said and then broke off, and listened with dawning astonishment. Then she interrupted him.

'Uncle John, why won't you let me speak to her?' Her temper was rising sharply. 'All right! Damn it. Here he is.' She covered the mouthpiece with her hand.

'He won't put me through to Mater, and he won't tell me anything. He only wants to speak to you.' Hector took the phone from her.

'John? It's me, Hector. What's going on?' There was a silence on the other end of the line, but then he heard the painfully laboured sounds of a grown man weeping. 'For God's sake, John. Speak to me.'

'I don't know what to do,' John sobbed. 'She's gone, and now there is nobody to take her place.'

'You're not making sense, John. Get a hold of yourself.'

'It's Grace. She is dead. You and Hazel have to come. Now. Immediately. Please, Hector. You must bring Hazel. I don't know what to tell her. I don't know what to do.' The line went dead. Hector looked at Hazel. She was deathly pale and her eyes were huge, and so dark blue that they were almost black.

'I heard,' she whispered, 'I heard what he said. My mother is dead.' She sobbed once as though she had taken an arrow through the heart and she reached for him with both arms. They hugged each other in the steaming waters of the bath. After a while Hazel rallied.

'Darling, I need a little time to recover from this. Will you please speak to Peter for me.' Peter Naughton was the captain of the BBJ. 'Tell him we must have an expedited takeoff for Cape Town. Tell him we will be at the airfield in two hours at the latest.'

They refuelled in Perth in Western Australia, but were air-borne again within an hour. Their next and last refuelling stop was on the island of Mauritius. They had tried repeatedly to contact Uncle John, but he was not answering his phone. Hazel sent him an SMS from Mauritius informing him of their ETA in Cape Town, but the reply was from Grace's secretary, who confirmed that there would be transport waiting at Thunder City for them. By the time they landed in Cape Town their nerves were ragged. Since leaving Japan they had spoken of very little else than Grace's death, and in the end Hector had to insist that Hazel take a sleeping draught. When they touched down she was still dulled by the drug. Hector had never seen her looking so drawn and haggard.

As soon as they were seated in the Maybach and heading into the mountains towards Dunkeld Hazel tried to pump the chauffeur for information. However, if he knew anything beyond the fact that Miss Grace was dead and that her body had been taken away in an ambulance, he was not saying. Clearly he had been gagged by somebody and the obvious somebody was Uncle John. In the end he let slip one small item.

'But at least the police have gone now, Miss Hazel.' Hazel leapt on this morsel of information and tried to wheedle more from him, but the chauffeur looked terrified and retreated behind a barrier of feigned ignorance. In the end even Hazel was forced to give up bullying the fellow.

Uncle John was waiting for them on the porch of the house. When he came down the steps to greet them they hardly recognized him. He seemed to have aged by twenty years. His features were ravaged. Hazel did not remember his hair as being so white. He moved like a very old man. She gave him a perfunctory kiss and then looked into his eyes,

'What are you up to, Uncle John?' she demanded. 'Why won't you tell me what has happened to Mater? I know she wasn't sick. How can she be dead?'

'Not out here, Hazel. Come inside, and I'll tell you all that we know.' When they were in the sitting room John led her to a sofa. 'Sit down, please. It's a shocking business. I cannot yet get to grips with it.'

'I can't wait any longer. Tell me, damn you.'

'Grace was murdered,' he blurted and began to sob. He slumped onto the seat beside her and his whole body convulsed with grief. Hazel's expression changed and she hugged him to try to comfort him. He clung to her like a bewildered child.

'Grace was my only sibling. She was all I had, and now she is gone.'

'Tell us what happened. Who killed her?' Hazel was gentle with him, controlling her own suffering.

'We don't know. There was an intruder. He poisoned the dogs, and somehow managed to short-circuit the alarm system. Then he got into her bedroom. I was sleeping only two doors away and I heard nothing.' Hazel stared at him dumbly. She left it to Hector to ask the next question.

'How did he do it, John? Did he strangle her? Club her to death?'

John shook his head. 'It's too horrible.' The old man bowed his head and sobbed.

'You have to tell us, John,' Hector insisted. John lifted his head slowly and his voice was so soft and tremulous that they could barely make out the words.

'He decapitated her. He cut off her head,' he said.

Hazel gasped. 'Oh God, no. Why would anybody do a thing like that?'

'Did he steal anything?' Hector demanded brusquely. His tone was hard and without emotion. John shook his head.

'So you are saying that he stole nothing? He took nothing from the house?' Hector insisted. John raised his head and looked directly at him for the first time.

'He took nothing, except—' He broke off again.

'Come on, John! Tell us. What did he take?'

'He took Grace's head.' Even Hector was speechless for a long moment.

'He took her head? Have the police found it?'

'No. It's gone. That's why I couldn't tell you before. It's too horrible.' Hector turned his head to look into Hazel's eyes. She read his expression and rose to her feet covering her mouth with one hand, staring at him.

'Sweet Christ!' he said softly. 'It's the Beast again!' She dropped her hand from her mouth.

'Cayla! Oh, God save my baby! Cayla!' She sank to her knees and buried her face in her cupped hands. 'I am so afraid for my baby. I have to go to her.' Hector put his arm around her and lifted her to her feet. He looked at John on the sofa.

'We have to go, John. I'm dreadfully sorry. However, the living must take precedence over the dead. Cayla is in mortal danger. Unless we can do our utmost to prevent it, the same thing may happen to her.' He started for the door, still guiding Hazel.

'You can't leave me. Please stay with me until after the funeral at least,' John cried after them. Hector had no reply for him. He and Hazel ran down the front steps to where the Maybach was still parked. He placed Hazel tenderly on the back seat and sat beside her with his arm around her. Then he snapped at the chauffeur,

'Take us back to the airport at once!'

• • •

As soon as they were airborne they made the first call on the speaker phone. It was to Cayla's mobile phone, but it went straight to voicemail. Hazel's next call was to Cayla's dorm at the Vet School in Denver. She was answered by a cheerful young female voice.

'Cayla Bannock? Okay! I haven't seen her today, but she must be around. Can you hold while I try to find her?' It was seven minutes of agonizing wait, before the girl came back on the line.

'She isn't in the common room. I knocked on the door of her bedroom, but there was no reply. None of the other girls in the dorm has seen her since Monday. Can you try the registrar at the main block? I'll give you the number.' They made four more calls before they found Simon Cooper at the Med School.

'Hello, Mrs Bannock. Excuse me! I forgot that you are married now. Hello, Mrs Cross.'

'Simon, I have to speak to Cayla. Do you know where she is?'

'Oh, I haven't seen her since last Friday evening. I have been studying for the examinations that are coming up. Cayla is not too pleased with me. She says I'm neglecting her. She hasn't called me, and she won't answer my calls. I think I'm being punished. I presumed she was with you in Houston for the holiday weekend.'

'No, Simon, we are not in Houston. We're travelling. Cayla is missing. Please try to find her. When you do find her please ask her to telephone me urgently, will you?'

'Of course I will, Mrs Cross.' Hazel broke the connection and she and Hector looked at each other.

'We mustn't jump to the worst conclusions.' He touched her arm.

'No,' she agreed. 'There's probably a perfectly logical explanation. I'll ring Agatha in Houston.' Hazel's PA came on the line after only a few rings. She had recognized Hazel's number on the screen at her end.

'Good evening, Mrs Cross,' she said in her usual businesslike tone. 'Or I expect it's not evening wherever you are.' Hazel had neither the time nor the fancy for pleasantries.

'Agatha, have you seen Cayla?'

'No, I'm afraid not. Not since the wedding in any event.'

'Please try to find her, and tell her to contact me urgently.' She disconnected and looked at Hector. Her eyes were filling with tears.

'She has disappeared,' she said miserably. 'And here we are stuck helplessly in this stupid damned machine over the Atlantic. What can we do?'

'Paddy is in Vancouver. He's attending a seminar there. He gave me his number.' He searched quickly through the names listed on his mobile phone. 'Here it is.' He dialled and within a very short time Paddy's familiar brogue echoed from the speakers.

'This is O'Quinn. Who is calling?'

'Paddy, this is Heck. We have a red alert.'

'I'm listening. Tell me about it, Heck.'

'Hazel's mother has been murdered in Cape Town. Her corpse was decapitated and her head was taken by her killer. The whole business stinks of the Beast. Now Cayla seems to be missing from her school at Denver. We are returning as fast as we can, but we have only just taken off from South Africa. You must take a charter flight to Denver, Colorado. That is where Cay was last seen four days ago. Go there and find her, Paddy!'

'Right away, boss,' said Paddy. 'First thing to do is file a Missing Persons. Who was the last person to see her?'

'As far as we know, it was her boyfriend, Simon Cooper.' Hector gave his phone number to Paddy.

'Tell Hazel not to worry. It never helps at all.'

'Call us every hour, Paddy, even if you have nothing to report.'

Within eight hours Paddy was with the Chief of Police in Denver. They had an all-points bulletin out for Cayla. All the local radio stations and TV stations were broadcasting appeals for information and displaying Cayla's photograph. Police officers had been sent out to grill Simon Cooper and all the other students in Cayla's class and dorm.

'Nothing definite yet, Hector. But everybody is working on it. Cayla hasn't slept in the dorm for the last three nights, nor has she attended her classes since Monday. I have just this minute spoken to the Chief of Police in Houston. He knows Hazel well. Big respect. He is sending out his people to visit all Cayla's usual haunts.' When the BBJ landed at Atlanta to clear customs and immigration Hector called Paddy immediately.

'We have to make a decision, Paddy. Do we fly to Houston or Denver? What is your advice?'

'Half an hour ago we received a tip from the local TV station. A caller thinks he recognized the photograph of Cayla. He thinks he saw a girl like her on the flight from Denver to Houston two days ago. So the main search moves to Houston.'

'Please God, let it be her,' Hazel breathed. 'Tell Peter to file a flight plan for Houston. I'll call Agatha to have a car for us at the airport. It will be after midnight before we arrive.' Both of them managed a few hours of broken sleep on the last leg of the flight, but they were exhausted when they at last reached the Bannock homestead. All the lights were on in the house and Agatha met them at the front door.

'Any news?' Hazel demanded.

'I'm so sorry, Mrs Cross. I have heard nothing more since we last spoke. They are trying to contact all the passengers on the flight that Cayla may have been on.' As soon as they were in the suite they called Paddy again.

'Nothing more for the moment,' he told Hector. 'Why don't the two of you try to get some sleep? It looks as though you are going to have a hectic time over the next few days. I will call you again the minute I have anything new to report. I promise you that.'

'All right. That's what we'll do, Paddy.'

• • •

Hector reached out in his sleep, but although the sheet was still warm from Hazel's body the bed beside him was empty. He was wide awake instantly and reached out to touch the pistol that always lay on the bedside table.

'Hazel!' he said sharply.

'I'm here.' She was standing by the window.

'Come to bed,' he ordered.

'I thought I heard something.'

'What was it? I heard nothing.'

'You were asleep,' she said. 'Perhaps I was dreaming.'

'Come to bed, my love.'

'I have to use the bathroom, before I burst.' She moved across the room, a slim silhouette against the moonlight coming through the windows. She went into the bathroom and switched on the light. She paused in surprise. There was something on her marble vanity top that had not been there when she went to bed. It was a large object with a loose white cloth draped over it. She crossed the room slowly and cautiously; then she saw that there was an envelope propped up against the package. It was embossed, the kind that usually contains a greeting card or a message from the giver, from a lover.

'Hector!' she whispered aloud. 'He knows me so well; how I love presents from him. The darling is trying to comfort me.' She picked up the envelope. It was not addressed, and the flap was not sealed. She opened it and slid out the card it contained, then stared at it in bewilderment. It was not written in English but in some eastern script.

'Arabic?' She was not certain. She looked down at the covered object, then reached out and took a corner of the cloth. She drew it aside, to reveal two large glass bell jars, the type in which laboratory specimens are preserved. Still puzzled, she stooped to make a closer inspection of the contents of the jars.

Then she screamed. It was an expression of the wildest, deepest anguish of the soul. She reeled backwards and fell to the white-tiled floor. On her hands and knees she scrambled to the further corner of the room and curled up there like a wild animal in a cage. She began to urinate in a hot gush down her legs. She opened her mouth to scream again, but a powerful projectile stream of yellow vomit shot out of her mouth and cascaded halfway across the tiled floor.

Her scream had electrified Hector. He bounded out of the bed and snatched up the pistol. As he raced across the bedroom he cycled a round of ammunition from the magazine into the breech. He burst into her bathroom with the pistol levelled in a double-handed grip. He crouched in the doorway covering the room. He saw her curled up in the corner, and smelled the reek of fresh vomit and urine in the air. He felt sick with dread.

She is hurt, he thought, *wounded*. He went quickly to her and knelt at her side. 'Hazel, what happened? Was there somebody here? Why are you so frightened?' He put out his hand to her but she shied away from him, shaking her head and pointing at the vanity shelf. He turned quickly, with the pistol aimed and his finger resting on the trigger guard ready for a snap shot.

Then he saw the two bell jars. It took him a moment to understand what he was looking at. A disembodied human head floated in each jar filled with colourless preservative spirit. In the lefthand one was the head of Grace Nelson. Her eyes were closed and her skin was yellow with age, bagging and pouched. The thin silver strands of her hair were plastered across her face like seaweed. She looked very old, as if she had been dead a hundred years.

In the righthand jar was the head of Cayla Bannock. Her eyes were open. They seemed to be looking directly at him.

They were no longer bright sparkling blue. They were dull and expressionless as pebbles. Her lips were slightly parted and her white teeth showed in the vestige of a cynical smile. Her skin was pale, but smooth and flawless. Her hair floated around her face in a golden cloud. It seemed as though she had just woken from a deep sleep. He knew if he looked upon her loveliness for another instant his heart would break.

He stooped and picked Hazel up in his arms and carried her through to the bed and laid her upon it. He picked up the bedside intercom and dialled Agatha. She answered almost immediately.

'Get the security guards to search the house and grounds for an intruder. Call the police. There has been a murder. Then we need a doctor for Hazel.' He paused. 'It's an emergency.' He stripped off Hazel's nightdress, and wiped her face and body with a damp towel. Then he covered her with a duvet, and came under it with her, taking her in his arms. She clung to him. Her whole body was shaking and her teeth chattered. Terrible, gut-wrenching sobs came up from deep inside her. He held her and whispered endearments to her until the doctor arrived.

'My wife has lost her daughter. It has been a terrible shock,' Hector explained.

The doctor gave her an injection that dropped her into a deep dark hole of unconsciousness. 'I want to take her to my clinic, and have a nurse attend her day and night until she recovers fully,' he said.

'Good!' Hector agreed. 'Things are going to happen here that she should not be involved in—' He broke off as they heard the police sirens racing through the paddocks towards the house.

'I will call for an ambulance right away.'

After Hazel was carried downstairs on a stretcher, Hector kissed her unconscious face and watched the ambulance drive away. Then he returned to the bathroom and covered the two pathetic heads with the white cloth. He opened the envelope and read the Arabic script on the card.

'The blood debt is four. Two heads taken and two more to take before the debt is paid in full.'

• • •

Seven days later the Denver police recovered the decapitated body of Cayla Bannock from a storm drain at the back of the sports arena in the grounds of the university. People had called to complain of the smell. The corpse was in an advanced stage of decomposition. The undertakers sealed it in a lead sheath and then laid it in a white marble sarcophagus along with the embalmed heads of Cayla and her grandmother. The lid of the sarcophagus was engraved with both their names. A charter flight delivered it to Steam Boat Springs and a hearse carried it up to the Bannock mausoleum on Spy Glass Mountain. On the same day in South Africa the remains of Grace Nelson's body were cremated and Uncle John scattered her ashes on the Dunkeld vineyards.

Only a handful of close family and friends attended the interment on Spy Glass Mountain. The sarcophagus was placed on a pink marble plinth to the right of Cayla's father. The priest who had baptized Cayla conducted the simple service. There were no speeches. Afterwards each of the mourners placed a single red rose upon the lid of the sarcophagus as they filed out. Simon Cooper was amongst them and he wept openly.

'I will never know another girl like her. We were going to be married and have a home and babies. She was wonderful.' He broke off. 'I'm sorry, Mrs Bannock, I didn't want to make a spectacle of myself.'

'I am so glad you came, Simon,' she told him.

When Hector and Hazel were alone they walked down the lawns and sat together on the stone bench. Hector looked up at the sky. Hazel smiled sadly.

'I'm afraid Henry isn't going to show,' she said. 'He hasn't the time to flit around in his goose persona. At the moment he has his hands too full with Cayla and Grace.'

'You read my thoughts. I was waiting for Henry,' Hector admitted. 'I think this is the first time I've seen you smile since it all started.'

'I am all cried out,' she told him. 'The weeping time is behind us. Let's leave Henry and Cayla alone for a while so they can get to know each other again.' She stood up and took his hand and they started down the mountain path to the house beside the lake. As they walked he kept glancing sideways at her face. *She is not like any other woman I have ever known*, he thought. *Those others would have been totally destroyed by such a cruel loss. But it is almost as if she has gained strength and resolve from it. I can see now how she has achieved so much in her short life. She is a fighter and she never gives up. She never succumbs to self-pity. She might always mourn for Cayla, but she will never let that debilitate her. She lost Henry at a critical time in her life. She misses him still but she fought on alone, and took over his legendary mantle. I feel deeply honoured to have received the gift of her love. It is my armour. With her at my side I shall never again know loneliness.*

Neither of them had any appetite for dinner. They sent the dishes back to the chef in his kitchen. Hector opened a bottle of claret and they took it and the glasses down to the end of the jetty and sat with their legs dangling over the water. They drank the wine in silence and watched the moon come up over the lake. Hazel spoke first.

'The police have not yet been able to trace the person or persons that placed those heads of my two poor darlings for us to find,' she sighed.

'That isn't surprising,' Hector replied. 'Your security on the Houston ranch is not very tight. There are literally hundreds of service people who have access: contract gardening service teams, delivery people bringing supplies, daily hired hands, meter readers, plumbers, painters, electricians and all the others.'

'But how could Adam have reached any of them from Africa so many thousands of miles away? Surely these people are all Americans.'

'Plus Latinos, Europeans, Asians, Africans and other immigrants of twenty different nationalities . . . including Somalians, from Puntland.' She turned to stare at him.

'Somalians? How is that possible?'

'Canada alone has over a quarter of a million Somalians who have entered that country legally, and the US–Canadian border is wide open. Your mother's country, South Africa, is flooded with refugees from the north of the continent. Not only Zimbabweans and Malawians but huge numbers of Nigerians and Somalians. Most of the Somalians are from Puntland and they are still under the sway of Tippoo Tip. If the police ever catch those involved in the murder of Grace and Cayla, they will be very small fish who will not even know who it was that ordered the killings.' Hector paused and put his arm around Hazel's shoulder. 'So you see, my darling, this is not the end of the business. Adam has only just begun. He has thousands of underlings to send against us. It is useless to cut off the tentacles of the Beast. They grow back swiftly. I have to go back to cut off its head.'

'Don't you see that is exactly what he is trying to force you to do? That is why he left that taunting warning about taking two more heads. You mustn't let him suck you in. You mustn't go.' She placed her hand on his forearm, and spoke earnestly and passionately. 'If I lose you, then I have lost everything.'

'We have no choice,' he told her.

'If you go, then I am going with you.' The tone of her voice was final, brooking no argument. A short silence fell.

'No, my sweet. I can't let you come. You know how it was last time. We will be on the Beast's home ground again.'

'Send Paddy then. That's what he's paid for. That's what he's good at,' she said.

'I can never send another man to do what I am afraid to do myself. If I don't go then the Beast will come after us as he has threatened.'

'Yes, that's the best solution. Let him come. Make him meet us on our home turf for a change. This time you can be ready for him.' Hector stared at her in the moonlight.

'Yes!' he said thoughtfully, then shook his head. 'No. He'll never come himself. He'll send hired assassins after us, just as he did before. There are those hordes of religious fanatics for him to call on.'

'Then we must place irresistible temptation in his way,' she said softly, 'something so tantalizing that he will not be able to resist it.'

'Are you suggesting we lay out a bait for him? It's a clever thought.' He nodded. 'But what is there that will bring him personally into the open?'

'The *Golden Goose*,' she replied.

'My God! You're right,' he whispered. 'We know he is greedy. We know he is vindictive. We also can deduce that he is puffed up with power and self-importance by his new station in life – the Sheikh of his clan. The *Golden Goose* might be the only thing we have to bring the Beast out of his cave.'

• • •

Now that they had something tangible to divert them from the despair of their bereavement, both Hector and Hazel were filled with renewed energy and determination. When Hector was able to contact him, Paddy was in the final departure lounge of Charles De Gaulle airport in Paris, waiting for his flight to Dubai and the Middle East.

'Change of plans, Paddy. We want you back at the Bannock Oil headquarters in Houston as soon as you are able to get there.'

'By Jesus, Heck! Something has brought you back to life again. I can hear it in your voice. You're no longer the sad and sorry bastard you were when I left you a few days ago.'

'Lock and load, my old son! You and I are hitting the warpath again,' Hector told him, and his tone was crisp and incisive.

Hazel and Hector had debated making either Abu Zara or Taipei the base for the operation. In the end they agreed that both of these locations were too close to the lair of the Beast and were susceptible to infiltration by Adam's agents. Finally they decided on Bannock House, the corporation headquarters in Houston. Bannock House was on Dallas Street, down the road from the Hyatt Hotel. The twenty-fifth floor at the top of the building overlooked the park. The entire floor was Hazel's personal domain. The security was ironclad, the amenities all-embracing and the comfort hedonistic. Hazel had pondered on the code-name for the operation. She had finally decided on 'Operation Lampos'. The Greek meaning of the word was 'Shining Light'. Lampos was not only the name of Hector's warhorse in the classical mythology of Virgil and Homer, but it was also the name that Cayla had chosen for her favourite palomino mare.

'The connection to both you and Cayla is strong,' Hazel explained. 'But only to those who know you intimately.'

'Operation Lampos, I like it. We have a name for it. Now we need the men for it. Paddy should be here tomorrow. Then we can discuss who else we need.'

When Hector propounded Operation Lampos to Paddy, he listened without comment and even when Hector finished speaking he did not immediately reply. He went on doodling on the notepad in front of him. At last he dropped the pencil and looked up.

'The *Golden Goose*? Who thought this up?' he asked, then his eyes swivelled to Hazel who had been sitting quietly at the end of the table. 'It has a feminine flavour.'

'Don't you like the idea, Paddy?' she asked.

'I love it. It's plain bloody brilliant.' He guffawed happily.

'Who do we need to bring in, Paddy?' Hector asked.

'The fewer the merrier,' Paddy replied, still chuckling. 'Dave Imbiss for a start. He is our IT geek and red-hot on planning and procurement of equipment and materials. Then we must have your old half-section, Tariq. We need a hard warrior, a born Arabic speaker who can think like the Beast, somebody who knows the enemy and the battleground intimately.'

'Where is Tariq now?' Hector asked. 'Can you contact him?'

Paddy nodded. 'Yes. Tariq and I have worked out a call sign. He is still undercover in Puntland but I can get him out very quickly.'

'Very well. So far it's Hazel, me, you, Dave Imbiss and Tariq. Who else do we take on board?'

'That will do for a start. The way I see it is that the four of us, and of course Hazel, will brainstorm the basic plan. As we add refinements we may have to call in experts to deal with the details. How long do we have before the *Golden Goose* is ready to sail?'

'She is scheduled to take on board her first load of natural gas from the Abu Zara field at the beginning of October,' Hazel answered.

'Four and a half months from now. We must move quickly,' Paddy said.

'Get Dave and Tariq here as soon as you can,' Hector ordered.

• • •

Dave Imbiss and Tariq Hakam came into Houston four days later on a flight from Dubai and Paris. Within an hour of their arrival the first planning session of Operation Lampos was under way on the top floor of Bannock House. Hector outlined the basic concept for them.

'The object of the exercise is to entice Adam out of the fortress at the Oasis of the Miracle. It will be easy enough to suck in his underlings, but if we are going to bring an end to this blood feud he is waging against us then we have to take him out.' He looked around their faces. They were all intent and serious. 'We know that the campaign of piracy being conducted against all foreign maritime traffic in the Indian Ocean is orchestrated and controlled by Sheikh Adam Tippoo Tip. This campaign has intensified and become more sophisticated since Adam succeeded his grandfather as Sheikh.' Hector pressed the control switch on the table top in front of him, and the screen on the wall facing them lit up and displayed rows of dates and figures. 'These are the statistics for the number of pirate attacks in the last year of his grandfather's rule. As you see there were twenty-eight attacks on shipping and all of these were localized to the Gulf of Aden. Of these only nine were successful, but they reaped ransom money of an estimated one hundred and twenty million dollars.' He changed the display on the screen.

'These are the statistics for the last twelve months.' David Imbiss whistled softly with surprise, and Hector went on, 'You may indeed whistle, Dave. One hundred and twenty-seven attacks, ninety-one of which were successful. The ransom money collected was an estimated one point two-five billion dollars.' They were stunned into silence. 'Yes, that's a lot of money. Almost all of it goes into Adam's coffers. The interesting thing is that Adam's attack boats are now operating as much as a thousand nautical miles offshore. And they are doing so with impunity. With all the cash he has Adam can now operate mother ships for his attack craft. We know from Tariq that he is using captured Taiwanese and Russian trawlers for this purpose. These all carry sophisticated electronic equipment, but more significantly he has built helicopter pads on their decks. He now has two, or possibly three, Bell Jet Ranger helicopters in service. This enables him to scour the waters for hundreds of miles around, to spot both dangerous naval warships and fat and juicy mercantile targets.'

'Why don't the navies of the Western powers destroy his attack boats wherever they find them?' asked Dave.

'Two reasons,' Hector replied. 'First off, it's not easy to find a small boat in hundreds of thousands of square miles of ocean. To do this effectively the cost of the surveillance assets they would have to deploy would be prohibitive. And even if they were able to find them, they would have to catch them actually red-handed in an act of piracy. They cannot simply blow Adam's ships out of the water as they lie at anchor in Gandanga Bay. They are hamstrung by the complex laws of the sea, and the old-maidish sensibilities of many of the stridently socialistic countries, who are more concerned with the human rights of pirates captured in the act of seizing ships on the high seas than they are for the victims. They fret that a captured pirate may not receive a fair trial, indeed may be shot out of hand. It's so big-hearted and politically correct of them. Meanwhile, Adam rampages across the oceans and puts billions of dollars into his piggy bank.

'The crews of the merchant ships are unarmed, in accordance with the terms of the owners' insurance policies, which forbid them to take up arms, and their own sense of self-preservation which tells them that if they shoot first the pirates are going to shoot back and they will have superior fire power. For Adam it's open season, Christmas and New Year every day of the week.' Hector let them think about that for a moment. 'So what are we going to do about it? Dave and Tariq, you have missed out on what has been decided so far, so I will go over it for your benefit.' Briefly he explained what they hoped to achieve by Operation Lampos.

'As you know, my wife has suffered the murder and horrible mutilation of both her mother and her only daughter. Tariq has also lost his wife Daliyah and their son at the hands of Adam's thugs. Adam has placed a price on the heads of my wife and myself and sworn an oath before Allah that he will have us killed, just as he killed the other innocent members of our families. We seek retribution for the dead, and we seek safety for ourselves and for all other law-abiding men and women who ply the oceans. We have been lulled into a false sense of security, believing that we were protected by distance from his little empire in Puntland, and protected also by the law enforcement of this land in which we live. Adam has shown us that he has the power to strike at us wherever we may be. He has left us no alternative but to kill him before he kills us.' They all made sounds of agreement.

'After much discussion it has been decided that we should not mount an expedition against Adam in his stronghold at the Oasis of the Miracle. We have tried that once already and we lost most of our good men, including Ronnie Wells. Tariq was lucky to survive the experience.' Hector smiled at him. 'How has your wound healed?'

'Very pretty scar,' Tariq said grimly. He no longer smiled readily.

'If we go into Puntland there will be too many imponderables. We have to get Adam and his lieutenant Uthmann Waddah to come into the open. We have to set a baited trap for the two of them.' Even Paddy who had sat in on the earlier discussions was intrigued by hearing it all set out in such orderly detail. He was nodding his agreement with the others around the table. 'We have considered what form of bait Adam will not be able to resist. My wife has suggested that we use the *Golden Goose*.' Dave and Tariq both looked mystified. Paddy spoke for them.

'I think you have got Dave and Tariq flummoxed, Heck. I know what you're talking about. Security in the Osaka shipyard is my responsibility, but you will have to explain it to them.'

Hector turned to Hazel. 'The *Goose* is your baby. Do you want to tell us about it, please, Hazel.'

'Okay, let me explain,' she said eagerly. 'It's quite simple, really. Bannock Oil is in the process of building one of the largest and most valuable vessels ever to sail the seas. It is a supertanker for the transport of natural gas. It has already been launched and has been moved to Taiwan for the final fitting of its equipment. So far we have managed to keep the project under wraps, which is why even you are in the dark. The ship has been named the *Golden Goose*. She has an insurance value in excess of a billion dollars.' Even Paddy looked deeply impressed. It was the first time he had been told the figures. 'Now Hector will tell you the rest of our plans.'

'Once the *Golden Goose* is ready for her maiden voyage we will arrange massive publicity, including coverage on Al Jazeera Arabic TV which must go straight to Adam. The first voyage of the tanker will be to France from the new gas fields in Abu Zara. The *Golden Goose* is far too large to negotiate the

Suez Canal so it cannot take the route through the Gulf of Aden under Adam's nose. However, we have already discussed Adam's use of mother ships for his attack boats and search helicopters, so we know he has the capacity to operate his attack boats as far as twelve hundred nautical miles off the Great Horn of Africa. The route the *Golden Goose* must take to reach the Cape of Good Hope from the mouth of the Persian Gulf will bring her as close as three hundred nautical miles from his base at Gandanga Bay. We will make sure that Adam knows when and where the *Golden Goose* will sail past his stronghold. He will know the value of the ship, and who the owners are. The opportunity will be irresistible. He must strike, and we will be ready for him.' They considered the enormity of the plot in silence. Then Tariq spoke softly.

'Adam will not come. Men say that he has grown cautious with wealth and power. He will not place himself in danger. He is a cowardly swine who delights in the torture and killing of women and children, but he no longer takes any risks himself.'

'You think that he will not attack the *Golden Goose*?' Hazel asked.

'No, he will not. Because he is a coward. Neither will Uthmann Waddah because as Hector knows well Uthmann is afraid of the sea. Adam will send his uncle Kamal Tippoo Tip, who is the commander of his attack flotilla. But Adam will not come himself to the seizing of the *Golden Goose*. He will remain safely at Gandanga Bay until they bring the prize to him. Only then will he go aboard to take possession of it.' The men sat back in their chairs uneasily, and Paddy and David exchanged glances. Hazel went to the window and stood looking down at the park. There were children frolicking on the lawns watched over by their doting parents and a marching band practising on the playing field. It all looked so peaceful and commonplace; so different from the savage reality they had been discussing. Hazel felt the sorrow of her bereavement welling up inside her once again, but she forced it down and turned back to face the men at the table.

'Very well. We must let Kamal capture the *Golden Goose* and take her into Gandanga Bay.' They went silent and still, staring at her in blank astonishment. She began to smile, and suddenly Hector burst out laughing.

'So! Hector's warhorse, Lampos, becomes the Trojan Horse! You are going to send Adam a little bit more than just a billion-dollar ship and a million cubic metres of natural gas.' At this Paddy slapped the table top and laughed out loud.

'Lovely! Only you could have dreamed that up, Mrs Cross. You are going to have to watch this lady wife of yours, Hector. Duplicity thy name is woman!'

Then Dave Imbiss saw what was happening, and he laughed along with Paddy. 'You are going to hide our men somewhere in the ship until Adam comes on board, then we all jump out shouting "Surprise! Surprise!"' he chortled. 'Once we have captured Adam we can launch a landing party. They will destroy all the pirate mother ships, the helicopters and the flotilla of attack boats. They will free all the captured foreign seamen from the stockades. We will put them on board their own ships, and we will cover them while they escape out to sea.'

But Tariq looked dubious.

'We will need a hundred or more men to do all these things that you are planning. Is there space on your ship to hide so many?'

'Tariq, this is probably the largest cargo ship ever built,' Hector explained. 'Wait until you see her! We could hide an army on board her.'

'By God! That gives me an idea. We can arm her with a concealed battery of artillery, just like the old Q-ships of the Second World War.' Paddy was exultant. 'We can bombard the town and sink any other vessels that try to resist or run from us.'

'No!' Hazel said sharply. 'No bombardment of the town. There are hundreds of women and children living there in make-shift houses. It would be a massacre. It would make us worse than Adam. However, I agree that we will have to send a landing party ashore to free the captive foreign seamen.'

'How much water will the *Golden Goose* draw when she is fully loaded?' Hector asked, and answered his own question. 'Probably more than a hundred feet. The pirates will not be able to bring the *Goose* within a mile of the beach. We can't send small boats in from that distance. They would be exposed to fire from the shore all the way in. It would be suicidal.'

'If the ship is that big, we could conceal a couple of AAVs in her holds,' David Imbiss said thoughtfully.

'AAVs?' Hazel asked. 'What are they?'

'Amphibious Assault Vehicles is the official designation. They are the new generation of the swimming tanks, like those that reinforced the Allied Forces when they went ashore on the Normandy beaches in 1944.'

'Is it possible to launch them from a high-sided ship?' Hazel persisted.

'Absolutely. They can make a splash entry from a height of thirty feet,' Dave assured her.

'Even fully laden the freeboard of the *Goose* will be greater than that. And then how would we recover them again?' Hazel wanted to know.

'We will equip the ship with hydraulic cranes on travelling gantries that lie inconspicuously flat on the cargo deck until they are deployed out over the ship's side. The AAVs can leave the *Goose* and return to her by this arrangement,' Hector said without looking up from the sketch of the idea he was drawing on his notepad.

'Right on!' Dave agreed. 'You wouldn't want to abandon the AAVs when we pull out of Gandanga Bay. They will cost a couple of hundred thousand dollars each.'

'Describe one of these toys to me,' Hazel said.

'It looks very much like a conventional battle tank with tracks and a turret, except it has much taller sides. The type we need is the personnel carrier, which can carry twenty-five fully equipped infantrymen, plus the crew of three. Its turret is armed with ring-mounted .50-calibre heavy machine guns and a grenade launcher. Its armour is proof to rifle and heavy machine gunfire. On land it has a speed of twenty-five miles an hour and on the water it is capable of almost ten mph.'

'Can you get a few of these machines for us, Dave?' Hazel wondered.

'It would be very difficult to get our hands on one straight off the factory floor. But I'm sure I could find a couple of them that have been in service for a few years, but which have been well maintained and are in good running order. South Korea, Taiwan, Indonesia and a number of other countries in the Far East all have them in use. I should be able to cut a deal with one of them.'

Hazel looked at Hector and Paddy. 'How many do we need?' she asked.

'If we can achieve complete surprise, and get fifty men ashore, we can take and hold the town for at least a day until the enemy are able to regroup,' Hector replied. 'Two AAVs should do it.'

'That leaves no latitude for mistake or accident,' Paddy demurred. 'Three vehicles and seventy-five men would cover all possible eventualities.'

'Paddy often pisses iced water.' Hector apologized for him.

'It's chilly on the willy, but at least it keeps me alive.' Paddy grinned back at him.

'Dave, please find Paddy his third AAV. We want him to go on staying alive.' Hazel laughed with them.

I am so proud of her strength and resilience, Hector thought with delight, *she has come alive again. She can laugh. The hurting has been thrust aside to make way for constructive thought. It will never go away completely, but now she has it under control. If you can meet with triumph and disaster and treat those two impostors just the same; old Rudyard could have written that with her in mind.*

Then he grew serious again. 'I think we have reached the stage when we need to call in a team of the Chinese design engineers from the Taipei shipyard, so we can reconfigure the *Goose*'s hull,' he said.

The three engineers arrived five days later bringing with them all the working drawings of the *Golden Goose* in a number of large black plastic tubes. Once the client's requirements were made clear to them, Hazel gave them a suite of rooms on the floor below hers and they set to work on the drawings with enormous single-minded energy. On the tenth day they re-emerged to present their new designs for consideration.

The empty gas cargo tank nearest to the high superstructure in the ship's stern was as cavernous as a large aircraft hangar. The designers had partitioned this off from the rest of the ship to form a covert area. Then they had divided this space laterally into three separate levels. The uppermost level was allocated to the storage of military supplies including munitions and firearms that would need to be unloaded swiftly. They had included a single smaller cabin, twelve feet square, in which were two narrow bunks one above the other, and a toilet and shower cabinet beyond a connecting doorway. This cabin was for use by Hazel and Hector. Next door to this was the open parking space for the three AAVs. Directly overhead the shuttered roof opened to allow the vehicles to be lifted to the deck above on a hydraulic hoist. This hoist was mounted on a travelling gantry which could carry the AAVs one at a time to the ship's side and lower them to the surface of the sea. Within fifteen minutes of opening the overhead hatch all three AAVs could be on the water and heading for the beach at ten miles an hour, carrying seventy-five heavily armed men to the attack.

The second level of the covert area of the hull comprised the men's living and sleeping quarters, the mess and the ablutions, the toilets and the air-conditioning units to maintain a constant supply of fresh air to all areas. Also on this level was the assembly area from which the men would disperse to their action stations. The bottom level would house the kitchens and refrigerated storage for foodstuffs. But most of the space on this level was taken up by the operational situation room and the electronic equipment. In every part of the ship above them concealed CCTV cameras and listening microphones would be installed. There was not a corner of the entire ship, from the bridge to the bilges, which could not be monitored from this position. One of the cameras would be sited on the stubby radio mast on top of the bridge. It would afford the men in the situation room far below a panoramic view of the ship's surroundings and her horizon.

Radiating out from the assembly area on the second tier was a network of hidden tunnels and ladders. They would be cunningly built in behind the bulkheads. By means of these tunnels combat-ready men could swiftly reach every part of the vessel without exposing themselves until they burst out of the disguised hatches to take the unsuspecting enemy off guard.

The five of them – Hazel, Paddy, Dave Imbiss, Tariq and Hector – sat at the long boardroom table facing the three Chinese and debated the merits and demerits of the planned layout. One of the considerations that received their full attention was the soundproofing of the clandestine spaces. One hundred and twenty-five men living in confined metal compartments would make some noise even simply moving around. These sounds could alert the enemy to their presence on board. Ceilings, bulkheads and particularly the decks would have to be lined with thick tiles of sound-proofed polyurethane. Every moving part within the covert area, the doors of the microwave ovens and the refrigerators, even the water taps and the flushing mechanisms of the toilets, had to be completely muffled. The men would eat off paper plates and use plastic mugs and utensils, so there would be no clink of metal on china. They would wear only soft-soled boots. When the order for 'Silent Ship' was given they would speak only when absolutely necessary, and then in whispers. The electronic equipment would all be muted, and the operators would wear headphones to listen in on all sounds in the other parts of the ship. The gas circulation pumps in the neighbouring cargo tanks would be automatically set to operate in continuous relays, so that they would drown out any small noises from the covert area amidships. Once all had been done to assure quiet operation, they turned their attention to the fitting of armaments and observation equipment. The CCTV cameras had to be completely disguised or concealed, but placed where they were able to cover every part of the ship. The same considerations applied to positioning the listening microphones.

The ship's bridge was at the very top of the stern tower almost one hundred feet above the cargo deck. It gave the captain, navigation officer and the helmsman a clear 360 degree view all round. On the tier below the bridge was the captain's accommodation, the communications and navigation room and the luxurious owner's suite. On the tier immediately below that were the cabins of the junior officers and ship's engineers, the ship's kitchen and mess. The designers proposed building an additional tier on top of the existing bridge and converting this upper level to become the main bridge, leaving the deck below empty. This empty space was to be sealed off entirely. The only access to it would be via the ladder tunnel leading up from the covert area below the main deck. Behind the blank steel walls of this upper deck would be mounted a pair of MK44 Bushmaster 40mm automatic light cannon capable of a rate of fire of 200 rounds per minute. At the throw of a handle the concealing panels dropped down and the cannons were unmasked and ready to go into immediate action, bringing their devastating fire power to bear on any hostile target.

Once all the plans were approved the team dispersed. Dave Imbiss flew out to South Korea where within three weeks he had procured as ex-army stock three AAVs and the pair of Bushmaster cannon. All this equipment was already en route to the port of Chi-Lun in Taiwan where it would be fitted into the covert areas of the *Golden Goose*. During the voyage from Taiwan to the Abu Zara gas field the drivers and crews selected to operate the AAV would be trained in the operation of these cumbersome-looking but extraordinarily effective machines. On the same leg of the voyage the gunners would be trained to serve the Bushmaster cannon.

All these men were to be selected from the force of 125 male personnel and one woman that Paddy was assembling at Sidi el Razig. Seventy of the men were flown in from the Cross Bow operations around the globe. The remainder were chosen from Paddy's extensive list of mercenaries and freelance guns-for-hire who were ready to accept even the most hazardous assignments, for the thrills and for the money. The single female member of the force was also carefully selected not only for her martial arts skills but more importantly for her remarkable resemblance to Hazel. She was a Russian girl who had been trained by Spetsnaz. Her name was Anastasia Voronova, but she answered to Nastiya.

Tariq flew to Mecca and from there joined a party of Muslim pilgrims returning to Puntland. He crossed with them on the ferry to Mogadishu and then travelled by bus to Gandanga Bay. Once he was there he blended in with the local population, disguised as an itinerant job seeker. He lived rough amongst the other tramps and beggars. His instructions from Hector were to write nothing down, but swiftly he obtained a mental map of the layout of the town and the bay. He studied the exact position where each of the pirated vessels was anchored. He located the stockades in which the captured seamen were being held. He observed and mentally logged the movements of Adam's mother ships and attack boats. One of his most important duties on this assignment was to observe the movements of his arch-enemy Uthmann Waddah. It was vital for Hector to know if Uthmann was ever aboard any of the pirate mother ships or attack boats when they left the Bay or returned from one of their raids. Hector's plans hinged on this information, because Uthmann would be the only one among the pirates able to recognize Hazel if he ever saw her again. However, Hector was almost certain that Uthmann would never go to sea. The simple reason for this was, as Tariq had pointed out earlier, that Uthmann Waddah, the invincible warrior, was pathologically terrified of open water. A chronic sufferer from sea sickness, a few hours on the ocean waves would reduce him to a prostrated moaning and vomiting wreck, unable to lift his head let alone stand upright on his two feet. Seawater was his one weakness.

In the few weeks he remained at Gandanga Bay, Tariq watched four large pirated merchant ships brought in by Kamal Tippoo Tip and witnessed the wild jubilation of the successful pirates and the crowds that lined the beach to welcome them back from their forays. Always Adam and Uthmann Waddah were on the beach at Gandanga Bay to watch the ships come in. However, when Sheikh Adam went out in his splendid royal barge to board the captured vessel and distribute largesse to the successful pirates, Uthmann remained on the beach. It was obvious that he was terrified even by the calm waters of the bay.

Hector and Hazel flew in the BBJ to Taipei where the *Goose's* captain was already on board. His name was Cyril Stamford. He had been retired from the US Navy only ten months previously at the mandatory age of sixty-two years. He had commanded a battle cruiser and was still of bright mind and in robust health, eager to continue working with big ships.

He was from a long line of fighting Americans. One of his direct ancestors had served in the war against the Barbary pirates in North Africa in 1800 to 1805. Cyril showed Paddy an old and treasured letter which his remote ancestor, Captain Thomas Stamford, had written to his wife from Tunisia in 1804. He read out to Paddy this sentence in yellowing ink:

"'It was written in their Koran, that all nations which had not acknowledged the Prophet were pagans, infidels and sinners, whom it was the right and duty of the faithful to plunder and enslave; and that every Mohammedan who was slain in this warfare was sure to go to paradise."

'The Stamfords have fought against tyranny, bigotry and lawlessness in two World Wars,' Cyril continued proudly. 'Most recently my eldest son Robert gave his life in the mountains of Afghanistan, after being captured by these people and tortured most horribly. My navy has put me out to grass but, by God, I would love to take one more crack at the murderous bastards.'

Before confirming his command of the *Golden Goose*, Hector explained what his clandestine role would be and the hazards that would confront him. Cyril accepted the job gleefully. He was given ten of the Cross Bow Security men from nautical backgrounds to train as his crew. The *Goose's* engine room and navigation bridge were equipped with such sophisticated electronic controls that a crew of this size would be perfectly able to operate and navigate her efficiently.

Dave Imbiss was also on board overseeing the final work on the *Golden Goose* – the installation of the cannon in the concealed emplacements and the reconfiguration of the bays in the hold to contain the three AAVs.

The *Golden Goose* was lying in one of the outer port basins and the security cloak that Paddy's men had thrown over it was all-embracing. Canvas screens had been rigged over the stern tower and all work was carried out behind this. The cannon, AAV and all other sensitive materials were brought in at night on low-loader transporters swathed in shapeless layers of black plastic sheeting.

When the work on the vessel was nearing completion and the accommodations aboard her were habitable, Paddy O'Quinn arrived in Taipei. Over the following few days the first forty men of his expeditionary force followed him into the city in small groups posing as tourists. These included the technicians who would operate the sophisticated electronic listening devices and CCTV. Then there followed the gunners to serve the Bushmaster cannon, and the twelve drivers and crewmen for the AAVs. The man Paddy had chosen to command the armour was a former officer who had served under him in the army. His name was Sam Hunter and he was a hard man with vast experience in the use of amphibious armoured vehicles.

Lastly but very far from least there was Nastiya Voronova. In a hired car Hector and Hazel picked up Paddy and the Russian girl from their hotel to drive them to the shipyards. At this first meeting the two women bridled at each other, acutely aware of the other's rival attributes. Hazel sensed at once that the other woman was a wildcat, all feline grace and pulchritude on the surface but sheer primeval ferocity at the core. From her side, Nastiya was unaccustomed to not being the most strikingly beautiful female in any gathering.

Hazel and Nastiya sat together in the back seat of the hire car and conversed guardedly. On the dockside while they waited for the ferry to take them out to the *Goose*'s mooring, Hazel took Hector's arm and led him a little aside to whisper in his ear, 'Paddy and the Russian are already into each other like a pair of beavers in springtime.'

'Good God! How do you know that? Did she tell you?'

'She didn't have to say a word, you silly man. The sweet odour of lust that hangs over the two of them is like the scent of orange blossom. Haven't you noticed?'

'Yes, but funnily enough I thought it really was orange blossom.' Hector laughed. The knowledge that Nastiya was deeply involved with Paddy softened Hazel's attitude towards her. Now she knew that she would not have to guard Hector from the other girl's extravagant attractions, she found herself beginning to take a liking to the Russian.

• • •

The first thing that Paddy's recruits had to become accustomed to was the sheer size of the ship. The cargo deck was as long as five football pitches. When they were taken down into the covert area in the reconstructed No. 1 cargo hold they found themselves in a maze of interconnecting compartments and steel tunnels. The tunnels were so ill-lit, poorly ventilated, low and narrow that in them a tall man had to stoop. Once in the tunnels there were no points of reference, and it was not difficult to become confused. For instance, to reach the bridge from the assembly point on the second level involved a claustrophobic vertical climb of over ninety feet, breathing stale air and passing identical exit hatches at the level of each intervening deck. In consequence the men arrived at the bridge level disoriented and short of breath.

Hector ordered the builders to install improved lighting and ventilation. In addition he ordered the interior of the tunnels to be clearly signed, with various colours of paint to demarcate each level. After that Hector turned his attention to the hatches. With the original design, opening these from the inside involved unwinding the twin locking handles. This was a noisy and protracted procedure that would give the enemy on the far side full warning. Hector devised a new system. The hinges of the hatches were spring-loaded, so that when a retaining pin was knocked out with a single hammer blow the hatch was thrown wide open with considerable force and the attackers were able to storm through it immediately afterwards, taking whoever was on the far side completely by surprise.

By the time that the *Goose* was ready to sail for Abu Zara all the men knew the layout of the ship intimately. As soon as they were out of sight of land Hector ordered Captain Stamford to heave to. While they drifted on a sluggish and oily swell Sam Hunter and his AAV crews took their battle stations and the drivers started the engines. Then from the situation room in the belly of the ship the hatches above the vehicles were opened remotely and the hydraulic hoist lifted the first AAV to the main deck, carried it to the ship's side and lowered it overboard.

The powerful diesel engines of the AAV roared and it surged forward with Sam in the turret, clearing the way for the other vehicles to follow. One behind the other they were lowered over the ship's side. They splashed into the water, sinking for a moment below the surface and then bursting out again in a flurry of white foam. In formation the three ungainly craft circled the *Goose* and then returned to her side, where they were hoisted up onto the cargo deck. When the last of them was safely lashed down and secured below deck, the hatch above them closed. The hoists were hinged to lie inconspicuously flat on the cargo deck until they were needed again. On each of the four following days the same training procedure was carried out a number of times. The gunners in the AAV turrets were given their chance of firing their heavy machine guns at floating targets from various ranges before they returned to the *Goose*.

When the ship was a hundred and fifty miles offshore from Taiwan and there was no other shipping showing on the radar screen, Hector ordered an exercise with the cannon on the gun deck beneath the bridge. On his command the gun captains released the steel doors that concealed the gun emplacement. The doors swung down on their hinges and revealed the two Bushmaster cannon, with their long barrels pointed forward.

The cannon were loaded with air-burst fragmentation shells. Each of these contained hundreds of steel balls. The timer in the nose of the shell was set electronically by the gun captain for the required range using the built-in computer. The gunner picked up his target in the lens of his optical sight and then squeezed the trigger handle. The computer began continually calculating the range of the target and feeding this information into the fuse of the shell. When the gunner released the trigger handle the range was locked in and at the same instant the cannon fired. The shell burst in the air precisely above the target.

While Hector, Paddy and the two women watched from the bridge, the crew of the ship dropped empty oil drums over the side to serve as targets. Each of the cannon in turn fired a five-round salvo over the drums. The results were spectacular. The cloud of flying tungsten balls turned the surface of the sea to a tall column of spume and spray, engulfing the drums and everything else around them for a distance of thirty yards in a storm of flying metal. When the spray fell back to the surface nothing remained except the ripples.

'By God and Begorrah!' Paddy cried. 'I can hardly wait to watch that happen to one of Adam's attack boats.'

'I would say we are almost ready to go and pay a visit to Gandanga Bay,' Hector remarked.

'You are ruddy well correct!' he agreed with a smile.

'Paddy actually said "ruddy",' said Hazel, nudging Hector. 'Have you noticed how Paddy never swears in front of Nastiya? You could take a lesson in manners from him, my boy.' Paddy looked dismayed. Up to this moment he had fondly believed that his burgeoning relationship with the nubile Russian was a top military secret. Standing at his shoulder, Nastiya kept her expression remote and inscrutable.

• • •

By necessity, Hazel and Nastiya spent many hours together in the owner's suite on the deck below the bridge, working to increase their physical resemblance. Hazel cut and blow-dried Nastiya's hair in the same style that she affected herself.

'How you are so good vith the scissors?' Nastiya asked, as she admired herself in the mirror.

'There was a time I had to do my own hair.' Nastiya looked puzzled, and Hazel went on to explain, 'I was broke. I could hardly afford to eat, let alone visit a beauty salon.'

'That is stupid! When you look like you do, is no need to be broke, never.'

'Perhaps I was too fussy.'

'Too fussy is also stupid.' Nastiya gave her sage opinion. Once they had perfected the hair styling Hazel opened the large cupboards on each side of the mirror that contained her cosmetics and she set to work. Nastiya's reserve broke and she giggled like a schoolgirl as she watched her own transformation taking place in the mirror. After that they turned their attention to choosing suitable clothing. Nastiya was entranced by the contents of Hazel's commodious walk-in wardrobe. It was a treasure house of silk, satin and lace. Of course, they were of similar dress and shoe sizes – Nastiya had been chosen for this resemblance. The Chanel and Hermès shoes looked almost as good on Nastiya's feet as on Hazel's.

When Hazel had finished kitting her out, they put on a little show for the men. Nastiya paraded around the lounge with the aplomb of the fashion model she had once been, and with the same disdainful expression on her lovely face. Hector and Paddy reclined in the easy chairs with whisky tumblers in hand and applauded her enthusiastically, while Hazel watched her creation with a proprietary pride.

Nastiya's assignment required her to mimic Hazel's mannerisms: her walk, the way she held her head and the expressive way she used her hands. The Russian was a natural actress and she swiftly fitted into the role. Finally Hazel attempted to polish her diction. This soon proved to be a waste of everybody's time. Thanks to her Spetsnaz training, Nastiya spoke the English language well enough, except for one or two small weaknesses. Her word order was often confused, and she could not prevent her tongue from transposing the letters W and V.

'You are very welcome' was a phrase Nastiya used often, if and when she spoke at all, and Hazel could barely contain her merriment whenever Nastiya enunciated clearly, 'You are werry velcome'.

One of her other idiosyncratic pronunciations was the word 'Okay' which from her pouting lips became 'Hokay!' Finally it was decided that she would have to keep her mouth closed during her period of captivity by the pirates. Fortunately this restriction would not inconvenience her inordinately. 'Silent Ship' was Nastiya's preferred mode of operation.

To make absolutely certain that Adam would attack the ship they had to lead him to believe that both Hazel and Hector were on board. They had to allow the TV crew from Al Jazeera to film the two of them on the ship when she arrived at the natural gas offshore terminal. Even after the *Goose* sailed from the terminal Hector would have to remain on board to command Operation Lampos. However, when he attempted to get Hazel to agree to leave the ship before she sailed and move to a place of safety far beyond Adam's reach, while Nastiya Voronova took her place, his arguments to this effect made as much impression on Hazel as a light drizzle of rain would make on Cleopatra's Needle.

'Please don't be daft, Hector Cross,' she said flatly.

Hector could not allow himself to be captured when the pirates boarded the ship. He could not command Operation Lampos while he was in chains and guarded by a gang of heavily armed pirates. So they had to choose a double to replace him too. There were a number of men amongst Paddy's recruits who could fit the role, in that they were dark-haired and well-built. In any event, it was generally acknowledged by all that to an Arab most Caucasians looked alike, and vice versa. When Hector's double was taken into captivity by the pirates they might beat him up, but Paddy helped Hector to choose Vincent Woodward, a hard man who could take punishment. As Paddy pointed out to Vincent, when he was captured, unlike Nastiya, he would at least be in no danger of rape. For an extra ten thousand dollars Vincent volunteered happily to become Hector's alter ego.

However, at this late juncture Hazel suddenly became squeamish about sending Nastiya into the jaws of hell in her place. The Russian girl had become her friend. She expressed her misgivings to Paddy.

'I truly have the utmost pity for any Arab who tries to lower Nastiya's knickers without her full agreement and cooperation,' said Paddy with a smile. This was not enough for Hazel and she insisted on a frank discussion and disclosure with Nastiya. They all met in the sitting room of the owner's suite. Hazel gave a long disquisition on the hazards that Nastiya would encounter if she allowed herself to be captured. She expressed the affection and respect she had developed for Nastiya, and offered her the chance to withdraw from the assignment. Nastiya sat silent, beautiful and inscrutable throughout the whole recital, watching Hazel intently.

When Hazel had finished she asked, 'So, hundred thousand dollars you are not going to pay me?'

'No, no,' Hazel replied, 'that is not fair to you, Nastiya. In view of the fact that you are going to risk your life for me I think I should pay you at least double that amount.'

Nastiya almost smiled. 'We all know that these people will not try to kill me whatever I do to them, as long as they believe I am really you, *Da* or *Nyet*?'

'We don't think they would kill you. They want the ransom. But they might try to hurt you. They might try to force you, to rape you.'

'Vell, they vill be werry velcome to try,' said Anastasia Voronova, which put an end to any further discussion on the subject.

Three days later the *Golden Goose* entered the Gulf of Oman and headed up towards the Strait of Hormuz and the entrance to the Persian Gulf. As soon as they were within easy range of land the Bannock Oil Corporation helicopter flew out to meet them. This was a large twenty-six-seater Sikorski, a replacement for the old Russian MIL-26 that had been lost in Puntland. It ferried Paddy's men ashore, and landed them at the training camp in a remote part of the Abu Zara desert where the rest of the troops were in intensive preparation for the Puntland expedition. Relieved of her supernumeraries the *Golden Goose* sailed on towards the natural gas terminal to take on her cargo.

• • •

The director of publicity for the Bannock Oil Corporation invited Al Jazeera Television to send a film crew to the new natural gas terminal in the Gulf offshore from the Emirate of Abu Zara to record the maiden voyage of the *Golden Goose*. They accepted with alacrity, and Bert Simpson placed the Sikorski at their disposal. It picked up the Al Jazeera camera crew when they arrived in Sidi el Razig and flew them down to intercept the *Golden Goose* as she passed through the Strait of Hormuz. As the TV crew circled the ship she was a truly impressive sight. Her gas tanks were empty, so she stood to her full height out of the water, a towering mountain of steel. The camera crew were delighted with the footage they obtained.

When the *Goose* docked at the gas terminal a succession of visitors came aboard. All the other Middle Eastern news media sent journalists to cover the event. When they had gone, the Emir and his entourage, including most of his ministers, arrived to attend the royal banquet that Hazel had ordered in his honour.

A large Bedouin tent was erected on the cargo deck of the *Golden Goose* and the deck itself was spread with colourful Turkish carpets. The Emir, his three gorgeously bejewelled wives and all the other guests were seated on silk cushions, and the most famed chef in Arabia with fifty assistants prepared the banquet. A string band played traditional music in the background. The foreign minister was one of the Emir's younger brothers. He was a graduate of Oxford University, and made a speech in beautifully modulated English extolling the virtues of the Bannock Oil Corporation and the role the company had played in the development of the Emirate's resources.

Then Hazel addressed the distinguished guests. She gave some information on the *Golden Goose* and her cargo capacity. She spoke of the cost and planning that had gone into the building and launching of the ship and what this would mean for Abu Zara. She explained that the ship was much too large to negotiate the Suez Canal and for her maiden voyage she would sail down the east coast of the African continent and round the Cape of Good Hope. Then she would head northwards up the Atlantic Ocean to the port of Brest in France to discharge her gas. Hazel told the assembly that she anticipated that the voyage would begin in fifteen days' time. She went on to say that for Bannock Oil this was such an important event that she and her husband Mr Hector Cross would sail on the ship as far as Cape Town on the southern tip of Africa.

The cameramen at the rear of the tent discreetly filmed the entire ceremony. In the situation room in the bowels of the ship Paddy and Nastiya followed the proceedings on the CCTV screens, and Nastiya mimicked to near-perfection every movement, every gesture that Hazel made.

Five evenings later Hector and Hazel sat together with Nastiya and Paddy in the situation room and watched as Al Jazeera TV broadcast a seven-minute programme which covered all the main elements of the *Golden Goose*'s voyage. The images of this enormous ship at sea were compelling, and the excerpts from Hazel's speech contained all the most vital elements: the enormous value of the ship and its cargo, its proposed route around Africa, its estimated date of departure and the fact that both Hazel Bannock and her husband would be on board for the first leg of the voyage as far as the Cape. At the end of the programme Hector looked across the situation room at Paddy.

'Well, what do you think?'

'I think Mrs Cross should go into film,' the Irishman replied. 'She could put Nicole Kidman out of work, so she could.'

'Thank you, Paddy,' Hazel said, smiling. 'From such a judge of womankind that is high praise indeed. So you think Adam will fall for it?'

'Head over heels and arse over tip, no doubt about it.'

'Vot means "arse over tip"?' Nastiya asked.

'Exactly the same thing as head over heels,' Hector explained, and Nastiya looked at Paddy pityingly.

'So vhy so many vords you must alvays be using?'

Hazel smiled at this demonstration of the authority that Nastiya was already wielding in their relationship.

• • •

Now fully laden with her cargo of gas and riding low in the water, the *Goose* went back through the Strait of Hormuz ostensibly to begin the outward leg of her voyage to France. As soon as they were out of sight of the shore the Sikorski began ferrying Paddy's men out from the desert camp and landing them on the cargo deck. As they arrived on board they were issued with their arms and equipment. Each man carried a Beretta 9mm automatic pistol and a Beretta SC 70/90 assault rifle. They were issued with body armour and each of them carried a compact shortwave Falcon hand-held battle radio. Those amongst them who had sailed in the ship from Taipei began an intensive indoctrination of the newcomers, who very quickly learned the layout of the covert tunnels and how to use them to reach any point aboard the *Goose* swiftly, quietly and unseen. They practised embarking in the AAVs and disembarking from them. The ship hove-to and the AAVs were once again deployed overboard but this time with a full complement of troops on board, then they were recovered and stowed below decks.

The men were already in top physical condition and Paddy kept them that way by using the expansive cargo deck as a training field. Every man ran twenty circuits of the deck twice a day, with Hector and Paddy close behind them chivying them on. Paddy divided them into teams of ten men who competed with each other in shooting competitions and boisterous games of touch rugby. Paddy held a daily relay race from the bottom tier of the cargo hold to the bridge and back, using the ladders in the steel tunnels. He timed them with a stopwatch, and Hazel put up a prize of a thousand dollars each day for the fastest team. She and Nastiya made up a ladies' team and they registered the best individual times on three consecutive days, to the deep chagrin of the men.

The *Golden Goose* was still six hundred nautical miles east of the Great Horn of Africa when her sirens sounded 'general quarters' in the middle of a keenly contested touch rugby match. There was a rush to clear the deck. Hector and Hazel reached the bridge within minutes.

'What is it?' Hector demanded of Captain Stamford.

'We have a radar contact at forty-two miles, bearing twenty-seven degrees. Looks like a slow-flying aircraft, almost certainly a light helicopter. It's heading this way.'

'It probably has already picked us up on its own radar,' Hector said. 'We make a large enough target. He couldn't miss us. Hold your course and speed, please, Cyril.' Then he turned to Hazel. 'If this is who we think it is, it might be a good idea for the two of us to show ourselves on the deck.'

'Shouldn't our doubles do that?'

'No, it's just possible Uthmann Waddah might be aboard the helicopter. He would spot the difference right away. Come on!' They hurried down to the deserted main deck and ran its full length to reach the bows. There they leaned against the rail and watched the distant speck materialize over the western horizon. The speck grew larger until it resolved itself into a Bell Ranger helicopter. They stared up at it. Hector was standing behind Hazel and he slipped his arms around her waist, and laughed and squeezed her, as she began to hum the theme from the movie *Titanic*, 'My Heart Will Go On'. They imitated the famous pose of DiCaprio and Winslet standing at the doomed liner's bowsprit in the film.

Hector had ordered a small section of the *Goose*'s hull amidships to be painted with red lead primer, and rope ladders and a workmen's cradle to be left dangling over the ship's side just above the water level as though the painting of the hull was a work in progress. The dangling equipment was an open invitation to a boarding party. This would certainly be noted by the pilot of the helicopter and reported to Kamal.

The helicopter circled the tanker once at low level. The pilot was the only occupant. He wore dark goggles and the lower part of his face was covered by a keffiyeh. Hazel waved up at him. He gave no acknowledgement but turned the machine back the way it had come and was soon lost to view. Paddy and Dave Imbiss were waiting for them on the bridge.

'All right. There is very little doubt that this is them, and that their main force is not far off,' Hector told them. 'The round-trip range of that helicopter is under a hundred and fifty miles. In less than an hour and a half from now it will be landing on the deck of the pirates' mother ship.' He was switching into battle-ready mode, his mind razor-sharp. 'From now on the main deck is off-limits to all personnel. Everyone must return to their quarters in the covert area and remain there until the enemy makes the next move. All the hidden hatches must be closed and checked. "Silent Ship" must be maintained at all times. Hazel and I will move out of the owner's suite and into the small cabin on the AAV deck. Nastiya and Vincent will take our places in the suite.'

'But, I sincerely hope, not to follow your behavioural patterns when they are ensconced there,' Paddy said sourly.

'You can keep an eye and an ear on them with the CCTV camera in the bedroom,' Hector suggested, and Paddy nodded thoughtfully. Although Paddy was too much of a gentleman to spy on the woman he loved, it was just by chance that a short time later, while he happened to be checking the correct function of the camera in the owner's suite, he witnessed an episode between Nastiya and Vincent Woodward as they settled in. With a deadly tone of voice Nastiya was making her position clear to Vincent.

'If you think you can treat me like a real vife, Wincent Voodvard, I vill tell Mr O'Quinn and he vill kill you, but first I vill remove by force those round things that hang between your legs and I will push them up your nose holes.'

Paddy was greatly heartened to overhear this moving expression of her feelings towards him.

• • •

Adam's uncle, Kamal Tippoo Tip, stood in the wheelhouse of the 110-foot captured Taiwanese trawler and watched his helicopter skimming the tops of the swells as it raced back from its reconnaissance. He turned the trawler's bows into the light breeze to facilitate the landing. The mast and most of the superstructure had been removed from the trawler not only to assist the operation of the helicopter, but also to offer a lesser target for the radar of other shipping. Forward of the wheelhouse a wooden landing platform had been laid on top of the deck. The choice of material was also to reduce radar echoes. Now the Bell Ranger hovered above this and then delicately lowered itself until it settled with a barely perceptible jolt onto the platform. The crew ran out with mooring lines to secure the machine.

Kamal nodded his approval. The pilot was an Iranian who had been trained by the airforce of that country and was an enthusiastic recruit in the Islamic jihad against the infidel. As soon as his aircraft was secured he shut down the engine and jumped down to the trawler's deck. He hurried back to the wheelhouse, pushing up his goggles and unwinding the scarf that covered his lower face.

'Praise and gratitude to Allah and his exalted Prophet,' he greeted Kamal.

'To them be all praise and devotion,' Kamal agreed. 'What news, Mustapha, my brother?'

'The infidel is delivered into your hands. The ship is only one hundred and fifteen miles ahead of us, and closing with us at a speed of well over twenty knots.'

'You are certain it is the ship we are hunting for?'

'There can be no other on all the oceans like her. She is bigger than a mountain and her name is on the bows and the stern. She is the *Golden Goose*. Praise be to Allah, his Prophet and all his saints.'

'All praise and devotion to Allah! Tell me all you have seen.'

'On her bridge three men were visible, but on her foredeck there were a man and a woman. The woman has yellow hair, and was not old. Her hair and her face were uncovered.'

'Praise Allah! It is the Bannock whore! What of the man?'

'He is tall and with dark hair. He was openly caressing the woman in the most obscene and shameless fashion.'

'It is the assassin Hector Cross! This time he will not escape our righteous wrath.' Mustapha went on to describe details of the ship's structure and possible weak points, not forgetting the workmen's cradle hanging conveniently over the side.

'I must inform the Sheikh at once of our great good fortune,' said Kamal, turning to the electronic array at the back of the wheelhouse and switching on the satellite telephone. There was a delay as his call was passed upwards but at last he heard the voice of his nephew.

'Who is this I speak to?'

'It is Kamal. Greetings and the blessing of Allah upon you, mighty Sheikh!'

'And on you also blessings, revered Uncle,' Adam answered.

'We have found that which you seek, my beloved Sheikh. It is delivered into your hands along with the man who murdered both your father and mine.'

'How do you know for certain that the pig Cross is on board the ship?' Adam demanded insistently.

'Mustapha saw him on the deck, with his whore, Allah be praised.'

'All praise to God and his Prophet. But there is no mistake? It is the Bannock woman? Are you certain?'

'It is certain, my Sheikh. Her head was uncovered. Her hair was yellow. It is her! The ship is fully laden and low in the water. Her cargo is worth almost as much as the vessel itself. The stupid infidel sailors have left rope ladders hanging over her side. It will be very easy to take her, my esteemed and beloved nephew and Sheikh.'

'If you do so you will make us both very rich, my uncle. When will you reach the prize?'

'She is on an interception course, sailing directly towards us at twenty knots. If Allah is kind we will be alongside her in less than five hours. By dawn tomorrow the ship and all its contents will be in your hands. The blood debt can at last be settled in full. As you do also, I mourn the murder of my father and your grandfather.'

'May Allah and Muhammad his Prophet bless our enter-prise, revered uncle. Make certain that the infidel dog Cross and his whore are brought to me alive. I wish to talk with them before they die.'

• • •

The only sounds in the situation room in the covert section of the *Golden Goose* were the soft rush of the sea along her hull, the thumping and wheezing of the gas pumps in the adjoining holds and the low hum of the electronic equipment. Hector, Paddy and David Imbiss were seated at the long table facing the computer screens. Tariq had pushed his chair back and crossed his arms over his chest. They spoke seldom and when they did it was in whispers. Hazel was curled up on the narrow padded bench at the rear of the cabin with a blanket around her shoulders. She was sleeping quietly. Most of the lighting came from the glow of the multiple CCTV screens. The clock on the wall above them showed ten minutes before midnight. Infrared sensors in each of the hidden cameras detected any live movement around the ship. When they did they automatically switched the camera on and gave it precedence on the screens. At the moment one screen showed the bridge and Cyril Stamford pacing up and down the deck, staring out into the darkness over the bows. The screen beside it showed two of his crew sitting in the mess, drinking coffee and smoking cigarettes. Another screen abruptly switched over to the camera in the bedroom of the owner's suite. The suite was in darkness, but the camera was in infrared mode. The images on the screen were in monochrome. Nastiya Voronova threw back the bedclothes and stood up. She wore a dark one-piece jump suit. As she crossed the deck to the door of the bathroom there was a glimpse of Vincent in the background. He was sleeping alone on the sofa against the far bulkhead.

'No cause for anxiety there, Paddy,' Hector murmured. Nastiya entered the bathroom and closed the door. The camera in that particular bathroom had been deactivated on Hazel's orders. It was like watching one of those reality TV programmes such as *Big Brother*, Hector thought, and every bit as boring. Paddy closed his eyes and put his head down on his folded arms on the table top in front of him. Hector stood up and stretched. He went to pour himself a mug of black coffee from the thermos flask and returned to his chair.

'Not much longer to wait. I can almost smell them,' he said softly to Paddy, who opened his eyes and nodded, then lowered his head again. Hector looked back at Hazel, and almost as though she could feel his eyes upon her she opened hers and smiled at him. Then she changed her position and adjusted the pillow under her head. In the owner's suite the door of the bathroom opened and Nastiya returned to the emperor-size bed. She pulled the cover over her head and disappeared from view.

'Does she always sleep like a mole in a hole?' Hector asked.

'Mind your own bloody business, Cross,' Paddy replied in mock indignation. Hector grinned and watched the red second-hand of the clock click relentlessly around the dial. It was now fifteen after midnight. Then suddenly one of the darkened screens at the end of the array lit up. It showed an infrared image of the tanker's main cargo deck. Hector straightened up in his chair, and his expression changed, his eyes narrowed and his lips compressed into a hard line. This camera, which was sited on the top of the stern tower, had detected live movement, but the image of the foredeck was dark, monochromatic and distant.

'Dave!' Hector said curtly. 'Pull focus on Number Four camera. There is movement there at the port deck rail.' Dave Imbiss blinked the sleep from his eyes, and tapped a message into the keyboard of the camera controls. He zoomed in on the deck below. Now they could make out the gantry from which the rope ladders and the workmen's cradle were suspended. Abruptly a man stepped out from behind the cable winch where he had been concealed. He was dressed all over in black and his features were hidden by a scarf wound around his face. He turned his head and looked behind him. He must have given a command or made a signal because immediately a string of similarly dressed figures swarmed up over the rail and raced down the deck towards the stern tower. Every one of them carried a weapon.

'The Beast has arrived,' Hector said softly. Paddy, Tariq and Hazel sprang up and crowded forward to the desk, from where they stared up at the screen in silence. Hector pressed the 'Send' button on his Falcon hand-held battle radio.

'Bridge! Cross!' he said into the microphone, and on one of the other TV screens Cyril Stamford stood up from his command chair and reached for his own set.

'Cross! This is Stamford.'

'They are on board,' said Hector, still staring up at the screen. 'Fifteen of them already, but more are coming up the ladder every second. I am losing count. Make no response. They must believe that they have achieved total surprise.' The order was redundant; Stamford and his crew had rehearsed this drill many times.

'Roger,' he said. 'Minimum retaliation and quick submission.'

'That's the medicine, Cyril,' Hector agreed and changed frequency on the radio. On another screen they saw Nastiya sit up from under the bedclothes and reach for her radio set.

'Voronova.'

'The pirates are aboard. They will be in your cabin in a few minutes. Do not switch on the lights. Get Vincent into the bed with you. Hurry.'

'Hokay!'

'Remember, no fighting back.'

'Hokay!' she said and Hector again changed the frequency. He grinned at Paddy.

'That wench of yours is a regular little chatterbox, isn't she?'

'One of her many virtues,' Paddy replied seriously. They turned their full attention back to the TV screens as they lit up in quick succession, following the pirates as they stormed up the companion-way of the stern tower towards the bridge. Five of them burst into the crew's quarters. The two men seated at the mess table were clubbed to the deck, and the others were dragged from their bunks and forced to their knees while their wrists were pinioned in front of them with nylon cable ties. Another gang of pirates swarmed into the bridge house howling threats and orders in Arabic.

Cyril Stamford sprang up and ran towards them shouting, 'Who the hell are you? You are not allowed here. Get out, damn you. Get out!' One of the pirates knocked him to the deck with the butt of his AK-47 and two others pounced on him and bound his wrists together with cable ties. The helmsman and the radio operator received the same treatment. One of the pirates went quickly to the control console and closed all the throttles.

'It will take at least ten miles for the ship to stop,' he said in Arabic, and removed his mask to reveal his face. His features were fierce and forbidding, his beard tinged with grey.

'It is Kamal Tippoo Tip!' Tariq exclaimed, staring up at the image. 'He is Adam's uncle and the commander of the pirate flotilla. I would know him anywhere.'

'We were expecting him,' Hector said. 'The one I'm worried about is Uthmann Waddah. He's the only one of the gang who will know that Nastiya is not Hazel, and that Vincent is not me. Keep an eye out for him.'

On the screen Kamal was still giving orders to his men. 'Find the Bannock whore and the Christian assassin. They will certainly be in one of the cabins in the deck below us. Secure them but do not hurt them. If you value your own life make sure they stay alive.' Five of his men hastened from the bridge to obey him. Kamal turned to his remaining men.

'Split up into groups of five. Spread out and search every part of the ship. Make certain there are no more of the infidel crew hiding anywhere aboard!' From the situation room they watched the pirates on the CCTV as they rampaged through the ship. If a door was locked they smashed it open. They tore the doors off the life-jacket lockers and storage bins. They fired AK bursts into the locked cupboards in the cabins. In the crew's quarters there was a crucifix fixed to the bulkhead above one of the bunks. A pirate ripped it off laughing and dumped it in the toilet bowl.

In the meantime the men Kamal had sent to the owner's suite had battered down the door with kicks and blows of their rifle butts. Once it was down they swarmed into the suite and raged through the cabins. With insensate violence they destroyed furniture and ornaments, until at last they burst into the bedroom where Nastiya and Vincent were huddled in a corner, feigning abject terror. Like the others they were hauled out and bound with cable ties. Then they were forced to squat on the floor in the middle of the main cabin. Two Arabs stood over them with their AKs pointed at their heads, while one of the others rushed back to the bridge and jubilantly reported to Kamal.

'Revered Prince, it is with great joy that we can inform you that we have captured the murderer of your sainted father and his whore. All thanks and praise to Allah and his Prophet!' Kamal glanced at the control panel to make certain that the ship was hove-to and drifting easily broadside to the wind, then said, 'I will go down to inspect the captives.' When he entered the cabin in the owner's suite he went directly to Vincent Woodward and kicked him in the face.

'You are the animal who killed my father and three of my brothers. When we reach port you will meet a death so exquisite that at the end you will go to it whimpering like a puppy and pleading for release from your agony.' Kamal spoke fluent but heavily accented English. His kick had broken Vincent's nose and a trickle of blood snaked over his lips and dripped from his unshaven chin. Vincent showed no emotion and stared back at Kamal. This irked Kamal unendurably. He yelled into Vincent's upturned face, 'You are silent now, but you will squeal loud enough when you feel the red-hot iron going up your anus.' He kicked at his face again, but Vincent dropped his chin and took it on his forehead. Kamal left him, went to where Nastiya was kneeling and stood over her. He took a handful of her thick blonde hair and twisted her head back. He stared into her face. His expression was gloating and vindictive. In the situation room Hazel watched what she had dreaded most beginning to materialize. She seized Hector's hand and shook it violently.

'We have to stop this! He's going to kill her,' she blurted.

'No! He won't do that. He's too much afraid of Adam,' Hector assured her. She suppressed her next protest, but her grip on his hand tightened with her anxiety as she watched Kamal stoop to stare into Nastiya's face.

'Her eyes are blue,' he said in Arabic. 'The eyes of a devil. This is what I was told to expect, but Uthmann Waddah should be here to make certain of this sow's identity.'

In the situation room Hector nodded and smiled grimly.

'Well, that takes care of my chief concern,' he said to his wife. 'Uthmann is not with the boarding party. There is nobody on board the ship who can recognize us.'

'How do we know that some of Kamal's thugs have not seen you and me on TV or seen our pictures in the press?' Hazel asked anxiously.

'We don't have to worry about that. There's no television coverage in Puntland, and no English-language press. Adam Tippoo Tip has all the media under his control, on pain of death.'

They all watched Kamal spit into Nastiya's upturned face.

'Look at her insolence, the bitch! I think I should let a few of my men drive the devil out of her with their meat rods.' The men around him smiled expectantly and moved closer to peer into Nastiya's face. She looked back at them so coldly that they dropped their eyes and backed off from her again.

'Dirty little whore!' Kamal put his hand over her face to shove her backwards. As fast as a crocodile snatching a drinking buck from the edge of his pool, Nastiya darted her head forward and clamped her teeth into his hand. Kamal howled with shock and pain. With his free hand he struck her across the face, trying to loosen her hold.

'You poisonous bitch. Let go or I will kill you!'

She smiled through her clenched teeth and his blood mingled with her saliva as it ran down her chin. He raised his free hand for another blow, but suddenly his wounded hand came free and he staggered backwards clutching it to his chest. He stared at it in horror. The two top joints of his little finger were missing. She had bitten them clean off.

'You cow! You pig sow,' he sobbed, 'you filthy animal.' Nastiya opened her mouth and spat his finger at his feet. She smiled at him again and his blood stained her teeth.

'She is a devil from hell.' Kamal backed away. 'Kill her! Cut her head off and feed it to the dogs.' Two of his men drew their daggers, but Kamal steadied himself and only just in time stopped them. 'Wait! No, do not kill her,' he panted. 'The Sheikh has commanded that she be brought to him alive.' He grimaced as he took the keffiyeh from around his neck and wrapped it around the stump of his finger. 'We will not kill her yet, but I will humiliate her and punish her. You men, draw lots and the winners will cover her as a dog does a bitch in heat. But first I will speak with the Sheikh. Now lock this man Cross in a separate cabin. Leave five men to guard the whore. Then I must get the ship under way again and on course for Gandanga Bay.' Kamal turned and holding his injured hand against his chest he left the owner's suite and returned to the bridge. He walked slowly and awkwardly, like an old man.

In the situation room they had watched the whole violent episode and were still staring at the CCTV screen. Hector broke the shocked silence.

'Minimum retaliation and quick submission.' He softly repeated the instructions he had given to Nastiya. 'Should I have said it in Russian for her to understand, Paddy?'

'Give the poor little lass a break. She was very restrained. You can't really complain. She only bit his finger off, for goodness' sake.'

'I thought she was splendid,' said Hazel in an awed tone. 'A little bit naughty not to obey you, but splendid nonetheless.'

'That was nothing. You should see her when she really gets angry. I think she must have Irish blood in her,' Paddy said proudly.

•   •   •

Kamal sat in the captain's chair on the bridge of the *Golden Goose*. His face was haggard with pain and he nursed his hand tenderly, as he ordered Cyril Stamford to be hauled in front of him.

'I am going to free your hands,' he told Cyril. 'If you make any attempt to escape you will be beaten. You will obey my orders. You will sail the ship where and how I command you. Do you understand?'

'If you take these ties off my hands, I will sail her,' Cyril agreed. Kamal nodded and ordered one of his men to cut the nylon cable tie from the captain's wrists. Cyril went to the control console and opened the throttles. Then he looked at Kamal.

'Give me a course to steer.'

'The course is two-eight-five degrees magnetic,' Kamal told him and Cyril confirmed and punched it into the navigational computer. He set the engine revolutions at 120 rpm. The *Goose* began to execute a stately turn to port onto the stipulated heading. Kamal checked the compass, and then beckoned to one of his men and snapped the fingers of his uninjured hand. Obediently the man handed him a portable satellite telephone. Kamal punched in some numbers and his call was answered almost immediately by Adam in person.

'We have captured the ship, mighty Sheikh!' Kamal stood up from the command seat and moved out onto the port wing of the bridge, where the reception from the satellite would be clearer.

'All thanks and praise to Allah!' Adam exulted. 'What of the Bannock whore and the villain Cross?'

'They are my prisoners. I am bringing them to you with the ship, my lord and master.'

'I shall reward you with whatsoever you ask of me, my uncle.'

'I crave one boon of you, great chieftain.'

'Ask and I will grant it.'

'The Bannock whore is a she-devil, a monster with the soul of a hellhound. She has bitten off my finger!' Adam laughed out loud and Kamal's tone rose sharply, as his anger boiled over. 'My Sheikh, I wish to punish her. I wish to humiliate her as she has humiliated me in front of all my men.' Adam stopped laughing.

'I have told you many times already that the execution of the woman is my prerogative alone, Uncle! It gives me pleasure to consider the manner of her death. At the moment I am undecided between hunting her with the dogs and having her stretched between two heavy trucks, a wrist and an ankle tied to each of them. When they are driven slowly apart her limbs will be plucked from her carcass like the wings of a roasted chicken.' Adam chuckled at the mental image. 'You will be beside me to watch it all.'

'It will be a very interesting and amusing sight to watch,' Kamal assured him. 'I am not asking your permission to kill her. I wish merely to punish her. I want to give her to my men to sport with. I will be there at all times to make sure that none of them take the play too far.'

'Why do you not wish to enjoy her yourself?' Adam teased him and Kamal shuddered at the thought. His nephew knew well that his preferences ran strongly to young boys, and the thought of again letting the whore come close enough to touch him made his injured finger throb most painfully, chilling any residual ardour Kamal might have been able to muster for a female.

'She is beneath my dignity, Master. I would rather rut with a rabid pig.'

'Very well, my revered uncle. Let the men take her by both her holes, back and front. However, you must stop them at once if she starts to bleed copiously.'

'My loyal thanks to you, my magnanimous Sheikh and master.'

• • •

'What the hell is Kamal up to now?' Hector wondered aloud as they watched him on one of the screens coming in from the wing of the bridge. From the situation room they had not been able to monitor his conversation with Adam. While they watched Kamal spoke to Cyril Stamford again.

'I am leaving four of my men here to watch your every move. You will not alter our speed or our course. Neither you nor any of your crew is to touch the electronic equipment to transmit any message. Do you understand?'

'I understand,' Cyril confirmed gruffly. In the situation room Hector nodded his approval.

'Good man, Cyril. At least somebody on board is following my orders.' They watched Kamal gather up the rest of his men and lead them down to the owner's suite on the deck below. The men were all laughing and chattering with excitement. When they crowded into the sitting room, Kamal seated himself in one of the leather armchairs and issued a string of instructions to his men. They dragged in the table from the dining salon next door, and placed it in front of their chief in the centre of the cabin. Once he was satisfied with the arrangement Kamal gave another order and four of the men went through to the bedroom suite where Nastiya was still kneeling in the centre of the cabin. Her guards watched over her warily. They had seen how Kamal had lost his finger. They had bayonets fixed on their rifles and they kept well clear of her, even though her hands were pinioned in front of her.

'Kamal has ordered us to bring the whore to him,' they told the guards, who looked relieved. Two of the Arabs moved in on Nastiya and at a signal they seized her arms and hoisted her to her feet. Then they ran with her into the sitting room and bundled her onto the table in the centre of the room. Still holding her arms they stretched her out on her back with her legs dangling over the end. While they held her down one of the others came to the table with his curved dagger in his right hand. He ran two fingers into the front opening of her black jump suit and holding the cloth away from her skin, slipped the point of his dagger into the opening and split the suit down to her crotch. Then he ripped the suit off her body and left her lying naked on the table. Her arms were still pinioned in front of her by the green nylon cable tie on her wrists. The watchers in the situation room far below were shocked into a strained silence as the scene unfolded on the TV screen.

Kamal was sitting forward in the easy chair stroking his curling beard and watching with fascination as his men prepared Nastiya for her punishment. From time to time he gave an order on how to proceed, and his men quickly obeyed. Under the overhead lights Nastiya's body was pale and sleekly muscled. Her hair was tangled around her face and her lips were swollen, and one of her eyes was half-closed, bruised and puffed up where Kamal had struck her. She seemed very young and fragile in comparison to the men standing over her. They were laughing and joking with each other, aroused by her nudity. The one who had cut away her clothing reached down and squeezed her breast, then tweaked her nipple and pulled it out, stretching it to the limit of her skin's elasticity. The others guffawed and then one by one they each took their turn to fondle and pinch her breasts. They howled with merriment as she lay quiescent in the grip of the two men restraining her. Her tormentors were egging each other on, clowning and trying to outdo each other. One of them took her nipple between his filthy fingernails. He pinched her so cruelly that a drop of blood welled up from the wound. He licked the blood off his fingers to the delight of his companions. Then another reached down to her pubic bush and seized one of the golden curls. With a savage jerk he pulled out a tuft, and sniffed it as though it were a bouquet of flowers. Then he passed it around for the others to savour. Nastiya did not move or cry out.

'She can do that,' Paddy whispered. 'Self-hypnosis. She can shut out the pain.'

'This is horrible,' Hazel said. 'I never bargained for this. I am totally to blame.'

'No!' Hector intervened. 'Not you. It's Kamal and Adam who are to blame. But there will soon be a reckoning.'

At a sharp command from Kamal the men who were gathered around Nastiya drew back and Kamal leaned forward and showed her his injured hand.

'Listen to me, you Christian whore. I am going to punish you for the wound you have inflicted on me. Every one of my men will rip into your filthy body and spurt you full of good Muslim sperm. You are going to bleed, whore. You are going to cry for my mercy, you dirty sow.' Nastiya did not look at him. He eyes were focused far away and her expression was calm and remote.

'She is preparing herself to act,' Paddy said almost under his breath. On the screen they saw that Kamal was becoming angry and frustrated at her isolated calm. He turned to his men with blazing eyes.

'Which of you will be the first to ride this filly?' he shouted.

'Bayhas, the lion!' they shouted. 'Bayhas of the mighty pole. He was the first to mount this whore's daughter at the Oasis. He must be first to plough the Mother Whore.' They pushed Bayhas forward. He chuckled and opened the front of his trousers and brought out his monstrous sexual organ. It stiffened and extended to its full length as he tugged and massaged it.

'Hold the she-dog,' he ordered the men around her. 'She will grow mad with lust when she feels this thing going into her. Open her legs.' The men on each side of the table pulled her thighs roughly apart, and Bayhas stepped between them. He spat in his hand and anointed the head of his penis with the saliva.

'I have to stop this,' Hazel burst out. 'We have to go in and bring her out of there.'

'Wait! You cannot stop the war with the first casualty,' Hector told her.

'Nastiya is not a soldier.' Hazel was angry.

'Oh, yes she is,' Paddy contradicted her. 'She would never forgive you if you pulled her out now. This is what she is trained for. This is her trade. Her profession. Watch her!' He pointed to the screen. Bayhas, the lion, was rubbing his lubricated penis along the opening of her sex, shifting his feet, steadying himself for the first thrust into her. Suddenly Nastiya's lithe body jack-knifed under him. She broke the grip that the two Arabs had on her ankles. Her knees folded back over her shoulders with seemingly effortless grace, then drove forward again with such power that they seemed to blur. Her naked heels smashed into the base of Bayhas's pubis. Over the microphones they clearly heard his pelvic bone break, cracking at the juncture of its symphysis into its two separate halves. His engorged penis was caught between Nastiya's heels and the sharp leading edge of his own pelvic girdle. It was crushed by the force of the blow and his corpora cavernosa, the blood-holding chambers of the penis, were ruptured so that as he was hurled backwards against the bulkhead his penis squirted blood instead of semen. He wailed as his knees buckled under him and he sagged down the bulkhead and fell onto the deck clutching his damaged organs.

Nastiya jack-knifed her body again but this time each of her legs hooked around the necks of the two men holding her shoulders down. Using her own momentum and the strength of those long athletic legs she swung forward again and hurled the men across the cabin as though they were stones from a catapult. They too crashed into the bulkhead. One of them went into it head-first and the front of his skull was stoved in. The other managed to throw up one arm to protect his face, but his elbow bore the brunt of the impact and the joint splintered. He rolled on the deck whimpering, and calling on his God for mercy.

Nastiya jack-knifed yet again and flipped forward onto her feet in perfect balance. She stooped over the body of the dead man and still with her wrists tied together she drew the dagger from the belt of the sprawling corpse and whirled around to face the charge of the other guards. She slashed the first of them across the belly and when he doubled over to try and prevent his innards bulging out of the long wound, she used the silver and rhinoceros-horn hilt of the dagger like a hammer into the base of his skull. He was dead before he sprawled on the deck. One of the other guards had come up behind her, urged on by Kamal's roars of rage. Nastiya did not turn to face him, but she shot out a backward mule kick that caught him under the chin and snapped his head back so violently that the vertebrae in his neck were crushed and he flopped down onto the deck like a discarded shirt. His comrades jammed in the doorway in their eagerness to escape from the suite.

With the dagger still clutched in her tied hands, Nastiya leapt over the first corpse and went for Kamal. He saw her coming and he sprang out of the chair, turned around and ran. He was the last man through the door. As he reached it Nastiya stabbed the point of the dagger through his tight jump-suit pants into his buttocks. With another howl of pain and rage he hurled himself through the open doorway and one of his men slammed the door shut behind him. Nastiya slid the lock on the door across, then came back into the salon, stepping daintily over the corpses, and perched on the edge of the table. She wedged the dagger between her knees, slipped the point of the blade under the cable tie and with one quick upward jerk of her bound wrists cut through the tough nylon. When her bonds fell away she massaged the welts around her wrists and then stood up and came towards where she knew the camera was placed. She stood before it stark naked and unashamed and she looked up at the watchers in the situation room in the depths of the ship. Her expression was calm and unfathomable. Then she drooped one eyelid in a conspiratorial wink before she smiled. The smile was angelic and serene as though she were totally uninvolved with the dead men scattered around the cabin deck like cuttings from a flowerbed made by a demented gardener.

Through all this the watchers in the situation room sat in astounded silence. At last Hazel found her voice.

'What is she doing now?' she asked as Nastiya turned her attention to the air-conditioning control panel on the bulkhead beside the door.

'She's turning down the temperature as far as it will go,' Paddy explained.

'Why would she do that?' Hazel was puzzled.

'She is very fastidious,' Paddy said in tones of high approbation. 'I expect she doesn't want the corpses to start stinking, not if she has to share the suite with them.'

'And I was fretting myself into a nervous breakdown over her safety!' Hazel laughed, almost hysterical with relief. 'She is unique!'

'Isn't she just perfect,' Paddy agreed. 'I was hesitating, but after that little performance I am seriously going to ask her to be my wife.'

Nastiya turned away from the air-conditioning controls and sauntered through to the bedroom of the suite, her buttocks oscillating like a pair of silk bags full of live serpents.

'God! She is just so cute,' Dave Imbiss said in tones of near-religious awe.

'Much too cute for you, my lad,' Paddy asserted. 'In future when you look at her, kindly keep your eyes firmly closed.'

As Nastiya entered the bedroom the next camera picked up her image again. She locked the door behind her and went to the vanity. She seated herself in front of the mirror and with one of Hazel's brushes she rearranged the hair style that Kamal had disturbed. When she was satisfied with her hair she powdered over her facial bruises, and helped herself to Hazel's Chanel lipstick and perfume. She was playing up to her hidden audience, fully aware that all their eyes were upon her. She stood up and went through into the walk-in wardrobe at the far end of the cabin. Unhurriedly she browsed through the trays of Hazel's underwear, and at last decided on a matching set of Janet Reger panties and bra in oyster silk and Venetian lace. She held the panties across her lower body and looked up at the camera with her golden head cocked on one side, obviously seeking approval of her choice. They could not break silence to applaud her, but Dave put two fingers in his mouth and gave an almost inaudible wolf whistle.

'Perfect! I couldn't have made a better choice myself,' Hazel murmured softly. Almost as though she were able to hear them, Nastiya smiled again.

• • •

One of the units in the electronic navigation array on top of the mast above the *Golden Goose*'s bridge contained a link to the situation room in the covert area. The operator in the bowels of the ship was able to monitor the radar and Global Positioning System. In the situation room they were as well advised of the ship's progress as were the men on the bridge.

An air of tension pervaded the entire covert area. The men spoke hardly at all and when they did it was in stage whispers. Mostly they passed the time checking and preparing their equipment: honing the edges on their trench knives, unloading the ammunition clips then polishing and lubricating each separate round to feed smoothly into the breach, cleaning the rifle bores until they gleamed and adjusting the trigger release until it was sweet and light as a maiden's sigh. Hector and his officers maintained their rapt attention in the situation room, monitoring the navigation displays and the CCTV screens.

Vincent Woodward was still locked in one of the smaller cabins on the same level as the owner's suite. His wrists were pinioned with cable ties and two heavily armed guards sat on the narrow bunk and covered him with their AK-47s. Another three guards were posted outside the cabin door. Twice during the day Kamal came down from the bridge to vent his choler on Vincent. He started by spitting on him and calling down the wrath of Allah on his filthy pagan head for having assassinated his father and his brothers, then he put the boot into him again, aiming for his belly and crotch. Vincent doubled himself into a ball to guard his vitals and he kept rolling to ride the main force of the blows. When at last Kamal tired he grabbed an AK from one of the guards who were delightedly following the performance, and finished the beating with two or three cracks with the steel-shod butt of the rifle aimed at Vincent's head. However, Kamal's damaged hand was so painful that the blows lacked real power. Vincent easily managed to deflect their main impact.

'Vincent is earning his ten thousand dollars,' David commented.

'I shall have to add a bonus to his pay cheque for services far beyond the call of duty,' said Hazel, shaken by the savagery of Kamal's temper.

'Nonsense!' Paddy demurred. 'For Vic a little tickle up like that's no more onerous than a kiss from an ugly wench.' He

thought about it for a moment, then added, 'He would probably prefer the beating to the ugly girl.'

There were another five men guarding the door to Nastiya's
cabin. None of them had dared to enter the salon where the
corpses of their comrades still lay. They had dead-locked the
door and piled heavy furniture against it to protect themselves.
Their trepidation was undisguised. They kept as far back from
the barricaded door as the bounds of the cabin allowed and
never took their eyes off it. With fingers on triggers, they were
poised to repel another sudden whirlwind of kicks, blows and
snapping teeth.

Kamal emerged from the opposite cabin where he had
been beating up Vincent and now he turned on his own men,
haranguing them furiously.

'Have you left the bodies of your valiant comrades in there
with that she-devil? Have you no respect for custom and law?
They must be buried or committed to the sea before nightfall.
Bring them out at once!' None of them seemed in any hurry
to lead another foray into the master suite, but at last they gar-
nered sufficient courage cautiously to remove the barricade and
open the door a crack. When they peered in cautiously and
found that Nastiya was not lying in wait for them they rushed
in together, seized the corpses and dragged them out by their
heels. Then they hastily relocked the door and piled the furniture back against it.

Meanwhile, in the inner cabin Nastiya lounged in one of
the black calf-skin leather chairs, eating chocolates from the
box she had found in the refrigerator of the kitchenette, and
idly turning the pages of one of the fashion magazines from
the stack on the coffee table. She hardly looked up when she
heard the Arabs in the next cabin retrieving their dead. Nastiya
was wearing a pair of pale green trousers, beautifully tailored in
pure new wool, and over them a vivid Emilio Pucci top from
Hazel's wardrobe.

'The lady has eccentric taste,' David Imbiss observed.

'She certainly does,' Hector agreed. 'She has paired up with Paddy, hasn't she? That makes eccentric seem mundane.'

• • •

There was one more significant incident that they were able to follow on the CCTV screens in the situation room. After his casualties had been dropped overboard with brief ceremony, Kamal was still restless. He took to leaving the bridge at odd times during the day and night. One of his lieutenants stood guard over Cyril Stamford while Kamal prowled around the rest of the ship examining the bulkheads between the compartments and the different tiers. Kamal seemed to have a nagging feeling that he had overlooked something important.

When he took to tapping sections of the hull with his dagger and listening intently to the echo, Hector gradually became alarmed. The tier below the bridge that had been converted to house the Bushmaster cannon came under Kamal's close scrutiny. He examined it carefully, even descending to the cargo deck to peer up at the blank outer bulkhead which hid the gun deck. When Kamal returned to the bridge Hector overheard a conversation between Kamal and Cyril Stamford about this section. As usual Cyril had a plausible but totally fictional explanation. He described how this area housed delicate machinery that managed the pumps in the depths of the ship. The pumps controlled the temperature and distribution of the gas in the cargo tanks. Over a certain temperature the gas became so volatile that it could spontaneously explode and destroy the entire ship. Cyril explained to Kamal that the machinery was controlled remotely by satellite from the Bannock Corporation's technical headquarters in the United States. Even he as ship's captain was unable to enter the sensitive area while the ship was at sea.

'So these people will be able to read our change of course?' Kamal asked.

'Does that worry you, Captain?' Cyril asked.

'Not at all.' Kamal smiled and shook his head. 'Within a few hours we will be safely in territorial waters. There is nothing they can do about it.'

However, his explorations continued, and he poked and pried into every odd corner. One afternoon he discovered the hatch that led down into the service tunnels which connected the separate gas holds, and housed the huge pumps which circulated and cooled the cargo of gas, transferring it from one tank to another to balance and trim the ship as necessary.

In Taiwan when the hull had been reconfigured to make room for the covert area, it had been necessary to move this access hatch from amidships to the port side of the stern tower. It was an awkward and unsatisfactory compromise that would attract the attention of a seaman of Kamal's calibre. Kamal opened the hatch and found his way down into the labyrinth of tunnels below the gas storage tanks, and he explored these exhaustively. The observers in the situation room just above his head followed his progress anxiously on the infrared sensors. At one stage Kamal tapped with the handle of his dagger on one of the gas pipes and the sound of his blows carried so clearly that it sounded as if he were in the room with them. They held their breaths until, much to their relief, it seemed that Kamal had at last decided that there was nothing sinister contained in this area of the *Golden Goose*. They heard his footfalls on the steel rungs of the ladder as he climbed back past the situation room to the cargo deck.

• • •

The *Goose* trod down the miles of glittering tropical waters under her gigantic bows and every hour brought them closer to the African mainland.

'Do we have an estimate of when we will reach Gandanga Bay?' Hazel asked as they sat at the mess table.

'The GPS gives an ETA of 0900 hours Thursday the fourteenth, that is in three days' time,' David answered her. They were eating Canadian bison fillets and potato chips with ketchup. Only Hector favoured the fiery jalapeño snake juice. Although this rustic meal was served on plastic plates and cutlery, the polystyrene cups were filled with a vintage Malconsorts Burgundy wine. Hazel had been keeping it for a very special occasion, and she had decided this was it. Hector tasted the wine reverently.

'One of the rarest and most heavenly wines on this earth,' he said sadly, 'drunk in the most insalubrious conditions on this same earth.'

'Eat, drink and be merry,' Paddy advised, 'For tomorrow we—'

'Do shut up, Paddy!' David interjected quickly.

'For tomorrow we flourish?' Hazel suggested as she raised her cup. 'Prosper? Thrive? Succeed?'

'For tomorrow the bad guys die,' Hector said and they all drank the toast with fitting solemnity. As they set down their cups, Tariq darted up the companionway from the situation room.

'Hector! Paddy! Come quick!'

'What is it, Tariq?' Hector demanded as he sprang to his feet.

'New radar contact. Strange ship closing with us. Smells like trouble.' They abandoned the meal, even the Malconsorts wine, and trooped down the companionway to the lower deck, where they gathered in front of the display screens. The contact that showed on the repeater from the ship's radar was bright and solid.

'Big ship,' said Dave. 'Let me get her speed.' He worked quickly with the ranger and then leaned back in his chair. 'Forty-three point six knots. Merchantmen don't burn gas like that. This is a warship.' He checked his other instruments. 'Cyril is holding a constant course and speed.'

'You bet he is!' Hector said grimly. 'No way can he run away from a greyhound like that one. I just hope this isn't the US cavalry charging in to rescue us, and trampling all over the roses.' Anxiously they watched the images being transmitted from the camera on the top of the *Goose*'s communications mast. The strange ship came swiftly up over the horizon. She was grey and austere, functional as the blade of a battle axe.

From the bridge of the *Golden Goose* the approaching ship was still below the horizon. Kamal did not have the same height advantage as the covert camera on the masthead, but he was studying the radar image avidly. When he was no longer in any doubt he turned to Cyril Stamford.

'You are Yankee, yes?' he demanded. Cyril was from south of the Mason-Dixon line but he did not think it wise to split hairs.

'I am American, yes.'

'The strange ship is going to intercept us. It is certainly an infidel warship; perhaps English or more likely American. You will speak to them.' He seized Cyril's shoulder and spun him around to glare into his face menacingly. 'If they wish to board and search us you will stop them. I don't care what or how, but you will tell them something to make them leave us. You understand, okay?'

'I understand, okay,' Cyril said quietly.

'If a boarding party comes across to us, you will be dead before it arrives.' Kamal drew his dagger and pricked Cyril's throat. A drop of bright blood welled up from the tiny wound. 'You understand that I am serious?'

'I understand,' Cyril agreed. He was standing very still but he swivelled his eyes and went on in the same quiet tone. 'The strange ship is in sight already.'

Kamal turned away quickly and stared over the starboard quarter. The approaching vessel's superstructure showed clearly above the horizon, and at that moment the marine frequency channel on 156.5 MHz crackled to life in the *Goose*'s radio room at the back of the bridge.

'Bulk tanker on the port bow! This is Commander Robins aboard the United States Navy destroyer USS *Manila Bay*. What ship are you?' Cyril glanced at Kamal.

'You wish me to reply?'

'Yes. But remember you will be the first to die if you make a mistake.'

Cyril nodded. He crossed the deck to the radio room and unhooked the microphone. He took his time. He did not want to appear over-willing or efficient. The other captain would expect a certain amount of slovenliness from a merchantman.

'Hi there! *Manila Bay*. This is the *Golden Goose*. Captain Stamford. En route Sidi el Razig in the Persian Gulf to Jedda in Saudi Arabia.' There was a long silence, then Robins came back on the line.

'Captain Stamford, sir! You wouldn't happen to be an American citizen by any chance?'

'Son of a gun! How d'you know that?' Cyril exaggerated his accent slightly. 'Darned right I'm an American. Cyril Stamford, late commanding the US Navy cruiser *Reno*. They put me out to grass for being too old and decrepit.' He chuckled. From the destroyer there was a momentary silence.

'What is your port of registry and the name of your owner?'

'My owner is Bannock Cargoes and the port of registry is Taipei.'

'Okay! That checks out. Captain Stamford, sir! Did you perhaps have a son graduate from Anapolis in 1996?'

'Sure did, Commander.'

'Is his first name Timothy?'

'You sure as hell know that it was not. His name was Bobby. And yours is Andy. You two were shipmates. Bobby brought you to our house for a barbecue one time. Have you forgotten?'

'No, sir, Captain. I remember pretty good. I was just making sure. Your wife cooks a great apple pie.'

'Thank you. She would have been pleased to hear that, Andy. But sadly she passed away four years ago.'

'I am so sorry, sir.'

'So am I, Andy.'

In the situation room Hector whistled softly. 'Where the hell did you find this guy, Paddy? He is a prince.'

'Sharp as a Samurai sword,' Paddy agreed. 'Let's see how he staves off a boarding party.' Delicately Andy Robins came back to the business in hand.

'Captain Stamford, are you in full command of your ship?'

Cyril laughed easily. 'I darned well hope so. Not senile yet, despite what the Navy thinks of me.'

'If you need me to do so, I could send a boarding party across to you to render any assistance, sir.'

'Very good of you, Andy, but that would disrupt both our routines. I assure you it is not necessary. Everything is under control. I am on a strict timetable.'

But Andy came back again. 'Are you aware that you are sailing into an area of the Indian Ocean which is a hotspot of pirate activity? Only four days ago a Japanese whaler was reported taken by the pirates in the Gulf of Aden.'

'I heard about that,' Cyril agreed. 'However, my owners have made arrangements with the government of Puntland. Puntland has guaranteed us free passage of its waters. We should be safe enough from molestation.'

'Do you trust the word of a pirate, Captain?'

'My owners do,' Cyril responded. 'That has to be good enough for me.'

'It's your call, sir,' Andy Robins acquiesced reluctantly. 'Bon voyage, Captain. But tell me before you go, how is my old pal Bobby?'

'The Taliban got him in Afghanistan, Andy.'

'Bastards!' said Andy quietly but intensely.

In the situation room they watched the *Manila Bay* turn away and head back in the direction from which she had appeared. Hector stood up and stretched.

'There you have it, my lady and gentlemen. Free passage to Gandanga Bay, compliments of Captain Cyril Stamford. Let's go and polish off that bottle of Malconsorts, before it too becomes pirate booty.'

• • •

Sheikh Adam decided to move his entire household from the Oasis of the Miracle to Gandanga Bay to welcome the *Golden Goose* when Kamal Tippoo Tip sailed the infidel booty into the bay. The arrival of captured prizes had become so common-place that Adam seldom stirred himself from the security and comfort of his fortress.

He had seven wives. Three more than the Koran allowed him. The mullah had assured him that a ruler of his stature could take more wives than a commoner. In addition to the wives he had over one hundred concubines. He was never sure of the exact number as it changed continually. His procurers scoured the entire country for nubile young girls. As Adam grew older his taste in females became increasingly paedo-philic. Any girl over thirteen years of age held little appeal. They interested him only until they began exhibiting the first signs of puberty. He liked to feel them tear open as he forced his way into them. He liked the feel of warm blood spreading over his belly and the sound of their screams and weeping. At the present time he had thirteen of these little things locked in his harem, awaiting his attentions. He only enjoyed them once, then he sent them back to their families in the villages, with a present for their fathers of one hundred dollars Americani. His peculiar tastes and his generosity were so widely known throughout Puntland that when his procurers arrived at any of the remote villages there were always several families waiting for them with all their youngest children on offer. Adam had discussed his treatment of the girls with the mullah, who had reassured him that all females had been placed on this earth by Allah for one reason only, and that was the gratification of all desires of men, including the provision of children but not limited to that duty alone.

Adam had assembled a personal bodyguard of almost two hundred men, enlisted and trained by Uthmann Waddah. His network of spies stretched across all of the Middle East, from Cairo to Jordan and beyond. He had a communications centre equipped with state-of-the-art electronics, through which he was in constant touch with his bankers and investment advisers in Iran, China, Taiwan and other Far Eastern countries which were beyond the thrall of the US Federal Reserve's watchdogs and other Western regulatory bodies. Adam had long ago learned how to open secret doors with large sums of money.

He had built an airstrip in the desert close to his fortress. Daily his personal jet flew in every indulgence and extravagance he could imagine or desire. There was very little reason why he should ever leave the Oasis and venture out into a world that he did not completely control. Especially as he was aware that Hector Cross and his American harlot were waiting out there for him with hot vengeance in their hearts. Very little reason indeed to venture abroad, except to welcome into Gandanga Bay the greatest prize that had ever sailed the oceans: the *Golden Goose* and his two most virulent enemies led before him in bonds and completely at his mercy.

His retainers had erected a city of colourful tents on the higher ground overlooking Gandanga Bay. All the closest members of his family, his most loyal household retainers and his bodyguards, his horses and hunting dogs and falcons with their handlers and four of his as-yet untapped little girls had all been moved down to the coast in a convoy of trucks. When they were settled into the city of tents and all was in readiness to receive him, Adam and Uthmann Waddah flew from the Oasis of the Miracle to Gandanga Bay in one of the Bell Jet Ranger helicopters. Uthmann was at the controls. He had taken instruction in Iran with the airforce of that country, which was well disposed to Puntland and its new Sheikh. The Iranians strongly approved of Adam's devotion to Islam and enthusiastically supported his undeclared war on the shipping of the infidel nations. Over the past years Uthmann had become a skilled helicopter pilot. He had shown a natural aptitude for the work, and he possessed the hand–eye coordination that it called for.

He circled the bay at low altitude, hovering over each one of the captured ships for Adam to admire them, while one of his militia officers seated in the rear of the helicopter reeled off their tonnages and the value of every hull and its cargo. There were several hundred million dollars' worth of shipping lying at anchor below them. However, Adam was not satisfied. He lifted his eyes from the ships and gazed out hungrily over the empty waters of the eastern ocean.

'Soon! Very soon Kamal will come, bringing me not only immense wealth but also the man who has murdered half my family. It will be the sweetest day of my life when I watch the *Golden Goose* sail into the bay. All else that I have ever achieved will be as nothing against this treasure.' He was consumed with impatience. He glanced sideways at Uthmann Waddah in the pilot's seat and considered ordering him to leave the bay and fly out to meet the tanker. They could land on the tanker's deck and he could begin to enjoy his triumph two days earlier. Then he shook his head. He knew it would be futile to ask Uthmann to fly out to sea. Uthmann was a highly capable and resourceful pilot. However, the intensity of his aquaphobia was such that if he ventured out beyond gliding distance from the shore he would become so paranoiac as to be almost completely incapable of rational thought or action. If it were possible, this terror would have been aggravated still further by the sight of the huge sharks cruising the waters of the bay below them. These scavengers had been attracted by the sewage and other rubbish that had been dumped overboard from the captured ships. Then Adam considered taking one of the high-speed attack boats and having a crew run him out to meet the tanker. If he were ten years younger he would not have hesitated, but of late he had become soft and accustomed to a safe and comfortable existence. A small fast boat in any kind of sea would be extremely unpleasant; he felt a sneaking sympathy for Uthmann's loathing of water.

No, he decided, there were many distractions in the tented camp ashore to allow him to pass the time pleasantly enough until Kamal's arrival. All the headmen and chieftains for a hundred miles around had already arrived to pay homage. Adam had developed an appetite for extravagant praise and cringing subservience. In addition Uthmann had promised the execution of a number of criminals who had been captured by his men, or brought in by the headmen who knew of his interest in the dispensation of justice and punishment. He could rely on Uthmann to be creative and inventive. This was in effect a dress rehearsal for the sentences that he would pass on Cross and his harlot. Uthmann would see to it that the hunting dogs were given a good run. When that sport palled there were always his little babies to play with. He wriggled in the seat of the helicopter with pleasure and then tapped Uthmann on the shoulder and pointed back to the assembly of multicoloured tents on the hillside. Uthmann nodded and banked the helicopter. Adam smiled as he saw the throng waiting on the ground to welcome him. They were dancing, waving flags and banners and discharging their weapons into the air in a *feu de joie*.

• • •

The sea under the *Goose*'s hull changed its colour and temperament as the ship approached the African continent. It lost the sapphire sparkle of deep water and became dun and sullen, the swells were steeper and they ran before the wind in closer ranks. There were clumps of seaweed and other flotsam drifting aimlessly with the current and seabirds hovering and diving over the seething shoals of small fish. As the sun set and quenched its flames in the waters the GPS showed the distance to run to the entrance of Gandanga Bay as sixty-eight nautical miles.

During the night, the fourth since the taking of the ship, Hector and Hazel were on watch in the situation room. One of the hidden cameras was focused on the bridge and they overheard Kamal ordering Cyril Stamford to reduce speed and alter course four degrees westward. Since Cyril had placated the captain of the American warship and sent him on his way, Kamal's treatment of his captives had become if not exactly magnanimous, at least slightly more lenient. For the last forty-eight hours he had not been down to the cabin in which Vincent Woodward was imprisoned to curse and kick him, and use the rifle butt on his head. He had even allowed the guards to give Vincent a mug of water and feed him a plate of slops. None of them dared to take food or drink to Nastiya. The doors to the suite remained locked and barricaded, but behind them Nastiya was comfortably ensconced. She had discovered several large cans of Beluga caviar in the refrigerator of the kitchenette, in addition to packets of sliced springbuck biltong, smoked salmon and Swiss chocolates.

On the bridge Cyril suggested to Kamal that he should send one of his men to the ship's dispensary to fetch the first-aid kit; he agreed and Cyril disinfected and bandaged the stump of Kamal's finger and made him swallow a handful of antibiotics and powerful painkillers. Kamal's mood improved quite dramatically. He actually took over the watch from Cyril Stamford, and allowed him to stretch out and sleep on the bunk in the radio room for a few hours. When he sent one of his men to rouse Cyril and order him back to his station, instead of forcing him to stand at gunpoint he allowed him to sit on the captain's stool, and chatted with him quite amiably about the sailing and handling characteristics of the *Golden Goose*, the operation of the navigational console and the engine configuration of the ship. He seemed particularly interested in the depth-sounding equipment. Now when he ordered the change of course and speed he condescended to discuss this move with Cyril.

'We are coming very close to our destination but I do not wish to arrive during darkness. The roads and entrance to the harbour are difficult to negotiate in the dark. Also my beloved Sheikh and many thousands of my people will be gathered to welcome our arrival. When they see the size and importance of this vessel they will be filled with happiness. I do not wish to deprive them of this pleasure. They must see the splendour of the prize I am bringing to them in full daylight, with the rising sun behind it. I must be able to bring it in as close to the beach as is safe.'

'I am very happy for you, sir.' Cyril had not made the fatal mistake of letting Kamal know that he was aware of his identity. 'However, can you tell me what will happen to my ship, my passengers, my crew and myself once we reach port?'

'Your passengers will become the honoured guests of my Sheikh.' Kamal smiled coolly at his own understatement. 'You, your crew and your ship will remain with us for a while, but only until arrangements can be made with your owners and their insurance company. When that is done you will be free to continue your voyage without suffering any harm. *Inshallah!*'

'If it is God's will,' Cyril agreed. Kamal looked startled and then smiled.

'I have enjoyed your company, Yankee. I shall regret our parting.'

'Perhaps if God is kind we will meet again?' Cyril smiled back at him. One of his front teeth had been knocked out when Kamal's pirate whipped him with the rifle butt. The empty hole in his mouth gave him a louche expression.

'I love him, don't you?' Hazel smiled as she watched Cyril on the video screen. 'He is so super cool, as Cayla might have said.'

'He is a hard case, is our lad,' Hector agreed. He was delighted to hear Hazel mention Cayla's name so naturally. Was she at last coming to terms with the fact that her daughter was gone, he wondered?

No! he said to himself in reply. *It won't be over, not for Hazel, not for me, until we have finished what we have come here to do.*

• • •

Although he now knew the exact time they would sail into Gandanga Bay, Hector let the troops sleep for four more precious hours. Forty minutes before sunrise he passed the word for 'Stand To'. Quietly each man woke the man on the far side of him and within ten minutes they were all gathered in full kit and body armour in the assembly area on the second level. They watched Hector's face avidly as he stood before their closely packed ranks. He gestured for them to insert the earpieces of their Falcon battle radios, then cupped his hands around the microphone of his own set and spoke into it quietly. Even though he was speaking directly into the earpieces of his men, there was no sound of a human voice to echo through the bulkheads and alert a listening pirate.

'We are about to enter the pirates' home harbour. You have all studied the maps that Tariq Hakam drew up for us, so in general you know what to expect. However, we cannot know the exact anchorage which Kamal will select for the *Goose*. Sam, it may be a long run in the AAVs to the beach but Dave's gunners will keep the enemy heads down until you are safely ashore. As you all know our main objective is to capture or neutralize two particular men. You have seen their faces on video many times already, but I am going to show them to you one last time. These fine gentlemen are the first prize.' Hector turned to the large video screen on the bulkhead behind him and started the projection. The first images to appear were from the archives of Cross Bow Security. There were several excellent shots of Uthmann Waddah, talking with Hector, giving a lecture on firearms on the firing range and drilling new recruits.

'Many of you know this man,' Hector told them. 'He was once a member of Cross Bow. He is extremely dangerous. Mark him well. There is a bounty of fifty thousand dollars on his head, dead or alive.' The watching men stirred with excitement. Hector changed the projected images. First there were several passport photographs he had obtained from his contact in French Interpol. They were full-face and side-view images of the subject.

'This person's name is Adam Tippoo Tip and he is a man of importance in Puntland; a sheikh and the head of his tribe. He is also the leader of the pirates,' Hector explained. 'Bear in mind that these pictures were taken almost seven years ago. Tariq has seen him recently and he says that his beard is now full and dark. Also he has put on some weight.'

Hector brought up another image on the screen. 'Now this video was taken a little over four years ago.' Hector started running the clip from the ransom demand that Adam had sent on Cayla's mobile phone. Blown up to full screen it was slightly grainy and blurred. Adam was looking into the camera and speaking, but the sound had been expunged from the recording, and Adam mouthed his threats silently. At the back of the assembly area Hazel stood up and ran from the room, unable to watch once again the face of Cayla's murderer. Hector ran the loop three times. Then he switched off the video machine and spoke into the microphone, directly into their ears.

'The bounty on Adam's head is one hundred thousand dollars.' His listeners smiled wolfishly and a few of them nodded and smiled. Hector looked them over with satisfaction. They were as hot as a pack of hounds with the smell of the game in their nostrils, eager to be slipped from the leash. He sent Tariq to fetch Hazel back and once she returned Hector went on speaking into the radio.

'I am switching now to the camera at the ship's masthead. This is real-time.' The image changed to a wide-angle view of the African coastline ahead of the *Golden Goose*. They were still four or five miles off. The time at the foot of the frame showed as 0617. The heat haze had not yet obscured the line of blue-glazed hills on the westerly horizon. The rising sun was highlighting them. They were looking into the wide, open mouth of an extensive natural harbour, guarded on either side by two low headlands. In the depths of the bay was an untidy assembly of shipping.

'So we come at last to the lovely pleasure resort of Gandanga Bay, Jewel of the African coast!' said Hector with heavy irony. 'There is even a meet-and-greet service on its way out to welcome you all.' A flotilla of pirate attack craft poured from the mouth of the bay and headed directly towards the *Goose* at high speed. The wakes left behind by the powerful outboard motors frothed the surface like boiling milk. Every boat was packed with bearded men with dark complexions. As they drew closer it became clear that they were dressed in jihadist militia uniform, baggy breeches and black turbans, and that they were brandishing either rifles or scimitars.

'Time to man your stations, gentlemen,' Hector told them. 'Remember! We will not spring the ambush until we have a positive fix on the exact whereabouts of both Uthmann Waddah and of his boss, Adam. This might take some time as there will be a lot of people milling around, but when we have them spotted in the throng we will have to move very fast. Try to take those two main targets alive. However, if they are escaping from you don't hesitate to kill them. You will still be up for the rewards.' Hector made a winding movement with his right arm. 'Okay! Move out in order of deployment!'

David Imbiss's gun crews formed up in an eerie silence and Dave led them into the entrance of the covert tunnel system. Swiftly they climbed the ladder to the gun platform below the bridge. Within minutes Dave reported back to Hector over the Falcon battle radio.

'Both guns loaded and manned, Heck.' Hector acknowledged and then spoke to Sam Hunter. Although they were in direct eye contact he used the battle radio to keep the noise level down to an absolute minimum.

'Okay, Sam. Get your men loaded into the AAVs. But the mode is still "Silent Ship". Do not start your engines until I give the order.' Sam acknowledged curtly, and then led the ninety men of the landing party up the companionway to the level beneath the cargo deck. It took a little longer than manning the guns, but at last Sam's voice came over the radio.

'All AAV crews loaded. Hoist cables attached and ready to lift. Turret hatches closed, and engines off. We are ready to launch.'

'Right-oh, Sam!' Hector approved. Then he looked over the men still remaining in the assembly area. These were his storm troopers. They would spearhead the assault on board the ship. Of course, Hector was in overall command but his lieutenants were Paddy and Tariq.

Hector's stick of six men was a mixed bag. There were twin brothers, Jacko and Bingo MacDuff from Glasgow, two Iraqis, an Aussie from Queensland and a German Afrikaner from Namibia. They were all fighters and killers. If luck was with the attackers, and Adam and Uthmann came out on the royal barge to welcome the *Goose*, and if they went directly up to the bridge to greet Kamal, it would simplify the matter a hundredfold. Hector and his stick could grab all of them in one fell swoop.

But whichever way it went, Hector and his stick must seize Kamal and the four jihadists with him on the bridge. Then they could release Cyril Stamford and the other crew members being held there. From the heights of the bridge Hector would then be in a position to overlook the entire bay and spot the whereabouts of Adam and his henchman. He would be able to direct Dave Imbiss's gunners onto these prime targets. After that they would destroy Kamal's fleet of attack boats and cover the landing of the three AAVs on the beach, and their return from the compounds escorting the seamen of the pirated ships.

Paddy and his team would attack the second level. Their first objective would be to subdue the guards in the owner's suite and in the smaller cabin on the same level where Nastiya and Vincent were being held. Once they had rescued these hostages they would be ready to move swiftly to any area of the ship where Hector needed them.

Tariq and his team would attack the lowest level of the *Goose*'s accommodation where the other crew members were being held by the pirates. Once they were in control of that level they would also have command of the main cargo deck. After Paddy's team had come down to reinforce them they would be able to concentrate all their forces on their primary task, which was to capture Adam wherever he might be at that time.

Considering his pathological aversion to seawater it seemed highly unlikely that Uthmann Waddah would accompany his Sheikh, but he must surely be on the beach to witness the triumphant entry of the *Golden Goose* to Gandanga Bay. Hector was confident that he would be able to spot him through the high-power telescopic lens of the camera at the ship's masthead. Then he might have to go after him and hunt him down.

At all times during the action Hazel and her four assistants would keep Hector and his officers informed of developments and of the exact whereabouts of every pirate aboard. The five of them would remain in the situation room to monitor all the cameras and listening equipment. The men under Hazel were all born Arabic speakers and would translate for her every word uttered by Kamal and his gang.

In the dawn the *Golden Goose* moved slowly and carefully between the sandy headlands of Gandanga Bay. Under Kamal's direction she was groping her way down the deep-water channel. Hector, Paddy and Tariq watched the scene ahead on the repeater screen on the bulkhead of the assembly area. The surface of the bay swarmed with small craft. The wolf pack of attack boats was already circling the tanker. The roar of outboard motors, the crackle of rifle fire and screaming and chanting was so loud that Hector was able to hear it even deep in the hull of the tanker.

Hector spoke into the microphone of his radio. 'Hazel! Have you spotted Adam? He should be coming out to us in his royal barge. According to Tariq he will be dressed in white robes with a golden headband around his turban. It should be easy to pick him out.'

'Negative, Hector. I cannot see anyone who answers that description,' Hazel replied. Hector had been absolutely certain that Adam would want to be the first to step aboard the *Golden Goose*. His whole plan was based on this premise, but now he felt the sharp stab of doubt.

Shit! If the very first thing goes wrong, he thought, *then everything afterwards goes wrong!* But he must not let his doubts affect the others, so he said calmly, 'Hazel! Where is Kamal? Do you have him on your screens?'

'Affirmative, Hector. Kamal is on the starboard wing of the bridge with three of his pirates. He is waving to the men in the small boats and they are cheering him. Cyril Stamford is at the ship's helm. It's all getting somewhat confused.'

'Okay, Hazel. Watch that swine Kamal. I cannot delay any longer. We have to deploy into the tunnels and take up our jump-off positions at the hatches.' Hector nodded to Paddy and Tariq. Then he went to the tunnel entrance and climbed swiftly. The ladder was only wide enough to admit one man at a time. The six men of his team followed him closely. As soon as the last of them disappeared into the tunnel Paddy led his team in behind them. They stopped at the level of the owner's suite. Paddy could see the soft para boots of the men of Hector's team on the steel rungs above his head. When he looked down he could see the top of Tariq's helmet. He was at the level of the crew's quarters and the cargo deck. The ladder was loaded with armed men primed for action.

• • •

Hector leaned his shoulder against the clandestine entrance to the bridge and whispered into his microphone.

'Hazel! Where's Kamal now?'

'Hector! He's come in from the wing. He's with Cyril at the con. I think he's preparing to drop anchor.'

'How far are we off the beach?' There was a pause while Hazel read the range finder.

'Seven hundred and thirty-four metres,' she said. 'Kamal has taken us in very close.' Hector was aware of a faint rumble and vibration and immediately Hazel went on, 'Yes! I can see that Kamal has let go the two bow anchors.'

'Still no sign of Adam's barge?'

'No. None.'

'Are any of the men from the attack boats coming aboard the *Goose*?'

'No. They are shouting and shooting in the air, but they are standing well off from our ship. It's almost as though they are waiting for something to happen.'

'Can you see any sign of Adam or his barge on the beach?'

'There are hundreds of people there, but I can't make out any sign of him or Uthmann Waddah.'

'Where the hell is the bastard? We can't do a thing until he shows himself,' Hector fretted.

'Hold on! Kamal has gone out on the wing of the bridge again,' Hazel said softly. 'He's making another call on his satphone.'

'You can bet all your money that he's talking to his master,' Hector guessed.

• • •

With the skirts of his robe tucked up between his knees, Uthmann Waddah squatted in the clearing on the periphery of the tent city above Gandanga Bay. He had the satphone pressed to his ear, and in front of him was a fine view out across the anchorage to where the great ship lay at anchor. Although he had watched it for over an hour as it came in sedately through the mouth of the bay and anchored off the beach, still he was amazed by its enormous size. It did not seem possible that anything of that magnitude would be capable of floating. Its open deck seemed larger than the new airfield that Adam had had built at the Oasis of the Miracle. That deck seemed sufficiently spacious for a 737 to land upon it, and furthermore the ship was less than a kilometre off the beach. Uthmann felt much more sanguine about the orders that Adam had given him. He was listening to Kamal's voice on the other end of the satphone, and occasionally acknowledging the orders he was receiving.

'As you say, noble prince!—I shall give him your message at once, Your Royal Highness.'

The titles were extravagant for such an unimportant scion of an undistinguished family of brigands, but Kamal seemed to accept them as his due. Uthmann ended the call and stood up. He adjusted his ammunition bandolier over his shoulder and hefted his assault rifle. Then he stepped out briskly towards the largest tent in the encampment. Adam looked up as Uthmann prostrated himself before him.

'Did you speak to my uncle?' Adam was seated on a cushion of snowy lamb's fleece. His robes were flowing and dazzling white. His turban was of the same cloth. And his headband was of eighteen-carat gold filigree.

'This very moment!' Uthmann replied. 'He has asked me to assure you that all is well. He has complete control of the ship. He has searched every inch of it, and there are no enemy hidden anywhere on board. All the infidel captives are bound and helpless. But the news that will light up your heart is that Hector Cross and his harlot, Hazel Bannock, are still his prisoners. They are totally subdued, helplessly awaiting your judgment and execution. Your uncle humbly begs you to come to him and take possession of the great treasure he has brought to you.'

'Are you still willing to fly me in the helicopter to the ship, Uthmann?'

'I am willing and eager to be of service to you in any way possible, my Sheikh.'

'You were not so willing yesterday and the day before,' Adam reminded him.

'Yesterday the ship was hundreds of leagues out in the ocean. I was fearful only for your safety, my Sheikh. If the machine had failed so far from the land you would have been in grave danger. But today the ship lies less than a kilometre from dry land. Your sacred person will be secure. Even if the helicopter engine should fail, I will be able to steer you to a safe touchdown on dry land.'

'I am deeply touched by your concern for my safety,' Adam sneered at him, and Uthmann prostrated himself once more to hide the anger in his own eyes. Adam took pleasure in taunting Uthmann about his terror of water. This single weakness somehow reduced him to the same level as Adam himself, no longer the perfectly intrepid and invincible warrior.

Adam had his black leather briefcase on his lap. It was almost part of his body. That case went everywhere with him. He never let it out of his sight. He trusted no one else to carry it. A stainless-steel chain was attached to the frame and dangling from it was a cuff of the same steel. Adam snapped the cuff onto his left wrist. Uthmann knew that it was a combination lock. Clutching the case, Adam rose to his feet and with his right hand made a regal gesture towards the entrance of the tent.

'Very well, Uthmann Waddah. You may take me to my blood enemy, Hector Cross. My vengeance has been too long delayed.'

• • •

'Hector! Things are moving.' Hazel's voice was soft in Hector's ear. 'Kamal has left the bridge. Cyril Stamford is being guarded by four militia. They've tied his wrists and his elbows together and forced him to sit on the deck. Kamal has gone down to the second level. His men have tied Vincent and led him out of his cabin. Now the whole gang are all gathered outside the owner's suite. There they go! They've forced the door and are pouring into the suite. Nastiya is standing in the middle of the cabin. She is making no move to defend herself. They are tying her arms behind her back at her elbows and wrists. Now they're holding her down and fixing a short hobble between her ankles. They're scared witless by those pretty little feet of hers. With that hobble Nastiya will hardly be able to walk. My God! Now they're looping a lead rope around her neck. Kamal is taking no more chances with her. Now six of his thugs are dragging her out of the suite. Two of them are holding her on the lead rope. Kamal has not ventured within ten paces of her. It looks like they are taking her and Vincent to the lift. Nastiya is behaving very docilely—'

Paddy's voice interrupted her transmission. 'Hector! I can hear them through the hatch. Kamal is no more than a few feet from where I am standing. I can hear his voice clearly. I could go in now and with one sweep take Kamal and all his men out of the game.'

'Negative, Paddy! I repeat negative! We must wait for Adam to show up before we move. Acknowledge that order!'

'Received and understood!' Paddy's voice was tormented. *Poor old bastard*, Hector thought, *they have got his woman and he is helpless*. Hector ached with him.

'Hector, they're descending in the lift,' Hazel broke in. 'They have left the second level deserted. Now they've reached the cargo deck level. Kamal's men are frogmarching the two prisoners out onto the open deck.'

'Paddy! Go back down the ladder to join Tariq's team on the level below you,' Hector ordered.

'Will comply!' Paddy answered formally. *He is truly pissed off with me*, Hector thought with a grim smile. Suddenly Hazel's voice stung his eardrum. Her tone was sharp with excitement.

'Hector, there's a helicopter approaching from the shore. It looks like the same machine that buzzed us before Kamal boarded the *Goose*.'

'Hazel, give me a running commentary,' Hector ordered. 'Can you see who is in the cockpit?'

'Negative! The sun is reflecting straight off the canopy into my lens. However, all the pirates in the attack boats are concentrating their full attention on the helicopter. They are waving their banners at it and screaming like a troop of baboons at feeding time. The four men Kamal left on the bridge to guard Cyril have all crowded to the wing of the bridge to watch the chopper and join in the tumult and the shouting!' Hazel caught her breath and then went on quickly, 'Hold on, the helicopter is banking across the sun. I can see into the cockpit now. Two men in the front seats. The pilot and a passenger. The passenger in the righthand seat is wearing a white turban and gold headband. I swear it's Adam!'

'Let us give thanks for that,' Hector said with relief. 'Now hear me, all of you. I am going to seize the bridge. If the men there are all looking the other way, I will be able to take them without any muss or fuss. From there I will be able to make the best judgement call. Paddy and Tariq, hold your present positions in the tunnel at the level of the cargo deck, but be ready to go in. Dave, stay on your toes. We will be needing your Bushmasters very soon now.'

They all acknowledged and Hector moved up onto the narrow ledge under the hatch. There was room for three of his men on the ledge with him, and the other three were crowded at the head of the steel ladder just below them. Hector loosened his trench knife in its sheath on his webbing and gave his men the thumbs-up sign, then slapped the shoulder of the hammer man at his side. He swung the hammer and with that single blow the retaining pin shot out of the lock and the steel hatch flew open. Hector led them through in a concerted rush. The four pirates were in a tight group on the far wing of the bridge. All their attention was on the approaching helicopter, and like their comrades in the attack boats they were hollering and whooping and shooting into the air. They were so absorbed that they had not even heard the hatch opening behind them. Hector was halfway across the bridge before one of the pirates turned and looked over his shoulder. He stared at Hector in blank astonishment. Before he could recover Hector chopped him across the side of his neck with the blade of his hand. He dropped to the deck and lay without even a twitch. Hector jumped over him and used the handle of his trench knife to bludgeon the Somalian leaning over the bridge rail beside him. He went down on top of Hector's first victim. The heavy knife handle left a depression the size and shape of an eggcup in the back of his skull. The men following Hector, the MacDuff brothers, knifed the two remaining pirates, but they botched the job a little. One pirate was down on the deck kicking in a spreading puddle of his own blood. The last one was staggering towards the companionway that led down to the next level. Blood spouted from the knife wound in his back and he was screeching wildly in Arabic, 'Beware! The infidels are here!'

He would be down the stairs before Hector could cross the wide bridge and catch him. Hector drew the 9mm pistol from its quick-release holster. It was like an extension of his own body and shot exactly wherever he was looking. He was barely aware of releasing the trigger, but it was a perfect brain shot. The pirate's head jerked and his whole body seemed to melt like a chocolate bar in a microwave. He slithered bonelessly down the stairs and collapsed on the first landing. From the break-in to Hector's pistol shot it had taken less than five seconds.

'Think they heard your shot?' asked the wiry little Scot at Hector's side as he wiped the blood-smeared blade on his trouser leg.

'I doubt it, Bingo.' Hector shook his head. 'Not with all those lads outside blazing away with their AKs.' Then he looked down at the pirate who was still whimpering and dragging himself across the deck on his belly. 'Tell your brother to finish off what he started. Then you can free Captain Stamford and his crew.'

Jacko bent over the wounded man and seized a handful of his beard. He wrenched his head back to expose his throat. Hector turned away and went out onto the wing of the bridge. Behind him he heard the Arab gasp and gurgle his last as Jacko slit his throat neatly.

Keeping well back out of sight under the bridge canopy, Hector searched the sky for the helicopter. He picked it up at low level coming in very slowly over the tanker's bows, its rotor buffeting as the pilot pulled up his collective and began a controlled descent. Hector watched the machine settle gently on the steel deck.

The door of the passenger cabin opened and a striking figure stepped down to the deck. It was a tall man in a shimmering white robe and turban. His beard was full, black and curling. His belly under the white robe was slightly protuberant. In his left hand he carried a small black leather briefcase. He lifted the other arm in a gesture of benediction as he advanced down the deck towards Kamal and his men. They all fell to their knees and dragged down the two captives with them.

'Hail, great Sheikh!' Kamal cried. 'Warrior son of mighty warriors!' On the wing of the bridge high above the gathering of pirates on the cargo deck, Hector placed his lips an inch from the microphone of his radio.

'Paddy, where are you?'

'I am with Tariq, in position at the Number One entry hatch!'

'The helicopter has landed. Adam has disembarked. Kamal is on the cargo deck to greet him. Nastiya and Vincent are down there with them. Kamal is going to present them to Adam. They are all of them off guard. This is the time to take them before they realize that Nastiya and Vincent are ringers. Go, Paddy! Go! Go! Go!'

'Roger that!' Paddy sang out with fierce joy. 'Here we go!'

Hector made a final check of the situation on the cargo deck below him. Very little had changed while he was speaking to Paddy, except that the pilot of Adam's helicopter had climbed down from the cockpit and was lounging against the fuselage. He was casually holding an assault rifle. Hector spared him one quick glance. Kamal and Adam were his main concern. Then belatedly he realized who the helicopter pilot was. His gaze darted back to the man, and an icicle seemed to pierce his heart.

'No! It's not possible. Uthmann can't fly a helicopter. But it's him. It's Uthmann!'

As he thought it, Kamal shouted an order and two of his men jumped up from the deck and dragged both Vincent and Nastiya to their feet and thrust them forward towards Adam as he approached.

'Behold, mighty Sheikh!' Kamal cried out. 'As you commanded me, I bring you the assassin Cross and his harlot.' Adam stopped and stared at the two captives uncertainly.

Then from behind him Uthmann Waddah yelled, 'That is not Cross! That is not Hazel Bannock! It is a trap, my Sheikh. Beware! The infidel is about to strike.' He did not wait for Adam to run back to the chopper, but hurled his rifle through the open door, and as quick as a ferret into a rabbit hole he followed it. He had left the engine running and the rotor revolving idly. Now he doubled over in the pilot's seat and kept his head well down as he grabbed the controls and gunned the engine. The helicopter lifted off the deck and turned on its axis to head towards the beach.

Adam was still running back down the deck screaming in Arabic, 'Wait for me, Uthmann! I command you. Do not leave me here at the mercy of Cross!' Uthmann never even raised his head to glance in his direction. Instead he lowered the nose of the machine and roared away, low over the waters of the bay.

Hector had a distorted view of the top few inches of Uthmann's head through the perspex canopy. The machine was climbing and banking steeply. The target was infinitesimal and the angles were impossible. In desperation, Hector fired and saw the perspex of the canopy shatter, leaving a gaping hole too far back to be effective in stopping Uthmann. The helicopter did not waver and raced away directly towards the beach, gaining altitude and speed. Hector lifted the microphone of his radio to his lips.

'Dave! Dave! Unmask your guns. Take that helicopter under fire. Uthmann is flying it. Don't let him escape. Shoot him down, for God's sake, shoot him!'

'Roger that!' Dave responded at once. From the deck below his feet Hector heard the crash as the steel doors that concealed the gun emplacement dropped down on their hinges and revealed the two Bushmaster cannon. But already the helicopter was approaching the shore 700 yards away. Hector watched it avidly. He heard Dave chanting his orders to his gunners on the deck below. Then there were the flashes and the stunning multiple cracks as the twin Bushmasters fired three-round bursts of fragmentation shells after the fleeing machine. Hector saw the puffs of smoke and flame of the airbursts appear in the sky above the machine. That one salvo was enough. He saw the helicopter trip and stagger in flight as the storm of steel balls ripped through its fuselage. The pilot must have been killed instantly, and the engine destroyed, for the rotor stopped dead in the air. The nose of the machine dropped and it began a powerless and uncontrolled plunge towards the surface of the sea.

Then the miracle occurred. Hector saw the helicopter come under control again, the nose lifted into the attitude for auto rotation. The rotor began spinning once more, but now the airflow over the blades was reversed. It was not driving the machine forward but braking its fall sharply. It was gliding towards the beach and Hector shouted an order into the mike for Dave to keep firing at the helicopter. There was no response. Hector's voice had been drowned by the thunder of cannon. David Imbiss had not picked up Hector's order. Instead he had switched his targets and both guns were firing at the circling pack of attack boats.

The fragmentation shells burst in the air above them and the steel balls tore the flimsy wooden hulls to splinters and scythed down the men in them. The surviving boats turned away at top speed and headed for the safety of the shore. The helicopter continued its auto rotation glide towards the beach but as Hector watched it fell only just short and plummeted into the water, kicking up a tall cloud of spray. For a few moments it disappeared, but then it bobbed back to the surface and floated onto its side.

Surely even Uthmann could not have survived that, Hector thought, but the topside door of the helicopter opened slowly and a human form crawled out and clung to the fuselage. It was too far to recognize a face but he knew it was Uthmann. His hands were empty. He had left his rifle in the cabin. Anyway the range was six or seven thousand yards, much too far even for the Beretta.

'The bastard can't swim and he is terrified of water.' Hector spoke aloud, but without any real conviction. He watched the distant figure tumble off the helicopter's fuselage into the sea, and expected to see him go under. But the water was only deep enough to reach to Uthmann's armpits. Helplessly Hector watched him as with frantic and uncoordinated movements he floundered towards the beach, and then staggered ashore.

Hector looked back at the cargo deck just as Paddy and Tariq's combined strike teams burst out of the lower doors of the stern tower and rushed at the group of Arabs who surrounded Kamal. Immediately both forces were locked in a struggling mêlée. They were almost equally matched in numbers, and the fighting was at close quarters and hand to hand. None of them could risk firing for fear of hitting their own men.

Hector saw Paddy trying to fight his way to Nastiya in the confusion, but a dozen men intervened and Paddy had to turn on them to protect himself. On the far side of the scrimmage Kamal had grabbed the end of the rope around Nastiya's neck and was hauling her away backwards, at the same time calling desperately to Adam in Arabic.

'This way, my Sheikh. Follow me. The helicopter and the boats have deserted us. Follow me!' One of Paddy's men grabbed a fold of Adam's flowing headcloth as he passed, but the Sheikh turned on him with his curved dagger and stabbed him in the eye. The man dropped with the cloth twisted around his fingers and Adam ran after Kamal and Nastiya bare-headed.

Hector was too high above the cargo deck to be able to intervene actively. He tried to work out what Kamal would do next, then saw him run to the hatch in the corner of the stern tower. Kamal knew very well that this was the access to the service tunnels between the natural gas tanks which housed the huge pumps that circulated the gas in the tanks. Only a few days previously they had watched on the CCTV in the situation room as Kamal explored this dank and twisting labyrinth in the bowels of the hull. Kamal must have decided to use this as his bolthole. He dragged Nastiya struggling on the end of the rope into the hatchway and Adam followed them, shoving Nastiya down the ladder after Kamal. He slammed and bolted the steel hatch behind them.

'Paddy!' Hector called him on the battle radio and saw him look up at the bridge. 'Kamal and Adam have taken Nastiya down into the pump service tunnel. Kamal has a rifle, but Adam has only a dagger. Put a guard on both ends of the service tunnel. There is no way out for Kamal and Adam. They're trapped down there. We can winkle them out later. But first you must launch Sam's AAVs and send them ashore to take the town and release the captured seamen from the stockades. I am handing over command of the *Golden Goose* to you. I'm going ashore to deal with Uthmann.' As he spoke Hector was stripping off his heavy body armour and all the other equipment that would weigh him down in the water. He kept only his knife, his radio and the Beretta 9mm pistol that were all attached to his webbing harness. He looked around to find Jacko MacDuff at his shoulder.

'I'm going ashore, Jacko. Take command of the stick. Our work up here is done. Go down and put yourself and the men under Paddy O'Quinn's command on the cargo deck. Good luck, Jacko,' said Hector. While they were speaking he was working out his next move. Most of the attack boats had made a run for the shore in an attempt to escape the fire of Dave Imbiss's Bushmasters. However, there were a few more crafty pirates who were using the *Golden Goose*'s own hull as a shield. They were hugging the sides of the ship so closely that the cannon set high up in the stern tower were unable to bring them under fire. At this moment one of these attack boats was hiding directly under where Hector was standing on the wing of the bridge. Although there was a fearsome drop from the bridge to the water, Hector did not hesitate. He backed up as far as the navigation console in the centre of the bridge. Bingo MacDuff had just released Cyril Stamford and he stood beside the console. Cyril understood at once what Hector was about to attempt, and his voice was gruff with respect.

'You have got a fine pair of balls, Mr Cross.'

'Look who's talking!' Hector smiled grimly at Cyril, and then started his run.

When he reached the rail at the wing of the bridge he was moving at the top of his speed. He dived as far out as all his strength and momentum could carry him. From this height he could not risk a head-first dive. If he turned over in the air and landed on his back his spine would snap like a pretzel. Instead, as soon as he was airborne he rolled himself into a ball, his knees tucked up against his chest, his head bowed and fingers of both hands locked together at the back of his neck. His guts swooped up under his ribs as he fell, and then he hit the surface of the water. The impact drove the air from his lungs and numbed his buttocks, which had struck first. He went under with the impetus of a cannonball. From deep down he looked up and saw above him the wavering silhouette of the longboat against the light. Fighting the urge to breathe he swam up towards it. He propelled himself upwards the last few feet and burst out alongside the low hull of the attack boat. He hooked his fingers over the gunwale and heaved himself over the side, at the same time drawing a mighty breath of sweet air.

There were two pirates in the boat. They were naked except for their grubby loin cloths and turbans. They stared at Hector in astonishment. One of them jumped to his feet with an assault rifle in his hands. Before he could raise the weapon Hector crashed into him with his shoulder and sent him hurtling over the side into the sea. Hector felt a fleeting regret that he had taken his rifle with him. The other man was squatting at the controls of the silver-and-red 200 horsepower outboard motor in the stern. He began to rise to his feet, but not fast enough. Hector jumped over the thwart and took two more flying paces towards him, then kicked him under his raised chin as though he were punting a football. The man's head snapped back and he sprawled over the cover of the huge outboard motor, then slipped down into the bottom of the longboat and flopped about in the bilges as helplessly as a stranded fish. Hector stooped over him, grabbed him by the heels and flipped him over the side. The pirate wallowed face-down in the water. Hector turned back to the outboard motor. It was still running, the exhaust burbling under the stern. He engaged the gear shift and twisted the throttle grip. The boat surged forward.

However, at that moment a human body plunged down the tall side of the tanker and splashed into the water just in front of the longboat's bows. Hector recognized the jumper as he flashed past. He closed the throttle and kicked the gear shift back into neutral, then ran forward and peered over the bows into the turbid water where the body had struck. He saw the man swimming up from the depths and then his head broke the surface. He was gasping for air.

'Tariq! You bloody fool, I could easily have chopped you to mincemeat in the prop.' He reached over the side and caught hold of Tariq's arm and hauled him on board. Then he ran back to the big outboard motor in the stern and twisted the throttle grip wide open. Under him the boat bounded forward and he lined it up with the wreck of the helicopter that was still wallowing on the edge of the beach. He looked back over the stern at the *Golden Goose* and with alarm saw the barrels of the two Bushmaster cannon swivelling towards them and beginning to range and track them.

He shouted at Tariq over the roar of the motor, 'Quickly! Stand up and give Dave Imbiss a wave. He's about to make a little mistake and blow us out of the water.' Tariq jumped to his feet and balanced in the dancing longboat as he waved both hands above his head. At once the cannon barrels lifted off them, and they saw Dave's head appear from behind the starboard cannon. He waved his helmet in the air in a gesture of apology. Then he disappeared back behind the blast shield and the cannon traversed right and resumed fire on some of the other attack boats which were scattering across the waters of the bay. Tariq crawled back along the bouncing and plunging longboat to Hector in the stern.

'What's going on, Hector? While I was still in the tunnel I heard you tell Dave to fire at a helicopter. You said that Uthmann was in it. But by the time I reached the cargo deck with Paddy I couldn't see any helicopter. I was mixed up in the fighting. Then I heard you warn Paddy on the radio that Kamal and Adam had escaped down into the pump service tunnel. By that time the other pirates had been subdued. There was no reason for me to stay, especially when I saw you jump off the wing of the bridge. Of course, I had to follow you.' Tariq looked anxious. 'Did I do the right thing, Hector?'

'Completely the right thing, as always, Tariq,' Hector replied in Arabic, and Tariq lapsed into the same language.

'Thank you, Hector. But where is Uthmann now? What happened to the helicopter? Where are we going?'

'Dave gunned the helicopter down, and it crashed on the edge of the shore.' He pointed ahead. 'There, you can see the wreckage floating in the surf.'

'But Uthmann? What has happened to him?'

'He escaped from the wreck. I saw him wading ashore. I jumped from the bridge to go after him.'

'I am glad I followed you. I want him even more than you do,' Tariq said softly.

'I know.' Hector nodded. 'He belongs to you. We will hunt him down together, but you will be the one to take vengeance.'

'Thank you, Hector.' Tariq drew a long breath to steady himself. 'Is he alone? Is he armed? Neither of us has a rifle.'

'Yes, Uthmann is alone. He had a rifle when he took off from the cargo deck, but after the helicopter crashed I saw him wade ashore. Too far off to be certain, but I don't think he was still carrying it. He probably panicked when he hit the water, and forgot all about his weapon. His only thought would have been to get to dry land. We will make a quick search of the helicopter cabin, if it's still afloat when we get there.'

They were tearing across the bay at fifty miles an hour, leaving a long straight creaming wake behind them as they headed for the wrecked machine. The sprawl of shanties which made up the town was half a mile further down the bay shore. Hector stood up and studied the terrain beyond the wreck into which Uthmann had escaped. It was devoid of any habitation, with rolling sand dunes covered in dense thickets of coarse salt scrub.

'Not a good place to track a wounded lion,' he decided. Uthmann was as dangerous as any wild animal. Hector slowed the longboat as they came up to the floating helicopter. The bows bumped against the wreckage. The air was heavy with the smell of spilt aviation fuel. Tariq scrambled up onto the battered fuselage and knelt to peer into the open doorway.

'There it is!' he called and disappeared through the door. He emerged again only seconds later brandishing a Beretta assault rifle.

'Ammunition?' Hector demanded.

'None,' Tariq answered, 'only what is in the magazine.'

'Maybe twenty rounds, if we're lucky. That should do.'

Hector put the outboard motor into gear and moved in slowly towards the beach. They both saw the string of footprints that Uthmann had left in the yellow sand. They ran from the edge of the water up the slope of the first dune and disappeared into the saltbush thicket on the crest. They wasted no time trying to moor the boat. Hector cut the motor, but let the boat drift. They jumped down into the knee-deep water and Hector led Tariq at a run to the foot of the first dune. Here they paused briefly to examine the spoor and then check the weapons they carried.

'Here, take this!' said Tariq, proffering the Beretta. 'You are a better rifle shot than I am. Let me have your pistol.' They exchanged weapons. Both rifle and pistol were soaked with saltwater. They shook it out of the magazines as best they could and made sure the barrels were free of sand or any other obstruction.

'That's the best we can do. They are designed to work in all the most extreme conditions,' Hector grunted. 'You lead, Tariq. Tracking is your job. I will be on your left side.' They climbed to the top of the first dune, where they found the spot where Uthmann had lain amongst the bushes. Tariq knelt beside the indentation his body had left. The loose dry sand was still trickling down into it. He must have watched them land on the beach, before he moved on. Something else caught Hector's eye: a pair of sandals lying under the nearest clump of scrub. They were still soaking wet, and the strap on one of them had snapped at the buckle. Uthman must have discarded them and gone on barefoot. The tracks he had left confirmed this.

'He is not very far ahead,' Tariq whispered. 'He is probably watching us again right now.'

'Go carefully. He might have lost his rifle, but he always has his blade,' Hector warned. For a brief moment they both thought of their four companions whose corpses they had left at the Oasis of the Miracle. Then they put from their minds everything but the job in hand. They went forward in overlapping formation so that each of them was able to cover the one flank as well as the immediate front. They could not afford to let their hatred override their respect for Uthmann as a fighter. They dared not let him get in close enough to use his blade.

The bush was dense, the hooked thorns tenacious. They had to move with the greatest care so as to make as little noise as possible. It took them six minutes ten seconds by Hector's wristwatch to cover the first hundred yards. There they came upon Uthmann's next lie-over, where he had waited for them to come up to him. If they had shown the slightest carelessness or given him any advantage at this stage they knew that this was where he would have taken them. But he had moved off again just ahead of them. The barefoot tracks he had left in the sand where he had squatted to wait for them were still settling.

Now he knows we aren't going to blunder in on top of him, Hector thought grimly. *His next trick will be to circle and try to get behind us.* He snapped his fingers softly and Tariq shot a quick glance at him. He made a circling motion to warn him. Tariq nodded; he understood the danger. They went on. Twice more they pushed Uthmann off his lie-over. Each time he moved away silently just ahead of them.

By now he will be thinking he has lulled us with repetition. This is when he will circle back on us. Hector changed his own tactics in anticipation. After every twenty slow paces he stopped and revolved slowly, studying the ground that he had already traversed from a fresh angle. Then he squatted on his haunches and studied the same ground behind them from a lower perspective, concentrating on the bases of the trees where the roots were bunched and twisted, behind which a man could lie with a thin sharp blade in his hand.

Suddenly Hector blinked as something alien caught his eye. He stared at it with all his concentration. It moved slightly and the whole picture jumped into focus. He was looking at a naked human foot that protruded from behind a bunch of the twisted roots. The sole of the foot was dusty pink, and the skin above it was tobacco brown. Hector felt the hair rise on the back of his neck. By God, Uthmann was close! He had almost walked on top of him.

He was lying not more than five long strides from where Hector was. Hector knew he could cover that distance with the speed of a hunting cheetah. He could almost feel Uthmann's eyes on him, watching him through one of the tiny chinks in the dense vegetation of the saltbush. Uthmann had a trick of keeping his eyes carefully slitted when he watched an enemy, his dark lashes veiling the tell-tale shine of the whites of his eyes. Hector saw the tendons in Uthmann's left foot standing out proud as he dug in his toes for purchase in the soft earth, prior to launching himself at Hector.

Hector was squatting on his haunches. The rifle was across his lap. There was a bullet in the breach, and the safety was off. His right hand was on the pistol grip, but he knew he could not get the rifle butt to his shoulder before Uthmann covered the gap and was on him. If that happened the rifle would be an encumbrance. He had to shoot out of hand, and he had to do it quickly. Uthmann's foot was all he had to aim at, and he had to fire without lifting the weapon from his lap. He could not aim the shot. He had to let his instinct take over completely. This was payback time for all those hundreds of hours spent on the firing range, he told himself. He made a slight movement as though he was about to rise upright, but the barrel of the rifle dropped slightly and swung through a narrow arc onto the target, and he fired as a reflex action. He saw the heel of Uthmann's bare foot ripped off in a burst of bone chips, flying tissue and blood.

Uthmann grunted as savagely as a gut-shot lion and he reared up from behind the saltbush. But the crippled foot pinned him to the spot. The pain forced him down on one knee. Hector saw the blade in his right hand, and the despair in his eyes. Uthmann knew he had lost, but he kept trying. He came up again on one leg, and tried to hop close enough to Hector to use the blade. But by now Hector was on his feet and charging in on him. He swung the rifle butt at Uthmann's elbow. It landed solidly and he felt the joint shatter. This time Uthmann screamed, and the blade spun out of his nerveless fingers. The crippled foot gave way and he sprawled in the loose sand. Tariq darted in behind him and seized the wrist of Uthmann's damaged arm. He wrenched it over and the broken bones grated upon each other. Tariq put his boot on the back of Uthmann's neck and forced his face into the sand. It filled his eyes and mouth and nose. He began to suffocate.

'Wait!' Hector ordered Tariq.

'You told me that vengeance was mine,' Tariq protested. He was sobbing wildly with the strength of his hatred.

'This is too good for him, Tariq.' Hector pulled him back. 'This is too quick. This creature burned your wife and your son. He murdered our comrades. He betrayed us to the Beast. He must pay for these sins in full measure.' Tariq shook his head and lifted the pistol, shoving the muzzle into the back of Uthmann's head.

'There is no fitting punishment. Anything we can do to him will not be enough.' He ground the muzzle of the loaded pistol into his scalp, but although Uthmann's face contorted with agony he refused to cry out.

'It was you who set fire to my home,' Tariq panted at him, 'you who burned Daliyah and my son! Deny it if you can, Uthmann Waddah.' Uthmann tried to smile but it was a painful travesty, and his voice was pain-racked. He spat the sand out of his mouth,

'They reeked like burning pork as they cooked,' he whispered, 'but I revelled in the stink of them.' Tariq sobbed and looked at Hector with the tears oozing down his cheeks.

'You heard him! What is there we can do to match such evil?'

'Water,' Hector replied quietly. 'Only seawater will wash away this stain from the face of the earth.' They saw the terror flare in Uthmann's eyes, and Tariq rejoiced.

'Of course, you are right, Hector. Seawater will do it. Up, Uthmann Waddah! Get on your feet. Your last walk will be down the beach and into the sea.' Tariq lowered the pistol and grabbed his wrist. He twisted it viciously against the shattered elbow joint. Uthmann shrieked again. His fierce defiance and his reckless courage were eroded by the threat of the one thing he feared above all else.

'I challenge you to do it here, if you have the stomach for it, Tariq. Shoot me and make an end to it, you gutless coward!'

'You are too hasty,' Tariq told him. 'This is the final act of your foul existence. You must savour every last moment of it. The taste of saltwater in the back of your throat, the burn of it in your lungs as they fill, the sting of it in your eyes as your vision fades.' He hauled on the broken arm and Uthmann could not resist the pressure. He allowed himself to be hoisted upright and tried to balance on his one good leg, but Hector seized his other arm and between the two of them they dragged him back to the beach. At last they looked down upon the bay from the crest of the final dune.

The *Golden Goose* lay at anchor where they had last seen her, but most of the surviving pirate longboats were abandoned along the shoreline like flotsam left behind the storm. The cannon on the *Golden Goose* were firing intermittently at targets that were out of sight to them from where they stood, and there was the distant rattle of automatic fire from the precincts of the town. A few of the buildings were on fire and the smoke drifted out over the bay. Just below them the longboat that they had abandoned was nudging the beach.

'Come on, Uthmann.' Tariq twisted his arm viciously. 'Not much further to go.' Uthmann fell to his knees, and now his terror had taken control of him completely. He was blubbering and gibbering barely coherently.

'No, Tariq! Shoot me here. Get it over with. There is something I want to tell you. I threw your brat into the flames first. Then I fucked your wife. I thought of you with every thrust I gave her. When I had finished I threw her on top of her bastard. Her long hair burned like a torch. Now you must shoot me. If you don't it will be a memory that will follow you all your days.' His voice rose in a despairing wail. Hector grabbed his other arm and the two of them dragged him on his belly, wailing and squealing down the dune and into the sea. When the water was knee-deep Hector rolled him face-down and lifted his ankles together behind him. Tariq strad-dled his shoulder and with his full weight forced his face below the surface. Uthmann was trying to hold his breath below the surface and at the same time give full voice to his terror. His movements grew wilder and less coordinated and then began to grow weaker. His mouth opened under the surface and a gust of silver bubbles broke past his lips. He was coughing and gasping and vomiting, the sounds muffled by the water over his head. When it seemed it was almost over, Hector dragged him out by his heels and laid him face-down on the wet sand. Tariq bounced on his back. Seawater and vomit gushed up out of his throat and he managed to draw a few short breaths before his whole body convulsed in another paroxysm of cough-ing. He vomited again and half of the yellow bile was sucked back into his lungs with his next breath. Slowly, very slowly, Uthmann managed to clear his lungs of water and vomit, but he was too exhausted to sit up or speak. Hector and Tariq squatted on each side of him and watched him struggle for his life.

'You heard him boast about what he did to Daliyah and my boy?' Tariq whispered.

'I heard.'

'There must be something we can do to match such hideous evil. A simple drowning is far too merciful.'

'There is something,' said Hector, nodding. 'There is an anchor rope in the longboat. Tie one end of it to that ring-bolt in the transom and bring the other end here.' It seemed that Tariq was about to ask a question but without voicing it he jumped up and ran to the longboat. He came back uncoiling the rope on the wet sand. Uthmann tried to sit up as Tariq stood over him, but Tariq kicked him over on his back and looked at Hector.

'Tie his wrists together,' Hector ordered, and Uthmann began to struggle and scream again. Tariq twisted his broken arm to subdue him while Hector slipped a loop of the rope over his wrists and tightened it until the hemp cut into his flesh.

'Do you know what you are now, Uthmann Waddah?' Hector asked quietly, and immediately answered his own question. 'You are live bait.'

'I don't understand,' Tariq admitted, and Hector went on to explain,

'All those captured boats have been lying at anchor for months out there in the bay. The men living on board have been throwing all their rubbish and sewage overboard. That attracts sharks, plenty of big sharks, tiger sharks mostly, for they are the scavengers, but others also – bronze whalers, Zambezi sharks and blacktips.' Tariq smiled and horror dawned in Uthmann's dark eyes.

'You are bleeding quite heavily, Uthmann.' Hector kicked his wounded foot, and Uthmann moaned. 'Did you know that sharks are attracted by blood? Let's go fishing!' They pushed the stranded longboat off the sand while Uthmann struggled weakly on the end of the anchor rope. Every time he managed to get up on his knees Tariq jerked his end of the rope and sent him sprawling again. As soon as the longboat was afloat Hector jumped on board and started the motor. He turned the bows away from the beach and opened the throttle gradually. Uthmann was pulled flat and dragged across the wet sand, screaming with pain and fear.

Tariq splashed out to the longboat and scrambled over the gunwale. He and Hector stared over the stern as Uthmann was hauled bodily into the low surf. The rope dragged him under the surface, but he came out in a flurry of water like a breaching whale, and then rolled under again. The pressure of seawater shot up his nose and down his throat. He managed to cough a little of it out of his mouth before he went under again, but now the rush of water into his right ear ruptured the eardrum. The agony must have been blinding, but he no longer had the breath to scream. The wake he left along the surface was tinted with blood and as the longboat entered the deepwater channel the first shark finned up in the blood slick. Hector saw the stripes across its broad back.

'Uthmann, there is a tiger shark coming up behind you,' he shouted. 'Not a very big one – a little less than three metres long. But big enough to bite a nice chunk out of you.'

The shark did not rush in at once, but it followed Uthmann cautiously until another larger shark rose out of the green waters. The one goaded the other and together they charged in. The larger shark opened its jaws in a cavernous gape and then bit down into Uthmann's shattered ankle. He screamed as he realized what was happening to him. The sharks dragged him under and Hector cut the outboard motor and drifted softly on the tide. He didn't want Uthmann to drown before the sharks were finished with him. It didn't take very long. Each time Uthmann came to the surface his struggles were weaker and his screams feebler. The water around him darkened with his blood. Tatters of his own flesh floated around him. Then he went under once more but he did not surface again. When Tariq hauled in the rope Uthmann's two disembodied hands were still fastened in the end noose. He tossed them back over the side. He went to squat beside Hector as he turned the longboat sharply and roared back across the bay towards the *Golden Goose*. They were both silent for a while then Hector raised his voice above the din of the engine.

'I could not ask before but tell me now, what was your son's name?'

'His name was Tabari.'

'We did what we had to do. But it doesn't help much, does it?' Hector mused. 'Vengeance is a tasteless dish.' Tariq nodded and turned his face away. He did not want even Hector to see too deeply into his soul where the ghosts of Daliyah and Tabari would live on for ever.

• • •

As they raced back under the towering hull of the *Golden Goose* Hector stood in the stern of the longboat balancing with a twist of the anchor rope around his wrist. He was figuring out the run of events that had taken place while he and Tariq had been engaged in the chase of Uthmann. He saw that the formation of three AAVs under Sam Hunter was approaching the beach in front of the town. He felt a quick flare of anger. By now they should have reached the prison stockade beyond town and freed the prisoners. He barked into the microphone of his battle radio, his tone reflecting his anger.

'Sam, what the bloody hell are you playing at? You are almost an hour behind schedule.'

'One of the hoists sustained damage from heavy machine-gun fire from the beach. It took time to get it working again. Sorry, Hector.'

'Okay, so now let's get our fingers out of our butts.' Hector broke the connection, and watched the AAVs. The water was breaking over their bows as they rode the shore chop. Small-arms fire from the shanties above the beach was thrashing the sea around them. However the hatches in the turrets were locked down, and the 50 calibre heavy machine guns were hosing tracer into the village. Shells from Dave Imbiss's Bushmasters were joining in the bombardment, bursting in the air above the rickety buildings. Some of the corrugated-iron roofs collapsed under the weight of shot and the surviving pirates scrambled out of the wreckage and fled back towards the hills. The gale of shrapnel burst overhead and most of them were knocked down.

As Hector watched all three AAVs reached the beach together and rolled ashore with their steel tracks churning up the sand, and hurtling them up the slope and into the village. The winding streets were too narrow for the huge armoured machines and they drove straight through the flimsy shacks without a check, flattening them and then disappearing from view as they raced for the stockades in which the captured seamen were imprisoned.

When Hector and Tariq arrived at the *Goose*'s side in the longboat the hoists that had launched the AAVs were still hanging at water level. They abandoned the boat and jumped across to the hoist cradle. Hector called the hoist operator on the Falcon radio. He lifted them to the cargo deck where Paddy was waiting to meet them. He was looking agitated.

'Fill me in with what has been happening, Paddy,' Hector ordered him.

'We have accounted for every one of Kamal's pirates that he brought on board. Eight of them are dead, including the four you took down on the bridge.' He paused and drew a sharp breath. 'As you know Adam and Kamal are holed up in the pump service tunnel. They have taken Nastiya in there with them. Hazel is tracking their movements on the infrared sensors.' Hector pressed the transmit button on his battle radio.

'Hazel, where are they now?'

'Hector, they are in the Number Two section, just beyond the main egress flow pipe intersection. They have not moved for the last twelve minutes.' Hector frowned. The service tunnel was the most difficult section of the ship to work in. Confined and claustrophobic, most of the space was taken up with banks of steel piping as well as the huge gas pumps. The noise of the pumps was deafening, and there was little ventilation. Down there a defender would have a clear advantage over an attacker who was trying to rout him out. They were all looking at Hector for orders; even Paddy seemed devoid of any suggestions as to how they should proceed. Hector was trying to visualize the layout of the area.

'Right!' He made his decision at last. 'There are only two entrances to the system and Paddy has got them both guarded, right?' Paddy nodded. 'Okay, so we'll work the tunnel from both ends simultaneously in two teams and try to catch Kamal and Adam between them. There is nearly a mile of tunnel down there. It will be a hell of a job to drive them out, unless—' Hector paused to think for a moment. 'Unless . . .' he repeated.

'Unless what?' Paddy demanded anxiously, but Hector did not answer directly.

'Come with me, quickly. We must waste no time,' Hector ordered, and two at a time he bounded up the stairs of the companionway that led up to the bridge. Paddy raced up behind him. Cyril Stamford was waiting for them on the bridge.

'Top of the morning to you, Captain,' Hector greeted him. 'Have you got your ship fully under your command again?'

'That I have.' Cyril's grin was lopsided. His face was still swollen and decorated with purple and green bruises where Kamal had used the rifle butt on him. 'Engines are running and we are shortened up on one anchor chain, ready to sail at your word.'

'A few chores to take care of first, Cyril. Please run Paddy and me through the firefighting procedures in the pump service tunnel.'

'I had a strange premonition you were going to ask me that, when I heard that was where Kamal had bolted with his boss and the charming Russian lady,' Cyril answered. 'Come to the chart room.'

The chart room was at the back of the bridge. Hector knew that the plans of the *Golden Goose*'s hull were stored flat in the wide drawers below the chart table. However, as soon as he entered the cabin Hector saw that Cyril had already spread out the drawings of the lower deck on the table. Hector and Paddy pored over them, while Cyril explained the layout of the eight compartments that made up the pump service tunnel.

'Each compartment can be sealed off with watertight and airtight doors, correct?' Hector knew the answer, but he asked for Paddy's benefit. 'You can also close off the electrical circuit, and shut down any lighting and ventilation in the tunnel?'

'Correct,' Cyril confirmed.

'And you can operate the doors from the bridge?'

In reply Cyril pointed through the open door. 'That's the control panel on the starboard bulkhead. Above the navigation console,' he stated.

'Can you also control the flow of CO_2 gas from here?'

'Affirmative!' Cyril nodded again. 'I can flood one compartment at a time, or all of them together.'

'CO_2 gas?' Paddy demanded. 'What the hell?'

'Fire control. It will snuff out the flames,' Hector answered brusquely, 'but it's also poisonous to humans.' He turned back to Cyril. 'Where do you keep the firefighting equipment?'

'On level one. We have fireproof suits—'

'We won't need those.' Hector cut him off. 'What about oxygen sets?'

'Yep! We have Draeger closed-circuit rebreathers. Four hours' life support in a toxic environment.'

'What about night-vision goggles?' Hector persisted.

'They are standard with the Draegers. They give you vision in total darkness or smoke.'

'How many suits do you have on board?'

'Two only.'

'Shit!' said Hector. 'So it's just you and me, Paddy.'

'I'm not sure what you have in mind, Heck. But hell's bells, I can do this on my own, standing on my head.'

'We all know that you have a powerful Russian motivation, but we do this together, Paddy.' Hector did not wait for the argument. 'Okay, Cyril, this is how it'll work. I'll go into the tunnel through the forward hatch. Paddy will go in at the stern hatch. He will hold his position as soon as he reaches the lowest deck. I will work my way back along the tunnel. You will flood each compartment with CO_2 as I come to it. Then you will close the watertight doors as I pass through them. Hazel will monitor the state of play from the situation room. She will keep us advised of the exact position of the fugitives and their hostage at all times.'

'I am so pleased that you remembered the existence of Nastiya. You are all heart,' said Paddy sarcastically. 'She is going to be down there in the gas. She will be unprotected. What is her survival time?'

'With Hazel directing us we will be able to stay in close contact with Nastiya and get to her very quickly. We will have a spare oxygen cylinder with us to give her.'

'That does not answer my question. How long will she have once the gas hits her?'

'Four or five minutes before she loses consciousness,' Hector replied quietly.

'And—?' Paddy insisted.

'And eight to twelve minutes before death.'

'Bugger your bloody gas, Hector Cross. I don't need it. Let me go in alone. I will take care of Kamal and bring Nastiya out without gassing her.'

'Sorry, Paddy. We do this my way.' Hector spoke with finality. 'We've wasted enough time yapping. Let's get on with it!'

• • •

Hector was in the anchor chain tier in the bows of the tanker. Tariq stood behind him and checked his weaponry; the placement of the Beretta pistol, the spare magazines and the knife in its sheath. He made certain they were all readily to Hector's hand.

On his hip Hector hung a small two-litre emergency oxygen bottle with a built-in face mask. It would give twenty minutes of grace to anybody caught in the CO_2 gas. Paddy was carrying an identical cylinder. One of them had to get to Nastiya before the CO_2 killed her.

The main Draeger oxygen rebreather was large and clumsy, and neither he nor Paddy had operated one before. However, one of Cyril's crewmen knew the equipment intimately, and had given them a brief introductory course. The helmet was extraterrestrial in appearance, and was rendered even more outlandish by the protruding eyes of the infrared night vision. The crewman plugged the Falcon radio into the extension mike inside the helmet.

'All ready to roll, sir,' he told Hector. 'Remember to switch on the oxygen tap before you close the face mask, not afterwards. You'd be surprised at how many novices forget that.' Hector nodded and called Hazel first.

'Hazel, I'm about to descend through the forward hatch now.'

'Hector, we have you on the screen. You're all clear ahead. The target is still stationary in the Number Two compartment.'

'Thank you, Hazel,' Hector acknowledged. 'Cyril, do you read me?'

'Loud and clear, Hector,' Cyril replied from the bridge.

'Paddy, do you read me?'

'Your dulcet tones ring sweetly in my ears, Heck.' Paddy's mood was obviously lightening with the promise of action, and the imminent rescue of Nastiya.

'Hold your position until I give you the word to move in.' Hector stepped onto the top rung of the steel ladder and gave Tariq and the crewman a thumbs-up. Then he swiftly descended the ladder to the lower level. The surroundings were cramped and confined, boxed in by raw steel painted a poisonous and forbidding green. Despite Hazel's assurance that the tunnel ahead was clear, he loosened the pistol in its holster and took it in a double-handed grip, pointing down the tunnel ahead of him.

'Okay, Cyril, you can kill the lights now.' Even though he had given the order the darkness was so sudden and intense that he had to stifle a gasp. He switched on his infrared night vision and his surroundings re-emerged in a dull and red monochrome.

'Hazel?' he asked.

'No change, Hector, the target is still stationary in Number Two.' Hector moved down the narrow tunnel. He was amazed at the length of the compartments. Walking fast, it took him over four minutes to reach the first watertight door. He stepped through and then called Cyril again.

'Cyril, I'm through the Number Eight hatch. Close it behind me.' He watched the hatch slide closed with a hydraulic hiss from the driving pistons.

'Should I gas the compartment behind you, Hector?' Cyril asked.

'Negative.' Hector stopped him. 'The compartment is deserted. No profit in gassing it.' He went on past another of the huge pumps. It was thumping and wheezing as it circulated the gas. Above it was a narrow vertical shaft that carried the egress pipe from the pump up to the top of the main tank. There was another ladder that ran up this shaft, but it was a dead end. There was no exit or escape through the upper end of the shaft.

Hector passed eight more of the massive pumps, and went through four more hatches. Each time he reached one of the hatches he called Hazel, and she told him that the target was still stationary in the No. 2 compartment. Hector went through the hatch into No. 4, and from the bridge Cyril closed it behind him. But when he reached the next hatchway and stepped into No. 3 there was an abrupt change. The hatch was sliding closed behind Hector, when Hazel called sharply over the radio.

'Hector, heads up! The target is splitting. Two subjects are stationary but the third is moving down the tunnel in your direction.' Hector was taken by surprise. Which one of them had broken away? It couldn't be Kamal; he would never abandon his hostage and go on alone. It couldn't be Nastiya for exactly the same reason; Kamal would never let her escape. It could only be Adam. What wild self-serving impulse had made him leave Kamal's protection? Probably the pitch darkness had worn down his nerves until they broke. That was why Hector had ordered Cyril to douse all the lights.

'Good!' Hector grunted. 'Cyril, open the hatch behind me again. Expedite!' As soon as it opened Hector went back through it into the compartment he had just vacated. 'Okay, Cyril. I am back inside the Number Four compartment. Close the hatch again.' He waited quietly for almost six minutes, then Hazel called again.

'Hector, the third man has reached your position. He is on the other side of the hatch from where you are standing. He seems to be examining the hatch, trying to find the lock and get the door open.'

'Okay, Hazel. I am sure the third man is Adam Tippoo Tip, and now we have got him where we want him. Cyril, close the hatch behind Adam, and let me know when you have done so.' Only a minute later Cyril came back on.

'Hatch is closed, Hector,' he reported. 'Adam is bottled up in Number Three compartment.'

'Okay, Cyril. Now flood the compartment with CO_2.' There was another long pause, and Cyril explained the delay.

'It takes time for the gas to permeate the whole compartment.' Nobody spoke again for a while, then Hazel called.

'Now it's working! Adam is running back the way he came in. He's obviously panicking. The CO_2 is getting to him.'

'Cyril, open the hatch and let me through.' Hector switched on the oxygen tap and closed his face mask. He stepped through the hatch into the CO_2-drenched compartment and ran down the catwalk in pursuit of Adam. He had to get to him before the gas killed him. He found him slumped against one of the gas pumps in an attitude of prayer, and recognized the white robes before he saw his face. When Hector turned him over he saw that he was already unconscious, but breathing in deep gasps. Hector saw that he had a black leather attaché case chained to his left wrist and tried to remove it, but the chain was stainless steel and the lock was of superior quality, similar to those used by diplomatic couriers. It would take a cutting torch to release it. There was no time to waste now, so he dragged Adam to one of the green steel gas pipes that ran horizontally along one side of the tunnel, and laid him facedown on top of it. He wrapped his limbs around the pipe, attaché case and all, and used cable ties to secure his wrists and ankles. Adam was pinned as securely to the gas pipe as a chunk of pork on a kebab skewer.

'That will hold you,' Hector said quietly and reached for the two-litre oxygen cylinder hanging from his belt. He placed the moulded polyurethane mask over Adam's nose and mouth and opened the tap. The oxygen hissed softly into Adam's gasping mouth. Hector secured the mask in place with the elastic strap around the back of Adam's head, then called Cyril.

'Sure enough, the runaway is Adam. I have him secured. He is still unconscious, but I have put the oxygen mask on him. He should come around again in a few minutes. Switch on the lights in this compartment and then run the ventilators to purge the CO_2.' As the oxygen began to take effect, Adam gulped and grimaced. He opened his eyes and groaned, his limbs convulsed and he struggled against his bonds. Then he looked up at Hector in his monstrous Draeger helmet and he screamed wildly and incoherently. He tried to throw off the oxygen mask, but when he found that he could not do so he sobbed into it,

'Where am I? What is happening to me?'

Hector ignored him. He waited for another ten minutes by his wristwatch and then opened his own face mask and tested the quality of the air. At low concentrations CO_2 is odourless, but at high concentrations it has a sharp acidic smell and a sour taste on the tongue. The ventilators had purged and cleansed the poisonous gas. The air was untainted.

Hector ripped the oxygen mask off Adam's face, and closed the tap before he hung it on his own belt again.

'Who are you? What are you going to do with me?' Adam's voice quavered.

'We will discuss that later,' Hector promised him in Arabic as he checked the cable ties on his ankles and wrists.

'I know who you are! You are the assassin, Hector Cross!' Adam's voice rose to a shriek. 'You killed my father and my grandfather, now you are going to kill me.'

'Yes. There is a good chance of that happening,' Hector agreed with him as he straightened up and called Cyril on the radio. 'Adam is secured and he has regained consciousness. Open the hatch into the Number Two compartment. I am going after Kamal and Nastiya now. Close the hatch after I've passed through.'

The hatch opened in front of him and he ducked through it into No. 2. There he paused.

'Hazel, where is Kamal?' he called.

'Hector, he has not moved. He is still in Number Two just ahead of you. I think he's found some secure hole in which to hide and he's waiting for you to come to him.'

'Then we mustn't disappoint him,' Hector told her. 'Okay, Cyril, close both hatches to Number Two compartment and be ready to flood it with gas at my command.'

'Roger, Hector. We have got Kamal boxed in. No way out for him.'

'Paddy, do you copy me?'

'Copy you, Hector.'

'Move up and wait at the Number Two hatch at your end. I will be waiting on my side. Cyril will pump in the gas and as soon as Kamal is incapacitated we will go in at the same time to grab Nastiya before the gas gets her.'

'You'll have to move fast to beat me, Cross. This is my girl you are monkeying with.'

'She's going to be all right, Paddy. She's too tough and beautiful to die young.'

'Stop yapping, Cross. Let's do it!'

'Hazel, last check. Where is the target?'

'Hector, they haven't moved. Still holed up in the middle of the compartment. I don't like this. I think Kamal has got a last trick in his hat. He's waiting for you. Please be careful, my love.'

'Careful is my middle name,' Hector assured her. 'But I think a whiff of CO_2 might make Kamal a little more friendly. Give him the gas, Cyril.'

'Roger, Hector. I am opening the CO_2 cylinders now!'

'Paddy, we go in exactly four minutes. By then Kamal should be down.'

'Sure, and so will Nastiya,' Paddy replied bitterly. Hector turned a deaf ear as he watched the luminous second hand of his Rolex. It moved around the dial with all the deliberation of an

Alpine glacier. It had reached the zenith and started its second circuit when Hazel spoke again, her voice taut with anxiety.

'We have lost contact! Kamal and Nastiya have disappeared off our screen.'

'That's not possible. Is the IR sensor in the tunnel still functioning? Perhaps Kamal has found it and disabled it.' Just when he was sure he had the situation well in hand, Hector felt it all beginning to unravel.

'Affirmative. It's still functioning, but Kamal has gone. No contact!' Hazel repeated urgently. Hector braced himself to ride the panic he felt rising to carry him away.

Think like the fox! he exhorted himself. *Think like Kamal! What is the bastard doing?* His intuition kicked in and he found the answer to his own question. He spoke into the battle radio. 'Paddy, Kamal has probably smelled the gas. That odour is unmistakable. He knows it's CO_2 and he knows it's heavier than air. He knows that to survive he must get above it. But how would he do that?' It took him another few seconds before he had the answer. 'The Number Two egress shaft! The bastard has climbed to the top of the shaft, and taken Nastiya with him. There is no IR sensor in the shaft, and the sweet air will be trapped in it. In there he can breathe and he has Nastiya as a shield. We can't fire up the shaft without hitting her.'

'We have to go in now, Hector!' Paddy's voice rose to a shout. 'Let me go! For Christ's sake let me go to her.'

'You're right, Paddy. We have to go in!' Hector said crisply. 'Cyril, open all the hatches! Then cut the gas off and start venting the compartment.' He drew a deep breath and then went on, 'Hazel, get the doctor down here. Somebody is going to get hurt.'

'I am coming with the doctor,' Hazel told him. Hector thought of arguing, but he knew from experience that was futile. Besides which the hatch was sliding open, and he had to go. He ducked through the open hatch and sprinted down the catwalk. There was no time for caution. He knew exactly where Kamal was. The egress shaft rose up from the centre of the compartment above the gas pump; at this rate he could reach it in two minutes. Without breaking his stride he called Paddy again.

'Paddy, when you reach it, take cover behind the gas pump. I will be on this side of it. Tell me when you are in position. We must work together on this. Don't you pull a Lone Ranger act on me.' Paddy did not respond and Hector saw the dark bulk of the gas pump looming just ahead of him. Above it the entrance to the egress shaft gaped like the mouth of a toothless monster. Hector slid in under the shelter of the pump and came up on his knees. The Beretta 9mm was in his hands and aimed up into the mouth of the shaft.

'Okay, Paddy, are you in position?' he asked softly and the reply came back instantly.

'In position, Hector!'

'Cyril, do you copy?'

'Copy you, Hector.'

'At my count of five, switch on all the lights. One. Two. Three. Four. Lights!' From utter darkness, the compartment was lit up with the bright electric glare. There was a 180-watt bulb in a wire cage at the top of the egress shaft. It back-lit Kamal and Nastiya like a stage effect. Kamal was crouched on the narrow steel landing. Nastiya was standing on the rung of the ladder below him. She had both her hands pinioned with cable ties in front of her. There was a rope around her neck. Kamal was holding the other end of the rope in one hand and an automatic rifle in the other. He was aiming the rifle down the shaft, and as soon as he saw Hector and Paddy in the shaft thirty feet below him he fired a burst at them with one hand. The moment before he fired they both ducked behind the pump.

The report of the rifle was ear-splitting in the enclosed area of the shaft. The bullets clanged off the steel bulkheads and the heavy gas pipes, throwing up bright showers of sparks. As soon as the rifle burst ceased, Hector risked a quick glance around the dome of the pump. There was no chance of a shot at Kamal. Nastiya's body screened him almost completely, yet he saw that she had somehow managed to twist a bight of Kamal's rope around her bound wrists. He could no longer use it as a garotte. She was balancing precariously on the rung of the ladder, without any handhold. Hector saw at once what she was planning to do, even before she yelled wildly, 'Catch me, Babu!' Then she threw herself backwards into the shaft. The rope jerked up tight but she took the strain on her wrists rather than with her neck. The end of it was whipped out of Kamal's hands and he was almost dislodged from his perch. He scrabbled wildly to keep his balance.

Who the hell is Babu? Hector thought irrelevantly. His unspoken question was answered at once as Paddy raced out from behind the gas pump and stood under the mouth of the shaft with his arms spread wide, looking up at Nastiya as she hurtled down towards him. She had balled her body, tucking in her elbows and knees, and the fall was almost thirty feet. She was accelerating to bone-shattering velocity, but Paddy did not flinch. He snatched her out of the air and into his arms, and was knocked down by her momentum onto the steel deck, absorbing most of the shock of the collision with his own body. The impact sounded like a sack of coal thrown from the back of a dray onto a cobbled street, and Hector heard the crackle of breaking bone. But Paddy never released his grip. He held Nastiya to his chest.

Hector did not spare even a glance at the two interlocked bodies under his feet, but he concentrated every last iota of mind and muscle on the figure high above him in the steel shaft.

Kamal was clinging to one of the ladder rungs, kicking and struggling to keep his balance. Hector's first shot with the Beretta ricocheted off a rung of the steel ladder directly beneath him. The deformed bullet lost only a little of its velocity as it tumbled in the air and then went up between Kamal's legs, piercing the perineum and burrowing deeply into his bowels. Kamal's whole body bucked and convulsed. He hung on to the ladder with a death grip, but could not maintain his hold on the rifle. It dropped, rattling against the bulkheads and bouncing on the rungs of the ladder. Hector ducked as it flew past his head, and then he fired three more shots in rapid succession. Every one of them tore through flesh, bone and vitals. Slowly Kamal's fingers opened until he lost his grip on the steel ladder and dropped down the shaft, his loose robes fluttering around him until he struck the deck at Hector's feet. Hector leaned over him and fired two more shots into his head, before he turned to where Paddy and Nastiya lay.

The tunnel was still flooded with CO_2 gas which had not yet been purged by the ventilators. Nastiya was at risk. Hector knelt beside her and unhooked the two-litre oxygen bottle from his belt. He opened the tap and clapped the mask over her nose and mouth.

'See to Paddy first!' Nastiya demanded and her voice was muffled by the plastic mask. Paddy was trying to sit up, but he was injured. His body was out of shape; his one shoulder drooping.

Collarbone gone and probably a couple of ribs, Hector thought. *Certainly a few sprains and torn muscles, but is there any brain damage?* Then he said aloud, 'Come along, Babu. Lady says I have to look after you.'

'One of these days you are going to go too far, Cross,' Paddy warned him but without real rancour. His face was twisted with a mixture of pain and adulation as Nastiya knelt over him and he looked up into her eyes.

'No brain damage. The lad is still hot as a pistol!' Hector said with a grin and switched on the mike of his radio. 'Now hear this all of you! Kamal is down and out. So is Uthmann Waddah. Adam is captured. Paddy has broken a couple of bones, but he is tough and they'll mend. Main thing is that Nastiya and I are just fine. So no real worries!'

• • •

Hector and Hazel stood together on the wing of the *Golden Goose*'s bridge. He had his arms around her and she was leaning back against his chest. In silence they watched the last boats coming off the beach, packed with the seamen that Sam Hunter's column had released from the prison stockades ashore. The men were being ferried out to their ships in the bay.

Sam's men were torching the buildings of the town, after making sure that no widows and orphans had been left behind by the fleeing populace. Hazel had been very definite about that. Already most of the pirated ships in the bay had the majority of their original crews on board, and they had started their engines in preparation for sailing. Eight ships that had been lying at anchor for many years had deteriorated to such an extent that their engines were rusted solid and their hulls were so riddled with rust that they were totally unseaworthy. Hector ordered them to be scuttled, to deprive the pirates of even these meagre rewards. When their seacocks were opened to flood the hulls many of them capsized, while others sank to the bottom in an upright position with only their rigging showing above the surface. At last Sam Hunter's squadron of AAVs trundled down the beach into the sea and started swimming back to the *Goose*, leaving the town in flames. Hazel broke their silence.

'So, my darling, the job is over and done,' she said in what was almost a whisper.

'Almost but not quite done. There is just one more thing we have to see to,' Hector replied, and she turned in the circle of his arms and looked up into his face.

'I know. I've been dreading this part of it.' She sighed. 'Where is he?'

'Tariq has him locked in the armoury in the covert area of the ship.'

'We should do it at once, and get it over with before I lose my nerve.'

'We will only do it once we are at sea,' he demurred. 'But neither of us will lose our nerve. We owe it to Cayla and Grace.'

'I know,' Hazel whispered and stirred against his chest, 'we must have justice for them. Without that none of us will ever have peace. When, my darling? When must we do it?'

'We sail this evening. We'll do it at dawn tomorrow, when we are out of sight of land.'

'Just you and me?' Hazel asked softly. 'Nobody else?'

'Others have suffered,' Hector reminded her. 'Tariq, Paddy and Nastiya.'

'Very well. But I have to do it. It's my sacred duty.'

The sun was setting, and there was only just enough light to make out the channel as the *Golden Goose* led the convoy of strangely assorted ships out of Gandanga Bay. They sailed southeast during the night. While it was still dark the next morning Hector and Hazel bathed and dressed in fresh clothes. Then they each drank a mug of strong black coffee, standing together in the kitchenette of the master suite without speaking. At precisely five o'clock Tariq knocked on the door and Hector opened it.

'Everything is ready,' Tariq told him.

'Thank you, old friend.' Hector left him at the door and went back to see Hazel sitting on the bed. She looked up at him. Her eyes were a shade of blue he had never seen them before, cold and sunless as an Arctic sea.

'Yes?' she asked.

'Yes!' he said and taking her hand he lifted her to her feet. He led her to the lift and they descended to the lowest level. When the doors opened he took her elbow and steered her out onto the stern deck. A section of the deck had been screened off with a heavy tarpaulin. Tariq walked ahead of them and held open the fly in the canvas. After they passed through he closed it behind them.

Paddy and Nastiya were waiting for them. Paddy was seated in a folding canvas chair. His chest was strapped with surgical tape and his left arm was in a sling. Nastiya stood beside him with one hand resting lightly on his shoulder. Hector and Hazel went to stand at Paddy's other side. Hector looked at Tariq.

'Fetch Adam,' he ordered. Tariq went out through the opening in the canvas screen and returned almost at once. Two of the Cross Bow men followed him. They had Adam between them. His legs were paralysed with terror. His guards were half-dragging, half-carrying him. They let him drop on his knees in front of Hazel. Hector nodded at them and they went to stand guard at the entrance to the enclosure.

Adam knelt facing Hector and Hazel and his eyes were dark and swimming with tears. The black attaché case was still chained to his wrist and with both hands he hugged it against his chest.

'Why does he still have that case? Take it away from him,' Hector demanded.

'There's a combination lock on the chain,' Tariq replied. 'He won't give it up. We cannot get it away from him.'

'Cut off his hand at the joint of the wrist, Tariq. The chain will slip off the stump easily enough,' Hector ordered. 'Use your trench knife.' Tariq stooped over Adam, drew the knife and grabbed his arm. Adam squealed like a piglet having its throat cut.

'No! Don't use that knife. I will give you the case.' He placed it in his lap and with shaking fingers tumbled the combination of the lock. At his second effort the chain fell from his wrist and he crawled across the deck and proffered the attaché case to Hector with both hands.

'You and I can strike a bargain,' he sobbed. 'I know you are a man of your word, Hector Cross. In this little bag there are the internet bank codes and passwords to almost two billion dollars deposited in twenty-six banks around the world. We can share it, you and I. Set me free and you can take half the money.'

'The money is not yours, Adam. You stole it from the people whose ships and goods you plundered.'

'Then, you can take all of it,' Adam pleaded. 'Two billion dollars! Take it all, but let me go.'

'Yes! I *am* going to take it all, Adam,' Hector said with a nod, 'and I'm going to let you go to Iblis, the evil jinnee. He is waiting for you. Take the case from him, Tariq.' Adam wailed and tried to resist, clinging to the chain. Tariq reversed his knife in its scabbard and whipped the hilt across his temple. Adam released the chain to clutch at his skull with both hands. Tariq handed the attaché case to Hector. He set it aside and concentrated his attention on the wretch cringing at his feet.

'Adam, you are the perpetrator of countless acts of piracy, rape and murder. Even under the Sharia law which you profess to honour, all these are capital crimes. You are in manifest guilt. However, one of your victims was a young woman named Cayla Bannock. You raped and tortured her without mercy. Finally you murdered Cayla and her grandmother Grace Nelson by ordering your minions to decapitate them. Then you sent the two heads to Hazel Cross with a mocking message. Hazel Cross, who is Grace Nelson's daughter and Cayla Bannock's mother, stands before you now demanding retribution.'

Adam raised his head and gazed at Hazel. Blood trickled down his cheek from the blow that Tariq had dealt him. He was weeping and the tears diluted the blood and dripped onto his white robe.

Hector went on quietly, 'Cayla Bannock's mother stands before you now. She claims from you the right of retaliation granted to her under Sharia law. A life for a life.'

'Please!' He cupped his hands and held them out to Hazel in supplication like a beggar. 'It was my duty. I only did what was my duty to Allah and my ancestors. Please understand. Please have mercy.' Hector looked across at Tariq and nodded. Tariq had a folded canvas sheet lying at his feet. Now he spread this on the deck. Then the two Cross Bow men carried in a heavy sandbag and placed it in the centre of the sheet.

'Adam, go to the sheet and lie upon it with your head on the sandbag,' Hector ordered.

'No!' Adam blubbered. 'I have given you the money. I have paid the blood debt under Sharia law, and you have accepted it. You must let me go free.'

Hector drew the pistol from the holster on his webbing, and he reversed his grip and handed it butt first to Hazel. She took it, pumped a round into the chamber and pointed the muzzle at the deck. Then Hector went to where Adam knelt. Adam's voice rose to a shriek.

'Mercy! I beg of you, mercy.'

Hector took hold of one of Adam's wrists and, seemingly without effort, twisted the hand up behind Adam's back and lifted him to his feet. He marched him to the spread canvas sheet and forced him belly down upon it.

'Place your head on the sandbag,' Hector ordered him quietly. 'It will stop the bullet after it has passed through your skull. Afterwards the sandbag will weigh your corpse down when it goes into the sea.'

Adam screamed, a formless incoherent sound. Hector forced him down until the scream was muffled by the sandbag. Then he looked up at Hazel.

'Are you ready?' he asked, and she nodded. She was weeping silently. She went and stood beside Hector and pointed the pistol down at Adam's head, but her shoulders were heaving and the pistol wavered and shook in her grip. She lifted it and pointed the muzzle at the sky. She was shaking her head and gasping for breath like a drowning woman. Nastiya Voronova left Paddy's side and came to her. She laid her hand gently on Hazel's shoulder.

'I vill do it for you, Hazel. I am trained for zis, and you are not,' Nastiya said; but Hazel shook her head again.

'No,' she whispered, 'it's my duty to God, my mother and my daughter.'

She lowered the pistol and aimed at the back of Adam's head. Her hands were suddenly rock steady and she was no longer sobbing. She fired a single shot. Afterwards there was no sound except the throbbing beat of the engines.

Hector took the pistol out of Hazel's hand and removed the magazine. He ejected the live round from the breach. Then he placed his arm around his wife's shoulder and said, 'Now it's over. It's done, and done well. Grace and Cayla are free and so are we.'

She buried her face against his chest and did not watch while Tariq and the two guards came forward. They rolled Adam and the sandbag into the canvas sheet and with a length of nylon cord trussed the bundle up neatly and securely. Then between them they carried the package to the stern rail and slid it over into the seething white wake of the ship. It disappeared without trace.

• • •

The USS *Manila Bay* intercepted the flotilla thirty nautical miles outside territorial waters. Commander Andrew Robins's tone was incredulous as he called up the *Golden Goose*.

'*Golden Goose*, this is *Manila Bay*. Is Captain Stamford available?'

'Hi there, Andy, this is Cyril Stamford.'

'Good to speak to you again, sir. There have been reports of some trouble in the Gulf of Aden. At a place named Gandanga Bay in particular.'

'Do tell, Andy! I wonder what that was about?'

'Well, sir, as long as you were not involved in any unpleasantness. I was a little worried for you.' There was a pause. 'I see you are sailing in company.'

'Darn funny thing, Andy, how these fellows latched onto me. Seems they lost their way.'

'How many are there, sir?'

'Nineteen at the last count.'

'My orders are to go to the aid of any vessels emerging from the Gulf of Aden who request assistance.'

'Then I will hand them all over to you, Andy, and get on my way.'

'Last time we spoke I thought you said you were bound for Jeddah in Saudi Arabia, Captain Stamford?'

'Change of plan, Andy. My owners just can't make up their minds where they want me to go. Now I am on my way around the Cape of Good Hope.'

'Seems that the rumour of trouble in Gandanga Bay was an exaggeration. The last satellite report is that the bay is totally deserted.'

'Just goes to show, Andy, that you can't believe everything you hear.'

'Shall we just score one up for your boy, Bobby?'

'God bless you, Andy Robins!'

'Calm seas and fair winds, Uncle Cyril!'

• • •

After long debate between Hazel, Hector and Paddy it was decided that regardless of the cost they should get rid of any incriminating equipment left on board the *Golden Goose*. Accordingly the Bushmaster cannon were dismounted from their emplacements and together with all the ammunition they were dumped into the Mascarene Basin in over five thousand feet of water. All three AAVs followed them with their turrets and seacocks wide open.

Once she was clean the *Golden Goose* stopped over in the roads of Dar es Salaam harbour and sent 146 men ashore by ferry. Each of the passengers was dressed in civilian clothes and carrying a fat cashier's cheque drawn on the Hongkong and Shanghai Banking Corporation. Bernie and Big Nella Vosloo were waiting at Dar es Salaam airport to fly them up to Qatar in the Hercules. From there they dispersed across the globe on commercial airline flights. Paddy was still not in any condition to travel so he remained on board, with his self-appointed Russian nurse. They sailed on down to Cape Town where the BBJ was waiting. It took Paddy and Nastiya up to Moscow, where Nastiya wanted to get her mother's approval for what the two of them had in mind.

Hector and Hazel stayed over at Dunkeld Estate for a week to sample Uncle John's latest vintage and render comfort and support over the loss of his beloved sister Grace. When he learned that the scores had been settled and that Hazel had carried out the execution in person John was well on the way to a full recovery. The BBJ returned from Moscow and flew Hector and Hazel back to Houston.

During the flight home they discussed what had to be done with the contents of Adam Tippoo Tip's attaché case. Finally they agreed that if the funds could be recovered from the bank accounts using the passwords and usernames they had acquired, then they would have to be returned to their rightful owners. As soon as they were back in Texas they made the first attempt at recovery. First they opened a numbered account in Switzerland. Then Hector went online and used his fluent Arabic to type in the username and password of Adam's account at the Central Bank of the Islamic Republic of Iran.

'Shit! It works!' he breathed as the files opened on the screen with miraculous rapidity.

'Don't swear, darling,' Hazel told him primly, 'it'll bring us bad luck.'

Hector pointed to the balance on the bank account. 'Do you think eight hundred and fifty-seven million US dollars is bad luck?'

'It will be, unless you can transfer it into the Swiss numbered account.'

'Hold your breath and pray,' he told her, and typed in the instructions. 'Here we go!' He hit the 'Submit' button, then let out a whoop of triumph. 'It has accepted the instruction! The money has been transferred!'

'Check that it's gone in,' Hazel suggested. Quickly he opened their Swiss account.

'It's there!' he gloated. 'Look at it! Eight hundred and fifty-seven million dollars!' He took her in his arms and waltzed her twice around the room.

'Now, let's be serious.' She stopped him at last. 'Let's get the rest of the lolly.' They sat down in front of the computer again, and worked away for the next three hours. At the end of that time they stared in awe at the screen.

'We've scooped the pot!' Hector said in sepulchrous tones. 'We've got the lot. Every last bloody dollar. A smidgen over two billion dollars.'

'Okay! Go ahead and swear. I was wrong. It does seem to bring us good luck.'

'There is a magnum of Roederer Cristal champagne in the fridge. What d'you think? Shall we?'

'I think it's obligatory,' she agreed. They toasted each other and absent friends, and then got down to the next item of business.

'Right!' said Hazel. 'Can we establish who paid the money into Adam's accounts?'

'Yes, of course. We just open Adam's bank statements. It's all there.'

'And we have their account numbers to return all the money to?' she asked.

'Not all of it. We have to reimburse Bannock Oil for all the expenditure of equipping and mounting the expedition to Gandanga Bay.'

'Yes, of course. But we must keep all of this at arm's length. We can never admit that we had any part in the raid on the pirates. We broke nearly every law in the book when we did that.'

'As for the refund of expenses to Bannock Oil, I will talk to Prince Mohammed in Abu Zara. We can route the money through him as oil royalties.'

'Will he do that for us?'

'Not for us, but for a nice little commission,' Hector said with a shrug. 'Apart from being the Prime Minister and Minister of Mines, he is also head of both the army and police force, and governor of the Central Bank of Abu Zara. People tend to do what Princey says without kicking up a fuss.'

Hazel laughed. 'He sounds like my kind of guy. But how do we get the money to the others that Adam Tippoo Tip robbed?'

'Have you got a really reliable lawyer?'

'A whole platoon of them,' she agreed.

'Your chosen lawyer will contact each of them separately under a confidentiality agreement. He will explain that his anonymous client has negotiated with the pirates and received a substantial refund of the extorted funds. If they sign a guarantee of secrecy, then they are in line for a distribution of a portion of this amount. You can bet that they will jump at the offer.'

Hector was right; Prince Mohammed channelled the money into the Bannock coffers, and the ship owners and insurance companies who had suffered losses performed like Olympic athletes jumping at their offer.

While all of this was in process Hector and Hazel found the time to fly to Moscow for the wedding of Nastiya Voronova and Paddy. On the way they picked up Cyril Stamford in Taiwan, where the *Golden Goose* was being refitted. Cyril was now officially employed as the full-time captain of the vessel, and Nastiya had particularly asked Hazel to see to it that he was present at the wedding. Hector could not see the reason why Cyril's presence was planned so carefully by the two girls. It was only when Nastiya introduced Cyril to her mother that matters became clearer. Galina Voronova was a tall and stately lady of fifty-seven years whose long hair had turned silver blonde. Looking at her it was obvious from whom Nastiya had inherited her own spectacular beauty.

Cyril and Galina shook hands and she said in excellent English, 'You are a sea captain. That is very romantic!'

Cyril stammered something unintelligible and paled beneath his tan. He seemed actually to sway on his feet as he stared at her. Hazel squeezed Hector's arm and murmured just loudly enough for only him to hear, 'Bingo!' Then she and Nastiya exchanged self-satisfied glances.

After the wedding ceremony in the Cathedral of Christ the Saviour, Hazel handed Nastiya her contract with Cross Bow Security. She had appointed Nastiya the new assistant chief director of the company. When Hector and Hazel flew back to Houston Cyril Stamford was not on board the jet. It would be at least another three months before the *Golden Goose* was ready for sea and he had that time to spare. For reasons which he fondly believed were known only to himself, Cyril had decided to stay over in Moscow for a while.

• • •

Hector and Hazel had a mountain of work awaiting their attention in Houston, including the Bannock Oil AGM and a Japanese delegation anxious to discuss deepwater drilling in the Mariana Trench in the Pacific Ocean, so it was almost a month after their return before they had the opportunity to fly to the ranch in Colorado. After breakfast on the first morning they walked up to the mausoleum on top of Spy Glass Mountain. Old Tom greeted them at the door.

'They told me you was coming, Miss Hazel and Mister Hector,' he said, 'so I got in the flowers. Arum lilies for Mister Henry and roses for Miss Cayla, like always.'

'You are a good man, Tom.' Hector watched from the doorway as Hazel arranged the flowers, and when it was done she called him. They knelt side by side on the purple velvet cushions that Tom had placed at the head of Cayla's marble sarcophagus.

'I'm not very good at this prayer business,' Hector warned her gently.

'I know. Leave this part to me,' she replied. She was very good at it. The tears welled up in Hector's eyes as he listened to her.

It was just a little short of two hours before they went out onto the lawn again. The sky was grey with dense snow clouds. They sat together on the stone bench. A snowflake settled lightly on Hazel's nose. It tickled, so she wiped it away.

'Winter's coming early this year,' she said. 'Dickie tells me that the geese have already flown south.'

'Cayla and Henry have gone with them,' Hector agreed. 'They weren't there today.' He looked back at the mausoleum.

'You also sensed that?'

'They won't be coming back, Hazel. They have gone for ever. Only the memory of them will remain with us.'

'I know.'

'Don't be sad, my darling.'

'I'm not sad. I'm happy for them. We've set them free at last.' She moved closer to him and he put his arm around her. The evening was coming on apace and it had turned very cold.

'Hector?' she said.

'I am still here,' he replied. 'No plans to go anywhere without you.'

'I stopped taking the pill this month.'

'Good God, what did you do that for?' He was astonished.

'I want another baby. This is my last chance. I am over forty years of age. Very soon it will be too late. I must have a baby. I must have a piece of you inside me. That will be the ultimate affirmation of our love. Oh! my darling, don't you understand? I need to have a baby to take the place of Cayla. Don't you want one also?'

'Hell! Yes! Of course I do,' he said.

'So you really aren't mad at me?'

'Hell! No!' He stood up and took both her hands in his and lifted her to her feet.

'Come along, woman!' he said.

'Where are we going?'

'Back to the Fatherland, where else? You and I have some important business to take care of.' Hand in hand they ran down Spy Glass Mountain, laughing all the way back to the house on Guitar Lake.

WILBUR SMITH

Readers' Club

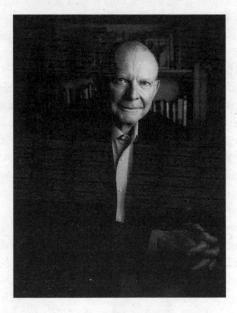

If you would like to hear more about my books, why not join the WILBUR SMITH READERS' CLUB by visiting www.bit.ly/WilburSmithClub. It only takes a few moments to sign up and we'll keep you up-to-date with all my latest news.